NOV 2 0 2003

LISLE LIBRARY DISTRICT
LISLE, ILLINOIS 60532
TEL: (630) 971-1675

DEMCO

EVERYMAN'S LIBRARY

EVERYMAN,

I WILL GO WITH THEE,

AND BE THY GUIDE,

IN THY MOST NEED

TO GO BY THY SIDE

FYODOR DOSTOEVSKY

The Adolescent

Translated from the Russian by
Richard Pevear and Larissa Volokhonsky

E V E R Y M A N ' S   L I B R A R Y
Alfred A. Knopf New York London Toronto

270

THIS IS A BORZOI BOOK

PUBLISHED BY ALFRED A. KNOPF

First included in Everyman's Library, 2003
Copyright © 2003 by Richard Pevear and Larissa Volokhonsky
Bibliography and Chronology Copyright © 2003 by Everyman's Library
Typography by Peter B. Willberg

All rights reserved under International and Pan-American Copyright Conventions. Published in the United States by Alfred A. Knopf, a division of Random House, Inc., New York, and simultaneously in Canada by Random House of Canada Limited, Toronto. Distributed by Random House, Inc., New York. Published in the United Kingdom by Everyman's Library, Gloucester Mansions, 140A Shaftesbury Avenue, London WC2H 8HD.

US website: www.randomhouse/everymans

ISBN: 1-4000-4118-X (US)
1-85715-270-0 (UK)

This translation has been made from the Russian text of the Soviet Academy of Sciences edition, volume 13 (Leningrad, 1975).

Dostoyevsky, Fyodor, 1821–1881.
[Podrostok. English]
The adolescent / Fyodor Dostoyevsky; translated from the Russian by Richard Pevear and Larissa Volokhonsky; with an introduction by Richard Pevear.
p. cm.—(Everyman's library)
Includes bibliographical references.
ISBN 1-4000-4118-X (alk. paper)
I. Pevear, Richard, 1943—. II. Volokhonsky, Larissa. III. Title.
PG3326.P5 2003
891.73′3—dc21 2003044885

A CIP catalogue reference for this book is available from the British Library

Book design by Barbara de Wilde and Carol Devine Carson

Typeset in the UK by AccComputing, North Barrow, Somerset
Printed and bound in Germany by GGP Media, Germany

LISLE LIBRARY DISTRICT
LISLE, ILLINOIS 60532

F
DOS

THE ADOLESCENT

23.00
B.T
11/18/03

CONTENTS

INTRODUCTION

In the early 1870s, the radical satirist M. E. Saltykov-Shchedrin declared that in Russia the family novel was dead: "The family, that warm and cosy element . . . which once gave the novel its content, has vanished from sight . . . The novel of contemporary man finds its resolution in the street, on the public way, anywhere but in the home." In 1875, however, two novels began to appear serially in rival journals: Tolstoy's *Anna Karenina* in the conservative *Russian Messenger*, and Dostoevsky's *The Adolescent* in the populist *Notes of the Fatherland*. Though they have nothing else in common, both are family novels *in excelsis*. Their appearance at that time suggests that, far from having vanished from sight, the family was still the mirror of Russian social life, and the fate of the family was a key to Russia's destiny.

Tolstoy defied the radicals by portraying the ordered life of his own class, the hereditary aristocracy, and the tragedy of its disruption – that is, by looking back at a world which, as Dostoevsky saw, had become a fantasy. "But you know," Dostoevsky wrote to his friend Apollon Maikov, "this is all landowner's literature. It has said everything it had to say (magnificently in Leo Tolstoy). But this word, a landowner's in the highest degree, was the last. A *new word*, replacing the landowner's, does not exist yet." In *The Adolescent*, which he conceived in part as an answer to Tolstoy, Dostoevsky found that new word, portraying what he calls the "accidental family" of his time, the reality behind Tolstoy's grand "mirage." In *Dostoevsky, His Life and Work*, Konstantin Mochulsky draws the ultimate conclusion about the family chronicle as Dostoevsky conceived it. The main theme of *The Adolescent*, he writes, is "*the problem of communion*: man is determined by his character, but his fate is defined in freedom, *in spite of his character*. The influence of one personality on another is limitless; the roots of human interaction go down into metaphysical depths; the violation of this organic collectivity is reflected in social upheavals and political catastrophes."* What Saltykov-Shchedrin saw taking place on the public way had its cause in what was taking place in the fundamental unity of the family, which could still serve as the image of Russian society in its inner, spiritual dimension.

The Adolescent is the fourth of the five major novels that Dostoevsky wrote after the turning point of *Notes from Underground* (1864). These novels in their sequence represent an ascending movement from "underground" towards the cold, clear light at the end of *The Brothers Karamazov. The Adolescent* is the next-to-last step in this ascent. And yet it is the least known of the five novels, the least discussed in the vast critical literature on Dostoevsky, simply omitted, for instance, from such major readings of his work as Vyacheslav Ivanov's *Freedom and the Tragic Life*, Romano Guardini's *Der Mensch und der Glaube* ("Man and Fate"), and the essays of the philosopher Lev Shestov. In *The Mantle of the Prophet*, the final volume of his critical biography of Dostoevsky, Joseph Frank refers to *The Adolescent* rather dismissively as "a curious hybrid of a novel" and "something of an anomaly among the great creations of Dostoevsky's last period." He finds that it lacks "the collision of conflicting moral-spiritual absolutes that invariably inspired his best work." Edward Wasiolek, editor and annotator of *The Notebooks for "A Raw Youth,"*† simply calls it "a failure."

It is true that *The Adolescent* lacks the dark intensity of *Crime and Punishment*, *The Idiot*, and *Demons*, the mephitic atmosphere, the whiff of brimstone that many readers consider Dostoevsky's

* "Organic collectivity" here is a translation of the nearly untranslatable Russian word *sobornost*, meaning a free, inner, organic "unity in multiplicity." It is a central term in Russian religious philosophy, which drew much inspiration from Dostoevsky. A profound exploration of the meaning of *sobornost*, and one extremely pertinent to *The Adolescent*, is to be found in *The Spiritual Foundations of Society*, by the Russian philosopher Semyon Frank, translated by Boris Jakim (Ohio University Press, 1987).

† Dostoevsky's title in Russian is *Podrostok*, which means "adolescent." Constance Garnett altered it to *A Raw Youth* in her translation, and that title has also been used most often in English critical writings on the novel.

essence. It is very different in tone from the preceding novels. But that difference is a sign of its special place in the unity of Dostoevsky's later work. *The Adolescent* is up to something else.

The distinctive tone of the novel is set by the adolescent narrator himself, that is, by the fact of his being an adolescent, speaking in the first person and writing as an amateur. Dostoevsky's notebooks show how carefully he weighed the question of point of view, and with what effect in mind. In September 1874, during the early stages of planning the novel, he notes: "In *the first person* it would be much more original, and show more love; also, it would require more artistic skill, and would be terribly bold, and shorter, easier to arrange; moreover, it would make the character of [the adolescent] as the main figure of the novel much clearer..." And a little further on: "A narrative *in the first person* is more original by virtue of the fact that the [adolescent] may very well keep skipping, in ultra-naïve fashion...to all kinds of anecdotes and details, proper to his development and immaturity, but quite impossible for an author conducting his narrative in regular fashion." A few days later, he repeats: "In *the first person* it would be more naïve, incomparably more original, and, in its deviations from a smooth and systematic narrative, even more delightful."

Dostoevsky had considered writing both *Crime and Punishment* and *The Idiot* in the first person, but had abandoned the idea. He came back to it in *The Adolescent*, which is his only novel with a first-person protagonist after *Notes from Underground*. The two have more than a little in common. For instance, both narrators, though they are constantly aware of the reader, deny any literary or artistic purpose and claim to be writing only for themselves. "I, however, am writing only for myself," asserts the man from underground, "and I declare once and for all that even if I write as if I were addressing readers, that is merely a form, because it's easier for me to write that way. It's a form, just an empty form, and I shall never have any readers. I have already declared as much..." The adolescent, Arkady Dolgoruky, begins his "notes" with the declaration that he is "not writing for the same reason everyone else writes, that is, for the sake of the reader's praises." Later he says:

> ...The reader will perhaps be horrified at the frankness of my confession and will ask himself simple-heartedly: how is it that the author doesn't blush? I reply that I'm not writing for publication; I'll probably have a reader only in some ten years, when everything is already so apparent, past and proven that there will no longer be any point in blushing. And therefore, if I sometimes address the reader in my notes, it's merely a device. My reader is a fantastic character.

Arkady also turns out to share some of the underground man's opinions, for instance about rational egoism and social progress. At a meeting of young radicals, he delivers a perfect "underground" tirade:

> Things are not at all clear in our society, gentlemen. I mean, you deny God, you deny great deeds, what sort of deaf, blind, dull torpor can make me act this way [i.e. nobly], if it's more profitable for me otherwise? You say, "A reasonable attitude towards mankind is also to my profit"; but what if I find all these reasonablenesses unreasonable, all these barracks and phalansteries? What the devil do I care about them, or about the future, when I live only once in this world? Allow me to know my own profit myself: it's more amusing. What do I care what happens to this mankind of yours in a thousand years, if, by your code, I get no love for it, no future life, no recognition of my great deed? No, sir, in that case I shall live for myself in the most impolite fashion, and they can all go to blazes!

The unaware reader would find it hard to tell which of the two is speaking.

But the differences between them are far more important. And the main difference is precisely Arkady's adolescence. The underground man is trapped in the endless alternation of "Long live the underground!" and "Devil take the underground!" and has sat in his corner like that for forty years. Arkady Dolgoruky is young, fresh, resilient. Time and again he falls asleep after some disastrous blunder or crushing humiliation, sleeps soundly and dreamlessly, and wakes up feeling heartier than ever. The underground man is inwardly fixed; Arkady is all inner movement, constantly going beyond himself. His experiences do not bind him as the underground man's do; they liberate him.

Why did Dostoevsky come to give such a privileged place

to adolescence in his work? A brief sketch jotted down in his notebook sometime in October or November of 1867, years before he began writing *The Adolescent*, may suggest an answer. Among plans that would later be realized, we find a heading all in capitals, "A THOUGHT (POEM) / THEME WITH THE TITLE: 'THE EMPEROR,'" followed by two pages of notes for a story based on the strange life of the Russian emperor Ivan VI, better known as Ivan Antonovich, who lived from 1740 to 1764. Ivan Antonovich was the son of Peter the Great's niece, the empress Anna Ivanovna. She died the year he was born, and he was immediately proclaimed emperor, but he never reigned. In 1741 Elizaveta Petrovna, the daughter of Peter the Great, seized the throne and had the one-year-old emperor imprisoned in the Schlüsselburg fortress, where he remained until 1764, when a certain Lieutenant Mirovich attempted to restore him to the throne by means of a coup. The plot failed, and Ivan Antonovich was killed.

As his notes make clear, what interested Dostoevsky was not so much the historical episode as the thought of this boy growing up in complete isolation from the world: "Underground, darkness, a young man not knowing how to speak, Ivan Antonovich, almost twenty years old. Description of his *nature.* His development. He develops by himself, fantastic frescoes and images, dreams, a young girl (in a dream). He imagines her, having seen her from the window. Elementary notions of all things. Extravagant imagination . . ." And then the catastrophic confrontation of this isolated consciousness with reality. Dostoevsky made only a few notes for the story and never came back to it, but in imagining the situation of Ivan Antonovich, he was preparing himself for the portrayal of Prince Myshkin, Alyosha Karamazov, and, above all, Arkady Dolgoruky.

In the notes, Mirovich "finally declares to [Ivan Antonovich] that he is the emperor, that everything is possible for him. Visions of power." "Everything is possible" – that is the link between Ivan Antonovich and the state of adolescence. "Visions of power" are certainly part of it in Arkady's case. He has his "Rothschild idea" of achieving power by accumulating money. He also has a document sewn into his coat which he believes gives him power over certain people who are central to his life. He even tells himself that the consciousness of power is enough, without the need to exercise it, and declaims, "enough for me / Is the awareness of it," quoting from Pushkin's *The Covetous Knight*. Further on he comments:

> They'll say it's stupid to live like that: why not have a mansion, an open house, gather society, exert influence, get married? But what would Rothschild be then? He'd become like everybody else. All the charm of the "idea" would vanish, all its moral force. As a child I had already learned by heart the monologue of Pushkin's covetous knight; Pushkin never produced a higher idea than that! I'm also of the same mind now.

Dostoevsky himself reread Pushkin's "little tragedy" during the summer of 1874, while staying at the German health spa of Ems and trying to start work on his new novel. "Please God only that I can begin the novel and draw up at least some plan," he wrote to his wife. "Beginning is already half the affair." But he read Pushkin instead and "grew intoxicated with ecstasy." Here, clearly, is the origin of Arkady's vision of power. And it is linked, through Pushkin, with the struggle between son and father. Mikhail Bakhtin notes in *Problems of Dostoevsky's Poetics* that, starting with *The Gambler* in 1866, *The Covetous Knight* "exercises a very fundamental influence on all of Dostoevsky's subsequent works, especially on *The Adolescent* and *The Brothers Karamazov*." The "Rothschild idea" is Arkady's underground. "My idea is – my corner," he says. "The whole goal of my 'idea' is – solitude... Yes, I've thirsted for power all my life, power and solitude." The formula is perfect and reveals the extent of Arkady's willed refusal of human communion. This refusal will be sorely tested in the course of the novel.

But if the phrase "everything is possible" suggests an abstract dream of power, it also describes adolescence in another way, as that state of uncertainty, ignorance, incompleteness, but also of richness and exuberance, in which everything is literally still possible. In fact, far more turns out to be possible than Arkady ever suspected. He keeps being astonished, keeps stumbling into situations he was unaware of, keeps speaking out of turn. This constant maladroitness sets the tone of the novel and also governs its events. This was the freshness and naïveté Dostoevsky was seeking, a sense of the world and the person being born at the same time.

Thus "adolescence" also determines the compositional method of the novel, which is characteristic of Dostoevsky's later work in general. Bakhtin was the first to define it clearly:

> The fundamental category in Dostoevsky's mode of artistic visualizing was not evolution, but *coexistence* and *interaction*. He saw and conceived his world primarily in terms of space, not time. Hence his deep affinity for the dramatic form. Dostoevsky strives to organize all available meaningful material, all material of reality, in one time-frame, in the form of a dramatic juxtaposition, and he strives to develop it extensively... For him, to get one's bearings on the world meant to conceive all its contents as simultaneous, and *to guess at their interrelationships in the cross-section of a single moment.*

The action of *The Adolescent* covers a period of some four months, but each of its three parts takes place in only three days: the 19th to 21st of September, the 15th to 17th of November, and "three fateful days" in December. Nothing takes shape over time; everything is already there and only waiting to be revealed. Arkady writes his notes a year after the start of events, and it is then that his real awakening occurs, as he says himself: "On finishing my notes and writing the last line, I suddenly felt that I had reeducated myself precisely through the process of recalling and writing down." In a notebook entry for 18 September 1874, Dostoevsky settled the problem of the lapse between the events and the time of writing. He had been considering a space of five years, but decided: "... better make it a year. In the tone of the narrative, the whole impact of a recent shock would still be apparent, and a good many things would still remain unclear, yet at the same time there would be this first line: 'A year, what a tremendous interval of time!' " All through the novel, Dostoevsky plays with fine humor on this "adolescent" sense of time, the double view of "what I was" and "what I am now," meaning "now that *so much* time has passed." The Russia of the 1870s thus appears as the sum of all the conflicts and contradictions that enter Arkady's consciousness in the space of those few days, as he comes to understand them, and insofar as he comes to understand them, a year later.

This simultaneity and juxtaposition of events in an extremely restricted time frame leads to a downplaying of the importance of the linear plot – the *fabula*, as he liked to call it – in Dostoevsky's novels. In *The Adolescent* the intrigue turns on the document sewn into Arkady's coat. It is melodramatic and highly improbable, and Dostoevsky exploits it to the last drop. But it is not what the novel is about.

Near the beginning of the first notebook for *The Adolescent*, Dostoevsky wrote and underlined: "*Disintegration is the principal visible idea of the novel.*" Later, after establishing a new plan, he returned to the same theme: "Title of the novel: 'Disorder.' The whole idea of the novel is to demonstrate that we have now general disorder, disorder everywhere and wherever you go, in society, in business, in guiding ideas (of which, for that very reason, there aren't any), in convictions (which, for the same reason, we don't have), in the disintegration of the family unit." Arkady Makarovich Dolgoruky is the illegitimate son of a bankrupt landowner by the name of Andrei Petrovich Versilov. He has been raised by foster parents and tutors, has seen his mother, a peasant woman from Versilov's estate, two or three times in his life and his father only once. His legal father, the peasant Makar Dolgoruky, he has never seen. On graduating from high school in Moscow, he goes to Petersburg, armed with his "Rothschild idea," to meet his family and above all to confront Versilov, whose love he longs for and of whose disgrace and wrongdoing he has all sorts of notions and even some evidence.

As father, husband, and lover, Versilov is the center of a complicated "accidental" family made up of his legitimate children by his deceased wife, his illegitimate children, Arkady and Liza, and their mother Sofya Andreevna, whom he lives with but cannot marry because her husband, Makar Dolgoruky, is still alive. There is also the so-called "aunt," Tatyana Pavlovna, who acts as a sort of fairy godmother to them all. Konstantin Mochulsky comments on the shift in emphasis from Dostoevsky's previous novel:

As in *Demons*, the action is concentrated around the hero, but the personality of Versilov is revealed differently than the personality of Stavrogin. The hero of *Demons* is connected with the other characters only ideologically; the personality of Versilov includes in itself the entire history of his family; *it is organically collective.** Stavrogin is the *ideological center* of the novel; Versilov is the *vital center.*

"The crisis of communion," as Mochulsky says, "is shown in that organic cell from which society grows – in the family." Within and around Versilov's accidental family, Dostoevsky juxtaposes all the "material of reality" in Russian society at that time. "The novel contains all the elements," he wrote in his notebook as early as September 1874, and he specifies:

The civilized and desperate, idle and skeptical higher intelligentsia – that's [Versilov].
Ancient Holy Russia – Makar's family.
What is holy, good about new Russia – the aunt.
A [great] family gone to seed – the young Prince (a skeptic, etc.)
High society – the funny and the abstractly ideal type.
The young generation – the [adolescent], all instinct, knows nothing.
Vasin – hopelessly ideal.
Lambert – flesh, matter, horror, etc.

If we add the swindler Stebelkov, the revolutionary populists (particularly the gentle suicide Kraft), and the young widow Akhmakov and her father, we will have a virtually complete list of the characters in *The Adolescent.* Together they make up an image of the general disorder, the "Russian chaos," that was Dostoevsky's main preoccupation in all his great novels.

Versilov is the "vital center" of the novel, and the essence of the disorder is reflected in him, but he is always Versilov as seen by his son, and thus he remains an elusive, mysterious, contradictory figure. Arkady's perception of him is constantly changing, going to extremes of condemnation and adoration, owing to his own ignorance and naïveté. But the contradictions are not only in Arkady's perception, but in Versilov himself. As Mochulsky observes: "Versilov the philosopher-deist and bearer of the idea of 'all-unity,' and Versilov shattered by two

* See note to p. xii.

loves – are one and the same man . . . Versilov suffers from all the infirmities of contemporary civilization: everything shifts, wavers, and doubles in his consciousness; ideas are ambiguous, truths – relative, faith – unbelief." By letting the adolescent do the talking, Dostoevsky is able to present two dramas at once: the drama of Versilov's life as the gradual revelation of the divided consciousness of his time, and the drama of Arkady's *coming to consciousness* of precisely that drama, in himself as well as in Versilov. Arkady calls it "breadth," as will Mitya Karamazov ("No, man is broad, even too broad, I would narrow him down. Devil knows even what to make of him, that's the thing!"). Olga Meerson, in her excellent study of *Dostoevsky's Taboos*, calls it "the many-storiedness of *any* human soul."

Dostoevsky has left us several portraits of liberal idealists from the generation of the 1840s – Ivan Ilyich Pralinsky in "A Nasty Anecdote," Stepan Trofimovich Verkhovensky in *Demons*, Pyotr Alexandrovich Miusov in *The Brothers Karamazov* – but the portrait of Versilov is by far the fullest, the most serious and searching. He was not invented out of nothing; among his prototypes were two of the most important figures of nineteenth-century Russian intellectual life: Alexander Herzen (1812–70) and Pyotr Yakovlevich Chaadaev (1794–1856). Herzen, the illegitimate son of a wealthy nobleman, attended Moscow University, where he joined a socialist circle and became an opponent of serfdom. He wrote several novels, was sent to internal exile for his views, and in 1847, having inherited a large fortune from his father, left Russia forever. The failure of the French revolution of 1848 disillusioned him with the West, and he lamented the death of Europe in a collection of letters entitled *From the Other Shore* (1850). Versilov shares his "nobleman's yearning" and his sorrow. Versilov also speaks with Arkady about a "high cultural type" that has developed only in Russia, calling it "the type of universal suffering for all" – a phrase that had been applied to Herzen by the critic Nikolai Strakhov. Versilov's "breadth" is also reminiscent of Herzen, who was both an aristocrat and a socialist, a defender of the workers and a connoisseur of beauty, an unbeliever but with a great nostalgia for Christianity, a permanent exile who repeatedly proclaimed his love of Russia.

The biographical parallels of Versilov and Chaadaev are even more striking, and in fact, during the earliest stages of his work on *The Adolescent*, Dostoevsky gave the name of Chaadaev to his protagonist. Chaadaev was a friend and slightly older contemporary of Pushkin's, a Guards officer of the high nobility, a handsome, intelligent, and spirited man, who took part in the Napoleonic campaigns of 1812 and the occupation of Paris, resigned his commission in 1821, and wandered in Europe before returning to Russia. In 1836, the publication of the first of his *Philosophical Letters Written to a Lady* (there were eight letters in all, written in French) caused an enormous scandal by its sharp criticism of Russia's backwardness and isolation among the nations of Europe, which he blamed partly on the Orthodox Church. The shock was so great that the emperor Nicholas I had Chaadaev declared mad, forbade the publication of the remaining letters, and kept their author under permanent surveillance until his death. But the *Letters* circulated in manuscript, and in 1862 the first three were published in Paris, where Dostoevsky bought and read them. Dostoevsky also knew Herzen's admiring portrait of Chaadaev in his book of reflections and reminiscences, *My Past and Thoughts* (1852–55). In *Dostoevsky and the Process of Literary Creation*, Jacques Catteau lists the convergent details of Chaadaev's and Versilov's biographies:

> Both are handsome and are pampered by women who admire them, protect them, and try to curb their prodigality. Both are inordinately proud, unconsciously egotistical, and of a wounding casualness. Both are remarkably intelligent and witty, profound and ironic. They have the same manners of the spoiled aristocrat, and the refined elegance of the dandy. They served in the same Guards regiment, haughtily refused to fight a duel, wandered for a long time in Europe, and underwent the fascination of Catholicism. Both fell in love with a whimsical and sick young girl... before becoming infatuated with a woman who reminds them of a world that is nobler and less empty than their own...

We might add that Chaadaev's *Philosophical Letters* are addressed to a lady, while Versilov is referred to ironically at one point as a "women's prophet." Versilov is a complex and original figure, not simply an amalgam of his prototypes, but he is one deeply rooted in the intellectual and spiritual life of the Russian intelligentsia.

The gradual emergence of Versilov in Arkady's consciousness is the overarching story of *The Adolescent.* It is varied by a number of inset stories, a technique that Dostoevsky would use even more extensively in *The Brothers Karamazov.* These are all spoken stories, each in a voice quite distinct from Arkady's written notes: the tragic story of the young student Olya told by her mother; the comic story of the big stone told by Arkady's landlord, Pyotr Ippolitovich; the three stories told by Makar Dolgoruky; and Versilov's account of his dream of the golden age and the last days of mankind. Coming from experiences very different from Arkady's, they form a counterpoint and something of a corrective to his "first person adolescent" point of view, as does the epilogue written by Arkady's former tutor, Nikolai Semyonovich.

Makar Dolgoruky, the wanderer, is himself an inset figure in the novel. He appeared suddenly and as if fully formed in Dostoevsky's early notes, and he also appears suddenly in Arkady's life, to die just as Arkady "resurrects." He is Dostoevsky's only full-length portrait of a Russian peasant, a slightly idealized figure out of the past of "Holy Russia," an image of peasant piety and strength, of mirth, and of spiritual beauty. In his notes, Dostoevsky worked especially on his voice, filling several pages with characteristic phrases and expressions, full of "scriptural sweetness" and cast in the half-chanting cadences of peasant speech. Makar Dolgoruky is the antithesis of Versilov. Arkady bears his name only by chance, but the old man becomes a spiritual father for him. After meeting him for the first time and talking with him only briefly, the adolescent bursts out feverishly: "I'm glad of you. Maybe I've been waiting for you a long time. I don't love any of them; they have no seemliness . . . I won't go after them, I don't know where I'll go, I'll go with you . . ." But later he makes the same declaration to Versilov, when the latter finally seems to welcome him as his son: " 'Now I have no need for dreams and reveries, now you are enough for me! I will follow you!' I said, giving myself to him with all my soul." Arkady stands between these two fathers, these embodiments of two very different Russias. He loses one and in the end saves the life of the other.

In the beginning, Arkady says of Versilov: "I absolutely had to find out the whole truth in the very shortest time, for I had come to judge this man." He learns in the course of the novel that it is very difficult to judge something as complex, as "many-storied," as another person, that what he – and we, too, of course – would have considered a moral failing may in fact be a higher kind of virtue. At one point, for instance, Versilov advises him: "My friend, always let a man lie a little – it's innocent. Even let him lie a lot. First, it will show your delicacy, and second, you'll also be allowed to lie in return – two enormous profits at once. *Que diable!* one must love one's neighbor!" The moral condemnation of lying is unexpectedly displaced by Christ's second commandment, and Versilov's ironic tone is only a cover for his sincerity. Again, Arkady thinks – as most of us do – that honesty implies speaking everything out, but when he asks Versilov to explain something during one of their conversations, Versilov demurs:

"In short, it's – one of those long stories that are very boring to begin, and it would be much better if we talked about other things, and still better if we were silent about other things."

"All you want to do is be silent."

"My friend, remember that to be silent is good, safe, and beautiful."

"Beautiful?"

"Of course. Silence is always beautiful, and a silent person is always more beautiful than one who talks."

These are dialogues of innocence and experience. The examples could be multiplied many times. Olga Meerson has shown that the question of speaking or keeping silent is of central importance in *The Adolescent.* Arkady learns to respect the silences of others. He finally comes to understand, as Meerson says, "that he *has no choice* but to keep silent about the scandalousness of this fallen world and of himself in it. The taboo on paying attention to this scandalousness is absolute because nobody imposes it on the character-narrator; he simply begins to perceive it as the only means for survival – moral, spiritual, psychological, or narrational." He learns the meaning of tactfulness, of attention, of not judging others; he learns the meaning of forgiveness. That is the beginning of his struggle for order in the disordered world around him.

When *The Adolescent* started to appear in *Notes of the Fatherland* in 1875, it caused considerable amazement. The journal, under the influence of the critic N. K. Mikhailovsky, had become the organ of the populists, who abandoned the extreme rationalism and negation of the nihilists of the 1860s and preached a "going to the land" and the communal values of the Russian peasantry. The editor of the journal at that time was the poet and publicist Nikolai Nekrasov, an old acquaintance of Dostoevsky's and his longtime ideological opponent. Dostoevsky's devastating attack on the nihilists in *Demons* (1871–72) had turned most of the radical intelligentsia against him. Though they may have had a lingering respect for him as the "prisoner of Omsk," who had served a ten-year term of hard labor and exile for his own "antigovernment" activities, they hardly expected to find him in their company. On the other hand, the publication of *The Adolescent* in such an extreme-left journal brought accusations of betrayal and opportunism from Dostoevsky's conservative friends, many of whom abandoned him. What explains this apparent switch of loyalties?

In April 1874, when Dostoevsky offered Mikhail Katkov, editor of *The Russian Messenger*, the plan for a new novel, Katkov turned it down. (Only later did Dostoevsky learn that Katkov already had a big novel coming in – Tolstoy's *Anna Karenina*, for which he was paying twice as much as Dostoevsky had asked.) Then, quite unexpectedly, Nekrasov came to him and offered to take the novel for *Notes of the Fatherland*. Dostoevsky's wife wrote in her memoirs: "My husband was very glad to renew friendly relations with Nekrasov, whose talent he rated very highly." Though she added that "Fyodor Mikhailovich could in no case give up his fundamental convictions." He remained somewhat skeptical of this sudden interest from his former enemies, and vowed that he "would not concede a line to their tendency," but in the end Nekrasov's enthusiastic response to the first parts won him over. "All night I sat and read, I was so captivated," the poet told him. "And what freshness, my dear fellow, what freshness you have! ... Such freshness no longer exists in our age, and not one writer has it." Thirty years before, Nekrasov had greeted Dostoevsky's first novel, *Poor Folk*, with the same enthusiasm and had been largely responsible for his initial success. This closing of the circle must have moved Dostoevsky deeply.

In fact, Nekrasov even has a certain presence in *The Adolescent*. The figure of Makar Dolgoruky is based in part on the description of the old peasant wanderer in Nekrasov's poem "Vlas," as Dostoevsky signals by having Versilov quote a line from it when he first describes Makar to Arkady. Dostoevsky had written an admiring article on "Vlas" in 1873, a year before he began work on the novel. But there is another more hidden presence. Towards the end of the tribute he wrote in 1877 on the occasion of Nekrasov's death, he speaks of a dark side to the poet's life, which he foretold in one of his earliest poems. And he quotes three stanzas describing the young provincial's arrival in the capital – "The lights of evening lighting up, / There was wind and soaking rain / ... on my shoulders a wretched sheepskin, / In my pocket fifteen groats" – and ending:

> No money, no rank, no family,
> Short of stature and funny looking,
> Forty years have passed since then –
> In my pocket I've got a million.

This was the adolescent poet's dream of power. "Money," Dostoevsky writes, "that was Nekrasov's demon! ... His was a thirst for a gloomy, sullen, segregated security with a view to dependence on no one." This soul that sympathized with all of suffering Russia also had its "Rothschild idea" and its underground – the same "breadth" that Arkady Dolgoruky was alarmed to discover not only in Versilov but in himself.

But there was something besides Nekrasov's invitation that drew Dostoevsky to *Notes of the Fatherland*. He was anxious not to lose touch with the younger generation, and saw that the shift in revolutionary ideology from nihilism to populism might allow for more inner movement in the youth of the seventies and offer a chance of reconciliation. In the last years of his life, Dostoevsky tried repeatedly to act as a mediator among the conflicting factions, generations, and classes in Russia, hoping that a restoration of communion might still be possible in that disintegrating world. That is the significance of Arkady's role in *The Adolescent*, and of his final attempt to become an "all-reconciler."

The tonal range of this high and serious comedy is remarkably broad, bordering at times on tragedy and at other times on farce. Dostoevsky was able to place himself unerringly in the mind and even the unconscious of a green nineteen-year-old and maintain his voice consistently. Arkady's leitmotif is the word "stupid" – the perfect adolescent word, repeated in countless variations: his fear of looking stupid, of saying something stupid, his judgments of the stupidity of other people, their stupid ideas, their stupid feelings, their stupid curtains. The play on "Dolgoruky" – the name of an ancient Russian princely family, while Arkady is not a prince but "simply Dolgoruky," and illegitimate at that – runs through the whole novel, coming to a hilarious climax in the police station. At the beginning of his notes, Arkady mentions that in Moscow he "lodged in the quarters of the unforgettable Nikolai Semyonovich." In the epilogue, Nikolai Semyonovich, who has read through the manuscript at Arkady's request, mockingly returns this rather pompous epithet to him: "And never, my unforgettable Arkady Makarovich, could you have employed your leisure time more usefully..." (Incidentally, he has just seen himself described as "something of a cold egoist, but unquestionably an intelligent man.")

The epilogue gives the crowning touch to this formal play. In it the "unforgettable" Nikolai Semyonovich, as requested, gives his reflections on Arkady's notes – that is, on Dostoevsky's novel, minus the epilogue. He comments on its themes – the present disorder, the longing for "seemliness," the lack of "beautiful finished forms" – and discusses the problems facing the contemporary Russian novelist (with allusions to both *War and Peace* and *Anna Karenina*). After a rather perceptive characterization of Versilov, he observes: "Yes, Arkady Makarovich, you are *a member of an accidental family*, as opposed to our still-recent hereditary types, who had a childhood and youth so different from yours. I confess, I would not wish to be a novelist whose hero comes from an accidental family! Thankless work and lacking in beautiful forms." Dostoevsky is, of course, precisely that novelist of the unfinished, the unfinalized, of possible exaggerations and oversights, who can only "guess... and be mistaken."

Richard Pevear

SELECT BIBLIOGRAPHY

MIKHAIL BAKHTIN, *Problems of Dostoevsky's Poetics*, edited and translated by Caryl Emerson, University of Minnesota Press, Minneapolis, 1985. The classic study of Dostoevsky's formal innovations and the place of his work in the traditions of Menippean satire and carnival humor.

JACQUES CATTEAU, *Dostoyevsky and the Process of Literary Creation*, tr. Audrey Littlewood, Cambridge University Press, Cambridge and New York, 1989. A translation of *La création littéraire chez Dostoïevski*, Institute d'Études Slaves, Paris, 1975. Contains seven central chapters on the composition of *The Adolescent.*

FYODOR DOSTOEVSKY, *Diary of a Writer*, tr. Kenneth Lantz, Northwestern University Press, Evanston, Ill., 1993. Dostoevsky's experiment in a new kind of journalism, written in the periods just preceding and following his work on *The Adolescent*, and often commenting directly or indirectly on the themes of the novel.

———, *The Notebooks for "A Raw Youth"* [*The Adolescent*], edited and introduced by Edward Wasiolek, tr. Victor Terras, University of Chicago Press, Chicago and London, 1969.

JOSEPH FRANK, *Dostoevsky: The Mantle of the Prophet, 1871–1881*, Princeton University Press, Princeton, N.J., 2002. The fifth and final volume of Frank's socio-cultural biography of Dostoevsky, covering the period of composition of *The Adolescent* and *The Brothers Karamazov.*

RENÉ GIRARD, *Deceit, Desire, and the Novel*, tr. Yvonne Freccero, Johns Hopkins University Press, Baltimore, 1990. A translation of *Mensonge romantique et vérité romanesque*, Grasset, Paris, 1961. Girard's major work on the novel, dealing mainly with Cervantes, Stendhal, Dostoevsky, and Proust.

———, *Resurrection from the Underground: Fedor Dostoevsky*, tr. James G. Williams, Crossroad, New York, 1997. A translation of *Dostoïevski, du double à l'unité* (Plon, Paris, 1963), especially interesting for its analysis of the erotic/mimetic aspects of Dostoevsky's work.

W. J. LEATHERBARROW, ed. *The Cambridge Companion to Dostoevsky*, Cambridge University Press, Cambridge and New York, 2002. A collection of essays by various hands dealing with Dostoevsky's works mainly in terms of their cultural context.

OLGA MEERSON, *Dostoevsky's Taboos*, Studies of the Harriman Institute,

Dresden University Press, Dresden-Munich, 1998. A penetrating study of the meta-psychology of tabooing and the meanings of the unsaid in Dostoevsky.

KONSTANTIN MOCHULSKY, *Dostoevsky, His Life and Work*, tr. Michael A. Minihan, Princeton University Press, Princeton, N.J., 1967. The work of a distinguished émigré scholar, first published in 1947 and still the best one-volume critical biography of Dostoevsky.

CHRONOLOGY

DATE	AUTHOR'S LIFE	LITERARY CONTEXT
1821	Born in Moscow.	
1823–31		Pushkin: *Evgeny Onegin.*
1825		
1830		Stendhal: *Le Rouge et le Noir.*
1833–7	At school in Moscow.	
1834	Family purchases estate of Darovoe.	Pushkin: *The Queen of Spades.*
1835		Balzac: *Le Père Goriot.*
1836		Gogol: *The Government Inspector.* Chaadaev: *Philosophical Letters.* Pushkin founds *The Contemporary.*
1837	Death of mother. Enters St. Petersburg Academy of Military Engineering.	Dickens: *Pickwick Papers.* Death of Pushkin in duel.
1839	Death of father, assumed murdered by serfs.	*Notes of the Fatherland* founded by Andrey Kraevsky. Stendhal: *La Chartreuse de Parme.*
1840		Lermontov: *A Hero of Our Time.*
1841		Death of Lermontov in duel.
1842		Gogol: *Dead Souls*, Part 1, and *The Overcoat.*
1844	Graduates, but resigns commission in order to pursue literary career.	
1845	Completes *Poor Folk* – acclaimed by the critic Belinsky.	
1846	Publication of *Poor Folk* and *The Double.*	
1847	Breaks with Belinsky. Joins Petrashevsky circle. "The Landlady", "A Novel in Nine Letters", "A Petersburg Chronicle".	Herzen: *Who Is to Blame?* Herzen leaves Russia. Goncharov: *An Ordinary Story.* Thackeray: *Vanity Fair* (to 1848).
1848	"A Faint Heart" and "White Nights".	Death of Belinsky.
1849	*Netochka Nezvanova.* Arrested and imprisoned in Peter and Paul Fortress. Mock execution. Sentenced to hard labor and Siberian exile.	Dickens: *David Copperfield* (to 1850).

Death of Alexander I and accession of Nicholas I. Decembrist revolt.
July revolution in France. Accession of Louis Philippe.

1840s and 1850s: Slavophile versus Westernizer debate among Russian intellectuals. Westernizers advocate progress by assimilating Western rationalism and civic freedom. Slavophiles assert spiritual superiority of Russia to the West and argue that future development should be based upon the traditions of the Orthodox Church and the peasant commune or *mir.*

Revolutions in Europe. *Communist Manifesto* published. Pan-Slav congress in Prague.
Russia invades Hungary.

DATE	AUTHOR'S LIFE	LITERARY CONTEXT
1850	Arrives at Omsk penal colony.	Turgenev: *A Month in the Country.* Herzen: *From the Other Shore.*
1851		
1852		Tolstoy: *Childhood.* Turgenev: *A Sportsman's Notebook.* Death of Gogol.
1853–6		
1854	Posted to Semipalatinsk.	
1855		
1856		Turgenev: *Rudin.* Aksakov: *A Family Chronicle.* Nekrasov: *Poems.*
1857	Marries Maria Dmitrievna Isaeva.	Flaubert: *Madame Bovary.* Baudelaire: *Les Fleurs du mal.*
1859	*The Friend of the Family.* Returns to St. Petersburg.	Turgenev: *A Nest of Gentlefolk.* Goncharov: *Oblomov.* Tolstoy: *Family Happiness.* Ostrovsky: *The Storm.* Darwin: *The Origin of Species.*
1860	Starts publication of *House of the Dead.*	Turgenev: *On the Eve, First Love.* George Eliot: *The Mill on the Floss.* Birth of Chekhov. Dickens: *Great Expectations* (to 1861).
1861	*Time* commences publication. *The Insulted and Injured.*	Herzen: *My Past and Thoughts* (to 1867).
1862	Travels in Europe. Affair with Polina Suslova.	Turgenev: *Fathers and Children.* Hugo: *Les Misérables.* Chernyshevsky arrested.
1863	Further travel abroad. *Time* closed. *Winter Notes on Summer Impressions.*	Tolstoy: *The Cossacks.* Chernyshevsky: *What Is to Be Done?*
1864	Launch of *The Epoch.* Death of wife and brother. *Notes from Underground.*	Nekrasov: *Who Can Be Happy and Free in Russia?* (to 1876). Dickens: *Our Mutual Friend* (to 1865).
1865	*The Epoch* closes. Severe financial difficulties.	Leskov: *Lady Macbeth of the Mtsensk District.*
1865–9		Tolstoy: *War and Peace.*
1866	*Crime and Punishment.* *The Gambler.*	*The Contemporary* and *The Russian Word* suppressed.
1867	Marries Anna Grigoryevna Snitkina. Flees abroad to escape creditors.	Turgenev: *Smoke.*

CHRONOLOGY

HISTORICAL EVENTS

World Exhibition at Crystal Palace, London. St. Petersburg–Moscow railway opens.
Louis Napoleon proclaimed Emperor of France.

Crimean War.

Death of Nicholas I. Accession of Alexander II.

Indian Mutiny: siege and relief of Lucknow.

Garibaldi captures Naples and Sicily.

Emancipation of serfs. Outbreak of American Civil War. Victor Emmanuel first king of Italy.
Bismarck becomes chief minister of Prussia.

Polish uprising.

The first International founded in London. Establishment of the Zemstva, organs of rural self-government and a significant liberal influence in Tsarist Russia.

Attempted assassination of Alexander II.

DATE	AUTHOR'S LIFE	LITERARY CONTEXT
1868	*The Idiot.* Birth and death of daughter, Sonya. Visits Switzerland and Italy.	Gorky born.
1869	Birth of daughter Liubov.	Goncharov: *The Precipice.* Flaubert: *L'Education sentimentale.*
1870	*The Eternal Husband.*	Death of Dickens and Herzen.
1871	Returns to St. Petersburg. Birth of son, Fyodor.	Ostrovsky: *The Forest.*
1871–2	*Demons (The Devils/The Possessed).*	
1872	Summer in Staraiâ Russa – becomes normal summer residence. Becomes editor of *The Citizen.*	Leskov: *Cathedral Folk.* Marx's *Das Kapital* published in Russia. George Eliot: *Middlemarch.*
1873	Starts *Diary of a Writer.*	
1874	Resigns from *The Citizen.* Seeks treatment for emphysema in Bad Ems.	
1875	*The Adolescent (A Raw Youth).* Birth of son, Alexey.	Saltykov-Shchedrin: *The Golovlyovs* (to 1880).
1875–8		Tolstoy: *Anna Karenina.*
1876		
1877		Turgenev: *Virgin Soil.*
1878	Death of Alexey. Visits Optina monastery with Vladimir Solovyov.	
1879		
1879–80	*The Brothers Karamazov.*	Tolstoy's religious crisis, during which he writes *A Confession.*
1880	Speech at Pushkin celebrations in Moscow.	Death of Flaubert and George Eliot.
1881	Dies of lung hemorrhage. Buried at Alexander Nevsky Monastery, St. Petersburg.	James: *The Portrait of a Lady.*

CHRONOLOGY

HISTORICAL EVENTS

Franco-Prussian War. Birth of V. I. Ulyanov (Lenin).

German Empire inaugurated. Capitulation of France. Defeat of Paris Commune.

Student unrest in Russian countryside.

New republican constitution passed in France.

Founding of Land and Freedom, first Russian political party openly to advocate revolution.
Russo-Turkish War (to 1878).
Mass trial of Populist agitators ("Trial of the 193").

Birth of Stalin. The People's Will, terrorist offshoot of Land and Freedom, founded.

Assassination of Alexander II. Accession of Alexander III. Severe repression of revolutionary groups. Reactionary ministers replace reformers.

TRANSLATORS' NOTES

LIST OF PRINCIPAL CHARACTERS

Russian names are composed of first name, patronymic (from the father's first name), and family name. Formal address requires the use of first name and patronymic; diminutives (Arkasha, Lizochka, Sonya) are commonly used among family and intimate friends. The following is a list of the principal characters in *The Adolescent*, with diminutives and epithets. In Russian pronunciation, the stressed vowel is always long and unstressed vowels are very short.

Dolgorúky, Arkády Makárovich (Arkásha, Arkáshenka, Arkáshka): the adolescent, "author" of the novel.

______, Makár Ivánovich: his legal father.

______, Sófya Andréevna (Sónya, Sophie): his mother.

______, Lizavéta Makárovna (Líza, Lízochka, Lizók): his sister.

Versílov, Andréi Petróvich: natural father of Arkady and Liza.

______, Ánna Andréevna: Versilov's daughter by his first marriage.

______, Andréi Andréevich: the kammerjunker, Versilov's son by his first marriage.

Akhmákov, Katerína Nikoláevna (Kátya): young widow of General Akhmakov.

______, Lýdia (no patronymic): her stepdaughter.

Sokólsky, Prince Nikolái Ivánovich: the old prince, Mme. Akhmakov's father.

Prutkóv, Tatyána Pávlovna: the "aunt," friend of the Versilov family.

Sokólsky, Prince Sergéi Petróvich (Seryózha): the young prince, no relation to Prince Nikolai Ivanovich.

Lambért, Mauríce: schoolfriend of Arkady's, a Frenchman.

Verdáigne, Alphonsíne de (Alphonsina, Alphonsinka): Lambert's girlfriend.

Dárya Onísimovna (no family name; her name changes to

Nastásya Egórovna in Part Three): mother of the young suicide Ólya (diminutive of Ólga).

Vásin, Grísha (diminutive of Grigóry; no patronymic): friend of Arkady's.

Stebelkóv (no first name or patronymic): Vasin's stepfather.

Pyótr Ippolítovich (no last name): Arkady's landlord.

Nikolái Semyónovich (no last name): Arkady's tutor in Moscow.

______, Márya Ivánovna: Nikolai Semyonovich's wife.

Trishátov, Pétya [i.e., Pyótr] (no patronymic): the pretty boy.

Andréev, Nikolái Semyónovich: *le grand dadais.*

Semyón Sídorovich (Sídorych; no last name): the pockmarked one.

A NOTE ON THE TOPOGRAPHY OF ST. PETERSBURG

The city was founded in 1703 by a decree of the emperor Peter the Great and built on the delta of the river Neva, which divides into three main branches – the Big Neva, the Little Neva, and the Nevka – as it flows into the Gulf of Finland. On the left bank of the Neva is the city center, where the Winter Palace, the Senate, the Admiralty, the Summer Garden, the theaters, and the main thoroughfares such as Nevsky Prospect, Bolshaya Millionnaya, and Bolshaya Morskaya are located. On the right bank of the Neva before it divides is the area known as the Vyborg side; the right bank between the Nevka and the Little Neva is known as the Petersburg side, where the Peter and Paul Fortress, the oldest structure of the city, stands; between the Little Neva and the Big Neva is Vassilievsky Island. To the south, some fifteen miles from the city, is the suburb of Tsarskoe Selo, where the empress Catherine the Great built an imposing palace and many of the gentry had summer houses.

THE ADOLESCENT

PART ONE

Chapter One

I

Unable to restrain myself, I have sat down to record this history of my first steps on life's career, though I could have done as well without it. One thing I know for certain: never again will I sit down to write my autobiography, even if I live to be a hundred. You have to be all too basely in love with yourself to write about yourself without shame. My only excuse is that I'm not writing for the same reason everyone else writes, that is, for the sake of the reader's praises. If I have suddenly decided to record word for word all that has happened to me since last year, then I have decided it as the result of an inner need: so struck I am by everything that has happened. I am recording only the events, avoiding with all my might everything extraneous, and above all—literary beauties. A literary man writes for thirty years and in the end doesn't know at all why he has written for so many years. I am not a literary man, do not want to be a literary man, and would consider it base and indecent to drag the insides of my soul and a beautiful description of my feelings to their literary marketplace. I anticipate with vexation, however, that it seems impossible to do entirely without the description of feelings and without reflections (maybe even banal ones): so corrupting is the effect of any literary occupation on a man, even if it is undertaken only for oneself. The reflections may even be very banal, because something you value yourself will quite possibly have no value in a stranger's eyes. But this is all an aside. Anyhow, here is my preface; there won't be anything more of its kind. To business; though there's nothing trickier than getting down to some sort of business—maybe even any sort.

II

I begin, that is, I would like to begin my notes from the nineteenth of September last year, that is, exactly from the day when I first met...

But to explain whom I met just like that, beforehand, when nobody knows anything, would be banal; I suppose even the tone is banal: having promised myself to avoid literary beauties, I fall into those beauties with the first line. Besides, in order to write sensibly, it seems the wish alone is not enough. I will also observe that it seems no European language is so difficult to write in as Russian. I have now reread what I've just written, and I see that I'm much more intelligent than what I've written. How does it come about that what an intelligent man expresses is much stupider than what remains inside him? I've noticed that about myself more than once in my verbal relations with people during this last fateful year and have suffered much from it.

Though I'm starting with the nineteenth of September, I'll still put in a word or two about who I am, where I was before then, and therefore also what might have been in my head, at least partly, on that morning of the nineteenth of September, so that it will be more understandable to the reader, and maybe to me as well.

III

I AM A HIGH-SCHOOL graduate, and am now going on twenty-one. My last name is Dolgoruky, and my legal father is Makar Ivanovich Dolgoruky,[1] a former household serf of the Versilov family. Thus I'm a legitimate, though in the highest degree illegitimate, son, and my origin is not subject to the slightest doubt. It happened like this: twenty-two years ago, the landowner Versilov (it's he who is my father), twenty-five years of age, visited his estate in Tula province. I suppose at that time he was still something rather faceless. It's curious that this man, who impressed me so much ever since my childhood, who had such a capital influence on my entire cast of mind and has maybe even infected my whole future with himself for a long time to come—this man even now remains in a great many ways a complete riddle to me. But of that, essentially, later. You can't tell it like that. My whole notebook will be filled with this man as it is.

He had become a widower just at that time, that is, in the twenty-fifth year of his life. He had married someone from high society, but not that rich, named Fanariotov, and had had a son and a daughter by her. My information about this spouse who abandoned him so early is rather incomplete and lost among my materials; then, too, much about the private circumstances of Versilov's life has escaped me, so proud he always was with me, so haughty, closed, and negligent, despite his moments of striking humility, as it were, before me. I mention, however, so as to mark it for the future, that he ran through three fortunes in his life, even quite big ones, some four hundred thousand in all, and maybe more. Now, naturally, he hasn't got a kopeck...

He came to the country then, "God knows why"—at least that was how he put it to me later. His little children were, as usual, not with him but with some relations; that was what he did with his children, legitimate and illegitimate, all his life. There was a significant number of household serfs on this estate; among them was the gardener Makar Ivanovich Dolgoruky. I will add here, to be rid of it once and for all: rarely can anyone have been so thoroughly angered by his last name as I was throughout my whole life. That was stupid, of course, but it was so. Each time I entered some school or met persons to whom I owed an accounting because of my age, in short, every little teacher, tutor, inspector, priest, anybody you like, they would ask my last name and, on hearing that I was Dolgoruky, would inevitably find it somehow necessary to add:

"Prince Dolgoruky?"

And each time I was obliged to explain to all these idle people: "No, *simply* Dolgoruky."

This *simply* began, finally, to drive me out of my mind. I will note with that, as a phenomenon, that I do not recall a single exception: everybody asked. Some of them seemingly had no need at all to ask; who the devil could have had any need of it, I'd like to know? But everybody asked, everybody to a man. Hearing that I was *simply* Dolgoruky, the asker ordinarily measured me with a dull and stupidly indifferent look, indicating thereby that he did not know himself why he had asked, and walked away. My schoolmates were the most insulting. How does a schoolboy question a newcomer? A lost and abashed newcomer, on the first day he enters school (no matter what kind), is a common victim: he is ordered around, he is teased, he is treated like a lackey. Some hale and fat boy suddenly stops right in front of his victim and looks at him point-blank for several moments with a long, stern, and arrogant gaze. The newcomer stands silently before him, looks askance, if he's not a coward, and waits for whatever is coming.

"What's your last name?"

"Dolgoruky."

"Prince Dolgoruky?"

"No, simply Dolgoruky."

"Ah, simply! Fool!"

And he's right; there is nothing stupider than to be called Dolgoruky without being a prince. I drag this stupidity around on my back without any guilt. Later on, when I began to get very angry, to the question "Are you a prince?" I always answered, "No, I'm the son of a household servant, a former serf."

Then, when I got angry in the last degree, to the question "Are you a prince?" I once answered firmly, "No, simply Dolgoruky, the illegitimate son of my former master, Mr. Versilov."

I had already thought that up when I was in the sixth class[2] in high school, and though I quickly became convinced beyond doubt that it was stupid, all the same I did not stop being stupid at once. I remember that one of my teachers—though he was the only one—found me "full of a vengeful and civic idea." Generally they took this escapade with a sort of offensive thoughtfulness. Finally, one of my classmates, a very sarcastic fellow, with whom I spoke only once a year, said to me with a serious air, but looking somewhat askance:

"Such feelings, of course, do you honor, and you undoubtedly have something to be proud of; but all the same, if I were in your place, I wouldn't celebrate my illegitimacy so much . . . you sound like a birthday boy!"

Since then I stopped *boasting* that I was illegitimate.

I repeat, it's very difficult to write in Russian: here I've scribbled a whole three pages on how I've spent all my life being angry over my last name, and meanwhile the reader has surely concluded that I'm angry precisely because I'm not a prince, but simply Dolgoruky. To explain again and justify myself would be humiliating for me.

IV

And so, among this household, of whom there were a great many besides Makar Ivanovich, there was a girl, and she was already about eighteen years old when the fifty-year-old Makar Dolgoruky suddenly showed the intention of marrying her. Marriages between domestics, as is known, were concluded in the time of serfdom with the permission of the masters, and sometimes even on their orders. There was an aunt about the estate then; that is, she wasn't my aunt, she was a landowner herself; yet, I don't know why, but all her life everybody called her aunt, not only mine, but in general, in Versilov's family as well, to which she was in fact almost related. This was Tatyana Pavlovna Prutkov. At that time she still had thirty-five souls of her own, in the same province and the same district. She didn't really manage Versilov's estate (of five hundred souls), but supervised it in a neighborly way, and that supervision, as I heard, was worth the supervision of some educated manager. However, I really don't care about her knowledge; I only want to add, setting aside all thought of flattery and fawning, that this Tatyana Pavlovna is a noble and even original being.

Now, she not only did not decline the marital inclinations of the gloomy Makar Dolgoruky (they say he was gloomy then), but, on the contrary, for some reason encouraged them in the highest degree. Sofya Andreevna (the eighteen-year-old serf girl, that is, my mother) had been an orphan for several years already; her deceased father, also a household serf, who had an extraordinary respect for Makar Dolgoruky and was obliged to him for something, as he was dying six years earlier, on his deathbed, they say even a quarter of an hour before his last breath, so that if need be it could have been taken for delirium, had he not been legally disqualified anyway as a serf, summoned Makar Dolgoruky, in front of all the servants and with a priest present, and spoke his will to him loudly and insistently, pointing to his daughter: "Bring her up and take her to wife." Everybody heard it. As for Makar Ivanovich, I don't know in what sense he later married her, that is, with great pleasure or only to fulfill his responsibility. Most likely he had an air of total indifference. This was a man who even then already knew how to "show himself." He was not exactly a Bible reader or literate man (though he knew the whole church service and especially the lives of certain saints, but more from hearsay), nor exactly a sort of household reasoner, so to speak; he simply had a stubborn character, sometimes even recklessly so; he spoke with pretension, judged irrevocably, and, in conclusion, "lived deferentially"—in his own amazing expression. That is how he was then. Of course, he achieved universal respect, but they say everyone found him unbearable. It was quite a different matter when he left the household: then people never referred to him otherwise than as some sort of saint and great sufferer. That I know for certain.

As for my mother's character, Tatyana Pavlovna kept her around herself until she was eighteen, despite the steward's urgings to send her to Moscow for an apprenticeship, and she gave her some education, that is, taught her to cut and sew, to walk in a ladylike way, and even to read a little. My mother never could write passably. In her eyes this marriage to Makar Ivanovich had long been a decided thing, and she found all that happened to her then excellent and the very best; she went to the altar with the calmest air possible on such an occasion, so that Tatyana Pavlovna herself called her a fish then. All this about my mother's character at that time I heard from Tatyana Pavlovna herself. Versilov came to the estate exactly six months after the wedding.

V

I ONLY WANT to say that I never could find out or make a satisfactory surmise as to precisely how it started between him and my mother. I'm fully prepared to believe, as he assured me himself last year, with a blush on his face, even though he told about it all with a most unconstrained and "witty" air, that there was not the least romance, and that it all happened *just so.* I believe it was just so, and that little phrase *just so* is charming, but still I always wanted to find out precisely how it came about with them. I myself have hated all this vileness all my life and hate it still. Of course, here it's by no means only shameless curiosity on my part. I will note that until last year I hardly knew my mother; from my infancy I had been handed over to other people, for Versilov's comfort, but of that later; and therefore I'm quite unable to imagine what her face could have been like at that time. If she was not really so good-looking, then what in her could have attracted such a man as Versilov was at that time? This question is important for me in that it highlights the man from an extremely curious side. That is why I ask it, and not out of depravity. He himself, this gloomy and closed man, with that sweet simpleheartedness he took from devil knows where (as if out of his pocket) when he saw it was necessary—he himself told me that he was quite a "silly young pup" then, not that he was sentimental, but *just so*, he had recently read *Anton the Wretch* and *Polinka Sachs*[3]—two literary works that had a boundless civilizing influence on our then rising generation. He added that it was perhaps because of *Anton the Wretch* that he had come to the estate then—and he added it extremely seriously. What form could the beginning between this "silly pup" and my mother have taken? It has just occurred to me that if I had at least one reader, he would probably burst out laughing at me, as at a most ridiculous adolescent who, having preserved his stupid innocence, barges with his reasonings and solutions into things he doesn't understand. Yes, indeed, I still don't understand, though I confess it not at all out of pride, because I know how stupid this inexperience at the age of twenty can be; only I will tell the gentleman that he himself does not understand, and I will prove it to him. True, I know nothing about women, and I don't want to know, because I'll spit on that all my life and I've given my word. But nevertheless I know for certain that one woman attracts you by her beauty, or whatever it is, from the first moment; another you have to chew over for half a year before you understand what's in her; and to make her out and fall in love with her, it's not enough to look and simply be ready for anything, on top of that you have to be somehow gifted. I'm convinced of that, even though I know nothing, and if it were otherwise, then all women would have to be reduced at once to the level of simple domestic animals and kept around only in that guise. Maybe a lot of people would like that.

I know positively from several hands that my mother was not a beauty, though I haven't seen her portrait from that time, which exists somewhere. That means it was impossible to fall in love with her at first sight. For mere "amusement," Versilov could have chosen another girl, and there was one like that, and unmarried besides, Anfisa Konstantinovna Sapozhkov, a house maid. And a man who arrived with *Anton the Wretch* and, on the basis of his rights as a landowner, violated the sacredness of marriage, even though it was of his household serf, would be very ashamed in his own eyes, because, I repeat, no more than a few months ago, that is, twenty years later, he spoke extremely seriously of this *Anton the Wretch*. Yet Anton only had a horse taken from him, and here it's a wife! It means something very peculiar happened, and that was why Mlle. Sapozhkov lost (or won, in my opinion). I bothered him with all these questions a couple of times last year, when it was possible to talk with him (because it was not always possible to talk with him), and I noticed that, despite all his worldliness and the space of twenty years, he somehow made an extremely wry face. But I insisted. At least I remember him once murmuring somehow strangely, with that air of worldly squeamishness he repeatedly allowed himself with me, that my mother was a person of the *defenseless* sort, whom you don't really fall in love with—on the contrary, not at all—but for some reason suddenly *fall to pitying*, for their meekness, is it, or for what, anyhow? No one ever knows, but you go on pitying for a long time; you pity and grow attached... "In short, my dear, it sometimes so happens that you cannot even rid yourself of it." That's what he told me; and if it really was so, then I'm forced to regard him as less of a stupid pup at that time than he gives himself out to have been. And that was just what I needed.

Anyhow, he started assuring me then that my mother fell in love with him out of "lowliness": he might just as well have said out of serfdom! He lied in order to show off, lied against conscience, against honor and nobility!

I've said all this, of course, in some sort of praise of my mother, and yet I've already stated that I knew nothing about how she was then. Moreover, I precisely know all the imperviousness of that milieu and of those pathetic notions in which she had hardened since childhood and in which she remained afterwards for the rest of her life. Nevertheless, the harm was done. Incidentally, I must correct myself: having soared into the clouds, I forgot about the fact which, on the contrary, ought to have been put forward first of all—namely, that it started between them directly with the *harm*. (I hope the reader will not put on airs to the extent of not understanding at once what I mean to say.) In short, it started between them precisely in a landowner's way, even though Mlle. Sapozhkov was bypassed. But here I'll step in and state beforehand that I am by no means contradicting myself. For what, O Lord, what could a man like Versilov possibly have talked about at that time with a person like my mother, even in the event of the most irresistible love? I've heard from depraved people that very often, when a man comes together with a woman, he starts in complete silence, which, of course, is the height of monstrosity and nausea; nevertheless, Versilov, even if he had wanted to, would have been unable to start in any other way with my mother. Could he have started by explaining *Polinka Sachs* to her? And moreover, they couldn't be bothered with Russian literature; on the contrary, according to his own words (he got carried away once), they hid in the corners, waited for each other on stairways, bounced away from each other like rubber balls, red-faced, if somebody passed by, and the "tyrant landowner" trembled before the least washer-woman, despite all his serf-owning rights. But though it started in a landowner's way, it turned out to be not quite so, and, essentially, it's still impossible to explain anything. There's even more darkness. The sheer dimensions to which their love developed already constitute a riddle, because the first condition of men like Versilov is to drop the girl immediately once the goal is achieved. That, however, is not how it turned out. For a depraved "young pup" (and they were all depraved, all of them to a man—both progressives and retrogrades) to sin with a pretty, flirtatious serving girl (and my mother was not flirtatious) was not only possible but inevitable, especially considering his novelistic status as a young widower, and his idleness. But to fall in love for one's whole life—that is too much. I can't guarantee that he loved her, but that he dragged her with him all his life is quite true.

I've posed many questions, but there is one most important question which, I'll note, I've never dared to ask my mother directly, though I've become quite close to her over the last year and, moreover, as a crude and ungrateful pup who finds them *guilty before him*, have been quite unceremonious with her. The question is the following: How could she, she herself, already married for half a year, and crushed, too, by all the notions of the legitimacy of marriage, crushed like a strengthless fly, she, who respected her Makar Ivanovich as nothing less than some sort of God, how could she, in a matter of two weeks, go so far as such a sin? For my mother wasn't a depraved woman, was she? On the contrary, I'll say now beforehand, that it is even difficult to imagine anyone being purer in soul, and that for all her life afterwards. The only possible explanation is that she did it unawares, that is, not in the sense that lawyers now affirm about their murderers and thieves, but under that strong impression which, given a certain simpleheartedness in the victim, takes over fatally and tragically. Who knows, maybe she fell desperately in love... with the fashion of his clothes, with the Parisian parting of his hair, with his French talk, precisely French, of which she understood not a sound, that romance he sang at the piano, fell in love with something she had never seen or heard before (and he was very handsome), and at the same time fell in love, to the point of prostration, with all of him, with all his fashions and romances. I've heard that that sometimes happened with serving girls in the time of serfdom, and with the most honest of them. I understand that, and he's a scoundrel who explains it by serfdom and "lowliness" alone! And so it means that this young man could have enough of that direct and seductive power in him to attract a being hitherto so pure and, above all, a being so completely different from himself, from a totally different world and different land, and to such obvious ruin? That it was to ruin—that I hope my mother has always understood; only when she went to it, she wasn't thinking of ruin at all; but it's always like that with these "defenseless" ones: they know it's ruin, and yet they get into it.

Having sinned, they immediately confessed. He wittily recounted to me how he had sobbed on Makar Ivanovich's shoulder, summoning him to his study on purpose for the occasion, and she—at the time she was lying unconscious somewhere in her maid's closet...

VI

BUT ENOUGH OF questions and scandalous details. Versilov, having bought out my mother from Makar Ivanovich, soon left, and since then, as I have already written above, began dragging her with him almost everywhere, except on those occasions when he was away for a long time; then he most often left her in the custody of the aunt, that is, Tatyana Pavlovna Prutkov, who always turned up from somewhere on such occasions. They lived in Moscow, lived in various other villages and cities, even abroad, and finally in Petersburg. Of all that later, if it's worth it. I'll say only that a year after Makar Ivanovich, I came into the world, then a year later my sister, and then, ten or eleven years later—a sickly boy, my younger brother, who died after a few months. The painful delivery of this child put an end to my mother's beauty, or so at least I was told: she quickly began to age and weaken.

But, all the same, connections with Makar Ivanovich were never broken off. Wherever the Versilovs were, whether they lived in one place for several years or moved about, Makar Ivanovich never failed to inform "the family" of himself. Some sort of strange relations took shape, somewhat solemn and almost serious. Among the gentry, something comical would inevitably have mixed into such relations, I know that; but here it didn't happen. Letters were sent twice a year, neither more nor less, and they were extremely like one another. I've seen them; there was little of anything personal in them; on the contrary, they contained, as far as possible, only solemn news about the most general events and the most general feelings, if one can say that about feelings: news of his own health first of all, then questions about health, then good wishes, solemn regards and blessings—that's all. This generality and impersonality seem precisely to constitute all the propriety of tone and all the highest knowledge of behavior in that milieu. "To my dearly beloved and esteemed spouse Sofya Andreevna I send my humblest salutations..." "To our beloved children I send my eternally steadfast parental blessing." The children would all be listed by name, as they accumulated, and I was there, too. I will note in this regard that Makar Ivanovich was clever enough never to refer to "his honor the most esteemed master Andrei Petrovich" as his "benefactor," though he invariably sent his humblest salutations, asking for his good favor and for God's blessing upon him. Replies were quickly sent to Makar Ivanovich by my mother, and were always written in exactly the same vein. Versilov, naturally, did not participate in this correspondence. Makar Ivanovich wrote from various ends of Russia, from towns and monasteries, in which he sometimes stayed for long stretches of time. He became what's known as a wanderer. He never asked for anything; on the other hand, about once every three years he unfailingly came home for a while and stayed right at my mother's, who, as always happened, had her own apartment separate from Versilov's apartment. I'll have to speak about that later, but here I'll only note that Makar Ivanovich did not sprawl on a sofa in the drawing room, but modestly settled somewhere behind a partition. He never stayed long—five days, a week.

I forgot to say that he was terribly fond and respectful of his last name, "Dolgoruky." Naturally, that was ridiculously stupid. The stupidest thing was that he liked his last name precisely because there were princes named Dolgoruky. An odd notion, completely upside down.

If I said the whole family was always together, that was without me, naturally. I was like an outcast and had been placed with other people almost from birth. But there was no special intention here, it simply turned out that way for some reason. When my mother gave birth to me, she was still young and beautiful, and that meant he needed her, and a howling baby would naturally have been a hindrance to everything, especially when traveling. That's why it happened that until I was twenty I saw almost nothing of my mother, except for two or three fleeting occasions. It came about not from my mother's feelings, but from Versilov's contempt for people.

VII

NOW ABOUT SOMETHING quite different.

A month earlier, that is, a month before the nineteenth of September, in Moscow, I decided to renounce them all and go into my own idea for good. I set it down like that: "go into my own idea," because this expression may signify almost my whole main thought—what I live for in the world. Of what this "my own idea" is, all too much will be said later. In the solitary dreaming of my many years of Moscow life, it took shape in me, from the sixth class of high school on, and since then has perhaps not left me for a moment. It swallowed up my whole life. I lived in dreams even before that, lived ever since childhood in a dreamlike realm of a certain hue; but with the appearance of this main idea that swallowed up everything in me, my dreams consolidated and all at once molded themselves into a certain form; from stupid they became reasonable. School did not interfere with dreams; nor did it interfere with the idea. I'll add, however, that I did poorly in the last year, whereas up to the seventh grade I had always been one of the first, and it happened owing to the same idea, owing to a conclusion, maybe a false one, that I drew from it. So it was not school that interfered with the idea, but the idea that interfered with school. It also interfered with the university. Having finished high school, I immediately intended not only to break radically with everyone, but, if need be, even with the whole world, though I was then only nineteen. I wrote to those I had to, through those I had to, in Petersburg, saying they should leave me in peace for good, not send me any more money for my keep, and, if possible, forget me entirely (that is, naturally, in case they remembered me at all), and finally—that I wouldn't go to the university, "not for anything." I was faced with an irrefutable dilemma: either the university and further education, or postpone putting the "idea" to work for another four years; I stood intrepidly for the idea, for I was mathematically convinced. Versilov, my father, whom I had seen only once in my life, for a moment, when I was only ten years old (and who in that one moment had managed to impress me), Versilov, in answer to my letter, which, incidentally, was not sent to him, summoned me to Petersburg himself in a letter written with his own hand, promising me a private post. This summons from a dry and proud man, contemptuous and negligent in my regard, who until now, having produced me and thrown me among strangers, not only did not know me at all, but never even repented of it (who knows, maybe he had a vague and imprecise notion of my very existence, because it turned out later that it was not he who paid for my upkeep in Moscow but others), a summons from this man, I say, who so suddenly remembered me and deigned to write to me in his own hand—this summons enticed me and decided my fate. Strangely, one of the things I liked in his little letter (one small page of small format) was that he didn't say a word about the university, did not ask me to alter my decision, did not reproach me for not wanting to study, in short, did not produce any parental folderol of that sort, as usually happens, and yet that was precisely bad on his part, in the sense that it testified still more to his negligence about me. I also decided to go because it didn't interfere in the least with my main dream: "I'll see what comes of it," I reasoned, "in any case, I'll be connected with him only for a time, maybe a very short time. But the moment I see that this step, even if it's conditional and small, still moves me further away from the *main thing*, I'll immediately break with them, drop everything, and withdraw into my shell." Precisely into a shell! "I'll hide in it like a turtle"—the comparison pleased me very much. "I won't be alone," I went on calculating, going around in a fuddle all those last days in Moscow, "I'll never be alone now as I was for all those terrible years before: I'll have my idea with me, which I'll never betray, even in the event that I like them all there, and they give me happiness, and I live with them for ten years!" It was this impression, I'll note beforehand, it was precisely this doubleness of my plans and aims, that was already determined in Moscow and that never left me for a moment in Petersburg (for I don't know if there was a single day in Petersburg that I didn't set up as my final date for breaking with them and going away)—this doubleness, I say, was also, it seems, one of the main reasons for my many imprudences committed that year, many abominations, even many low acts and, naturally, stupid ones.

Of course, a father had suddenly appeared, whom I had never had before. This thought intoxicated me both while I was packing in Moscow and on the train. The fact of a father was nothing, and I disliked tender feelings, but this man did not want to know me and humiliated me, while all those years I had dreamed long and hard of him (if one can say that about dreaming). Each of my dreams since childhood had echoed with him, had hovered around him, had in the final result come down to him. I don't know whether I hated or loved him, but he filled all my future, all my reckoning in life, with himself—and that happened on its own, it went together with my growing up.

Yet another powerful circumstance influenced my departure from Moscow, yet another temptation, which even then, three months before leaving (that is, when there had not yet been any mention of Petersburg), made my heart heave and pound! I was also drawn into this unknown ocean because I could enter it directly as the lord and master even of other people's destinies, and what people! But it was magnanimous and not despotic feelings that seethed in me—I warn you beforehand, so there will be no mistaking my words. Versilov might think (if he deigned to think about me) that this was a little boy coming, a recent high-school student, an adolescent, for whom the whole world was a marvel. And yet I already knew all his innermost secrets and had a most important document on me, for which (now I know it for certain) he would have given several years of his life, if I had revealed the whole secret to him then. However, I notice that I'm setting a lot of riddles. Feelings can't be described without facts. Besides, more than enough will be said about all that in its place; that's why I've taken up the pen. And to write this way is like raving or a cloud.

VIII

FINALLY, IN ORDER to go on definitively to the nineteenth, I'll meanwhile say briefly and, so to speak, in passing, that I found them all, that is, Versilov, my mother, and my sister (whom I was seeing for the first time in my life), in difficult circumstances, almost destitute or verging on destitution. I had already learned of that in Moscow, but I had never supposed what I saw. Ever since childhood I had been used to picturing this man, this "future father of mine," almost in some sort of halo, and couldn't imagine him otherwise than in the forefront everywhere. Versilov had never lived in the same apartment with my mother, but had always rented a separate one for her; he did it, of course, out of those mean "proprieties" of theirs. But here they were all living together in the same wooden wing, in a lane of the Semyonovsky quarter.[4] All their things had been pawned, so that I even gave my mother, in secret from Versilov, my secret sixty roubles. Precisely *secret*, because I had saved them from my pocket money, the five roubles a month allotted me, over the course of two years; the saving began from the first day of my idea, and therefore Versilov was not to know even a word of this money. I trembled over it.

This help was a mere drop. My mother worked, my sister also took in sewing; Versilov lived idly, was capricious, and went on living with a great many of his former, rather expensive habits. He grumbled terribly, especially at dinner, and all his manners were completely despotic. But my mother, my sister, Tatyana Pavlovna, and the whole family of the late Andronikov (a certain department head, deceased three months earlier, who at the time had managed Versilov's affairs), which consisted of countless women, stood in awe of him as of an idol. I could never have pictured such a thing. I'll note that nine years earlier he had been incomparably more elegant. I've already said that he remained with some sort of halo in my dreams, and therefore I could not imagine how it was possible to become so aged and shabby only some nine years later: I at once felt sadness, pity, shame. The sight of him was one of the most painful of my first impressions on arrival. However, he was by no means an old man yet, he was only forty-five; and as I studied him further, I found something even more striking in his good looks than what had survived in my memory. There was less brilliance than then, less of the external, even of the elegant, but it was as if life had imprinted on his face something much more interesting than was there before.

And yet destitution was only the tenth or twentieth part of his misfortunes, and I knew it only too well. Besides destitution, there was something immeasurably more serious—not to mention that there was still hope of winning the litigation over an inheritance that Versilov had started a year before against the Princes Sokolsky, and Versilov might receive in the nearest future an estate worth seventy thousand and maybe a bit more. I've already said above that this Versilov had run through three inheritances in his life, and here he was going to be rescued again by an inheritance! The case was to be decided in court in the shortest time. That was why I came. True, no one gave out money on hope, there was nowhere to borrow, and meanwhile they bore with it.

But Versilov did not go to anyone, though he sometimes left for the whole day. Over a year ago, he had already been *driven out* of society. That story, despite all my efforts, remained unclear to me in its main points, despite my whole month of life in Petersburg. Was Versilov guilty or not—that was what mattered to me, that was what I had come for! Everybody turned away from him, including, by the way, all the influential nobility, with whom he had been especially able to maintain relations all his life, owing to rumors of a certain extremely low and—what's worst of all in the eyes of the "world"—scandalous act he was supposed to have committed over a year before in Germany, and even of a slap in the face he had received then, much too publicly, precisely from one of the Sokolsky princes, and to which he had not responded with a challenge. Even his children (the legitimate ones), his son and daughter, turned away from him and lived separately. True, both the son and the daughter floated in the highest circle, through the Fanariotovs and old Prince Sokolsky (Versilov's former friend). However, looking at him more closely during that whole month, what I saw was an arrogant man, whom society had not excluded from its circle, but rather who had himself driven society away from him—so independent an air he had. But did he have the right to that air—that's what troubled me! I absolutely had to find out the whole truth in the very shortest time, for I had come to judge this man. My own power I still concealed from him, but I had either to acknowledge him, or to spurn him altogether. And the latter would be all too painful for me, and I suffered. I'll finally make a full confession: this man was dear to me!

And meanwhile I lived in the same apartment with them, worked, and barely refrained from being rude. In fact, I did not refrain. Having lived with them for a month, I became more convinced every day that I simply couldn't turn to him for final explanations. The proud man stood right in front of me as a riddle that insulted me deeply. He was even nice and jocular with me, but I sooner wanted a quarrel than such jokes. All my conversations with him always bore some sort of ambiguity in them, that is, quite simply some strange mockery on his part. At the very beginning, he did not meet me seriously when I came from Moscow. I could in no way understand why he did that. True, he achieved the result that he remained impenetrable to me; but I could not have lowered myself to beg for serious treatment from him. And besides, he had astonishing and irresistible ways about him, which I didn't know how to deal with. In short, he treated me like the greenest adolescent—something I was almost unable to bear, though I knew it would be like that. Consequently, I myself stopped speaking seriously and waited; I even almost stopped speaking entirely. I was waiting for a certain person, on whose arrival in Petersburg I could definitively learn the truth; in that lay my last hope. In any case, I was prepared to break with him definitively and had already taken all the measures. I pitied my mother, but... "either him or me"—that was what I wanted to suggest to her and my sister. Even the day had been fixed; but meanwhile I went to work.

Chapter Two

I

ON THAT NINETEENTH day of the month, I was also to receive my first pay for the first month of my Petersburg service at my "private" post. They never even asked me about this post, but simply sent me there, it seems, on the very first day of my arrival. That was very crude, and I was almost obliged to protest. The post turned out to be in the house of old Prince Sokolsky. But to protest right then would have meant breaking with them at once, which, though it didn't frighten me at all, would have harmed my essential aims, and therefore I accepted the post silently for the time being, my silence protecting my dignity. I'll explain from the outset that this Prince Sokolsky, a rich man and a privy councillor,[5] was in no way related to those Princes Sokolsky from Moscow (impoverished wretches for several generations in a row) with whom Versilov had his lawsuit. They were merely namesakes. Nevertheless, the old prince took great interest in them and especially liked one of these princes, the head of the family, so to speak—a young officer. Still recently, Versilov had had enormous influence on this old man's affairs and had been his friend, a strange friend, because the poor prince, as I noticed, was terribly afraid of him, not only at the time when I entered, but, it seems, throughout their friendship. However, they hadn't seen each other for a long time; the dishonorable act Versilov was accused of concerned precisely the prince's family; but Tatyana Pavlovna turned up, and it was through her mediation that I was placed with the old man, who wanted to have "a young man" in his office. It so happened that he also wanted terribly much to do Versilov a good turn, to make, so to speak, a first step, and Versilov *allowed* it. The old prince made the arrangements in the absence of his daughter, a general's widow, who probably would not have allowed him this step. Of that later, but I'll note that it was this strangeness of his relations with Versilov that struck me in his favor. It stood to reason that if the head of the insulted family still went on respecting Versilov, it meant that the rumor spread about Versilov's baseness was absurd or at least ambiguous. It was partly this circumstance that forced me not to protest at taking the post: in taking it, I precisely hoped to verify all that.

This Tatyana Pavlovna played a strange role at the time when I found her in Petersburg. I had almost forgotten about her entirely and had never expected that she had such significance. Previously, she had come my way three or four times in my Moscow life, appearing from God knows where, on somebody's instructions, each time I had to be settled somewhere—on entering Touchard's little boarding school,[6] or two and a half years later, when I was transferred to high school and lodged in the quarters of the unforgettable Nikolai Semyonovich. Having appeared, she'd spend the whole day with me, inspecting my linen, my clothes, drive with me to Kuznetsky and downtown, buy me everything I needed, in short, set up my whole trousseau to the last little box and penknife; and she would hiss at me all the while, scold me, reprimand me, quiz me, hold up to me the example of some other fantastic boys, her acquaintances and relations, who supposedly were all better than I was, and, really, she even pinched me and positively shoved me, even several times, and painfully. Once she had settled me and installed me in place, she would vanish without a trace for several years. So it was she who, just as I arrived, appeared and got me installed again. She was a small, dry little figure, with a sharp, birdlike little nose and sharp, birdlike little eyes. She served Versilov like a slave, and bowed down to him as to a pope, but out of conviction. But I soon noticed with astonishment that she was decidedly respected by everyone and everywhere, and, above all—decidedly everywhere and everyone knew her. Old Prince Sokolsky treated her with extraordinary deference; so did his family; so did those proud Versilov children; so did the Fanariotovs—and yet she lived by doing sewing, washing some sort of lace, taking work from a shop. She and I quarreled from the first word, because she decided to hiss at me at once, as she had done six years before; after that we kept quarreling every day; but that did not prevent us from talking occasionally, and, I confess, by the end of the month I began to like her—for the independence of her character, I suppose. However, I did not inform her of that.

I understood at once that I had been assigned a post with this ailing old man solely in order to "amuse" him, and that the whole job lay in that. Naturally, that humiliated me, and I was going to take measures at once; but soon afterwards the old eccentric produced a sort of unexpected impression in me, something like pity, and by the end of the month I grew somehow strangely attached to him, or at least I dropped my intention to be rude. He was, incidentally, no more than sixty. Here a whole story came out. A year and a half earlier he had suddenly had a fit; he had gone somewhere and had lost his mind on the way, so that something like a scandal had occurred, which was talked about in Petersburg. As is proper in such cases, he was immediately taken abroad, but about five months later he suddenly reappeared, and in perfect health, though he did leave government service. Versilov maintained seriously (and with notable warmth) that there was no insanity involved, but merely some sort of nervous fit. I immediately noticed this warmth of Versilov's. However, I will note that I myself all but shared his opinion. The old man just seemed awfully lightminded at times, which didn't go with his years, and they said he hadn't been that way at all before. They said that before he had been some sort of adviser somewhere and had once somehow distinguished himself greatly in some mission he had been charged with. Having known him for a whole month, I would never have supposed any special ability in him for being an adviser. They noticed (though I did not) that after his fit a sort of special inclination developed in him to get married quickly, and that he supposedly set about this idea more than once in that year and a half. This was supposedly known in society, and was of interest to the right people. But since this impulse was far too discordant with the interests of certain persons around the prince, the old man was watched on all sides. His own family was small; he had been a widower for twenty years and had only one daughter, the general's widow, who was now expected any day from Moscow, a young person whose character he unquestionably feared. But he had no end of various distant relations, mostly on his deceased wife's side, who were all but destitute; besides, there was a multitude of various wards, male and female, who received his benefactions, and who all expected a share of his inheritance, and so they all assisted the general's widow in supervising the old man. On top of that, ever since he was a young man, he had had a certain quirk—only I don't know whether it was ridiculous or not—of marrying off impoverished girls. He had been marrying them off for twentyfive years on end—distant relations, or stepdaughters of his wife's cousins, or his goddaughters; he even married off his doorkeeper's daughter. He started by taking them into his house while they were still little girls, brought them up with governesses and Frenchwomen, then educated them in the best schools, and in the end gave them away with a dowry. All this constantly crowded around him. The wards, naturally, once they married, would produce more girls, all the girls thus produced also aimed at becoming wards, he had to go everywhere to baptisms, all this showed up with congratulations on his birthdays, and he found it all extremely agreeable.

On entering his service, I noticed at once that a certain painful conviction had nested in the old man's mind—and it was quite impossible not to notice it—that everyone in society had supposedly begun to look at him strangely, that everyone had supposedly begun to treat him differently than before, when he had been in good health; this impression did not leave him even in the merriest social gatherings. The old man became insecure, began noticing something in everyone's eyes. The thought that he was still suspected of insanity obviously tormented him; even me he sometimes studied with mistrust. And if he had learned that someone was spreading or maintaining this rumor about him, I believe this gentlest of men would have become his eternal enemy. It is this circumstance that I ask you to take note of. I will add that this also decided me from the first day not to be rude to him; I was even glad if I sometimes had the chance to cheer him up or divert him; I don't think this confession can cast a shadow on my dignity.

The greater part of his money was invested. After his illness, he had joined a big shareholding company, a very solid one, by the way. And though the business was conducted by the others, he was also very interested in it, came to the shareholders' meetings, was elected a founding member, sat on the board, delivered long speeches, refuted, made noise, all with obvious pleasure. He very much liked making speeches: at least everyone could see his intelligence. And in general he began to be terribly fond of inserting especially profound things and bons mots into his conversation, even in his most intimate private life; that I understand only too well. In his house, downstairs, something like a home office was set up, and a clerk took care of the business, the accounts, and the bookkeeping, and also managed the household. This clerk, who served, besides, in a government post, would have been quite enough by himself; but, at the wish of the prince, they added me as well, as if to assist the clerk; but I was transferred at once to the study and often had no work in front of me, no papers, no books, not even for pretense.

I'm writing now like a man who has long since sobered up, and in many respects almost like an outsider; but how shall I depict my sadness of that time (which I vividly recall right now), as it lodged itself in my heart, and, above all, my agitation of that time, which would reach such a troubled and fervid state that I even didn't sleep at night—from my impatience, from the riddles that I set myself.

II

ASKING FOR MONEY is a vile affair, even when it's your salary, if you feel somewhere in the folds of your conscience that you haven't quite earned it. Meanwhile, the day before, my mother and sister were whispering together, in secret from Versilov ("so as not to upset Andrei Petrovich"), intending to go to a pawnshop with an icon from her icon stand, which for some reason was very dear to her. I was working for fifty roubles a month, but I had no idea how I would receive it; when I was appointed here, nobody told me anything. Some three days earlier, meeting the clerk downstairs, I had asked him who was responsible for the salaries here. The man looked at me with the smile of one astonished (he didn't like me):

"But do you get a salary?"

I thought that right after my reply he would add:

"And what for, sir?"

But he only answered drily that he "knew nothing" and buried himself in his ruled notebook, in which he was copying out accounts from some scraps of paper.

He was not unaware, however, that I did do something. Two weeks earlier I had sat for exactly four days over a job he himself had given me, making a copy from a rough draft, and it had almost come down to rewriting it. It was a whole crowd of the prince's "thoughts," which he had prepared to submit to the shareholders' committee. I had to put it together into a whole and touch up the style. Afterwards I spent a whole day sitting over this paper with the prince, and he argued with me very vehemently, though he remained pleased; only I don't know whether he submitted the paper or not. I won't even mention the two or three letters, also on business, which I wrote at his request.

It was also vexing for me to ask for my salary, because I had already decided to give up my position, anticipating that I'd be forced to leave here as well, owing to ineluctable circumstances. Waking up that morning and getting dressed upstairs in my little closet, I felt my heart pound, and though I spat as I entered the prince's house, I again felt the same agitation: that morning the person was to arrive here, the woman from whose arrival I expected an explanation of all that tormented me! This was precisely the prince's daughter, General Akhmakov's widow, the young woman of whom I have already spoken and who was at bitter enmity with Versilov. At last I've written that name! Of course, I had never seen her, and could not imagine how I would speak to her, or whether I would; but I imagined to myself (perhaps on sufficient grounds) that her arrival would disperse the darkness that surrounded Versilov in my eyes. I couldn't remain firm: it was terribly vexing that from the very first step I was so pusillanimous and awkward; it was terribly curious, and above all disgusting—three full impressions. I remember that whole day by heart!

My prince knew nothing as yet about the probable arrival of his daughter, and assumed she would return from Moscow maybe in a week. But I learned of it the evening before, quite by accident: Tatyana Pavlovna, who had received a letter from the general's widow, let it slip to my mother in my presence. Though they whispered and used remote phrases, I guessed it. Of course, I wasn't eavesdropping; I simply couldn't help listening when I saw my mother suddenly become so agitated at the news of this woman's arrival. Versilov was not at home.

I didn't want to inform the old man of it, because I couldn't help noticing in all that time how afraid he was of her coming. He had even let slip three days earlier, though timidly and remotely, that he was afraid of her coming on account of me—that is, that on account of me he would get a scolding. I must add, however, that in family relations he still maintained his independence and domination, especially in managing money. My first conclusion about him was that he was a real woman; but then I had to reconclude, in the sense that, even if he was a woman, all the same there remained in him at times a sort of stubbornness, if not real courage. There were moments when it was almost impossible to do anything with his apparently cowardly and susceptible character. Versilov explained it to me later in more detail. I mention now, with curiosity, that he and I hardly ever spoke of the general's widow—that is, avoided speaking, as it were; I especially avoided it, and he in turn avoided speaking of Versilov, and I surmised at once that he wouldn't answer me, if I were to ask any of the ticklish questions that interested me so much.

If anyone wants to know what we talked about during that whole month, I will reply that, essentially, it was about everything in the world, but all of it somehow strange. I very much liked the extreme artlessness with which he treated me. I sometimes studied the man with extreme perplexity, asking myself, "Where was he sitting before? He's just right for our high school, and for the fourth class at that—he'd make the nicest schoolmate." I also wondered more than once at his face: it looked extremely serious (almost handsome) and dry; thick, gray, curly hair, an open gaze; and his whole figure was lean, of a good height; but his face had a sort of unpleasant, almost indecent property of changing suddenly from the extraordinarily serious to the much-too-playful, so that someone seeing it for the first time would never expect it. I spoke of it with Versilov, who heard me out with curiosity; it seemed he hadn't expected me to be able to make such observations; yet he observed in passing that this property had appeared in the prince after his illness and maybe only quite recently.

We talked for the most part about two abstract subjects: about God and his being—that is, whether he exists or not—and about women. The prince was very religious and sentimental. In his office hung an enormous icon case with an icon lamp. But something would come over him—and he'd suddenly begin to doubt God's existence and say astonishing things, obviously challenging me to reply. My attitude to this idea was rather indifferent, generally speaking, but even so the two of us would get carried away, and always sincerely. Generally, even now I recall all those conversations with pleasure. But the sweetest thing of all for him was to chat about women, and since I, given my dislike of conversations on that topic, could not be a good interlocutor, he would sometimes even get upset.

He had just begun talking in this vein as I came in that morning. I found him in a playful mood, while the previous evening I had left him extremely sad for some reason. Yet I absolutely had to be done that day with the matter of my salary—before the arrival of certain persons. I calculated that we would be *interrupted* that day without fail (not for nothing was my heart pounding)—and then perhaps I wouldn't venture to talk about money. But since one couldn't just start talking about money, I naturally got angry at my own stupidity and, as I remember it now, vexed at some much-too-merry question he asked me, I fired all my views of women at him at once, and that with extreme ardor. But the result was that he got still more carried away, worse luck for me.

III

". . . I DON'T LIKE WOMEN, because they're rude, because they're awkward, because they're not independent, and because they wear indecent clothes," I concluded my lengthy tirade incoherently.

"Have mercy, dear heart!" he cried, terribly amused, which made me still angrier.

I'm yielding and trifling only in trifles, but I will never yield in the main thing. In trifles, in certain social manners, one can do God knows what with me, and I've always cursed this trait in myself. Out of some stinking goodnaturedness, I have sometimes been ready to yes even some society fop, seduced solely by his courtesy, or to get into an argument with a fool, which is most unpardonable. All from lack of self-control and from having grown up in a corner. You go away angry and swearing that tomorrow it won't be repeated, but tomorrow the same thing happens again. That's why I've sometimes been taken almost for a sixteen-year-old. But instead of acquiring self-control, I prefer even now to shut myself up still more in a corner, though it be in the most misanthropic way: "Maybe I'm awkward, but—farewell!" I say that seriously and forever. However, I am by no means writing this apropos of the prince, and not even apropos of our conversation that time.

"I am by no means saying it for your amusement," I almost shouted at him, "I am simply voicing a conviction."

"But how is it that women are rude and indecently dressed? That's novel."

"They're rude. Go to the theater, go for a promenade. Every man knows the right side, they come towards each other and pass each other, he on the right and I on the right. A woman, that is, a lady—I'm speaking of ladies—comes stomping straight at you, without even noticing you, as if it were your unfailing duty to jump aside and yield her the way. I'm ready to yield, as to a weaker being, but why is it her right, why is she so sure I must do it—that's what's offensive! I always spit when I run into them. And after that they cry that they're humiliated and demand equality; what kind of equality is it, if she tramples me down or stuffs my mouth full of sand!"

"Sand!"

"Yes. Because they're indecently dressed; only a depraved man can fail to notice that. They shut the doors in courts when a case gets to indecency; why then do they allow it in the streets, where there are a lot more people? They pad themselves quite openly with some frou-frou behind, to show that they're belles-femmes. Openly! I can't help noticing it, and any young man will notice it, and a child, a beginning little boy, will also notice it. It's base. Let old philanderers admire it and run after them with their tongues hanging out, but there are pure young people who must be protected. The only thing left to do is spit. She goes down the boulevard and leaves a four-foot train behind her sweeping the dust; how about the one behind her: you either have to run ahead or jump aside, otherwise she'll stuff five pounds of sand in your nose and mouth. Besides, it's silk, and she frays it on the stones for three miles, just for the sake of fashion, and her husband earns five hundred roubles a year in the Senate:[7] there's where the bribes are sitting! I always spit on it, I spit and berate them out loud."

Though I'm writing down this conversation somewhat humorously here, and in a way characteristic of me then, the thinking is still mine.

"And get away with it?" the prince became curious.

"I spit and walk away. Naturally, she feels it, but she doesn't let it show, she stomps on majestically without turning her head. And there was only one time that I berated a couple of them quite seriously, both with trains, on the boulevard—naturally, not in nasty words, I merely observed out loud that trains were offensive."

"That's how you put it?"

"Of course. First, she's trampling on social conventions, and second, she's raising dust; and the boulevard is for everybody: I walk there, another person walks there, a third, Fyodor, Ivan, it makes no difference. So I spoke it all out. And generally I don't like the female gait, if you look from behind; I spoke that out, too, but in a hint."

"My friend, you could have gotten into a serious incident: they could have dragged you to the justice of the peace!"

"They could have done nothing at all. There were no grounds for complaint: a man walks by and talks to himself. Every man has the right to voice his conviction into the air. I was speaking abstractly, I wasn't addressing them. They themselves did the pestering: they started berating me, they were much nastier than I was: milksop, ought to go without dinner, nihilist, hand him over to the police, and that I started pestering them because they were alone and weak women, and that if there had been a man with them, I'd have put my tail between my legs at once. I told them coolly that they should stop bothering me, and that I would cross to the other side. And in order to prove to them that I'm not afraid of their men and am ready to accept their challenge, I will follow twenty steps behind them right to their house, then stand in front of their house and wait for their men. And so I did."

"Really?"

"Of course, it was stupid, but I was worked up. They dragged me for over three miles, in hot weather, as far as the institutes, went into a one-story wooden house—quite a decent one, I must admit—and you could see lots of flowers inside, two canaries, three lapdogs, and some framed prints. I stood in the middle of the street in front of the house for about half an hour. They peeked out on the sly three times or so, and then drew all the blinds. Finally, an official came out of the gate, an elderly man; judging by his looks, he had been asleep and had been awakened on purpose; he was wearing, not quite a house robe, but something very informal; he stood by the gate, put his hands behind his back, and started looking at me, and I at him. He would glance away, then look at me again, and suddenly he began to smile at me. I turned around and left."

"My friend, this is something Schilleresque![8] It has always surprised me: you've got ruddy cheeks, your face is bursting with health, and—such a, one might say, aversion to women! How is it possible that at your age a woman does not make a certain impression? When I was just eleven, *mon cher*, my tutor observed to me that I gazed too much at the statues in the Summer Garden."[9]

"You'd like terribly for me to go and visit some local Josephine and come to let you know. There's no need. I myself, when I was just thirteen, saw a woman's nakedness, all of it; since then I've felt this loathing."

"Seriously? But, *cher enfant*, a beautiful, fresh woman smells just like an apple, what's there to loathe?"

"In my former little boarding school, at Touchard's, even before high school, I had a comrade—Lambert. He used to beat me, because he was more than three years older, and I served him and took his boots off. When he went to confirmation, the abbé Rigaud visited him to congratulate him on his first communion,[10] and the two rushed in tears to embrace each other, and the abbé Rigaud started pressing him to his breast terribly hard, with various gestures. I also wept and was very envious. When his father died, he left school, and I didn't see him for two years, but after two years I met him in the street. He said he would come to see me. I was already in high school and was living with Nikolai Semyonovich. He came in the morning, showed me five hundred roubles, and told me to come with him. Though he had beaten me two years earlier, he had always needed me, not only for his boots; he used to tell me everything. He told me that he had stolen the money that day from his mother's cashbox, having duplicated the key, because his father's money was all his by law, and she dared not keep it from him, and that the abbé Rigaud had come the day before to admonish him—came in, stood over him and started whimpering, portraying horror, and raising his arms to the sky, "and I pulled my knife and said I'd cut his throat" (he pronounced it *thghroat*). We drove to Kuznetsky. On the way, he told me that his mother had relations with the abbé Rigaud, and that he had noticed it, and that he spat on it all, and that everything they said about communion was rubbish. He said a lot more, and I was frightened. In Kuznetsky he bought a double-barreled shotgun, a game bag, cartridges, a horsewhip, and then also a pound of candy. We drove out of town to shoot, and on our way met a birdcatcher with his cages; Lambert bought a canary from him. In the woods he let the canary out, because it couldn't fly far after being in a cage, and began shooting at it, but missed. It was the first time in his life he had shot a gun, but he had been wanting to buy a gun for a long time, still at Touchard's, and we had long dreamed of a gun. He was as if spluttering. His hair was terribly black, his face white and red-cheeked like a mask, his nose long and aquiline, such as Frenchmen have, his teeth white, his eyes black. He tied the canary to a branch with a thread, and with both barrels, point-blank, from four inches away, blasted it twice, and it scattered into a hundred little feathers. Then we went back, stopped at a hotel, took a room, began eating and drinking champagne; a lady came... I was very struck, I remember, by how magnificently she was dressed, in green silk. Here I saw all that... what I told you about... Afterwards, when we started drinking again, he began to taunt her and abuse her; she was sitting there without her dress; he had taken her dress away, and when she began cursing and asking for her dress, so that she could put it on, he started whipping her as hard as he could on her bare shoulders with the whip. I stood up and seized him by the hair, so deftly that I threw him to the floor at once. He seized a fork and stuck it into my thigh. Then people rushed in, hearing the shouting, and I managed to escape. Since then the memory of nakedness has been loathsome to me; believe me, she was a beauty."

As I talked, the prince's face changed from playful to very sad.

"*Mon pauvre enfant!** I've always been convinced that there were a great many unhappy days in your childhood."

"Please don't worry."

"But you were alone, you told me so yourself, though there was this Lambert. The way you described it: the canary, the confirmation with tears on each other's breasts, and then, after a year or so, he speaks of his mother and this abbot . . . *O, mon cher*, this children question of our time is simply frightful: while these little golden heads, with their curls and innocence, in their earliest childhood, flutter before you and look at you with their bright laughter and bright little eyes—they're like God's angels or lovely little birds; but later . . . but later it so happens that it would be better for them not to grow up at all!"

"How unnerved you are, Prince! As if you had children yourself. You don't have children and never will."

"*Tiens!*"† His face changed instantly. "In fact, Alexandra Petrovna—the day before yesterday, heh, heh!—Alexandra Petrovna Sinitsky—I think you must have met her here about three weeks ago—imagine, suddenly, the day before yesterday, to my cheerful remark that if I marry now, at least I can rest assured that I won't have children—suddenly she says to me, and even with a sort of spite, 'On the contrary, you precisely will, such a one as you will *unfailingly* have children, even in the very first year, you'll see.' Heh, heh! And everybody imagined for some reason that I'd suddenly get married; but, though it's spiteful, you must agree it's witty."

"Witty, but offensive."

"Well, *cher enfant*, one cannot be offended by just anybody.

*My poor boy!
†Well!

What I appreciate most of all in people is wittiness, which is evidently disappearing, and what Alexandra Petrovna is going to say—who can take that into account!"

"What, what did you say?" I latched on. "Not by just anybody . . . precisely so! Not everybody's worth paying attention to—an excellent rule! That is precisely what I need. I'll write it down. You occasionally say the nicest things, Prince."

He beamed all over.

"*N'est-ce pas?** *Cher enfant*, true wit is disappearing more and more. *Eh, mais . . . C'est moi qui connais les femmes.*† Believe me, every woman's life, whatever she may preach, is an eternal search for someone to submit to . . . a thirst for submission, so to speak. And note—without a single exception."

"Perfectly true, splendid!" I cried in delight. At another time we would have launched at once into philosophical reflections on the subject, for a whole hour, but it was as if something suddenly bit me, and I blushed all over. I imagined that, by praising his bons mots, I was sucking up to him on account of the money, and that he would be sure to think of that when I began to ask. I mention it now on purpose.

"Prince, I humbly request that you pay me right now the fifty roubles you owe me for this month," I blurted out all at once, irritated to the point of rudeness.

I remember (just as I remember that whole morning in minute detail) that a scene then took place between us that was most vile in its real truth. At first he didn't understand me, looked for a long time and did not understand what money I was talking about. It was only natural that he never imagined I should receive a salary—and what for? True, he started assuring me later that he had forgotten, and, when he grasped it, he instantly started taking out the fifty roubles, but he became hurried and even turned red. Seeing how things were, I stood up and declared sharply that I could not accept the money now, that I had obviously been told of the salary either mistakenly or deceitfully, so that I would not reject the post, and that I now understood only too well that I had no reason to be paid, because there wasn't any work. The prince became frightened and started assuring me that I had worked terribly much, and that I would have still more work, and that fifty roubles

*Isn't it so?

†Eh, but . . . I'm the one who knows women.

was so insignificant that he, on the contrary, would increase it, because it was his duty, and that he himself had negotiated with Tatyana Pavlovna, but had "unpardonably forgotten all about it." I flared up and announced definitively that it would be mean of me to receive a salary for scandalous stories of how I had accompanied two trains to the institutes, that I had not been hired to amuse him, but to occupy myself with business, but since there was no business, it must be terminated, etc., etc. I couldn't even have imagined that it was possible to be as frightened as he was after these words of mine. Naturally, the end was that I stopped objecting, and he did stick me with the fifty roubles: to this day I blush to recall that I accepted it! Things always end in meanness in this world, and, worst of all, he almost managed to convince me then that I had unquestionably earned it, and I had the foolishness to believe it, and with that it was somehow decidedly impossible not to take it.

"*Cher, cher enfant!*" he exclaimed, kissing and embracing me (I confess, I myself was about to weep, devil knows why, though I instantly restrained myself, and even now, as I write, color comes to my face). "Dear friend, you're now like one of my own; in this month you've become like a piece of my own heart! In 'society' there is only 'society' and nothing more; Katerina Nikolaevna" (his daughter) "is a brilliant woman, and I'm proud of it, but she often offends me, my dear, very, very often... Well, and these girls (*elles sont charmantes**) and their mothers, who come on birthdays—they only bring their embroidery, but they don't know how to say anything. I've accumulated sixty pillows with their embroidery, all dogs and deer. I love them very much, but with you I'm almost as if with my own—and not with a son, but a brother, and I especially like it when you object; you're literary, you've read, you know how to admire..."

"I've read nothing and am not literary at all. I've read whatever happened along, but in the past two years I haven't read at all and don't intend to."

"Why not?"

"I have other goals."

"*Cher*... it's a pity to say at the end of your life, as I do, *je sais tout, mais je ne sais rien de bon.*† I decidedly do not know why

*They are charming.

†I know everything, but I don't know anything worthwhile.

I've lived in the world! But...I owe you so much...and I even wanted..."

He broke off somehow suddenly, went limp, and became pensive. After a shock (and with him the shocks could come every other minute, God knows why), he usually seemed to lose his good sense for a while and be unable to control himself; however, he would soon put himself to rights, so it was all harmless. We sat for a minute. His lower lip, which was very thick, hung down...Most of all, I was surprised that he had suddenly mentioned his daughter, and with such candor. Of course, I ascribed it to his being upset.

"*Cher enfant*, you're not angry that I address you familiarly, are you?" suddenly escaped him.

"Not in the least. I confess, in the beginning, the first few times, I was slightly offended and also wanted to address you familiarly, but I saw it was stupid, because you surely don't do it to humiliate me."

He was no longer listening and had forgotten his question.

"Well, how's your *father*?" he suddenly raised his pensive eyes to me.

I simply jumped. First, he had designated Versilov as my *father*—something he had never allowed himself with me; and, second, he had begun speaking of Versilov, something that had never happened before.

"Sits without money and mopes," I replied briefly, burning with curiosity myself.

"Yes, about money. Their case is to be decided today in the district court, and I'm waiting for Prince Seryozha and what he'll come with. He promised to come to me straight from court. Their whole destiny is involved; it's sixty or eighty thousand. Of course, I've also always wished the best for Andrei Petrovich" (Versilov, that is), "and it seems he'll come out the winner and the princes will be left with nothing. Law!"

"In court today?" I exclaimed, struck.

The thought that Versilov had neglected to inform me even of that struck me in the extreme. "That means he said nothing to mother, or maybe to anybody," it occurred to me all at once. "What character!

"And is Prince Sokolsky in Petersburg?" another thought suddenly struck me.

"Since yesterday. Straight from Berlin, especially for this day."

Another extremely important piece of news for me. "And he'll come here today, this man who gave *him* a slap!"

"Well, what of it?" The prince's whole face suddenly changed. "He still preaches God as he used to, and, and . . . maybe still goes after the girls, after unfledged little girls? Heh, heh! Right now, too, there's a most amusing anecdote hatching . . . Heh, heh!"

"Who preaches? Who goes after the girls?"

"Andrei Petrovich! Would you believe, he pestered us all back then like a burr—what do we eat, what do we think?—or almost like that. Frightened us and purified us: 'If you're religious, why don't you go and become a monk?' He demanded almost that. *Mais quelle idée!** Even if it's right, isn't it too severe? It was me especially that he liked to frighten with the Last Judgment, me of all people."

"I haven't noticed any of that, and I've lived with him for a month now," I replied, listening impatiently. It was terribly vexing that he hadn't quite come to his senses and mumbled so incoherently.

"He just doesn't say it now, but, believe me, it's so. The man is clever, indisputably, and deeply educated; but is that the right kind of intelligence? It all happened to him after his three years abroad. And, I confess, he shocked me very much . . . he shocked everybody . . . *Cher enfant, j'aime le bon Dieu*† . . . I believe, I believe as much as I can, but—I was certainly beside myself then. Suppose I used a frivolous method, but I did it on purpose, in vexation—and besides, the essence of my objection was as serious as it has been from the beginning of the world: 'If there is a supreme being,' I say to him, 'and it exists *personally*, and not in the form of some sort of spirit poured over creation in the form of a liquid or whatever (because that is still more difficult to understand)—where, then, does it live?' My friend, *c'était bête*,‡ undoubtedly, but that's what all objections boil down to. *Un domicile*§ is an important matter. He was terribly angry. He converted to Catholicism there."

"I've also heard about that idea. Nonsense, surely."

"I assure you by all that's holy. Look at him well . . . However, you say he's changed. Well, but at that time he tormented us all so! Would you believe, he behaved as if he were a saint and his

*But what an idea!
†Dear boy, I love God . . .
‡It was stupid.
§A residence.

relics were about to be revealed.[11] He demanded an account of our behavior from us, I swear to you! Relics! *En voilà une autre!** Well, let him be a monk or an anchorite—but here's a man going around in a tailcoat and all the rest... and then suddenly—his relics! A strange wish for a man of the world and, I confess, a strange taste. I don't say anything about it: of course, it's all holy, and anything can happen... Besides, it's all *de l'inconnu*,† but for a man of the world it's even indecent. If it should somehow happen to me, or they should offer it to me, I swear I'd refuse. Why, suddenly I'm dining today in a club, and then suddenly—I *reveal* myself! No, I'd be a laughing-stock! I told him all that then... He wore chains."[12]

I turned red with anger.

"Did you see the chains yourself?"

"I didn't myself, but..."

"Then I declare to you that it's all a lie, a tissue of vile machinations and enemy slander, that is, of one enemy, the chiefest and most inhuman one, because he has only one enemy—your daughter!"

The prince flushed in his turn.

"*Mon cher*, I beg you and I insist that in the future my daughter's name never be mentioned again in my presence together with this vile story."

I rose slightly. He was beside himself; his chin was trembling.

"*Cette histoire infâme!*‡ ... I didn't believe it, I never wanted to believe it, but... they tell me: believe it, believe it, I..."

Here the valet suddenly came in again and announced a visitor. I sank back down on my chair.

IV

TWO LADIES CAME in, both young, one the stepdaughter of one of the cousins of the prince's late wife, or something of the sort, his ward, for whom he had already allotted a dowry, and who (I note it for the future) had money of her own; the other was Anna Andreevna Versilov, Versilov's daughter, three years older than I, who lived with her brother at Mme. Fanariotov's and whom before

*There's another one!
†Unknown.
‡This infamous story!

then I had seen only once in my life, fleetingly in the street, though I had already had a skirmish with her brother, also fleetingly, in Moscow (quite possibly I'll mention that skirmish later on, if there's room, though essentially it's not worth it). This Anna Andreevna had been a special favorite of the prince's since childhood (Versilov's acquaintance with the prince began terribly long ago). I was so embarrassed by what had just transpired that I didn't even stand up when they came in, though the prince stood up to meet them; and afterwards I thought it embarrassing to stand up, and remained in my place. Above all, I was thrown off, because the prince had been shouting at me just three minutes before, and I still didn't know whether I should leave or not. But my old man had already forgotten everything completely, as was his wont, and was all pleasantly animated at the sight of the girls. He even managed, with a quick change of physiognomy and a sort of mysterious wink, to whisper to me hastily, just before they came in:

"Take a look at Olympiada, look closely, closely . . . I'll tell you later . . ."

I looked at her quite closely and found nothing special: not a very tall girl, plump, and with extremely ruddy cheeks. Her face, however, was rather pleasant, the kind that the materialists like. Her expression was kind, perhaps, but with a wrinkle. She could not have been especially brilliant intellectually, at least not in a higher sense, but one could see cunning in her eyes. No more than nineteen years old. In short, nothing remarkable. We'd have called her a "pillow" in high school. (If I describe her in such detail, it's solely because I'll need it in the future.)

By the way, everything I've been describing so far, with such apparently unnecessary detail, all leads to the future and will be needed there. It will all echo in its own place: I've been unable to avoid it; and if it's boring, I beg you not to read it.

Versilov's daughter was quite a different sort of person. Tall, even slightly lean; an elongated and remarkably pale face, but black, fluffy hair; big, dark eyes, a profound gaze; small and red lips, a fresh mouth. The first woman whose gait did not fill me with loathing; however, she was thin and lean. The expression of her face was not entirely kind, but imposing; twenty-two years old. Hardly a single external feature resembling Versilov, and yet, by some miracle, an extraordinary resemblance to him in her facial expression. I don't know if she was good-looking; that's a matter of taste. Both women were dressed very modestly, so it's not worth describing. I expected to be offended at once by some look or gesture from Miss Versilov, and I prepared myself; for her brother had offended me in Moscow, at our very first confrontation in life. She couldn't have known me by my face, but she had certainly heard that I visited the prince. Everything the prince proposed or did aroused interest and was an event among that whole heap of his relations and "expectant ones"—the more so his sudden partiality for me. I knew positively that the prince was very interested in the fate of Anna Andreevna and was seeking a fiancé for her. But it was more difficult to find a fiancé for Miss Versilov than for the ones who embroidered on canvas.

And so, contrary to all expectation, Miss Versilov, having shaken the prince's hand and exchanged some cheerful social phrases with him, looked at me with extraordinary curiosity and, seeing that I was also looking at her, suddenly bowed to me with a smile. True, she had just walked in and her bow was in greeting, but her smile was so kind that it was obviously deliberate. And I recall that I experienced an extraordinarily pleasant feeling.

"And this . . . this is my dear and young friend Arkady Andreevich Dol . . ."—the prince murmured, noticing that she had bowed to me, while I was still sitting—and suddenly broke off: perhaps he became embarrassed that he was introducing me to her (that is, essentially, a brother to a sister). The pillow also gave me a bow; but I suddenly flew into a stupid rage and jumped up from my seat: a surge of affected pride, completely senseless, all from self-love!

"Excuse me, Prince, I am not Arkady Andreevich, but Arkady Makarovich," I cut off cuttingly, quite forgetting that I ought to have responded to the ladies' bows. Devil take that indecent moment!

"*Mais . . . tiens!*" the prince cried out, striking himself on the forehead with his finger.

"Where did you study?" I heard beside me the silly and drawn-out question of the pillow, who had come over to me.

"In a high school in Moscow."

"Ah! So I heard. And do they teach well there?"

"Very well."

I went on standing, and spoke like a soldier reporting.

The girl's questions were indisputably unresourceful, but, nevertheless, she did manage to cover up my stupid escapade and to ease the embarrassment of the prince, who listened at the same time with a merry smile to something Miss Versilov was merrily whispering to him—evidently not about me. A question, though: why should this girl, a total stranger to me, volunteer to cover up my stupid escapade and all the rest? At the same time, it was impossible to imagine that she had addressed me just like that; there was an intention here. She looked at me all too curiously, as if she also wanted me to take as much notice of her as possible. I figured it all out afterwards and was not mistaken.

"What, today?" the prince cried suddenly, leaping up from his place.

"So you didn't know?" Miss Versilov was surprised. "*Olympe!* The prince didn't know that Katerina Nikolaevna would be here today. We came to see her, we thought she took the morning train and had long been at home. We only just met her on the porch; she came straight from the station and told us to go to you, and that she would come presently... Here she is!"

The side door opened and—*that woman appeared!*

I already knew her face from an astonishing portrait that hung in the prince's office; I had studied that portrait all month. In her presence, I spent some three minutes in the office and not for one second did I tear my eyes from her face. But if I hadn't known the portrait and had been asked, after those three minutes, "What is she like?"—I wouldn't have been able to answer, because everything became clouded in me.

I only remember from those three minutes a truly beautiful woman, whom the prince was kissing and making crosses over, and who suddenly—just as soon as she entered—quickly began looking at me. I clearly heard how the prince, obviously pointing to me, murmured something, with a sort of little laugh, about a new secretary, and spoke my last name. She somehow jerked her face up, gave me a nasty look, and smiled so insolently that I suddenly made a step, went up to the prince, and murmured, trembling terribly, without finishing a single word and, I think, with chattering teeth:

"From then on I... my own affairs now... I'm going."

And I turned and went out. No one said a word to me, not even the prince; they all merely looked. The prince later told me that I turned so pale that he was "simply frightened."

Well, who could care!

Chapter Three

I

PRECISELY, WHO COULD CARE? The highest consideration absorbed all trifles, and one powerful feeling satisfied me for everything. I went out in a sort of rapture. Stepping into the street, I was ready to start singing. As if on purpose, it was a lovely morning, sun, passersby, noise, movement, joy, the crowd. But hadn't this woman insulted me? From whom would I have borne such a look and such an insolent smile without an immediate protest, even the stupidest—it makes no difference—on my part? Note that she was coming just so as to insult me the sooner, without ever having seen me: in her eyes, I was "Versilov's agent," and she was convinced even then and for a long time afterwards that Versilov held her entire fate in his hands and had the means to ruin her at once, if he wished to, by means of a certain document; she suspected as much at least. This was a duel to the death. And here—I was not insulted! There was an insult, but I didn't feel it! Far from it! I was even glad; having come to hate her, I even felt I was beginning to love her. "I don't know, can a spider hate the fly it has picked out and wants to catch? Sweet little fly! It seems to me that one loves one's victim; at least one may. You see, I love my enemy: I find it terribly pleasing, for instance, that she's so beautiful. I find it terribly pleasing, madam, that you are so haughty and majestic; if you were a bit meeker, the satisfaction wouldn't be so great. You spat upon me, but I'm triumphant; if you were actually to spit in my face with real spit, I really might not get angry, because you are my victim—*mine*, and not *his*. What a fascinating thought! No, the secret awareness of power is unbearably more enjoyable than manifest domination. If I were worth a hundred million, I think I'd precisely enjoy going around in my old clothes, so as to be taken for the measliest of men, who all but begs for alms, and be pushed around and despised; for me, the consciousness alone would be enough."

That was how I would have translated my thoughts and my joy at that time, and much of what I felt. I will add only that here, in what I've just written, it has come out more light-minded: in reality, I was more profound and modest. Maybe even now I'm more modest in myself than in my words and deeds. God grant it!

Maybe I've done a very bad thing in sitting down to write; there is immeasurably more left inside than what comes out in words. Your thought, even a bad one, while it is with you, is always more profound, but in words it is more ridiculous and dishonorable. Versilov told me that the complete opposite happens only with the worst people. They just lie, it's easy for them; while I'm trying to write the whole truth, which is terribly hard!

II

On this nineteenth day of the month, I took one more "step."

For the first time since my arrival, I had money in my pocket, because my sixty roubles, which I had saved up over two years, I had given to my mother, as I mentioned above; but several days earlier I had resolved that, on the day I got my salary, I would make a "test" I had long been dreaming of. Just the day before, I had cut out an address from a newspaper—an announcement by "the bailiff of the St. Petersburg Civil Court," and so on and so forth, that "on the nineteenth of September instant, at twelve noon, in the Kazan quarter, such-and-such precinct, etc., etc., at house number whatever, the sale of the movable property of Mrs. Lebrecht will take place," and that "the description, value, and property itself can be seen on the day of the sale," etc., etc.

It was just past one o'clock. I hurried on foot to the address. It was over two years since I'd taken a cab—I gave my word (otherwise I wouldn't have saved sixty roubles). I never went to auctions, I couldn't *afford* it yet; and though my present "step" was only *tentative*, even this step I had resolved to resort to only when I had finished school, when I had broken with everyone, when I had shrunk into my shell and become completely free. True, I was still far from being in a "shell" and far from being free; but I resolved to take the step only as a test—just so, in order to see, almost to dream a little, as it were, and then perhaps not to come for a long time, until it was a serious beginning. For everyone else it was only a small, stupid little auction, but for me it was the first log for the ship in which Columbus went to discover America. Those were my feelings at the time.

Reaching the place, I went into the courtyard indicated on the announcement, and entered Mrs. Lebrecht's apartment. The apartment consisted of a front hall and four not very big, not very high-ceilinged rooms. In the first room beyond the hall there was a crowd of up to thirty people, of whom half were buyers and the rest, judging by their looks, were either curious, or amateurs, or sent from Mrs. Lebrecht; there were both merchants and Jews, who had their eye on the gold things, and there were several people dressed "properly." Even the physiognomies of some of these gentlemen are imprinted on my memory. In the room to the right, in the open doorway, a table had been placed squarely between the doorposts, so that it was impossible to enter that room: the objects being perquisitioned and sold were there. To the left was another room, but the doors to it were closed, though they kept opening every moment by a little crack, through which someone could be seen peeking out—it must have been one of Mrs. Lebrecht's numerous family, who naturally felt very ashamed at the moment. At the table between the doors, facing the public, Mr. Bailiff sat on a chair, wearing a badge, and carried out the sale of the objects. I found the business almost half over already; as soon as I entered, I made my way through the crowd to the table. Bronze candlesticks were being sold. I began to look.

I looked and at once began to think: what can I buy here? And what was I going to do right now with bronze candlesticks, and would I achieve my goal, and was this how things were done, and would my calculation succeed? And wasn't my calculation childish? I thought of all this and waited. It was the same sort of sensation as at the gambling table, at the moment when you haven't played a card yet, but have come over with the intention of playing: "I'll play if I want, and I'll leave if I want—it's my choice." Your heart isn't pounding yet, but somehow hesitates and thrills slightly—a sensation not without pleasure. But indecision quickly begins to weigh you down, and you somehow turn blind: you reach out, you take a card, but mechanically, almost against your will, as if someone else was guiding your hand; finally you make up your mind and play—here the sensation is quite different, tremendous. I'm writing not about the auction, but only about myself: who else would have a pounding heart at an auction?

There were some who got excited, there were some who kept silent and bided their time, there were some who bought and regretted it. I felt no pity at all for a gentleman who, by mistake, having misheard, bought a nickel silver pitcher instead of a silver one, for five roubles instead of two; I even began to feel rather merry. The bailiff varied the objects: after the candlesticks came earrings, after the earrings, an embroidered morocco pillow, followed by a box—probably for the sake of diversity or in line with the buyers' demands. I didn't even hold out for ten minutes, was tending towards the pillow, then towards the box, but each time I stopped at the decisive moment: the objects seemed quite impossible to me. Finally, an album turned up in the bailiff's hands.

"A family album, bound in red morocco, worn, with drawings in watercolor and ink, in a carved ivory case with silver clasps—the starting price is two roubles!"

I went up: the object looked refined, but there was a flaw in one place in the ivory carving. I was the only one who went up, everybody was silent; there were no competitors. I could have unfastened the clasps and taken the album out of the case to examine it, but I didn't exercise my right and only waved a trembling hand, as if to say: "It makes no difference."

"Two roubles, five kopecks," I said, again, I believe, with chattering teeth.

It fell to me. I took out the money at once, paid, snatched the album, and went into a corner of the room; there I took it out of the case and feverishly, hurriedly, began to examine it: excepting the case, it was the trashiest thing in the world—a little album the size of small-format letter paper, thin, with worn gilt edges—exactly the kind that girls used to start keeping in the old days, as soon as they left the institute. Temples on hills, cupids, a pond with swans floating on it, were drawn in watercolors and ink; there were verses:

> I am setting out for far away,
> I am leaving Moscow for many a day,
> To all my dear ones I say good-bye,
> By stagecoach to the Crimee I fly.

(They've been preserved in my memory!) I decided that I had "failed"; if there was anything nobody needed, this was precisely it.

"Never mind," I decided, "you always lose on the first card; it's even a good omen."

I was decidedly cheerful.

"Ah, I'm too late! It's yours? Did you acquire it?" I suddenly heard beside me the voice of a gentleman in a dark blue coat, well dressed and of an imposing air. He was too late.

"I'm too late. Ah, what a pity! How much?"

"Two roubles, five kopecks."

"Ah, what a pity! Won't you let me have it?"

"Let's step out," I whispered to him, my heart skipping a beat.

We went out to the stairway.

"I'll let you have it for ten roubles," I said, feeling a chill in my spine.

"Ten roubles! Good heavens, how can you!"

"As you wish."

He stared wide-eyed at me; I was well dressed, in no way resembled a Jew or a retailer.

"Merciful heavens, it's a trashy old album, who needs it? The case is in fact quite worthless, you won't sell it to anybody."

"You want to buy it."

"But mine is a special case, I found out only yesterday, *I'm* the only one like that! Good heavens, how can you!"

"I should have asked twenty-five roubles; but since there was a risk that you'd let it go, I asked only ten so as to be sure. I won't go down even a kopeck."

I turned and walked away.

"Take four roubles," he overtook me in the courtyard, "or make it five."

I said nothing and walked on.

"All right, here!" He took out ten roubles, and I gave him the album.

"But you must agree it's dishonest! Two roubles and ten—eh?"

"Why dishonest? It's the market!"

"What kind of market is this?" (He was angry.)

"Where there's demand, there's the market. If you hadn't asked, I wouldn't have been able to sell it for forty kopecks."

Though I wasn't laughing out loud and looked serious, I did laugh my head off inwardly, not really with delight, but I don't know why myself, slightly out of breath.

"Listen," I murmured quite irrepressibly, but amiably and loving him terribly, "listen: when James Rothschild,[13] the late one, in Paris, the one who left seventeen hundred million francs" (the man nodded), "while still a young man, when he chanced to learn a few hours ahead of everybody else about the murder of the Duke of Berry, he rushed off at once to inform the right people, and with that one trick, in one instant, made several million—that's the way to do it!"

"So you're Rothschild, are you?" he shouted at me indignantly, as at a fool.

I quickly left the house. One step—and I'd made seven roubles, ninety-five kopecks! The step was meaningless, child's play, I agree, but even so it coincided with my thought and couldn't help stirring me extremely deeply... However, there's no point in describing feelings. The ten-rouble bill was in my waistcoat pocket, I stuck two fingers in to feel it—and walked along that way, without taking my hand out. Having gone about a hundred steps down the street, I took it out to look at it, looked, and wanted to kiss it. A carriage suddenly clattered at the porch of a house; the doorkeeper opened the door, and a lady came out of the house to get into the carriage, magnificent, young, beautiful, rich, in silk and velvet, with a five-foot train. Suddenly a pretty little pocketbook dropped from her hand and fell on the ground; she got in; the valet bent down to pick up the little thing, but I ran over quickly, picked it up, and handed it to the lady, tipping my hat. (It was a top hat, I was dressed like a young gentleman, not so badly.) With restraint, but smiling most pleasantly, the lady said to me, "*Merci, m'sieu.*" The carriage clattered off. I kissed the ten-rouble bill.

III

THAT SAME DAY I had to see Efim Zverev, one of my former high-school comrades, who had dropped out of school and enrolled in some specialized higher institute in Petersburg. He himself is not worth describing, and in fact I wasn't friends with him; but I had looked him up in Petersburg; he could (owing to various circumstances that are also not worth talking about) tell me the address of a certain Kraft, a man I needed very much, once he came back from Vilno. Zverev expected him precisely that day or the next, and had informed me of it two days before. I had to walk to the Petersburg side, but I wasn't tired at all.

I found Zverev (who was also about nineteen years old) in the courtyard of his aunt's house, where he was living temporarily. He had just had dinner and was walking around the courtyard on stilts; he informed me at once that Kraft had arrived the day before and stopped off at his former apartment, also there on the Petersburg side, and that he wished to see me himself as soon as possible, to inform me immediately of something necessary.

"He's going away again," Efim added.

Since in my present circumstances it was of capital importance for me to see Kraft, I asked Efim to take me at once to his apartment, which turned out to be two steps away in a lane. But Zverev declared that he had met Kraft an hour before and that he had gone to see Dergachev.[14]

"So let's go to Dergachev's, why do you keep making excuses—are you scared?"

Indeed, Kraft might spend a long time at Dergachev's, and then where was I to wait for him? I wasn't scared of going to Dergachev's, but I didn't want to, though this was already the third time Efim tried to drag me there. And this "scared" he always pronounced with the nastiest smile on my score. It wasn't a matter of being scared, I declare beforehand, and if I was afraid, it was of something quite different. This time I decided to go; it was also just two steps away. As we went, I asked Efim whether he still intended to run away to America.

"I may wait a little," he answered with a slight laugh.

I didn't much like him, I even didn't like him at all. His hair was very blond, he had a full, much too white face, even indecently white, to the point of infantility, and he was even taller than I, but you wouldn't have taken him for more than seventeen years old. I had nothing to talk about with him.

"And what's there? Always a crowd?" I asked for the sake of solidity.

"But why do you keep getting scared?" he laughed again.

"Go to the devil!" I got angry.

"Not a crowd at all. Only acquaintances come, and all our people, rest assured."

"But what the devil business is it of mine whether they're all your people or not? Am I one of your people? Why should they go and trust me?"

"I'm bringing you, and that's enough. They've even heard about you. Kraft can also speak for you."

"Listen, will Vasin be there?"

"I don't know."

"If he is, nudge me as soon as we go in and point to Vasin—as soon as we go in, you hear?"

I had heard a lot about Vasin and had long been interested.

Dergachev lived in a little wing in the courtyard of a wooden house that belonged to a merchant's widow, but the whole wing was at his disposal. There were three good rooms in all. The four windows all had their blinds lowered. He was a technician and had a job in Petersburg; I had heard in passing that he had been offered a profitable private post in the provinces and that he was about to set off.

As soon as we went into the tiny front hall, we heard voices; there seemed to be a heated argument and someone shouted: "*Quae medicamenta non sanant, ferrum sanat; quae ferrum non sanat, ignis sanat.*"*[15]

I was actually somewhat worried. Of course, I wasn't used to company, even whatever it might be. In high school I had addressed all my comrades informally, but I was comrades with almost none of them; I had made myself a corner and lived in my corner. But that was not what troubled me. In any case, I had promised myself not to get into any arguments and to say only what was most necessary, so that no one could draw any conclusions about me; above all—don't argue.

In the room, which was even much too small, there were some seven people, ten including the women. Dergachev was twenty-five years old, and he was married. His wife had a sister and another female relation; they also lived at Dergachev's. The room was furnished haphazardly, though sufficiently, and was even clean. On the wall hung a lithographic portrait, but a very cheap one, and in the corner an icon without a casing, but with a lighted icon lamp. Dergachev came over to me, shook hands, and invited me to sit down.

"Sit down, they're all our people here."

"Be so kind," a young woman added at once. She was rather pretty, very modestly dressed, and having bowed slightly to me, she at once went out. This was his wife, and it seemed by the look of it that she, too, had been arguing, but had now gone to nurse the baby. The other two ladies remained in the room—one very short, about twenty years old, in a black dress, and also not a bad-looking sort, while the other was about thirty, dry and sharp-eyed. They sat, listened very much, but did not enter into the conversation.

*What is not cured by medicines, will be cured by iron; what is not cured by iron, will be cured by fire.

As far as the men were concerned, they were all standing, and the only ones seated, apart from me, were Kraft and Vasin. Efim pointed them out to me at once, because I was now seeing Kraft as well for the first time in my life. I got up from my seat and went over to make their acquaintance. I'll never forget Kraft's face: no special beauty, but something as if all too meek and delicate, though personal dignity showed everywhere. Twenty-six years old, rather lean, of above-average height, blond, his face grave but soft; overall there was something gentle in him. And yet, if you had asked me, I would never have traded my maybe even very banal face for his face, which I found so attractive. There was something in his face that I wouldn't want to have in mine, something all too calm in a moral sense, something like a sort of secret, unconscious pride. However, I was probably unable to judge so literally then; it seems to me now that I judged that way then, that is, after the event.

"I'm very glad you've come," said Kraft. "I have a letter that concerns you. We'll sit here a while and then go to my place."

Dergachev was of medium height, broad-shouldered, very dark-haired, with a big beard; in his glance once could see quick-wittedness and restraint in everything, a certain constant wariness; though he was mainly silent, he was obviously in control of the conversation. Vasin's physiognomy did not impress me very much, though I had heard he was extremely intelligent: blond, with big light gray eyes, a very open face, but at the same time there was something as if excessively hard in it: one sensed little sociability, but his gaze was decidedly intelligent, more intelligent than Dergachev's, more profound—the most intelligent in the room; however, maybe I'm exaggerating it all now. Of the rest, I recall only two faces among all those young men: one tall, swarthy man with black side-whiskers, who talked a lot, about twenty-seven years old, a teacher or something of that sort, and also a young fellow of my age, in a long Russian vest—with a wrinkle in his face, taciturn, a listener. He turned out later to be of peasant stock.

"No, that's not the way to put it," began the teacher with black side-whiskers, who was the most excited of them all, obviously taking up the previous argument again. "I'm not saying anything about mathematical proofs, but this idea, which I'm ready to believe even without mathematical proofs..."

"Wait, Tikhomirov," Dergachev interrupted loudly, "the latest arrivals don't understand. This, you see," he suddenly turned to me alone (and, I confess, if his intention was to examine me as a newcomer or make me speak, the method was very clever on his part; I immediately sensed it and prepared myself), "this, you see, is Mr. Kraft, whose character and solid convictions are quite well-known to us all. Starting from a rather ordinary fact, he has arrived at a rather extraordinary conclusion, which has surprised everybody. He has deduced that the Russian people are a second-rate people..."

"Third-rate," someone cried.

"...second-rate, whose fate is to serve merely as material for a more noble race, and not to have its own independent role in the destinies of mankind. In view of this possibly correct deduction of his, Mr. Kraft has come to the conclusion that any further activity of any Russian man should be paralyzed by this idea, so to speak, that everyone should drop their hands and..."

"Permit me, Dergachev, that's not the way to put it," Tikhomirov again picked up impatiently (Dergachev yielded at once). "In view of the fact that Kraft has done serious research, has deduced deductions on the basis of physiology, which he considers mathematical, and has killed maybe two years on his idea (which I would quite calmly accept *a priori*), in view of that, that is, in view of Kraft's anxieties and seriousness, this matter presents itself as a phenomenon. A question arises from all this which Kraft cannot comprehend, and that is what we should occupy ourselves with, that is, Kraft's incomprehension, because it is a phenomenon. We should decide whether this is a clinical phenomenon, as a singular case, or is a property that may normally be repeated in others; this is of interest in view of the common cause. I shall believe Kraft about Russia and even say that I am perhaps also glad; if this idea were adopted by everyone, it would unbind hands and free many from patriotic prejudice..."

"It's not out of patriotism," said Kraft, as if with strain. This whole debate seemed disagreeable to him.

"Patriotism or not, that can be left aside," said Vasin, who was very silent.

"But, tell me, how could Kraft's deduction weaken the striving for the general human cause?" shouted the teacher (he alone shouted, all the rest spoke quietly). "Suppose Russia is destined to be second-rate; but it is possible not to work for Russia alone. And, besides, how can Kraft be a patriot, if he has ceased to believe in Russia?"

"Anyhow he's German," a voice was heard again.

"I'm Russian," said Kraft.

"That question is not directly related to the matter," Dergachev pointed out to the one who had interrupted.

"Abandon the narrowness of your idea." Tikhomirov wouldn't listen to anything. "If Russia is only material for nobler races, why shouldn't she serve as such material? It's a handsome enough role. Why not settle on this idea with a view to broadening the task? Mankind is on the eve of its regeneration, which has already begun. Only blind men can deny the forthcoming task. Leave Russia, if you've lost faith in her, and work for the future—for the future of a still unknown people, but which will be composed of all mankind, with no distinction of races. Even without that, Russia will die one day; peoples, even the most gifted of them, live no more than fifteen hundred, two thousand years at most; what difference does it make, two thousand or two hundred years? The Romans didn't survive even fifteen hundred years as a living entity, and they also became material. They're long gone, but they left an idea, and it entered into the destinies of mankind as an element of things to come. How can you tell a man there's nothing to do? I can't imagine a situation in which there could ever be nothing to do! Do it for mankind and don't worry about the rest. There's so much to do that a lifetime won't be enough, if you look around attentively."

"We must live by the law of nature and truth,"[16] Mrs. Dergachev said from behind the door. The door was slightly ajar, and she could be seen standing there, holding the baby to her breast, with her breast covered, and listening ardently.

Kraft listened, smiling slightly, and finally said, as if with a somewhat weary look, though with great sincerity:

"I don't understand how it's possible, while under the influence of some dominant idea, to which your mind and heart are totally subject, to live by anything that lies outside that idea."

"But if you're told logically, mathematically, that your deduction is mistaken, that the whole thought is mistaken, that you do not have the least right to exclude yourself from general useful activity only because Russia is predestined to be second-rate; if you are shown that, instead of a narrow horizon, an infinity is open to you, that instead of a narrow idea of patriotism..."

"Eh!" Kraft quietly waved his hand, "but I told you it's not a matter of patriotism."

"There's obviously a misunderstanding here," Vasin suddenly mixed in. "The mistake is that for Kraft it's not just a logical deduction, but, so to speak, a deduction that has turned into a feeling. Not all natures are the same; for many, a logical deduction sometimes turns into the strongest feeling, which takes over their whole being, and which it is very difficult to drive out or alter. To cure such a person, it's necessary in that case to change the feeling itself, which can be done only by replacing it with another that is equally strong. That is always difficult, and in many cases impossible."

"Mistake!" the arguer yelled. "A logical deduction in itself already breaks down prejudices. An intelligent conviction generates the same feeling. Thought proceeds from feeling and, installing itself in a person in its turn, formulates the new!"

"People are very varied: some change their feelings easily, others with difficulty," replied Vasin, as if not wishing to prolong the argument; but I was delighted with his idea.

"It's precisely as you say!" I suddenly turned to him, breaking the ice and suddenly beginning to speak. "It's precisely necessary to put one feeling in the place of another, so as to replace it. Four years ago, in Moscow, a certain general... You see, gentlemen, I didn't know him, but... Maybe he, indeed, could not inspire respect on his own... And besides, the fact itself might seem unreasonable, but... However, you see, his child died, that is, as a matter of fact, two girls, one after the other, of scarlet fever... Well, he was suddenly so crushed that he was sad all the time, so sad that he went around and you couldn't even look at him—and he ended by dying in about half a year. That he died of it is a fact! What, then, could have resurrected him? Answer: a feeling of equal strength! Those two girls should have been dug up from the grave and given to him—that's all, or something of the sort. So he died. And meanwhile you could have presented him with beautiful deductions: that life is fleeting, that everyone is mortal; presented him with calendar statistics,[17] how many children die of scarlet fever... He was retired..."

I stopped, breathless, and looked around.

"That's not it at all," someone said.

"The fact you cite, though not of the same kind as the given case, still resembles it and clarifies the matter," Vasin turned to me.

IV

HERE I MUST confess why I was delighted with Vasin's argument about the "idea-feeling," and along with that I must confess to an infernal shame. Yes, I was scared to go to Dergachev's, though not for the reason Efim supposed. I was scared because I had already been afraid of them in Moscow. I knew that they (that is, they or others of their sort—it makes no difference) were dialecticians and would perhaps demolish "my idea." I was firmly convinced in myself that I would not betray or tell my idea to them; but they (that is, again, they or their sort) might tell me something on their own that would make me disappointed in my idea, even without my mentioning it to them. There were questions in "my idea" that I hadn't resolved yet, but I didn't want anyone to resolve them except me. In the last two years I had even stopped reading books, afraid of coming across some passage that would not be in favor of the "idea," that might shake me. And suddenly Vasin resolves the problem at a stroke and sets me at peace in the highest sense. Indeed, what was I afraid of, and what could they do to me with no matter what dialectics? Perhaps I was the only one there who understood what Vasin said about the "idea-feeling"! It's not enough to refute a beautiful idea, one must replace it with something equally beautiful; otherwise, in my heart, unwilling to part with my feeling for anything, I will refute the refutation, even by force, whatever they may say. And what could they give me instead? And therefore I should have been braver, I was obliged to be more courageous. Delighted with Vasin, I felt shame, felt myself an unworthy child!

This resulted in yet another shame. Not the vile little urge to boast of my intelligence that had made me break the ice there and start talking, but also a desire to "throw myself on their necks." This desire to throw myself on people's necks so that they recognize me as good and start embracing me or something like that (swinishness, in short), I consider the most loathsome of all my shames, and I had suspected it in myself for a very long time—namely, ever since the corner I had kept myself in for so many years, though I don't regret it. I knew that I had to be gloomier among people. What comforted me, after each such disgrace, was simply that the "idea" was with me all the same, in secret as always, and that I hadn't betrayed it to them. With a sinking feeling, I sometimes imagined that once I had spoken my idea to someone, I would suddenly have nothing left, so that I'd become like everybody else, and might even abandon the idea; and so I preserved and cherished it and trembled at the thought of babbling. And then at Dergachev's, almost with the first encounter, I had been unable to hold out, I hadn't betrayed anything, of course, but I had babbled inadmissibly; the result was disgrace. A nasty recollection! No, it's impossible for me to live with people; I think so even now; I say it for forty years to come. My idea is—my corner.

V

As soon as Vasin praised me, I suddenly felt an irrepressible urge to speak.

"In my opinion, each of us has the right to have his own feelings... if it's from conviction... so that no one should reproach him for them," I addressed Vasin. Though I spoke glibly, it was as if it wasn't me, but as if somebody else's tongue was moving in my mouth.

"Re-e-eally, sir?" a voice picked up at once, drawling ironically, the same that had interrupted Dergachev and had shouted to Kraft that he was a German.

Considering him a total nonentity, I turned to the teacher, as if it was he who had shouted.

"My conviction is that I cannot judge anyone," I trembled, already knowing that I was going to fly off.

"Why such secrecy?" the nonentity's voice rang out again.

"Each of us has his idea," I looked point-blank at the teacher, who, on the contrary, was silent and studied me with a smile.

"Do you?" shouted the nonentity.

"It's too long to tell... But part of my idea is precisely that I should be left in peace. As long as I've got two roubles, I want to live alone, not depending on anybody (don't worry, I know the objections), and not doing anything—even for that great future of mankind for which Mr. Kraft has been invited to work. Personal freedom, I mean my own, sir, is foremost, and I do not want to know anything beyond that."

My mistake was that I got angry.

"That is, you preach the placidity of a sated cow?"

"Let it be so. There's no insult in a cow. I don't owe anyone anything, I pay society money in the form of fiscal impositions, so that I won't be robbed, beaten, or killed, and no one dares to demand anything more from me. I personally may have other ideas, and would like to serve mankind, and will, and maybe even ten times more than all the preachers, but I only want it to be so that no one *dares to demand* it of me, or forces me, like Mr. Kraft; my full freedom, even if I don't lift a finger. And to run around throwing yourself on other people's necks out of love for mankind, and burn with tears of tenderness—that is merely a fashion. And why should I necessarily love my neighbor or your future mankind, which I'll never see, which will not know about me, and which in its turn will rot without leaving any trace or remembrance (time means nothing here), when the earth in its turn will become an icy stone and fly through airless space together with an infinite multitude of identical icy stones, that is, more meaningless than anything one can possibly imagine! There's your teaching! Tell me, why should I necessarily be noble, especially if it all lasts no more than a minute?"

"B-bah!" shouted the voice.

I had fired all this off nervously and spitefully, snapping all the ropes. I knew I was falling into a pit, but I hurried for fear of objections. I sensed only too well that I was pouring as if through a sieve, incoherently, and skipping ten thoughts to get to the eleventh, but I was in a hurry to convince and reconquer them. This was so important for me! I'd been preparing for three years! But, remarkably, they suddenly fell silent, said absolutely nothing, and listened. I went on addressing the teacher:

"Precisely, sir. A certain extremely intelligent man said, among other things, that there is nothing more difficult than to answer the question, 'Why must one necessarily be noble?' You see, sir, there are three sorts of scoundrels in the world: naïve scoundrels, that is, those who are convinced that their meanness is the highest nobility; ashamed scoundrels, that is, those who are ashamed of their meanness, but fully intend to go through with it anyway; and, finally, sheer scoundrels, purebred scoundrels. With your permission, sir: I had a friend, Lambert, who at the age of sixteen said to me that when he was rich, his greatest pleasure would be to feed dogs bread and meat, while the children of the poor were dying of hunger, and when they had no wood for their stoves, he would buy a whole lumberyard, stack it up in a field, and burn it there, and give not a stick to the poor. Those were his feelings! Tell me, what answer should I give this purebred scoundrel when he asks, 'Why should I necessarily be noble?' And especially now, in our time, which you have so refashioned. Because it has never been worse than it is now. Things are not at all clear in our society, gentlemen. I mean, you deny God, you deny great deeds, what sort of deaf, blind, dull torpor can make me act this way, if it's more profitable for me otherwise? You say, 'A reasonable attitude towards mankind is also to my profit'; but what if I find all these reasonablenesses unreasonable, all these barracks and phalansteries?[18] What the devil do I care about them, or about the future, when I live only once in this world? Allow me to know my own profit myself: it's more amusing. What do I care what happens to this mankind of yours in a thousand years, if, by your code, I get no love for it, no future life, no recognition of my great deed? No, sir, in that case I shall live for myself in the most impolite fashion, and they can all go to blazes!"

"An excellent wish!"

"However, I'm always ready to join in."

"Even better!" (This was still that same voice.)

The rest went on being silent, they went on peering at me and studying me; but tittering gradually began to come from different ends of the room, still quiet, but they all tittered right in my face. Only Vasin and Kraft did not titter. The one with the black side-whiskers also grinned; he looked at me point-blank and listened.

"Gentlemen," I was trembling all over, "I won't tell you my idea for anything, but, on the contrary, I will ask you from your own point of view—don't think it's mine, because it may be that I love mankind a thousand times more than all of you taken together! Tell me—and you absolutely must answer me now, you are duty bound, because you're laughing—tell me, how will you entice me to follow you? Tell me, how will you prove to me that with you it will be better? Where are you going to put the protest of my person in your barracks? I have long wished to meet you, gentlemen! You will have barracks, communal apartments, *stricte necessaire*,* atheism, and communal wives without children—that's your finale, I know it, sirs. And for all that, for that small share of middling profit that your reasonableness secures for me, for a crust and some warmth, you take my whole person in exchange! With your

*The strictly necessary.

permission, sir: say my wife is taken away; are you going to subdue my person so that I won't smash my rival's head in? You'll say that I myself will become more reasonable then; but what will the wife of such a reasonable husband say, if she has the slightest respect for herself? No, it's unnatural, sirs; shame on you!"

"And you're what—a specialist in the ladies' line?" the gleeful voice of the nonentity rang out.

For a moment I had the thought of throwing myself at him and pounding him with my fists. He was a shortish fellow, red-haired and freckled... but, anyhow, devil take his looks!

"Don't worry, I've never yet known a woman," I said curtly, addressing him for the first time.

"Precious information, which might have been given more politely, in view of the ladies!"

But they all suddenly began stirring densely; they all started taking their hats and preparing to leave—not on account of me, of course, but because the time had come; but this silent treatment of me crushed me with shame. I also jumped to my feet.

"Allow me, however, to know your name, you did keep looking at me," the teacher suddenly stepped towards me with the meanest smile.

"Dolgoruky."

"Prince Dolgoruky?"

"No, simply Dolgoruky, the son of the former serf Makar Dolgoruky and the illegitimate son of my former master, Mr. Versilov. Don't worry, gentlemen, I'm not saying it so that you'll throw yourselves on my neck and we'll all start lowing like calves from tenderness!"

A loud and most unceremonious burst of laughter came at once, so that the baby who had fallen asleep behind the door woke up and squealed. I was trembling with fury. They all shook hands with Dergachev and left, paying no attention to me.

"Let's go," Kraft nudged me.

I went up to Dergachev, squeezed his hand as hard as I could, and shook it several times, also as hard as I could.

"I apologize for the constant insults from Kudriumov" (that was the red-haired one), Dergachev said to me.

I followed Kraft out. I wasn't ashamed of anything.

VI

Of course, between me as I am now and me as I was then there is an infinite difference.

Continuing to be "not ashamed of anything," I caught up with Vasin while still on the stairs, having left Kraft behind as second-rate, and with the most natural air, as if nothing had happened, asked:

"It seems you know my father—that is, I mean to say, Versilov?"

"We're not, in fact, acquainted," Vasin answered at once (and without a whit of that offensive, refined politeness assumed by delicate people when speaking with someone who has just disgraced himself), "but I know him slightly; I've met him and listened to him."

"If you've listened to him, then, of course, you know him, because you are—you! What do you think of him? Forgive the hasty question, but I need to know. Precisely what *you* would think, *your own* proper opinion is necessary."

"You're asking a lot of me. It seems to me that the man is capable of placing enormous demands on himself and, perhaps, of fulfilling them—but he renders no account to anyone."

"That's right, that's very right, he's a very proud man! But is he a pure man? Listen, what do you think of his Catholicism? However, I forgot that you may not know..."

If I hadn't been so excited, I naturally would not have fired off such questions, and so pointlessly, at a man I had never spoken with, but had only heard about. It surprised me that Vasin seemed not to notice my madness.

"I've also heard something about that, but I don't know how correct it might be," he answered as calmly and evenly as before.

"Not a bit! It's not true about him! Do you really think he can believe in God?"

"He's a very proud man, as you just said yourself, and many very proud people like to believe in God, especially those who are somewhat contemptuous of people. In many strong people there seems to be a sort of natural need—to find someone or something to bow down to. It's sometimes very hard for a strong man to bear his own strength."

"Listen, that must be terribly right!" I cried out again. "Only I wish I could understand..."

"Here the reason is clear: they choose God so as not to bow down before people—naturally, not knowing themselves how it comes about in them: to bow down before God is not so offensive. They become extremely ardent believers—or, to put it more correctly, they ardently desire to believe; but they take the desire for belief itself. In the end they very often become disappointed. As for Mr. Versilov, I think there are also extremely sincere traits of character in him. And generally he interests me."

"Vasin!" I cried out, "you make me so glad! I'm not surprised at your intelligence, I'm surprised that you, a man so pure and so immeasurably far above me—that you can walk with me and speak so simply and politely, as if nothing had happened!"

Vasin smiled.

"You praise me too much, and all that happened there was that you're too fond of abstract conversation. You were probably silent for a very long time before this."

"I was silent for three years, I've been preparing to speak for three years... To you, naturally, I couldn't have seemed a fool, because you are extremely intelligent yourself, though it would be impossible to behave more stupidly than I did—but a scoundrel!"

"A scoundrel?"

"Yes, undoubtedly! Tell me, don't you secretly despise me for saying that I was Versilov's illegitimate son... and boasting that I was the son of a serf?"

"You torment yourself too much. If you find that you spoke badly, you need only not speak that way the next time; you still have fifty years ahead of you."

"Oh, I know I should be very silent with people. The meanest of all debauches is to throw yourself on people's necks; I just said it to them, and here I am throwing myself on yours! But there's a difference, isn't there? If you've understood that difference, if you were capable of understanding it, I'll bless this moment!"

Vasin smiled again.

"Come and see me, if you want to," he said. "I have work now and am busy, but you'll give me pleasure."

"I concluded earlier, from your physiognomy, that you were all too firm and uncommunicative."

"That may very well be so. I knew your sister, Lizaveta Makarovna, last year in Luga... Kraft has stopped and seems to be waiting for you; he has to turn there."

I firmly shook Vasin's hand and ran to join Kraft, who had gone ahead of us while I was talking with Vasin. We silently went as far as his quarters; I did not want to speak to him yet, and could not. One of the strongest traits of Kraft's character was his delicacy.

Chapter Four

I

KRAFT USED TO be in government service somewhere, and along with that had also helped the late Andronikov (for a remuneration from him) to conduct some private affairs, which the latter had always engaged in on top of his government work. For me the important thing was that Kraft, owing to his particular closeness to Andronikov, might be informed of much that so interested me. But I knew from Marya Ivanovna, the wife of Nikolai Semyonovich, with whom I lived for so many years while I was in school—and who was the niece, the ward, and the favorite of Andronikov—that Kraft had even been "charged" with delivering something to me. I had been waiting for him that whole month.

He lived in a small two-room apartment, completely separate, and at the present moment, having only just returned, was even without a servant. The suitcase, though unpacked, had not been put away; things were strewn over chairs, and laid out on the table in front of the sofa were a valise, a traveling strongbox, a revolver, and so on. Coming in, Kraft was extremely pensive, as if he had totally forgotten about me; he may not even have noticed that I hadn't spoken to him on the way. He at once began looking for something, but, glancing into the mirror in passing, he stopped and studied his face closely for a whole minute. Though I noticed this peculiarity (and later recalled it very well), I was sad and very confused. I couldn't concentrate. There was a moment when I suddenly wanted to up and leave and thus abandon all these matters forever. And what were all these matters essentially? Weren't they simply self-inflicted cares? I was beginning to despair that I was maybe spending my energy on unworthy trifles out of mere sentimentality, while I had an energetic task before me. And meanwhile my incapacity for serious business was obviously showing itself, in view of what had happened at Dergachev's.

"Kraft, will you go to them again?" I suddenly asked him. He slowly turned to me, as if he hadn't quite understood me. I sat down on a chair.

"Forgive them!" Kraft said suddenly.

To me, of course, this seemed like mockery; but, looking at him attentively, I saw such a strange and even astonishing ingenuousness in his face, that I was even astonished at how seriously he had asked me to "forgive" them. He moved a chair and sat down beside me.

"I myself know that I'm maybe a rag-bag of all the vanities and nothing more," I began, "but I don't ask forgiveness."

"And there's no one to ask," he said softly and seriously. He spoke softly and very slowly all the time.

"Let me be guilty before myself... I like being guilty before myself... Kraft, forgive me for babbling here with you. Tell me, can it be that you're also in that circle? That's what I wanted to ask."

"They're no more stupid than others, nor more intelligent; they're crazy, like everybody."

"So everybody's crazy?" I turned to him with involuntary curiosity.

"Among the better sort of people now, everybody's crazy. Only mediocrity and giftlessness are having a heyday... However, that's all not worth..."

As he spoke, he somehow stared into space, began phrases and broke them off. Especially striking was a sort of despondency in his voice.

"Can it be that Vasin's with them? Vasin has a mind, Vasin has a moral idea!" I cried.

"There aren't any moral ideas now; suddenly not one can be found, and, above all, it looks as if there never were any."

"Before there weren't?"

"Better drop that," he said with obvious fatigue.

I was touched by his woeful seriousness. Ashamed of my egoism, I started to fall into his tone.

"The present time," he began himself, after a couple of minutes of silence and still staring somewhere into space, "the present time is a time of the golden mean and insensibility, a passion for ignorance, idleness, an inability to act, and a need to have everything ready-made. No one ponders; rarely does anyone live his way into an idea."

He broke off again and was silent for a little while. I listened.

"Now they're deforesting Russia, exhausting her soil, turning it into steppe, and preparing it for the Kalmyks.[19] If a man of hope were to appear and plant a tree, everyone would laugh: 'Do you think you'll live so long?' On the other hand, those who desire the good talk about what will be in a thousand years. The binding idea has disappeared completely. Everyone lives as if in a flophouse, and tomorrow it's up and out of Russia; everyone lives only so far as there's enough for him..."

"Excuse me, Kraft, you said, 'They're concerned about what will be in a thousand years.' Well, but your despair... about the fate of Russia... isn't it the same sort of concern?"

"That... that is the most urgent question there is!" he said irritably and quickly got up from his place.

"Ah, yes! I forgot!" he said suddenly in a completely different voice, looking at me in bewilderment. "I invited you on business, and meanwhile... For God's sake, forgive me."

It was as if he suddenly came out of some sort of dream, almost embarrassed; he took a letter from a briefcase that lay on the table and gave it to me.

"That is what I was to deliver to you. It is a document having a certain importance," he began with attentiveness and with a most businesslike air.

Long afterwards I was struck when I remembered this ability of his (at such a time for him!) to treat another's business with such heartfelt attentiveness, to tell of it so calmly and firmly.

"This is a letter of that same Stolbeev, following whose death a case arose between Versilov and the Princes Sokolsky over his will. That case is now being decided in court and will surely be decided in Versilov's favor; the law is with him. Meanwhile, in this letter, a personal one, written two years ago, the testator himself sets forth his actual will, or, more correctly, his wish, and sets it forth rather in the princes' favor than in Versilov's. At least the points that the Princes Sokolsky base themselves on in disputing the will gain much strength from this letter. Versilov's opponents would give a lot for this document, which, however, has no decisive legal significance. Alexei Nikanorovich (Andronikov), who was handling Versilov's case, kept this letter and, not long before his death, gave it to me, charging me to 'stow it away'—perhaps fearing for his papers in anticipation of his death. I have no wish now to judge Alexei Nikanorovich's intentions in this matter, and, I confess, after his death I was painfully undecided about what to do with this document, especially in view of the impending decision of the court case. But Marya Ivanovna, in whom Alexei Nikanorovich seems to have confided very much while he lived, brought me out of this difficulty: three weeks ago she wrote to me very resolutely that I should give the document precisely to you, and that this would also *seem* (her expression) to coincide with Andronikov's will. So here is the document, and I'm very glad that I can finally deliver it."

"Listen," I said, puzzled by such unexpected news, "what am I going to do now with this letter? How am I to act?"

"That's as you will."

"Impossible, I'm terribly unfree, you must admit! Versilov has been waiting so for this inheritance... and, you know, he'll die without this help—and suddenly there exists such a document!"

"It exists only here in this room."

"Can it be so?" I looked at him attentively.

"If you yourself can't find how to act in this case, what advice can I give you?"

"But I can't turn it over to Prince Sokolsky either; I'll kill all Versilov's hopes and, besides that, come out as a traitor before him... On the other hand, by giving it to Versilov, I'll reduce innocent people to poverty, and still put Versilov in an impossible position: either to renounce the inheritance or to become a thief."

"You greatly exaggerate the significance of the matter."

"Tell me one thing. Does this document have a decisive, definitive character?"

"No, it doesn't. I'm not much of a jurist. The lawyer for the opposing side would, of course, know how to put this document to use and derive all possible benefit from it; but Alexei Nikanorovich found positively that this letter, if presented, would have no great legal significance, so that Versilov's case could be won anyway. This document sooner represents, so to speak, a matter of conscience..."

"But that's the most important thing of all," I interrupted, "that's precisely why Versilov will be in an impossible position."

"He can destroy the document, however, and then, on the contrary, he'll deliver himself from any danger."

"Do you have special grounds for supposing that of him, Kraft? That's what I want to know, it's for that that I'm here!"

"I think anyone in his place would do the same."

"And you yourself would do the same?"

"I'm not getting an inheritance, and therefore don't know about myself."

"Well, all right," I said, putting the letter in my pocket. "The matter's finished for now. Listen, Kraft. Marya Ivanovna, who, I assure you, has revealed a lot to me, told me that you and you alone could tell the truth about what happened in Ems a year and a half ago between Versilov and the Akhmakovs. I've been waiting for you like a sun that would light up everything for me. You don't know my position, Kraft. I beseech you to tell me the whole truth. I precisely want to know what kind of man *he* is, and now—now I need it more than ever!"

"I'm surprised that Marya Ivanovna didn't tell you everything herself; she could have heard all about it from the late Andronikov and, naturally, has heard and knows maybe more than I do."

"Andronikov himself was unclear about the matter, that's precisely what Marya Ivanovna says. It seems nobody can clear it up. The devil would break a leg here! I know, though, that you were in Ems yourself then..."

"I didn't witness all of it, but what I know I'll willingly tell you, if you like—only will that satisfy you?"

II

I WON'T QUOTE his story word for word, but will give only the brief essence of it.

A year and a half ago, Versilov, having become a friend of the Akhmakovs' house through old Prince Sokolsky (they were all abroad then, in Ems), made a strong impression, first, on Akhmakov himself, a general and not yet an old man, but who, in the space of three years of marriage, had lost all the rich dowry of his wife, Katerina Nikolaevna, at cards, and had already had a stroke from his intemperate life. He had recovered from it and was convalescing abroad, but was living in Ems for the sake of his daughter from his first marriage. She was a sickly girl of about seventeen, who suffered from a weak chest, and was said to be extremely beautiful, but at the same time also fantastical. She had no dowry; hopes were placed, as usual, in the old prince. Katerina Nikolaevna was said to be a good stepmother. But the girl, for some reason, became especially attached to Versilov. He was then preaching "something passionate," in Kraft's expression, some new life, "was in a religious mood in the loftiest sense"—in the strange, and perhaps also mocking, expression of Andronikov, which was reported to me. But, remarkably, everyone soon took a dislike to him. The general was even afraid of him. Kraft in no way denies the rumor that Versilov somehow managed to instill it into the sick husband's mind that Katerina Nikolaevna was not indifferent to the young Prince Sokolsky (who had then absented himself from Ems to Paris). And he did it not directly, but, "as was his wont"—by slander, hints, and various meanderings, "at which he was a great master," as Kraft put it. Generally, I will say that Kraft considered him, and wished to consider him, sooner a crook and a born intriguer than a man indeed imbued with anything lofty or at least original. I knew even apart from Kraft that Versilov, who first exercised an extraordinary influence on Katerina Nikolaevna, gradually went so far as to break with her. What the whole game consisted of, I could not get from Kraft, but everyone confirmed the mutual hatred that arose between them after their friendship. Then a strange circumstance occurred: Katerina Nikolaevna's sickly stepdaughter apparently fell in love with Versilov, or was struck by something in him, or was inflamed by his talk, or I have no idea what else; but it is known that for some time Versilov spent almost every day near this girl. It ended with the girl suddenly announcing to her father that she wished to marry Versilov. That this actually happened, everyone confirms—Kraft and Andronikov and Marya Ivanovna—and once even Tatyana Pavlovna let something slip about it in my presence. It was also affirmed that Versilov himself not only wished but even insisted on marrying the girl, and that this concord of two dissimilar beings, an old one and a young one, was mutual. But the father was frightened at the thought; to the extent that he was turning away from Katerina Nikolaevna, whom he had formerly loved very much, he had begun almost to idolize his daughter, especially after his stroke. But the most violent opponent of the possibility of such a marriage was Katerina Nikolaevna herself. There took place an extreme number of some sort of secret, extremely unpleasant family confrontations, arguments, grievances, in short, all kinds of nastiness. The father finally began to give in, seeing the persistence of his daughter, who was in love with and "fanaticized" by Versilov—Kraft's expression. But Katerina Nikolaevna continued to rebel with implacable hatred. And here begins the tangle that no one understands. Here, however, is Kraft's direct conjecture, based on the given facts, but still only a conjecture.

Versilov supposedly managed to instill into the young person, *in his own way*, subtly and irrefutably, that the reason why Katerina Nikolaevna would not consent was that she was in love with him herself and had long been tormenting him with her jealousy, pursuing him, intriguing, had already made him a declaration, and was now ready to burn him up for loving another woman—in short, something like that. The worst of it was that he supposedly also "hinted" it to the father, the husband of the "unfaithful" wife, explaining that the prince was only an amusement. Naturally, there began to be real hell in the family. According to some versions, Katerina Nikolaevna loved her stepdaughter terribly, and now, being slandered before her, was in despair, to say nothing of her relations with the sick husband. But then, next to that there exists another version, in which, to my sorrow, Kraft fully believed, and in which I also believed myself (I had already heard about all that). It was affirmed (Andronikov is said to have heard it from Katerina Nikolaevna herself) that, on the contrary, Versilov, still earlier, before the beginning of the young girl's feelings, had offered Katerina Nikolaevna his love; that she, being his friend, and even in exaltation over him for some time, though constantly disbelieving and contradicting him, met this declaration of Versilov's with extreme hatred and mocked him venomously. She formally drove him away from her, because the man had proposed directly that she be his wife, in view of her husband's supposedly impending second stroke. Thus Katerina Nikolaevna must have felt a particular hatred for Versilov when she saw afterwards that he was openly seeking her stepdaughter's hand. Marya Ivanovna, conveying all this to me in Moscow, believed both the one variant and the other, that is, all of it together: she precisely affirmed that it could all occur at once, that it was something like *la haine dans l'amour*,* an offended love's pride on both sides, etc., etc., in short, something in the way of some most subtle novelistic entanglement, unworthy of any serious and sober-minded person, and with meanness to boot. But Marya Ivanovna herself had been stuffed with novels from childhood and read them day and night, despite her excellent character. As a result, Versilov's obvious meanness was displayed, a lie and an intrigue, something black and vile, the more so in that the end was indeed tragic: they say the poor inflamed girl poisoned herself with phosphorus matches; however, I don't know even now whether this last rumor was accurate; at least they tried their best to stifle it. The girl was sick for no more than two weeks and then died. The matches thus remained in doubt, but Kraft firmly believed in them as well. Soon after that, the girl's father also died—of grief, they say, which caused a second stroke, though

*Hate in love.

not before three months had passed. But after the girl's funeral, the young Prince Sokolsky, having returned to Ems from Paris, gave Versilov a slap in the face publicly in the garden, and the latter did not respond with a challenge; on the contrary, the very next day he appeared at a promenade as if nothing had happened. It was then that everyone turned away from him, in Petersburg as well. Versilov, though he continued to have acquaintances, had them in a totally different circle. His society acquaintances all accused him, though, incidentally, very few of them knew all the details; they only knew something about the novelistic death of the young lady and about the slap. Only two or three persons had possibly full information; the late Andronikov, who had long had business connections with the Akhmakovs, and particularly with Katerina Nikolaevna on a certain matter, knew most of all. But he kept all these secrets even from his own family, and only revealed something to Kraft and Marya Ivanovna, and that out of necessity.

"Above all, there's now a certain document involved," Kraft concluded, "which Mme. Akhmakov is extremely afraid of."

And here is what he told me about that as well.

Katerina Nikolaevna had had the imprudence, while the old prince, her father, was abroad and had already begun to recover from his fit, to write to Andronikov in great secret (Katerina Nikolaevna trusted him fully) an extremely compromising letter. At that time, they say, the recuperating prince indeed showed an inclination to spend his money and all but throw it to the winds: while abroad he started buying totally unnecessary but valuable objects, paintings, vases; gave and donated large sums to God knows what, even to various institutions there; he almost bought a ruined estate, encumbered with litigations, from a Russian society squanderer, sight unseen, for an enormous sum; finally, he seemed indeed to begin dreaming of marriage. And so, in view of all that, Katerina Nikolaevna, who never left her father's side during his illness, sent to Andronikov, as a lawyer and an "old friend," the inquiry, "Would it be possible legally to declare the prince under guardianship or somehow irresponsible; and if so, what would be the best way to do it without a scandal, so that no one could accuse anyone and her father's feelings would be spared, etc., etc." They say Andronikov brought her to reason then and advised against it; and afterwards, when the prince had fully recovered, it was no longer possible to go back to the idea; but the letter stayed with Andronikov. And now he dies. Katerina Nikolaevna remembered at once about the letter. If it should be discovered among the deceased's papers and get into the hands of the old prince, he would undoubtedly throw her out for good, disinherit her, and not give her a kopeck while he lived. The thought that his own daughter had no faith in his reason, and even wanted to declare him mad, would turn this lamb into a savage beast. While she, having become a widow, was left without any means, thanks to her gambler husband, and had only her father to count on; she fully hoped to get a new dowry from him as rich as the first one!

Kraft knew very little about the fate of this letter, but he observed that Andronikov "never tore up necessary papers" and, besides, was a man not only of broad intelligence, but also of "broad conscience." (I even marveled then at such an extraordinarily independent view on the part of Kraft, who had so loved and respected Andronikov.) But all the same Kraft was certain that the compromising document had fallen into the hands of Versilov, through his closeness to Andronikov's widow and daughters. It was known that they had presented Versilov at once and dutifully with all the papers the deceased had left behind. He also knew that Katerina Nikolaevna was informed that Versilov had the letter, and that this was what she feared, thinking that Versilov would at once go to the old prince with the letter; that, having returned from abroad, she had already searched for the letter in Petersburg, had visited the Andronikovs, and was now continuing to search, since the hope still remained in her that the letter was perhaps not with Versilov, and, in conclusion, that she had also gone to Moscow solely with that aim and had pleaded with Marya Ivanovna there to look among the papers she had kept. She had found out about Marya Ivanovna's existence and her relations with the late Andronikov quite recently, on returning to Petersburg.

"Do you think she didn't find it at Marya Ivanovna's?" I asked, having a thought of my own.

"If Marya Ivanovna didn't reveal anything even to you, then maybe she doesn't have anything."

"So you suppose that Versilov has the document?"

"Most likely he does. However, I don't know, anything is possible," he said with visible fatigue.

I stopped questioning him. What was the point? All the main things had become clear to me, in spite of this unworthy tangle; everything I was afraid of—had been confirmed.

"That's all like dreams and delirium," I said in profound sorrow, and took my hat.

"Is this man very dear to you?" Kraft asked with visible and great sympathy, which I read on his face at that moment.

"I anticipated," I said, "that I wouldn't learn the full story from you anyway. Mme. Akhmakov is the one remaining hope. I did have hope in her. Maybe I'll go to see her, and maybe not."

Kraft looked at me in some perplexity.

"Good-bye, Kraft! Why foist yourself on people who don't want you? Isn't it better to break with it all—eh?"

"And then where?" he asked somehow sternly and looking down.

"To yourself, to yourself! Break with it all and go to yourself!"

"To America?"

"To America! To yourself, to yourself alone! That's the whole of 'my idea,' Kraft!" I said ecstatically.

He looked at me somehow curiously.

"And you have this place: 'to yourself'?"

"I do. Good-bye, Kraft. I thank you, and I'm sorry to have troubled you! In your place, since you've got such a Russia in your head, I'd send everybody to the devil: away with you, scheme, squabble among yourselves—what is it to me!"

"Stay a while," he said suddenly, having already seen me to the front door.

I was a little surprised, went back, and sat down again. Kraft sat down facing me. We exchanged smiles of some sort, I can see it all as if it were now. I remember very well that I somehow wondered at him.

"What I like about you, Kraft, is that you're such a polite man," I said suddenly.

"Oh?"

"It's because I'm rarely able to be polite myself, though I'd like to be able... But then, maybe it's better that people insult us. At least they deliver us from the misfortune of loving them."

"What time of day do you like best?" he asked, obviously not listening.

"What time? I don't know. I don't like sunset."

"Oh?" he said with a sort of special curiosity, but at once lapsed into thought again.

"Are you going somewhere again?"

"Yes... I am."

"Soon?"

"Soon."

"Do you really need a revolver to get to Vilno?" I asked without the least second thought: it didn't even enter my thoughts! I just asked, because the revolver flashed there, and I was at pains to find something to talk about.

He turned and looked intently at the revolver.

"No, I just do it out of habit."

"If I had a revolver, I'd have hidden it somewhere under lock and key. You know, by God, it's tempting! Maybe I don't believe in epidemics of suicides, but if that sticks up in front of your eyes—really, there are moments when it might be tempting."

"Don't speak of that," he said, and suddenly got up from his chair.

"I don't mean me," I added, also getting up. "I wouldn't use it. You could give me three lives—it would still be too little."

"Live more," as if escaped from him.

He smiled distractedly and, strangely, walked straight to the front hall, as if leading me out personally, naturally without knowing what he was doing.

"I wish you all luck, Kraft," I said, going out to the stairs.

"That may be," he replied firmly.

"See you later!"

"That also may be."

I remember his last look at me.

III

SO THIS WAS the man after whom my heart had been throbbing for so many years! And what had I expected from Kraft, what new information?

When I left Kraft, I had a strong wish to eat; evening was already falling, and I had not had lunch. I went into a small tavern right there on the Petersburg side, on Bolshoi Prospect, intending to spend some twenty kopecks, twenty-five at the most—not for anything would I have allowed myself to spend more then. I ordered soup and, I remember, having finished it, I sat looking out the window. The room was full of people; there was a smell of burnt grease, tavern napkins, and tobacco. It was vile. Above my head, a voiceless nightingale, glum and brooding, tapped the bottom of its cage with its beak. The billiard room on the other side of the wall was noisy, but I sat and thought intensely. The setting sun (why was Kraft surprised that I didn't like sunset?) inspired in me some new and unexpected sensations, quite out of place. I kept imagining my mother's gentle look, her dear eyes that had gazed at me so timidly for a whole month now. Lately I had been very rude at home, mostly to her; I wished to be rude to Versilov, but, not daring with him, out of my mean habit, I tormented her. I even thoroughly intimidated her: she often looked at me with such imploring eyes, when Andrei Petrovich came in, fearing some outburst from me... It was very strange that now, in the tavern, I realized for the first time that Versilov addressed me familiarly, and she—formally. I had wondered about it before, and not favorably for her, but here I realized it somehow particularly—and all sorts of strange thoughts came pouring into my head one after another. I went on sitting there for a long time, till it was completely dark. I also thought about my sister...

A fateful moment for me. I had to decide at all costs! Can it be that I'm incapable of deciding? What's so hard about breaking with them, if on top of it they don't want me themselves? My mother and my sister? But I won't leave them in any case—whatever turn things take.

It's true that the appearance of this man in my life, that is, for a moment, in early childhood, was the fateful push with which my consciousness began. If he hadn't come my way then, my mind, my way of thinking, my fate, would surely have been different, even despite the character fate determined for me, which I couldn't have escaped anyway.

But it now turned out that this man was only my dream, my dream since childhood. I had thought him up that way, but in fact he turned out to be a different man, who fell far below my fantasy. I had come to a pure man, not to this one. And why had I fallen in love with him, once and for all, in that little moment when I saw him while still a child? This "for all" had to go. Someday, if I find room, I'll describe our first meeting: it's a most empty anecdote, from which precisely nothing could come. But for me a whole pyramid came from it. I began on that pyramid while still under my child's blanket, when, as I was falling asleep, I would weep and dream—about what?—I myself don't know. About being abandoned? About being tormented? But I was tormented only a little, for just two years, while I was at Touchard's boarding school, where he tucked me away then and left forever. After that nobody tormented me; even the contrary, I myself looked proudly at my comrades. And I can't stand this orphanhood whining about itself! There's no more loathsome role than when orphans, illegitimate children, all these cast-offs, and generally all this trash, for whom I have not the slightest drop of pity, suddenly rise up solemnly before the public and start their pitiful but admonitory whining: "Look at how we've been treated!" I'd thrash all these orphans. Not one of all that vile officialdom understands that it's ten times nobler for him to keep silent, and not to whine, and not *deign* to complain. And since you've started to deign, it serves you right, love-child. That's what I think!

But what is ridiculous is not that I used to dream "under the blanket," but that I came here for him, once again for this thought-up man, all but forgetting my main goals. I was coming to help him to smash slander, to crush his enemies. The document Kraft spoke of, that woman's letter to Andronikov, which she is so afraid of, which can smash her life and reduce her to poverty, and which she supposes to be in Versilov's possession—this letter was not in Versilov's possession, but in mine, sewn into my side pocket! I had sewn it myself, and no one in the whole world knew of it yet. That the novelistic Marya Ivanovna, who "had charge" of the document, found it necessary to turn it over to me and no one else, was merely her view and her will, and I'm not obliged to explain it; maybe someday I'll tell about it by the way; but, being so unexpectedly armed, I could not but be tempted by the wish to come to Petersburg. Of course, I proposed to help this man not otherwise than secretly, without showing off or getting excited, without expecting either his praise or his embraces. And never, never would I *deign* to reproach him with anything! And was it his fault that I had fallen in love with him and made him into a fantastic ideal? Maybe I didn't even love him at all! His original mind, his curious character, his intrigues and adventures of some sort, and the fact that my mother was with him—all this, I thought, could not stop me now; it was enough that my fantastic doll was smashed and that I could perhaps not love him anymore. And so, what was stopping me, what was I stuck on? That was the question. The upshot of it all was that I was the only stupid one, and nobody else.

But, since I demand honesty of others, I'll be honest myself: I must confess that the document sewn into my pocket did not only arouse in me a passionate desire to fly to Versilov's aid. That is all too clear to me now, though even then I already blushed at the thought. I kept imagining a woman, a proud high-society being, whom I would meet face to face; she would despise me, laugh at me as at a mouse, not even suspecting that I was the master of her fate. This thought intoxicated me still in Moscow, and especially on the train as I was coming here; I've already confessed that above. Yes, I hated this woman, yet I already loved her as my victim, and this is all true, this was all actually so. But it was all such childishness as I hadn't expected even from someone like myself. I'm describing my feelings at that time, that is, what went through my head as I sat in the tavern under the nightingale and decided to break with them ineluctably that same evening. The thought of today's meeting with this woman suddenly brought a flush of shame to my face. A disgraceful meeting! A disgraceful and stupid little impression and—above all—the strongest proof of my inability to act! It proved simply, as I thought then, that I was unable to hold out even before the stupidest enticements, whereas I had just told Kraft that I had "my own place," my own business, and that if I had three lives, even that would be too little for me. I had said it proudly. That I had dropped my idea and gotten drawn into Versilov's affairs—that could still be excused in some way; but that I rush from side to side like a startled hare and get drawn into every trifle, that, of course, was only my own stupidity. What the deuce pushed me to go to Dergachev's and pop up with my stupid talk, if I had long known that I'm unable to tell anything intelligently and sensibly, and that the most advantageous thing for me is to be silent? And then some Vasin brings me to reason by saying that I still have "fifty years of life ahead of me, and so there's nothing to be upset about." His objection is splendid, I agree, and does credit to his indisputable intelligence; it's splendid already in that it's the simplest, and what is simplest is always understood only in the end, once everything cleverer or stupider has been tried; but I knew this objection myself even before Vasin; I had deeply sensed this thought more than three years ago; moreover, "my idea" partly consists in it. That's what I was thinking about in the tavern then.

I felt vile when I reached the Semyonovsky quarter that evening, between seven and eight, weary from walking and thinking. It was already quite dark, and the weather changed; it was dry, but a nasty Petersburg wind sprang up at my back, biting and sharp, and blew dust and sand around. So many sullen faces of simple folk, hurrying back to their corners from work and trade! Each had his own sullen care on his face, and there was perhaps not a single common, all-uniting thought in that crowd! Kraft was right: everybody's apart. I met a little boy, so little that it was strange that he could be alone in the street at such an hour; he seemed to have lost his way; a woman stopped for a moment to listen to him, but understood nothing, spread her arms, and went on, leaving him alone in the darkness. I went over to him, but for some reason he suddenly became frightened of me and ran off. Nearing the house, I decided that I would never go to see Vasin. As I went up the stairs, I wanted terribly to find them at home alone, without Versilov, to have time before he came to say something kind to my mother or my dear sister, to whom I had hardly addressed a single special word for the whole month. It so happened that he was not at home...

IV

AND BY THE WAY: bringing this "new character" on stage in my "Notes" (I'm speaking of Versilov), I'll give a brief account of his service record, which, incidentally, is of no significance. I do it to make things clearer for the reader, and because I don't see where I might stick this record in further on in the story.

He studied at the university, but went into the guards, into a cavalry regiment. He married Miss Fanariotov and resigned. He went abroad and, returning, lived in Moscow amidst worldly pleasures. On his wife's death, he came to his country estate; here occurred the episode with my mother. Then for a long time he lived somewhere in the south. During the war with Europe,[20] he again went into military service, but did not get to the Crimea and never saw action all that while. When the war ended, he resigned, went abroad, and even took my mother, whom, however, he left in Königsberg. The poor woman occasionally told with a sort of horror and shaking her head of how she had lived for a whole six months then, alone as could be, with a little daughter, not knowing the language, as if in a forest, and in the end also without any money. Then Tatyana Pavlovna came to fetch her and took her back to somewhere in Nizhny-Novgorod province. Later Versilov joined the arbiters of the peace at the first call-up,[21] and they say he performed his duties splendidly; but he soon quit and in Petersburg began to occupy himself with conducting various private civil suits.

Andronikov always thought highly of his capacities, respected him very much, and said only that he didn't understand his character. Later he also dropped that and went abroad again, this time for a long period, for several years. Then began his especially close connections with old Prince Sokolsky. During all this time his financial means underwent two or three radical changes: first he fell into poverty, then he suddenly got rich and rose again.

But anyhow, now that I've brought my notes precisely to this point, I've decided to tell about "my idea" as well. I'll describe it in words for the first time since its conception. I've decided to, so to speak, disclose it to the reader, also for the clarity of the further account. And not only the reader, but I myself am beginning to get entangled in the difficulty of explaining my steps without explaining what led me and prompted me to them. Because of this "figure of omission," I, in my lack of skill, have fallen back into those novelistic "beauties" that I myself derided above. On entering the door of my Petersburg novel, with all my disgraceful adventures in it, I find this preface necessary. But it was not "beauties" that tempted me to omission up to now, but also the essence of the matter, that is, the difficulty of the matter; even now, when all the past has already passed, I feel an insurmountable difficulty in telling about this "thought." Besides that, I undoubtedly should explain it in the form it had then, that is, in the way it took shape and conceived itself in me at that time, and not now, and that is a new difficulty. It's almost impossible to tell about certain things. Precisely those ideas that are the simplest, the clearest—precisely those are also hard to understand. If Columbus, before the discovery of America, had started telling his idea to others, I'm sure he wouldn't have been understood for a terribly long time. And in fact he wasn't. In saying this, I have no thought of equating myself with Columbus, and if anybody concludes that, he should be ashamed, that's all.

Chapter Five

I

MY IDEA IS—to become Rothschild. I invite the reader to calmness and seriousness.

I repeat: my idea is to become Rothschild, to become as rich as Rothschild; not simply rich, but precisely like Rothschild. Why, what for, precisely what goals I pursue—of that I shall speak later. First, I shall merely prove that the achievement of my goal is mathematically assured.

The matter is very simple, the whole secret lies in two words: *persistence* and *continuity*.

"We've heard all that," I'll be told, "it's nothing new. Every *Vater* in Germany repeats it to his children, and yet your Rothschild" (that is, the late James Rothschild, the Parisian, he's the one I'm speaking of) "was only one, while there are millions of *Vaters*."

I would answer:

"You assure me that you've heard it all, and yet you haven't heard anything. True, you're also right about one thing: if I said that this was a 'very simple' matter, I forgot to add that it's also the most difficult. All the religions and moralities in the world come down to one thing: 'We must love virtue and flee from vice.' What, it seems, could be simpler? So go and do something virtuous and flee from at least one of your vices, give it a try—eh? It's the same here."

That's why your countless *Vaters* in the course of countless ages can repeat these two astonishing words, which make up the whole secret, and yet Rothschild remains alone. Which means it's the same and not the same, and the *Vaters* are repeating quite a different thought.

No doubt they, too, have heard about persistence and continuity; but to achieve my goal, it's not *Vater* persistence and *Vater* continuity that are needed.

Already this one word, that he's a *Vater*—I'm not speaking only of Germans—that he has a family, that he lives like everybody else, has expenses like everybody else, has duties like everybody else—here you don't become Rothschild, but remain only a moderate man. I understand all too clearly that, having become Rothschild, or even only wishing to become him, not in a *Vater*-like way, but seriously—I thereby at once step outside of society.

A few years ago I read in the newspapers that on the Volga, on one of the steamboats, a certain beggar died, who had gone about in tatters, begging for alms, and was known to everybody there. After his death, they found as much as three thousand in banknotes sewn into his rags. The other day I again read about a certain beggar, from the nobility, who went around the taverns hat in hand. They arrested him and found as much as five thousand roubles on him. Two conclusions follow directly from this: first, *persistence* in accumulating, even by kopecks, produces enormous results later on (time means nothing here); and, second, that the most unsophisticated but *continuous* form of gain mathematically assures success.

And yet there are people, perhaps quite a few of them, who are respectable, intelligent, and restrained, but who (no matter how they try) do not have either three or five thousand, but who nevertheless want terribly much to have it. Why is that so? The answer is clear: because, despite all their wanting, not one of them *wants* to such a degree, for instance, as to become a beggar, if there's no other way of getting money; or is persistent to such a degree, even having become a beggar, as not to spend the very first kopecks he gets on an extra crust for himself or his family. And yet, with this method of accumulation, that is, with begging, one has to eat nothing but bread and salt in order to save so much money; at least that's my understanding. That is surely what the two abovementioned beggars did, that is, ate nothing but bread and lived all but under the open sky. There is no doubt that they had no intention of becoming Rothschild: these were Harpagons or Plyushkins[22] in the purest form, nothing more; but conscious money-making in a completely different form, and with the goal of becoming Rothschild, will call for no less wanting and strength of will than with these two beggars. A *Vater* won't show such strength. There is a great diversity of strengths in the world, strengths of will and wanting especially. There is the temperature of boiling water, and there is the temperature of red-hot iron.

Here it's the same as a monastery, the same ascetic endeavor. Here's it's a feeling, not an idea. What for? Why? Is it moral, and is it not ugly, to go about in sackcloth and eat black bread all your life, while carrying such huge money on you? These questions are for later, but now I'm only talking about the possibility of achieving the goal.

When I thought up "my idea" (and it consists of red-hot iron), I began testing myself: am I capable of the monastery and asceticism? To that end I spent the whole first month eating nothing but bread and water. It came to no more than two and a half pounds of black bread a day. To carry it out, I had to deceive the clever Nikolai Semyonovich and the well-wishing Marya Ivanovna. I insisted, to her distress and to a certain perplexity in the most delicate Nikolai Semyonovich, that dinner be brought to my room. There I simply destroyed it: the soup I poured out the window into the nettles or a certain other place, the beef I either threw out the window to the dog, or wrapped in paper, put in my pocket, and took out later, well, and all the rest. Since they served much less than two and a half pounds of bread for dinner, I bought myself more bread on the sly. I held out for that month, only I may have upset my stomach somewhat; but the next month I added soup to the bread, and drank a glass of tea in the morning and evening—and, I assure you, I spent a whole year that way in perfect health and contentment, and morally—in rapture and continuous secret delight. Not only did I not regret the meals, I was in ecstasy. By the end of the year, having made sure that I was able to endure any fast you like, I began to eat as they did and went back to having dinner with them. Not satisfied with this test, I made a second one: apart from my upkeep, which was paid to Nikolai Semyonovich, I was allocated a monthly sum of five roubles for pocket money. I decided to spend only half of it. This was a very hard test, but in a little over two years, when I came to Petersburg, I had in my pocket, apart from other money, seventy roubles saved up solely by this economy. The result of these two experiments was tremendous for me: I learned positively that I was able to want enough to achieve my goal, and that, I repeat, is the whole of "my idea." The rest is all trifles.

II

HOWEVER, LET US examine the trifles as well.

I have described my two experiments; in Petersburg, as is already known, I made a third—went to the auction and, at one stroke, made a profit of seven roubles, ninety-five kopecks. Of course, that wasn't a real experiment, but just a game, for fun: I wanted to steal a moment from the future and experience how I would go about and behave. But generally, still at the very beginning, in Moscow, I postponed the real setting out in business until I was completely free; I understood only too well that I at least had, for instance, to finish high school first. (I sacrificed the university, as is already known.) Indisputably, I went to Petersburg with repressed wrath: I had just finished high school and become free for the first time, when I suddenly saw that Versilov's affairs would again distract me from starting business for an unknown period! But though I was wrathful, I still went completely at ease about my goal.

True, I knew nothing of practical life; but I had been thinking it over for three years on end and could not have any doubts. I had imagined a thousand times how I would set about it: I suddenly turn up, as if dropped from the sky, in one of our two capitals[23] (I chose to begin with our capitals, and namely with Petersburg, to which, by a certain reckoning, I gave preference), and so, I've dropped from the sky, but am completely free, not dependent on anybody, healthy, and have a hundred roubles hidden in my pocket for an initial working capital. It's impossible to begin without a hundred roubles, otherwise the very first period of success would be delayed for too long. Besides a hundred roubles, I have, as is already known, courage, persistence, continuity, total solitude, and secrecy. Solitude is the main thing: I terribly disliked till the very last minute any contact or association with people; generally speaking, I decided absolutely to begin the "idea" alone, that was *sine qua*. People are a burden to me, and I would be troubled in spirit, which would harm my goal. And generally all my life till now, in all my dreams of how I would deal with people—I always have it come out very intelligent; as soon as it's in reality—it's always very stupid. And I confess this with indignation and sincerely, I have always betrayed myself with words and hurried, and therefore I resolved to cancel people. The gain was independence, peace of mind, clarity of goal.

Despite the terrible Petersburg prices, I determined once and for all that I would not spend more than fifteen kopecks on food, and I knew I would keep my word. I had pondered this question of food thoroughly and for a long time; I proposed, for instance, to eat only bread and salt for two days in a row, so as to spend the money saved in two days on the third day; it seemed to me that it would be more profitable for my health than an eternally regular fast on the minimum of fifteen kopecks. Then I needed a corner to live in, literally a corner, only to have a good night's sleep or take refuge on a particularly nasty day. I proposed to live in the street, and if necessary I was prepared to sleep in night shelters, where, on top of a night's lodging, they give you a piece of bread and a glass of tea. Oh, I'd be only too able to hide my money, so that it wouldn't be stolen in my corner or in the shelter; they wouldn't even catch a glimpse of it, I promise you! "Steal from me? No, the real fear is that I'll steal from them!"—I heard this merry phrase once from some rascal in the street. Of course, I apply only the prudence and cunning to myself, and have no intention of stealing. Moreover, still in Moscow, maybe from the very first day of the "idea," I decided that I would not be a pawnbroker or a usurer: there are Yids for that, and those Russians who lack both intelligence and character. Pawnbroking and usury are for mediocrities.

As for clothes, I proposed to have two outfits: an everyday one and a decent one. Once I had them, I was sure I'd wear them for a long time; I purposely spent two and a half years learning how to wear clothes and even discovered a secret: for suits to stay always new and not wear out, they should be cleaned with a brush as often as possible, five or six times a day. Cloth has no fear of the brush, believe me, what it fears is dust and dirt. Dust is the same as stones, looked at under a microscope, while even the stiffest brush is, after all, almost wool itself. I also learned how to wear boots evenly: the secret is that you must carefully put your foot down with the whole sole at once, avoiding as far as possible bringing it down on the side. It can be learned in two weeks, after which it becomes unconscious. In this way boots can be worn, on the average, one-third longer. Two years' experience.

Then the activity itself begins.

I started from this consideration: I have a hundred roubles. In Petersburg there are so many auctions, sales, small shops at flea markets, and people in need of things, that it's impossible, once you've bought an object for such-and-such a price, not to sell it for a little more. With the album I made a profit of seven roubles, ninety-five kopecks on a capital expenditure of two roubles, five kopecks. This enormous profit was taken without risk: I saw from his eyes that the buyer wouldn't back out. Naturally, I understand very well that it was mere chance: but those are the kinds of chances I seek, that's why I decided to live in the street. Well, granted such chances may even be extremely rare; all the same, my main rule will be not to risk anything, and the second—to be sure to earn at least something each day over and above the minimum spent on my subsistence, so that the accumulation doesn't stop for a single day.

They'll tell me: these are all dreams, you don't know the street, and you'll be cheated from the first step. But I have will and character, and street science is a science like any other, it yields to persistence, attention, and ability. In high school I was among the first right up to the final grade; I was very good at mathematics. Well, as if experience and street science should be extolled to such an idolizing degree as to predict certain failure! The only ones who say it are always those who have never experimented with anything, never started any life, and went on vegetating with everything provided. "If one gets his nose smashed, another will do the same." No, I won't get my nose smashed. I have character, and with my attentiveness, I'll learn everything. Well, is it possible to imagine that with constant persistence, constant keen-sightedness, and constant reflection and calculation, with boundless activity and running around, you will not attain finally to a knowledge of how to earn an extra twenty kopecks a day? Above all, I decided never to aim at the maximum profit, but always to remain calm. Later on, once I've already made a thousand or two, I will, of course, inevitably get out of trading and street dealing. Of course, I still know very little about the stock exchange, shares, banking, and all the rest. But, instead of that, I know, like the back of my hand, that in my own time I'll learn and master all this exchanging and banking like nobody else, and that this study will come quite easily to me, merely because matters will reach that point. Does it take so much intelligence? Is it some kind of wisdom of Solomon? All I need is character; skill, adroitness, knowledge will come by themselves. So long as I don't stop "wanting."

Above all, take no risks, and that is precisely possible only with character. Just recently, when I was already in Petersburg, there was a subscription for railway shares; those who managed to subscribe made a lot. For some time the shares were going up. And then suppose, suddenly, somebody who didn't manage to subscribe, or just turned greedy, seeing me with the shares in my hand, offered to buy them from me, with a premium of so much percent. Why, I'd certainly sell them to him at once. They'd start laughing at me, of course, saying: if you'd waited, you would have made ten times more. Right, sirs, but my premium is more certain, since it's already in my pocket, while yours is still flying around. They'll say you can't make much that way; excuse me, but there's your mistake, the mistake of all these Kokorevs, Polyakovs, Gubonins.[24] Know the truth: constancy and persistence in making money and, above all, in accumulating it, are stronger than momentary profits, even of a hundred percent!

Not long before the French Revolution, a man named Law[25] appeared in Paris and undertook a project that was brilliant in principle (afterwards, in fact, it crashed terribly). All Paris was astir; Law's shares were snapped up, there was a stampede. Money came pouring from all over Paris, as if from a sack, into the house where the subscription was announced; but the house, finally, was not enough: the public crowded in the street—all estates, conditions, ages; bourgeois, nobility, their children, countesses, marquises, public women—everything churned up into a raging, half-crazed mass of people bitten by a rabid dog; ranks, prejudices of breeding and pride, even honor and good name—everything was trampled in the same mud; everyone sacrificed (even women) in order to obtain a few shares. The subscription finally passed into the street, but there was nowhere to write. Here one hunchback was asked to lend his hump for a time, as a table for subscribing to shares. The hunchback accepted—you can imagine for what price! Some time later (very little), it all went bankrupt, it all crashed, the idea went to the devil, and the shares lost all value. Who profited? Only the hunchback, precisely because he did not take shares, but cash in louis d'ors. Well, sirs, I am that very same hunchback! Didn't I have strength enough not to eat and to save up seventy-two roubles out of kopecks? I'll also have enough to restrain myself, right in the whirl of the fever that overcomes everybody, to prefer sure money to big money. I'm trifling only in trifles, but in great things I'm not. I often lacked the character for a small forbearance, even after the "idea" was born, but for a big one I'll always have enough. When my mother served me cold coffee in the morning before I went to work, I got angry and was rude to her, and yet I was the same man who survived a whole month on nothing but bread and water.

In short, not to make money, not to learn how to make money, would be unnatural. It would also be unnatural, with continuous and regular accumulation, with continuous attention and sober-mindedness, restraint, economy, with ever-increasing energy, it would be unnatural, I repeat, not to become a millionaire. How did the beggar make his money, if not by fanaticism of character and persistence? Am I worse than that beggar? "And, finally, suppose I don't achieve anything, suppose my calculation is wrong, suppose I crash and fail—all the same, I'm going. I'm going because I want it that way." That's what I said still in Moscow.

They'll tell me there's no "idea" here, and precisely nothing new. But I say, and for the last time now, that there's incalculably much idea and infinitely much that's new.

Oh, I did anticipate how trivial all the objections would be, and how trivial I myself would be, explaining the "idea": well, what have I said? I didn't say even a hundredth part; I feel that it came out petty, crude, superficial, and even somehow younger than my years.

III

It remains to answer the "what for" and "why," the "moral or not," and so on, and so forth. I've promised to answer that.

I feel sad to disappoint the reader at once, sad but glad as well. Be it known that the goals of my "idea" have absolutely no feeling of "revenge," nothing "Byronic"—no curse, no orphaned complaints, no tears of illegitimacy, nothing, nothing. In short, a romantic lady, if she were to come across my "Notes," would be crestfallen at once. The whole goal of my "idea" is—solitude.

"But one can achieve solitude without any bristling up about becoming Rothschild. What has Rothschild got to do with it?"

"Just this, that, besides solitude, I also need power."

I'll preface that. The reader will perhaps be horrified at the frankness of my confession and will ask himself simpleheartedly: how is it that the author doesn't blush? I reply that I'm not writing for publication; I'll probably have a reader only in some ten years, when everything is already so apparent, past and proven, that there will no longer be any point in blushing. And therefore, if I sometimes address the reader in my notes, it's merely a device. My reader is a fantastic character.

No, it was not the illegitimacy for which they taunted me so much at Touchard's, not my sad childhood years, not revenge or the right to protest that was the beginning of my "idea"; my character alone is to blame for it all. From the age of twelve, I think, that is, almost from the birth of proper consciousness, I began not to like people. Not so much not to like, but they somehow became oppressive to me. It was sometimes all too sad for me myself, in my pure moments, that I could in no way speak everything out even to those close to me, that is, I could, but I didn't want to, I restrained myself for some reason; that I was mistrustful, sullen, and unsociable. Then, too, I had long noticed a feature in myself, almost from childhood, that I all too often accuse others, that I'm all too inclined to accuse them; but this inclination was quite often followed immediately by another thought, which was all too oppressive for me: "Is it not I myself who am to blame, instead of them?" And how often I accused myself in vain! To avoid resolving such questions, I naturally sought solitude. Besides, I never found anything in the company of people, however I tried, and I did try; at least all my peers, all my comrades to a man, proved to be inferior to me in thinking; I don't remember a single exception.

Yes, I'm glum, I'm continually closed. I often want to leave society. I may also do good to people, but often I don't see the slightest reason for doing good to them. And people are not at all so beautiful that they should be cared for so much. Why don't they come forward directly and openly, and why is it so necessary that I should go and foist myself on them? That's what I asked myself. I'm a grateful being, and I've already proved it by a hundred follies. I would instantly respond with openness to an open person and begin to love him at once. And so I did; but they all cheated me at once and closed themselves to me in mockery. The most open of them was Lambert, who used to beat me badly in childhood; but he, too, was merely an open scoundrel and robber; and here, too, his openness came merely from stupidity. These were my thoughts when I came to Petersburg.

Having left Dergachev's then (God knows what pushed me to go there), I approached Vasin and, on a rapturous impulse, praised him to the skies. And what then? That same evening I already felt that I liked him much less. Why? Precisely because, by praising him, I had lowered myself before him. Yet it seems it should have been the opposite: a man so just and magnanimous as to give another his due, even to his own detriment, such a man is almost superior in his personal dignity to everyone else. And what, then—I knew this, and still I liked Vasin less, even much less, I purposely give an example already familiar to the reader. Even Kraft I remembered with a bitter and sour feeling, because he brought me out to the front hall himself, and so it remained right up to another day, when everything about Kraft became perfectly clear and it was impossible to be angry. From the very lowest grade in school, as soon as any of my comrades got ahead of me in studies, or in witty answers, or in physical strength, I at once stopped keeping company with him and speaking to him. Not that I hated him or wished him to fail; I simply turned away, because such was my character.

Yes, I've thirsted for power all my life, power and solitude. I dreamed of them even at such an age that decidedly anyone would have laughed in my face if he had made out what I had inside my skull. That is why I came to love secrecy so much. Yes, I dreamed with all my might and to a point where I had no time to talk; this led to the conclusion that I was unsociable, and my absentmindedness led to a still worse conclusion in my regard, but my rosy cheeks proved the contrary.

I was especially happy when, going to bed and covering myself with a blanket, I began, alone now, in the most complete solitude, with no people moving around and not a single sound from them, to re-create life in a different key. The fiercest dreaming was my companion until I discovered the "idea," when all my dreams went at once from stupid to reasonable, and from a dreamy form of novel passed on to the rationalistic form of reality.

Everything merged into a single goal. However, they weren't so stupid even before, though there were myriad upon myriad and thousand upon thousand of them. But I had some favorites... However, there's no point bringing them in here.

Power! I'm convinced that a great many people would find it very funny to learn that such "trash" was aiming at power. But I'll amaze them still more: maybe from my very first dreams, that is, almost from my very childhood, I was unable to imagine myself otherwise than in the first place, always and in all turns of life. I'll add a strange confession: maybe that goes on even to this day. And I'll also note that I'm not apologizing.

In this lies my "idea," in this lies its strength, that money is the only path that will bring even a nonentity to the *first place*. Maybe I'm not a nonentity, but I know from the mirror, for instance, that my appearance does me harm, because my face is ordinary. But if I were as rich as Rothschild—who would question my face, and wouldn't thousands of women rush to me with their charms if I merely whistled? I'm even certain that, in the end, they themselves would quite sincerely find me handsome. Maybe I'm also intelligent. But even if I had a forehead seven inches wide, there would inevitably turn up in society a man with a forehead eight inches wide, and that would be the end of me.

Whereas if I were Rothschild—would this smarty with the eight-inch forehead mean anything next to me? He wouldn't even be allowed to speak next to me! Maybe I'm witty; yet here next to me is Talleyrand or Piron[26]—and I'm put in the shade; but once I'm Rothschild—where is Piron, and maybe even Talleyrand? Money is, of course, a despotic power, but at the same time it's also the highest equalizer, and that is its chief strength. Money equalizes all inequalities. I had already decided all that in Moscow.

You will, of course, see nothing in this thought but impudence, violence, the triumph of nonentity over talent. I agree that it's a bold thought (and therefore sweet). But so what, so what? Do you think I wished for power then in order to crush unfailingly, to take revenge? That's just the point, that the ordinary man would unfailingly behave that way. Moreover, I'm certain that if Rothschild's millions were heaped on them, the thousands of talents and smarties, who are so above it all, would lose control at once and behave like the most banal of ordinary men, and crush more than anybody else. My idea is not that. I'm not afraid of money; it won't crush me and won't make me crush others.

I don't need money, or, better, it's not money that I need; it's not even power; I need only what is obtained by power and simply cannot be obtained without power: the solitary and calm awareness of strength! That is the fullest definition of freedom, which the world so struggles over! Freedom! I have finally inscribed that great word... Yes, the solitary awareness of strength is fascinating and beautiful. I have strength, and I am calm. Jupiter holds thunderbolts in his hand, and what then? He's calm. Do we often hear him thunder? A fool might think he was asleep. But put some writer or foolish peasant woman in Jupiter's place—oh, what thunder, what thunder there will be!

If only I had power, I reasoned, I'd have no need at all to use it; I assure you that I myself, of my own free will, would take the last place everywhere. If I were Rothschild, I'd go about in an old coat and carry an umbrella. What do I care if I'm jostled in the street, if I'm forced to go skipping through the mud so as not to be run over by cabs? The awareness that it was I, Rothschild himself, would even amuse me at that moment. I know that I can have a dinner like nobody else, and from the world's foremost chef, and it's enough for me that I know it. I'll eat a piece of bread and ham and be satisfied with my awareness. I think so even now.

It's not I who will get in with the aristocracy, but they who will get in with me; it's not I who will chase after women, but they who will flow to me like water, offering me everything a woman can offer. The "banal" ones will come running for money, but the intelligent ones will be drawn by curiosity to a strange, proud, closed being, indifferent to everything. I'll be nice to the ones and to the others, and maybe give them money, but I won't take anything from them myself. Curiosity gives rise to passion, maybe I'll also inspire passion. They'll go away with nothing, I assure you, except perhaps a few presents. I'll only become twice as curious for them.

...enough for me
Is the awareness of it.[27]

The strange thing is that this picture (a correct one, by the way) tempted me when I was no more than seventeen.

I don't want to crush or torment anyone and I won't; but I know that if I did want to ruin such-and-such a person, my enemy, no one would keep me from doing it, but everyone would be obliging; and again, enough. I wouldn't even take revenge on anyone. I was always surprised at how James Rothschild could agree to become a baron! Why, what for, when he's superior to everyone in the world without that? "Oh, let this insolent general offend me at the posting station, where we're both waiting for horses; if he knew who I was, he'd run to hitch them up himself and jump out and hasten to seat me in my modest tarantass! They wrote that a certain foreign count or baron, at a certain Viennese railway station, before the public, helped a certain local banker into his shoes, and the man was so ordinary that he allowed it. Oh, let her, let this fearsome beauty (precisely fearsome, there are such!)—the daughter of this magnificent and high-born aristocratic lady, having met me by chance on a steamboat or wherever, look askance and, turning up her nose, wonder scornfully how this humble and puny little man with a newspaper or book in his hands could dare to show up beside her in first class! But if she only knew who was sitting next to her! And she will know—she will know, and will sit down next to me, obedient, timid, gentle, seeking my eyes, glad of my smile..." I have purposely introduced these early pictures in order to express my idea more vividly, but the pictures are pale and perhaps trivial. Reality alone justifies everything.

They'll say it's stupid to live like that. Why not have a mansion, an open house, gather society, exert influence, get married? But what would Rothschild be then? He'd become like everybody else. All the charm of the "idea" would vanish, all its moral force. As a child I had already learned by heart the monologue of Pushkin's covetous knight; Pushkin never produced a higher idea than that! I'm also of the same mind now.

"But your ideal is too low," they'll say with scorn. "Money, riches! A far cry from social usefulness and humane endeavors!"

But who knows how I'll use my riches? What is immoral, what is low, in having these millions flow out of a multitude of dirty and pernicious Jewish hands, into the hands of a sober and firm ascetic, who keenly studies the world? Generally, all these dreams of the future, all these conjectures—all this is still like a novel now, and maybe I shouldn't be writing it down; it should have stayed inside my skull; I also know that maybe no one will read these lines; but if anyone does, would he believe that maybe I, too, was unable to endure the Rothschildian millions? Not because they would crush me, but in quite a different sense, the opposite. In my dreams, I had more than once seized on that moment in the future when my consciousness would be too well satisfied and power would seem all too little. Then—not from boredom, and not from aimless anguish, but because I will desire something boundlessly greater—I will give all my millions away to people; let society distribute all my riches, and I—I will once more mingle with nonentity! Maybe I'll even turn into that beggar who died on the steamboat, with this difference, that they won't find anything sewn into my rags. The awareness alone that I had had millions in my hands and had flung them into the mud, would feed me in my wilderness like a raven.[28] I'm prepared to think so even now. Yes, my "idea" is that fortress in which I can always and in any case hide from all people, be it even like the beggar who died on the steamboat. This is my poem! And know that I need precisely my *whole* depraved will—solely to prove *to myself* that I'm strong enough to renounce it.

They'll undoubtedly object that this is poetry, and that I'll never let go of millions, if I've got them, and will not turn into a Saratov beggar. Maybe I won't let go; I've merely traced out the ideal of my thought. But I'll add seriously now: if, in the accumulation of wealth, I should reach the same figure as Rothschild, then it might indeed end with my flinging it to society. (However, it would be hard to do that before the Rothschildian figure.) And I wouldn't give away half, because then it would be nothing but a banality: I'd only become twice poorer and nothing more; but precisely all,

all to the last kopeck, because, having become a beggar, I'd suddenly become twice as rich as Rothschild! If they don't understand that, it's not my fault; I won't explain.

"Fakirism, the poetry of nonentity and impotence," people will decide, "the triumph of untalentedness and mediocrity!" Yes, I admit that it's partly the triumph of both untalentedness and mediocrity, but hardly of impotence. I liked terribly to imagine a being, precisely an untalented and mediocre one, standing before the world and telling it with a smile: you are Galileos and Copernicuses, Charlemagnes and Napoleons, you are Pushkins and Shakespeares, you are field marshals and hofmarshals, and here I am—giftlessness and illegitimacy, and all the same I'm superior to you, because you submit to it yourselves. I confess, I've pushed this fantasy to such a verge that I've even ruled out education. It seemed to me that it would be more beautiful if this person was even filthily uneducated. This already exaggerated dream even influenced my results then in the final grade of high school; I stopped studying precisely out of fanaticism: it was as if lack of education added beauty to the ideal. Now I've changed my convictions on this point; education doesn't hurt.

Gentlemen, can it be that independence of mind, even the least bit of it, is so painful for you? Blessed is he who has his ideal of beauty, even if it's a mistaken one! But I believe in mine. Only I've explained it improperly, clumsily, primitively. Ten years from now, of course, I'll explain it better. And this I'll keep as a memento.

IV

I've finished the "idea." If the description is banal, superficial—I'm to blame, and not the "idea." I've already warned you that the simplest ideas are the hardest to understand; I'll now add that they are also the hardest to explain, the more so as I've described the "idea" still in its former shape. There is also an inverse law for ideas: banal, hasty ideas are understood extraordinarily quickly, and invariably by a crowd, invariably by the whole street; moreover, they are considered the greatest and most brilliant, but only on the day of their appearance. What's cheap is not durable. Quick understanding is only a sign of the banality of what is understood. Bismarck's idea was instantly regarded as brilliant, and Bismarck himself as a brilliant man;[29] but this quickness is precisely suspicious: I wait for Bismarck ten years from now, and then we'll see what's left of his idea, and maybe of Mr. Chancellor himself. Of course, I haven't introduced this highly extraneous and inappropriate observation for the sake of comparison, but also as a reminder. (An explanation for the overly crude reader.)

And now I'll tell two anecdotes, so as to finish with the "idea" altogether, and not have it interfere in any way with the story.

In the summer, in July, two months before I came to Petersburg, and when I was already completely free, Marya Ivanovna asked me to go to Troitsky Posad to see a certain old maid who had settled there, on an errand too uninteresting to mention in detail. Coming back that same day, I noticed a certain puny young man on the train, not badly but uncleanly dressed, with blackheads, a dark-haired, dirtily swarthy type. He was distinguished by the fact that, at every station, large or small, he unfailingly got off and drank vodka. By the end of the journey, a merry little circle had formed around him—an utterly trashy company, incidentally. There was a shopkeeper, also slightly drunk, who was especially admiring of the young man's ability to drink continuously while remaining sober. There was yet another very pleased young fellow, terribly stupid and terribly talkative, dressed in German fashion, who gave off a rather nasty smell—a lackey, as I learned later; this one even struck up a friendship with the drinking young man and, each time the train stopped, got him to his feet with the invitation, "Time now for some vodka"—and the two would go out in each other's embrace. The drinking young man hardly said a word, but more and more interlocutors sat down around him; he merely listened to them all, grinning continuously with a slobbery titter and producing from time to time, but always unexpectedly, a sort of sound like "tir-lir-li!" and placing a finger on his nose in a very caricaturish way. It was this that delighted the merchant, and the lackey, and all of them, and they laughed extremely loudly and casually. It's impossible to understand why people laugh sometimes. I, too, went over—and I don't understand why I also found this young man likable, as it were; maybe by his all-too-spectacular violation of conventional and banalized proprieties; in short, I failed to discern the fool in him; anyhow, we were on familiar terms there and then, and as we got off the train, I learned from him that he would be coming to Tverskoy Boulevard that evening after eight. He turned out to be a former student. I went to the boulevard, and here's what trick he taught me: we went around all the boulevards together, and later on, the moment we spotted a woman of a decent sort walking along, but so that there was no public close by, we'd immediately start pestering her. Without saying a word to her, we'd place ourselves, he on one side, I on the other, and with the most calm air, as if not noticing her at all, would begin a most indecent conversation between ourselves. We called things by their real names with a most unperturbed air, as if it was quite proper, and went into such details, explaining various vile and swinish things, as the dirtiest imagination of the dirtiest debaucher could not have thought up. (I, of course, had already acquired all this knowledge at school, even before high school, but only in words, not in deeds.) The woman would be very frightened and hurriedly walk away, but we would also quicken our pace and—go on with our thing. For the victim, of course, it was impossible to do anything; she couldn't shout: there were no witnesses, and it would somehow be strange to complain. Some eight days were spent on these amusements; I don't understand how I could have liked it; and in fact I didn't like it, I just did it. At first I found it original, as if it went outside everyday trite conventions; besides, I can't stand women. I once told the student that Jean-Jacques Rousseau admits in his *Confessions*[30] that, as a youth, he liked to expose himself on the sly, from around the corner, uncovering the usually covered parts of the body, and waited like that for passing women. The student answered me with his tir-lir-li. I noticed that he was frightfully ignorant and interested in surprisingly little. There was no trace of the hidden idea I had hoped to find in him. Instead of originality, I found only an overwhelming monotony. I disliked him more and more. Finally it all ended quite unexpectedly. Once when it was already quite dark, we began to pester a girl who was walking quickly and timidly down the boulevard, a very young girl, maybe only sixteen or even less, dressed very neatly and modestly, who maybe lived by her own labor and was going home from work to her old mother, a poor widow with children; however, there's no need to fall into sentimentality. The girl listened for some time, walking faster and faster, her head lowered and her face covered by a veil, afraid and trembling, but suddenly she stopped, threw back the veil from her very pretty, as far as I remember, but thin face, and with flashing eyes cried to us:

"Ah, what scoundrels you are!"

Maybe she would also have burst into tears here, but something else happened: she swung her small, skinny arm and planted a slap on the student's face, than which a more deft has maybe never been given. What a smack! He cursed and rushed at her, but I held him back, and the girl had time to run away. Left there, we began quarreling at once. I told him everything that had been smoldering in me all that time; I said he was nothing but a pathetic giftlessness and ordinariness, and that there had never been the least sign of an idea in him. He called me a... (I had explained to him once about my being illegitimate), then we spat at each other, and I've never seen him since. That evening I was very vexed, the next day less so, the third day I almost forgot all about it. And so, though I sometimes remembered this girl afterwards, it was just by chance and fleetingly. It was only on arriving in Petersburg some two weeks later that I suddenly remembered that whole scene—remembered, and then felt so ashamed that tears of shame literally poured down my cheeks. I suffered all evening, all night, I'm partly suffering now as well. I couldn't understand at first how it had been possible to fall so low and disgracefully then, and above all—to forget the incident, not to be ashamed of it, not to be repentant. Only now did I realize what was the matter: the "idea" was to blame. In short, I draw the direct conclusion that if you have in mind something fixed, perpetual, strong, something terribly preoccupying, it is as if you thereby withdraw from the whole world into a desert, and everything that happens takes place in passing, apart from the main thing. Even impressions are received wrongly. And besides that, the main thing is that you always have an excuse. However much I tormented my mother all that time, however much I neglected my sister: "Ah, I have my 'idea,' those are all trifles"—that's what I seemed to say to myself. I'd get insulted myself, and painfully—I'd go out insulted and then suddenly say to myself, "Ah, I'm base, but all the same I have an 'idea,' and they don't know about it." The "idea" comforted me in my disgrace and nonentity; but all my abominations were also as if hiding under the idea; it eased everything, so to speak, but it also clouded everything over before me; and such a blurred understanding of events and things may, of course, even harm the "idea" itself, to say nothing of the rest.

Now the other anecdote.

On the first of April last year, Marya Ivanovna had a name-day party. In the evening some guests came, a very few. Suddenly Agrafena comes in, breathless, and announces that there's a foundling baby squealing in the entry, by the kitchen door, and that she doesn't know what to do. Excited by the news, we all went and saw a basket, and in the basket a three- or four-week-old squealing girl. I took the basket, brought it to the kitchen, and at once found a folded note: "Dear benefactors, render your well-wishing aid to the baptized girl Arina, and with her we will ever send up our tears to the throne of God for you, and we congratulate you on your angel's day. People unknown to you." Here Nikolai Semyonovich, whom I so respect, upset me very much: he made a very serious face and decided to send the girl to the orphanage immediately. I felt very sad. They lived very economically, but had no children, and Nikolai Semyonovich was always glad of it. I carefully took Arinochka out of the basket and held her up by her little shoulders; the basket gave off a sort of sour and sharp smell, as of a long-unwashed nursing baby. After some arguing with Nikolai Semyonovich, I suddenly announced to him that I was taking the girl at my own expense. He began to object with a certain severity, despite all his mildness, and though he ended with a joke, he left his intention about the orphanage in full force. It worked out my way, however: on the same courtyard, but in another wing, lived a very poor cabinetmaker, already an old man and a drunkard, but his wife, a very healthy woman and not old at all, had just lost her nursing baby, and above all her only one, who had been born after eight years of childless marriage, also a girl, and by strange luck also named Arinochka. I say luck, because as we were arguing in the kitchen, this woman, hearing about the incident, came running to see, and when she learned that it was Arinochka, her heart melted. Her milk was not gone yet; she opened her bodice and put the baby to her breast. I fell before her and began begging her to take Arinochka with her, and said I'd pay her monthly. She feared her husband wouldn't allow it, but took her for the night. In the morning, the husband allowed it for eight roubles a month, and I counted them out to him for the first month in advance. He drank up the money at once. Nikolai Semyonovich, still smiling strangely, agreed to vouch for me to the cabinetmaker that the money, eight roubles a month, would be paid regularly. I tried to give Nikolai Semyonovich my sixty roubles in cash, by way of security, but he wouldn't take it; however, he knew I had the money and trusted me. This delicacy on his part smoothed over our momentary quarrel. Marya Ivanovna said nothing, but was surprised at my taking on such a care. I especially appreciated their delicacy in that neither of them allowed themselves the slightest mockery of me, but, on the contrary, began to treat the matter with the proper seriousness. I ran by Darya Rodionovna's every day, three times a day or so, and a week later I gave her personally, in her own hand, on the quiet from her husband, three more roubles. For another three I bought swaddling clothes and a little blanket. But ten days later, Rinochka suddenly got sick. I brought a doctor at once, he prescribed something, and we spent the whole night fussing about and tormenting the tiny thing with his nasty medicine, but the next day he declared that it was too late, and to my entreaties—though they seemed more like reproaches—he said with noble evasiveness, "I am not God." The girl's tongue, lips, and whole mouth got covered with a sort of fine white rash, and towards evening she died, gazing at me with her big dark eyes, as if she already understood. I don't understand how it didn't occur to me to take a photograph of her dead. Well, would you believe that I did not weep but simply howled that evening, something I had never allowed myself to do, and Marya Ivanovna was forced to comfort me—and again, totally without mockery either on her own or on his part. The cabinetmaker made a little coffin; Marya Ivanovna trimmed it with ruche and put a pretty little pillow in it, and I bought flowers and strewed them over the little baby; and so they took away my poor little wisp, whom, believe me, to this day I cannot forget. A while later, though, this whole almost unexpected occurrence even made me reflect a lot. Of course, Rinochka had not cost me much—thirty roubles in all, including the coffin, the burial, the doctor, the flowers, and the payments to Darya Rodionovna. I reimbursed myself for this money, as I was leaving for Petersburg, from the forty roubles Versilov had sent me for my trip, and by selling some things before I left, so that my whole "capital" remained intact. "But," I thought, "if I can be sidetracked like that, I won't get very far." From the story with the student, it followed that the "idea" can fascinate one to the point of a blurring of impressions and distract one from the flow of actualities. From the story with Rinochka the opposite followed, that no "idea" can be so intensely fascinating (for me, at least) that I cannot stop suddenly before some overwhelming fact and sacrifice to it at once all that I had done for the idea during years of toil. Both conclusions were nonetheless correct.

Chapter Six

I

My hopes were not fully realized; I didn't find them alone: though Versilov wasn't there, my mother was sitting with Tatyana Pavlovna—an outsider after all. Half of my magnanimous mood fell off of me at once. It's astonishing how quick I am to turn about on such occasions; a hair or a grain of sand is enough to disperse the good and replace it with the bad. But my bad impressions, to my regret, are not so soon driven out, though I'm not rancorous. As I entered, it flashed in me that my mother at once and hastily broke off the thread of her conversation with Tatyana Pavlovna, which seemed quite animated. My sister had returned from work just a minute before me and had not come out of her little closet yet.

This apartment consisted of three rooms. The one in which everyone usually sat, our middle room, or drawing room, was rather large and almost decent. There were soft red sofas in it, though very shabby ones (Versilov couldn't stand slipcovers), rugs of some sort, several tables and needless little tables. Then to the right was Versilov's room, small and narrow, with one window; in it stood a pathetic writing table, on which several unused books and forgotten papers were scattered, and in front of the table, a no less pathetic soft armchair, with a broken spring sticking out at an angle, which often made Versilov groan and curse. His bed was made up in this same study, on a soft and also shabby sofa; he hated this study of his and, it seems, did nothing in it, but preferred to sit idly in the drawing room for hours at a time. To the left of the drawing room was exactly the same sort of room, in which my mother and sister slept. The entrance to the drawing room was from the corridor, which ended with the entrance to the kitchen, where lived the cook Lukerya, who, when she cooked, mercilessly filled the whole apartment with the smoke of burnt oil. There were moments when Versilov loudly cursed his life and his fate because of this kitchen smoke, and in that alone I fully sympathized with him; I also hate such smells, though they did not penetrate to me: I lived upstairs in a little room under the roof, which I climbed to by an extremely steep and creaky little staircase. Noteworthy in my place were the fan-window, the terribly low ceiling, the oilcloth sofa, on which Lukerya spread a sheet and put a pillow for me at night, while the rest of the furniture was just two objects—the simplest plank table and a wicker chair with a hole in it.

However, our place still preserved the remains of a certain former comfort; in the drawing room, for instance, there was a rather good china lamp, and on the wall hung a fine, big engraving of the Dresden Madonna[31] and just opposite on the other wall, an expensive photograph, of huge dimensions, showing the cast bronze doors of the Florentine cathedral.[32] In a corner of the same room hung a big case with old family icons, one of which (of All Saints) had a big gilt-silver casing, the same one they had wanted to pawn, and another (of the Mother of God) a velvet casing embroidered with pearls. Before the icons hung an icon lamp that was lit for every feast. Versilov was obviously indifferent to the icons, in the sense of their meaning, and merely winced sometimes, visibly restraining himself, at the light of the icon lamp reflected in the gilt casing, complaining slightly that it hurt his eyes, but all the same he did not keep my mother from lighting it.

I usually entered silently and sullenly, looking somewhere into a corner, and sometimes without any greeting. I always came home earlier than this time, and had my dinner served upstairs. As I came in now, I suddenly said, "Hello, mama," something I had never done before, though somehow this time, too, out of shyness, I still could not force myself to look at her, and sat down at the opposite side of the room. I was very tired, but wasn't thinking of that.

"This ignoramus still comes into your house like a boor, just as he used to," Tatyana Pavlovna hissed at me; she had allowed herself abusive words before as well, and it had become a custom between us.

"Hello..." my mother answered, as if immediately at a loss because I had greeted her. "Dinner has been ready for a long time," she added, almost abashed, "if only the soup isn't cold, and I'll tell them right now about the cutlets..." She hurriedly started getting up to go to the kitchen, and maybe for the first time in the whole month, I suddenly felt ashamed that she should jump up so promptly to serve me, though before that was just what I myself had demanded.

"I humbly thank you, mama, I've already had dinner. If I'm not bothering you, I'll rest here."

"Ah... well, then... stay, of course..."

"Don't worry, mama, I'm not going to be rude to Andrei Petrovich anymore," I said abruptly...

"Ah, Lord, how magnanimous on his part!" cried Tatyana Pavlovna. "Sonya, darling, can it be that you still address him formally? Who is he that he should receive such honors, and that from his own mother! Look at you getting all abashed in front of him, what a shame!"

"It would be very nice for me, mama, if you addressed me informally."

"Ah... well, all right, then, I will," my mother hastened to say. "I—I didn't always... well, from now on I'll know."

She blushed all over. Decidedly her face could be extremely attractive on occasion... She had a simplehearted face, but not at all simpleminded, slightly pale, anemic. Her cheeks were very gaunt, even hollow, and little wrinkles were beginning to accumulate on her forehead, but there were none around her eyes yet, and her eyes, rather big and wide open, always shone with a gentle and quiet light, which had attracted me to her from the very first day. I also liked it that there was nothing sad or pinched in her face; on the contrary, its expression would even have been gay, if she hadn't been so frequently alarmed, sometimes for no reason, getting frightened and jumping up sometimes over nothing at all, or listening fearfully to some new conversation, until she was reassured that all was still well. With her, "all was well" meant precisely that "all was as before." If only nothing changed, if only nothing new happened, even something fortunate!... One might think she had somehow been frightened in childhood. Besides her eyes, I liked the elongated shape of her face, and, I believe, if her cheekbones had only been a little less wide, she might have been considered a beauty, not only in her youth, but even now as well. Now she was no more than thirty-nine years old, but her dark blond hair was already strongly streaked with gray.

Tatyana Pavlovna looked at her with decided indignation.

"Before such a whelp? To tremble like that before him! You're a funny one, Sofya; you make me angry, that's what!"

"Ah, Tatyana Pavlovna, why are you like this with him now! Or maybe you're joking, eh?" my mother added, noticing something like a smile on Tatyana Pavlovna's face. Indeed, Tatyana Pavlovna's abuse was sometimes impossible to take seriously, but she smiled (if she did smile), of course, only at my mother, because she loved her kindness terribly and had undoubtedly noticed how happy she was just then at my submissiveness.

"I, of course, can't help feeling it, if you yourself fall upon people, Tatyana Pavlovna, and precisely now, when I came in and said, 'Hello, mama,' which is something I've never done before," I finally found it necessary to point out to her.

"Just imagine," she boiled up at once, "he considers it a great deed? Should we go down on our knees to you or something, because you've been polite for once in your life? And as if that's politeness! Why do you look off into the corner when you come in? As if I don't know how you storm and rage at her! You might greet me as well, I swaddled you, I'm your godmother."

Naturally, I disdained to reply. Just then my sister came in, and I quickly turned to her:

"Liza, I saw Vasin today, and he asked me about you. You're acquainted?"

"Yes, we met in Luga last year," she answered quite simply, sitting down next to me and looking at me affectionately. I don't know why, but I thought she'd just turn bright red when I told her about Vasin. My sister was a blonde, a light blonde; her hair was quite unlike her mother's and her father's, but her eyes and the shape of her face were almost like her mother's. Her nose was very straight, small, regular; however, there was another peculiarity—small freckles on her face, something my mother didn't have at all. Of Versilov there was very little, perhaps only her slender waist, her tall stature, and something lovely in her gait. And not the least resemblance to me; two opposite poles.

"I knew himself for three months," Liza added.

"You're saying *himself* about Vasin, Liza? You ought to say *him*, and not *himself*. Excuse me, sister, for correcting you, but it distresses me that your education seems to have been quite neglected."

"It's mean on your part to make such observations in front of your mother," Tatyana Pavlovna flared up, "and you're wrong, it hasn't been neglected."

"I'm not saying anything about my mother," I put in sharply. "You should know, mama, that I look upon Liza as a second you; you've made of her the same loveliness of kindness and character as you surely were yourself, and are now, to this day, and will be eternally... What I meant was external polish, all that society stupidity, which is nevertheless indispensable. I'm only indignant that Versilov, if he heard you say *himself* instead of *him* about

Vasin, probably wouldn't correct you at all—he's so haughty and indifferent with us. That's what infuriates me!"

"He's a bear cub himself, and here he's teaching us about polish. Don't you dare, sir, to say 'Versilov' in front of your mother, or in my presence either—I won't stand for it!" Tatyana Pavlovna flashed fire.

"Mama, I received my salary today, fifty roubles, here, take it please!"

I went over and gave her the money; she became alarmed at once.

"Ah, I don't know how I can take it!" she said, as if afraid to touch the money. I didn't understand.

"For pity's sake, mama, if you both regard me as a son and a brother in the family, then..."

"Ah, I'm guilty before you, Arkady; I should confess certain things to you, but I'm so afraid of you..."

She said it with a timid and ingratiating smile; again I didn't understand and interrupted her:

"By the way, do you know, mama, that the case between Andrei Petrovich and the Sokolskys was decided today in court?"

"Ah, I know!" she exclaimed, pressing her hands together fearfully in front of her (her gesture).

"Today?" Tatyana Pavlovna gave a great start. "But it can't be, he would have told us. Did he tell you?" she turned to my mother.

"Ah, no, not that it was today, he didn't tell me about that. I've been so afraid all week. Even if he loses, I'd pray only so as to have it off our shoulders and be as we were before."

"So he didn't tell you either, mama!" I exclaimed. "What a fellow! There's an example of his indifference and haughtiness; what did I just tell you?"

"Decided how, how was it decided? And who told you?" Tatyana Pavlovna flung herself about. "Speak!"

"But here's the man himself! Maybe he'll tell us," I announced, hearing his footsteps in the corridor, and quickly sat down near Liza.

"Brother, for God's sake, spare mama, be patient with Andrei Petrovich..." my sister whispered to me.

"I will, I will, I came back with that in mind." I pressed her hand.

Liza looked at me very mistrustfully, and she was right.

II

He came in very pleased with himself, so pleased that he didn't find it necessary to conceal his state of mind. And in general he had become accustomed, lately, to opening himself up before us without the least ceremony, and not only to the bad in him, but even to the ridiculous, something everyone is afraid of; yet he was fully aware that we would understand everything to the last little jot. In the past year, by Tatyana Pavlovna's observation, he had gone very much to seed in his dress; his clothes were always decent, but old and without refinement. It's true that he was prepared to wear the same linen for two days, which even made mother upset; they considered it a sacrifice, and this whole group of devoted women looked upon it as outright heroism. The hats he wore were always soft, wide-brimmed, black; when he took his hat off in the doorway, the whole shock of his very thick but much-graying hair just sprang up on his head. I always liked looking at his hair when he took his hat off.

"Hello. Everybody's gathered, even including him? I could hear his voice in the front hall—denouncing me, it seems?"

One of the signs that he was in a merry mood was that he began sharpening his wit on me. I didn't reply, naturally. Lukerya came in with a whole bag of purchases and put it on the table.

"Victory, Tatyana Pavlovna! The suit is won, and, of course, the princes won't decide to appeal. The case is mine! I at once found where to borrow a thousand roubles. Sofya, put your work down, don't strain your eyes. Just home from work, Liza?"

"Yes, papa," Liza replied with an affectionate look. She called him father; I wouldn't submit to that for anything.

"Tired?"

"Yes."

"Leave work, don't go tomorrow; and drop it completely."

"It's worse for me that way, papa."

"I ask you to . . . I dislike it terribly when women work, Tatyana Pavlovna."

"How can they be without work? As if a woman shouldn't work! . . ."

"I know, I know, that's all splendid and right, and I agree beforehand; but—I mean hand work mainly. Imagine, it seems to be one of my morbid, or, better, one of my incorrect impressions from childhood. In the vague memories from when I was five or six years old, I most often remember—with disgust, of course—a conclave of clever women at a round table, stern and severe, scissors, fabrics, patterns, and a fashion plate. They all divine and opine, shaking their heads slowly and gravely, measuring and calculating, as they prepare for the cutting out. All those affectionate faces, which love me so much, suddenly become unapproachable. If I should start acting up, I'd be taken away at once. Even my poor nanny, who holds me with one hand and doesn't respond to my crying and pulling, is mesmerized, gazing and listening as if to a bird of paradise. It's that sternness of clever faces and gravity before the start of cutting out that I find it painful to picture, for some reason, even now. You, Tatyana Pavlovna, are terribly fond of cutting out! Aristocratic as it may be, I still much prefer a woman who doesn't work at all. Don't take it to your own account, Sofya... Not that you could! A woman is a great power even without that. However, you know that, too, Sonya. What's your opinion, Arkady Makarovich? You probably protest?"

"No, not really," I replied. "It's particularly well put, that a woman is a great power, though I don't know why you connect it with work. And that one can't help working when one has no money—you know yourself."

"But now it's enough," he turned to my mother, who was beaming all over (when he addressed me, she gave a start), "at least for right now, I don't want to see any hand work, I ask for my own sake. You, Arkady, as a youth of our time, are surely a bit of a socialist. Well, would you believe it, my friend, those who have the greatest love of idleness are from the eternally laboring people!"

"Maybe not idleness, but rest."

"No, precisely idleness, total do-nothingness, that's the ideal! I knew one eternally laboring man, though not from the people; he was a rather developed man and able to generalize. All his life, maybe every day, he dreamed passionately and sweetly of the most total idleness, carrying his ideal to the absolute—to the boundless independence, to the eternal freedom of dreaming and idle contemplation. It went on like that till he broke down completely at work. He couldn't mend; he died in the hospital. I'm sometimes seriously ready to conclude that the notion of the delights of labor was thought up by idle people, of the virtuous sort, naturally. It's one of those 'Geneva ideas' from the end of the last century.[33] Tatyana

Pavlovna, two days ago I cut out an advertisement from the newspaper. Here it is." He took a scrap of paper from his waistcoat pocket. "It's from one of those endless students, who know classical languages and mathematics and are ready to relocate, live in a garret, or anywhere. Now listen: 'Female teacher prepares for all institutions of learning' (for all, listen to that) 'and gives lessons in arithmetic'—just one line, but a classic! Prepares for institutions of learning—of course, that also means in arithmetic? No, she mentions arithmetic separately. This—this is pure starvation, this is the ultimate degree of need. The touching thing here is precisely this lack of skill: obviously she never prepared herself to be a teacher, and is hardly able to teach anything. But it's either drown herself, or drag her last rouble to the newspaper and advertise that she prepares for all institutions of learning and, on top of that, gives lessons in arithmetic. *Per tutto mondo e in altri siti.*"*

"Ah, Andrei Petrovich, she must be helped! Where does she live?" exclaimed Tatyana Pavlovna.

"Oh, there are lots of them!" He put the address in his pocket. "This bag is full of all sorts of treats—for you, Liza, and for you, Tatyana Pavlovna; Sofya and I don't like sweets. You, too, if you please, young man. I bought it all myself at Eliseevs' and Ballet's.[34] For too long we've been 'sitting hungry,' as Lukerya says." (N.B. None of us ever sat hungry.) "There are grapes, bonbons, duchesse pears, and a strawberry tart; I even bought some excellent liqueur; also nuts. It's curious, Tatyana Pavlovna, ever since childhood I've loved nuts, you know, the simplest kinds. Liza takes after me: she also likes to crack nuts like a squirrel. But there's nothing lovelier, Tatyana Pavlovna, than chancing sometimes, among your childhood memories, to imagine yourself momentarily in the woods, in the bushes, when you were gathering nuts... The days are almost autumnal, but clear, sometimes so fresh, you hide in the thicket, you wander off into the forest, there's a smell of leaves... Do I see something sympathetic in your look, Arkady Makarovich?"

"The first years of my childhood were also spent in the country."

"Why, no, I believe you were living in Moscow... if I'm not mistaken."

"He was living with the Andronikovs in Moscow when you came that time; but before then he lived with your late aunt, Varvara Stepanovna, in the country," Tatyana Pavlovna picked up.

*Throughout the world and other places.

"Sofya, here's the money, put it away. They promised to give me five thousand one of these days."

"So there's no more hope for the princes?" asked Tatyana Pavlovna.

"None whatsoever, Tatyana Pavlovna."

"I've always sympathized with you, Andrei Petrovich, and all of yours, and have been a friend of your house; but, though the princes are strangers to me, by God, I feel sorry for them. Don't be angry, Andrei Petrovich."

"I have no intention of sharing, Tatyana Pavlovna."

"Of course, you know my thinking, Andrei Petrovich. They would have stopped the litigation if you had offered to go halves with them at the very beginning; now, of course, it's too late. However, I won't venture to judge... I say it because the deceased certainly wouldn't have cut them out of his will."

"Not only wouldn't have cut them out, he'd certainly have left everything to them and cut out just me alone, if he'd been able to do it and had known how to write a will properly; but now the law is with me—and it's finished. I cannot and do not want to share, Tatyana Pavlovna, and the matter ends there."

He uttered this even with anger, which he rarely allowed himself. Tatyana Pavlovna quieted down. Mother lowered her eyes somehow sadly: Versilov knew that she approved of Tatyana Pavlovna's opinion.

"It's the slap in Ems!" I thought to myself. The document procured by Kraft, which I had in my pocket, would fare badly if it fell into his hands. I suddenly felt that it was all still hanging on my neck; this thought, in connection with all the rest, of course, had an irritating effect on me.

"Arkady, I wish you'd dress better, my friend; you're not dressed badly, but in view of things to come, there's a good Frenchman I might recommend to you, a most conscientious man, and with taste."

"I beg you never to make me such offers," I suddenly ripped out.

"Why's that?"

"I, of course, do not find it humiliating, but we are not in such agreement; on the contrary, we even disagree, because one day, tomorrow, I'll stop going to the prince's, seeing not the least work to do there..."

"But the fact that you go there, that you sit with him—is already work!"

"Such notions are humiliating."

"I don't understand; however, if you're so ticklish, don't take money from him, just go there. You'll upset him terribly; he's already stuck on you, you can be sure... However, as you wish..."

He was obviously displeased.

"You tell me not to ask for money, but thanks to you I did a mean thing today. You didn't warn me, and today I demanded my month's salary from him."

"So you've already taken care of it; and, I'll confess, I thought you'd never begin to ask. How adroit you've all now become, though! There are no young people these days, Tatyana Pavlovna."

He was terribly irritated; I also became terribly angry.

"I ought to have settled accounts with you... it was you who made me do it—now I don't know how to be."

"By the way, Sophie, give Arkady back his sixty roubles immediately; and you, my friend, don't be angry at the hasty reckoning. I can guess from your face that you have some enterprise in mind, and that you're in need of... working capital... or something like that."

"I don't know what my face expresses, but I never expected of mama that she would tell you about that money, since I asked her not to." I looked at my mother, flashing my eyes. I can't even express how offended I was.

"Arkasha, darling, forgive me, for God's sake, there was no way I couldn't tell him..."

"My friend, don't hold it against her that she revealed your secrets," he turned to me. "Besides, she did it with good intentions—a mother simply wanted to boast of her son's feelings. But believe me, I'd have guessed that you're a capitalist even without that. All your secrets are written on your honest face. He has 'his idea,' Tatyana Pavlovna, I told you so."

"Let's forget my honest face," I went on ripping out. "I know you often see through things, though in other cases no further than a chicken's nose—and your perceptive abilities have surprised me. Well, yes, I do have my 'idea.' The fact that you put it that way is, of course, accidental, but I'm not afraid to admit it: I have an 'idea.' I'm not afraid and not ashamed."

"Above all, don't be ashamed."

"But all the same I won't ever reveal it to you."

"That is, you won't deign to reveal it. No need, my friend, I know the essence of your idea even so; in any case, it's this: 'To the desert I withdraw...'[35] Tatyana Pavlovna! I think he wants... to become

Rothschild, or something like that, and withdraw into his grandeur. Naturally, he will magnanimously grant you and me a pension—or maybe he won't grant me one—but in any case, that will be the last we see of him. He's like a new moon—it no sooner appears than it sets."

I shuddered inside. Of course, it was all chance: he knew nothing and wasn't speaking of that at all, though he did mention Rothschild. But how could he have defined my feelings so accurately: to break with them and withdraw? He had guessed it all and wanted to dirty the tragedy of the fact beforehand with his cynicism. There was no doubt that he was terribly irritated.

"Mama, forgive me my outburst, the more so as it's impossible to hide anything from Andrei Petrovich anyway!" I laughed insincerely, trying to move it all towards joking at least for a moment.

"The best thing, my dear, is that you laughed. It's hard to imagine how much every person gains by that, even in appearance. I'm speaking in the most serious way. You know, Tatyana Pavlovna, he always looks as if he has something so important on his mind that he's even ashamed of this circumstance himself."

"I beg you seriously to be more restrained, Andrei Petrovich."

"You're right, my friend; but it needs to be spoken out once and for all, so that we don't keep touching on it later. You came to us from Moscow in order to rebel at once—that's what we know so far about the purpose of your coming. Of the fact that you came in order to astonish us with something—of that I naturally make no mention. Then, you've been with us and snorting at us for a whole month—yet you're obviously an intelligent man and in that quality might have left such snorting to those who have no other way of taking revenge on people for their nonentity. You always close yourself up, whereas your honest air and red cheeks testify directly that you could look everyone in the eyes with perfect innocence. He's a hypochondriac, Tatyana Pavlovna; I don't understand, why are they all hypochondriacs now?"

"If you didn't even know where I grew up—how could you know what makes a man a hypochondriac?"

"There's the solution: you're offended that I could forget where you grew up!"

"Not at all! Don't ascribe stupidities to me. Mama, Andrei Petrovich just praised me for laughing, so let's laugh—why sit like this! Shall I tell you funny stories about myself? The more so as Andrei Petrovich knows nothing of my adventures?"

It was all smoldering in me. I knew we'd never sit together again like now, and that, having left this house, I would never come back, and therefore, on the eve of all that, I couldn't restrain myself. He himself had challenged me to such a finish.

"That's very nice, of course, if it really will be funny," he observed, peering at me keenly. "You turned a bit crude, my friend, wherever it was that you grew up, but, anyhow, you're still decent enough. He's quite nice today, Tatyana Pavlovna, and it's an excellent thing that you're finally untying that bag."

But Tatyana Pavlovna was frowning; she didn't even turn at his words and went on untying the bag and putting the treats on plates that had been brought. Mother also sat in complete bewilderment, of course, understanding and sensing that things were turning out wrong with us. My sister again touched my elbow.

III

"I SIMPLY WANT to tell you all," I began with the most casual air, "about how a certain father met his own dear son for the first time; this took place precisely 'where he grew up'..."

"But, my friend, won't this be... boring? You know: *tous les genres*..."*[36]

"Don't frown, Andrei Petrovich, it's not at all what you think. I precisely want everyone to laugh."

"Then may God hear you, my dear. I know you love us all and... you won't want to upset our evening," he murmured somehow affectedly, negligently.

"Here, too, of course, you've guessed by my face that I love you?"

"Yes, partly by your face."

"Well, and I've long guessed by Tatyana Pavlovna's face that she's in love with me. Don't look at me so ferociously, Tatyana Pavlovna, it's better to laugh! Better to laugh!"

She suddenly turned quickly to me and peered at me piercingly for half a minute.

"You watch out!" She shook her finger at me, but so seriously that it could no longer refer to my stupid joke, but was a warning about something else: "Does he intend to start something?"

*All genres...

"So, Andrei Petrovich, you really don't remember how you and I met for the first time in our lives?"

"By God, I've forgotten, my friend, and I apologize from the bottom of my heart. I only remember that it was somehow very long ago and took place somewhere..."

"Mama, do you remember visiting the village where I grew up, I think it was before I was six or seven, and above all, did you really come to that village once, or did I only imagine, as in a dream, that I saw you there for the first time? I've long wanted to ask you, but I kept putting it off. Now the time has come."

"Why, yes, Arkashenka, yes! I visited Varvara Stepanovna there three times; the first time I came when you were only one year old, the second when you were already going on four, and then when you were just turning six."

"Well, there, I've been wanting to ask you about it all month."

Mother simply glowed from the quick rush of memories, and she asked me with feeling:

"Arkashenka, do you really remember me from then?"

"I don't remember and don't know anything, only something of your face has remained in my heart all my life, and, besides that, the knowledge remained that you were my mother. I see that village now as in a dream, I even forget my nanny. I have a drop of recollection of Varvara Stepanovna, only because she eternally had her cheek bound from toothache. I also remember huge trees near the house, lindens, I think, then strong sunlight sometimes coming through the open windows, a front garden with flowers, a path, and you, mama, I remember clearly only at one moment, when you took me to communion in the church there, and lifted me up to receive the gifts and kiss the chalice; that was in summer, and a dove flew across under the cupola, from window to window..."

"Lord! That's just how it all was," my mother clasped her hands, "and I remember that little dove as if it were now. You gave a start just at the chalice and cried, 'A dove, a little dove!'"

"Your face, or something of it, its expression, remained so well in my memory that five years later, in Moscow, I recognized you at once, though no one told me then that you were my mother. And when I first met Andrei Petrovich, I was taken from the Andronikovs; before that, I had quietly and cheerfully vegetated with them for five years on end. I remember their government apartment in detail, and all those ladies and girls, who have all now aged so much here, and the house full of everything, and

Andronikov himself, how he himself brought all the provisions from town in bags—fowl, perch, and suckling pig—and at table ladled out the soup for us, in place of his wife, who was too uppish, and the whole table always laughed at that, and he first of all. The young ladies there taught me French, but most of all I loved Krylov's fables,[37] learned many of them by heart, and recited one to Andronikov each day, going straight to his tiny study, whether he was busy or not. Well, so it was through a fable that you and I became acquainted, Andrei Petrovich . . . I see you're beginning to remember."

"I remember a thing or two, my dear, namely, that you recited something to me then . . . a fable, I believe, or a passage from *Woe from Wit*?[38] What a memory you have, though!"

"Memory! What else! I've remembered only this all my life."

"Well, well, my dear, you even liven me up."

He even smiled, and right after him my mother and sister began to smile. Trustfulness was returning; but Tatyana Pavlovna, having arranged the treats on the table and sat down in the corner, went on piercing me with her nasty gaze.

"It so happened," I went on, "that suddenly, one bright morning, a friend of my childhood appeared, Tatyana Pavlovna, who always appeared unexpectedly in my life, as in the theater, and took me in a carriage, and brought me to a grand house, to a magnificent apartment. You were then staying with Mme. Fanariotov, Andrei Petrovich, in her empty house, which she had once bought from you; she was abroad at the time. I had always worn short jackets; here suddenly I was dressed in a pretty blue frock coat and excellent linen. Tatyana Pavlovna fussed over me all that day and brought me many things; and I kept walking through the empty rooms, looking at myself in all the mirrors. In this way, at around ten o'clock the next morning, wandering about the apartment, I suddenly walked, quite by chance, into your study. I'd already seen you the day before, when I was brought there, but only fleetingly, on the stairs. You were coming down the stairs to get into a carriage and go somewhere; you had arrived in Moscow alone then, after an extremely long absence, and for a short time, so that you were snapped up by everybody and almost didn't live at home. Meeting me and Tatyana Pavlovna, you only drew out a long 'Ah!'—and didn't even stop."

"He describes it with particular love," observed Versilov, turning to Tatyana Pavlovna; she turned away and didn't answer.

"I can see you then as if it were now, flourishing and handsome. It's surprising how you've managed to age and lose your good looks in these nine years—forgive my frankness; however, back then you were already around thirty-seven, but I even gazed at you in wonder: you had such astonishing hair, almost perfectly black, with a lustrous shine, and not a trace of gray; moustache and side-whiskers of a jeweler's finish—there's no other way to put it; your face was matte pale, not the sickly pale that it is now, but like the face of your daughter Anna Andreevna, whom I had the honor of meeting today; burning dark eyes and gleaming teeth, especially when you laughed. You precisely burst out laughing as you looked me over when I came in; I had little discernment then, only my heart rejoiced at your smile. That morning you were in a dark blue velvet jacket, on your neck a scarf of bright Solferino crimson over a magnificent shirt with Alençon lace, standing in front of a mirror with a notebook in your hand and rehearsing, declaiming Chatsky's last monologue, and especially his last cry:

'My carriage, my carriage!' "

"Ah, my God," cried Versilov, "but he's right! Despite the shortness of my stay in Moscow, I had undertaken then to play Chatsky in Alexandra Petrovna Vitovtov's home theater, because Zhileiko was sick!"[39]

"Had you really forgotten?" laughed Tatyana Pavlovna.

"He's reminded me! And I confess, those few days in Moscow were perhaps the best moment of my whole life! We were all still so young then . . . and everyone was so ardently expectant . . . In Moscow then I unexpectedly met so many . . . But go on, my dear, you did very well this time to recall it in such detail . . ."

"I stood, looked at you, and suddenly cried, 'Ah, how good, the real Chatsky!' You suddenly turned to me and asked, 'So you already know Chatsky?'—and sat down on the sofa and turned to your coffee in the most charming mood—I could have kissed you. Then I told you that at Andronikov's everybody read a lot, and the young ladies knew many poems by heart and played scenes from *Woe from Wit* among themselves, and that last week we all read *A Hunter's Sketches*[40] aloud together, and that I loved Krylov's fables most of all and knew them by heart. You told me to recite something by heart, and I recited 'The Fussy Bride' for you: 'A maiden-bride was thinking on a suitor.' "

"Precisely, precisely, now I remember everything," Versilov cried again, "but, my friend, I remember you clearly, too: you were such a nice boy then, even a nimble boy, and, I swear to you, you've also lost a bit in these nine years."

Here everybody, even Tatyana Pavlovna herself, burst out laughing. Clearly, Andrei Petrovich was joking and had "paid" me in my own coin for my barb about his having aged. Everybody cheered up; and it had indeed been well put.

"As I recited, you were smiling, but before I reached the middle, you stopped me, rang the bell, and, when the servant came in, told him to send for Tatyana Pavlovna, who came running with such a cheerful look that, though I had seen her the day before, I almost didn't recognize her now. In front of Tatyana Pavlovna, I began 'The Fussy Bride' again and finished brilliantly, even Tatyana Pavlovna smiled, and you, Andrei Petrovich, you even shouted 'Bravo!' and observed warmly that if I had recited 'The Grasshopper and the Ant,' it wouldn't have been so surprising, that any sensible boy my age could read it sensibly, but that this fable:

> A maiden-bride was thinking on a suitor.
> In that there's yet no sin...

'Just listen to how he articulates: "In that there's yet no sin"!' In short, you were delighted. Here you suddenly began speaking to Tatyana Pavlovna in French, and she instantly frowned and began to object to you, even very vehemently; but since it was impossible to contradict Andrei Petrovich if he suddenly wanted something, Tatyana Pavlovna hurried me off to her rooms; there my face and hands were washed again, my shirt was changed, my hair was pomaded and even curled. Then towards evening Tatyana Pavlovna herself got dressed up quite magnificently, even more so than I could have expected, and took me with her in a carriage. I found myself in a theater for the first time in my life, at an amateur performance at Mme. Vitovtov's: candles, chandeliers, ladies, military men, generals, young ladies, a curtain, rows of chairs—I had never seen anything like it before. Tatyana Pavlovna took a most modest seat in one of the back rows and sat me down beside her. Naturally, there were other children like me there, but I no longer looked at anything and waited with a fainting heart for the performance. When you came out, Andrei Petrovich, I was rapturous, rapturous to the point of tears—why, over what, I don't understand myself. Why tears of rapture?—that's what I've found so wild, remembering it all these nine years! I followed the comedy with bated breath; of course, the only thing I understood about it was that *she* was unfaithful to *him*, that stupid people not worth his little finger laughed at him. When he declaimed at the ball, I understood that he was humiliated and insulted, that he was reproaching all these pathetic people, but that he was great, great! Of course, my preparation at the Andronikovs' contributed to my understanding, but—so did your acting, Andrei Petrovich! I was seeing the stage for the first time! In the final scene, when Chatsky cries, 'My carriage, my carriage!' (and you cried it remarkably well), I tore from my seat and, together with the whole audience, which burst into applause, I clapped and shouted 'Bravo!' with all my might! I vividly remember at that same moment a furious pinch from Tatyana Pavlovna piercing me from behind, 'below the lower back,' but I paid no attention! Naturally, right after *Woe from Wit*, Tatyana Pavlovna brought me home: 'You can't stay for the dancing, and it's only because of you that I can't stay,' you, Tatyana Pavlovna, hissed at me all the way in the carriage. All night I was delirious, and the next day at ten o'clock I was already standing by your study, but the study was closed. You had people with you, you were busy with them; then you suddenly drove off for the whole day, till late at night—and so I didn't see you! What it was that I wanted to tell you then—I've forgotten, of course, and didn't know then, but I had a burning desire to see you as soon as possible. But the next morning, by eight o'clock, you were so good as to leave for Serpukhov: you had just sold your Tula estate in order to pay off your creditors, but you were still left holding a handsome sum, that was why you had come to Moscow, which you couldn't visit before then for fear of creditors; and there was only this one boor from Serpukhov, alone of all your creditors, who refused to take half the debt instead of the whole. Tatyana Pavlovna wouldn't even respond to my questions: 'It's nothing to you, and the day after tomorrow I'll be taking you to boarding school; get ready, gather your notebooks, put your books in order, and get into the habit of packing your own trunk, you're not to grow up into a do-nothing, sir!' and this and that—oh, how you drummed away at me for those three days, Tatyana Pavlovna! It ended with my being taken to Touchard's boarding school, in love with you and innocent, Andrei Petrovich, and it may have been the stupidest incident, this whole encounter with you, but, would you believe it, six months later I wanted to run away from Touchard's to you!"

"You've told it beautifully and reminded me so vividly of everything," Versilov pronounced distinctly, "but what chiefly strikes me in your account is the wealth of certain strange details, about my debts, for instance. To say nothing of a certain impropriety in these details, I don't understand how you could even have gotten hold of them."

"Details? How I got hold of them? But, I repeat, the only thing I've done is get hold of details about you all these nine years."

"A strange confession and a strange pastime!"

He turned, half reclined in his armchair, and even yawned slightly—whether on purpose or not, I don't know.

"So, then, shall I go on with how I wanted to run away to you from Touchard's?"

"Forbid him, Andrei Petrovich, suppress him, and throw him out," Tatyana Pavlovna snapped.

"Impossible, Tatyana Pavlovna," Versilov answered her imposingly. "Arkady obviously has something in mind, and therefore we absolutely must allow him to finish. Well, and let him! He'll tell it and get it off his chest, and for him the main thing is to get it off his chest. Begin your new story, my dear—that is, I'm only calling it new; don't worry, I know the ending."

IV

"I RAN AWAY, that is, I wanted to run away to you, very simply. Tatyana Pavlovna, you remember how Touchard wrote you a letter two weeks after I was installed there, don't you? Marya Ivanovna showed me the letter later, it also wound up among the late Andronikov's papers. Touchard suddenly thought he had asked too little money, and in his letter announced to you 'with dignity' that, in his institution, princes and senators' children were educated, and that he considered it beneath his institution to keep a pupil with such an origin as mine, unless he was paid extra."

"*Mon cher*, you might..."

"Oh, never mind, never mind," I interrupted, "I'll tell only a little about Touchard. You replied to him from the provinces, Tatyana Pavlovna, two weeks later, and sharply refused. I remember him then, all purple, coming into our classroom. He was a very short and very stocky little Frenchman of about forty-five, and indeed of Parisian origin, from cobblers, of course, but from time immemorial he had held a government post in Moscow as a teacher of

French, and even had some rank, which he was extremely proud of—a profoundly uneducated man. We, his pupils, were only six in number; among us there was indeed some nephew of a Moscow senator, and we all lived there in a completely family situation, more under the supervision of his wife, a very affected lady, the daughter of some Russian official. During those two weeks I put on airs terribly in front of my comrades, boasting of my dark blue frock coat and my papa, Andrei Petrovich, and their questions—why was I Dolgoruky and not Versilov—didn't embarrass me in the least, precisely because I didn't know why myself."

"Andrei Petrovich!" cried Tatyana Pavlovna in an almost threatening voice. My mother, on the contrary, could not tear her eyes from me, and obviously wanted me to continue.

"*Ce Touchard*... indeed, I recall him now, was small and fidgety," Versilov said through his teeth, "but he was recommended to me then from the best side..."

"*Ce Touchard* came in holding the letter, went over to our big oak table, at which all six of us were grinding away at something, seized me firmly by the shoulder, raised me from my chair, and told me to pick up my notebooks.

"'Your place is not here, but there.' He pointed to a tiny room to the left of the front hall, in which stood a simple table, a wicker chair, and an oilcloth sofa—exactly as I have now in my little room upstairs. I went there with astonishment and greatly intimidated; never before had I been treated rudely. Half an hour later, when Touchard left the classroom, I began exchanging glances and laughter with my comrades; they, of course, were laughing at me, but I didn't guess that and thought we were laughing because we were having fun. Here Touchard fell on me all at once, seized me by the forelock, and started pulling.

"'You dare not sit together with noble children, you're of mean origin and the same as a lackey!'

"And he hit me painfully on my plump red cheek. He liked that at once and hit me a second and a third time. I wept and sobbed, I was terribly astonished. For a whole hour I sat, covering my face with my hands, and wept and wept. Something had taken place that I could in no way understand. I don't understand how someone like Touchard, a foreigner, who was not a wicked man, who even rejoiced at the emancipation of the Russian peasants, could beat such a stupid child as I. However, I was only astonished, not insulted; I was still unable to be insulted. It seemed to me that I had done some mischief, but when I improved, I'd be forgiven, and we'd all suddenly become merry again, go and play in the yard, and have the best possible life."

"My friend, if I'd only known..." Versilov drawled with the careless smile of a somewhat weary man. "What a scoundrel this Touchard was, though! However, I still haven't lost hope that you'll somehow gather your strength and finally forgive us for it all, and again we'll have the best possible life."

He decidedly yawned.

"But I'm not accusing anybody, not at all, and, believe me, I'm not complaining about Touchard!" I cried, somewhat thrown off. "And he beat me only for two months or so. I remember I kept wanting to disarm him in some way, rushed to kiss his hands, and kissed them and kept weeping and weeping. My comrades laughed at me and despised me, because Touchard started using me as a servant, ordered me to hold his clothes while he dressed. Here my lackey character was instinctively of use to me. I tried as hard as I could to cater to him, and wasn't insulted in the least, because I understood none of it yet, and I'm even astonished to this day that I was so stupid then as not to understand how unequal I was to them all. True, my comrades had already explained a lot to me—it was a good schooling. Touchard ended by preferring to kick me from behind with his knee, rather than slap my face; and six months later he even began to be gentle with me at times; only now and then, but once a month for certain, he would give me a beating, so that I wouldn't forget myself. Soon I was also seated together with the other children and allowed to play with them, but not once in two and a half years did Touchard forget the difference in our social position, and he still went on using me as a servant, though not too much—I think precisely as a reminder to me.

"As for my running away, that is, my wanting to run away, that was five months after those first two months. And generally all my life I've been slow to make decisions. When I went to bed and covered myself with the blanket, I at once began dreaming of you, Andrei Petrovich, of you alone; I don't know at all why it worked out that way. I even saw you in my sleep. Above all, I dreamed passionately that you would suddenly walk in, and I'd rush to you, and you would take me out of that place and bring me to your house, to that study, and we'd go to the theater again, well, and so on. Above all, we wouldn't part—that was above all! And when I had to wake up in the morning, then suddenly the boys' mockery and scorn would begin. One of them would begin straight off by beating me and making me bring him his boots; he would abuse me in the nastiest terms, especially trying to explain my origin to me, to the delight of all the listeners. And when Touchard himself suddenly appeared, something unbearable started in my soul. I felt that I'd never be forgiven here—oh, I was gradually beginning to understand precisely what would not be forgiven and precisely where my fault lay! And so I finally resolved to run away. I dreamed of it terribly for a whole two months, and finally decided; it was September then. I waited till all my comrades went away for the weekend, and meanwhile, on the sly, I carefully tied myself up a little bundle of the most necessary things. I had two roubles. I was going to wait till it got dark. 'I'll creep down the stairs,' I thought, 'and go out, and then go on.' Where? I knew that Andronikov had already been transferred to Petersburg, so I decided to find Mme. Fanariotov's house on the Arbat. 'I'll spend the night walking or sitting somewhere, and in the morning I'll ask somebody in the courtyard: where is Andrei Petrovich now, and if not in Moscow, then in what city or country? They'll surely tell me, I'll leave, and then in another place somewhere I'll ask somebody which gate to take in order to go to such and such city, and so I'll go out, and go on, go on. I'll keep on going; I'll spend the nights somewhere under the bushes, and I'll eat nothing but bread, and for two roubles I'll have enough bread for a very long time.' On Saturday, however, I didn't manage to run away; I had to wait for the next day, Sunday, and, as if on purpose, Touchard and his wife went somewhere on Sunday; Agafya and I were the only ones left in the whole house. I waited for night in terrible anguish, I remember, sitting in our classroom by the window and looking at the dusty street with its little wooden houses and the rare passersby. Touchard lived on the outskirts, and the city gate could be seen from the windows: is that the one? I kept imagining. The setting sun was so red, the sky was so cold, and a sharp wind, just like today, blew the sand about. It finally became completely dark. I stood in front of an icon and began to pray, only quickly, quickly, I was in a hurry; I seized my little bundle and tiptoed down the creaky stairs, terribly afraid that Agafya would hear me from the kitchen. The door was locked, I opened it, and suddenly—dark, dark night stood black before me like an endless and dangerous unknown, and the wind tore at my visored cap. I went out; from across the pavement came the hoarse, drunken bellowing of an abusive passerby; I stood, looked, and quietly turned back, quietly went upstairs, quietly undressed, put down my bundle, and lay facedown, without tears and without thoughts, and it was from that very moment, Andrei Petrovich, that I began to think! From that very moment, when I realized that, besides being a lackey, I was also a coward, my real and correct development began!"

"And at this very moment I see through you once and for all!" Tatyana Pavlovna suddenly jumped up from her place, and even so unexpectedly that I was quite unprepared for it. "Not only were you a lackey then, you're a lackey now, you have a lackey soul! What would it have cost Andrei Petrovich to send you to be a cobbler? He'd even have done a good deed, teaching you a craft! Who would ask or demand that he do any more for you? Your father, Makar Ivanych, did not so much ask as almost demand that you, his children, not be taken from the lower estates. No, you don't appreciate that he got you as far as the university, and that through him you acquired rights.[41] The boys teased him, you see, and so he swore to take revenge on mankind . . . Scum that you are!"

I confess, I was astounded by this outburst. I stood up and stared for some time, not knowing what to say.

"Why, Tatyana Pavlovna has indeed told me something new," I finally turned firmly to Versilov. "I'm indeed so much of a lackey that I can in no way be satisfied merely with the fact that Versilov did not send me to be a cobbler; even 'rights' didn't appease me, but give me, say, the whole of Versilov, give me my father . . . that's what I was demanding—am I not a lackey? Mama, it has been on my conscience for eight years, how you came alone to Touchard's to visit me, and how I received you then, but there's no time for that now, Tatyana Pavlovna won't let me tell it. Till tomorrow, mama, maybe you and I can still see each other. Tatyana Pavlovna! Well, what if I'm once again a lackey to such a degree that I cannot even allow a man whose wife is still living to marry yet another wife? And that's nearly what happened with Andrei Petrovich in Ems! Mama, if you don't want to stay with a husband who might marry another woman tomorrow, remember that you have a son, who promises to be a respectful son forever—remember, and let's go, only with the understanding that it's 'either him or me.' Do you want to? I'm not asking for an answer now; I know it's impossible to answer such questions straight off . . ."

But I couldn't finish, first of all, because I became excited and confused. My mother turned all pale and her voice seemed to fail her: she couldn't utter a word. Tatyana Pavlovna was saying a lot and very loudly, so that I couldn't even make it out, and twice she shoved me on the shoulder with her fist. I only remember her shouting that my words were "affected, fostered in a petty soul, dug out with a finger." Versilov sat motionless and very serious, not smiling. I went to my room upstairs. The last look to accompany me out of the room was my sister's look of reproach; she sternly shook her head behind me.

Chapter Seven

I

I'M DESCRIBING ALL these scenes without sparing myself, in order to recall it all clearly and restore the impression. Going upstairs to my room, I had absolutely no idea whether I should be ashamed of myself or triumphant, like someone who has done his duty. If I had been a bit more experienced, I would have guessed that the least doubt in such a matter should be interpreted for the worse. But I was thrown off by another circumstance: I don't understand what I was glad about, but I was terribly glad, in spite of my doubts and the clear awareness that I had flunked it downstairs. Even the fact that Tatyana Pavlovna had abused me so spitefully struck me as only ridiculous and amusing, but didn't anger me at all. Probably that was all because I had broken the chain anyway and for the first time felt myself free.

I also felt that I had harmed my situation: still greater darkness surrounded the question of how I should now act with the letter about the inheritance. They would now decidedly take it as a wish to be revenged on Versilov. But while still downstairs, during all those debates, I had resolved to submit the matter of the letter about the inheritance to arbitration, and to appeal to Vasin as arbiter, and, failing Vasin, to yet another person, I already knew whom. Once, this time only, I'll go to Vasin, I thought to myself, and then—disappear from them all for a long time, for several months, and I'll even especially disappear from Vasin; only maybe I'll see my mother and sister every once in a while. All this was disorderly; I felt I had done something, though not in the right way, and—and I was pleased; I repeat, all the same I was glad of something.

I had decided to go to bed early, foreseeing a lot of running around the next day. Besides renting an apartment and moving, I took a few other decisions which I resolved to carry out in one way or another. But the evening was not to end without its curiosity, and Versilov did manage to astonish me greatly. He had decidedly never come up to my little room, and suddenly, I hadn't been there an hour when I heard his footsteps on the little stairs: he called me to light his way. I brought a candle and, reaching out my hand, which he seized, helped him to drag himself up.

"*Merci*, friend, I never once crept up here, not even when I was renting the apartment. I sensed it was something like this, but all the same I never supposed it was quite such a kennel," he stood in the middle of my room, looking around with curiosity. "Why, it's a coffin, a perfect coffin!"

Indeed, it had a certain resemblance to the inside of a coffin, and I even marveled at how correctly he had defined it with a single word. It was a long and narrow closet; at the height of my shoulder, not more, the angle between the wall and the roof began, the top of which I could touch with my palm. For the first minute, Versilov instinctively stooped, for fear of bumping his head on the ceiling, though he didn't and ended by sitting down quite calmly on my sofa, where my bed was already made up. As for me, I did not sit down and looked at him in deep astonishment.

"Your mother tells me she didn't know if she should take the money you offered her today for your monthly upkeep. In view of this coffin, not only should the money not be taken, but, on the contrary, a deduction should be made from us in your favor! I've never been here and... can't imagine that it's possible to live here."

"I'm used to it. But what I can't get used to is seeing you here after all that went on downstairs."

"Oh, yes, you were considerably rude downstairs, but... I also have my particular goals, which I'll explain to you, though, anyhow, there's nothing extraordinary in my visit. Even what took place downstairs is also perfectly in the order of things. But explain this to me, for Christ's sake: what you told us there, downstairs, and which you prepared for us and set about so solemnly—can that be all you intended to reveal or tell? Was there nothing else?"

"That was all. That is, let's say it was all."

"A bit lacking, my friend; I confess, judging by the way you set about it, and how you invited us to laugh—in short, seeing how anxious you were to tell it, I expected more."

"But isn't it all the same to you?"

"I'm concerned, essentially, with the sense of measure: it wasn't worth such noise, and so the measure was upset. For a whole month you were silent, making ready, and suddenly—nothing!"

"I wanted to go on longer, but I'm ashamed that I told even that much. Not everything can be told in words, certain things it's better never to tell. I did tell enough, though, but you didn't understand me."

"Ah! so you, too, suffer sometimes because a thought won't go into words! It's a noble suffering, my friend, and granted only to the chosen; a fool is always pleased with what he says, and, besides, he always says more than he needs to; they like extras."

"As I did downstairs, for instance. I also said more than I needed to; I demanded 'the whole of Versilov,' which is much more than I need. I don't need any Versilov at all."

"My friend, I see you want to make up for what you lost downstairs. You're obviously repentant, and since with us to repent means immediately to fall upon someone again, you don't want to miss the mark with me a second time. I came early, you haven't cooled off yet, and, besides, you have difficulty putting up with criticism. But sit down, for God's sake, I've come to tell you something; that's right, thank you. From what you said to your mother downstairs, on your way out, it's only too clear that it will be better, even in any case, if we live separately. I've come in order to persuade you to do it as softly as possible and without a scandal, so as not to upset or frighten your mother still more. Even the fact that I've come here myself has already cheered her up; she somehow believes that we'll still manage to be reconciled, well, and everything will go as before. I think if you and I laughed loudly now once or twice, we'd fill their timid hearts with delight. They may be simple hearts, but they are sincerely and artlessly loving, why shouldn't we pamper them on occasion? Well, that's one thing. Second: why should we necessarily part still with a thirst for vengeance, with a grinding of teeth, with curses, and so on? Without any doubt, it won't do at all for us to go hanging on each other's necks, but we can part, so to speak, with mutual respect, isn't that true, eh?"

"That's all nonsense! I promise I'll move out without a scandal—and enough. Are you going to this trouble because of my mother? Yet to me it seems that my mother's peace makes decidedly no difference to you, and you're only saying it."

"You don't believe me?"

"You speak to me decidedly as to a child!"

"My friend, I'm ready to ask your forgiveness for it a thousand times, and for all you've laid to my account, for all those years of your childhood and so on, but, *cher enfant*, what will come of it? You're intelligent enough not to want to wind up in such a stupid position. I say nothing of the fact that even up to this moment I quite fail to understand the character of your reproaches: indeed, what is it, essentially, that you blame me for? That you weren't born a Versilov? Or what? Bah! you laugh scornfully and wave your arms—does that mean no?"

"Believe me, no. Believe me, I find no honor in being named Versilov."

"Let's leave honor out of it; besides, your answer was bound to be democratic. But if so, what do you blame me for?"

"Tatyana Pavlovna just said everything I needed to know and never could understand before: that you didn't send me to be a cobbler, consequently I should be grateful. I fail to understand why I'm not grateful even now, when I've been brought to reason. Or is it your proud blood speaking, Andrei Petrovich?"

"Probably not. And, besides, you must agree that all your outbursts downstairs, instead of falling on me, as you meant, only tyrannized and tormented her. Yet it seems it's not for you to judge her. And how is she guilty before you? Explain to me also, by the way, my friend: why was it and with what purpose that you spread it around in school, and in high school, and all your life, and in front of every first comer, as I've heard, that you are illegitimate? I've heard that you did it with a sort of special eagerness. And yet it's all nonsense and vile slander: you are legitimate, a Dolgoruky, the son of Makar Ivanych Dolgoruky, a respectable man, remarkable for his intelligence and character. And if you have received higher education, that is in fact owing to your former master, Versilov, but what of it? Above all, by proclaiming your illegitimacy, which in itself is a slander, you thereby revealed your mother's secret and, out of some sort of false pride, dragged your mother to judgment before the first scum to come along. My friend, that is very ignoble, the more so as your mother is not personally guilty of anything: hers is the purest character, and if she is not Mrs. Versilov, it is solely because she is still married."

"Enough, I agree with you completely, and I believe so much in your intelligence that I fully hope you will stop this already too-lengthy scolding of me. You have such a love of measure; and yet everything has its measure, even your sudden love of my mother. This will be better: since you've ventured to come to me and sit here for a quarter or half an hour (I still don't know what for; well, let's suppose it's for my mother's peace of mind)—and, moreover, you talk to me with such eagerness, in spite of what happened downstairs, it would be better if you told me about my father—

this Makar Ivanovich, the wanderer.[42] I'd like to hear about him precisely from you; I've long meant to ask you. Since we're parting, and maybe for a long time, I'd also like very much to get an answer from you to this question: how is it possible that in this whole twenty years you could have no effect on my mother's prejudices, and now also my sister's, enough to dispel with your civilizing influence the surrounding darkness of her original milieu? Oh, I'm not talking about her purity! Even without that she has always been infinitely superior to you morally, forgive me, but... this is merely an infinitely superior corpse. Only Versilov lives, and all the rest around him, and everything connected with him, vegetates under the unfailing condition that it has the honor of nourishing him with its forces, its living juices. But wasn't she alive once? Wasn't there something you loved in her? Wasn't she a woman once?"

"My friend, if you like, she never was," he answered me, twisting at once into that former manner he had had with me, which I remembered so well, and which infuriated me so much; that is, he was apparently the most sincere simpleheartedness, but look—and everything in him was just the deepest mockery, so that sometimes I couldn't figure out his face at all, "she never was! A Russian woman can never be a woman."

"And a Polish woman, a French woman, can be? Or an Italian, a passionate Italian woman, there's what's capable of captivating a civilized Russian man of a higher milieu like Versilov?"

"Well, who would have expected to run into a Slavophile?"[43] Versilov laughed.

I remember his story word for word; he even began talking with great eagerness and obvious pleasure. It was all too clear to me that he had by no means come to me for a chat, and not at all so as to calm my mother, but probably with other goals in mind.

II

"All these twenty years, your mother and I have lived in complete silence," he began his palaver (affected and unnatural in the highest degree), "and all that has been between us has taken place in silence. The main quality of our twenty-year-long liaison has been—speechlessness. I don't think we even quarreled once. True, I often went away and left her alone, but in the end I always came back. *Nous revenons toujours*,* that's a fundamental quality of men; it's owing to their magnanimity. If the matter of marriage depended on women alone, no marriage would stay together. Humility, meekness, lowliness, and at the same time firmness, strength, real strength—that is your mother's character. Note that she's the best of all the women I've met in the world. And that there is strength in her—that I can testify to; I've seen how that strength nourishes her. Where it's a matter, I wouldn't say of convictions, there can be no proper convictions here, but of what they consider convictions, which, to their minds, also means sacred, there even torture would be to no avail. Well, but you can judge for yourself: do I look like a torturer? That's why I preferred to be silent about almost everything, not only because it's easier, and, I confess, I don't regret it. In this way everything went over by itself, broadly and humanely, so that I don't even ascribe to myself any praise for it. I'll say, by the way, in parenthesis, that for some reason I suspect she never believed in my humaneness, and therefore always trembled; but while trembling, at the same time she never yielded to any culture. They somehow know how to do it, and there's something here that we don't understand, and generally they know better than we how to manage their own affairs. They can go on living in their own way in situations that are most unnatural for them, and remain completely themselves in situations that are most not their own. We can't do that."

"They who? I don't quite understand you."

"The people, my friend, I'm speaking of the people. They have demonstrated this great, vital force and historical breadth both morally and politically. But to return to what we were saying, I'll observe about your mother that she's not always silent; your mother occasionally says things, but says them in such a way that you see straight off that you've only wasted your time talking, even if you've spent five years beforehand gradually preparing her. Besides, her objections are quite unexpected. Note once again that I don't consider her a fool at all; on the contrary, there's a certain kind of intelligence here, and even a most remarkable intelligence; however, maybe you won't believe me about her intelligence..."

"Why not? I only don't believe that you really believe in her intelligence yourself, and are not pretending."

"Oh? You consider me such a chameleon? My friend, I allow

*We always come back.

you a bit too much . . . as a spoiled son . . . but let it remain so for this time."

"Tell me about my father—the truth, if you can."

"Concerning Makar Ivanovich? Makar Ivanovich is, as you already know, a household serf, who had, so to speak, a desire for a certain glory . . ."

"I'll bet that at this moment you envy him for something!"

"On the contrary, my friend, on the contrary, and, if you wish, I'm very glad to see you in such whimsical spirits; I swear that precisely now I am in a highly repentant humor, and precisely now, at this moment, and maybe for the thousandth time, I impotently regret all that happened twenty years ago. Besides, as God is my witness, it all happened quite inadvertently . . . well, and afterwards, as far as it was in my power, also humanely; at least so far as I then understood the endeavor of humaneness. Oh, we were all boiling over then with the zeal to do good, to serve civic goals, high ideas; we condemned ranks, our inherited rights, estates, and even moneylenders, at least some of us did . . . I swear to you. We weren't many, but we spoke well and, I assure you, we sometimes even acted well."

"That was when you wept on his shoulder?"

"My friend, I agree with you in everything beforehand; by the way, you heard about the shoulder from me, which means that at this moment you are making wicked use of my own simple-heartedness and trustfulness; but you must agree that that shoulder really wasn't as bad as it seems at first sight, especially for that time; we were only beginning then. I was faking, of course, but I didn't know I was faking. Don't you ever fake, for instance, in practical cases?"

"Just now, downstairs, I waxed a little sentimental, and felt very ashamed, as I was coming up here, at the thought that you might think I was faking. It's true that on some occasions, though your feelings are sincere, you sometimes pretend; but downstairs just now it was all natural."

"That's precisely it; you've defined it very happily in a single phrase: 'though your feelings are sincere, all the same you pretend.' Well, that's exactly how it was with me: though I was pretending, I wept quite sincerely. I won't dispute that Makar Ivanovich might have taken that shoulder as an added mockery, if he had been more clever; but his honesty then stood in the way of his perspicacity. Only I don't know whether he pitied me then or not; I remember I very much wanted that."

"You know," I interrupted him, "you're mocking now, too, as you say that. And generally all the time, whenever you spoke to me during this whole month, you did it mockingly. Why did you always do that when you spoke to me?"

"You think so?" he replied meekly. "You're very suspicious. However, if I do laugh, it's not at you, or at least not at you alone, rest assured. But I'm not laughing now, and back then—in short, I did all I could then, and, believe me, not for my own benefit. We, that is, the beautiful people, as opposed to the common folk, did not know at all how to act for our own benefit then; on the contrary, we always mucked things up for ourselves as much as possible, and I confess, among us then we considered that some sort of 'higher benefit of our own'—in a higher sense, naturally. The present generation of advanced people is much more grasping than we were. At that time, even before the sin, I explained everything to Makar Ivanovich with extraordinary directness. I now agree that much of it didn't need to be explained at all, still less with such directness; to say nothing of humaneness, it would simply have been more polite. But try restraining yourself when you're dancing away, and want to perform a nice little step! And maybe such are the demands of the beautiful and the lofty[44] in reality, all my life I've been unable to resolve that. However, it's too profound a theme for our superficial conversation, but I swear to you that I sometimes die of shame when I remember it. I offered him three thousand roubles then, and, I remember, he said nothing, I alone did the talking. Imagine, I fancied he was afraid of me, that is, of my serf-owning rights, and, I remember, I tried as hard as I could to encourage him; I persuaded him not to be afraid of anything and to voice all his wishes, and even with all possible criticism. As a guarantee, I gave him my word that if he didn't accept my conditions, that is, the three thousand, freedom (for him and his wife, naturally), and that he should go off on a journey any which way (without his wife, naturally)—he should tell me so directly, and I would at once grant him his freedom, let him have his wife, reward them both with the same three thousand, I believe, and it would not be they who would go off any which way, but I myself would go away to Italy for three years, all alone. *Mon ami*, I wouldn't have taken Mlle. Sapozhkov to Italy, I assure you; I was extremely pure at that time. And what then? This Makar understood excellently well that I would do just what I said; but he went on saying nothing, and only when I was about to fall down before him a third time, he drew back, waved his arm, and went out even somewhat unceremoniously, I assure you, which even surprised me then. I saw myself for a moment in the mirror then, and cannot forget it. In general, when they don't say anything, it's worst of all, and he was a gloomy character, and, I confess, not only did I not trust him, when I summoned him to my study, but I was even terribly afraid: there are characters in that milieu, and terribly many of them, who contain in themselves, so to speak, the incarnation of unrespectability, and that is something one fears more than a beating. *Sic.* And what a risk, what a risk I took! What if he had shouted for the whole yard to hear, howled, this provincial Uriah[45]—well, how would it have been then for me, an undersized David, and what could I have done? That was why I resorted to the three thousand first, it was instinctive, but, fortunately, I was mistaken; this Makar Ivanovich was something quite different..."

"Tell me, was there a sin? You said you sent for the husband even before the sin?"

"That depends, you see, on how you understand..."

"Meaning there was. You just said you were mistaken about him, that he was something different. What was different?"

"Precisely what, I don't know even now. But it was something else, and, you know, even quite respectable; I conclude that because by the end I felt three times more ashamed in his presence. The very next day he agreed to go on a journey, without a word—naturally, not forgetting any of the rewards I had offered."

"He took the money?"

"What else! You know, my friend, on this point he even quite surprised me. Naturally, I didn't happen to have three thousand in my pocket at the time, but I got hold of seven hundred roubles and handed them to him to start with. And what then? He requested the remaining two thousand three hundred from me, just to be sure, in the form of a promissory note in the name of some merchant. Two years later he used this letter to request the money from me through the court, and with interest, so that he surprised me again, the more so as he literally went about collecting money for building a church of God, and since then he's been wandering for twenty years. I don't understand why a wanderer needs so much money for himself... money's such a worldly thing... At that moment, of course, I offered it sincerely and, so to speak, with an initial fervor, but later, when so much time had passed, I naturally might have thought better of it... and I hoped he would at least spare me... or, so to speak, spare *us*, her and me, would at least wait. However, he didn't even wait..."

(I'll make a necessary *nota bene* here: if my mother should happen to outlive Mr. Versilov, she would be left literally without a kopeck in her old age, if it weren't for that three thousand of Makar Ivanovich's, which had long been doubled by interest, and which he left to her in its entirety, to a rouble, last year in his will. He had divined Versilov even then.)

"You once said that Makar Ivanovich came to visit you several times, and always stayed in my mother's apartment?"

"Yes, my friend, and I confess, at first I was terribly afraid of those visits. In all this period, in twenty years, he came only six or seven times, and on the first occasions, if I was at home, I hid myself. I didn't even understand at first what it meant and why he came. But then, owing to certain considerations, it seemed to me that it was not at all that stupid on his part. Then, by chance, I decided out of curiosity to go and look at him, and, I assure you, my impression was most original. This was his third or fourth visit, precisely at the time when I was about to become an arbiter of the peace and when, naturally, I was setting out with all my strength to study Russia. I even heard a great many new things from him. Besides, I met in him precisely what I had never expected to meet: a sort of good humor, an evenness of character, and, most surprisingly, all but mirth. Not the slightest allusion to *that* (*tu comprends**), and, in the highest degree, an ability to talk sense and to talk excellently well, that is, without that stupid homegrown profundity, which, I confess, I cannot stand, despite all my democratism, and without all those strained Russicisms in which 'real Russian people' speak in novels or on stage. With all that, extremely little about religion, unless you brought it up yourself, and even quite nice stories of their own sort about monasteries and monastery life, if you yourself became curious. And above all—deference, that modest deference, precisely the deference that is necessary for the highest equality, moreover, without which, in my opinion, one cannot attain to superiority. Precisely here, through the lack of the least arrogance, one attains to the highest respectability, and there appears a person who undoubtedly respects himself, and precisely whatever the situation he finds himself in, and whatever his destiny happens to be. This

*You understand.

ability to respect oneself in one's own situation—is extremely rare in the world, at least as rare as a true sense of one's own dignity... You'll see for yourself, once you've lived. But what struck me most afterwards, precisely afterwards, and not at the beginning" (Versilov added), "was that this Makar was of extremely stately appearance and, I assure you, was extremely handsome. True, he was old, but

Dark-faced, tall, and straight,[46]

simple and grave; I even marveled at how my poor Sofya could have preferred me *then*; he was fifty then, but was still such a fine fellow, and I was such a whirligig beside him. However, I remember he was already unpardonably gray then, which meant he was just as gray when he married her... That might have had an influence."

This Versilov had the most scoundrelly high-toned manner: having said (when it was impossible not to) several quite clever and beautiful things, suddenly to end on purpose with some stupidity like this surmise about Makar Ivanovich's gray hair and its influence on my mother. He did it on purpose, probably not knowing why himself, from a stupid society habit. To listen to him—it seemed he was speaking very seriously, and yet within himself he was faking or laughing.

III

I DON'T UNDERSTAND why I was suddenly overcome then by terrible anger. Generally, I recall some of my outbursts in those minutes with great displeasure. I suddenly got up from my chair.

"You know what," I said, "you say you came mainly so that my mother would think we've made peace. Enough time has passed for her to think that; would you kindly leave me alone?"

He blushed slightly and got up from his place.

"My dear, you are extremely unceremonious with me. However, good-bye; love can't be forced. I'll allow myself only one question: do you really want to leave the prince?"

"Aha! I just knew you had special goals..."

"That is, you suspect I came to persuade you to stay with the prince, because I stand to profit from it myself. But, my friend, you don't think I also invited you from Moscow with some sort of profit in mind, do you? Oh, how suspicious you are! On the contrary, I wished for your own good in everything. And even now, when my means have improved so much, I wish that, at least occasionally, you would allow your mother and me to help you."

"I don't like you, Versilov."

"And it's even 'Versilov.' By the way, I regret very much that I couldn't pass this name on to you, for in fact my whole fault consists only in that, if it is a fault, isn't that so? But, once again, I couldn't marry a married woman, judge for yourself."

"That's probably why you wanted to marry an unmarried one?"

A slight spasm passed over his face.

"You mean Ems. Listen, Arkady, you allowed yourself that outburst downstairs, pointing the finger at me in front of your mother. Know, then, that precisely here you went widest of the mark. You know exactly nothing of the story of the late Lydia Akhmakov. Nor do you know how much your mother herself participated, yes, even though she wasn't there with me; and if I ever saw a good woman, it was then, as I looked at your mother. But enough, this is all still a mystery, and you—you say who knows what and in somebody else's voice."

"The prince said precisely today that you were an amateur of unfledged girls."

"The prince said that?"

"Yes. Listen, do you want me to tell you exactly why you came to me now? I've been sitting all this while asking myself what was the secret of this visit, and now, it seems, I've finally guessed it."

He was already on his way out, but he stopped and turned his head to me in expectation.

"Earlier I let slip in passing that Touchard's letter to Tatyana Pavlovna got in with Andronikov's papers and wound up, after his death, with Marya Ivanovna in Moscow. I saw something suddenly twitch in your face, and only now did I guess why, when something just twitched in your face again in exactly the same way: it occurred to you then, downstairs, that if one of Andronikov's letters had already wound up with Marya Ivanovna, why shouldn't another do the same? And Andronikov might have left some highly important letters, eh? Isn't that so?"

"And I came to you wanting to make you blab about something?"

"You know it yourself."

He turned very pale.

"You didn't figure that out on your own; there's a woman's

influence here. And how much hatred there is in your words—in your coarse guess!"

"A woman's? And I saw that woman just today! Maybe you want to have me stay with the prince precisely in order to spy on her?"

"Anyhow, I see you'll go extremely far on your new road. Mightn't this be 'your idea'? Go on, my friend, you have unquestionable ability along the sleuthing line. Given talent, one must perfect it."

He paused to catch his breath.

"Beware, Versilov, don't make me your enemy!"

"My friend, in such cases no one speaks his last thoughts, but keeps them to himself. And now give me some light, I beg you. You may be my enemy, but not so much, probably, as to wish me to break my neck. *Tiens, mon ami*,* imagine," he continued, going down, "all this month I've been taking you for a good soul. You want so much to live and thirst so much to live, that it seems if you were given three lives, it wouldn't be enough for you; it's written on your face. Well, and such men are most often good souls. And see how mistaken I've been!"

IV

I CAN'T EXPRESS how my heart was wrung when I was left alone: as if I had cut off a piece of my own living flesh! Why I had suddenly gotten so angry, and why I had offended him like that—so intensely and deliberately—I couldn't tell now, of course, or then either. And how pale he had turned! And what, then? Maybe that paleness was an expression of the most sincere and pure feelings and the deepest grief, and not of anger and offense. It always seemed to me that there were moments when he loved me very much. Why, why should I not believe that now, the more so as so much has now been completely explained?

But maybe indeed I grew angry all at once and drove him out because of the sudden guess that he had come to me hoping to find out whether any more of Andronikov's letters had been left to Marya Ivanovna? That he must have been looking for those letters and was looking for them—that I knew. But who knows, maybe then, precisely at that moment, I was terribly mistaken! And who

*Say, my friend.

knows, maybe it was I, by that very mistake, who prompted him afterwards in the thought of Marya Ivanovna and the possibility of her having letters?

And, finally, again a strange thing: again he had repeated word for word my own thought (about three lives), which I had told to Kraft earlier that day and, above all, in my own words. The coincidence of words was once again chance, but all the same how well he knows the essence of my character: what insight, what perception! But if he understands one thing so well, why doesn't he understand another at all? And can it be that he wasn't faking, but was indeed unable to guess that what I needed was not Versilovian nobility, that it was not my birth that I couldn't forgive him, but that all my life I've needed Versilov himself, the whole man, the father, and that this thought has already entered my blood? Can it be that such a subtle man can be so dull and crude? And if not, then why does he enrage me, why does he pretend?

Chapter Eight

I

THE NEXT MORNING I tried to get up as early as possible. Ordinarily we got up at around eight o'clock, that is, my mother, my sister, and I; Versilov indulged himself till half-past nine. Precisely at half-past eight my mother would bring me coffee. But this time, not waiting for coffee, I slipped out of the house at exactly eight o'clock. The evening before, I had made up a general plan of action for this whole day. In this plan, despite my passionate resolve to set about fulfilling it at once, I sensed that there was a great deal that was unstable and uncertain at the most important points; that was why almost all night I had been as if in half-sleep, delirious, had an awful lot of dreams, and hardly a moment of proper sleep. Nevertheless I got up brisker and fresher than ever. I especially did not want to meet my mother. I couldn't talk to her otherwise than on a certain subject, and I was afraid to distract myself from the goals I had set myself by some new and unexpected impression.

The morning was cold, and a damp, milky fog lay upon everything. I don't know why, but I always like the busy early morning in Petersburg, despite its extremely nasty look, and all these egoistic and ever-pensive folk, hurrying about their business around eight in the morning, have some special attraction for me. I especially like, as I hurry on my way, either to ask somebody something businesslike, or to have somebody ask me something: both question and answer are always brief, clear, sensible, given without stopping, and are almost always friendly, and the readiness to respond is greatest at that hour. The Petersburger becomes less communicative in the middle of the day or towards evening, and is ready to abuse or deride at the least opportunity; it's quite different in the early morning, before work, at the most sober and serious time. I've noticed that.

I was again heading for the Petersburg side. Since I absolutely had to be back on the Fontanka by twelve to see Vasin (who could most often be found at home at twelve), I hurried and didn't stop, in spite of a great urge to have coffee somewhere. Besides, I also had absolutely to catch Efim Zverev at home; I was going to him again and in fact almost came too late; he was finishing his coffee and getting ready to go out.

"What brings you so often?" he met me without getting up from his place.

"I'm about to explain that."

Any early morning, a Petersburg one included, has a sobering effect on man's nature. Some flaming night's dream even evaporates completely with the coming of morning's light and cold, and I myself have happened of a morning to recall some of my night's only just-passed reveries, and sometimes also acts, with reproach and shame. However, I'll observe in passing that I consider the Petersburg morning, seemingly the most prosaic on the whole earth, to be all but the most fantastic in the world. That is my personal view, or, better to say, impression, but I'll stand up for it. On such a Petersburg morning, foul, damp, and foggy, the wild dream of some Pushkinian Hermann from the "Queen of Spades" (a colossal character, an extraordinary, perfectly Petersburgian type—a type from the Petersburg period!)[47]—it seems to me, should grow still stronger. A hundred times, in the midst of this fog, a strange but importunate reverie has come to me: "And if this fog breaks up and lifts, won't this whole foul, slimy city go with it, rise up with the fog and vanish like smoke, and leave only the former Finnish swamp, and in the middle, perhaps, for the beauty of it, a bronze horseman on a hot-breathed, overridden steed?"[48] In short, I can't convey my impressions, because it's all finally fantasy, poetry, and therefore rubbish. Nevetheless, one totally meaningless question has often come to me and comes to me now: "Here they all are rushing and throwing themselves about, and who knows, maybe it's all somebody's dream, and there's not a single true, genuine person here, not a single real act? The somebody whose dream it is will suddenly wake up—and everything will suddenly vanish." But I'm getting carried away.

I'll say beforehand: there are projects and dreams in every life so seemingly eccentric that at first sight they might unmistakably be taken for madness. It was with one of these fantasies that I went that morning to Zverev—to Zverev, because I had no one else in Petersburg to whom I could turn this time. And yet Efim was precisely the last person to whom, if I had had a choice, I would have turned with such a suggestion. When I sat down facing him, it even seemed to me myself that I, the incarnation of fever and delirium, was sitting down facing the incarnation of the golden mean and prose. But on my side was an idea and a right feeling, while on his there was only the practical conclusion that it's never done that way. In short, I explained to him, briefly and clearly, that apart from him I had absolutely no one in Petersburg whom I could send, in view of an urgent matter of honor, to act as a second; that he was an old comrade and therefore did not even have the right to refuse, and that I wanted to challenge the lieutenant of the guards, Prince Sokolsky, on the grounds that, a little more than a year ago, in Ems, he had given my father, Versilov, a slap in the face. I'll note, at the same time, that Efim knew even in great detail all my family circumstances, my relations with Versilov, and almost all that I myself knew of Versilov's history; I had told it to him myself at various times, except, of course, for certain secrets. He sat and listened, as he usually did, ruffled up like a sparrow in a cage, silent and serious, puffy-faced, with his disheveled flaxen hair. A motionless, mocking smile never left his lips. This smile was the nastier in that it was involuntary and not at all deliberate; it was evident that he really and truly considered himself at that moment vastly superior to me in intelligence and character. I also suspected that, besides that, he also despised me for yesterday's scene at Dergachev's; that was as it should have been: Efim was the crowd, Efim was the street, and that always bows down only to success.

"And Versilov doesn't know of it?" he asked.

"Of course not."

"Then what right do you have to interfere in his affairs? That's the first thing. And, second, what do you want to prove by it?"

I knew the objections and at once explained to him that it was not at all as stupid as he supposed. First, it would be proved to the insolent prince that there were still people of our estate who understood honor, and, second, Versilov would be shamed and learn a lesson. And, third, and most important, even if Versilov, owing to certain convictions of his own, was right not to have challenged the prince and to have decided to bear with the slap, he would at least see that there was a being who was able to feel his offense so strongly that he took it as his own, and was ready even to lay down his life for his interests . . . in spite of the fact that he had parted with him forever . . .

"Wait, don't shout, my aunt doesn't like it. Tell me, is it the same Prince Sokolsky that Versilov is in litigation with over an inheritance? In that case, it will be a totally new and original way of winning in court—by killing your opponents in a duel."

I explained to him *en toutes lettres** that he was simply stupid and insolent, and that if his mocking smile spread wider and wider, that only proved his smugness and ordinariness, that he couldn't really suppose that the thought of the litigation had not been in my head right from the very start, but had deigned to visit only his much-thinking head. Then I told him that the litigation had already been won, and besides, that it had been conducted not against Prince Sokolsky, but against the Princes Sokolsky, so that if one prince was killed, the others would remain, but that the challenge would undoubtedly have to be put off till after the period of appeal (though the princes would not appeal), solely for the sake of decency. Once the period was over, the duel would follow; but I had come now because the duel would not be at once, but I had to secure a second, because I didn't have one, I didn't know anybody, so as to find one at least by the time I needed him, if he, Efim, refused. That's why I came, I said.

"Well, come back and talk then, there's no point rolling ten miles for nothing."

He got up and took his cap.

"And you'll go then?"

"Naturally not."

"Why?"

"I won't go for this reason alone, that if I agree now to go then, you'll spend the whole period of appeal dragging yourself to me every day. And the main thing is that it's all nonsense, and that's that. Why should I ruin my career because of you? The prince would up and ask me, 'Who sent you?' 'Dolgoruky.' 'And what has Dolgoruky got to do with Versilov?' So then I should explain your genealogy to him? He'll just laugh!"

"Then give him one in the mug!"

"Well, that's all fairy tales."

"Afraid? You're so tall; you were the strongest one in high school."

"Afraid, of course I'm afraid. The prince won't fight, because they only fight with equals."

"I'm also a gentleman by development, I have the right, I'm equal... on the contrary, it's he who's unequal."

"No, you're little."

"Why little?"

*Spelling it all out.

"You're just little; we're both little, but he's big."

"You're a fool! By law I could have gotten married a year ago."

"So go and get married, and even so you're a pipsqueak; you're still growing!"

I realized, of course, that he had decided to jeer at me. Undoubtedly this whole stupid anecdote could have gone untold, and it would be even better if it died unknown; besides, it's disgusting in its pettiness and uselessness, though it had quite serious consequences.

But to punish myself still more, I'll tell it in full. Having perceived that Efim was jeering at me, I allowed myself to give him a shove on the shoulder with my right hand, or, better to say, with my right fist. He then took me by the shoulders, turned me face to the field, and—really proved to me that he was indeed the strongest one in our high school.

II

The reader, of course, will think that I was in a terrible mood going out of Efim's, and yet he will be mistaken. I realized only too well that it was childish, a schoolboy incident, but the seriousness of the matter remained intact. I had my coffee only on Vassilievsky Island, purposely skipping my yesterday's tavern on the Petersburg side; both the tavern and the nightingale had become doubly hateful to me. A strange quality: I'm capable of hating places and objects as if they were people. On the other hand, there are also several happy places in Petersburg, that is, places where, for some reason, I was happy—and I cherish those places and purposely don't visit them for as long as possible, so that later, when I'm quite alone and unhappy, I can go there to grieve and recall. Over coffee I did full justice to Efim and his common sense. Yes, he was more practical than I, but hardly more realistic. Realism that is limited to the end of one's nose is more dangerous than the most insane fantasticality, because it's blind. But in doing justice to Efim (who at that moment probably thought I was going down the street cursing him), I still did not yield anything of my convictions, as I haven't up till now. I've seen people who, at the first bucket of cold water, renounce not only their actions, but even their idea, and begin to laugh at something they considered sacred only an hour before. Oh, how easily it's done with them! Grant that Efim, even in the essence of the matter, was more right than I, and I was stupider than all that's stupid and merely clowning, but still, in the very depth of the matter, there lay a point, standing upon which I, too, was right, there was something correct on my side, too, and, above all, something that they could never understand.

I wound up at Vasin's, on the Fontanka by the Semyonovsky Bridge, almost exactly at twelve o'clock, but I didn't find him at home. He had his work on Vassilievsky, and came home strictly at certain hours, among others almost always before twelve. Since, besides that, it was some holiday, I had supposed I would be sure to find him; not finding him, I settled down to wait, despite the fact that I had come to see him for the first time.

I reasoned like this: the matter of the letter about the inheritance was a matter of conscience, and I, in choosing Vasin as a judge, was thereby showing him the whole depth of my respect, which, of course, should be flattering to him. Naturally, I was truly concerned about this letter and really convinced of the necessity for arbitration; but I suspect, nevertheless, that even then I could have wriggled out of the difficulty without any outside help. And, above all, I knew it myself; to wit: I had only to hand the letter over to Versilov personally, and he could do whatever he wanted; that was the solution. And to make myself the supreme judge and arbiter in a matter like this was even quite wrong. In removing myself by handing the letter over, and that precisely silently, I would profit at once by that very thing, putting myself in a higher position than Versilov, for by renouncing all profit from the inheritance, so far as it concerned me (because, being Versilov's son, I would, of course, have something coming to me, if not now, then later), I would forever preserve for myself a superior moral view of Versilov's future action. And, again, no one could reproach me for ruining the princes, because the document had no decisive legal significance. All this I thought over and figured out completely, while sitting in Vasin's empty room, and it even entered my head that I had come to see Vasin so desirous of his advice about what to do, with the sole purpose of letting him see what a highly noble and umercenary man I was, and thus taking revenge on him for my humiliation before him yesterday.

Having realized all that, I felt great vexation; nevertheless, I did not leave but stayed, though I knew for certain that my vexation would only grow greater every five minutes.

First of all, I began to take a terrible dislike to Vasin's room.

"Show me your room, and I'll know your character"—you really can say that. Vasin lived in a furnished room, renting from tenants, obviously poor ones, who earned their living that way and had other lodgers. I was acquainted with these narrow little rooms, hardly filled with furniture, and yet with pretensions to a comfortable look; here was the inevitable soft sofa from the flea market, which it was dangerous to move, the washstand, and the iron bed behind a screen. Vasin was obviously the best and most reliable tenant. A landlady is sure to have one such best tenant, who receives special favors for it: his room is cleaned and swept more thoroughly, some lithograph gets hung over the sofa, a consumptive little rug gets spread under the table. People who like this musty cleanness and, above all, the landlady's obsequious deference—are themselves suspect. I was convinced that the title of best tenant flattered Vasin. I don't know why, but the sight of those two tables piled high with books gradually began to infuriate me. Books, papers, an inkstand—everything was in the most disgusting order, the ideal of which coincides with the worldview of a German landlady and her maid. There were quite a few books—not magazines or newspapers, but real books—and he obviously read them, and probably sat down to read or began to write with an extremely grave and precise look. I don't know, but I like it better when books are scattered about in disorder, when studies are at least not turned into a sacred rite. Probably this Vasin is extremely polite with visitors, but probably his every gesture tells the visitor, "I'll now sit with you for an hour and a half or so, and then, when you leave, I'll get down to business." Probably you can start up an extremely interesting conversation with him and hear something new, but—"I'm now going to have a talk with you, and I'll get you very interested, but when you leave I'll get down to what's most interesting . . ." And, nevertheless, I still didn't leave, but sat there. By then I was thoroughly convinced that I had no need at all of his advice.

I had already been sitting for an hour and more, and was sitting by the window on one of the two wicker chairs that stood by the window. It also infuriated me that time was passing and I still had to find quarters before evening. I wanted to pick up some book out of boredom, but I didn't; the very thought of amusing myself made it doubly disgusting. The extraordinary silence had gone on for more than an hour, and then suddenly, somewhere very close by, behind the door screened by the sofa, I began to make out, involuntarily and gradually, a whispering that grew louder and louder. Two voices were speaking, obviously women's by the sound of them, though it was quite impossible to make out their words; and nevertheless, out of boredom, I somehow began to listen. It was clear that they were speaking animatedly and passionately, and that the talk was not about patterns: they were arranging or arguing about something, or one voice persuaded and begged while the other disobeyed and objected. Must have been some other tenants. I soon got bored and my ear grew accustomed to it, so that, though I went on listening, I did so mechanically, sometimes even quite forgetting that I was listening, when suddenly something extraordinary happened, just as if someone had jumped from a chair with both feet or had suddenly jumped up from his place and stamped; then came a groan and a sudden cry, not even a cry, but a shriek, animal, angry, that no longer cared whether other people heard it or not. I rushed to the door and opened it; at the same time another door opened at the end of the corridor, the landlady's as I learned afterwards, from which two curious heads peeked out. The cry, however, subsided at once; then suddenly the door next to mine, the women neighbors', opened, and a young woman, as it seemed to me, quickly burst out of it and ran down the stairs. The other woman, an elderly one, wanted to hold her back, but couldn't, and only moaned behind her:

"Olya, Olya, where are you going? Oh!"

But, seeing our two open doors, she quickly closed hers, leaving a crack and listening through it to the stairs, till the sound of Olya's running footsteps died away completely. I went back to my window. Everything was quiet. A trifling incident, and maybe also ridiculous. I stopped thinking about it.

Around a quarter of an hour later, a loud and brash male voice rang out in the corridor, just by Vasin's door. Somebody grasped the door handle and opened it enough so that I could make out some tall man in the corridor, who obviously also saw me and was even already studying me, though he did not yet come into the room, but, still holding the door handle, went on talking with the landlady all the way down the corridor. The landlady called out to him in a thin and gay little voice, and one could tell by her voice that she had long known the visitor, and respected and valued him as both a solid guest and a merry gentleman. The merry gentleman shouted and cracked jokes, but the point was only that Vasin was not at home, that he never could find him at home, that it had been so ordained, and that he would wait again, as the other time, and all this undoubtedly seemed the height of wittiness to the landlady. Finally the visitor came in, thrusting the door fully open.

This was a well-dressed gentleman, obviously from one of the best tailors, in "high-class fashion," as they say, and yet he had very little of the high-class about him, and that, it seemed, despite a considerable desire to have it. He was not really brash, but somehow naturally insolent, which was in any case less offensive than insolence that rehearsed itself in front of a mirror. His hair, dark blond gone slightly gray, his black eyebrows, big beard, and big eyes, not only did not personalize his character, but seemed precisely to endow it with something general, like everyone else. Such a man laughs, and is ready to laugh, yet for some reason you never feel merry with him. He passes quickly from a laughing to a grave look, from a grave to a playful or winking one, but it is all somehow scattered and pointless... However, there's no sense describing it beforehand. Later I came to know this gentleman much better and more closely, and therefore I have involuntarily presented him now more knowingly than then, when he opened the door and came into the room. Though now, too, I would have difficulty saying anything exact or definite about him, because the main thing in these people is precisely their unfinishedness, scatteredness, and indefiniteness.

He had not yet had time to sit down, when I suddenly fancied that this must be Vasin's stepfather, a certain Mr. Stebelkov, of whom I had already heard something, but so fleetingly that I could not have said precisely what: I only remembered that it was not something nice. I knew that Vasin had lived for a long time as an orphan under his authority, but that he had long since gotten out from under his influence, that their goals and their interests were different, and that they lived separately in all respects. I also remembered that this Stebelkov had some capital, and that he was even some sort of speculator and trafficker; in short, it may be that I already knew something more specific about him, but I forget. He sized me up at a glance, though without any greeting, placed his top hat on the table in front of the sofa, pushed the table aside peremptorily with his foot, and did not so much sit as sprawl directly on the sofa, on which I had not ventured to sit, so that it let out a creak, dangled his legs, and, lifting up the right toe of his patent leather boot, began to admire it. Of course, he turned to me at once and again sized me up with his big, somewhat immobile eyes.

"I never find him at home!" he nodded his head to me slightly.

I said nothing.

"Unpunctual! His own view of things. From the Petersburg side?"

"You mean that you have come from the Petersburg side?" I returned the question.

"No, I'm asking you."

"I . . . I came from the Petersburg side, but how did you find out?"

"How? Hm." He winked, but did not deign to explain.

"That is, I don't live on the Petersburg side, but I was on the Petersburg side just now and then came here."

He went on silently smiling some sort of significant smile, which I disliked terribly. There was something stupid in this winking.

"At Mr. Dergachev's?" he said finally.

"What, at Dergachev's?" I opened my eyes wide.

He looked at me victoriously.

"I don't even know him."

"Hm."

"As you wish," I replied. I was beginning to find him repulsive.

"Hm, yes, sir. No, sir, pardon me; you buy something in a shop, in another shop next to it another buyer buys something else, and what do you think it is? Money, sir, from a merchant who is known as a moneylender, sir, because money's also a thing, and the moneylender is also a merchant . . . Do you follow?"

"Perhaps so."

"A third buyer walks past and, pointing at one of the shops, says, 'That's substantial,' then, pointing at another of the shops, says, 'That's insubstantial.' What conclusion can I draw about this buyer?"

"How should I know?"

"No, sir, pardon me. I'll give an example; man lives by good example. I go down Nevsky Prospect and notice that on the other side of the street, walking down the sidewalk, is a gentleman whose character I should like to determine. We reach, on different sides, the same turn onto Morskaya Street, and precisely there, where the English shop is, we notice a third pedestrian who has just been run over by a horse. Now get this: a fourth gentleman passes by and wishes to determine the character of the three of us, including the run-over one, in the sense of practicality and substantiality . . . Do you follow?"

"Excuse me, but with great difficulty."

"Very well, sir; just as I thought. I'll change the subject. I've been more than once to the spas in Germany, mineral water spas, it makes no difference which. I walk on the waters and see Englishmen. As you know, it's hard to strike up an acquaintance with an Englishman; but then, after two months, having finished the cure, we're all in a mountainous region, a whole company, with alpenstocks, going up a mountain, this one or that, it makes no difference. At a turn, that is, at a stopping-place, precisely where the monks make Chartreuse liqueur—note that—I met a native, standing solitarily, gazing silently. I wish to conclude about his substantiality: what do you think, could I turn for a conclusion to the crowd of Englishmen, with whom I was proceeding solely because I was unable to strike up a conversation with them at the spa?"

"How should I know? Excuse me, but I find it very hard to follow you."

"Hard?"

"Yes, you tire me."

"Hm." He winked and made some sort of gesture with his hand, probably meant to signify something very triumphant and victorious; then, quite solidly and calmly, he drew from his pocket a newspaper, obviously just bought, opened it, and began reading the last page, apparently leaving me completely alone. For some five minutes he didn't look at me.

"The Brest-Graevs[49] didn't go bust, eh? They took off, they keep going! I know many that went bust straightaway."

He looked at me from the bottom of his heart.

"I understand little about the stock exchange as yet," I replied.

"Denial?"

"Of what?"

"Money, sir."

"I don't deny money, but . . . but, it seems to me, first comes the idea, and then money."

"That is, pardon me, sir . . . here stands a man, so to speak, before his own capital . . ."

"First a lofty idea, and then money, but without a lofty idea along with money, society will collapse."

I don't know why I began to get heated. He looked at me somewhat dully, as if confused, but suddenly his whole face extended into the merriest and slyest smile:

"That Versilov, eh? He snapped it up, snapped it right up! It was decided yesterday, eh?"

I suddenly and unexpectedly perceived that he had long known who I was, and maybe knew much more as well. Only I don't understand why I suddenly blushed and stared most stupidly, without taking my eyes off him. He was visibly triumphant, he looked at me merrily, as if he had found me out and caught me at something in the slyest manner.

"No, sir," he raised both eyebrows, "you're now going to ask me about Mr. Versilov! What did I just tell you about substantiality? A year and a half ago, on account of that baby, he could have brought off a perfect little deal—yes, sir, but he went bust, yes, sir."

"On account of what baby?"

"On account of a nursing baby that he's now nurturing on the side, only he won't get anything through that... because..."

"What nursing baby? What is this?"

"His baby, of course, his very own, sir, by Mademoiselle Lydia Akhmakov... 'A lovely maiden did caress me...'[50] Those phosphorus matches—eh?"

"What nonsense, what wildness! He never had a baby by Miss Akhmakov!"

"Go on! And where have I been then? I'm both a doctor and a male midwife. Name's Stebelkov, haven't you heard? True, I had long ceased to practice by then, but I could give practical advice in a practical matter."

"You're a male midwife... you delivered Miss Akhmakov's baby?"

"No, sir, I didn't deliver Miss Akhmakov's anything. In that suburb there was a Doctor Granz, burdened with a family, they paid him half a thaler, that's the situation there with doctors, and on top of that nobody knew him, so he was there in my place... It was I who recommended him, for the darkness of the unknown. Do you follow? And I only gave one piece of practical advice, to a question from Versilov, sir, Andrei Petrovich, to a most highly secret question, sir, eye to eye. But Andrei Petrovich preferred two birds."

I was listening in profound amazement.

"You can't kill two birds with one stone, says a folk, or, more correctly, a simple-folk's proverb. But I say exceptions that constantly repeat themselves turn into a general rule. He tried to hit a second bird, that is, translating it into Russian, to chase after another lady—and got no results. Once you grab something, hold on to it. Where things need speeding up, he hems and haws.

Versilov is a 'women's prophet,' sir—that's how young Prince Sokolsky beautifully designated him to me then. No, you should come to me! If you want to learn a lot about Versilov, come to me."

He obviously admired my mouth gaping in astonishment. Never had I heard a thing up till then about a nursing baby. And it was at that moment that the neighbors' door suddenly banged and somebody quickly went into their room.

"Versilov lives in the Semyonovsky quarter, on Mozhaiskaya Street, at Mrs. Litvinov's house, number seventeen, I went to the address bureau myself!" an irritated female voice cried loudly. We could hear every word. Stebelkov shot up his eyebrows and raised a finger over his head.

"We talk about him here, and there he's already... There's those exceptions that constantly repeat themselves! *Quand on parle d'une corde** ..."

With a quick jump, he sat up on the sofa and began listening at the door where the sofa stood.

I was also terribly struck. I realized that this woman shouting was probably the same one who had run out earlier in such agitation. But how did Versilov figure in it? Suddenly someone shrieked again as earlier, the furious shriek of a person turned savage with wrath, who is not being given something or is being held back from something. The only difference from the previous time was that the cries and shrieks went on longer. A struggle could be heard, some words, rapid, quick: "I don't want to, I don't want to, give it back to me, give it back to me right now!" or something like that—I can't quite remember. Then, as the other time, someone rushed swiftly to the door and opened it. Both women ran out to the corridor, one of them, as earlier, obviously holding the other back. Stebelkov, who had long ago jumped up from the sofa and was listening delightedly, now darted to the door and quite frankly jumped out to the corridor, right onto the neighbors. Naturally, I also ran to the door. But his appearance in the corridor was like a bucket of cold water: the women quickly disappeared and noisily slammed the door behind them. Stebelkov was about to leap after them, but paused, raising his finger, smiling, and thinking; this time I discerned something extremely bad, dark, and sinister in his smile. Having spotted the landlady, who was again standing by her door, he quickly ran to her on tiptoe down the corridor; after

*When you speak of a rope [in the hanged man's house].

exchanging whispers with her for about two minutes and certainly receiving information, he came back to the room, imposingly and resolutely now, took his top hat from the table, looked fleetingly in the mirror, ruffled up his hair, and, with self-confident dignity, not even glancing at me, went to the neighbors. He listened at the door for a moment, putting his ear to it and winking victoriously to the landlady, who shook her finger at him and wagged her head as if to say, "Ah, naughty boy, naughty boy!" Finally, with a resolute but most delicate look, even as if hunched over with delicacy, he rapped with his knuckles on the neighbors' door. A voice was heard:

"Who's there?"

"Will you allow me to come in on most important business?" Stebelkov pronounced loudly and imposingly.

They did open, albeit slowly, just a little at first, a quarter; but Stebelkov firmly seized the handle at once and would not have let the door close again. A conversation began. Stebelkov spoke loudly, trying all the while to push his way into the room; I don't remember his words, but he spoke about Versilov, saying that he could inform them, could explain everything—"no, ma'am, just ask me," "no, ma'am, just come to me"—along that line. They very soon let him in. I went back to the sofa and tried to eavesdrop, but I couldn't make out everything, I only heard that Versilov was mentioned frequently. By the tone of his voice, I guessed that Stebelkov was already in control of the conversation, was already speaking not insinuatingly but peremptorily, and sprawling as earlier with me: "do you follow," "now kindly get this," and so on. However, he must have been extraordinarily affable with the women. Twice already I had heard him guffaw loudly and, probably, quite inappropriately, because along with his voice, and sometimes overpowering his voice, I heard the voices of the two women, which expressed no gaiety at all, mainly the young woman's, the one who had shrieked earlier; she spoke a lot, nervously, quickly, apparently denouncing something and complaining, seeking justice and a judge. But Stebelkov would not leave off, raised his voice more and more, and guffawed more and more often; such people cannot listen to others. I soon left the sofa, because it seemed shameful to me to eavesdrop, and moved to my old place on the wicker chair by the window. I was convinced that Vasin considered this man as nothing, but that if I were to declare the same opinion, he would at once defend him with serious dignity and observe didactically that he was "a practical man, one of those present-day businesslike people, who cannot be judged from our general and abstract points of view." At that moment, however, I remember that I was all somehow morally shattered, my heart was pounding, and I was undoubtedly expecting something. Some ten minutes went by, and suddenly, right in the middle of a rolling burst of laughter, someone shot up from the chair, exactly as earlier, then I heard the cries of the two women, I heard Stebelkov jump up as well and start saying something in a completely different voice, as if vindicating himself, as if persuading them to listen to him... But they didn't listen; wrathful shouts came: "Out! you blackguard, you shameless man!" In short, it was clear that he was being driven out. I opened the door just at the moment when he leaped into the corridor from the neighbors' room, literally pushed, it seemed, by their hands. Seeing me, he suddenly shouted, pointing at me:

"Here's Versilov's son! If you don't believe me, then here's his son, his own son! If you please!" And he seized me peremptorily by the arm.

"This is his son, his own son!" he repeated, bringing me to the ladies, adding nothing more, however, by way of explanation.

The young woman was standing in the corridor, the elderly one a step behind her, in the doorway. I only remember that this poor girl was not bad-looking, about twenty years old, but thin and sickly, with reddish hair and a face that somewhat resembled my sister's; this feature flashed and remained in my memory; only Liza had never been and certainly never could be in such a wrathful frenzy as this person who now stood before me: her lips were white, her pale gray eyes flashed, she was trembling all over with indignation. I also remember that I myself was in an extremely stupid and undignified position, because I was decidedly unable to find anything to say, thanks to this insolent fellow.

"So what if he's his son! If he's with you, he's a blackguard. If you are Versilov's son," she suddenly turned to me, "tell your father from me that he's a blackguard, that he's an unworthy, shameless man, that I don't need his money... Take it, take it, take it, give him this money at once!"

She quickly pulled several banknotes out of her pocket, but the elderly woman (that is, her mother, as it turned out later) seized her by the hand:

"Olya, maybe it's not true, maybe he's not his son!"

Olya quickly looked at her, understood, looked at me scornfully, and went back into the room, but before slamming the door, standing on the threshold, she once again shouted in frenzy at Stebelkov:

"Out!"

And she even stamped her foot at him. Then the door slammed and this time was locked. Stebelkov, still holding me by the shoulder, raised his finger and, extending his mouth into a long and pensive smile, rested his questioning gaze on me.

"I find your action with me ridiculous and unworthy," I muttered in indignation.

But he wasn't listening to me, though he didn't take his eyes off me.

"This ought to be in-ves-tigated!" he said pensively.

"But, anyhow, how dared you drag me out? What is this? Who is that woman? You seized me by the shoulder and led me—what's going on here?"

"Eh, the devil! Some sort of lost innocence... 'the oft-repeated exception'—do you follow?"

And he rested his finger on my chest.

"Eh, the devil!" I pushed his finger away.

But he suddenly and quite unexpectedly laughed softly, inaudibly, lengthily, merrily. In the end he put on his hat and, his face changed and now glum, observed, furrowing his brows:

"And the landlady ought to be instructed... they ought to be driven out of the apartment—that's what, and as soon as possible, otherwise they'll... You'll see! Remember my words, you'll see! Eh, the devil!" he suddenly cheered up again, "so you're waiting for Grisha?"

"No, I won't wait any longer," I answered resolutely.

"Well, it's all one..."

And without adding another sound, he turned, walked out, and went down the stairs without even deigning to look at the landlady, who was obviously waiting for explanations and news. I also took my hat and, after asking the landlady to report that I, Dolgoruky, had been there, ran down the stairs.

III

I HAD MERELY wasted time. On coming out, I set off at once to look for an apartment; but I was distracted, I wandered the streets for several hours and, though I stopped at five or six places with rooms to let, I'm sure I went past twenty without noticing them. To my still greater vexation, I had never imagined that renting lodgings was so difficult. The rooms everywhere were like Vasin's, and even much worse, and the prices were enormous, that is, not what I had reckoned on. I directly requested a corner,[51] merely to be able to turn around, and was given to know that in that case I should go "to the corners." Besides, there was a multitude of strange tenants everywhere, whom by their looks alone I would have been unable to live next to; I would even have paid not to live next to them. Some gentlemen without frock coats, in waistcoats only, with disheveled beards, casual and curious. There were about ten of them sitting in one tiny room over cards and beer, and I was offered the room next door. In other places, I myself gave such absurd answers to the landlords' questions that they looked at me in astonishment, and in one apartment I even had a quarrel. However, I can't really describe all these worthless things; I only want to say that, having gotten very tired, I ate something in some cookshop when it was already almost dark. I made a final resolve that I would go right now, by myself and alone, give Versilov the letter about the inheritance (without any explanations), pack my things upstairs into a suitcase and a bundle, and move at least for that night to a hotel. I knew that at the end of Obukhovsky Prospect, by the Triumphal Arch, there were inns where I could even get a separate little room for thirty kopecks; I decided to sacrifice for one night, only so as not to spend it at Versilov's. And then, going past the Technological Institute, it suddenly occurred to me for some reason to call on Tatyana Pavlovna, who lived just there, across from the Institute. In fact, the pretext for calling was the same letter of inheritance, but the insuperable impulse to call on her had, of course, other reasons, which, however, I'm unable to explain even now: there was some confusion of mind here about a "nursing baby," about "exceptions that make up the general rule." Whether I wanted to tell, or to show off, or to fight, or even to weep—I don't know, only I did go up to Tatyana Pavlovna's. Till then I had only visited her once, when I had just come from Moscow, on some errand from my mother, and I remember that, having come and given what I was charged with, I left after a minute, without even sitting down, and without her inviting me to.

I rang the bell, and the cook opened for me at once and silently let me in. All these details are precisely needed, to make it possible to understand how the crazy adventure could take place, which had such enormous influence on all that came afterwards. And, first, about the cook. She was a spiteful, snub-nosed Finn, who seemed to hate her mistress, Tatyana Pavlovna, who, on the contrary, could not part with her, owing to some sort of partiality, something like what old maids feel for wet-nosed pugs or eternally sleeping cats. The Finn was either angry and rude, or, having quarreled, would be silent for weeks on end in order to punish her lady. I must have hit on one of those silent days, because even to my question, "Is the lady at home?"—which I positively remember having asked her—she gave no reply and silently went to her kitchen. After which, naturally convinced that the lady was at home, I went in and, finding no one, began to wait, supposing that Tatyana Pavlovna would presently come out of the bedroom; otherwise why would the cook have let me in? I did not sit down and waited for two or three minutes; it was almost evening, and Tatyana Pavlovna's dark little apartment looked still more cheerless because of the endless chintz that hung everywhere. Two words about this vile little apartment, in order to understand the terrain where the thing happened. Tatyana Pavlovna, with her stubborn and imperious character, and as a result of her old landowning preferences, could not have lived in furnished rooms along with other tenants, and rented this parody of an apartment only so as to live separately and be her own mistress. These two rooms were exactly like two canary cages placed side by side, one smaller than the other, on the third floor, with windows facing the courtyard. Entering the apartment, you stepped directly into a narrow little corridor less than four feet wide, to the left were the above-mentioned canary cages, and straight down the corridor, at the bottom of it, was the door to the tiny kitchen. There might have been in these little rooms the ten cubic feet of air a man needs for twelve hours, but hardly more. They were grotesquely low, but the stupidest thing was that the windows, the doors, the furniture—all, all of it was hung or upholstered with chintz, fine French chintz, and adorned with little festoons; but this made the room seem twice as dark and like the interior of a traveling coach. In the room where I was waiting, you could still turn around, though it was all cluttered with furniture, and, by the way, not bad furniture: there were various little inlaid tables with bronze fittings, chests, an elegant and even costly toilet table. But the next room, from which I expected her to come, the bedroom, separated from this room by a heavy curtain, consisted, as it turned out later, literally of nothing but a bed. All these details are necessary in order to understand the stupid thing I did.

And so I was waiting and suspecting nothing, when the bell rang. I heard the cook pass through the corridor with unhurried steps and silently, exactly as with me earlier, let the people in. They were two ladies, and both were talking loudly, but what was my amazement when I recognized by their voices that one of them was Tatyana Pavlovna and the other precisely the woman whom I was least of all prepared to meet now, and in such circumstances at that! I couldn't be mistaken: I had heard that sonorous, strong, metallic voice yesterday, for only three minutes, true, but it had remained in my soul. Yes, it was "yesterday's woman." What was I to do? I'm not asking the reader this question, I'm only imagining that moment to myself, and I'm utterly unable to explain even now how it happened that I suddenly rushed behind the curtain and found myself in Tatyana Pavlovna's bedroom. In short, I hid, and barely had time to jump there as they came in. Why I didn't go to meet them, but hid myself—I don't know. It all happened accidentally, in the highest degree unaccountably.

Having jumped into the bedroom and stumbled over the bed, I noticed at once that there was a door from the bedroom to the kitchen, which meant a way out of my trouble and a possibility of escape, but—oh, horror!—the door was locked and the key was not in the lock. I lowered myself onto the bed in despair; I saw clearly that it meant I would now be eavesdropping, and from the first phrases, from the first sounds of the conversation, I realized that it was a secret and ticklish one. Oh, of course, an honest and noble person ought to have gotten up, even now, come out and said loudly, "I'm here, wait!"—and, despite his ridiculous position, walked past; but I did not get up and come out; I didn't dare, I turned coward in the meanest way.

"My dear Katerina Nikolaevna, you upset me deeply," Tatyana Pavlovna implored. "Calm yourself once and for all, it doesn't even suit your character. Wherever you are, there is joy, and now suddenly... At least me, I think, you continue to trust, knowing how devoted I am to you. Surely no less than to Andrei Petrovich, to whom, once again, I do not conceal my eternal devotion... Well, believe me, then, I swear to you on my honor, he doesn't have this document in his hands, and maybe no one does; and he's incapable of such skulduggery, it's sinful of you even to suspect it. The two of you have simply invented this hostility..."

"The document exists, and he is capable of anything. Why, I came in yesterday and the first thing I met was *ce petit espion** that he foisted on the prince."

"Eh, *ce petit espion*. First of all, he's not an *espion* at all, because it was I, I who insisted on placing him with the prince, otherwise he'd go crazy in Moscow, or starve to death—that was how they attested him from there; and above all, the crude brat is even a perfect little fool, how could he be a spy?"

"Yes, some little fool, which, however, doesn't prevent him from becoming a scoundrel. I was vexed yesterday, otherwise I'd have died of laughter: he turned pale, rushed to me, bowed and scraped, spoke French. And in Moscow, Marya Ivanovna assured me he was a genius. That this unfortunate letter has survived and exists somewhere in a most dangerous place—that I concluded mainly from Marya Ivanovna's face."

"My beauty! But you yourself said she had nothing!"

"The thing is that she has, she's merely lying, and what a crafty one she is, let me tell you! Back before Moscow I still had hopes that no papers had been left, but here, here..."

"Ah, my dear, on the contrary, they say she's a kind and sensible being, Andronikov valued her above any of his nieces. True, I don't know her that well, but—you could seduce her, my beauty! It's nothing for you to win people over, I'm an old woman and here I am in love with you, and in a minute I'll start kissing you... Well, what would it cost you to seduce her!"

"I tried to seduce her, Tatyana Pavlovna, I did, I even sent her into raptures, but she's also very clever... No, there's a whole character here, and a special one, a Moscow one... And imagine, she advised me to address a certain man here, Kraft, Andronikov's former assistant, she said he might know something. I already have an idea of this Kraft, and I even remember him fleetingly; but when she told me about this Kraft, I became convinced at once that it wasn't simply that she didn't know, but that she was lying and knew everything."

"But why, why? Anyway, perhaps it might be possible to consult him! He's German, this Kraft, not a babbler, and, as I recall, a

*This little spy.

most honest man—really, why not question him! Only it seems he's not in Petersburg now..."

"Oh, he came back yesterday, I was just at his place... I've come precisely to you in such anxiety, my arms and legs are trembling, I wanted to ask you, my angel, Tatyana Pavlovna, since you know everybody, couldn't we find out from his papers at least, because surely he left some papers, so where would they go now from him? Perhaps they'll fall into dangerous hands again? I've come running to ask your advice."

"What papers do you mean?" Tatyana Pavlovna did not understand. "And you say you yourself were just at Kraft's?"

"I was, I was, just now, but he shot himself. Yesterday evening."

I jumped up from the bed. I could sit it out when they called me a spy and an idiot; and the further they went in their conversation, the less possible it seemed for me to appear. It would have been unimaginable! I had decided to myself that I would sit it out, with a sinking heart, until Tatyana Pavlovna sent her visitor away (if I was lucky and she didn't come into the bedroom earlier for something), and later, once Mme. Akhmakov was gone, I might just have a fight then with Tatyana Pavlovna!... But suddenly now, when I heard about Kraft, I jumped up from the bed, I was all seized as if by a convulsion. Not thinking of anything, not reasoning or imagining, I took a step, raised the portière, and appeared before the two of them. There was still enough light for them to make me out, pale and trembling... They both screamed. How could they not?

"Kraft?" I murmured, addressing Mme. Akhmakov. "Shot himself? Yesterday? At sunset?"

"Where were you? Where did you come from?" shrieked Tatyana Pavlovna, and she literally clutched my shoulder. "Have you been spying? Eavesdropping?"

"What was I just telling you?" Katerina Nikolaevna got up from the sofa, pointing at me.

I lost my temper.

"Lies, nonsense!" I interrupted her furiously. "You just called me a spy, oh, God! Is it worth not only spying, but even living in the world alongside such people as you? A magnanimous man commits suicide; Kraft has shot himself—because of an idea, because of Hecuba... However, you don't know about Hecuba![52]... And here—go and live amidst your intrigues, hang around with your lies, deceptions, snares... Enough!"

"Slap his face! Slap his face!" cried Tatyana Pavlovna, and since Katerina Nikolaevna, though she looked at me (I remember it all down to the smallest trace) without taking her eyes away, didn't move from her place, Tatyana Pavlovna would probably have carried out her own advice in a moment, so that I inadvertently raised my hand to protect my face; and from this gesture it seemed to her that I was swinging my own arm.

"Yes, hit me, hit me! Prove you're a born lout! You're stronger than women, why stand on ceremony!"

"Enough of your slander, enough!" I cried. "I've never raised my hand against a woman! You're shameless, Tatyana Pavlovna, you've always despised me. Oh, one must deal with people without respecting them! You, Katerina Nikolaevna, are probably laughing at my figure; yes, God hasn't given me a figure like your adjutants. And, nevertheless, I don't feel humiliated before you, but, on the contrary, exalted... Well, it makes no difference how it's expressed, only I'm not to blame! I wound up here accidentally, Tatyana Pavlovna, the one to blame is your Finnish cook, or, better to say, your partiality for her: why did she refuse to answer my question and bring me straight here? And then, you must agree, it seemed so *monstrueuse** to me to come jumping out of a woman's bedroom, that I decided sooner to endure your spitting silently than to show myself... You're laughing again, Katerina Nikolaevna?"

"Get out, get out, go away!" cried Tatyana Pavlovna, almost pushing me. "Don't take his pack of lies for anything, Katerina Nikolaevna, I told you they attested him as crazy there!"

"As crazy? There? Who would that be, and from where? Enough, it makes no difference. Katerina Nikolaevna! I swear to you by all that's holy, this conversation and all that I've heard will remain between us... Is it my fault that I learned your secrets? The more so as I'm ending my work with your father tomorrow, so that, as regards the document you're looking for, you may be at peace!"

"What's that?... What document are you talking about?" Katerina Nikolaevna was at a loss, so much so that she even turned pale, or maybe it just seemed so to me. I realized that I had said too much.

I left quickly; they followed me silently with their eyes, and there was the highest degree of astonishment in their gaze. In short, I had set them a riddle...

*Monstrous.

Chapter Nine

I

I WAS HURRYING home and—wondrous thing—I was very pleased with myself. Of course, one doesn't speak that way with women, and with such women at that—or, more precisely, with such a woman, because I didn't count Tatyana Pavlovna. Maybe it's quite impossible to tell a woman of that category to her face: "I spit on your intrigues," but I had said it and was pleased precisely with that. Not to mention other things, I was sure at least that by that tone I had blotted out all that was ridiculous in my position. But I had no time to think very much about it: Kraft was sitting in my head. Not that he tormented me so much, but all the same I was shaken to my foundations; and even to the point that the ordinary human feeling of a certain pleasure at another's misfortune, that is, when somebody breaks a leg, loses his honor or a beloved being, and so on, even that ordinary feeling of mean satisfaction yielded in me without a trace to another extremely wholesome sensation, namely grief, regret for Kraft, that is, I don't know whether it was regret, but some very strong and kindly feeling. I was also very pleased by that. It's astonishing how many extraneous thoughts can flash through your mind precisely when you're all shaken by some colossal news, which in reality, it seems, ought to overpower all other feelings and scatter all extraneous thoughts, especially petty ones; but it's the petty ones, on the contrary, that get at you. I also remember that I was gradually overcome by a rather palpable nervous trembling, which went on for several minutes, and even all the while I was at home and having a talk with Versilov.

This talk took place under strange and extraordinary circumstances. I have already mentioned that we lived in a separate wing in the yard; this apartment bore the sign of number thirteen. Even before I went through the gate, I heard a woman's voice asking someone loudly, with impatience and vexation, "Where's apartment number thirteen?" It was a lady asking, just by the gate, opening the door of a grocery shop; but it seems they gave her no reply or even chased her away, and she was coming down the steps in distress and anger.

"But where's the caretaker here?" she cried, stamping her foot. I had long since recognized the voice.

"I'm going to apartment number thirteen," I went up to her, "whom do you want?"

"For a whole hour I've been looking for the caretaker, I've asked everybody, climbed all the stairs."

"It's in the yard. Don't you recognize me?"

But she had already recognized me.

"You want Versilov; you have business with him, and so do I," I went on. "I've come to say good-bye to him forever. Come along."

"Are you his son?"

"That means nothing. However, let's suppose I am his son, though my name is Dolgoruky. I'm illegitimate. This gentleman has endless illegitimate children. When conscience and honor demand, a son can leave home. It's in the Bible.[53] Besides, he got an inheritance, but I don't want my share, I go by the labor of my hands. When need be, a magnanimous man even sacrifices his life; Kraft shot himself, Kraft, because of an idea, imagine, a young man, who gave one hopes... This way, this way! We're in a separate wing. It's in the Bible that children leave their fathers and start their own nest... If an idea beckons... if there's an idea! The idea's the main thing, the idea's everything..."

I babbled to her like that all the while we were climbing up to our place. The reader has probably noticed that I don't spare myself much and, where needed, give myself an excellent attestation: I want to learn to tell the truth. Versilov was at home. I came in, but didn't take off my coat, and neither did she. Her clothes were terribly flimsy: over a dark dress hung a scrap of something intended to be a cape or a mantilla; on her head was an old, peeling sailor hat, very unbecoming to her. When we entered the drawing room, my mother was sitting in her usual place over her work, and my sister came out of her room and stopped in the doorway. Versilov was doing nothing, as usual, and rose to meet us; he fixed me with a stern, questioning look.

"I have nothing to do with it." I hastened to wave it away and stood to one side. "I met this person by the gate; she was looking for you, and nobody could direct her. I've come on business of my own, which I shall have the pleasure of explaining after her..."

Versilov nevertheless went on looking at me curiously.

"Permit me," the girl began impatiently. Versilov turned to her. "I've long been thinking about why you decided to leave money with me yesterday... I... in short... Here's your money!" she almost shrieked, as earlier, and flung a wad of banknotes on the table. "I had to look for you through the address bureau, otherwise I'd have brought it sooner. Listen, you!" She suddenly turned to my mother, who became all pale. "I don't want to insult you, you have an honest look and maybe this is even your daughter. I don't know if you're his wife, but you should know that this gentleman cuts out newspaper advertisements that governesses and teachers publish with their last money, and goes to these unfortunate women, looking for a dishonorable profit and getting them into trouble through money. I don't understand how I could have taken money from him yesterday! He looked so honest!... Away, not one word! You're a blackguard, my dear sir! Even if you had honest intentions, I don't want your charity. Not a word! Not a word! Oh, how glad I am to have exposed you now in front of your women! A curse on you!"

She quickly ran out, but turned on the threshold for a moment, only to shout:

"They say you've received an inheritance!"

And then she vanished like a shadow. I remind you once more: she was beside herself. Versilov was deeply struck; he stood as if pondering and trying to understand; at last he turned suddenly to me:

"You don't know her at all?"

"Earlier today I accidentally saw her raging in the corridor at Vasin's, shrieking and cursing you; but I didn't get into conversation with her and know nothing, and just now we met by the gate. She's probably yesterday's teacher 'who gives lessons in arithmetic'?"

"The very same. Once in my life I did a good deed and... But, anyhow, what have you got?"

"Here's this letter," I answered. "I consider it unnecessary to explain: it comes from Kraft, who got it from the late Andronikov. You'll find out from the contents. I'll add that no one in the whole world knows of this letter now except me, because Kraft, having given me the letter yesterday, shot himself just after I left..."

While I spoke, breathless and hurrying, he took the letter and, holding it out in his left hand, watched me attentively. When I announced Kraft's suicide to him, I peered into his face with particular attention to see the effect. And what?—the news didn't make the slightest impression on him; he didn't even raise his eyebrows! On the contrary, seeing that I had stopped, he pulled out his lorgnette, which never left him and hung on a black ribbon, brought the letter over to a candle, and, after glancing at the signature, began to study it closely. I can't express how I was even offended by this arrogant unfeelingness. He must have known Kraft very well; besides, it was in any case such extraordinary news! Finally, I naturally wanted it to produce an effect. Having waited for half a minute, and knowing that the letter was long, I turned and went out. My suitcase had long been ready, I only had to pack several things into a bundle. I thought of my mother and that I had not gone over to her. Ten minutes later, when I was quite ready and wanted to go for a cab, my sister came into my room.

"Here, mama sends you your sixty roubles and again asks you to forgive her for having told Andrei Petrovich about it, and there's another twenty roubles. You gave her fifty roubles yesterday for your keep; mother says it's simply impossible to take more than thirty from you, because she hadn't spent fifty on you, so she's sending you twenty roubles in change."

"Well, thanks, if only she's telling the truth. Good-bye, sister, I'm going away!"

"Where to now?"

"To an inn for the time being, only so as not to spend the night in this house. Tell mama that I love her."

"She knows that. She knows that you also love Andrei Petrovich. You ought to be ashamed to have brought that unfortunate girl!"

"I swear to you, it wasn't me; I met her by the gate."

"No, you brought her."

"I assure you..."

"Think, ask yourself, and you'll see that you, too, were the reason."

"I was only very glad that Versilov was disgraced. Imagine, he has a nursing baby by Lydia Akhmakov... however, why am I telling you..."

"He has? A nursing baby? But it's not his baby! Where did you hear such a lie?"

"Well, as if you'd know."

"Who else should know? It was I who took care of this baby in Luga. Listen, brother: I saw long ago that you know nothing about anything, and yet you insult Andrei Petrovich, well, and mama, too."

"If he's right, then I'll be wrong, that's all, and I don't love you any less. Why did you blush so, sister? And still more now! Well, all right, but even so I'll challenge that princeling to a duel for Versilov's slap in Ems. The more so if Versilov was in the right with Miss Akhmakov."

"Brother, come to your senses, really!"

"Since the court has now closed the case . . . Well, and now you've turned pale."

"But the prince won't fight a duel with you," Liza smiled a pale smile through her fright.

"Then I'll disgrace him publicly. What's wrong, Liza?"

She became so pale that she couldn't stand on her feet and lowered herself onto the sofa.

"Liza!" mother called from downstairs.

She put herself to rights and stood up; she was smiling tenderly at me.

"Brother, leave these trifles, or wait for a while, till you learn much more: you know so terribly little."

"I'll remember, Liza, that you turned pale when you learned I'd be going to a duel!"

"Yes, yes, remember that, too!" she smiled once more in farewell and went downstairs.

I called a cab and, with the driver's help, carried my things out of the apartment. None of my family opposed me or stopped me. I did not go to say good-bye to my mother, so as not to meet Versilov. When I was already sitting in the cab, a thought suddenly flashed in me.

"To the Fontanka, the Semyonovsky Bridge," I ordered suddenly, and went to Vasin's again.

II

It suddenly occurred to me that Vasin already knew about Kraft, and maybe a hundred times more than I did; and that's how it turned out to be. Vasin at once and dutifully told me all the details—without great warmth, however; I concluded that he was tired, and so he was. He had been at Kraft's himself that morning. Kraft had shot himself with a revolver (that same one) the night before, in full darkness, as was made clear by his diary. The last entry in the diary was made just before the shot, and he notes in it that he was writing almost in the dark, barely making out the letters; and he didn't want to light a candle for fear of leaving a fire behind him. "And I don't want to light it, only to put it out again before the shot, like my life," he added strangely in almost the last line. He had undertaken this death diary two days earlier, as soon as he returned to Petersburg, before the visit to Dergachev; after I left, he wrote in it every quarter of an hour; the very last three or four entries were written every five minutes. I voiced my surprise that Vasin, having had this diary under his eyes for so long (it was given him to read), had not made a copy, the more so as it was no more than a printer's sheet in all, and the entries were short—"at least the last page!" Vasin observed to me with a smile that he remembered it as it was, and moreover the notes were without any system, about whatever came to mind. I tried to argue that that was the precious thing in this case, but dropped it and began pestering him to remember at least something, and he remembered several lines, about an hour before the shot, saying "that he had chills; that he contemplated drinking a glass in order to warm up, but the thought that it would perhaps cause a bigger hemorrhage stopped him."—"It's almost all that sort of thing," concluded Vasin.

"And you call that trifles!" I exclaimed.

"When did I call it that? I simply didn't make a copy. But though it's not trifles, the diary is actually quite ordinary, or, rather, natural, that is, precisely as it ought to be in this case..."

"But it's his last thoughts, his last thoughts!"

"Last thoughts can sometimes be extremely insignificant. One such suicide precisely complains in the same sort of diary that at such an important hour at least one 'lofty thought' should have visited him, but, on the contrary, they were all petty and empty."

"And that he had chills is also an empty thought?"

"That is, you mean the chills proper, or the hemorrhage? Yet it's a known fact that a great many of those who are capable of contemplating their imminent death, self-willed or not, are quite often inclined to be concerned with the handsome appearance in which their corpse will be left. In this sense, Kraft, too, feared an excessive hemorrhage."

"I don't know whether that's a known fact... or whether it's so," I murmured, "but I'm surprised that you consider it all so natural, and yet was it long ago that Kraft spoke, worried, sat among us? Can it be that you're not at least sorry for him?"

"Oh, of course I'm sorry for him, and that's quite another matter;

but in any case Kraft himself pictured his death as a logical conclusion. It turns out that everything said about him at Dergachev's was correct: he left behind a notebook this big, full of learned conclusions, based on phrenology, craniology, and even mathematics, proving that the Russians are a second-rate breed of people, and that, consequently, it's not at all worth living as a Russian. If you wish, what's most characteristic here is that it's possible to draw any logical conclusion you like, but to up and shoot oneself as the result of a conclusion—that, of course, doesn't happen all the time."

"At least we must give credit to his character."

"And maybe not only that," Vasin observed evasively, but clearly he had in mind stupidity or weakness of reason. All this irritated me.

"You yourself spoke about feelings yesterday, Vasin."

"Nor do I deny them now; but in view of the accomplished fact, something in him presents itself as so badly mistaken that a severe view of the matter somehow unwillingly drives out pity itself."

"You know, I could tell earlier by your eyes that you would revile Kraft, and so as not to hear it, I decided not to seek your opinion; but you've voiced it yourself, and I'm unwillingly forced to agree with you; but still I'm displeased with you! I feel sorry for Kraft!"

"You know, we've gone too far..."

"Yes, yes," I interrupted, "but it's comforting at least that in such cases those who are left alive, the judges of the deceased, can always say of themselves, 'Though the man who shot himself was worthy of all regret and indulgence, we're still left, and therefore there's no point in grieving too much.'"

"Yes, naturally, if you see it from that angle... Ah, yes, it seems you were joking! And most wittily. This is my tea time and I'll have it brought at once—you'll probably keep me company."

And he went out, measuring my suitcase and bundle with his eyes.

I actually had wanted to say something malicious, in revenge for Kraft; and I had said it as I could, but, curiously, he had first taken my thought that "the likes of us are left" as serious. But be that as it may, he was still more right than I in everything, even feelings. I admitted all that without any displeasure, but I decidedly felt that I did not like him.

When tea was brought, I explained to him that I was asking for his hospitality for only one night, and that if it was impossible, he should say so and I would move to the inn. Then I briefly told him my reasons, stating simply and directly that I had quarreled definitively with Versilov, without going into details. Vasin listened attentively, but without any emotion. Generally, he only answered questions, though he answered affably and with sufficient fullness. I passed over in total silence the letter with which I had come to him previously to ask for advice; and I explained my previous call as a simple visit. Having given Versilov my word that no one would know of the letter besides me, I considered myself as no longer having the right to tell anyone about it. For some reason it became particularly repugnant to me to inform Vasin of certain things. Of certain things, but not of others: I still managed to get him interested in my stories about those scenes in the corridor and with the women in the neighboring room, culminating in Versilov's apartment. He listened with great attention, especially about Stebelkov. He asked me to repeat twice how Stebelkov inquired about Dergachev, and he even fell to pondering; however, he still smiled in the end. It suddenly seemed to me at that moment that nothing could ever disconcert Vasin; however, the first thought of it, I remember, presented itself to me in a form quite flattering to him.

"Generally, I couldn't gather much from what Mr. Stebelkov said," I concluded about Stebelkov. "He speaks somehow confusedly... and there seemed to be something light-minded in him..."

Vasin immediately assumed a serious look.

"He indeed has no gift of eloquence, but that's only at first sight. He has managed to make extremely apt observations; and generally—these are more people of business, of affairs, than of generalizing thought; they should be judged from that angle..."

Exactly as I had guessed earlier.

"Anyhow he acted up terribly at your neighbors', and God knows how it might have ended."

About the neighbors, Vasin told me that they had lived there for about three weeks and had come from somewhere in the provinces; that their room was extremely small, and everything indicated that they were very poor; that they were sitting and waiting for something. He didn't know that the young one had advertised in the newspapers as a teacher, but he had heard that Versilov had visited them; this had happened while he was away, and the landlady had told him. The neighbors, on the contrary, avoided everybody, even the landlady herself. In the last few days he had begun to notice that something was indeed not right with them, but there had been no such scenes as today's. All this talk of ours about the neighbors I recall now with a view to what followed; meanwhile a dead silence reigned behind their door. Vasin listened with particular interest when I said that Stebelkov thought it necessary to talk with the landlady about them, and that he had twice repeated, "You'll see, you'll see!"

"And you will see," Vasin added, "that it didn't come into his head for nothing; he has a very keen eye in that regard."

"So, then, in your opinion, the landlady should be advised to throw them out?"

"No, I'm not saying they should be thrown out, but so that some sort of story doesn't happen... However, all such stories end one way or another... Let's drop it."

As for Versilov's visit to the women, he resolutely refused to offer any conclusion.

"Everything is possible; the man felt money in his pocket... However, it's also probable that he simply offered charity; it suits his tradition, and maybe also his inclination."

I told him what Stebelkov had babbled that day about the "nursing baby."

"Stebelkov in this case is completely mistaken," Vasin said with particular seriousness and particular emphasis (and that I remember all too well).

"Stebelkov," he went on, "sometimes trusts all too much in his practical sense, and because of that rushes to a conclusion in accordance with his logic, which is often quite perspicacious; yet the event may in fact have a much more fantastic and unexpected coloration, considering the characters involved. And so it happened here: having partial knowledge of the matter, he concluded that the baby belongs to Versilov; however, the baby is not Versilov's."

I latched on to him, and here is what I learned, to my great astonishment: the baby was Prince Sergei Sokolsky's. Lydia Akhmakov, either owing to her illness, or simply because of her fantastic character, sometimes behaved like a crazy woman. She became infatuated with the prince still before Versilov, and the prince "had no qualms about accepting her love," as Vasin put it. The liaison lasted only a moment: they quarreled, as is already known, and Lydia chased the prince away, "of which, it seems, the man was glad."

"She was a very strange girl," Vasin added, "it's even very possible that she was not always in her right mind. But, as he was leaving for Paris, the prince had no idea of the condition in which he had left his victim, and he didn't know it to the very end, until his return. Versilov, having become the young person's friend, offered to marry her precisely in view of the emergent circumstance (which it seems the parents did not suspect almost to the end). The enamored girl was delighted, and saw in Versilov's proposal 'not only his self-sacrifice,' which, however, she also appreciated. However, he certainly knew how to do it," Vasin added. "The baby, a girl, was born a month or six weeks before term, was placed somewhere in Germany, then Versilov took it back, and it is now somewhere in Russia, maybe in Petersburg."

"And the phosphorus matches?"

"I know nothing about that," concluded Vasin. "Lydia Akhmakov died two weeks after the delivery; what happened there—I don't know. The prince, only just returned from Paris, found out that there was a baby, and, it seems, did not believe at first that it was his... Generally, the story is kept secret on all sides even to this day."

"But how about this prince!" I cried in indignation. "How about the way he behaved with the sick girl!"

"She wasn't so sick then... Besides, she chased him away herself... True, maybe he was unnecessarily quick to take advantage of his dismissal."

"You vindicate such a scoundrel?"

"No, I merely don't call him a scoundrel. There's much else here besides direct meanness. Generally, it's a very ordinary affair."

"Tell me, Vasin, did you know him closely? I'd especially like to trust your opinion, in view of a circumstance that concerns me greatly."

But here Vasin's answers became somehow all too restrained. He knew the prince, but with obvious deliberateness he said nothing about the circumstances under which he had made his acquaintance. Next he said that his character was such that he merited a certain indulgence. "He's full of honest inclinations and he's impressionable, but he possesses neither the sense nor the strength of will to sufficiently control his desires. He's an uneducated man; there is a host of ideas and phenomena that are beyond him, and yet he throws himself upon them. For instance, he would insistently maintain something like this: 'I am a prince and a descendant of Rurik,[54] but why shouldn't I be a shoemaker's apprentice, if I have to earn my bread and am incapable of doing anything else? My shingle will say: "Prince So-and-so, Shoemaker"—it's even noble.' He'll say it, and he'll do it—that's the main thing," Vasin added, "and yet there's no strength of conviction here, but just the most light-minded impressionability. But afterwards repentance would undoubtedly come, and then he would always be ready for some totally contrary extreme; and so for his whole life. In our age many people come a cropper like that," Vasin concluded, "precisely because they were born in our time."

I involuntarily fell to thinking.

"Is it true that he was thrown out of his regiment earlier?" I inquired.

"I don't know if he was thrown out, but he did indeed leave the regiment on account of some unpleasantness. Is it known to you that last autumn, precisely being retired, he spent two or three months in Luga?"

"I . . . I knew that you were living in Luga then."

"Yes, I, too, for a while. The prince was also acquainted with Lizaveta Makarovna."

"Oh? I didn't know. I confess, I've spoken so little with my sister . . . But can it be that he was received in my mother's house?" I cried.

"Oh, no. He was too distantly acquainted, through a third house."

"Yes, what was it my sister told me about this baby? Wasn't the baby in Luga as well?"

"For a while."

"And where is it now?"

"Undoubtedly in Petersburg."

"Never in my life will I believe," I cried in extreme agitation, "that my mother participated in any way in this story with this Lydia!"

"Apart from all these intrigues, which I don't undertake to sort out, the personal role of Versilov in this story had nothing particularly reprehensible about it," Vasin observed, smiling condescendingly. It was apparently becoming hard for him to speak with me, only he didn't let it show.

"Never, never will I believe," I cried again, "that a woman could give up her husband to another woman, that I will not believe! . . . I swear that my mother did not participate in it!"

"It seems, however, that she didn't oppose it."

"In her place, out of pride alone, I wouldn't have opposed it!"

"For my part, I absolutely refuse to judge in such a matter," Vasin concluded.

Indeed, Vasin, for all his intelligence, may have had no notion of women, so that a whole cycle of ideas and phenomena remained unknown to him. I fell silent. Vasin was working temporarily in a joint-stock company, and I knew that he brought work home. To my insistent question, he confessed that he had work then, too, some accounts, and I warmly begged him not to stand on ceremony with me. That seemed to afford him pleasure; but before sitting down with his papers, he began to make a bed for me on the sofa. First of all he tried to yield me his bed, but when I didn't accept, that also seemed to please him. He obtained a pillow and a blanket from the landlady. Vasin was extremely polite and amiable, but it was somehow hard for me to see him going to such trouble on my account. I had liked it better when once, about three weeks ago, I had chanced to spend the night on the Petersburg side, at Efim's. I remember him concocting a bed for me, also on a sofa and in secret from his aunt, supposing for some reason that she would get angry on learning that his comrades came to spend the night. We laughed a lot, spread out a shirt instead of a sheet, and folded an overcoat for a pillow. I remember Zverev, when he had finished work, giving the sofa a loving flick and saying to me:

*"Vous dormirez comme un petit roi."**

Both his stupid gaiety and the French phrase, which suited him like a saddle on a cow, had the result that I slept with extreme pleasure then at this buffoon's place. As for Vasin, I was extremely glad when he finally sat down to work, his back turned to me. I sprawled on the sofa and, looking at his back, thought long and about much.

III

AND THERE WAS plenty to think about. My soul was very troubled, and there was nothing whole in it; but some sensations stood out very definitely, though no one of them drew me fully to itself, owing to their abundance. Everything flashed somehow without connection or sequence, and I remember that I myself had

*You'll sleep like a little king.

no wish to stop at anything or introduce any sequence. Even the idea of Kraft moved imperceptibly into the background. What excited me most of all was my own situation, that here I had already "broken away," and my suitcase was with me, and I wasn't at home, and was beginning everything entirely anew. Just as if up to now all my intentions and preparations had been a joke, and only "now, suddenly and, above all, *unexpectedly*, everything had begun in reality." This idea heartened me and, however troubled my soul was about many things, cheered me up. But... but there were other sensations as well; one of them especially wanted to distinguish itself from the others and take possession of my soul, and, strangely, this sensation also heartened me, as if summoning me to something terribly gay. It began, however, with fear: I had been afraid for a long while, since that very moment earlier when, in my fervor and taken unawares, I had told Mme. Akhmakov too much about the document. "Yes, I said too much," I thought, "and perhaps they'll guess something... that's bad! Naturally, they won't leave me in peace if they begin to suspect, but... let them! Perhaps they won't even find me—I'll hide! But what if they really start running after me..." And then I began to recall down to the last detail and with growing pleasure how I had stood before Katerina Nikolaevna and how her bold but terribly astonished eyes had looked straight at me. And I had gone out leaving her in that astonishment, I recalled; "her eyes are not quite black, however... only her eyelashes are very black, that's what makes her eyes, too, look so dark..."

And suddenly, I remember, it became terribly loathsome for me to recall... and I was vexed and sickened, both at them and at myself. I reproached myself for something and tried to think about other things. "Why is it that I don't feel the least indignation at Versilov for the story with the woman next door?" suddenly came into my head. For my part, I was firmly convinced that his role here had been amorous and that he had come in order to have some fun, but that in itself did not make me indignant. It even seemed to me that he couldn't be imagined otherwise, and though I really was glad that he had been disgraced, I didn't blame him. That was not important for me. What was important for me was that he had looked at me so angrily when I came in with the woman, looked at me as he never had before. "He finally looked at me *seriously*!" I thought, and my heart stood still. Oh, if I hadn't loved him, I wouldn't have been so glad of his hatred!

I finally dozed off and fell sound asleep. I only remember through my sleep that Vasin, having finished his work, put things away neatly, gave my sofa an intent look, undressed, and blew out the candle. It was past midnight.

IV

ALMOST EXACTLY TWO hours later I awoke with a start like a halfwit and sat up on my sofa. Dreadful cries, weeping and howling, were coming from behind the neighbors' door. Our door was wide open, and in the already lighted corridor people were shouting and running. I was about to call Vasin, but guessed that he was no longer in bed. Not knowing where to find matches, I felt for my clothes and hurriedly began to dress in the darkness. The landlady, and maybe also the tenants, had obviously come running to the neighbors' room. One voice was screaming, however, that of the elderly woman, while yesterday's youthful voice, which I remembered only too well, was completely silent; I remember that that was the first thought that came to my head then. Before I had time to dress, Vasin came hurrying in; instantly, with an accustomed hand, he found the matches and lighted the room. He was only in his underwear, dressing gown, and slippers, and he immediately began to dress.

"What's happened?" I cried to him.

"A most unpleasant and troublesome business!" he replied almost angrily. "This young neighbor, the one you were telling me about, has hanged herself in her room."

I let out a cry. I can't convey how much my heart was wrung! We ran out to the corridor. I confess, I didn't dare go into the women's room, and I saw the unfortunate girl only later, when she had been taken down, and then, to tell the truth, at some distance, covered with a sheet, from under which the two narrow soles of her shoes stuck out. For some reason I never looked at her face. The mother was in a dreadful state; our landlady was with her, not much frightened, however. All the tenants of the apartments came crowding around. There weren't many: only one elderly sailor, always very gruff and demanding, though now he became very quiet; and some people from Tver province, an old man and woman, husband and wife, quite respectable and civil-service people. I won't describe the rest of that night, the fuss, and then the official visits; till dawn I literally shivered and considered it my duty not to go to bed, though, anyhow, I didn't do anything. And everybody had an extremely brisk look, even somehow especially brisk. Vasin even drove off somewhere. The landlady turned out to be a rather respectable woman, much better than I had supposed her to be. I persuaded her (and I put it down to my credit) that the mother couldn't be left like that, alone with her daughter's corpse, and that she should take her to her room at least till the next day. She agreed at once and, no matter how the mother thrashed and wept, refusing to leave the corpse, in the end, nevertheless, she still moved in with the landlady, who at once ordered the samovar prepared. After that, the tenants went to their rooms and closed the doors, but I still wouldn't go to bed and sat for a long time at the landlady's, who was even glad of an extra person, and one who could, for his part, tell a thing or two about the matter. The samovar proved very useful, and generally the samovar is a most necessary Russian thing, precisely in all catastrophes and misfortunes, especially terrible, unexpected, and eccentric ones; even the mother had two cups, of course after extreme entreaties and almost by force. And yet, sincerely speaking, I had never seen more bitter and outright grief than when I looked at this unfortunate woman. After the first bursts of sobbing and hysterics, she even began speaking eagerly, and I listened greedily to her account. There are unfortunate people, especially among women, for whom it is even necessary that they be allowed to speak as much as possible in such cases. Besides, there are characters that are, so to speak, all too worn down by grief, who have suffered all their lives long, who have endured extremely much both from great griefs and from constant little ones, and whom nothing can surprise anymore, no sort of unexpected catastrophes, and who, above all, even before the coffin of the most beloved being, do not forget a single one of the so-dearly-paid-for rules of ingratiating behavior with people. And I don't condemn them; it's not the banality of egoism or coarseness of development; in these hearts maybe one can find even more gold than in the most noble-looking heroines; but the habit of longtime abasement, the instinct of self-preservation, a long intimidation and inhibition finally take their toll. The poor suicide did not resemble her mother in this. Their faces, however, seemed to resemble each other, though the dead girl was positively not bad-looking. The mother was not yet a very old woman, only about fifty, also blond, but with hollow eyes and cheeks, and with big, uneven yellow teeth. And everything in her had some tinge of yellowness: the skin of her face and hands was like parchment; her dark dress was so threadbare that it also looked quite yellow; and the nail on the index finger of her right hand was, I don't know why, plastered over thoroughly and neatly with yellow wax.

The poor woman's story was incoherent in some places. I'll tell it as I understood it and as I have remembered it.

V

THEY CAME FROM Moscow. She had long been a widow, "though the widow of a court councillor,"[55] her husband had been in the service, left almost nothing "except two hundred roubles, though, in a pension. Well, what is two hundred roubles?" She raised Olya, though, and had her educated in high school... "And how she studied, how she studied; she was awarded a silver medal at graduation..." (Long tears here, naturally.) The deceased husband had lost nearly four thousand in capital with one merchant here in Petersburg. Suddenly this merchant became rich again. "I had papers, got some advice, they said, 'Make a claim, you're sure to get everything...' So I began, and the merchant started to agree. 'Go in person,' they said. Olya and I made ready and came a month ago now. Our means were only so much; we took this room because it was the smallest, and we saw it was an honorable house, and that was the most important thing for us. We're inexperienced women, anybody can offend us. Well, we paid you for a month, with one thing and another, Petersburg's expensive, our merchant flatly refused us. 'I don't know who you are,' and the paper I had was not in order, I understood that myself. So they advise me, 'Go to this famous lawyer, he was a professor, not simply a lawyer, but a jurist, he'll tell you for certain what to do.' I took my last fifteen roubles to him; the lawyer came out, and didn't listen to me for even three minutes: 'I see,' he says, 'I know,' he says, 'if he wants to,' he says, 'the merchant will pay you back, if he doesn't, he won't, but if you start a case, you may have to pay more, best of all is to make peace.' And he made a joke from the Gospel: 'Agree with thine adversary,' he says, 'whiles thou art in the way, till thou hast paid the uttermost farthing.'[56] He sends me away, laughing. That was the end of my fifteen roubles! I came to Olya, we sit facing each other, I began to weep. She doesn't weep, she sits there proud, indignant. And she's always been like that, all her life, even when she was little, she never sighed, never wept, so she sits, glaring terribly, it's even eerie to look at her. And, would you believe it, I was afraid of her, completely afraid, long afraid; and I'd feel like whining now and then, but I don't dare in front of her. I went to the merchant for a last time, wept my fill there. 'All right,' he says, and doesn't even listen. Meanwhile, I must confess, since we hadn't counted on staying so long, we'd already been without money for some time. I gradually began to pawn my clothes, and we lived on that. We pawned everything we had, she began giving up her last bit of linen, and here I started weeping bitter tears. She stamped her foot, jumped up, and ran to the merchant herself. He's a widower; he talked to her: 'Come the day after tomorrow at five o'clock,' he said, 'maybe I'll tell you something.' She came back cheered up: 'See,' she says, 'maybe he'll tell me something.' Well, I was glad, too, only my heart somehow went cold in me: what's going to happen, I think, but I don't dare ask her. Two days later she came back from the merchant pale, all trembling, threw herself on the bed—I understood everything, but I don't dare ask. What do you think: he gave her fifteen roubles, the robber, 'and if I meet with full honor in you,' he says, 'I'll add another forty roubles.' That's what he said right to her face, shamelessly. She rushed at him then, she told me, but he pushed her back and even locked himself away from her in another room. And meanwhile, I confess to you in all conscience, we have almost nothing to eat. We took and sold a jacket lined with rabbit fur, and she went to the newspaper and advertised: preparation in all subjects, and also arithmetic. 'They'll pay at least thirty kopecks,' she says. And towards the very end, dear lady, I even began to be horrified at her: she says nothing to me, sits for hours on end at the window, looking at the roof of the house opposite, and suddenly shouts: 'At least to do laundry, at least to dig the earth!' She'd shout just some word like that and stamp her foot. And we have no acquaintances here, there's nobody to go to: 'What will become of us?' I think. And I keep being afraid to talk to her. Once she slept in the afternoon, woke up, opened her eyes, looked at me; I sit on the chest, also looking at her; she got up silently, came over to me, embraced me very, very tightly, and then the two of us couldn't help ourselves and wept, we sit and weep, without letting go of each other's arms. It was the first time like that in her whole life. So we're sitting like that with each other, and your Nastasya comes in and says, 'There's some lady asking to see you.' This was just four days ago. The lady comes in. We see she's very well dressed, speaks Russian, but with what seems like a German accent: 'You advertised in the newspaper,' she says, 'that you give lessons?' We were so glad then, asked her to sit down, she laughs so sweetly: 'It's not me,' she says, 'but my niece has small children; if you like, kindly come to see us, we'll discuss things there.' She gave the address, by the Voznesensky Bridge, number such-and-such, apartment number such-and-such. She left. Olechka set off, she went running that same day, and what then? She came back two hours later in hysterics, thrashing. Later she told me: 'I asked the caretaker,' she says, 'where apartment number such-and-such was. The caretaker looked at me,' she says. '"And what," he says, "do you want with that apartment?" He said it so strangely that I might have thought better of it.' But she was imperious, impatient, she couldn't stand these questions and rudeness. 'Go,' he says, jabbing his finger towards the stairs, turned and went back to his lodge. And what do you think? She goes in, asks, and women come running at once from all sides: 'Come in, come in!'—all the women, laughing, painted, foul, piano-playing, rush to her and pull her. 'I tried to get out of there,' she says, 'but they wouldn't let me go.' She got frightened, her legs gave way under her, they don't let her go, and then it's all sweet talk, coaxing her, they opened a bottle of port, give it to her, insist. She jumped up, shouting with all her might, trembling: 'Let me go, let me go!' She rushed to the door, they hold the door, she screams; then the one that had come to us ran up to her, slapped my Olya twice in the face, and shoved her out the door: 'You're not worthy, you slut,' she says, 'to be in a noble house!' And another shouts after her on the stairs: 'You came here yourself, since you've got nothing to eat, but we wouldn't even look at such a mug!' All that night she lay in a fever, raving, and the next morning her eyes flashed, she'd get up and pace: 'To court,' she says, 'I'll take her to court!' I said nothing: well, I thought, what can you do about it in court, what can you prove? She paces, she wrings her hands, her tears pour down, her lips are pressed together, unmoving. And since that same time, her whole face turned dark till the very end. On the third day she felt better, she was silent, she seemed to have calmed down. It was then, at four o'clock in the afternoon, that Mr. Versilov paid us a visit.

"And I'll say it outright: I still can't understand how Olya, mistrustful as she was, could have begun to listen to him then almost from the first word. What attracted us both most of all then was that he had such a serious look, stern even, he speaks softly, thoroughly, and so politely—ever so politely, even respectfully, and yet there's no self-seeking to be seen in him: you see straight off that the man has come with a pure heart. 'I read your advertisement in the newspaper,' he says. 'You didn't write it correctly, miss,' he says, 'and you may even do yourself harm by it.' And he began to explain, I confess I didn't understand, there was something about arithmetic, only I can see Olya blushed, and became as if animated, she listens, gets into conversation so willingly (he really must be an intelligent man!), I hear how she even thanks him. He asked her about everything so thoroughly, and you could see he'd lived a long time in Moscow, and, it turned out, knew the directress of her high school personally. 'I'm sure I'll find lessons for you,' he says, 'because I have many acquaintances here and can even appeal to many influential persons, so that if you want a permanent position, then that, too, can be kept in view... and meanwhile,' he says, 'forgive me one direct question to you: may I not be of use to you right now in some way? It will not be I who give you pleasure,' he says, 'but, on the contrary, you who give it to me, if you allow me to be of use to you in any way at all. Let it be your debt,' he says, 'and once you get a position, you can pay it back to me in the shortest time. And, believe me on my honor, if I ever fell into such poverty afterwards, while you were provided with everything—I'd come straight to you for a little help, I'd send my wife and daughter...' That is, I don't remember all his words, only at this point I shed a few tears, because I saw Olya's lips quiver with gratitude. 'If I accept,' she answers him, 'it's because I trust an honorable and humane man who could be my father...' She said it to him so beautifully, briefly and nobly: 'a humane man,' she says. He stood up at once: 'I'll find lessons and a post for you without fail, without fail,' he says, 'I'll busy myself with it starting today, because you have quite enough qualifications for that...' And I forgot to say that at the very beginning, when he came in, he looked over all her documents from high school, she showed them to him, and he examined her in various subjects... 'He examined me in some subjects, mama,' Olya says to me later, 'and how intelligent he is,' she says, 'it's not every day you get to talk with such a developed and educated man...' And she's just beaming all over. The money, sixty roubles, is lying on the table. 'Put it away, mama,' she says, 'we'll get a post and pay it back to him first thing, we'll prove that we're honest, and that we're delicate he's already seen.' She fell silent then, I see, she's breathing so deeply: 'You know, mama,' she suddenly says to me, 'if we were coarse people, maybe we wouldn't have accepted it out of pride, but now that we've accepted it, we've proved our delicacy to him, showing that we trust him in everything, as a respectable, gray-haired man, isn't it true?' At first I didn't understand right and said, 'Why not accept the benevolence of a noble and wealthy man, Olya, if on top of that he's kindhearted?' She frowned at me: 'No, mama,' she says, 'it's not that, we don't need his benevolence, what's precious is his "humaneness." And as for the money, it would even be better not to take it, mama. Since he's promised to find me a position, that would be enough ... though we are in need.' 'Well, Olya,' I say, 'our need is such that we simply can't refuse'—I even smiled. Well, in myself I'm glad, only an hour later she slipped this in for me: 'You wait, mama,' she says, 'and don't spend the money.' She said it so resolutely. 'What?' I say. 'Just don't,' she said, broke off, and fell silent. She was silent the whole evening; only past one o'clock at night I wake up and hear Olya tossing on her bed. 'You're not asleep, mama?' 'No,' I say, 'I'm not.' 'Do you know,' she says, 'that he wanted to insult me?' 'How can you, how can you?' I say. 'It has to be so; he's a mean man, don't you dare spend one kopeck of his money.' I tried to talk to her, I even cried a little right there in bed—she turned to the wall: 'Be quiet,' she says, 'let me sleep!' The next morning I watch her, she goes about not looking herself; and believe me or not, I'll say it before God's judgment seat: she wasn't in her right mind then! Ever since they insulted her in that mean house, she got troubled in her heart ... and in her mind. I look at her that morning and I have doubts about her; I feel frightened; I won't contradict her, I thought, not in a single word. 'Mama,' she says, 'he didn't even leave his address.' 'Shame on you, Olya,' I say, 'you heard him yourself yesterday, you praised him yourself afterwards, you were about to weep grateful tears yourself.' As soon as I said it, she shrieked, stamped her foot: 'You're a woman of mean feelings,' she says, 'you're of the old upbringing on serfdom!' ... and despite all I said, she snatched her hat, ran out, and I shouted after her. 'What's the matter with her,' I think, 'where has she run to?' And she ran to the address bureau, found out where Mr. Versilov lived, came back. 'Today,' she says, 'right now, I'll bring him the money and fling it in his face; he wanted to insult me,' she says, 'like Safronov' (that's our merchant); 'only

Safronov insulted me like a crude peasant, and this one like a cunning Jesuit.' And here suddenly, as bad luck would have it, that gentleman from yesterday knocked: 'I heard you speaking about Versilov, I can give you information.' When she heard about Versilov, she fell on the man, totally beside herself, she talks and talks, I look at her, wondering: she's so taciturn, she never speaks like that with anyone, and here it's a complete stranger. Her cheeks are burning, her eyes flashing... And he up and says, 'You're perfectly right, miss,' he says. 'Versilov,' he says, 'is exactly like these generals here, that they describe in the newspapers; the general would deck himself out with all his medals and go calling on governesses who advertise in the newspapers, he'd go about and find what he wanted; and if he didn't find what he wanted, he'd sit and talk and promise heaps of things, and go away—even so he provides himself with entertainment.' Olya even burst out laughing, only so spitefully, and this gentleman, I see, takes her hand, puts it to his heart. 'I, too, miss,' he says, 'have capital of my own, and I could always offer it to a beautiful girl, but it's better,' he says, 'if I first kiss her sweet little hand...' And I see him pulling her hand to kiss it. She just jumped up, but here I jumped up with her, and the two of us chased him out. Then, before evening, Olya snatched the money from me, ran out, comes back: 'Mama,' she says, 'I took revenge on the dishonorable man!' 'Ah, Olya, Olya,' I say, 'maybe we've missed our chance, you've insulted a noble, benevolent man!' I wept from vexation at her, I couldn't help myself. She shouts at me: 'I don't want it,' she shouts, 'I don't want it! Even if he's the most honorable man, even then I don't want his charity! If anybody pities me, even that I don't want!' I lay down, and there was nothing in my thoughts. How many times I had looked at that nail in your wall, left over from the mirror—it never occurred to me, never once occurred to me, not yesterday, not before, and I never thought of it, never dreamed of it at all, and never, ever expected it of Olya. I usually sleep soundly, I snore, it's the blood flowing to my head, but sometimes it goes to my heart, I cry out in my sleep, so that Olya wakes me up in the night: 'You sleep so soundly, mama,' she says, 'it's even impossible to wake you up if I need to.' 'Oh, Olya,' I say, 'soundly, so soundly!' So I must have started snoring last night, she waited a while, and then she was no longer afraid, and she got up. This long strap from the suitcase was there all the time, this whole month, I was still thinking about it yesterday morning: 'Put it away, finally, so that it doesn't lie about.' And the chair she must have pushed away with her foot, and she spread her skirt beside it so that it wouldn't make any noise. And I must have woken up long, long after, a whole hour or more. 'Olya!' I call, 'Olya!' I suspected something at once. I call her. It was either that I couldn't hear her breathing in bed, or perhaps I made out in the darkness that her bed was empty—only I suddenly got up and felt with my hand: there was no one in the bed, and the pillow was cold. My heart just sank, I stand where I am as if senseless, my mind goes dim. 'She went out,' I thought—took a step, and I see her there by the bed, in the corner, near the door, as if she's standing there herself. I stand, silent, look at her, and she also seems to be looking at me out of the darkness, without stirring... 'Only why,' I think, 'did she get up on a chair?' 'Olya,' I whisper, getting scared, 'Olya, do you hear?' Only suddenly it was as if it all dawned on me, I took a step, thrust both arms out, straight at her, put them around her, and she sways in my arms, I clutch her, and she sways, I understand everything, and I don't want to understand... I want to cry out, but no cry comes... 'Ah!' I think. I dropped to the floor, and then I cried out..."

"Vasin," I said in the morning, already past five o'clock, "if it hadn't been for your Stebelkov, maybe this woudn't have happened."

"Who knows, it probably would. It's impossible to judge like that here, it was all prepared for even without that... True, this Stebelkov sometimes..."

He didn't finish and winced very unpleasantly. Before seven he went out again; he kept bustling about. I was finally left completely alone. Dawn had broken. My head was spinning slightly. I kept imagining Versilov; this lady's story presented him in a totally different light. To think it over more comfortably, I lay down on Vasin's bed, as I was, dressed and with my boots on, for a moment, with no intention of sleeping—and suddenly fell asleep. I don't even remember how it happened. I slept for nearly four hours; nobody woke me up.

Chapter Ten

I

I WOKE UP at around half-past ten and for a long time could not believe my eyes: on the sofa where I had slept the night before sat my mother, and beside her—the unfortunate neighbor, the mother of the suicide. They were holding each other's hands, speaking in whispers, probably so as not to wake me up, and both were weeping. I got out of bed and rushed straight to kiss mama. She beamed all over, kissed me, and crossed me three times with her right hand. We had no time to say a word: the door opened, and Versilov and Vasin came in. Mama stood up at once and took the neighbor with her. Vasin gave me his hand, but Versilov didn't say a word to me and lowered himself into an armchair. He and mama had evidently been there for some time. His face was somber and preoccupied.

"I regret most of all," he began saying measuredly to Vasin, obviously continuing a conversation already begun, "that I didn't manage to settle it last evening, and—surely this dreadful thing wouldn't have come about! And there was time enough: it wasn't eight o'clock yet. As soon as she ran away from us last night, I at once resolved mentally to follow her here and reassure her, but this unforeseen and urgent matter, which, however, I could very well have put off until today...or even for a week—this vexatious matter hindered and ruined everything. That things should come together like that!"

"But maybe you wouldn't have managed to reassure her; even without you, it seems a lot was seething and smoldering there," Vasin remarked in passing.

"No, I'd have managed, I'd surely have managed. And the thought occurred to me of sending Sofya Andreevna in my place. It flashed, but only flashed. Sofya Andreevna alone would have won her over, and the unfortunate girl would have remained alive. No, never again will I meddle...with 'good deeds'...Just once in my life I tried meddling! And here I'm thinking that I haven't lagged behind your generation and understand contemporary youth. Yes, our old folk grow old almost before they mature. Incidentally, there are actually an awful lot of people nowadays who, out of habit, still consider themselves the younger generation, because yesterday they still were, and they don't notice that they're already *verbannte*."*

"A misunderstanding occurred here, all too clear a misunderstanding," Vasin observed sensibly. "Her mother says that after the cruel insult in the public house, it was as if she lost her mind. Add to that the surroundings, the original insult from the merchant... all this could have happened in the same way in former times, and I don't think it's in any way especially characteristic of present-day youth."

"They're a bit impatient, these present-day youth, and besides, naturally, there's little understanding of actualities, which, though it's characteristic of any youth at any time, is somehow especially so of our youth... Tell me, and what mischief did Mr. Stebelkov do here?"

"Mr. Stebelkov," I suddenly cut in, "is the cause of it all. If it hadn't been for him, nothing would have happened; he poured oil on the fire."

Versilov listened, but he didn't look at me. Vasin frowned.

"I also reproach myself for one ridiculous circumstance," Versilov went on unhurriedly and drawing the words out as before. "It seems that I, as is my nasty habit, allowed myself a certain sort of merriment then, this light-minded little laugh—in short, I was insufficiently sharp, dry, and gloomy, three qualities that seem to be of great value among the contemporary younger generation... In short, I gave her reasons to take me for a wandering Céladon."[57]

"Quite the contrary," I again cut in abruptly, "her mother affirms in particular that you made an excellent impression precisely by your seriousness, sternness even, sincerity—her own words. The deceased girl praised you for it after you left."

"D-did she?" Versilov mumbled, giving me a fleeting glance at last. "Take this scrap of paper, it's necessary to the case"—he handed a tiny bit of paper to Vasin. The latter took it and, seeing that I was looking with curiosity, gave it to me to read. It was a note, two uneven lines scrawled with a pencil and maybe in the dark.

"Mama dear, forgive me for having stopped my life's debut. Your distressing Olya."

"It was found only in the morning," Vasin explained.

"What a strange note!" I exclaimed in astonishment.

*On the way out.

"Strange in what way?" asked Vasin.

"How can one write in humorous expressions at such a moment?"

Vasin looked at me questioningly.

"And the humor's strange," I went on, "the conventional high-school language among schoolmates... Well, at such a moment and in such a note to an unfortunate mother—and it turns out she did love her mother—who could write 'stopped my life's debut'!"

"Why can't one write it?" Vasin still didn't understand.

"There's no humor here at all," Versilov finally observed. "The expression is, of course, inappropriate, totally in the wrong tone, and indeed might have come from high-school talk or some sort of conventional language among schoolmates, as you said, or from some sort of feuilletons, but the deceased girl used it in this terrible note quite simpleheartedly and seriously."

"That can't be, she completed her studies and graduated with a silver medal."

"A silver medal means nothing here. Nowadays there are many who complete their studies."

"Down on the youth again," Vasin smiled.

"Not in the least," Versilov replied, getting up from his place and taking his hat. "If the present generation is not so literary, then it undoubtedly possesses... other virtues," he added with extraordinary seriousness. "Besides, 'many' is not 'all,' and I don't accuse you, for instance, of poor literary development, and you're also still a young man."

"Yes, and Vasin didn't find anything wrong in 'debut'!" I couldn't help observing.

Versilov silently gave Vasin his hand; the latter also seized his cap to go out with him, and shouted good-bye to me. Versilov left without noticing me. I also had no time to lose: I had at all costs to run and look for an apartment—now I needed it more than ever! Mama was no longer with the landlady, she had left and taken the neighbor with her. I went outside feeling somehow especially cheerful... Some new and big feeling was being born in my soul. Besides, as if on purpose, everything seemed to contribute: I ran into an opportunity remarkably quickly and found a quite suitable apartment; of this apartment later, but now I'll finish about the main thing.

It was just getting past one o'clock when I went back to Vasin's again for my suitcase and happened to find him at home again. Seeing me, he exclaimed with a merry and sincere air:

"How glad I am that you found me, I was just about to leave! I can tell you a fact that I believe will interest you very much."

"I'm convinced beforehand!" I cried.

"Hah, how cheerful you look! Tell me, did you know anything about a certain letter that had been kept by Kraft and that Versilov got hold of yesterday, precisely something to do with the inheritance he won? In this letter the testator clarifies his will in a sense opposite to yesterday's court decision. The letter was written long ago. In short, I don't know precisely what exactly, but don't you know something?"

"How could I not? Two days ago Kraft took me to his place just for that . . . from those gentlemen, in order to give me that letter, and yesterday I gave it to Versilov."

"Did you? That's what I thought. Then imagine, the business Versilov mentioned here today—which kept him from coming last evening and persuading that girl—this business came about precisely because of that letter. Last evening Versilov went straight to Prince Sokolsky's lawyer, gave him the letter, and renounced the entire inheritance he had won. At the present moment this renunciation has already been put in legal form. Versilov isn't giving it to them, but in this act he recognizes the full right of the princes."

I was dumbstruck, but delighted. In reality I had been completely convinced that Versilov would destroy the letter. Moreover, though I did talk with Kraft about how it would not be noble, and though I had repeated it to myself in the tavern, and that "I had come to a pure man, not to this one"—still deeper within myself, that is, in my innermost soul, I considered that it was even impossible to act otherwise than to cross out the document completely. That is, I considered it a most ordinary matter. If I were to blame Versilov later, I'd do it only on purpose, for appearances, that is, to retain my superior position over him. But, hearing about Versilov's great deed now, I was sincerely delighted, fully so, condemning with repentance and shame my cynicism and my indifference to virtue, and that instant, having exalted Versilov infinitely above me, I nearly embraced Vasin.

"What a man! What a man! Who else would have done that?" I exclaimed in ecstasy.

"I agree with you that a great many would not have done it . . . and that, indisputably, the act is highly disinterested . . ."

" 'But'? . . . finish what you're saying, Vasin, you have a 'but'?"

"Yes, of course there's a 'but.' Versilov's act, in my opinion, is a little bit hasty and a little bit not so straightforward," Vasin smiled.

"Not straightforward?"

"Yes. There's something like a 'pedestal' here. Because in any case he could have done the same thing without hurting himself. If not half, then still, undoubtedly, a certain portion of the inheritance could go to Versilov now, too, even taking the most ticklish view of the matter, the more so as the document did not have decisive significance, and he had already won the case. That is the opinion held by the lawyer of the opposite side; I've just spoken with him. The act would remain no less handsome, but owing solely to a whim of pride it has happened otherwise. Above all, Mr. Versilov became overexcited and—needlessly over-hasty. He said himself today that he could have put it off for a whole week..."

"You know what, Vasin? I can't help agreeing with you, but... I like it better this way! It pleases me better this way!"

"Anyhow, it's a matter of taste. You challenged me yourself; I would have kept silent."

"Even if there is a 'pedestal' here, that's all the better," I went on. "A pedestal's a pedestal, but in itself it's a very valuable thing. This 'pedestal' is the same old 'ideal,' and it's hardly better that it's missing from some present-day souls. Let it be, even with a slight deformity! And surely you think so yourself, Vasin, my dear heart Vasin, my darling Vasin! In short, I've talked my head off, of course, but you do understand me. That's what makes you Vasin; and in any case I embrace you and kiss you, Vasin!"

"With joy?"

"With great joy! For this man 'was dead and is alive again, was lost and is found!'[58] Vasin, I'm a trashy little brat and not worthy of you. I confess it precisely because there are some moments when I'm quite different, higher and deeper. Two days ago I praised you to your face (and praised you only because you had humiliated and crushed me), and for that I've hated you for two whole days! I promised myself that very night that I would never go to you, and I came to you yesterday morning only from spite, do you understand: *from spite*. I sat here on a chair alone and criticized your room, and you, and each of your books, and your landlady, trying to humiliate you and laugh at you..."

"You shouldn't be saying this..."

"Yesterday evening, concluding from one of your phrases that you didn't understand women, I was glad to have been able to catch you in that. Earlier today, catching you on the 'debut,' I was again terribly glad, and all because I myself had praised you the other time..."

"Why, how could it be otherwise!" Vasin finally cried (he still went on smiling, not surprised at me in the least). "No, that's how it always happens, with almost everybody, and even first thing; only nobody admits it, and there's no need to, because in any case it will pass and nothing will come of it."

"Can it be the same with everybody? Everybody's like that? And you say it calmly? No, it's impossible to live with such views!"

"And in your opinion:

> Dearer to me than a thousand truths
> Is the falsehood that exalts?"[59]

"But that's right!" I cried. "Those two lines are a sacred axiom!"

"I don't know; I wouldn't venture to decide whether those two lines are right or not. It must be that the truth, as always, lies somewhere in between; that is, in one case it's a sacred truth, in another it's a lie. I only know one thing for certain: that this thought will remain for a long time one of the chief points of dispute among people. In any case, I notice that you now want to dance. So, dance then: exercise is good for you, and I've had an awful lot of work piled on me all at once this morning... and I'm late because of you!"

"I'm going, I'm going, I'm off! Only one word," I cried, seizing my suitcase. "If I just 'threw myself on your neck' again, it's solely because when I came in, you told me about this fact with such genuine pleasure and 'were glad' that I came in time to find you here, and that after yesterday's 'debut'; by that genuine pleasure you all at once turned my 'young heart' in your favor again. Well, good-bye, good-bye, I'll try to stay away for as long as possible, and I know that will be extremely agreeable to you, as I see even by your eyes, and it will even be profitable for both of us..."

Babbling like this and nearly spluttering from my joyful babble, I dragged my suitcase out and went with it to my apartment. I was, above all, terribly pleased that Versilov had been so unquestionably angry with me earlier, had not wanted to speak or look. Having transported my suitcase, I immediately flew to my old prince. I confess, it had even been somewhat hard for me those two days without him. And he had surely already heard about Versilov.

II

I JUST KNEW he'd be terribly glad to see me, and I swear I'd have called on him today even without Versilov. I was only frightened, yesterday and today, at the thought that I might somehow meet Katerina Nikolaevna; but now I no longer feared anything.

He embraced me joyfully.

"And Versilov? Have you heard?" I began straight off with the main thing.

"*Cher enfant,* my dear friend, it's so sublime, it's so noble—in short, even Kilyan" (that clerk downstairs) "was tremendously impressed! It's not sensible on his part, but it's brilliant, it's a great deed! We must value the ideal!"

"Isn't it true? Isn't it true? You and I always agreed about that."

"My dear, you and I have always agreed. Where have you been? I absolutely wanted to go to you myself, but I didn't know where to find you... Because all the same I couldn't go to Versilov... Though now, after all this... You know, my friend, it was with this, it seems, that he used to win women over, with these features, there's no doubt of it..."

"By the way, before I forget, I've saved this precisely for you. Yesterday one most unworthy buffoon, denouncing Versilov to my face, said of him that he's a 'women's prophet'; what an expression, eh? the expression itself? I saved it for you..."

"A 'women's prophet'! *Mais... c'est charmant!** Ha, ha! But it suits him so well, that is, it doesn't suit him at all—pah!... But it's so apt... that is, it's not apt at all, but..."

"Never mind, never mind, don't be embarrassed, look at it just as a bon mot!"

"A splendid bon mot, and, you know, it has a most profound meaning... a perfectly right idea! That is, would you believe... In short, I'll tell you a tiny secret. Did you notice that Olympiada? Would you believe it, her heart aches a little for Andrei Petrovich, and to the point that she even seems to be nurturing some..."

"Nurturing! How would she like this?" I cried out, making a fig[60] in my indignation.

"*Mon cher*, don't shout, it's just so, and perhaps you're right from

*But... that's charming!

your point of view. By the way, my friend, what was it that happened to you last time in front of Katerina Nikolaevna? You were reeling... I thought you were going to fall down and was about to rush to support you."

"Of that some other time. Well, in short, I simply got embarrassed for a certain reason..."

"You're blushing even now."

"Well, and you have to go smearing it around at once. You know there's hostility between her and Versilov... well, and all that, well, and so I got excited: eh, let's drop it, another time!"

"Let's drop it, let's drop it, I'm glad to drop it myself... In short, I'm extremely guilty before her, and, remember, I even murmured in front of you then... Forget it, my friend; she'll also change her opinion of you, I have a real presentiment... But here's Prince Seryozha!"

A young and handsome officer came in. I looked at him greedily, I had never seen him before. That is, I say handsome, just as everybody said it of him, yet there was something in that young and handsome face that was not entirely attractive. I precisely note this as the impression of the very first moment, of my first glance at him, which remained in me ever after. He was lean, of a fine height, dark blond, with a fresh face, though slightly yellowish, and with a resolute gaze. His fine dark eyes had a somewhat stern look, even when he was quite calm. But his resolute gaze precisely repelled one, because one felt for some reason that this resoluteness cost him all too little. However, I don't know how to put it... Of course, his face was able to turn suddenly from a stern to a surprisingly gentle, meek, and tender expression, the transformation being, above all, unquestionably simplehearted. And this simpleheartedness was attractive. I'll note another feature: despite the gentleness and simpleheartedness, this face never showed mirth; even when the prince laughed with all his heart, you still felt as if there was never any genuine, bright, easy mirth in his heart... However, it's extremely hard to describe a face like his. I'm quite incapable of it. The old prince straightaway rushed to introduce us, as was his stupid habit.

"This is my young friend, Arkady Andreevich Dolgoruky" (again that "Andreevich"!).

The young prince turned to me at once with a doubly polite expression on his face, but it was clear that my name was totally unknown to him.

"He's . . . a relation of Andrei Petrovich," my vexatious prince murmured. (How vexatious these little old men sometimes are with their habits!) The young prince caught on at once.

"Ah! I heard so long ago . . ." he said quickly. "I had the great pleasure of making the acquaintance of your sister, Lizaveta Makarovna, last year in Luga . . . She also spoke to me about you . . ."

I was even surprised: a decidedly sincere pleasure shone in his face.

"Excuse me, Prince," I babbled, putting both hands behind my back, "I must tell you sincerely—and I'm glad to be speaking before our dear prince—that I even wished to meet you, and wished it still recently, only yesterday, but with an entirely different intent. I say it directly, however surprised you may be. In short, I wanted to challenge you for insulting Versilov a year and a half ago in Ems. And though you, of course, might not accept my challenge, because I'm only a high-school boy and an underage adolescent, nevertheless, I would make the challenge anyway, however you might take it and whatever you might do . . . and, I confess, I'm still of the same intent."

The old prince told me afterwards that I had managed to say it extremely nobly.

Sincere grief showed in the prince's face.

"Only you didn't let me finish," he replied imposingly. "If I turned to you with words that came from the bottom of my heart, the reason was precisely my present genuine feelings for Andrei Petrovich. I'm sorry that I cannot tell you all the circumstances right now, but I assure you on my honor that for a long, long time I have looked upon my unfortunate act in Ems with the deepest regret. As I was preparing to come to Petersburg, I decided to give Andrei Petrovich all possible satisfaction, that is, directly, literally, to ask his forgiveness, in whatever form he indicated. The loftiest and most powerful influences were the cause of the change in my view. The fact that we had a lawsuit would not have influenced my decision in the least. His action towards me yesterday shook my soul, so to speak, and even at this moment, believe me, it's as if I still haven't come back to myself. And now I must tell you—I precisely came to the prince in order to tell him about an extraordinary circumstance: three hours ago, that is, exactly at the time when he and his lawyer were putting together this act, a representative of Andrei Petrovich's came to bring me a challenge from him . . . a formal challenge on account of the incident in Ems . . ."

"He challenged you?" I cried, and felt my eyes begin to glow and the blood rush to my face.

"Yes, he did. I accepted the challenge at once, but I decided that before our encounter I would send him a letter in which I would explain my view of my act, and all my regret for this terrible mistake... because it was only a mistake—an unfortunate, fatal mistake! I'll note that my position in the regiment made this risky; for such a letter before an encounter, I'd be subjecting myself to public opinion... you understand? But in spite even of that, I resolved on it, only I had no time to send the letter, because an hour after the challenge, I again received a note from him in which he asked me to forgive him for having troubled me and to forget the challenge, adding that he regretted this 'momentary impulse of pusillanimity and egoism'—his own words. So he has now made the step with the letter quite easy for me. I haven't sent it yet, but I precisely came to tell the prince a word or two about it... And believe me, I myself have suffered from the reproaches of my conscience far more, maybe, than anybody else... Is this explanation sufficient for you, Arkady Makarovich, at least now, for the time being? Will you do me the honor of believing fully in my sincerity?"

I was completely won over. I saw an unquestionable straightforwardness, which for me was highly unexpected. Nor had I expected anything like it. I murmured something in reply and held out both hands to him; he joyfully shook them in his. Then he took the prince away and talked with him for about five minutes in his bedroom.

"If you want to give me particular pleasure," he addressed me loudly and openly, as he was leaving the prince, "come with me now, and I'll show you the letter I'm about to send to Andrei Petrovich, along with his letter to me."

I agreed with extreme willingness. My prince began bustling about as he saw me off, and also called me to his bedroom for a moment.

"*Mon ami*, how glad I am, how glad... We'll talk about it all later. By the way, I have two letters here in my portfolio: one needs to be delivered and explained personally, the other is to the bank—and there, too..."

And here he charged me with two supposedly urgent errands, which supposedly called for extraordinary effort and attention. I had to go and actually deliver them, sign, and so on.

"Ah, you sly fox!" I cried, taking the letters. "I swear it's all nonsense, and there's nothing to it, but you invented these two errands to convince me that I'm working and not taking money for nothing!"

"*Mon enfant*, I swear to you, you're mistaken about that: these are two most urgent matters... *Cher enfant!*" he cried suddenly, waxing terribly emotional, "my dear youth!" (He placed both hands on my head.) "I bless you and your destiny... let us always be pure in heart, like today... kind and beautiful, as far as possible... let us love all that's beautiful... in all its various forms... Well, *enfin... enfin rendons grâce... et je te bénis!*"*

He didn't finish and began whimpering over my head. I confess, I almost wept, too; at least I embraced my old eccentric sincerely and with pleasure. We kissed warmly.

III

PRINCE SERYOZHA (that is, Prince Sergei Petrovich, and so I shall call him) brought me to his apartment in a jaunty droshky, and, first thing, I was surprised at the magnificence of his apartment. That is, not really magnificence, but this was an apartment such as the most "respectable people" have, with high, big, bright rooms (I saw two, the others were shut up), and the furniture once again was not God knows what Versailles or Renaissance, but soft, comfortable, abundant, in grand style; rugs, carved wood, figurines. Yet everyone said they were destitute, that they had precisely nothing. I had heard in passing, though, that this prince raised dust wherever he could, here, and in Moscow, and in his former regiment, and in Paris, that he even gambled and had debts. The frock coat I had on was wrinkled and moreover covered with down, because I had slept without undressing, and my shirt was going on its fourth day. However, my frock coat was still not totally bad, but, finding myself at the prince's, I remembered Versilov's offer to have clothes made for me.

"Imagine, on the occasion of a certain suicide, I slept in my clothes all night," I remarked with an absentminded air, and since he paid attention at once, I briefly told him about it. But he was obviously occupied most of all with his letter. Above all, I found it strange

*Well, finally... finally let's give thanks... and I bless you!

that he not only had not smiled, but had not shown the smallest reaction in that sense, when I had told him directly earlier that I wanted to challenge him to a duel. Though I should have been able to prevent him from laughing, still it was strange from a man of his sort. We sat down facing each other in the middle of the room, at his enormous writing table, and he gave me an already finished fair copy of his letter to Versilov to read through. This document was very much like all he had told me earlier at my prince's; it was even ardently written. True, I didn't know yet how I should finally take this apparent straightforwardness and readiness for everything good, but I was already beginning to yield to it, because, in fact, why shouldn't I have believed it? Whatever sort of man he was and whatever people told about him, he still could have good inclinations. I also looked through the last little seven-line note from Versilov—renouncing his challenge. Though he actually wrote about his "pusillanimity" and "egoism" in it, the note as a whole was as if distinguished by a certain arrogance . . . or, better, this whole action showed a sort of disdain. However, I didn't say so out loud.

"You, though, how do you look at this renunciation?" I asked. "You don't think he turned coward?"

"Of course not," the prince smiled, but with a somehow very serious smile, and generally he was becoming more and more preoccupied. "I know all too well that he's a courageous man. Here, of course, there's a special view . . . his own disposition of ideas . . ."

"Undoubtedly," I interrupted warmly. "A certain Vasin says that his action with this letter and the renouncing of the inheritance are a 'pedestal' . . . In my opinion, such things aren't done for show, but correspond to something basic, inner."

"I know Mr. Vasin very well," remarked the prince.

"Ah, yes, you must have seen him in Luga."

We suddenly looked at each other and, I remember, it seems I blushed a little. In any case he broke off the conversation. I, however, wanted very much to talk. The thought of one meeting yesterday tempted me to ask him some questions, only I didn't know how to approach it. And in general I was somehow quite out of sorts. I was also struck by his astonishing courtesy, politeness, ease of manner—in short, all that polish of their tone, which they assume almost from the cradle. In his letter I found two gross errors in grammar. And generally, in such encounters, I never belittle myself, but become more curt, which sometimes may be bad. But in the present case it was especially aggravated by the thought that I was covered with down, so that several times I even blundered into familiarity... I noticed on the sly that the prince occasionally studied me very intently.

"Tell me, Prince," I suddenly popped out with a question, "don't you find it ridiculous within yourself that I, who am still such a 'milksop,' wanted to challenge you to a duel, and for somebody else's offense at that?"

"One can be very offended by an offense to one's father. No, I don't find it ridiculous."

"And to me it seems terribly ridiculous... in someone else's eyes... that is, of course, not in my own. The more so as I'm Dolgoruky and not Versilov. And if you're not telling me the truth or are softening it somehow from the decency of social polish, then does it mean you're also deceiving me in everything else?"

"No, I don't find it ridiculous," he replied terribly seriously. "How can you not feel your father's blood in you?... True, you're still young, because... I don't know... it seems someone who is not of age cannot fight a duel, and his challenge cannot be accepted... according to the rules... But, if you like, there can be only one serious objection here: if you make a challenge without the knowledge of the offended person, for whose offense you are making the challenge, you are thereby expressing, as it were, a certain lack of respect for him on your own part, isn't that true?"

Our conversation was suddenly interrupted by a footman, who came to announce something. Seeing him, the prince, who seemed to have been expecting him, stood up without finishing what he was saying and quickly went over to him, so that the footman made his announcement in a low voice, and I, of course, didn't hear what it was.

"Excuse me," the prince turned to me, "I'll be back in a minute."

And he went out. I was left alone; I paced the room and thought. Strangely, I both liked him and terribly disliked him. There was something in him that I could not name myself, but something repellent. "If he's not laughing at me a bit, then without doubt he's terribly straightforward, but if he was laughing at me... then maybe he'd seem more intelligent..." I thought somehow strangely. I went over to the table and read Versilov's letter once more. I was so absorbed that I even forgot about the time, and when I came to my senses, I suddenly noticed that the prince's little minute had indisputably lasted a whole quarter of an hour already. That began to trouble me a little; I paced up and down once more, finally took my hat and, I remember, decided to step out so as to meet someone, to send for the prince, and, when he came, to take leave of him at once, assuring him that I had things to do and could not wait any longer. It seemed to me that this would be most proper, because I was slightly pained by the thought that, in leaving me for so long, he was treating me negligently.

The two closed doors to this room were at two ends of the same wall. Having forgotten which door we came in by, or, rather, out of absentmindedness, I opened one of them and suddenly saw, sitting on a sofa in a long and narrow room—my sister Liza. There was no one there except her, and she was, of course, waiting for someone. But before I had time even to be surprised, I suddenly heard the voice of the prince, talking loudly to someone and going back to his study. I quickly closed the door, and the prince, coming in through the other door, noticed nothing. I remember he started apologizing and said something about some Anna Fyodorovna... But I was so confused and astounded that I made out almost none of it, and only muttered that I had to go home, and then insistently and quickly left. The well-bred prince, of course, must have looked at my manners with curiosity. He saw me off to the front hall and kept talking, but I did not reply and did not look at him.

IV

GOING OUTSIDE, I turned left and started walking at random. Nothing added up in my head. I walked slowly and, it seems, had gone quite far, some five hundred steps, when I suddenly felt a light tap on my shoulder. I turned and saw Liza: she had caught up with me and tapped me lightly with her umbrella. There was something terribly gay and a bit sly in her shining eyes.

"Well, how glad I am that you went this way, otherwise I wouldn't have met you today!" She was slightly breathless from walking quickly.

"How breathless you are."

"I ran terribly to catch up with you."

"Liza, was it you I just met?"

"Where?"

"At the prince's... Prince Sokolsky's..."

"No, not me, you didn't meet me..."

I said nothing, and we walked on some ten paces. Liza burst into loud laughter:

"Me, me, of course it was me! Listen, you saw me yourself, you looked into my eyes, and I looked into your eyes, so how can you ask whether you met me? Well, what a character! And you know, I wanted terribly to laugh when you stared into my eyes there, it was terribly funny the way you stared."

She laughed terribly. I felt all the anguish leave my heart at once.

"But, tell me, how did you wind up there?"

"I was at Anna Fyodorovna's."

"What Anna Fyodorovna?"

"Stolbeev. When we lived in Luga, I sat with her for whole days; she received mama at her place and even called on us. And she called on almost nobody there. She's a distant relation of Andrei Petrovich's and a relation of the Princes Sokolsky; she's some sort of grandmother to the prince."

"So she lives with the prince?"

"No, the prince lives with her."

"So whose apartment is it?"

"It's her apartment, the apartment has been all hers for a whole year now. The prince has just arrived and is staying with her. And she herself has only been four days in Petersburg."

"Well . . . you know what, Liza, God be with the apartment, and the woman herself . . ."

"No, she's wonderful . . ."

"Let her be, and in spades. We're wonderful ourselves! Look, what a day, look, how good! How beautiful you are today, Liza. However, you're a terrible child."

"Arkady, tell me, that girl, the one yesterday."

"Ah, what a pity, Liza, what a pity!"

"Ah, what a pity! What a fate! You know, it's even sinful that you and I go along so merrily, and her soul is now flying somewhere in the darkness, in some bottomless darkness, sinner that she is, and offended . . . Arkady, who's to blame for her sin? Ah, how frightful it is! Do you ever think about that darkness? Ah, how afraid I am of death, and how sinful that is! I don't like the dark, I much prefer this sun! Mama says it's sinful to be afraid . . . Arkady, do you know mama well?"

"Little so far, Liza, I know her very little."

"Ah, what a being she is; you must, must get to know her! She has to be understood in a special way . . ."

"But see, I didn't know you either, and now I know the whole of you. I came to know the whole of you in one minute. Though you're afraid of death, Liza, it must be that you're proud, bold, courageous. Better than I, much better than I! I love you terribly, Liza! Ah, Liza! Let death come when it must, and meanwhile—live, live! We'll pity that unfortunate girl, but even so we'll bless life, right? Right? I have an 'idea,' Liza. Liza, do you know that Versilov renounced the inheritance?"

"How could I not know! Mama and I already kissed each other."

"You don't know my soul, Liza, you don't know what this man has meant for me..."

"Well, how could I not know, I know everything."

"You know everything? Well, what else! You're intelligent; you're more intelligent than Vasin. You and mama—you have penetrating, humane eyes, that is, looks, not eyes, I'm wrong... I'm bad in many ways, Liza."

"You need to be taken in hand, that's all."

"Take me, Liza. How nice it is to look at you today. Do you know that you're very pretty? I've never seen your eyes before... Only now I've seen them for the first time... Where did you get them today, Liza? Where did you buy them? How much did you pay? Liza, I've never had a friend, and I look upon the idea as nonsense; but with you it's not nonsense... If you want, let's be friends! You understand what I want to say?..."

"I understand very well."

"And you know, without any conditions, any contract—we'll simply be friends!"

"Yes, simply, simply, only with one condition: if we ever accuse each other, if we're displeased with something, if we ourselves become wicked, bad, if we even forget all this—let's never forget this day and this very hour! Let's promise ourselves. Let's promise that we will always remember this day, when we walked hand in hand, and laughed so, and were so merry... Yes? Yes?"

"Yes, Liza, yes, and I swear it; but, Liza, it's as if I'm hearing you for the first time... Liza, have you read a lot?"

"He never asked till now! Only yesterday, when I made a slip in speaking, he deigned to pay attention for the first time, my dear sir, Mister Wise Man."

"But why didn't you start talking to me yourself, since I was such a fool?"

"I kept waiting for you to become smarter. I saw through you from the very beginning, Arkady Makarovich, and once I saw through you, I began to think like this: 'He'll come, he'll surely end up by coming'—well, and I supposed it was better to leave that honor to you, so that it was you who made the first step: 'No,' I thought, 'now you run after me a little!'"

"Ah, you little coquette! Well, Liza, confess outright: have you been laughing at me all this month or not?"

"Oh, you're very funny, you're terribly funny, Arkady! And you know, it may be that I loved you most of all this month because you're such an odd duck. But in many ways you're also a silly duck—that's so you don't get too proud. Do you know who else laughed at you? Mama laughed at you, mama and I together: 'What an odd duck,' we'd whisper, 'really, what an odd duck!' And you sat there and thought all the while that we're sitting there and trembling before you."

"Liza, what do you think of Versilov?"

"I think a great many things about him; but you know, we're not going to talk about him now. There's no need to talk about him today, right?"

"Perfectly right! No, you're terribly intelligent, Liza! You're certainly more intelligent than I am. You just wait, Liza, I'll finish with all this, and then maybe I'll tell you something..."

"Why are you frowning?"

"I'm not frowning, Liza, I'm just... You see, Liza, it's better to be direct: I have this feature, I don't like it when someone puts a finger on certain ticklish things in my soul... or, better to say, if you keep letting out certain feelings for everybody to admire, it's shameful, isn't it? And so I sometimes prefer to frown and say nothing. You're intelligent, you must understand."

"Not only that, I'm the same way myself; I understand you in everything. Do you know that mama is the same way, too?"

"Ah, Liza! If only we could live longer in this world! Eh? What did you say?"

"No, I didn't say anything."

"You're just looking?"

"Yes, and you're looking, too. I look at you and love you."

I took her almost all the way home and gave her my address. Saying good-bye, I kissed her for the first time in my life...

V

AND ALL THAT would have been fine, but there was one thing that wasn't fine: one oppressive idea had been throbbing in me since nightfall and would not leave my mind. This was that when I had met that unfortunate girl by the gate last evening, I had told her that I myself was leaving my home, my nest, that one could leave wicked people and start one's own nest, and that Versilov had many illegitimate children. These words about a father from a son had most certainly confirmed in her all her suspicions about Versilov and about his having insulted her. I had accused Stebelkov, but maybe it was I myself, above all, who had poured oil on the fire. This thought was terrible, it's terrible even now... But then, that morning, though I was already beginning to suffer, it had still seemed nonsense to me: "Eh, even without me, a lot was 'seething and smoldering' there," I repeated at times. "Eh, never mind, it'll pass! I'll come right! I'll make up for it... by some good deed... I've still got fifty years ahead of me!"

But the idea still throbbed.

PART TWO

Chapter One

I

I FLY OVER a space of nearly two months; let the reader not worry: everything will be clear from the further account. I sharply mark off the day of the fifteenth of November—a day all too memorable to me for many reasons. And first of all, nobody would have recognized me who had seen me two months earlier, at least externally; that is, they'd have recognized me, but wouldn't have known what to make of it. I'm dressed like a fop—that's the first thing. That "conscientious Frenchman and with taste," whom Versilov once wanted to recommend me to, had not only already made all my clothes, but had already been rejected by me: other tailors stitch for me, higher class, the foremost, and I even have an account with them. I also have an account in a certain famous restaurant, but here I'm still afraid, and the moment I have money I pay it at once, though I know it's *mauvais ton** and that I compromise myself by it. A French barber on Nevsky Prospect is on familiar terms with me, and when he does my hair, he tells me anecdotes. I confess, I practice my French with him. Though I know the language, and even quite decently, I'm still somehow afraid to start speaking it in grand society; besides, my pronunciation must be far from Parisian. I have Matvei, a coachman with a trotter, and he appears to serve me when I send for him. He has a light bay stallion (I don't like grays). There are, however, also some irregularities: it's the fifteenth of November, and the third day since winter settled in, but my fur coat is old, a raccoon from Versilov's shoulders, worth twenty-five roubles if I were to sell it. I must buy a new one, but my pockets are empty, and besides, I must provide myself with money for this evening, and that at all costs—otherwise I'm "wretched and forlorn," those were my own utterances at the time. Oh, meanness! What then, where have they suddenly come from, these thousands, these trotters, and *les Borel*?[1] How could I so suddenly forget everything and change so much? Disgrace! Reader, I am now beginning the history of my

*Bad tone.

shame and disgrace, and nothing in life can be more shameful for me than these memories!

I speak thus as a judge, and I know that I'm guilty. In that whirl in which I then spun, though I was alone, without guide or counselor, I swear, I was already aware of my fall, and therefore had no excuse. And yet all those two months I was almost happy—why almost? I was only too happy! And even to the point that the consciousness of disgrace, flashing at moments (frequent moments!), which made my soul shudder—that very awareness—will anyone believe me?—intoxicated me still more: "And so what, if I fall, I fall; but I won't fall, I'll get out! I have my star!" I was walking on a slender bridge made of splinters, without railings, over an abyss, and it was fun for me to walk like that; I even peeked into the abyss. It was risky, and it was fun. And the "idea"? "The idea" later, the idea was waiting; all that was going on—"was only a deviation to the side": "why not amuse myself?" The bad thing about "my idea," I'll repeat it once more, is that it allows for decidedly all deviations; had it not been so firm and radical, I might have been afraid to deviate.

And meanwhile I still continued to occupy my wretched little apartment, to occupy it, but not to live in it: there lay my suitcase, bag, and some things; my main residence was at Prince Sergei Sokolsky's. I sat there, slept there, and did so for whole weeks even... How it happened, I shall tell presently, but meanwhile I'll tell about this wretched little apartment. It was already dear to me: here Versilov came to see me, of himself, for the first time after that quarrel, and later came many times. I repeat, this was a time of terrible disgrace, but also of enormous happiness... And everything turned out so well then, everything smiled at me! "And why all that former gloom?" I thought in some rapturous moments. "Why all those old, morbid strains, my lonely and sullen childhood, my stupid dreams under the blanket, vows, calculations, and even the 'idea'? I had imagined and invented all that, and it turned out that the world wasn't like that at all; here I am feeling so joyful and light: I have a father—Versilov; I have a friend—Prince Seryozha; I also have..." But let's drop that "also." Alas, it was all done in the name of love, magnanimity, honor, and later it turned out ugly, impudent, dishonorable.

Enough.

II

He came to see me for the first time on the third day after our breakup then. I wasn't at home, and he stayed to wait. When I came into my tiny closet, even though I had been waiting for him all those three days, my eyes clouded over, as it were, and my heart gave such a throb that I even stopped in the doorway. Fortunately, he was sitting with my landlord, who found it necessary, so that the visitor would not be bored waiting, to become acquainted at once and begin telling him heatedly about something. He was a titular councillor,[2] about forty years old, very pockmarked, very poor, burdened with a consumptive wife and a sick child; of an extremely gregarious and placid character, though also rather tactful. I was glad of his presence, and he even helped me out, because what would I have said to Versilov? I knew, seriously knew, all those three days, that Versilov would come on his own, first—exactly as I wanted, because I would not have gone to him first for anything in the world, and not out of contrariness, but precisely out of love for him, out of some sort of jealous love—I don't know how to express it. And generally the reader won't find any eloquence in me. But though I had been waiting for him all those three days, and had imagined to myself almost continuously how he would come in, still I had been quite unable to picture beforehand, though I tried as hard as I could to picture it, what he and I would suddenly start talking about after all that had happened.

"Ah, here you are." He held out his hand to me amicably, without getting up from his seat. "Sit down with us. Pyotr Ippolitovich tells the most interesting story about this stone, near the Pavlovsky barracks . . . or somewhere there . . ."

"Yes, I know that stone," I answered quickly, lowering myself into a chair beside them. They were sitting at the table. The whole room was precisely two hundred square feet. I took a deep breath.

A spark of pleasure flashed in Versilov's eyes: it seemed he had doubts and thought I might want to make gestures. He calmed down.

"Start again from the beginning, Pyotr Ippolitovich." They were already addressing each other by first name and patronymic.

"So, this happened under the late sovereign,[3] sir," Pyotr Ippolitovich addressed me, nervously and somewhat painfully, as if suffering ahead of time over the success of the effect. "You know that stone—a stupid stone in the street, why, what for, it's in everybody's way, right, sir? The sovereign drove by many times, and each time there was this stone. In the end, the sovereign didn't like it, and indeed, a whole mountain, a mountain is standing in the street, ruining the street: 'The stone must not be!' Well, he said it must not be—you understand what 'it must not be' means? Remember the late tsar? What to do with the stone? Everybody's at their wit's end, including the Duma,[4] and mainly, I don't remember who precisely, but it was one of the foremost courtiers of the time who was charged with it. So this courtier listens: they say it would cost fifteen thousand, not less, in silver, sir (because paper banknotes had just been converted to silver under the late sovereign). 'How come fifteen thousand, that's wild!' First the Englishmen wanted to bring rails up to it, put it on rails, and take it away by steam; but what would that have cost? There were no railroads yet then, except for the one to Tsarskoe Selo[5] . . ."

"Well, look, they could have sawed it in pieces." I was beginning to frown; I was terribly vexed and ashamed in front of Versilov, but he listened with visible pleasure. I understood that he, too, was glad of the landlord, because he also felt abashed with me, I could see it; for me, I remember, that even seemed touching in him.

"Precisely saw it in pieces, sir, they precisely hit upon that idea, and it was precisely Montferrand; he was then building St. Isaac's Cathedral.[6] Saw it up, he says, and then take it away. Yes, sir, but what will that cost?"

"It won't cost anything. Simply saw it up and take it away."

"No, pardon me, but here you'd have to set up a machine, a steam engine, and then again, take it away where? And then again, such a mountain? Ten thousand, they say, you won't get away with less, ten or twelve thousand."

"Listen, Pyotr Ippolitovich, that's nonsense, it wasn't like that . . ." But just then Versilov winked at me inconspicuously, and in that wink I saw such delicate compassion for the landlord, even commiseration with him, that I liked it terribly much, and I burst out laughing.

"Well, so, so," rejoiced the landlord, who hadn't noticed anything and was terribly afraid, as such storytellers always are, that he would be thrown off by questions, "only just then some tradesman comes up to them, still a young man, well, you know, a Russian, wedge-shaped beard, in a long-skirted kaftan, and on the verge of being a little drunk... though, no, not drunk, sir. So this tradesman stands there while they're talking about it, the Englishmen and Montferrand, and this person who's in charge also drives up in a carriage, listens, and gets angry: how is it they keep deciding and can't decide? And suddenly he notices this little tradesman standing some distance away and smiling sort of falsely, that is, not falsely, I got it wrong, but how should I say..."

"Mockingly," Versilov put in cautiously.

"Mockingly, sir, that is, slightly mockingly, with this kindly Russian smile, you know; well, the person, of course, takes it with vexation, you know: 'You in the beard, what are you waiting here for? Who are you?'

"'Oh,' he says, 'I'm just looking at this little stone, Your Highness.' Precisely, I believe, 'Your Highness'—it was all but Prince Suvorov of Italy, a descendant of the generalissimo[7]... Though, no, not Suvorov, and it's a pity I've forgotten precisely who, only you know, though he's a highness, he's such a pure Russian man, this Russian type, a patriot, a developed Russian heart, so he guessed it: 'What are you going to do,' he says, 'take the stone away? What are you grinning at?' 'More at the Englishmen, Your Highness, the price they're asking is way out of proportion, sir, because the Russian purse is fat, and they've got nothing to eat at home. Allot me a hundred little roubles, Your Highness, and by tomorrow night we'll remove this little stone.' Well, can you imagine such an offer? The Englishmen, of course, want to eat him up; Montferrand laughs; only this highness prince, he's a Russian heart: 'Give him a hundred roubles!' he says. 'So,' he says, 'you'll really take it away?' 'By tomorrow night it'll be to your satisfaction, Your Highness.' 'And how will you do it?' 'That—no offense to Your Highness—is our secret, sir,' he says, and you know, in such Russian language. This was liked: 'Eh, give him everything he asks for!' Well, so they left him there; and what do you think he did?"

The landlord paused and began looking at us with a sweet gaze.

"I don't know," Versilov smiled. I was frowning deeply.

"Here's what he did, sir," the landlord said with such triumph as if he had done it himself. "He hired some peasants with spades, simple Russian ones, and started digging a hole right by the stone, at the very edge; they dug all night, made an enormous hole, exactly the size of the stone, only a couple of inches deeper, and when they were done, he told them to gradually and carefully dig the ground from under the stone. Well, naturally, when they dug away under it, the stone had no support, and the balance got tipsy; and once the balance got tipsy, they pushed the stone from the other side with their hands, with a hurrah, Russian-style: the stone plopped right into the hole! They straight away shoveled the dirt back over it, tamped it down with a tamper, paved it over—smooth, the stone vanished!"

"Fancy that!" said Versilov.

"I mean, people, people come running, untold numbers of them; those Englishmen, who had guessed long ago, stand there angry. Montferrand arrives: This is a peasant job, he says, it's too simple, he says. But that's the whole trick, that it's simple, and it didn't occur to you fools! And I'll tell you, that superior, that state personage, he just gasped, hugged him, kissed him: 'And where might the likes of you be from?' 'Yaroslavl province, Your Highness, myself I'm a tailor by trade, but in summer I come to the capital to sell fruit, sir.' Well, it reached the authorities; the authorities ordered a medal hung on him; he went around like that with the medal on his neck, and later they say he drank himself up; you know, a Russian man, can't help himself! That's why the foreigners prey on us to this day, yes, sir, so there, sir!"

"Yes, of course, the Russian mind..." Versilov began.

But here, fortunately for him, the storyteller was summoned by his ailing wife, and he ran off, otherwise I couldn't have stood it. Versilov was laughing.

"My dear, he entertained me for a whole hour before you came. That stone... that's everything there is of the most patriotically indecent among such stories, but how interrupt him? You saw him, he was melting with pleasure. And besides, the stone, it seems, is still standing there, unless I'm mistaken, and isn't buried in a hole at all..."

"Ah, my God!" I cried, "but that's true. How did he dare!..."

"What's with you? No, come now, it seems you're quite indignant. And he actually got it confused: I heard some such story about a stone back in the time of my childhood, only, naturally, it wasn't the same and wasn't about that stone. Good heavens, 'it reached the authorities.' His whole soul sang at that moment when it 'reached the authorities.' In this sorry milieu, it's impossible to do without such anecdotes. They have a host of them—above all from their lack of restraint. They haven't studied anything, they don't know anything precisely, well, and besides cards and promotions, they want to talk about something generally human, poetic... What is he, who is he, this Pyotr Ippolitovich?"

"The poorest of beings, and also unfortunate."

"Well, so you see, maybe he doesn't even play cards! I repeat, while telling this rubbish, he satisfies his love for his neighbor: you see, he wanted to make us happy as well. The feeling of patriotism is also satisfied; for instance, they also have an anecdote that the English offered Zavyalov[8] a million only so that he wouldn't stamp his brand on his products..."

"Ah, my God, I've heard that anecdote."

"Who hasn't heard it, and he knows perfectly well, as he tells it, that you've certainly heard it already, but still he tells it, *deliberately* imagining that you haven't. It seems the vision of the Swedish king[9] has become outdated with them; but in my youth they repeated it with gusto, and in a mysterious whisper, as well as the one about somebody at the beginning of the century supposedly kneeling before the senators in the Senate.[10] There were also many anecdotes about Commandant Bashutsky[11] and how the monument was taken away. They're terribly fond of anecdotes about the court; for instance, the stories about Chernyshov,[12] a minister in the previous reign, how as a seventy-year-old man he made himself up so that he looked like a thirty-year-old, so much so that the late sovereign was astonished at his receptions..."

"I've heard that, too."

"Who hasn't? All these anecdotes are the height of indecency, but you should know that this type of the indecent is much deeper and more widespread than we think. Even in our most decent society, you meet with the wish to lie with the purpose of making your neighbor happy, for we all suffer from this unrestraint of the heart. Only with us the stories are of a different kind; what they tell about America alone is something awful, and that's even statesmen! I confess, I myself belong to this indecent type and have suffered from it all my life..."

"I've told the story about Chernyshov several times myself."

"Have you really?"

"There's another tenant here besides me, a clerk, also pockmarked, and already old, but he's a terribly prosaic man, and as soon as Pyotr Ippolitovich starts talking, he immediately sets about confusing and contradicting him. And he's driven him to such a state that Pyotr Ippolitovich serves him like a slave and humors him, only so as he listens."

"That's already another type of the indecent, and maybe even more loathsome than the first. The first is all rapture! 'Just let me tell you a lie—you'll see how well it comes out.' The second is all spleen and prose: 'I won't let you lie—when, where, in what year?' In short, he has no heart. My friend, always let a man lie a little—it's innocent. Even let him lie a lot. First, it will show your delicacy, and second, you'll also be allowed to lie in return—two enormous profits at once. *Que diable!** one must love one's neighbor! But it's time I left. You've settled in quite nicely," he added, getting up from his chair. "I'll tell Sofya Andreevna and your sister that I called and found you in good health. Good-bye, my dear."

What, could that be all? No, this was by no means what I needed; I was waiting for something else, the *main thing*, though I understood perfectly well that it couldn't be otherwise. I began showing him to the stairs with a candle; the landlord also jumped over, but, in secret from Versilov, I seized his arm with all my strength and shoved him away fiercely. He looked at me in amazement, but effaced himself at once.

"These stairs..." Versilov mumbled, drawing out the words, evidently so as to say something, and evidently for fear I might say something, "these stairs—I'm not used to them, and you're on the third floor, but, anyhow, I'll find my way now... Don't trouble yourself, my dear, you'll catch cold."

But I didn't leave. We were going down the second flight of stairs.

"I've been waiting for you all these three days," escaped me suddenly, as if of itself; I was breathless.

"Thank you, my dear."

"I knew you wouldn't fail to come."

"And I knew you knew I wouldn't fail to come. Thank you, my dear."

He fell silent. We had already reached the front door, and I was still walking behind him. He opened the door; the wind burst in at once and blew out my candle. Here I suddenly seized him by the hand; it was completely dark. He gave a start, but said nothing. I bent to his hand and suddenly began kissing it greedily, several times, many times.

"My dear boy, what makes you love me so much?" he said, but now in a quite different voice. His voice trembled, and something quite new rang in it, as if it was not he who was speaking.

*What the devil!

I wanted to answer something but couldn't, and ran upstairs. He waited without moving from the spot, and only when I reached my apartment did I hear the street door downstairs open and slam shut noisily. I slipped into my room past the landlord, who for some reason turned up there again, fastened the latch, and, without lighting a candle, threw myself onto the bed, face to the pillow, and—wept, wept. It was the first time I had wept since Touchard's! Sobs burst from me with such force, and I was so happy . . . but why describe it!

I've written this down now without being ashamed, because maybe it was all good, despite all its absurdity.

III

BUT, OH, DID he get it from me for that! I became a terrible despot. Needless to say, we never mentioned this scene afterwards. On the contrary, we met three days later as if nothing had happened—what's more, I was almost rude that second evening, and he was also as if dry. It happened at my place again; for some reason I still wouldn't go to him myself, despite my desire to see my mother.

We talked all this time, that is, for these two whole months, only about the most abstract subjects. And that surprises me: all we did was talk about abstract subjects—the generally human and most necessary ones, of course, but not concerned in the least with the essential. Yet much, very much, of the essential needed to be defined and clarified, even urgently so, but of those things we didn't speak. I even said nothing about mother and Liza and . . . well, and finally about myself, about my whole story. Whether that was all from shame, or from some sort of youthful stupidity—I don't know. I suppose it was from stupidity, because shame could still have been surmounted. And I despotized him terribly and more than once even drove it as far as insolence, and even against my own heart: it was all done somehow of itself, uncontrollably, I couldn't control myself. His tone was of a subtle mockery, as before, though always extremely affectionate despite all. It also struck me that he much preferred coming to me himself, so that in the end I began to see mama terribly seldom, once a week, not more, especially in the most recent time, when I got into quite a whirl. He would come in the evening, sit in my room and chat; he was also very fond of chatting with the landlord; this last infuriated me in such a man as he. The thought also came to me: can it be that he has no one to go to except me? But I knew for certain that he had acquaintances; lately he had even renewed many former connections in high society circles, which he had abandoned during that last year; but it seems he wasn't especially tempted by them, and many were renewed only officially, while he preferred coming to me. It sometimes touched me very much that, on coming in of an evening, he seemed to grow timid almost every time as he opened the door, and in the first moment always peeked into my eyes with a strange anxiousness, as if to say, "Won't I be bothering you? Tell me and I'll go away." He even said it sometimes. Once, for instance, precisely in the most recent time, he came in when I was already fully dressed in a suit I had just received from the tailor and was about to go to "Prince Seryozha," so as to set off with him where I had to go (I'll explain where later). But he came in and sat down, probably not noticing that I was about to leave; there were moments when he was overcome by an extremely strange absent-mindedness. As if on purpose, he began talking about the landlord. I blew up:

"Eh, devil take the landlord!"

"Ah, my dear," he suddenly got up from his place, "it seems you're about to go out, and I'm bothering you... Forgive me, please."

And he humbly hastened to leave. This humility towards me from such a man, from such a worldly and independent man, who had so much of his own, at once resurrected in my heart all my tenderness for him and all my trust in him. But if he loved me so, why didn't he stop me then in the time of my disgrace? A word from him then—and maybe I would have held back. However, maybe not. But he did see this foppishness, this fanfaronade, this Matvei (once I even wanted to give him a ride in my sledge, but he wouldn't get in, and it even happened several times that he didn't want to get in), he did see that I was throwing money around—and not a word, not a word, not even out of curiosity! That astonishes me to this day, even now. And I, naturally, was not the least bit ceremonious with him then and let everything show, though, of course, also without a word of explanation. He didn't ask, and I didn't speak.

However, two or three times it was as if we did also start speaking about the essential. I asked him once, at the beginning, soon after he renounced the inheritance, how he was going to live now.

"Somehow, my friend," he said with extraordinary calm.

Now I know that even Tatyana Pavlovna's tiny capital of about five thousand was half spent on Versilov in these last two years.

Another time we somehow began talking about mama:

"My friend," he suddenly said sadly, "I often said to Sofya Andreevna at the beginning of our union—at the beginning, and the middle, and the end as well, however: 'My dear, I'm tormenting you, and I'll torment you thoroughly, and I'm not sorry, as long as you're before me; but if you should die, I know I'd do myself in with punishment.' "

However, I remember he was especially open that evening:

"If only I were a weak-tempered nonentity and suffered from the awareness of it! But no, I know that I'm infinitely strong, and what do you think my strength is? Precisely this spontaneous power of getting along with anything, which is so characteristic of all intelligent people of our generation. Nothing can destroy me, nothing can exterminate me, nothing can astonish me. I'm as tenacious as a yard dog. I can feel in the most comfortable way two contrary feelings at the same time—and that, of course, not by my own will. But nonetheless I know it's dishonest, mainly because it's all too reasonable. I've lived to be nearly fifty, and so far I don't know whether it's good that I've done so, or bad. Of course, I love life, and that follows directly from things, but for a man like me, to love life is base. Lately something new has begun, and the Krafts don't survive, they shoot themselves. But it's clear that the Krafts are stupid; well, and we're intelligent—so it's impossible to draw any analogy here, and the question still remains open. And can it be only for such as we that the earth stands? Yes, in all likelihood; but that is too cheerless an idea. However... however, the question still remains open."

He spoke with sadness, and even so I didn't know whether he was sincere or not. There was always some wrinkle in him that he wouldn't drop for anything.

IV

I SHOWERED HIM with questions then, I threw myself on him like a hungry man on bread. He always answered me readily and straightforwardly, but in the final end he always brought it down to the most general aphorisms, so that, in essence, nothing could be drawn from it. And yet all these questions had troubled me all my life, and, I confess frankly, while still in Moscow, I postponed their resolution precisely until our meeting in Petersburg. I even told it to him directly, and he didn't laugh at me—on the contrary, I remember, he shook my hand. On general politics and social questions, I could extract almost nothing from him, and it was these questions that troubled me most, in view of my "idea." Of the likes of Dergachev, I once tore the observation from him "that they were beneath any criticism," but at the same time he added strangely that he "reserved for himself the right not to attach any importance to his opinion." Of how the contemporary states and world would end and what would bring about a renewal of the social world, he kept silent for terribly long, but one day I finally tortured a few words out of him:

"I think it will all come about somehow in an extremely ordinary way," he said once. "Quite simply, all the states, despite all balancing of budgets and 'absence of deficits,' *un beau matin** will become utterly confused, and each and every one of them will refuse to pay up, so that each and every one of them will be renewed in a general bankruptcy. Meanwhile, all the conservative elements of the whole world will be opposed to that, for it will be they who are the shareholders and creditors, and they will not want to allow the bankruptcy. Then, of course, there will begin a general oxidation, so to speak; the Yid will arrive in quantity, and a kingdom of Yids will begin; but all those who never had any shares, and generally never had anything, that is, all the beggars, naturally will not want to participate in the oxidation... A struggle will begin, and after seventy-seven defeats, the beggars will annihilate the shareholders, take their shares from them, and sit in their place—as shareholders, of course. And maybe they'll say something new, or maybe not. Most likely they'll also go bankrupt. Beyond that, my friend, I can't predict anything in the destinies that will change the face of this world. However, look in the Apocalypse..."

"But can it all be so material? Can the present-day world end only because of finances?"

"Oh, naturally, I've taken only one little corner of the picture, but that corner is connected with everything by, so to speak, indissoluble bonds."

"What, then, is to be done?"

*One fine morning.

"Ah, my God, don't be in a hurry; it won't all come so soon. Generally, it's best to do nothing; at least your conscience is at peace, since you haven't taken part in anything."

"Eh, come on, talk business. I want to know precisely what I'm to do and how I'm to live."

"What are you to do, my dear? Be honest, never lie, don't covet your neighbor's house, in short, read the ten commandments: everything's written there for all time."

"Come on, come on, that's all so old, and besides—it's just words, and I need action."

"Well, if you're quite overcome with boredom, try loving someone, or something, or even simply becoming attached to something."

"You just laugh! And besides, what am I alone to do with your ten commandments?"

"But if you fulfill them, despite all your questions and doubts, you'll be a great man."

"Unknown to anyone."

"Nothing is secret, that shall not be made manifest."[13]

"No, you're decidedly laughing!"

"Well, if you take it so much to heart, then it would be best to try and specialize quickly, take up construction or law; then you'll be occupied with real and serious business, and you can settle down and forget about trifles."

I said nothing—well, what could I get from that? And yet after each such conversation, I was more troubled than before. Besides, I saw clearly that there was always as if some mystery left in him; it was this that drew me to him more and more.

"Listen," I interrupted him one day, "I always suspected that you were saying all this just so, from spite and out of suffering, but secretly, within yourself, it's you who are a fanatic of some higher idea and are only hiding it or ashamed to admit it."

"Thank you, my dear."

"Listen, there's nothing higher than being useful. Tell me, how can I be of greatest use at this given moment? I know you can't decide that; but I'm only seeking your opinion: you tell me, and I'll go and do as you tell me, I swear to you! Well, what is the great thought?"

"Well, to turn stones into bread—there's a great thought."[14]

"The greatest? No, truly, you've pointed out a whole path; tell me, then: is it the greatest?"

"A very great one, my friend, a very great one, but not the greatest; great, but secondary, and only great in the given moment. Man eats and doesn't remember it; on the contrary, he'll say at once: 'Well, so I've eaten, and now what do I do?' The question remains eternally open."

"You once talked about 'Geneva ideas.' I didn't understand—what are 'Geneva ideas'?"

"Geneva ideas—it's virtue without Christ, my friend, today's ideas, or, better to say, the idea of the whole of today's civilization.[15] In short, it's—one of those long stories that are very boring to begin, and it would be much better if we talked about other things, and still better if we were silent about other things."

"All you want to do is be silent!"

"My friend, remember that to be silent is good, safe, and beautiful."

"Beautiful?"

"Of course. Silence is always beautiful, and a silent person is always more beautiful than one who talks."

"But to talk as you and I do is, of course, the same as being silent. Devil take that sort of beauty, and furthermore, devil take that sort of profit!"

"My dear," he said to me suddenly, in a somewhat changed tone, even with feeling and with a sort of special insistence, "my dear, I by no means want to seduce you with any sort of bourgeois virtue instead of your ideals, nor do I insist that 'happiness is better than heroism'; on the contrary, heroism is higher than any happiness, and the capacity for it alone already constitutes happiness. So that's settled between us. I respect you precisely for being able, in our soured time, to cultivate some sort of 'idea of your own' in your soul (don't worry, I remember it very well). But all the same it's impossible not to think about measure, too, because now you precisely want a resounding life, to set something on fire, to smash something, to rise higher than all Russia, to sweep over like a storm cloud and leave everyone in fear and admiration, and disappear into the North American States. Surely there's something of that kind in your soul, and that's why I consider it necessary to warn you, because I've sincerely come to love you, my dear."

What could I get from that as well? Here there was only a worry about me, about my material fate; it spoke for the father, with his prosaic though kindly feelings; but was that what I needed, in view of the ideas for which every honest father should send his son even to his death, as the ancient Horatius sent his sons for the idea of Rome?[16]

I often pestered him with religion, but here the fog was thickest of all. To the question, What am I to do in this sense? he replied in the stupidest way, as to a little boy: "You must believe in God, my dear."

"Well, and what if I don't believe in all that?" I once cried in irritation.

"Splendid, my dear."

"How, splendid?"

"A most excellent sign, my friend; even the most trustworthy, because our Russian atheist, if only he's a true atheist and has a bit of intelligence, is the best man in the whole world and always inclined to treat God nicely, because he's unfailingly kind, and he's kind because he's immeasurably pleased that he's an atheist. Our atheists are respectable people and trustworthy in the highest degree, the support, so to speak, of the fatherland..."

That, of course, was something, but not what I wanted; only once did he speak his mind, only so strangely that he surprised me most of all then, especially in view of all these Catholicisms and chains I had heard about in connection with him.

"My dear," he said to me once, not at home, but one time in the street, after a long conversation; I was seeing him off. "My friend, to love people as they are is impossible. And yet one must. And therefore do good to them, clenching your feelings, holding your nose, and shutting your eyes (this last is necessary). Endure evil from them, not getting angry with them if possible, 'remembering that you, too, are a human being.' Naturally, you're in a position to be severe with them, if it's been granted you to be a little bit smarter than the average. People are mean by nature and love to love out of fear; don't give in to such love and don't cease to despise it. Somewhere in the Koran, Allah bids the prophet to look upon the 'recalcitrant' as mice, to do good to them and pass by—somewhat arrogant, but right. Know how to despise them even when they're good, for most often it's just here that they're nasty. Oh, my dear, I'm judging by myself in saying that! He who is only a little bit better than stupid cannot live and not despise himself—whether he's honest or dishonest makes no difference. To love one's neighbor and not despise him is impossible. In my opinion, man is created with a physical inability to love his neighbor. There's some mistake in words here, from the very beginning, and 'love for mankind' should be understood as just for that mankind which you yourself have created in your soul (in other words, you've created your own self and the love for yourself), and which therefore will never exist in reality."

"Never exist?"

"My friend, I agree that this would be rather stupid, but here the blame isn't mine; and since I wasn't consulted at the time of the creation of the world, I reserve for myself the right to have my own opinion about it."

"How can they call you a Christian after that," I cried, "a monk with chains, a preacher? I don't understand!"

"But who calls me that?"

I told him; he listened very attentively, but stopped the conversation.

I simply can't remember what occasioned this conversation, which was so memorable for me; but he even became irritated, which almost never happened with him. He had spoken passionately and without mockery, as if he weren't saying it to me. But once again I didn't believe him: could he really speak seriously about such things with the likes of me?

Chapter Two

I

On that morning, the fifteenth of November, I precisely found him with "Prince Seryozha." It was I who brought him together with the prince, but they had enough points of contact even without me (I'm speaking of those former stories abroad and so on). Besides that, the prince had given his word to allot him at least one-third of the inheritance, which would certainly come to about twenty thousand. To me, I remember, it was terribly strange then that he allotted him only a third and not a whole half; but I said nothing. The prince gave this promise then on his own; Versilov had no part in it, never mentioned it by half a little word; the prince himself popped up with it, and Versilov only allowed it silently and never once recalled it afterwards, never even showed by a look that he remembered anything at all about the promise. I'll note incidentally that the prince was decidedly charmed by him at first, especially by his talk, he even went into raptures and several times spoke of it to me. Sometimes, alone with me, he exclaimed about himself, almost in despair, that he was "so uneducated, that he was on such a false path!..." Oh, we were still such friends then!... I kept trying then to instill only good things about the prince into Versilov, I defended his failings, though I saw them myself; but Versilov kept silent or smiled.

"If he does have failings, he has at least as many virtues as failings!" I once exclaimed, alone with Versilov.

"God, how you flatter him," he laughed.

"How do you mean, flatter?" I didn't understand at first.

"As many virtues! Why, then his relics will be revealed,[17] if he has as many virtues as he has failings!"

But, of course, this was not an opinion. Generally he somehow avoided speaking about the prince then, as he generally did about all essentials; but about the prince especially. I already suspected even then that he went to see the prince without me as well, and that they had special relations, but I allowed for that. I also wasn't jealous that he talked with him as if more seriously than with me, more positively, so to speak, and was less given to mockery; but I was so happy then that it even pleased me. I also excused it by the fact that the prince was slightly limited, and therefore liked precision in words, and even didn't understand certain witticisms at all. And then, recently, he somehow began to emancipate himself. His feelings towards Versilov began to change, as it were. The sensitive Versilov noticed it. I'll also say beforehand that at that time the prince changed towards me as well, even all too visibly; there remained only some dead forms of our original, almost ardent friendship. Yet I still kept going to see him; I could hardly not go, however, having been drawn into all that. Oh, how unskillful I was then, and can it be that stupidity of heart alone can drive a person to such incompetence and humiliation? I took money from him and thought that it was nothing, that it was even right. Not so, however; I knew even then that it was wrong, but—I simply gave it little thought. It wasn't for money that I went to see him, though I needed money terribly. I knew that I didn't go there because of money, but I realized that I came every day to take money. But I was in a whirl and, besides all that, something else was in my soul then—was singing in my soul!

When I came in, at around eleven o'clock in the morning, I found Versilov just finishing some long tirade; the prince was listening, pacing the room, and Versilov was sitting down. The prince seemed to be somewhat agitated. Versilov could almost always make him agitated. The prince was an extremely susceptible being, naïvely so, which on many occasions made me look on him condescendingly. But, I repeat, in the last few days something spitefully tooth-baring had appeared in him. He stopped when he saw me, and something as if twitched in his face. I knew in myself what explained that shadow of displeasure that morning, but I hadn't expected his face to twitch so much. It was known to me that he had accumulated all sorts of troubles, but the disgusting thing was that I knew only the tenth part of them—the rest was a hard and fast secret for me. Therefore it was disgusting and stupid that I got at him so often with my consolations, with advice, and even grinned condescendingly at his weakness of getting beside himself "over such trifles." He said nothing, but it was impossible for him not to hate me terribly at such moments; I was in all too false a position and didn't even suspect it. Oh, God is my witness, I didn't suspect the main thing!

Nevertheless, he politely offered me his hand, and Versilov nodded his head without interrupting his speech. I sprawled on the sofa. What tone I had then, what manners! I pranced still more, treating his acquaintances as my own... Oh, if it were possible to do it all over again now, I'd know how to behave myself very differently!

Two words, so as not to forget: the prince was living in the same apartment then, but occupied almost all of it; the owner of the apartment, Mrs. Stolbeev, had stayed for only a month and gone off somewhere again.

II

THEY WERE TALKING about the nobility. I'll note that this idea sometimes troubled the prince very much, despite all his air of progressism, and I even suspect that much that was bad in his life came and originated from this idea; valuing his princehood and being destitute, he squandered money all his life out of false pride and got entangled in debts. Versilov hinted to him several times that this was not what made for princehood, and wanted to implant a higher notion in his heart; but in the end it was as if the prince began to be offended at being taught. Evidently there had been something of the sort that morning, but I didn't catch the beginning. Versilov's words seemed retrograde to me at first, but then he got better.

"The word 'honor' means duty," he said (I'm conveying only the sense, as far as I remember it). "When the state is ruled by a dominant estate, the land stands firm. The dominant estate always has its honor and its profession of honor, which may also be wrong, but which almost always serves to bind and strengthen the land; it is useful morally, but more so politically. But the slaves suffer, that is, all who do not belong to that estate. So that they won't suffer, they are granted equal rights. That has been done with us as well, and it's splendid. But by all experience, everywhere so far (in Europe, that is), with the equalizing of rights has come a lowering of the sense of honor and therefore of duty. Egoism has replaced the former binding idea, and everything has broken down into the freedom of persons. Set free, left without a binding thought, they have finally lost all higher connection to such a degree that they have even stopped defending the freedom they obtained. But the Russian type of nobility has never resembled the European. Even now our nobility, having lost its rights, could remain a higher estate as the guardian of honor, light, science, and the higher idea, and, above all, without shutting itself up in a separate caste, which would be the death of the idea. On the contrary, the gateway to this estate was thrown open with us all too long ago; and now the time has come to open it definitively. Let every deed of honor, science, and valor give anyone the right to join the higher category of people. In this way the estate turns by itself into what is merely a gathering of the best people, in the literal and true sense, and not in the former sense of a privileged caste. In this new or, better, renewed form, the estate might hold out."

The prince bared his teeth:

"What kind of nobility would it be then? That's some sort of Masonic lodge you're planning, not a nobility."

I repeat, the prince was terribly uneducated. I even swung around on the sofa in vexation, though I did not quite agree with Versilov. Versilov understood only too well that the prince was showing his teeth.

"I don't know in what sense you spoke of Masonry," he replied, "however, if even a Russian prince rejects such an idea, then, naturally, its time hasn't come yet. The idea of honor and enlightenment as the covenant of each one who wants to join the estate, which is open and continually renewed, is of course a utopia, but why is it impossible? If this thought still lives, though only in a few heads, it's not lost yet, but shines like a fiery spot in the deep darkness."

"You love to use the words 'higher thought,' 'great thought,' 'binding idea,' and so on. I'd like to know, what essentially do you mean by the words 'a great thought'?"

"I really don't know how to answer you on that, my dear prince." Versilov smiled subtly. "If I confess to you that I'm unable to answer it myself, that would be more accurate. A great thought is most often a feeling that sometimes goes without definition for too long. I know only that it was always that from which living life flowed—that is, not mental and contrived, but, on the contrary, amusing and gay; so that the higher idea from which it flows is decidedly necessary, to the general vexation, of course."

"Why vexation?"

"Because it's boring to live with ideas, and without ideas it's always fun."

The prince ate the pill.

"And what, in your opinion, is this living life?" (He was obviously angry.)

"I don't know that either, Prince; I only know that it must be something terribly simple, most ordinary, staring us in the face every day and every minute, and so simple that we just can't believe it could be so simple, and naturally we've been passing it by for many thousands of years now without noticing or recognizing it."

"I only wanted to say that your idea of the nobility is at the same time a denial of the nobility," said the prince.

"Well, since you're so insistent, maybe the nobility never existed among us."

"This is all terribly obscure and vague. If you speak, then, in my opinion, you have to develop..."

The prince furrowed his brow and glanced fleetingly at the wall clock. Versilov got up and took his hat.

"Develop?" he said. "No, better not develop, and what's more it's my passion—to speak without developing. That's really so. And here's another strange thing: if it happens that I begin to develop a thought I believe in, the result is almost always that by the end of the explanation I myself have ceased to believe in what I've explained. I'm afraid I'll fall into that now, too. Good-bye, dear Prince; I'm always unpardonably garrulous with you."

He left. The prince politely saw him off, but I felt offended.

"What are you so ruffled up for?" he suddenly shot out, not looking and walking past me to the desk.

"I'm ruffled up," I began with a tremor in my voice, "because, finding such a strange change in your tone towards me and even towards Versilov, I... Of course, Versilov maybe did begin in a somewhat retrograde way, but he got better and... his words maybe contained a profound thought, but you simply didn't understand and..."

"I simply don't want anybody popping up to teach me and considering me a little boy!" he snapped almost with wrath.

"Prince, such words..."

"Please, no theatrical gestures—do me a favor. I know that what I'm doing is mean, that I'm a squanderer, a gambler, maybe a thief... yes, a thief, because I lost my family's money at gambling, but I don't want any judges over me. Don't want it and won't allow it. I'm my own judge. And why these ambiguities? If he wanted to say something to me, then speak directly and don't prophesy in a foggy muddle. But to say that to me, you've got to have the right, you've got to be honorable yourself..."

"First of all, I didn't catch the beginning and don't know what you were talking about, and second, how is Versilov dishonorable, may I ask?"

"Enough, I beg you, enough. Yesterday you asked for three hundred roubles—here it is..." He put the money on the table in front of me, and himself sat in an armchair, leaned back nervously, and crossed one leg over the other. I stopped in embarrassment.

"I don't know..." I murmured, "I did ask you... and I need the money very badly now, but in view of such a tone..."

"Forget the tone. If I said anything sharp, forgive me. I assure you, I have other things on my mind. Listen to this: I've received a letter from Moscow; my brother Sasha—he's still a child, you know—died four days ago. My father, as you're also aware, has been paralyzed for two years, and now they write that he's worse, can't say a word, and doesn't recognize anybody. They're glad of the inheritance there and want to take him abroad; but the doctor writes to me that it's unlikely he'll live even two weeks. Which means that mother, my sister, and I are left, and that means I'm almost alone now... Well, in short, I'm alone... This inheritance... This inheritance—oh, maybe it would be better if it didn't come at all! But here's precisely what I wanted to tell you: I promised Andrei Petrovich a minimum of twenty thousand from this inheritance... And meanwhile, imagine, owing to formalities, so far it's been impossible to do anything. I even... we, that is... that is, my father hasn't come into possession of this estate yet. Meanwhile, I've lost so much money these last three weeks, and that scoundrel Stebelkov charges such interest... I've now given you almost the last..."

"Oh, Prince, if so..."

"I don't mean that, I don't mean that. Stebelkov is sure to bring some today, and I'll have enough to tide me over, but devil knows about this Stebelkov! I begged him to get me ten thousand, so that I could at least give ten thousand to Andrei Petrovich. My promise to allot him a third torments me, tortures me. I gave my word and I must keep it. And, I swear to you, I'm dying to free myself of obligations at least on that side. They're a burden to me, a burden, unbearable! This burdensome connection... I can't see Andrei Petrovich, because I can't look him straight in the eye... Why, then, does he abuse it?"

"What does he abuse, Prince?" I stopped before him in amazement. "Has he ever as much as hinted to you?"

"Oh, no, and I appreciate that, but I've hinted to myself. And, finally, I'm getting sucked in deeper and deeper... This Stebelkov..."

"Listen, Prince, please calm down. I see that the longer you go on, the more troubled you become, and yet maybe it's all just a mirage. Oh, I've gotten in deep myself, unpardonably, meanly; but I know it's only temporary... I just need to win back a certain figure, and then tell me, with this three hundred, I owe you about two thousand five hundred, is that right?"

"I don't believe I asked you for it," the prince suddenly snarled.

"You say: ten thousand to Versilov. If I do borrow from you now, then, of course, this money will be credited against Versilov's twenty thousand; I won't allow it otherwise. But... but I'll probably pay it back myself... No, can you possibly think Versilov comes to you for money?"

"It would be easier for me if he did come to me for money," the prince uttered mysteriously.

"You speak of some 'burdensome connection'... If you mean with Versilov and me, then, by God, that is offensive. And, finally, you say, why isn't he like what he teaches—that's your logic! And, first of all, it's not logic, allow me to inform you of that, because even if he weren't, he could still preach the truth... And, finally, what is this word 'preaches'? You say 'prophet.' Tell me, was it you who called him a 'women's prophet' in Germany?"

"No, it wasn't."

"Stebelkov told me it was you."

"He lied. I'm no expert at giving mocking nicknames. But if a man preaches honor, let him be honorable himself—that's my logic, and if it's wrong, it makes no difference. I want it to be so, and it will be so. And no one, no one dares to come and judge me in my own house and consider me a baby! Enough," he cried, waving his hand to keep me from going on. "Ah, at last!"

The door opened and Stebelkov came in.

III

HE WAS STILL the same, dressed in the same foppish clothes, thrust his chest out in the same way, looked with the same stupid gaze, had the same fancy about his own slyness, and was greatly pleased with himself. This time, as he came in, he looked around somehow strangely; there was something peculiarly cautious and keen in his gaze, as if he wanted to guess something from our physiognomies. However, he instantly calmed down, and a self-confident smile shone on his lips, that "ingratiatingly insolent" smile, which I still found unutterably vile.

I had long known that he tormented the prince greatly. He had already come once or twice while I was there. I . . . I also had had one contact with him that past month, but this time, for a certain reason, I was slightly surprised at his coming.

"One moment," the prince said to him without greeting him, and, turning his back to us, began taking the necessary papers and accounts out of his desk. As for me, I was decidedly offended by the prince's last words; the allusion to Versilov being dishonorable was so clear (and so astonishing!) that it was impossible to let it go without a radical explanation. But this was impossible in front of Stebelkov. I sprawled on the sofa again and opened a book that was lying in front of me.

"Belinsky, part two![18] That's something new; you wish to enlighten yourself?" I called out to the prince—very affectedly, it seems.

He was very busy and hurried, but he suddenly turned at my words.

"Leave that book alone, I beg you," he said sharply.

This was going beyond the limits, and above all—in front of Stebelkov! As if on purpose, Stebelkov grinned slyly and disgustingly, and nodded furtively to me towards the prince. I turned away from the stupid fellow.

"Don't be angry, Prince; I yield you up to the most important person, and efface myself for the time being . . ."

I decided to be casual.

"Is that me—the most important person?" Stebelkov picked up, merrily pointing his finger at himself.

"Yes, you; the most important person is you, and you know it yourself."

"No, sir, excuse me. There's a second person everywhere in the world. I am a second person. There's a first person, and there's a second person. The first person acts, and the second person takes. Which means the second person comes out as the first person, and the first person as the second person. Is that so or not?"

"It may be so, only as usual I don't understand you."

"Excuse me. There was a revolution in France and everybody was executed. Napoleon came and took everything. The revolution is the first person, and Napoleon the second person. But it turned out that Napoleon became the first person, and the revolution became the second person. Is that so or not?"

I'll note, incidentally, that in his speaking to me about the French Revolution, I saw something of his earlier slyness, which amused me greatly: he still continued to regard me as some sort of revolutionary, and each time he met me, he found it necessary to speak about something of that sort.

"Let's go," said the prince, and they both went out to the other room. Left alone, I decided definitively to give him back his three hundred roubles as soon as Stebelkov left. I had extreme need of this money, but I decided.

They stayed there for about ten minutes quite unheard, and suddenly began talking loudly. They both began talking, but the prince suddenly started to shout, as if in strong irritation, reaching the point of fury. He could sometimes be very hot-tempered, so that even I let it pass. But at that moment a footman came in to announce someone; I pointed him to their room, and everything instantly quieted down there. The prince quickly came out with a preoccupied face, but smiling; the footman rushed off, and half a minute later the prince's visitor came in.

This was an important visitor, with aiguillettes and a coronet, a gentleman of no more than thirty, of a high-society and rather stern appearance. I warn the reader that Prince Sergei Petrovich did not yet belong in any real sense to Petersburg high society, despite all his passionate desire (I knew about the desire), and so he must have terribly appreciated such a call. This acquaintance, as I was informed, had only just begun, after great efforts on the prince's part; the guest was now returning a visit, but unfortunately he had caught the host unawares. I saw with what suffering and what a lost look the prince turned for an instant to Stebelkov; but Stebelkov endured his gaze as if nothing was wrong and, without the slightest thought of effacing himself, casually sat down on the sofa and began ruffling his hair with his hand, probably as a token of independence. He even made some sort of important face—in short, he was decidedly impossible. As for me, I was certainly able to behave myself by then and, of course, would not have disgraced anyone, but what was my amazement when I caught that same lost, pitiful, and spiteful gaze of the prince on myself as well: it meant he was ashamed of us both and put me on a par with Stebelkov. This idea drove me to fury; I sprawled still more and began flipping through the book with such an air as if nothing concerned me. Stebelkov, on the contrary, goggled his eyes, leaned forward, and began listening to their conversation, probably supposing that this was both polite and amiable. The guest glanced once or twice at Stebelkov—and also at me, incidentally.

They began talking of family news; this gentleman had once known the prince's mother, who belonged to a well-known family. As far as I could conclude, the guest, despite his amiability and seeming ingenuousness of tone, was very stiff and, of course, valued himself enough to consider his visit a great honor even for whoever it might be. If the prince had been alone—that is, without us—I'm sure he would have been more dignified and resourceful; now, though, something peculiarly tremulous in his smile, maybe much too amiable, and some strange distractedness betrayed him.

They had not yet been sitting for five minutes when suddenly another guest was announced and, as if on purpose, also of a compromising sort. I knew this one well and had heard a lot about him, though he didn't know me at all. He was still a very young man, though already about twenty-three years old, charmingly dressed, of a good family, and a handsome fellow himself, but—unquestionably of bad society. A year ago he had still been serving in one of the most distinguished horse-guard regiments, but he had been forced to retire, and everyone knew the reasons why. His relations even published in the newspapers that they were not answerable for his debts, but he continued his carousing even now, obtaining money at ten percent a month, gambling terribly in the gambling houses, and squandering all he had on a notorious Frenchwoman. The thing was that about a week earlier he had managed to win some twelve thousand in one evening, and he was triumphant. He was on a friendly footing with the prince; they often gambled together as partners; but the prince even gave a start on seeing him, I noticed it from where I sat: this boy was as if in his own home everywhere, spoke loudly and gaily, was unembarrassed by anything, and said whatever came to his mind, and naturally it would never have come into his head that our host was trembling so before his guest on account of his company.

He came in, interrupting their conversation, and at once began telling about yesterday's gambling, even before he sat down.

"I believe you were also there," he turned at the third phrase to the important guest, taking him for one of his circle, but, seeing better immediately, he cried, "Ah, forgive me, but I took you also for someone from yesterday!"

"Alexei Vladimirovich Darzan, Ippolit Alexandrovich Nashchokin," the prince hastily introduced them. The boy could, after all, be presented: the family name was good and well-known, but he hadn't introduced us earlier, and we went on sitting in our corners. I decidedly did not want to turn my head to them; but Stebelkov, at the sight of the young man, began to grin joyfully and obviously threatened to start talking. I was even beginning to find it all amusing.

"I met you often last year at Countess Verigin's," said Darzan.

"I remember you, but then, I believe, you were in uniform," Nashchokin replied benignly.

"Yes, in uniform, but thanks to... Ah, Stebelkov, so you're here? What brings him here? It's precisely thanks to these fine sirs that I'm no longer in uniform," he pointed straight at Stebelkov and burst out laughing. Stebelkov, too, laughed joyfully, probably taking it as a compliment. The prince blushed and hastily turned to Nashchokin with some question, while Darzan went over to Stebelkov and began talking to him very vehemently about something, but now in a low voice.

"It seems you became very well acquainted with Katerina Nikolaevna Akhmakov abroad?" the guest asked the prince.

"Oh, yes, I knew..."

"It seems there will be some news here soon. They say she's going to marry Baron Bjoring."

"That's right!" cried Darzan.

"You... know it for certain?" the prince asked Nashchokin, visibly agitated and uttering his question with particular emphasis.

"I was told so; it seems people are already talking about it; however, I don't know for certain."

"Oh, it's certain!" Darzan went over to them. "Dubasov told me yesterday; he's always the first to know such news. And the prince ought to know..."

Nashchokin paused for Darzan and again addressed the prince: "She rarely appears in society now."

"Her father has been sick this last month," the prince observed somehow drily.

"She seems to be an adventurous lady!" Darzan blurted out suddenly.

I raised my head and straightened up.

"I have the pleasure of knowing Katerina Nikolaevna personally and take upon myself the duty of assuring you that all the scandalous rumors are nothing but lies and infamy . . . and have been invented by those . . . who circled around but didn't succeed."

Having broken off so stupidly, I fell silent, still looking at them all with a flushed face and sitting bolt upright. They all turned to me, but suddenly Stebelkov tittered; Darzan was struck at first, but then grinned.

"Arkady Makarovich Dolgoruky," the prince indicated me to Darzan.

"Ah, believe me, *Prince*," Darzan addressed me frankly and goodnaturedly, "I'm not speaking for myself; if there was any gossip, it wasn't I who spread it."

"Oh, I didn't mean you!" I answered quickly, but Stebelkov had already burst into inadmissible laughter, and that precisely, as became clear later, because Darzan had called me "prince." My infernal last name mucked things up here as well. Even now I blush at the thought that I—from shame, of course—did not dare at that moment to pick up this stupidity and declare aloud that I was simply Dolgoruky. It was the first time in my life that this had happened. Darzan gazed in perplexity at me and at the laughing Stebelkov.

"Ah, yes! Who was that pretty thing I just met on your stairs, sharp-eyed and fair-haired?" he suddenly asked the prince.

"I really don't know," the latter answered quickly, blushing.

"Then who would know?" Darzan laughed.

"Though it . . . it might have been . . ." the prince somehow faltered.

"It . . . but it was precisely his sister, Lizaveta Makarovna!" Stebelkov suddenly pointed at me. "Because I also met her earlier . . ."

"Ah, indeed!" the prince picked up, but this time with an extremely solid and serious expression on his face. "It must have been Lizaveta Makarovna, a close friend of Anna Fyodorovna Stolbeev, whose apartment I'm now living in. She must have come calling today on Darya Onisimovna, who is also a good friend of Anna Fyodorovna's and in charge of the house in her absence . . ."

That was all exactly how it was. This Darya Onisimovna was the mother of poor Olya, whose story I have already told and whom Tatyana Pavlovna finally sheltered with Mrs. Stolbeev. I knew perfectly well that Liza used to visit Mrs. Stolbeev and later occasionally visited poor Darya Onisimovna, whom they all came to love very much; but suddenly, after this, incidentally, extremely sensible statement from the prince, and especially after Stebelkov's stupid outburst, or maybe because I had just been called "prince," suddenly, owing to all that, I blushed all over. Fortunately, just then Nashchokin got up to leave; he offered his hand to Darzan as well. The moment Stebelkov and I were left alone, he suddenly started nodding to me towards Darzan, who was standing in the doorway with his back to us. I shook my fist at Stebelkov.

A minute later Darzan also left, having arranged with the prince to meet the next day without fail at some place they had already settled on—a gambling house, naturally. On his way out he shouted something to Stebelkov and bowed slightly to me. As soon as he went out, Stebelkov jumped up from his place and stood in the middle of the room with a raised finger:

"Last week that little squire pulled off the following stunt: he gave a promissory note and falsified Averyanov's name on it. And the nice little note still exists in that guise, only one doesn't do such things! It's criminal. Eight thousand."

"And surely it's you who have this note?" I glanced at him ferociously.

"I have a bank, sir, I have a *mont-de-piété*,* not promissory notes. Have you heard of such a *mont-de-piété* in Paris? Bread and charity for the poor. I have a *mont-de-piété* ..."

The prince stopped him rudely and spitefully:

"What are you doing here? Why did you stay?"

"Ah!" Stebelkov quickly began nodding with his eyes. "And that? What about that?"

"No, no, no, not that," the prince shouted and stamped his foot, "I told you!"

"Ah, well, if so ... then so ... Only it's not so ..."

He turned sharply and, inclining his head and rounding his back, suddenly left. The prince called after him when he was already in the doorway:

"Be it known to you, sir, that I am not afraid of you in the least!"

He was highly vexed, made as if to sit down, but, having glanced at me, did not. It was as if his glance was also saying to me, "Why are you also sticking around?"

"Prince," I tried to begin ...

"I really have no time, Arkady Makarovich, I'm about to leave."

*Pawn shop.

"One moment, Prince, it's very important to me; and, first of all, take back your three hundred."

"What's this now?"

He was pacing, but he paused.

"It's this, that after all that's happened... and what you said about Versilov, that he's dishonorable, and, finally, your tone all the rest of the time... In short, I simply can't accept."

"You've been *accepting* for a whole month, though."

He suddenly sat down on a chair. I stood by the table, flipping through Belinsky's book with one hand and holding my hat with the other.

"The feelings were different, Prince... And, finally, I'd never have brought it as far as a certain figure... This gambling... In short, I can't!"

"You simply haven't distinguished yourself in anything, and so you're frantic. I beg you to leave that book alone."

"What does 'haven't distinguished yourself' mean? And, finally, you almost put me on a par with Stebelkov in front of your guests."

"Ah, there's the answer!" he grinned caustically. "Besides, you were embarrassed that Darzan called you 'prince.'"

He laughed maliciously. I flared up:

"I don't even understand... I wouldn't take your princehood gratis..."

"I know your character. It was ridiculous the way you cried out in defense of Mme. Akhmakov... Leave the book alone!"

"What does that mean?" I also shouted.

"Le-e-eave the book alo-o-one!" he suddenly yelled, sitting up fiercely in his armchair, as if ready to charge.

"This goes beyond all limits," I said and quickly left the room. But before I reached the end of the hall, he called out to me from the door of the study:

"Come back, Arkady Makarovich! Come ba-a-ack! Come ba-a-ack right now!"

I paid no attention and walked on. He quickly overtook me, seized my arm, and dragged me back to the study. I didn't resist!

"Take it!" he said, pale with agitation, handing me the three hundred roubles I had left there. "You absolutely must take it... otherwise we... you absolutely must!"

"How can I take it, Prince?"

"Well, I'll ask your forgiveness, shall I? Well, forgive me!..."

"Prince, I always loved you, and if you also..."

"I also; take it..."

I took it. His lips were trembling.

"I understand, Prince, that you were infuriated by this scoundrel... but I won't take it, Prince, unless we kiss each other, as with previous quarrels..."

I was also trembling as I said it.

"Well, what softheartedness," the prince murmured with an embarrassed smile, but he leaned over and kissed me. I shuddered: in his face, at the moment of the kiss, I could decidedly read disgust.

"Did he at least bring you the money?..."

"Eh, it makes no difference."

"It's for you that I..."

"He did, he did."

"Prince, we used to be friends... and, finally, Versilov..."

"Well, yes, yes, all right!"

"And, finally, I really don't know ultimately, this three hundred..."

I was holding it in my hands.

"Take it, ta-a-ake it!" he smiled again, but there was something very unkind in his smile.

I took it.

Chapter Three

I

I TOOK IT because I loved him. To whoever doesn't believe it, I'll reply that at least at the moment when I took this money from him, I was firmly convinced that, if I had wanted to, I could very well have gotten it from another source. And therefore it means that I took it not out of extremity, but out of delicacy, only so as not to offend him. Alas, that was how I reasoned then! But even so I felt very oppressed on leaving him: I had seen an extraordinary change towards me that morning; there had never yet been such a tone; and against Versilov there was positive rebellion. Stebelkov, of course, had vexed him greatly with something earlier, but he had started even before Stebelkov. I'll repeat once more: it had been possible to notice a change compared with the beginning in all those recent days, but not like that, not to such a degree—that's the main thing.

The stupid news about this imperial aide-de-camp Baron Bjoring might have had an influence as well... I also left in agitation, but... That's just it, that something quite different was shining then, and I let so much pass before my eyes light-mindedly: I hastened to let it pass, I drove away all that was gloomy and turned to what was shining...

It was not yet one in the afternoon. From the prince, my Matvei drove me straight—will you believe to whom?—to Stebelkov! That's just it, that earlier that day he had surprised me not so much by his calling on the prince (because he had promised him to come), as by the fact that, though he winked at me out of his stupid habit, it was not at all on the subject I had expected. The evening before, I had received from him, through the city mail, a note I found quite mysterious, in which he urgently requested that I visit him precisely today, between one and two o'clock, and "that he could inform me of things I was not expecting." And yet just now, there at the prince's, he hadn't let anything show about the letter. What secrets could there be between Stebelkov and me? The idea was even ridiculous; but in view of everything that had happened, as I was going to him now, I even felt a little excited.

Of course, I turned to him for money once a couple of weeks before, and he was about to give it, but for some reason we had a falling-out then, and I didn't take it; he began muttering something vaguely then, as he usually does, and it seemed to me that he wanted to offer something, some special conditions; and since I treated him with decided condescension each time I met him at the prince's, I proudly cut off any thought of special conditions and left, despite the fact that he chased after me to the door. That time I borrowed from the prince.

Stebelkov lived completely by himself, and lived prosperously: an apartment of four splendid rooms, fine furniture, male and female servants, and some sort of housekeeper, rather elderly, however. I came in wrathfully.

"Listen, my dear fellow," I began from the doorway, "what, first of all, is the meaning of this note? I don't allow for any correspondence between myself and you. And why didn't you tell me what you wanted to earlier, right there at the prince's? I was at your service."

"And why did you also keep silent earlier and not ask?" he extended his mouth into a most self-satisfied smile.

"Because it's not I who have need of you, but you who have need of me," I cried, suddenly getting angry.

"Then why have you come to me, in that case?" he nearly jumped up and down with pleasure. I turned instantly and was about to leave, but he seized me by the shoulder.

"No, no, I was joking. It's an important matter; you'll see for yourself."

I sat down. I confess I was curious. We were sitting by the edge of a big writing table, facing each other. He smiled slyly and raised his finger.

"Please, without your sly tricks and without the finger, and above all without any allegories, but straight to business—otherwise I'm leaving!" I cried again in wrath.

"You're... proud!" he pronounced with some sort of stupid reproach, swinging himself towards me in his armchair and raising all the wrinkles on his forehead.

"One has to be with you!"

"You... took money from the prince today, three hundred roubles. I have money. My money's better."

"How do you know I took money?" I was terribly surprised. "Can he have told you that himself?"

"He told me. Don't worry, it was just so, side talk, it came up by the way, only just by the way, not on purpose. He told me. But it was possible not to take it from him. Is that so or not?"

"But I hear you fleece people at an unbearable rate."

"I have a *mont-de-piété*, but I don't fleece. I keep it only for friends, I don't lend to others. For others the *mont-de-piété* ..."

This *mont-de-piété* was the most ordinary lending of money on pledges, under some other name, in a different apartment, and it was flourishing.

"But I lend large sums to friends."

"What, is the prince such a friend of yours?"

"A frie-e-end; but... he talks through his hat. And he dare not talk through his hat."

"Why, is he so much in your hands? Does he owe a lot?"

"He... owes a lot."

"He'll pay you back; he's come into an inheritance..."

"That's not his inheritance. He owes me money, and he owes me other things. The inheritance isn't enough. I'll lend to you without interest."

"Also as 'to a friend'? How have I deserved it?" I laughed.

"You will deserve it." He again thrust his whole body towards me and was about to raise his finger.

"Stebelkov! No fingers, or else I leave."

"Listen... he may marry Anna Andreevna!" And he squinted his left eye infernally.

"Listen here, Stebelkov, the conversation is taking on such a scandalous character... How dare you mention the name of Anna Andreevna?"

"Don't be angry."

"I'm only listening unwillingly, because I clearly see some sort of trick here and want to find out... But I may lose control, Stebelkov!"

"Don't be angry, don't be proud. Don't be proud for a little while and listen; then you can be proud again. You do know about Anna Andreevna? That the prince may marry her... you do know?"

"I've heard about this idea, of course, and I know everything, but I've never said anything to the prince about this idea. I only know that this idea was born in the mind of old Prince Sokolsky, who is still sick; but I've never said anything or taken part in anything. As I'm telling you that solely by way of explanation, I'll allow myself to ask you, first: what made you start talking with me about this? And, second, can it be that the prince talks about such things with *you*?"

"He doesn't talk with me; he doesn't want to talk with me, but I talk with him, and he doesn't want to listen. He started yelling earlier."

"What else! I approve of him."

"Prince Sokolsky, the little old man, will give a big dowry with Anna Andreevna. She pleases him. Then Prince Sokolsky the suitor will pay me back all the money. And the non-money debt as well. He's sure to! But now he has no means to pay it back."

"But me, what do you need me for?"

"For the main question: you're an acquaintance; you know everybody there. You can find everything out."

"Ah, the devil... find what out?"

"Whether the prince wants it, whether Anna Andreevna wants it, whether the old prince wants it. Find out for certain."

"And you dare suggest that I be your spy, and do it for money!" I cried in indignation.

"Don't be proud, don't be proud. For just a little longer, don't be proud, for another five minutes." He sat me down again. He was evidently not afraid of my gestures and exclamations; but I decided to listen to the end.

"I need to find out soon, very soon, because... because soon it may be too late. Did you see how he ate the pill earlier, when the officer began talking about the baron and Mme. Akhmakov?"

It was decidedly humiliating to listen further, but my curiosity was invincibly enticed.

"Listen, you... you worthless man!" I said resolutely. "If I sit here and listen and allow you to speak of such persons... and even answer you myself, it's not at all because I allow you that right. I simply see some sort of meanness... And, first of all, what hopes can the prince have regarding Katerina Nikolaevna?"

"None, but he's frantic."

"That's not true."

"Frantic. Which means that Mme. Akhmakov is now—a pass. He's lost a trick here. Now he's only got Anna Andreevna. I'll give you two thousand... with no interest and no promissory note."

Having said this, he leaned back resolutely and importantly in his chair and goggled his eyes at me. I was also all eyes.

"Your suit comes from Bolshaya Millionnaya;[19] you need money,

money; my money's better than his. I'll give you more than two thousand."

"But what for? What for, devil take it?"

I stamped my foot. He leaned towards me and said expressively:

"So that you won't interfere."

"But it's no concern of mine anyway," I cried.

"I know you're keeping quiet. That's good."

"I don't need your approval. For my own part, I very much wish for it, but I consider that it's none of my business, and that it would even be indecent of me."

"You see, you see—indecent!" he raised his finger.

"See what?"

"Indecent... Heh!" and he suddenly laughed. "I understand, I understand that it's indecent for you, but... you're not going to interfere?" he winked, but in this winking there was something so insolent, even jeering, base! He precisely supposed some sort of baseness in me and was counting on that baseness... That was clear, but I still didn't understand what it was about.

"Anna Andreevna is also your sister, sir," he uttered imposingly.

"Don't you dare speak of that. And generally don't you dare speak of Anna Andreevna."

"Don't be proud, just for one more little minute! Listen: he'll get the money and provide for everybody," Stebelkov said weightily, "everybody, *everybody*, you follow?"

"So you think I'll take money from him?"

"Aren't you taking it now?"

"I'm taking my own!"

"What's your own?"

"This is Versilov's money; he owes Versilov twenty thousand."

"Versilov, not you."

"Versilov's my father."

"No, you're Dolgoruky, not Versilov."

"That makes no difference!"

Indeed, I was able to reason like that then. I knew it made a difference, I wasn't so stupid, but I reasoned like that then, again, out of "delicacy."

"Enough!" I cried. "I understand precisely nothing. And how dared you summon me for such trifles?"

"Can it be you really don't understand? Are you doing it on purpose or not?" Stebelkov said slowly, staring at me piercingly and with some sort of mistrustful smile.

"By God, I don't!"

"I say he can provide for everybody, *everybody*, only don't interfere and don't talk him out of it..."

"You must have lost your mind! What's this 'everybody' you keep trotting out? Is it Versilov he'll provide for?"

"You're not the only one in it, nor is Versilov... there are others. And Anna Andreevna is as much a sister to you *as Lizaveta Makarovna*!"

I stared at him goggle-eyed. Suddenly something like pity for me flashed in his vile gaze:

"You don't understand, and so much the better! It's good, it's very good that you don't understand. It's praiseworthy... if you really don't understand."

I became completely furious:

"Away with you and your trifles, you crazy man!" I cried, seizing my hat.

"They're not trifles! So it's a deal? But, you know, you'll come again."

"No," I snapped from the doorway.

"You'll come, and then... then there'll be a different talk. That will be the main talk. Two thousand, remember!"

II

HE MADE SUCH a filthy and murky impression on me that, going out, I even tried not to think of it and only spat. The idea that the prince could speak with him about me and this money pricked me as if with a pin. "I'll win and pay him back today," I thought resolutely.

Stupid and tongue-tied as Stebelkov was, I had seen a blazing scoundrel in all his splendor, and, above all, there certainly was some intrigue here. Only I had no time to go into any intrigues, and that was the main reason for my hen-blindness! I glanced worriedly at my watch, but it wasn't even two yet; that meant I could still make one visit, otherwise I'd have died of excitement before three o'clock. I drove to see Anna Andreevna Versilov, my sister. I had long ago become close with her at my little old prince's, precisely during his illness. The thought that I hadn't seen him for three or four days now nagged at my conscience, but it was precisely Anna Andreevna who helped me out: the prince was extremely taken with her and, to me, even called her his guardian angel. Incidentally, the thought of marrying her to Prince Sergei Petrovich had indeed been born in the old man's head, and he had even told me of it more than once, in secret, of course. I had conveyed this idea to Versilov, having noticed before that, for all the essential things to which Versilov was so indifferent, nevertheless he was always somehow especially interested when I told him something about my meetings with Anna Andreevna. Versilov had muttered to me then that Anna Andreevna was all too intelligent and, in such a ticklish matter, could do without other people's advice. Naturally, Stebelkov was right that the old man would give her a dowry, but how could he dare to count on anything here? Today the prince had shouted after him that he wasn't afraid of him at all. Had Stebelkov indeed talked with him in his study about Anna Andreevna? I can imagine how infuriated I'd have been in his place.

Lately I had even been at Anna Andreevna's quite often. But here one strange thing always happened: it was always she herself who invited me to come, and she certainly always expected me, but when I entered, she unfailingly made it seem that I had come unexpectedly and unintendedly. I noticed this feature in her, but I became attached to her all the same. She lived with Mme. Fanariotov, her grandmother, as her ward, of course (Versilov gave nothing to provide for them)—but in a far different role from that in which wards are usually described in the houses of aristocratic ladies, for instance, the old countess's ward in Pushkin's "Queen of Spades."[20] Anna Andreevna was like a countess herself. She lived completely separately in this house, that is, on the same floor and in the same apartment as the Fanariotovs, but in two separate rooms, so that, for instance, coming and going, I never once met any of the Fanariotovs. She had the right to receive whomever she wanted, and to use her time however she liked. True, she was already going on twenty-three. During the last year, she had almost stopped appearing in society, though Mme. Fanariotov did not stint on expenses for her granddaughter, whom, as I heard, she loved very much. On the contrary, I precisely liked in Anna Andreevna the fact that I always found her in such modest dresses, always busy with something, with a book or handwork. There was something of the nunnery, almost nunlike, in the way she looked, and I liked that. She was not loquacious, but always spoke with weight, and was terribly good at listening, something I never knew how to do. When I told her that, though they didn't have a single feature in common, she nevertheless bore a great resemblance to Versilov, she always blushed slightly. She blushed often and always quickly, but always only slightly, and I came to like very much this particularity of her face. With her I never called Versilov by his last name, but always Andrei Petrovich, and that came about somehow by itself. I even noticed very well that, generally, at the Fanariotovs', they must have been somehow ashamed of Versilov; I noticed it, however, from Anna Andreevna alone, though once again I don't know if one can use the word "ashamed" here; anyhow, there was something of the sort. I also talked to her about Prince Sergei Petrovich, and she listened very much and, it seemed to me, was interested in this information; but somehow it always happened that I told her things myself, while she never asked. Of the possibility of a marriage between them, I never dared to speak with her, though I often wished to, because I partly liked the idea myself. But in her room I stopped somehow venturing to talk about terribly many things, and, on the contrary, I found it terribly good to be in her room. I also liked it very much that she was very educated and had read a lot, and even serious books; she had read much more than I had.

She herself invited me to come the first time. I understood even then that she was maybe counting on occasionally worming a thing or two out of me. Oh, many people could have wormed a great many things out of me then! "But what of it," I thought, "she's not receiving me for that alone." In short, I was even glad that I could be of use to her, and... and when I sat with her, it aways seemed to me within myself that it was my sister sitting near me, though, incidentally, we never once spoke of our relation to each other, not a word, not a hint, as if it simply didn't exist. Sitting at her place, it seemed to me somehow quite unthinkable to start talking about it, and, really, looking at her, an absurd thought sometimes came to my head, that she maybe didn't know about this relation at all—so far as the way she behaved with me went.

III

On entering, I suddenly found Liza with her. It almost struck me. I was very well aware that they had seen each other before; it had happened at the "nursing baby's." I may tell later, if there's space, about this fantasy of the proud and modest Anna Andreevna's to see this baby, and about her meeting Liza there; but all the same I never expected that Anna Andreevna would ever invite Liza to her place. This struck me pleasantly. Not letting it show, naturally, I greeted Anna Andreevna and, warmly pressing Liza's hand, sat down beside her. The two women were busy with *work*: on the table and on their knees lay an evening dress of Anna Andreevna's, expensive but old, that is, worn three times, which she wanted to alter somehow. Liza was a great "expert" in such matters and had taste, and so a solemn council of "wise women" was taking place. I remembered Versilov and laughed; and anyhow I was in the most radiant spirits.

"You're very cheerful today, and that's very pleasant," said Anna Andreevna, articulating the words imposingly and distinctly. Her voice was a dense and sonorous contralto, but she always spoke calmly and softly, always lowering her long lashes slightly, and with a smile barely flitting over her pale face.

"Liza knows how unpleasant I am when I'm not cheerful," I replied cheerfully.

"Maybe Anna Andreevna knows about that, too," the mischievous Liza needled me. The dear! If only I had known what was in her heart then!

"What are you doing now?" asked Anna Andreevna. (I'll note that she had precisely even asked me to call on her today.)

"I'm now sitting here and asking myself: why is it always more pleasant for me to find you over a book than over handwork? No, really, handwork doesn't suit you for some reason. In that sense I take after Andrei Petrovich."

"You still haven't made up your mind to enter the university?"

"I'm only too grateful that you haven't forgotten our conversations; that means you think of me occasionally; but... I haven't formed my idea yet concerning the university, and besides I have goals of my own."

"That is, he has his secret," observed Liza.

"Drop your jokes, Liza. A certain intelligent man said the other day that, with all this progressive movement of ours in the last twenty years, we've proved first of all that we're filthily uneducated. Here, of course, he was also speaking of our university men."

"Well, surely papa said that; you repeat his thoughts terribly often," observed Liza.

"Liza, it's as if you don't believe I have a mind of my own."

"In our time it's useful to listen to the words of intelligent people and remember them," Anna Andreevna defended me a little.

"Precisely, Anna Andreevna," I picked up hotly. "Whoever doesn't think about Russia's present moment is not a citizen! Maybe I look at Russia from a strange viewpoint: we lived through the Tartar invasion, then through two centuries of slavery,[21] and that, certainly, because both the one and the other were to our liking. Now we've been given freedom, and we have to endure freedom. Will we be able to? Will freedom prove as much to our taste? That's the question."

Liza glanced quickly at Anna Andreevna, who looked down at once and began searching for something around her; I saw that Liza was trying as hard as she could to control herself, but somehow accidentally our eyes suddenly met, and she burst out laughing. I flared up:

"Liza, you're inconceivable!"

"Forgive me!" she said suddenly, ceasing to laugh and almost with sadness. "I've got God knows what in my head..."

And it was as if tears suddenly trembled in her voice. I felt terribly ashamed; I took her hand and kissed it hard.

"You're very kind," Anna Andreevna observed to me softly, seeing me kiss Liza's hand.

"I'm glad most of all, Liza, that I find you laughing this time," I said. "Would you believe it, Anna Andreevna, these past few days she met me each time with some strange look, and in this look there was as if a question: 'So, have you found anything out? Is everything going well?' Really, there's something like that with her."

Anna Andreevna gave her a slow and keen look. Liza dropped her eyes. I could see very well, however, that the two were much better and more closely acquainted than I'd have supposed when I came in earlier. The thought pleased me.

"You just said I was kind; you won't believe how the whole of me changes for the better with you, and how pleasant it is for me to be with you, Anna Andreevna," I said with feeling.

"And I'm very glad you say that to me precisely now," she replied meaningly. I must say that she never talked to me about my disorderly life and of the abyss I had plunged into, though I knew she not only knew about it all, but even made inquiries indirectly. So that now it was like a first hint, and—my heart turned to her still more.

"How's our invalid?" I asked.

"Oh, he's much better. He's walking, and he went for a ride

yesterday and today. But didn't you go to see him today either? He's waiting so much for you."

"I'm guilty towards him, but you visit him now and have fully replaced me. He's a great traitor and has exchanged me for you."

She made a very serious face, very possibly because my joke was trivial.

"I was at Prince Sergei Petrovich's today," I began to mutter, "and I... By the way, Liza, did you go to see Darya Onisimovna today?"

"Yes, I did," she answered somehow curtly, not raising her head. "It seems you go to see the sick prince every day?" she asked somehow suddenly, maybe in order to say something.

"Yes, I go to see him, only I don't get there," I smiled. "I go in and turn left."

"Even the prince has noticed that you go to see Katerina Nikolaevna very often. He mentioned it yesterday and laughed," said Anna Andreevna.

"At what? What did he laugh at?"

"He was joking, you know. He said that, on the contrary, a young and beautiful woman always produces an impression of indignation and wrath in a young man your age..." Anna Andreevna suddenly laughed.

"Listen... you know, that was a terribly apt remark he made," I cried. "Probably it wasn't he, but you who said it to him?"

"Why so? No, it was he."

"Well, but if this beauty pays attention to him, despite his being so insignificant, standing in the corner, angry at being 'little,' and suddenly prefers him to the whole crowd of surrounding admirers, what then?" I asked suddenly, with a most bold and defiant look. My heart began to pound.

"Then you'll just perish right in front of her," Liza laughed.

"Perish?" I cried. "No, I won't perish. I don't believe I'll perish. If a woman stands across my path, then she must follow after me. You don't block my path with impunity..."

Liza once said to me in passing, recalling it long afterwards, that I uttered this phrase then terribly strangely, seriously, and as if suddenly growing pensive; but at the same time "so ridiculously that it was impossible to control oneself." Indeed, Anna Andreevna again burst out laughing.

"Laugh, laugh at me!" I exclaimed in intoxication, because I was terribly pleased with this whole conversation and the direction it had taken. "From you it only gives me pleasure. I love your laughter, Anna Andreevna! You have this feature: you keep silent and suddenly burst out laughing, instantly, so that even an instant earlier one couldn't have guessed it by your face. I knew a lady in Moscow, distantly, I watched her from a corner. She was almost as beautiful as you are, but she couldn't laugh the way you do, and her face, which was as attractive as yours—lost its attraction; but yours is terribly attractive... precisely for that ability... I've long been wanting to tell you."

When I said of the lady that "she was as beautiful as you are," I was being clever: I pretended that it had escaped me accidentally, as if I hadn't even noticed; I knew very well that women value such "escaped" praise more highly than any polished compliment you like. And much as Anna Andreevna blushed, I knew it pleased her. And I invented the lady; I didn't know any such lady in Moscow, it was only so as to praise Anna Andreevna and please her.

"One truly might think," she said with a charming smile, "that you've been under the influence of some beautiful woman recently."

It was as if I were flying off somewhere... I even wanted to reveal something to them... but I restrained myself.

"And by the way, not long ago you spoke of Katerina Nikolaevna quite hostilely."

"If I ever said anything bad," I flashed my eyes, "the blame for it goes to the monstrous slander against her that she was Andrei Petrovich's enemy; the slander against him, too, that he was supposedly in love with her, had proposed to her, and similar absurdities. This idea is as outrageous as another slander against her, that, supposedly while her husband was still alive, she had promised Prince Sergei Petrovich that she would marry him when she was widowed, and then didn't keep her word. But I know firsthand that all this wasn't so, but was only a joke. I know it firsthand. Abroad there, once, in a joking moment, she indeed told the prince 'maybe,' in the future; but what could it have signified besides just a light word? I know only too well that the prince, for his part, cannot attach any value to such a promise, and he has no intentions anyway," I added, catching myself. "He seems to have quite different ideas," I put in slyly. "Today Nashchokin said at his place that Katerina Nikolaevna is supposedly going to marry Baron Bjoring: believe me, he bore this news in the best possible way, you may be sure."

"Nashchokin was there?" Anna Andreevna suddenly asked weightily and as if in surprise.

"Oh, yes. He seems to be one of those respectable people..."

"And Nashchokin spoke with him about this marriage to Bjoring?" Anna Andreevna suddenly became very interested.

"Not about the marriage, but just so, of the possibility, as a rumor; he said there was supposedly such a rumor in society; as for me, I'm sure it's nonsense."

Anna Andreevna pondered, and bent over her sewing.

"I like Prince Sergei Petrovich," I suddenly added warmly. "He has his shortcomings, indisputably, I've already told you—namely, a certain one-idea-ness—but his shortcomings also testify to a nobility of soul, isn't it true? Today, for instance, he and I nearly quarreled over an idea: his conviction that if you speak about nobility, you should be noble yourself, otherwise all you say is a lie. Well, is that logical? And yet it testifies to the lofty demands of honor in his soul, of duty, of justice, isn't it true?... Ah, my God, what time is it?" I suddenly cried, happening to glance at the face of the mantelpiece clock.

"Ten minutes to three," she said calmly, glancing at the clock. All the while I spoke of the prince, she listened to me, looking down with a sort of sly but sweet smile: she knew why I was praising him so. Liza listened, her head bent over her work, and for some time had not interfered in the conversation.

I jumped up as if burnt.

"Are you late somewhere?"

"Yes... no... I am late, though, but I'll go right now. Just one word, Anna Andreevna," I began excitedly, "I can't help telling you today! I want to confess to you that I've already blessed several times the kindness and delicacy with which you have invited me to visit you... Being acquainted with you has made a very strong impression on me. It's as if here in your room my soul is purified and I go away better than I am. It's really so. When I sit beside you, I not only can't speak about bad things, but I can't even have bad thoughts; they disappear in your presence, and if I remember something bad in your presence, I'm at once ashamed of this bad thing, grow timid, and blush in my soul. And, you know, it was especially pleasing to me to meet my sister here with you today... It testifies to such nobility of your... to such a beautiful attitude... In short, it speaks for something so *brotherly*, if you will allow me to break this ice, that I..."

As I spoke, she was rising from her seat, turning more and more red; but it was as if she was suddenly frightened by something, by some line that ought not to have been overleaped, and she quickly interrupted me:

"Believe me, I shall know how to appreciate your feelings with all my heart... I understood them without words... and already long ago..."

She paused in embarrassment, pressing my hand. Suddenly Liza tugged at my sleeve unobserved. I said good-bye and went out; but in the next room Liza caught up with me.

IV

"LIZA, WHY DID you tug at my sleeve?" I asked.

"She's nasty, she's cunning, she's not worth... She keeps you in order to worm things out of you," she whispered in a quick, spiteful whisper. I'd never seen her with such a face before.

"Liza, God help you, she's such a lovely girl!"

"Well, then I'm nasty."

"What's the matter with you?"

"I'm very bad. She's maybe the loveliest of girls, but I'm bad. Enough, drop it. Listen: mama asks you about something 'that she doesn't dare speak of,' as she said. Arkady, darling! Stop gambling, dear, I beseech you... mama, too..."

"Liza, I know it myself, but... I know it's a pathetic weakness, but... it's only trifles and nothing more! You see, I got into debt, like a fool, and I want to win only so as to pay it back. It's possible to win, because I played without calculation, off the cuff, like a fool, but now I'll tremble over each rouble... I won't be myself if I don't win! I haven't taken to it; it's not the main thing, it's just in passing, I assure you! I'm too strong not to stop when I want to. I'll pay back the money, and then I'm yours undividedly, and tell mama that I'll never leave you..."

"Those three hundred roubles today cost you something!"

"How do you know?" I gave a start.

"Darya Onisimovna heard everything..."

But at that moment Liza suddenly pushed me behind the curtain, and the two of us found ourselves in what's known as a "lantern," that is, a round, bay-windowed little room. Before I managed to come to my senses, I heard a familiar voice, the clank of spurs, and guessed at the familiar stride.

"Prince Seryozha," I whispered.

"Himself," she whispered.

"Why are you so frightened?"

"I just am. I don't want him to meet me for anything..."

"*Tiens*, he's not dangling after you, is he?" I grinned. "He'll get it from me if he is. Where are you going?"

"Let's leave. I'll go with you."

"Did you say good-bye in there?"

"Yes, my coat's in the front hall..."

We left. On the stairs an idea struck me:

"You know, Liza, he may have come to propose to her!"

"N-no...he won't propose..." she said firmly and slowly, in a low voice.

"You don't know, Liza, I did quarrel with him today—since you've already been told of it—but, by God, I love him sincerely and wish him good luck here. We made peace today. When we're happy, we're so kind...You see, he has many splendid inclinations...and humaneness...The rudiments at least...and in the hands of such a firm and intelligent girl as Miss Versilov, he'd straighten out completely and be happy. It's too bad I have no time...ride with me a little, I could tell you something..."

"No, ride alone, I'm not going that way. Will you come for dinner?"

"I'll come, I'll come, as promised. Listen, Liza, a certain rotter—in short, the vilest of beings, well, Stebelkov, if you know him—has a terrible influence on his affairs...promissory notes...well, in short, he's got him in his hands, and has him so cornered, and he feels so humiliated himself, that the two of them see no other solution than to propose to Anna Andreevna. She really ought to be warned. However, it's nonsense, she'll set the whole matter to rights later. But will she refuse him? What do you think?"

"Good-bye, I have no time," Liza cut me off, and I suddenly saw so much hatred in her fleeting glance that I at once cried out in fright:

"Liza, dear, why that look?"

"It's not at you; only don't gamble..."

"Ah, you mean gambling! I won't, I won't."

"You just said, 'when we're happy'—so you're very happy?"

"Terribly, Liza, terribly! My God, it's already three o'clock, and past!...Good-bye, Lizok. Lizochka, dear, tell me: can one keep a woman waiting? Is that permissible?"

"At a rendezvous, you mean?" Liza smiled faintly, with some sort of dead, trembling little smile.

"Give me your hand for luck."

"For luck? My hand? Not for anything!"

And she quickly walked away. And, above all, she had cried out so seriously. I jumped into my sledge.

Yes, yes, and this "happiness" was the main reason why I, like a blind mole, neither understood nor saw anything except myself then!

Chapter Four

I

NOW I'M EVEN afraid to tell about it. It was all long ago; but now, too, it's like a mirage for me. How could such a woman arrange a rendezvous with such a vile little brat as I was then?—that's how it was at first sight! When I left Liza and rushed off, my heart pounding, I thought I'd simply lost my mind; the idea of an *appointed* rendezvous suddenly seemed to me such a glaring absurdity that it was impossible to believe it. And yet I had no doubts at all, even to this extent: the more glaring the absurdity, the more strongly I believed in it.

That it had already struck three worried me: "If I've been granted a rendezvous, how can I be late for the rendezvous?" I thought. Stupid questions also flashed, such as, "Which is better for me now—boldness or timidity?" But it all only flashed, because in my heart there was one main thing, and such as I couldn't define. What had been said the day before was this: "Tomorrow at three o'clock I'll be at Tatyana Pavlovna's"—that was all. But, first, she had always received me alone, in her room, and she could have told me all she liked without moving to Tatyana Pavlovna's; so why appoint another place at Tatyana Pavlovna's? And again a question: will Tatyana Pavlovna be at home, or won't she? If it's a rendezvous, then it means Tatyana Pavlovna won't be at home. And how to accomplish that without explaining it all to Tatyana Pavlovna beforehand? Which means that Tatyana Pavlovna is also in on the secret? This thought seemed wild to me and somehow unchaste, almost crude.

And, finally, she might simply have wanted to visit Tatyana Pavlovna and told me yesterday without any purpose, and I imagined all sorts of things. And it had been said so much in passing, carelessly, calmly, and after a rather boring séance, because all the while I had been at her place yesterday, I had been thrown off for some reason: I sat, mumbled, and didn't know what to say, grew terribly angry and timid, and she was going out somewhere, as it turned out afterwards, and was visibly glad when I got up to leave. All these considerations crowded in my head. I decided, finally, that I would go, ring the bell, the cook would open the door, and I would ask, "Is Tatyana Pavlovna at home?" If she wasn't, it meant "rendezvous." But I had no doubts, no doubts!

I ran up the stairs and—on the stairs, in front of the door, all my fear vanished. "Well, come what may," I thought, "only quickly!" The cook opened the door and, with her vile phlegm, grumbled that Tatyana Pavlovna was not at home. "And is there anyone else waiting for Tatyana Pavlovna?" I was about to ask, but didn't. "Better see for myself," and, muttering to the cook that I would wait, I threw off my coat and opened the door...

Katerina Nikolaevna was sitting by the window and "waiting for Tatyana Pavlovna."

"She's not here?" she suddenly asked me, as if with worry and vexation, the moment she saw me. Both her voice and her face corresponded so little with my expectations that I simply got mired on the threshold.

"Who's not here?" I murmured.

"Tatyana Pavlovna! Didn't I ask you yesterday to tell her I'd call on her at three o'clock?"

"I... I haven't seen her at all."

"You forgot?"

I sat down as if crushed. So that's how it turned out! And, above all, everything was as clear as two times two, and I—I still stubbornly believed.

"I don't even remember your asking me to tell her. And you didn't; you simply said you'd be here at three o'clock," I cut her short impatiently. I wasn't looking at her.

"Ah!" she suddenly cried. "So, if you forgot to tell her, and yet knew yourself that I would be here, so then what did you come here for?"

I raised my head. There was neither mockery nor wrath in her face, there was only her bright, cheerful smile and some sort of additional mischievousness in her expression—her perpetual expression, however—an almost childlike mischievousness. "There, you see, I've caught you out. Well, what are you going to say now?" her whole face all but said.

I didn't want to answer, and again looked down. The silence lasted for about half a minute.

"Are you just coming from *papà*?" she suddenly asked.

"I'm just coming from Anna Andreevna, and I wasn't at Prince Nikolai Ivanovich's at all... and you knew that," I suddenly added.

"Did anything happen to you at Anna Andreevna's?"

"That is, since I now have such a crazy look? No, I had a crazy look even before Anna Andreevna's."

"And you didn't get smarter at her place?"

"No, I didn't. Besides, I heard there that you were going to marry Baron Bjoring."

"Did she tell you that?" she suddenly became interested.

"No, I told her that, and I heard Nashchokin say it to Prince Sergei Petrovich today when he came to visit."

I still wouldn't raise my eyes to her; to look at her meant to be showered with light, joy, happiness, and I didn't want to be happy. The sting of indignation pierced my heart, and in a single instant I made a tremendous decision. Then I suddenly began to speak, I scarcely remember what about. I was breathless and mumbled somehow, but now I looked boldly at her. My heart was pounding. I began talking about something totally unrelated, though maybe it made sense. At first she listened with her steady, patient smile, which never left her face, but, little by little, astonishment and then even alarm flashed in her intent gaze. Her smile still didn't leave her, but the smile, too, as if trembled at times.

"What's the matter?" I suddenly asked, noticing that she was all atremble.

"I'm afraid of you," she replied almost anxiously.

"Why don't you leave? Look, since Tatyana Pavlovna isn't here now, and you knew she wouldn't be, doesn't that mean you should get up and leave?"

"I wanted to wait, but now... in fact..."

She made as if to rise.

"No, no, sit down," I stopped her. "There, you just trembled again, but you smile even when you're afraid... You always have a smile. There, now you're smiling completely..."

"Are you raving?"

"Yes."

"I'm afraid..." she whispered again.

"Of what?"

"That you'll... start breaking down the walls..." She smiled again, but this time indeed timidly.

"I can't bear your smile!..."

And I started talking again. It was just as if I was flying. As if something was pushing me. I had never, never talked with her like that, but always timidly. I was terribly timid now, too, but I went on talking; I remember I began talking about her face.

"I can't bear your smile anymore!" I suddenly cried. "Why did I imagine you as menacing, magnificent, and with sarcastic society phrases while I was in Moscow? Yes, in Moscow; I talked about you with Marya Ivanovna while I was still there, and we imagined you, how you must be... Do you remember Marya Ivanovna? You visited her. As I was coming here, I dreamed of you all night on the train. Before you arrived, I spent a whole month here looking at your portrait in your father's study, and guessed nothing. The expression of your face is childlike mischievousness and infinite simpleheartedness—there! I've marveled at that terribly all the while I've been coming to see you. Oh, you know how to look proud and crush one with your gaze. I remember how you looked at me at your father's when you came from Moscow then... I saw you then, and yet if I had been asked then, when I left, what you were like—I wouldn't have been able to tell. I couldn't even have said how tall you were. I saw you and just went blind. Your portrait doesn't resemble you at all: your eyes aren't dark, but light, and only seem dark because of your long lashes. You're plump, of average height, but your plumpness is firm, light, the plumpness of a healthy young village girl. And you have a perfect village face, the face of a village beauty—don't be offended, it's good, it's better—a round, ruddy, bright, bold, laughing, and... shy face! Really, it's shy. The shy face of Katerina Nikolaevna Akhmakov! Shy and chaste, I swear! More than chaste—childlike!—that's your face! I've been struck all this while, and all this while I've asked myself: is this that woman? I know now that you're very intelligent, but in the beginning I thought you were a bit simple. Your mind is gay, but without any embellishments... Another thing I like is that the smile never leaves you; that's my paradise! I also like your calmness, your quietness, and that you articulate your words smoothly, calmly, and almost lazily—I precisely like that laziness. It seems that if a bridge collapsed under you, even then you'd say something smooth and measured... I imagined you as the height of pride and passion, yet you've talked with me these two whole months like student to student... I never imagined your forehead was like that: it's slightly low, as in statues, but it's white and delicate as marble under your fluffy hair. You have a high bosom, a light step, you're of extraordinary beauty, yet you have no pride at all. I've come to believe it only now, I didn't believe it before!"

She listened wide-eyed to this whole wild tirade; she saw that I was trembling myself. She raised her gloved little hand several times in a sweet, cautious gesture, so as to stop me, but each time withdrew it in perplexity and fear. Now and then she even recoiled quickly with her whole body. Two or three times a smile glimmered again on her face; one time she blushed very much, but in the end she was decidedly frightened and began to turn pale. As soon as I paused, she reached out her hand and said in a sort of pleading but still smooth voice:

"You cannot speak like that . . . it's impossible to speak like that . . ."

And she suddenly got up from her place, unhurriedly taking her scarf and sable muff.

"You're going?" I cried.

"I'm decidedly afraid of you . . . you abuse . . ." she drew out as if with regret and reproach.

"Listen, by God, I won't break down any walls."

"But you've already started," she couldn't help herself and smiled. "I don't even know if you'll let me pass." And it seemed she truly was afraid that I wouldn't let her go.

"I'll open the door for you myself, you can go, but know this: I've made a tremendous decision; and if you want to give light to my soul, come back, sit down, and listen to just two words. But if you don't want to, then go, and I myself will open the door for you."

She looked at me and sat down.

"With what indignation another woman would have left, but you sat down!" I cried in ecstasy.

"You never allowed yourself to talk like this before."

"I was always timid before. Now, too, I walked in not knowing what to say. Do you think I don't feel timid now? I do. But I suddenly made a tremendous decision, and I feel I'll carry it out. And as soon as I made this decision, I lost my mind at once and began saying all that . . . Listen, here are my two words: am I your spy or not? Answer me—there's the question!"

Color quickly poured over her face.

"Don't answer yet, Katerina Nikolaevna, but listen to everything and then tell me the whole truth."

I broke all the barriers at once and flew off into space.

II

"TWO MONTHS AGO I stood here behind the curtain...you know...and you were talking with Tatyana Pavlovna about the letter. I ran out, beside myself, and said too much. You knew at once that I knew something...you couldn't help understanding...you were looking for an important document and were apprehensive about it... Wait, Katerina Nikolaevna, hold off from speaking yet. I declare to you that there were grounds for your suspicions: this document exists...that is, it did...I saw it; it's your letter to Andronikov, right?"

"You saw that letter?" she asked quickly, embarrassed and agitated. "Where did you see it?"

"I saw it...I saw it at Kraft's...the one who shot himself..."

"Really? You saw it yourself? What happened to it?"

"Kraft tore it up."

"In your presence? You saw it?"

"In my presence. He tore it up, probably, before his death... I didn't know then that he was going to shoot himself..."

"So it's destroyed, thank God!" she said slowly, with a sigh, and crossed herself.

I didn't lie to her. That is, I did lie, because the document was with me and had never been with Kraft, but that was merely a detail, while in the main thing I didn't lie, because the moment I lied, I promised myself to burn the letter that very evening. I swear, if I'd had it in my pocket at that moment, I'd have taken it out and given it to her; but I didn't have it with me, it was at home. However, maybe I wouldn't have given it to her, because I would have been very ashamed to confess to her then that I had it and that I had been watching her for so long, waiting and not giving it to her. It's all one: I'd have burned it at home in any case, and I wasn't lying! I was pure at that moment, I swear.

"And if so," I went on, almost beside myself, "then tell me, did you attract me, treat me nicely, receive me, because you suspected I had knowledge of the document? Wait, Katerina Nikolaevna, don't speak for one more little minute, but let me finish everything. All the while I've been visiting you, all this time I've suspected that you were being nice to me only in order to coax this letter out of me, to drive me to a point where I'd confess...Wait one more minute: I suspected, but I suffered. Your duplicity was unbearable for me, because... because in you I found the noblest of beings! I'll say it straight out, straight out: I was your enemy, but in you I found the noblest of beings! Everything was vanquished at once. But the duplicity, that is, the suspicion of duplicity, tormented me... Now everything must be resolved, must be explained, the time has come; but wait a little more, don't speak, learn how I myself look at all this, precisely now, at the present moment. I'll say it straight out: even if it was so, I won't be angry... that is, I meant to say—won't be offended, because it's all so natural, I do understand. What could be unnatural and bad here? You're suffering over a letter, you suspect that so-and-so knows everything, why, then you might very well wish that so-and-so would speak... There's nothing bad in that, nothing at all. I say it sincerely. But all the same I need you to tell me something now... to confess (forgive me the word). I need the truth. For some reason I need it! And so, tell me, were you being nice to me just to coax the document out of me... Katerina Nikolaevna!"

I spoke as if I were plunging down, and my forehead was burning. She listened to me without alarm now; on the contrary, there was feeling in her face, but she looked somehow shy, as if ashamed.

"Just for that," she said slowly and softly. "Forgive me, I was to blame," she suddenly added, raising her hands towards me slightly. I had never expected that. I had expected anything but those words, even from her whom I already knew.

"And you say to me, 'I'm to blame!' Straight out like that: 'I'm to blame!'" I cried.

"Oh, long ago I began to feel that I was to blame before you... and I'm even glad that it's come out now..."

"Felt it long ago? Why didn't you say so sooner?"

"I didn't know how to say it," she smiled. "That is, I did know," she smiled again, "but I somehow came to feel ashamed... because, actually, in the beginning I 'attracted' you, as you put it, only for that, but then very soon it became disgusting to me... and I was tired of all this pretending, I assure you!" she added with bitter feeling. "And of all this fuss as well!"

"And why, why wouldn't you ask then in a direct way? You should have said, 'You know about the letter, why are you pretending?' And I'd have told you everything at once, I'd have confessed at once!"

"I was... a little afraid of you. I confess, I also didn't trust you. And it's true: if I was sly, you were, too," she added with a smile.

"Yes, yes, I was unworthy!" I cried, astounded. "Oh, you don't know yet all the abysses of my fall!"

"Well, now it's abysses! I recognize your style." She smiled quietly. "That letter," she added sadly, "was the saddest and most thoughtless act of my life. The awareness of that act has always been a reproach to me. Under the influence of circumstances and apprehensions, I doubted my dear, magnanimous father. Knowing that this letter might fall . . . into the hands of wicked people . . . having all the grounds for thinking so," she added hotly, "I trembled for fear they might make use of it, show it to *papà* . . . and it might make an extreme impression on him . . . in his state . . . on his health . . . and he would stop loving me . . . Yes," she added, looking brightly into my eyes and probably catching something in my gaze, "yes, I also feared for my own lot: I feared that he . . . under the influence of his illness . . . might also deprive me of his favor . . . That feeling was also part of it, but here I'm probably to blame before him, too: he's so kind and magnanimous that he would of course have forgiven me. That's all there was. But the way I acted with you—that should not have happened," she concluded, suddenly abashed again. "You make me feel ashamed."

"No, you have nothing to be ashamed of!" I cried.

"I was actually counting . . . on your ardor . . . and I admit it," she said, lowering her eyes.

"Katerina Nikolaevna! Who, tell me, who is forcing you to make such confessions to me aloud?" I cried as if drunk. "Well, what would it have cost you to stand up and prove to me, like two times two, in the choicest expressions and in the subtlest way, that while it did happen, all the same it didn't happen—you understand, the way you people in high society know how to manage the truth? I'm crude and stupid, I'd have believed you at once, I'd have believed anything you said! It wouldn't have cost you anything to do that, would it? You're not really afraid of me! How could you have humiliated yourself so willingly before an upstart, before a pathetic adolescent?"

"In this at least I haven't humiliated myself before you," she uttered with extreme dignity, evidently not understanding my exclamation.

"Oh, on the contrary, on the contrary! That's just what I'm shouting! . . ."

"Ah, it was so bad and so thoughtless on my part!" she exclaimed, raising her hand to her face and as if trying to cover herself with it. "I was already ashamed yesterday, that's why I was so out of sorts when you were sitting with me... The whole truth is," she added, "that my circumstances have now come together in such a way that I absolutely needed, finally, to know the whole truth about the fate of that unfortunate letter, otherwise I had already begun to forget about it... because I didn't receive you only on account of that," she added suddenly.

My heart trembled.

"Of course not," she smiled with a subtle smile, "of course not! I... You remarked on it very aptly earlier, Arkady Makarovich, that you and I often talked as student to student. I assure you that I'm sometimes very bored with people; it has become especially so after the trip abroad and all those family misfortunes... I even go out very little now, and not only from laziness. I often want to leave for the country. I could reread my favorite books there, which I set aside long ago, otherwise I can't find time to read them. Remember, you laughed that I read Russian newspapers, two newspapers a day?"

"I didn't laugh..."

"Of course, because it stirred you in the same way, but I confessed to you long ago: I'm Russian, and I love Russia. You remember, we kept reading the 'facts,' as you called them" (she smiled). "Though very often you're somehow... strange, yet you sometimes became so animated that you were always able to say an apt word, and you were interested in precisely what interested me. When you're a 'student,' you really are sweet and original. But other roles seem little suited to you," she added with a lovely, sly smile. "You remember, we sometimes spent whole hours talking about nothing but figures, counting and estimating, concerned about the number of schools we have and where education is headed. We counted up the murders and criminal cases, made comparisons with the good news... wanted to know where it was all going and what, finally, would happen with us ourselves. I met with sincerity in you. In society they never talk with us women like that. Last week I tried to talk with Prince ——v about Bismarck, because it interested me very much, but I couldn't make up my own mind, and, imagine, he sat down beside me and began telling me, even in great detail, but all of it with some sort of irony, and precisely with that condescension I find so unbearable, with which 'great men' usually speak to us women when we meddle in what is 'not our business'... And do you remember how you and I nearly quarreled over Bismarck?

You were proving to me that you had an idea of your own that went 'way beyond' Bismarck's," she suddenly laughed. "I've met only two people in my life who have talked quite seriously with me: my late husband, a very, very intelligent and . . . noble man," she said imposingly, "and then—you yourself know who . . ."

"Versilov!" I cried. I held my breath at each word she said.

"Yes. I liked very much to listen to him, and in the end I became fully . . . perhaps overly candid with him, but it was then that he didn't believe me!"

"Didn't believe you!"

"Yes, but then nobody ever believed me."

"But Versilov! Versilov!"

"It's not simply that he didn't believe me," she said, lowering her eyes and smiling somehow strangely, "but he decided that I had 'all vices' in me."

"Of which you don't have a single one!"

"No, I do have some."

"Versilov didn't love you, that's why he didn't understand you," I cried, flashing my eyes.

Something twitched in her face.

"Drop that and never speak to me of . . . that man . . ." she added hotly and with strong emphasis. "But enough; it's time to go." (She got up to leave.) "So, do you forgive me or not?" she said, looking at me brightly.

"Me . . . forgive . . . you! Listen, Katerina Nikolaevna, and don't be angry! Is it true that you're getting married?"

"That's not at all decided yet," she said, as if afraid of something, with embarrassment.

"Is he a good man? Forgive me, forgive me the question!"

"Yes, very good . . ."

"Don't answer any more, don't deign to answer me! I know that such questions are impossible from me! I only wanted to know whether he's worthy or not, but I'll find out about him myself."

"Ah, listen!" she said in alarm.

"No, I won't, I won't. I'll pass by . . . But I'll only say this: may God grant you every happiness, every one that you choose . . . for having given me so much happiness now, in this one hour! You are now imprinted on my soul forever. I have acquired a treasure: the thought of your perfection. I suspected perfidy, coarse coquetry, and I was unhappy . . . because I couldn't connect that notion with you . . . during these last days I've been thinking day and night; and suddenly it all becomes clear as day! Coming in here, I thought I'd go away with Jesuitism, cunning, a worming-out serpent, but I found honor, glory, a student!... You laugh? Go on, go on! But you're a saint, you can't laugh at what is sacred..."

"Oh, no, I'm only laughing that you use such terrible words... Well, what is a 'worming-out serpent'?" she laughed.

"You let drop one precious word today," I went on in rapture. "How could you possibly say in front of me 'that you were counting on my ardor'? Well, so you're a saint and confess even to that, because you imagined some sort of guilt in yourself and wanted to punish yourself... Though, incidentally, there wasn't any guilt, because even if there was, everything that comes from you is holy! But still you might not have said precisely that word, that expression!... Such even unnatural candor only shows your lofty chastity, your respect for me, your faith in me," I exclaimed incoherently. "Oh, don't blush, don't blush!... And who, who could slander and say that you are a passionate woman? Oh, forgive me, I see a pained expression on your face, forgive the frenzied adolescent his clumsy words! As if it were a matter of words and expressions now? Aren't you higher than all expressions?... Versilov once said that Othello killed Desdemona and then himself not because he was jealous, but because his ideal was taken from him... I understood that, because today my ideal has been given back to me!"

"You praise me too much: I'm not worthy of it," she said with feeling. "Do you remember what I said to you about your eyes?" she said jokingly.

"That I don't have eyes, but two microscopes instead, and that I exaggerate every fly into a camel! No, ma'am, there's no camel here!... What, you're leaving?"

She was standing in the middle of the room, with her muff and shawl in her hand.

"No, I'll wait till you go, and I'll go myself afterwards. I still have to write a couple of words to Tatyana Pavlovna."

"I'll leave right now, right now, but once more: be happy, alone or with the one you choose, and may God be with you! And I—I only need an ideal!"

"Dear, kind Arkady Makarovich, believe me, of you I... My father always says of you: 'A dear, kind boy!' Believe me, I'll always remember your stories about the poor boy abandoned among strangers, and about his solitary dreams... I understand only too well how your soul was formed... But now, though we're students," she added with a pleading and bashful smile, pressing my hand, "it's impossible for us to go on seeing each other as before, and, and... surely you understand that?"

"Impossible?"

"Impossible, for a long time... it's my fault... I see that it's now quite impossible... We'll meet sometimes at *papa*'s..."

"You're afraid of the 'ardor' of my feelings? You don't trust me?" I was about to cry out, but she suddenly became so abashed before me that the words would not come out of my mouth.

"Tell me," she suddenly stopped me right at the door, "did you yourself see that... the letter... was torn up? Do you remember it well? How did you know then that it was that same letter to Andronikov?"

"Kraft told me what was in it and even showed it to me... Good-bye! Each time I was with you in your boudoir, I felt timid in your presence, and when you left I was ready to throw myself down and kiss the spot on the floor where your foot had stood..." I suddenly said unaccountably, not knowing how or why myself, and, without looking at her, quickly left.

I raced home; there was rapture in my soul. Everything flashed through my mind like a whirlwind, and my heart was full. Driving up to my mother's house, I suddenly remembered Liza's ungratefulness towards Anna Andreevna, her cruel, monstrous words earlier, and my heart suddenly ached for them all! "How hard of heart they all are! And Liza, what's with her?" I thought, stepping onto the porch.

I dismissed Matvei and told him to come for me, to my apartment, at nine o'clock.

Chapter Five

I

I WAS LATE for dinner, but they hadn't sat down yet and were waiting for me. Maybe because in general I dined with them rarely, certain special additions had even been made: sardines appeared as an entrée, and so on. But, to my surprise and grief, I found them all as if preoccupied, frowning about something; Liza barely smiled when she saw me, and mama was obviously worried; Versilov was smiling, but with effort. "Can they have been quarreling?" it occurred to me. However, at first everything went well: Versilov only winced a little at the soup with dumplings, and grimaced badly when the stuffed meatcakes were served.

"I have only to warn you that my stomach can't stand a certain dish, for it to appear the very next day," escaped him in vexation.

"But what are we to think up, Andrei Petrovich? There's no way to think up any sort of new dish," mama answered timidly.

"Your mother is the direct opposite of some of our newspapers, for which whatever is new is also good." Versilov had meant to joke playfully and amicably, but somehow it didn't come off, and he only frightened mama still more, who naturally understood nothing in the comparison of her with a newspaper, and she looked around in perplexity. At that moment Tatyana Pavlovna came in and, announcing that she had already had dinner, sat down beside mama on the sofa.

I still hadn't managed to gain this person's favor; even the contrary, she had begun to attack me still more for each and every thing. Her displeasure with me had especially intensified of late: she couldn't abide my foppish clothes, and Liza told me she almost had a fit when she learned I had a coachman. I ended by avoiding meeting her as far as possible. Two months ago, after the return of the inheritance, I ran over to her to chat about Versilov's act, but I didn't meet with the least sympathy; on the contrary, she was awfully angry: it displeased her very much that it had all been returned, and not just half. To me she observed sharply at the time:

"I'll bet you're convinced that he returned the money and challenged him to a duel solely so as to better himself in the opinion of Arkady Makarovich."

And she had almost guessed right: in essence I actually felt something of that sort at the time.

I understood at once, as soon as she came in, that she was bound to throw herself upon me; I was even slightly convinced that she had, in fact, come for that, and therefore I suddenly became extraordinarily casual; and it didn't cost me anything, because, after what had just taken place, I still went on being in joy and radiance. I'll note once and for all that never in my life has casualness suited me, that is, it has never made me look good, but, on the contrary, has always covered me with shame. So it happened now as well: I instantly made a blunder; without any bad feeling, but purely from thoughtlessness, having noticed that Liza was terribly dull, I suddenly blurted out, not even thinking what I was saying:

"Once a century I have dinner here, and as if on purpose, Liza, you're so dull!"

"I have a headache," Liza answered.

"Ah, my God," Tatyana Pavlovna latched on, "so what if you're sick? Arkady Makarovich has deigned to come for dinner, so you must dance and be merry."

"You are decidedly the bane of my existence, Tatyana Pavlovna; never will I come here when you're here!"—and I slapped the table with my hand in sincere vexation. Mama gave a start, and Versilov looked at me strangely. I suddenly laughed and begged their pardon.

"I take back the word 'bane,' Tatyana Pavlovna," I turned to her, going on with my casualness.

"No, no," she snapped, "it's far more flattering for me to be your bane than the opposite, you may be sure."

"My dear, one should know how to endure the small banes of life," Versilov murmured, smiling. "Without them, life's not worth living."

"You know, sometimes you're an awful retrograde!" I exclaimed with a nervous laugh.

"Spit on it, my friend."

"No, I won't spit on it! Why don't you tell an ass outright that he's an ass?"

"You don't mean yourself, do you? First of all, I will not and cannot judge anyone."

"Why won't you, why can't you?"

"Laziness and distaste. An intelligent woman told me once that I had no right to judge others, because I 'don't know how to suffer,' and in order to be a judge of others, you must gain the right to judge through suffering. It's a bit high-flown, but applied to me it may also be true, so that I even submitted willingly to the judgment."

"Can it be Tatyana Pavlovna who said that to you?" I exclaimed.

"How could you tell?" Versilov glanced at me with some surprise.

"I guessed from Tatyana Pavlovna's face; she suddenly twitched so."

I had guessed by chance. The phrase, as it turned out later, had indeed been spoken to Versilov by Tatyana Pavlovna the day before in a heated conversation. And in general, I repeat, it was the wrong time for me to fly at them with my joy and expansiveness: each of them had his own cares, and very heavy ones.

"I don't understand anything, because it's all so abstract with you; and here's a trait: you have this terrible love of speaking abstractly, Andrei Petrovich. It's an egoistic trait; only egoists love to speak abstractly."

"Not stupidly put, but don't nag."

"No, excuse me," I got at him with my expansiveness, "what does it mean 'to gain the right to judge through suffering'? Whoever's honest can be a judge—that's what I think."

"You'll come up with very few judges, in that case."

"I already know one."

"Who's that?"

"He's now sitting and talking to me."

Versilov chuckled strangely, leaned over right to my ear, and, taking me by the shoulder, whispered to me, "He lies to you all the time."

To this day I don't understand what he had in mind then, but obviously at that moment he was in some extreme anxiety (owing to a certain piece of news, as I figured out later). But this phrase, "He lies to you all the time," was spoken so unexpectedly and so seriously, and with such a strange, not at all jocular, expression, that I somehow shuddered all over nervously, almost frightened, and looked at him wildly; but Versilov hastened to laugh.

"Ah, thank God!" said mama, frightened because he had whispered in my ear. "And I was beginning to think... Don't you be angry with us, Arkasha, there will be intelligent people without us, but who's going to love you if we don't have each other?"

"That's why love among relations is immoral, mama, because it's unearned. Love has to be earned."

"Who knows when you'll earn it, but here we love you for nothing."

Everyone suddenly laughed.

"Well, mama, maybe you didn't mean to shoot, but you hit the bird!" I cried out, also laughing.

"And you really imagined there was something to love you for," Tatyana Pavlovna fell upon me again. "Not only do they love you for nothing, but they love you through revulsion!"

"Ah, not so!" I cried gaily. "Do you know who, maybe, talked today about loving me?"

"Talked while laughing at you!" Tatyana Pavlovna picked up suddenly with some sort of unnatural spite, as if she had been waiting for precisely those words from me. "A delicate person, and especially a woman, would be filled with loathing just from your inner filth alone. You've got a part in your hair, fine linen, a suit from a French tailor, but it's all filth! Who clothes you, who feeds you, who gives you money to play roulette? Remember who you're not ashamed to take money from!"

Mama got so flushed, I'd never yet seen such shame on her face. I cringed all over.

"If I spend, I spend my own money, and I owe nobody an accounting," I snapped, turning all red.

"Whose own? What's your own?"

"If not mine, then Andrei Petrovich's. He won't refuse me . . . I've taken from the prince against his debt to Andrei Petrovich . . ."

"My friend," Versilov suddenly said firmly, "not a cent of that money is mine."

The phrase was terribly significant. I stopped short on the spot. Oh, naturally, recalling my whole paradoxical and devil-may-care mood then, I would, of course, have gotten out of it by some "most noble" impulse, or catchy little word, or whatever, but I suddenly noticed a spiteful, accusing expression on Liza's frowning face, an unfair expression, almost mockery, and it was as if the devil pulled at my tongue:

"You, madam," I suddenly addressed her, "seem to visit Darya Onisimovna frequently in the prince's apartment? Be so good as to personally convey to him this three hundred roubles, for which you roasted me so much today!"

I produced the money and held it out to her. Will anyone believe that I spoke those mean words then without any purpose, that is, without the slightest allusion to anything? And there could have been no such allusion, because at that moment I knew precisely nothing. Maybe I just had a wish to needle her with something comparatively terribly innocent, something like, say, a young lady mixing in what was not her business, so here, since you absolutely want to mix in it, be so good as to go yourself to meet this prince, a young man, a Petersburg officer, and give it to him, "since you wish so much to meddle in young men's affairs." But what was my amazement when mama suddenly stood up and, raising her finger in front of me and shaking it at me, cried:

"Don't you dare! Don't you dare!"

I could never have imagined anything like that from her, and I myself jumped up from my place, not really frightened, but with some sort of suffering, with some sort of painful wound in my heart, suddenly realizing that something grave had taken place. But mama couldn't bear it for long; she covered her face with her hands and quickly left the room. Liza, not even glancing in my direction, went out after her. Tatyana Pavlovna gazed at me silently for about half a minute:

"Can it be that you really wanted to blurt something out?" she exclaimed enigmatically, gazing at me with the deepest astonishment, but, not waiting for my reply, she also ran to them. Versilov, with an inimical, almost spiteful look, rose from the table and took his hat from the corner.

"I suppose you're not all that stupid, but merely innocent," he murmured mockingly. "If they come back, tell them not to wait for me with dessert: I'll take a little stroll."

I was left alone. At first I felt strange, then offended, but then I saw clearly that I was to blame. However, I didn't know what in fact I was to blame for, but only sensed something. I sat by the window and waited. After waiting for some ten minutes, I also took my hat and went upstairs to my former room. I knew they were there—that is, mama and Liza—and that Tatyana Pavlovna had already gone. And so I found the two of them together on my sofa, whispering about something. When I appeared, they immediately stopped whispering. To my surprise, they were not angry with me; mama at least smiled at me.

"I'm to blame, mama . . ." I began.

"Well, well, never mind," mama interrupted, "only love each other and don't ever quarrel, and God will send you happiness."

"He'll never offend me, mama, I can tell you that!" Liza said with conviction and feeling.

"If only it hadn't been for this Tatyana Pavlovna, nothing would have happened," I cried. "She's nasty!"

"Do you see, mama? Do you hear?" Liza pointed at me to her.

"I'll tell you both this," I pronounced, "if it's vile in the world, the only vile thing is me, and all the rest is lovely!"

"Arkasha, don't be angry, dear, but what if you really did stop..."

"Gambling, is it? Gambling? I will, mama; I'm going today for the last time, especially now that Andrei Petrovich himself has announced, and aloud, that not a cent of that money is his. You won't believe how I blush... I must talk with him, however... Mama, dear, the last time I was here I said... something awkward... mama, darling, I lied: I sincerely want to believe, it was just bravado, I love Christ very much..."

The last time we had indeed had a conversation of that sort; mama had been very upset and alarmed. Hearing me now, she smiled at me as at a child:

"Christ will forgive everything, Arkasha: he will forgive your abuse, and he will forgive more than that. Christ is our father, Christ needs nothing and will shine even in the deepest darkness..."

I said good-bye to them and left, reflecting on my chances of seeing Versilov that same day; I needed very much to have a talk with him, but just now it had been impossible. I strongly suspected that he was waiting for me at my place. I went on foot; after the warmth it had turned slightly frosty, and it was very pleasant to take a stroll.

II

I LIVED NEAR the Voznesensky Bridge, in an enormous house, on the courtyard. Almost going through the gateway, I bumped into Versilov, who was leaving my place.

"As is my custom, I walked as far as your lodgings, and even waited for you at Pyotr Ippolitovich's, but I got bored. They're eternally quarreling, and today his wife has even kept to her bed, weeping. I looked in and left."

I became vexed for some reason.

"Can it be that I'm the only one you go to see, and besides me and Pyotr Ippolitovich, you have nobody in all Petersburg?"

"My friend... but it makes no difference."

"Where to now?"

"No, I won't go back to your place. If you like, we can stroll a bit, it's a nice evening."

"If, instead of abstract reasonings, you had talked to me like a human being and, for instance, had only so much as hinted to me about this cursed gambling, maybe I wouldn't have gotten drawn into it like a fool," I said suddenly.

"You regret it? That's good," he said, sifting his words. "I've always suspected that gambling isn't the main thing with you, but only a tem-po-rary deviation... You're right, my friend, gambling is swinishness, and what's more, one can lose."

"And lose someone else's money."

"Have you lost someone else's money as well?"

"I've lost yours. I took from the prince against your account. Of course, it was awfully preposterous and stupid on my part... to regard your money as my own, but I kept wanting to win it back."

"I warn you once again, my dear, that none of that money is mine. I know the young man is in a squeeze himself, and I don't count on him at all, despite his promises."

"In that case, I'm in twice as bad a position... I'm in a comical position! And why on earth should he give to me or I take from him, then?"

"That's your business... But you really don't have the slightest reason for taking from him, eh?"

"Besides comradeship..."

"No, besides comradeship? There isn't anything that would make it possible for you to take from him, eh? Well, for whatever considerations?"

"What considerations? I don't understand."

"So much the better if you don't understand, and, I confess, my friend, I was sure of that. *Brisons là, mon cher*,* and try somehow not to gamble."

"If only you'd told me beforehand! Even now you talk to me as if you're mumbling."

"If I'd told you beforehand, we would only have quarreled, and you wouldn't have been so willing to let me call on you in the evenings. And know, my dear, that all this saving advice beforehand is only an intrusion into another's conscience at the other's expense. I've done enough jumping into other people's consciences and in

*Let's break it off there, my dear.

the end suffered nothing but flicks and mockery. Of course, I spit on flicks and mockery, but the main thing is that you achieve nothing by this maneuver: nobody will listen to you, for all your intruding... and everybody will dislike you."

"I'm glad you've begun to talk with me about something besides abstractions. I want to ask you about one more thing, I've long wanted to, but somehow with you it was always impossible. It's good that we're in the street. Remember that evening at your place, the last evening, two months ago, how we sat in my 'coffin' and I asked you about mama and Makar Ivanovich—remember how 'casual' I was with you then? Could a young pup of a son be allowed to speak of his mother in such terms? And what, then? You didn't let it show by one little word; on the contrary, you 'opened yourself up' to me, and made me even more casual."

"My friend, it's all too pleasant for me to hear... such feelings from you... Yes, I remember very well, I was actually waiting then for your face to turn red, and if I added to it myself, maybe it was precisely to push you to the limit..."

"And all you did was deceive me then, and trouble the pure spring in my soul still more! Yes, I'm a pathetic adolescent and don't know myself from minute to minute what's evil and what's good. If you had shown me just a bit of the way then, I would have guessed and jumped at once onto the right path. But you only made me angry then."

"*Cher enfant*, I've always sensed that you and I would become close in one way or another: this 'red' in your face did come to you of itself and without my directions, and that, I swear, is the better for you... I notice, my dear, that you've acquired a lot lately... could it be in the company of this little prince?"

"Don't praise me, I don't like it. Don't leave the painful suspicion in my heart that you're praising me out of Jesuitism, to the detriment of truth, so that I won't stop liking you. But recently... you see... I've been calling on women. I'm very well received, for instance, at Anna Andreevna's, did you know that?"

"I know it from her, my friend. Yes, she's very sweet and intelligent. *Mais brisons là, mon cher.* I feel somehow strangely vile today—spleen, or what? I ascribe it to hemorrhoids. How are things at home? All right? Naturally, you made peace there and there were embraces. *Cela va sans dire.** It's somehow sad to go

*That goes without saying.

back to them sometimes, even after the nastiest walk. Truly, at times I make an unnecessary detour in the rain, only to put off going back to those lower depths... And the boredom, the boredom, oh, God!"

"Mama..."

"Your mother is the most perfect and lovely being, *mais* ... In short, I'm probably not worthy of them. By the way, what's with them today? Lately they've all been somehow sort of... You know, I always try to ignore it, but today they've got something brewing there... You didn't notice anything?"

"I know decidedly nothing and wouldn't even have noticed anything, if it hadn't been for that cursed Tatyana Pavlovna, who can't keep from biting. You're right: there's something there. Today I found Liza at Anna Andreevna's; there, too, she was somehow... she even surprised me. You do know that she's received at Anna Andreevna's?"

"I do, my friend. And you... when were you at Anna Andreevna's—that is, at precisely what hour? I need that for the sake of a certain fact."

"From two to three. And imagine, as I was leaving, the prince came..."

Here I told him about my whole visit in extreme detail. He listened to it all silently: about the possibility of the prince proposing to Anna Andreevna he didn't utter a word; to my rapturous praises of Anna Andreevna he again mumbled that "she's sweet."

"I managed to astonish her extremely today by telling her the most fresh-baked society news about Katerina Nikolaevna Akhmakov marrying Baron Bjoring," I said suddenly, as if something in me had come unhinged.

"Oh? Imagine, she told me that same 'news' earlier today, before noon, that is, much earlier than you could have astonished her with it."

"What?" I just stopped in my tracks. "But how could she have found out? Though what am I saying? Naturally, she could have found out before me, but imagine: she listened to me say it as if it was absolute news! Though... though what am I saying? Long live breadth! One must allow for breadth of character, right? I, for instance, would have blurted it all out at once, but she locks it up in a snuffbox... And so be it, so be it, nonetheless she's the loveliest being and the most excellent character!"

"Oh, no doubt, to each his own! And what's most original of

all: these excellent characters are sometimes able to puzzle you in an extremely peculiar way. Imagine, today Anna Andreevna suddenly takes me aback with the question, 'Do you love Katerina Nikolaevna Akhmakov, or not?'"

"What a wild and incredible question!" I cried out, dumbfounded again. My eyes even went dim. Never yet had I ventured to talk with him on this subject, and—here he himself...

"What did she formulate it with?"

"With nothing, my friend, absolutely nothing; the snuffbox was locked up at once and still tighter, and, above all, notice, I had never allowed even the possibility of such conversations with me, nor had she... However, you say yourself that you know her, and therefore you can imagine how such a question suits her... You wouldn't happen to know anything?"

"I'm as puzzled as you are. Some sort of curiosity, or maybe a joke?"

"Oh, on the contrary, a most serious question, and not a question, but almost, so to speak, an inquiry, and evidently for the most extreme and categorical reasons. Won't you be going there? Mightn't you find something out? I'd even ask you to, you see..."

"But the possibility, above all—the possibility alone of supposing that you love Katerina Nikolaevna! Forgive me, I'm still dumbfounded. I've never, never allowed myself to speak with you on this or any similar subject..."

"And you've done wisely, my dear."

"Your former intrigues and relations—no, the subject is, of course, impossible between us, and it would even be stupid on my part; but, precisely in this last period, in the last few days, I've exclaimed to myself several times: what if you had loved this woman once, even for a moment? Oh, you would never have made such an awful mistake regarding her in your opinion of her as the one that came out afterwards! Of what came out, I do know: of your mutual enmity and your mutual, so to speak, aversion for each other, I do know, I've heard, I've heard only too well, I heard still in Moscow; but it's precisely here first of all that the fact of a bitter aversion leaps to the surface, the bitterness of hostility, precisely of *non-love*, and yet Anna Andreevna suddenly puts it to you, 'Do you love her?' Can she be so poorly renseigneered?* It's a wild thing! She was laughing, I assure you, she was laughing!"

*Distortion of French *renseignée*, "informed."

"But I notice, my dear," something nervous and soulfelt suddenly sounded in his voice, something that went to the heart, which happened terribly rarely with him, "I notice that you yourself speak of it all too ardently. You just said that you call on women . . . of course, for me to question you is somehow . . . on this subject, as you put it . . . But doesn't 'that woman' also figure on the list of your newer friends?"

"That woman . . ." My voice suddenly trembled. "Listen, Andrei Petrovich, listen: that woman is what you said today at the prince's about 'living life'—remember? You said that this living life is something so direct and simple, which looks at you so directly, that precisely because of this directness and clarity it's impossible to believe it could be precisely what we seek so hard all our lives . . . Well, so with such views you met the ideal woman, and in perfection, in the ideal, you recognized—'all vices'! There you are!"

The reader can judge what a frenzy I was in.

" 'All vices'! Ho, ho! I know that phrase!" exclaimed Versilov. "And if it's gone so far as telling you such a phrase, shouldn't you be congratulated for something? It means such intimacy between you that you may even have to be praised for your modesty and secrecy, which a young man is rarely capable of . . ."

A sweet, friendly, affectionate laughter sparkled in his voice . . . there was something inviting and sweet in his words, in his bright face, as far as I could tell at night. He was surprisingly excited. Involuntarily, I sparkled all over.

"Modesty! Secrecy! Oh, no, no!" I exclaimed, blushing and at the same time squeezing his hand, which I had somehow managed to seize and, without noticing it, would not let go of. "No, not for anything! . . . In short, there's nothing to congratulate me for, and never, never can anything happen here." I was breathless and flying, and I so wanted to be flying, it felt so good to me. "You know . . . well, let it be so just once, for one little time! You see, my darling, my nice papa—you'll let me call you papa—it's impossible, not only for a father and son, but for anyone, to talk with a third person about his relations with a woman, even the purest of them! Even the purer they are, the more forbidden it ought to be. It's forbidding, it's coarse, in short—a confidant is impossible! But if there's nothing, absolutely nothing, then it's possible to talk, isn't it?"

"As your heart dictates."

"An indiscreet, a very indiscreet question. You've known women in your life, you've had liaisons? . . . I'm asking generally, generally, not in particular!" I was blushing and spluttering with rapture.

"Let's suppose there were lapses."

"So here's an occasion, and you explain it to me, as a more experienced person: a woman, while taking leave of you, suddenly says somehow by chance, looking away, 'Tomorrow at three o'clock I'll be at such and such place' . . . well, say, at Tatyana Pavlovna's," I came unhinged and flew off definitively. My heart gave a throb and stopped; I even stopped talking, I couldn't. He was listening terribly.

"And so the next day I'm at Tatyana Pavlovna's at three o'clock, I go in and reason like this: 'If the cook opens the door'—you know her cook?—'I'll ask her first off: is Tatyana Pavlovna at home? And if the cook says Tatyana Pavlovna isn't at home, but some lady visitor's sitting and waiting—what should I have concluded, tell me, if you . . . In short, if you . . .' "

"Quite simply that you had an appointed rendezvous. But that means it took place? And took place today? Yes?"

"Oh, no, no, no, nothing, nothing! It took place, but it wasn't that; a rendezvous, but not for that, and I announce it first of all, so as not to be a scoundrel, it happened, but . . ."

"My friend, all this is beginning to become so curious, that I suggest . . ."

"Myself, I used to give a tenner or a twenty-fiver to solicitors. For a dram. Just a few kopecks, it's a lieutenant soliciting, a former lieutenant asking!" The tall figure of a solicitor, maybe indeed a retired lieutenant, suddenly blocked our way. Most curious of all, he was quite well dressed for his profession, and yet he had his hand out.

III

I PURPOSELY DO not want to omit this most paltry anecdote about the insignificant lieutenant, because I now recall the whole of Versilov not otherwise than with all the minutest circumstantial details of that moment so fateful for him. Fateful, but I didn't know it!

"If you do not leave us alone, sir, I shall immediately call the police," Versilov, stopping before the lieutenant, suddenly raised his voice somehow unnaturally. I could never have imagined such wrath from such a philosopher, and for such an insignificant reason. And note that we interrupted the conversation at the moment most interesting for him, as he said himself.

"So you really don't even have a fifteener?" the lieutenant cried rudely, waving his arm. "On what sort of canaille can you find a fifteener nowadays? Rabble! Scoundrels! He's all in beaver, yet he makes a state problem out of a fifteener!"

"Police!" shouted Versilov.

But there was no need to shout; a policeman was standing just at the corner and had heard the lieutenant's abuse himself.

"I ask you to be a witness to the insult, and you I ask to kindly come to the police station," said Versilov.

"E-eh, it's all the same to me, you'll prove decidedly nothing! Your intelligence least of all!"

"Don't let go of him, officer, and take us there," Versilov concluded insistently.

"Must we go to the police station? Devil take him!" I whispered to him.

"Absolutely, my dear. This presumptuousness in our streets is beginning to be tiresomely outrageous, and if each of us did his duty, it would be useful for all. *C'est comique, mais c'est ce que nous ferons.*"*

For about a hundred steps the lieutenant was very hot-tempered, spirited, and brave. He assured us that "this was impossible," that it was all "'cause of a fifteener," and so on, and so forth. But he finally started whispering something to the policeman. The policeman, a sensible fellow and clearly an enemy of street nervousness, seemed to be on his side, but only in a certain sense. To his questions, he murmured in a half-whisper that "it's impossible now," that "the thing's under way," and that "if, for instance, you were to apologize, and the gentleman would agree to accept your apology, then maybe..."

"Well, li-i-isten he-e-re, my dear sir, so, where are we going? I ask you, where are we trying to get to and what's so clever about it?" the lieutenant cried loudly. "If a man unlucky in his misfortunes agrees to offer an apology...if, finally, you need his humiliation...Devil take it, we're not in a drawing room, we're in the street! For the street, this is apology enough..."

Versilov stopped and suddenly rocked with laughter; I even

*It's comical, but that's what we're going to do.

thought for a moment that he had gone ahead with this whole story for the fun of it, but that wasn't so.

"I pardon you completely, Mr. Lieutenant, and I assure you that you have abilities. Act this way in a drawing room, and soon it will be quite enough for the drawing room as well, but meanwhile here's forty kopecks for you, have a drink and a bite to eat. Pardon me for the trouble, officer, I'd reward you, too, for your labors, but you're all on such a noble footing now... My dear," he turned to me, "there's an eatery here, in fact a terrible cesspool, but one can have tea there, and I'd suggest to you... here it is now, come on."

I repeat, I had never seen him in such excitement, though his face was cheerful and shone with light; but I noticed that when he was taking the two twenty-kopeck pieces from his purse to give to the lieutenant, his hands shook and his fingers wouldn't obey at all, so that he finally asked me to take them out and give them to the man. I can't forget that.

He brought me to a little tavern on the canal, in the basement. The customers were few. A hoarse little organ was playing out of tune, it smelled of dirty napkins; we sat down in the corner.

"Maybe you don't know? I like sometimes, out of boredom, out of terrible inner boredom... to go into various cesspools like this one. These furnishings, this stuttering aria from *Lucia*,[22] these waiters in costumes that are Russian to the point of indecency, this stench of tobacco, these shouts from the billiard room—all this is so banal and prosaic that it borders almost on the fantastic. Well, so what, my dear? This son of Mars stopped us at the most interesting place, it seems... But here's our tea; I like the tea here... Imagine, Pyotr Ippolitovich has now suddenly started assuring that other lodger, the pockmarked one, that in the last century a committee of jurists was especially appointed in the English Parliament to examine the whole trial of Christ before the high priest and Pilate,[23] solely in order to find out how it would go now, by our laws, and that it was all done with all solemnity, with lawyers, prosecutors, and the rest... well, and that the jury had to hand down a guilty verdict... Amazing—eh, what? That fool of a lodger started arguing, got angry, quarreled, and announced that he was moving out the next day... the landlady bursts into tears, because she's losing money... *Mais passons.** Sometimes they have nightingales in these taverns. Do you know the old Moscow

*But let's drop that.

anecdote *à la* Pyotr Ippolitovich? A nightingale is singing in a Moscow tavern. A merchant comes in, the 'out o' me way' type: 'How much is the nightingale?' 'A hundred roubles.' 'Roast it and serve it.' They roasted it and served it. 'Cut me ten kopecks' worth.' I once told it to Pyotr Ippolitovich, but he didn't believe it and even got indignant..."

He said a lot more. I quote these fragments as a sample. He interrupted me continually, as soon as I opened my mouth to begin my story, and began talking some sort of completely peculiar and inappropriate nonsense; he talked excitedly, gaily; laughed at God knows what, and even tittered—something I had never seen him do. He drank a glass of tea at one gulp and poured another. Now I understand: he was then like a man who has received a precious, curious, and long-awaited letter, which he places before him and doesn't open on purpose; on the contrary, he turns it over in his hands for a long time, studies the envelope, the seal, goes to another room to give orders, puts off, in short, the most interesting moment, knowing that it won't get away from him for anything, and all this for the greater fullness of pleasure.

I, naturally, told him everything, everything from the very beginning, and it took me maybe about an hour. And how else could it be? I had been longing to talk all the while. I began from our very first meeting, at the prince's that time, on her arrival from Moscow; then I told how it all went on gradually. I didn't leave anything out, and I couldn't have: he led me on himself, guessed, prompted me. At moments it seemed to me that something fantastic was happening, that he had been sitting somewhere or standing behind the door, each time, for all those two months: he knew beforehand my every gesture, my every feeling. I took a boundless pleasure in making this confession to him, because I saw in him such heartfelt gentleness, such deep psychological subtlety, such an astonishing ability to guess from a quarter of a word. He listened tenderly, like a woman. Above all, he managed to make it so that I wasn't ashamed of anything; at times he suddenly stopped me at some detail; he often stopped me and repeated nervously, "Don't forget the small things, above all, don't forget the small things—the smaller the trace, the more important it sometimes is." And he interrupted me several times in the same way. Oh, naturally, I began haughtily in the beginning, haughtily towards her, but I quickly came down to the truth. I told him sincerely that I was ready to throw myself down and kiss the place on the floor where her foot had stood. The most beautiful, the brightest thing of all was that he understood in the highest degree that she "could suffer from fear over the document" and at the same time remain a pure and irreproachable being, as she had revealed herself to me that same day. He understood in the highest degree the word "student." But as I was finishing, I noticed that, through his kind smile, something all too impatient began to flash in his eyes, something as if distracted and sharp. When I came to the "document," I thought to myself, "Shall I tell him the real truth or not?"—and I didn't, despite all my rapture. I note it here to remember it all my life. I explained the matter to him in the same way I had to her, that is, by Kraft. His eyes lit up. A strange wrinkle flitted across his forehead, a very dark wrinkle.

"You firmly recall, my dear, about that letter, that Kraft burned it in a candle? You're not mistaken?"

"I'm not mistaken," I confirmed.

"The thing is that that piece of writing is very important for her, and if it had been in your hands today, then even today you might..." But "might" what, he didn't finish saying. "And so, it's not in your hands now?"

I shuddered inwardly, but not outwardly. Outwardly I didn't betray myself in any way, didn't bat an eye; but still I couldn't believe the question.

"How not in my hands? In my hands *now*? If Kraft burned it then?"

"Yes?" he aimed a fiery, fixed gaze at me, a gaze I remembered. However, he was smiling, but all his goodnaturedness, all the femininity of expression he had had till then, suddenly disappeared. What came was something indefinite and disconnected; he was becoming more and more distracted. If he had been more in control of himself then, as he had been up to that moment, he wouldn't have asked me that question about the document; if he did, it was probably because he was in a frenzy himself. However, I say it only now; but at that time it took me a while to perceive the change that had taken place in him. I still went on flying, and there was the same music in my soul. But the story was over; I looked at him.

"An amazing thing," he said suddenly, when I had spoken everything out to the last comma, "a very strange thing, my friend: you say you were there from three to four, and that Tatyana Pavlovna wasn't at home?"

"Exactly from three till half-past four."

"Well, imagine, I stopped to see Tatyana Pavlovna at exactly half-past three to the minute, and she met me in the kitchen—I almost always come to see her by the back entrance."

"What, she met you in the kitchen?" I cried, drawing back in amazement.

"Yes, and she told me she couldn't receive me; I stayed with her a couple of minutes, and I had only come to invite her to dinner."

"Maybe she just came back from somewhere?"

"I don't know; though—of course not. She was in her housecoat. This was exactly at half-past three."

"But . . . Tatyana Pavlovna didn't tell you I was there?"

"No, she didn't tell me you were there . . . Otherwise I'd have known and wouldn't be asking you about it."

"Listen, this is very important . . ."

"Yes . . . depending on one's point of view; and you've even turned pale, my dear; but, anyhow, what's so important?"

"I've been laughed at like a child!"

"She was simply 'afraid of your ardor,' as she put it to you herself—well, and so she enlisted Tatyana Pavlovna."

"But, my God, what a trick it was! Listen, she let me say all that with a third person there, with Tatyana Pavlovna there—who, consequently, heard everything I said! It's . . . it's even terrible to imagine!"

"*C'est selon, mon cher!** And besides, you yourself mentioned earlier the 'breadth' of view of women in general, and exclaimed, 'Long live breadth!'"

"If I were Othello and you Iago, you couldn't have done it better . . . however, I'm laughing! There can't be any Othello, because there are no such relations. And how not laugh! So be it! I still believe in what is infinitely higher than I am, and I haven't lost my ideal! . . . If it's a joke on her part, I forgive her. A joke on the pathetic adolescent—so be it! I didn't get myself up as anything, and the student—the student was and remains anyway, no matter what, he was in her soul, he exists and will go on existing! Enough! Listen, what do you think: shall I go to her now, to learn the whole truth, or not?"

I said, "I'm laughing," but there were tears in my eyes.

"Why not? Go, my friend, if you want to."

"It's as if I've dirtied my soul by telling you all this. Don't be

*That depends, my dear!

angry, dear heart, but it's impossible to tell a third person about a woman, I repeat, about a woman. No confidant will understand; not even an angel will understand. If you respect a woman, don't take a confidant; if you respect yourself, don't take a confidant! I don't respect myself now. Good-bye; I can't forgive myself..."

"Come, my dear, you're exaggerating. You say yourself 'there was nothing.'"

We went out to the canal and began saying good-bye.

"Will you never kiss me from the heart, as a child, as a son kisses his father?" he said to me with a strange tremor in his voice. I kissed him warmly.

"My dear... always be as pure of heart as you are now."

I had never kissed him before in my life, I could never have imagined he would want me to.

Chapter Six

I

"Go, of course!" I decided, hurrying home. "Go at once. Quite possibly I'll find her at home alone—alone or with someone, it makes no difference—I can call her away. She'll receive me; she'll be surprised, but she'll receive me. And if she doesn't, I'll insist that she receive me, I'll send to tell her it's extremely necessary. She'll think it's something about the document and receive me. And I'll find out all about Tatyana. And then... and then what? If I'm wrong, I'll make it up to her, and if I'm right, and she's to blame, then it's all over! In any case—it's all over! What can I lose? I can't lose anything. Go! Go!"

And then—I'll never forget it and I remember it with pride—I *didn't* go! No one will ever know it, it will just die, but it's enough that I know it and that at such a moment I was capable of the noblest impulse! "This is a temptation, and I'll pass it by," I decided finally, thinking better of it. "They frightened me with a fact, but I didn't believe it and didn't lose faith in her purity! And why go, why ask? Why should she believe so unfailingly in me as I did in her, believe in my 'purity,' not be afraid of my 'ardor,' not enlist Tatyana? I haven't deserved it yet in her eyes. Let her not, let her not know that I do deserve it, that I don't yield to 'temptations,' that I don't believe wicked calumnies about her; but I myself know it and will respect myself for it. Respect my feeling. Oh, yes, she allowed me to speak myself out with Tatyana there, she allowed Tatyana, she knew that Tatyana was sitting and eavesdropping (because she couldn't help eavesdropping), she knew that she was laughing at me—it's terrible, terrible! But... but what if it was impossible to avoid? What could she have done in her position today, and how can she be blamed for it? No, I myself lied to her about Kraft, I deceived her, because it was also impossible to avoid it, and I lied involuntarily, innocently. My God," I suddenly exclaimed, blushing painfully, "and I, what have I just done myself? Haven't I just dragged her before the same Tatyana, haven't I just told everything to Versilov? Though—what's the matter with me?—there's a difference here. Here it was only about the document; essentially, I just told Versilov about the document, because there was nothing more to tell about, and there couldn't be. Wasn't I the first to inform him and cry that 'there couldn't be'? He's a man of understanding. Hm... But what hatred there is in his heart for this woman, though, even now! And what a drama must have taken place between them then and from what? Of course, from self-love! *Versilov can't be capable of any other feeling except boundless self-love!*"

Yes, this last thought escaped me then, and I didn't even notice it. It was such thoughts that raced through my head then one after another, and I was straightforward with myself then: I wasn't being sly, I wasn't deceiving myself; and if there was something I didn't comprehend then at that moment, it was just because I didn't have brains enough, and not from Jesuitism with myself.

I returned home in a terribly excited and, I don't know why, a terribly merry state of mind, though a very unclear one. But I was afraid to analyze and tried with all my might to divert myself. I went to my landlady at once; indeed, a terrible falling out was under way between her and her husband. She was a very consumptive clerk's wife, maybe even a kind one, but, like all consumptives, extremely capricious. I at once began to make peace between them, went to see the tenant, a very coarse, pockmarked fool, an extremely vain clerk who served in a bank, Chervyakov, whom I myself disliked very much, but with whom, anyhow, I got along well, because I often had the baseness to join him in teasing Pyotr Ippolitovich. I at once persuaded him not to move out, and he himself would not have ventured to actually move out. In the end I reassured the landlady definitively and, on top of that, managed to straighten the pillow under her head excellently. "Pyotr Ippolitovich can never manage like that," she concluded maliciously. Then I busied myself with her mustard plasters in the kitchen, and with my own hands prepared two superb plasters for her. Poor Pyotr Ippolitovich only looked at me with envy, but I didn't let him touch them and was rewarded literally by tears of gratitude from her. And then, I remember, I suddenly got bored with it all, and I suddenly realized that I was by no means looking after the sick woman out of the goodness of my heart, but just so, for some reason, for something else entirely.

I waited nervously for Matvei. That evening I decided to try my luck for the last time and... and, apart from luck, I felt a terrible need to gamble; otherwise it would have been unbearable. If I hadn't had to go anywhere, maybe I wouldn't have held out and would have gone to her. Matvei was to come soon, but suddenly the door opened and an unexpected visitor came in—Darya Onisimovna. I winced and was surprised. She knew my lodgings because she had come once on an errand from mama. I sat her down and began looking at her questioningly. She said nothing, but only looked me straight in the eye and smiled submissively.

"Have you come from Liza?" it occurred to me to ask.

"No, just so, sir."

I warned her that I would be leaving presently; again she answered that she had come "just so" and would leave presently herself. For some reason I suddenly felt sorry for her. I'll note that she had seen much sympathy from us all, from mama and especially from Tatyana Pavlovna, but once she was placed with Mrs. Stolbeev, we all somehow began to forget her, except perhaps for Liza, who often visited her. She herself, it seems, was the cause of that, because she had a capacity for withdrawing and effacing herself, despite all her submissive and ingratiating smiles. Personally I very much disliked those smiles, and the fact that she always obviously falsified her face, and I even thought once that she had not grieved long over her Olya. But this time for some reason I felt sorry for her.

And then suddenly, without saying a word, she bent forward, looked down, and, suddenly thrusting out both arms, put them around my waist and leaned her face against my knees. She seized my hand, I almost thought she was going to kiss it, but she pressed it to her eyes, and a flood of hot tears poured over it. She was all shaking with sobs, but she wept quietly. My heart was wrung, despite the fact that I was also as if vexed. But she embraced me with complete trust, not afraid in the least that I would get angry, despite the fact that she had smiled at me so timorously and servilely just before. I began asking her to calm down.

"Dear heart, darling, I don't know what to do with myself. When it gets dark, I can't stand it; when it gets dark, I can't stand it any more, I'm drawn outside, into the darkness. What draws me, mainly, is a dream. There's this dream born in my mind, that just as I step out, I'll meet her in the street. I walk and it's as if I see her. That is, it's somebody else walking, but I walk behind on purpose and think: isn't it her, there now, I think, isn't that my Olya? And I think and think. I get stupefied in the end, only knocking into people, it's sickening. Knocking about like I'm drunk, and people abuse me. I keep it to myself, I don't go to anyone. Or if I do, it's more sickening. I was passing by your place and thought, 'Why don't I drop in; he's the kindest of them all, and he was there then.' Dear heart, forgive a useless woman; I'll leave now and go away..."

She suddenly got up and began to hurry. Just then Matvei arrived; I put her into the sledge and took her home to Mrs. Stolbeev's apartment on the way.

II

MOST RECENTLY I had started going to play roulette at Zershchikov's. Before that I had gone to three houses, always with the prince, who had "introduced" me in those places. In one of those houses the game was predominantly faro, and they played for very significant money. But I didn't like it there; I saw it was only good there if you had big money, and besides, it was frequented by too many insolent people and "thundering" youth from high society. That was what the prince liked; he liked to gamble, but he also liked to hobnob with those rakehells. I noticed on those evenings that, though he sometimes came in with me, he somehow distanced himself from me during the evening and didn't introduce me to any of "his people." I looked around like a perfect savage, sometimes even so much so that I happened to attract attention. At the gambling table I sometimes even had to speak with one or another of them; but once, the next day, right there in those rooms, I tried to greet one little sir with whom I had not only talked but even laughed the day before, sitting next to him, and I had even guessed two cards for him, and what then?—he didn't recognize me at all. Worse than that: he looked at me as if with sham perplexity and walked past smiling. Thus I soon dropped the place and got into the habit of going to a certain cesspool—I don't know what else to call it. It was a roulette house, rather insignificant, paltry, kept by a certain kept woman, though she never appeared in the room herself. It was a terribly unbuttoned place, and though officers frequented it, and rich merchants, everything came out a bit dirtily, which many, however, found attractive. Besides, I often had luck there. But I dropped that place, too, after a certain repulsive incident that occurred at the height of a game and ended in a fight between two players, and started going to Zershchikov's, where, again, I was introduced by the prince. The owner was a retired cavalry staff-captain, and the tone at his evenings was quite tolerable, military, ticklishly irritable in observing the forms of honor, clipped and businesslike. Jokers and big carousers, for instance, didn't show up there. Besides, the faro bank was hardly a joking matter. They played faro and roulette. Up to that evening, the fifteenth of November, I had gone there twice in all, and Zershchikov, it seemed, already knew my face; but I didn't have any acquaintances yet. As if on purpose, the prince and Darzan showed up that evening only at around midnight, returning from the faro of those society rakehells that I had dropped. Thus, on that evening I was like a stranger in an alien crowd.

If I had a reader and he had read all that I've already written about my adventures, doubtless there would be no point in explaining to him that I am decidedly not created for any society whatever. Above all, I'm totally unable to behave myself in society. When I walk in somewhere where there are many people, it always feels to me that all their looks electrify me. I decidedly begin to cringe, cringe physically, even in such places as the theater, to say nothing of private houses. At all these roulettes and gatherings I decidedly failed to acquire any kind of bearing: first I sit and reproach myself for my unnecessary softness and politeness, then suddenly I get up and commit some rudeness. And meanwhile such blackguards, compared with me, managed to behave themselves there with astonishing bearing—and that was what infuriated me most of all, so that I lost my coolheadedness more and more. I'll say straight out that, not only now, but then as well, this whole society—and even winning itself, if all be told—finally became repugnant and tormenting to me. Decidedly tormenting. Of course, I experienced an extreme pleasure, but that pleasure came by way of torment; all of it, that is, these people, the gambling, and, above all, I myself there with them, seemed terribly dirty to me. "The moment I win, I'll spit on it all at once!" I said to myself each time, falling asleep at dawn in my lodgings after the night's gambling. And then again this winning: take just the fact that I had no love of money at all. That is, I'm not going to repeat the vile pronouncements usual in such explanations, that I gambled, say, for the sake of gambling, for the sensation, for the pleasure of risk, passion, and so on, and not at all for gain. I needed money terribly, and though it was not my way, not my idea, somehow or other I still decided then, as an experiment, to try this way, too. One strong thought kept throwing me off here: "You've already figured out that you can unfailingly become a millionaire only if you have a suitably strong character. You've already tested your character; show yourself here as well: does roulette call for more character than your idea?" That's what I repeated to myself. And since even to this day I hold the conviction that in games of chance, given a complete calmness of character, which preserves all the subtlety of intelligence and calculation, it is impossible not to overcome the crudeness of blind luck and win—so, naturally, I had to grow more and more vexed, seeing that at every moment I failed to sustain my character and got carried away like a perfect little brat. "I, who could endure hunger, cannot endure such a stupid thing!" That's what irked me. What's more, the awareness I have that no matter how ridiculous and humiliated I may seem, there lies within me that treasure of strength which will someday make them all change their opinion of me, this awareness—almost since the humiliated years of my childhood—then constituted the only source of my life, my light and my dignity, my weapon and my consolation, otherwise I might have killed myself while still a child. And therefore how could I not be irritated with myself, seeing what a pathetic being I turned into at the gaming table? That was why I could no longer leave off gambling; now I see it all clearly. Besides that main thing, my petty self-love also suffered. Losing humiliated me before the prince, before Versilov, though he never deigned to say anything, before everybody, even before Tatyana—so it seemed, so it felt to me. Finally, I'll make yet another confession: I was already corrupted then; it was already hard for me to give up a seven-course dinner in the restaurant, Matvei, the English shop, my perfumer's opinion—well, and all that. I was aware of it then, too, only I waved it away; now, though, in writing it down, I blush.

III

ARRIVING ALONE AND finding myself in an unfamiliar crowd, I first settled myself at the corner of the table and began staking small sums, and sat like that for about two hours without stirring. In those two hours, terrible rubbish went on—neither this nor that. I missed astonishing chances and tried not to get angry, but to succeed by coolheadedness and confidence. The end was that in the whole two hours I neither lost nor won: of the three hundred roubles, I lost some ten or fifteen. This insignificant result angered me, and what's more a most unpleasant vileness occurred. I know that there sometimes happen to be thieves at these roulette tables—that is, not from the street, but simply among the well-known gamblers. I'm certain, for instance, that the well-known gambler Aferdov is a thief; to this day he cuts a figure around town: I met him recently driving a pair of his own ponies; but he's a thief and he stole from me. This story is still to come; what happened that evening was just a prelude: I sat for the whole two hours at the corner of the table, and next to me all the while, on the left, was some rotten little fop—a Yid, I think; he participates somewhere, however, even writes something and gets it published. At the very last moment I suddenly won twenty roubles. Two red banknotes lay in front of me, and suddenly I see this little Yid reach out and quite calmly take one of my notes. I tried to stop him, but he, with a most insolent air and without raising his voice in the least, suddenly declares to me that it was his winnings, that he had just staked and won; he even refused to continue the conversation and turned his back. As if on purpose, I was in a most stupid state of mind at that moment: I had conceived a grand idea, and so I spat, got up quickly, and walked away, not even wanting to argue and making him a gift of the ten roubles. And it would have been hard to carry on with this story of the insolent pilferer, because the moment had been lost; the game had already gone ahead. And that was a huge mistake on my part, which had its consequences: three or four players next to us noticed our altercation and, seeing me give up so easily, probably took me for the same sort. It was exactly midnight; I went to another room, thought a bit, figured out a new plan, and, returning, exchangd my notes for half-imperials. I was now in possession of over forty pieces. I divided them into ten parts and decided to stake on *zéro* ten times in a row, four half-imperials each time, one after another. "If I win, I'm in luck; if I lose, so much the better; I'm never going to play anymore." I'll note that *zéro* hadn't come up even once in those two hours, so that in the end nobody even staked on it.

I played standing up, silently frowning and clenching my teeth. On the third stake, Zershchikov loudly announced *zéro*, which hadn't come up all day. They counted me out a hundred and forty half-imperials in gold. I still had seven stakes left, and I went on, and meanwhile everything around me began to spin and dance.

"Move over here!" I called the whole length of the table to one of the players who had been sitting next to me earlier, a gray-haired man with a big moustache and a purple face, wearing a tailcoat, who for several hours already, with inexpressible patience, had been staking small sums and losing time after time. "Move over here! The luck's here!"

"Are you speaking to me?" the moustache responded with some sort of menacing surprise from the other end of the table.

"Yes, you! You'll lose everything over there!"

"It's none of your business, and I beg you not to interfere with me!"

But I could no longer control myself. Across the table from me sat an elderly officer. Looking at my pile, he murmured to his neighbor:

"Strange: *zéro*. No, I won't venture on *zéro*."

"Venture it, Colonel!" I cried, placing another stake.

"I beg you to leave me in peace as well, sir, without your advice," he snapped sharply. "You shout too much here."

"I'm giving you good advice. Well, if you want to bet that *zéro* will come up again right now—here, I'll stake ten gold pieces, are you game?"

And I put up ten half-imperials.

"Bet ten gold pieces? That I can," he said drily and sternly. "I bet you that *zéro* won't come up."

"Ten louis d'ors, Colonel."

"Ten louis d'ors?"

"Ten half-imperials, Colonel, or, in high style—louis d'ors."

"Say half-imperials, then, and kindly do not joke with me."

I certainly had no hope of winning the bet: there were thirty-six chances to one that *zéro* wouldn't come up; but I proposed it, first, because I was showing off, and second, because I wanted to attract them all to me with something. I could see very well that for some reason nobody there liked me, and they took special pleasure in letting me know it. The roulette wheel spun—and what was the general amazement when *zéro* came up again! There was even a general outcry. Here the glory of winning befuddled me completely. Again they counted me out a hundred and forty half-imperials. Zershchikov asked me whether I wanted to take part of it in banknotes, but I mumbled something in reply, because I literally could no longer express myself calmly and coherently. My head was spinning, my legs were weak. I suddenly felt that I was about to start taking awful risks; besides, I wanted to undertake something else, propose another bet, count out a few thousand to somebody. Mechanically, I raked in the little pile of banknotes and gold pieces with my palm and couldn't bring myself to count them. At that moment I suddenly noticed the prince and Darzan behind me. They had just come from their faro, having lost their shirts there, as I learned afterwards.

"Ah, Darzan," I cried to him, "the luck's here! Stake on *zéro*!"

"I've lost everything, I have no money," he answered drily. And as for the prince, it was as if he decidedly did not notice or recognize me.

"There's money here!" I cried, pointing to my pile of gold. "How much do you want?"

"Devil take it!" cried Darzan, turning all red. "I don't believe I asked you for money."

"You're being called," Zershchikov pulled me by the sleeve.

I had been called, several times now and almost with curses, by the colonel, who had lost a bet of ten imperials to me.

"Kindly take it!" he cried, all purple with anger. "I'm not obliged to stand over you, and later you may say you didn't get it. Count it up."

"I trust you, I trust you, Colonel, without counting; only please don't shout at me like that and don't be angry." And I raked in his pile of gold pieces with my hand.

"My dear sir, I beg you, get at someone else with your raptures, and not at me," the colonel shouted sharply. "I didn't herd swine with you!"

"It's strange to let such people in—who is he?—some youngster," came low-voiced exclamations.

But I wasn't listening, I was staking at random, no longer on *zéro*. I staked a whole wad of hundred-rouble notes on the first eighteen numbers.

"Let's go, Darzan," the prince's voice came from behind me.

"Home?" I turned to them. "Wait for me, let's leave together, I'm through here."

My stake won; it was a big win.

"*Basta!*" I cried, and with trembling hands began raking up and pouring gold into my pockets, without counting and somehow clumsily crumpling the piles of banknotes with my fingers, wanting to stuff them all together into my side pocket. Suddenly the plump, signet-ringed hand of Aferdov, who was sitting next to me on the right and also staking large sums, reached for my three hundred-rouble notes and covered them with his palm.

"Excuse me, sir, that is not yours," he pronounced sternly and distinctly, though in a rather soft voice.

That was the prelude which, a few days later, was destined to have such consequences. Now I swear on my honor that those three hundred-rouble notes were mine, but, to my ill fate, though I was certain they were mine, I still had a lingering fraction of a doubt, and for an honest man that is everything; and I am an honest man. Above all, I did not yet know for certain then that Aferdov was a thief; I did not yet know his last name then, so that at that moment I could actually think that I was mistaken and that those three hundred-rouble notes were not among the ones just counted out to me. I hadn't counted my pile of money all the while and had only raked it in with my hands, but money had also been lying in front of Aferdov all the while, and right next to mine, albeit in good order and counted up. Finally, Aferdov was known there, was considered a rich man, was treated with respect. All this influenced me, and once again I didn't protest. A terrible mistake! The main swinishness consisted in the fact that I was in ecstasy.

"It's a great pity that I don't remember for certain, but it seems terribly likely to me that it's mine," I said, my lips trembling with indignation. These words at once aroused a murmur.

"In order to say such things, one needs to remember *for certain*, but you yourself have been so good as to declare that you do *not* remember for certain," Aferdov said with insufferable haughtiness.

"But who is he?—but how can it be permitted?" came several exclamations.

"It's not the first time for him; earlier there was an incident with Rechberg over a ten-rouble note," some mean little voice said beside me.

"Well, enough, enough!" I exclaimed, "I won't protest, take it! Prince... where are the prince and Darzan? Gone? Gentlemen, did you see where the prince and Darzan went?" and, having finally picked up all my money, and holding in my hand several half-imperials I hadn't had time to put in my pocket, I started after the prince and Darzan. The reader can see, I believe, that I'm not sparing myself and that I'm recollecting all of myself as I was at that moment, to the last vileness, so that what came afterwards will be understood.

The prince and Darzan had already gone downstairs, not paying the least attention to my calls and cries. I caught up with them, but paused for a second before the doorman and put three half-imperials in his hand, devil knows why; he looked at me in perplexity and didn't even thank me. But it was all the same to me, and if Matvei had been there, I surely would have dished out a whole fistful of gold pieces, and it seems that's what I wanted to do, but, running out to the porch, I suddenly recalled that I had dismissed him earlier. At that moment the prince's trotter drove up, and he got into the sledge.

"I'm coming with you, Prince, to your place!" I cried, seized the flap and flung it open so as to get into his sledge; but Darzan suddenly jumped into the sledge past me, and the driver, tearing the flap from my hands, covered the two gentlemen.

"Devil take it!" I cried in frenzy. It came out as if I had unfastened the flap for Darzan, like a lackey.

"Home!" cried the prince.

"Stop!" I bellowed, clutching at the sledge, but the horse pulled, and I tumbled into the snow. It even seemed to me that they laughed. Jumping up, I instantly grabbed the first cab that came along and raced to the prince's, urging my nag on every second.

IV

As if on purpose, the nag crawled on for an unnaturally long time, though I had promised a whole rouble. The driver kept whipping her up and, of course, whipped her enough for a rouble. My heart was sinking; I tried to start talking with the driver, but I couldn't even get the words out, and mumbled some sort of nonsense. That was the state I was in when I ran up to the prince's. He had just returned; he had taken Darzan home and was alone. Pale and angry, he was pacing his study. I repeat once more: he had lost terribly. He looked at me with some sort of distracted perplexity.

"You again!" he said, frowning.

"So as to have done with you, sir!" I said breathlessly. "How dared you act that way with me?"

He looked at me questioningly.

"If you were going with Darzan, you might just have told me you were going with Darzan, instead of which you started the horse, and I..."

"Ah, yes, it seems you fell in the snow," and he laughed in my face.

"The response to that is a challenge, and therefore we shall first finish with our accounts..."

And with a trembling hand I began taking my money out and placing it on the sofa, on a little marble table, and even into some open book, in piles, handfuls, wads; several coins rolled onto the carpet.

"Ah, yes, it seems you won?... One can tell it by your tone."

Never before had he spoken so impudently with me. I was very pale.

"Here... I don't know how much... has to be counted. I owe you up to three thousand... or how much?... more or less?"

"I don't believe I'm forcing you to pay."

"No, sir, I myself want to pay, and you should know why. I know there's a thousand roubles in this wad—here!" And I started counting with trembling hands, but stopped. "Never mind, I know it's a thousand. So I'm taking this thousand for myself, and all the rest, these piles, you can take for my debt, part of my debt. I think there's as much as two thousand here, or maybe more!"

"But you're still keeping a thousand for yourself?" the prince bared his teeth.

"Do you need it? In that case... I wanted... I thought you wouldn't want... but if you need it—here..."

"No, no need," he turned away from me contemptuously and again began pacing the room.

"And devil knows what makes you pay it back," he suddenly turned to me with a frightful challenge in his face.

"I'm paying it back in order to demand an accounting from you!" I yelled in my turn.

"Get out of here with your eternal words and gestures!" He suddenly stamped his feet at me as if in frenzy. "I wanted to throw you out long ago, you and your Versilov."

"You're out of your mind!" I cried. And it did look like it.

"The two of you have worn me out with your catchy phrases, nothing but phrases, phrases, phrases! About honor, for instance! Pah! I've long wanted to break... I'm glad, glad that the moment has come. I considered myself bound, and I blushed at being obliged to receive you... both! But now I don't consider myself bound by anything, not by anything, know that! Your Versilov set me on to attack Mme. Akhmakov and disgrace her... Don't you dare speak to me about honor after that. Because you're dishonorable people... both, both! And weren't you ashamed to take money from me?"

Everything went dark in my eyes.

"I took it from you as a comrade," I began terribly softly. "You yourself offered, and I trusted in your goodwill..."

"I'm not your comrade! I didn't give you money for that, and you yourself know what it was for."

"I took it against Versilov's money; of course, it was stupid, but I..."

"You couldn't have taken it against Versilov's money without his permission, and I couldn't have given you his money without his permission... I gave you my own, and you knew it—knew it and took it—and I suffered this hateful comedy in my own house!"

"What did I know? What comedy? Why did you give me the money?"

"*Pour vos beaux yeux, mon cousin!*"* he guffawed right in my face.

"Ah, the devil!" I yelled, "take all of it, here's the thousand for you! We're quits now, and tomorrow..."

And I hurled the wad of banknotes at him that I had been keeping for my further needs. The wad hit him right in the waistcoat and dropped to the floor. In three huge strides, he quickly came up close to me.

"Do you dare to tell me," he said ferociously and distinctly, syllable by syllable, "that while you were taking my money all this month, you didn't know that your sister is pregnant by me?"

"What? How?" I cried, and my legs suddenly became weak, and I sank strengthlessly onto the sofa. He himself told me later that I literally turned as pale as a sheet. My mind became addled. I remember we went on gazing silently into each other's faces. Fear seemed to pass over his face; he suddenly bent down, seized me by the shoulders, and began to support me. I remember very well his fixed smile; there was mistrust and astonishment in it. No! He had never expected his words would have such an effect, because he was convinced of my guilt.

It ended with my fainting, but only for a minute; I recovered, got to my feet, gazed at him and reflected—and suddenly the whole truth was revealed to my long-sleeping reason! If someone had told me beforehand and asked, "What would you do to him at that moment?" I would probably have answered that I would

*For your pretty eyes, my cousin!

tear him to pieces. But something quite different took place, and totally beyond my will: I suddenly covered my face with both hands, and wept and sobbed bitterly. It came out that way of itself! The little child suddenly betrayed himself in the young man. Which meant that the little child was still living in my soul by a whole half. I fell on the sofa weeping. "Liza! Liza! Poor, unfortunate girl!" The prince suddenly and completely believed me.

"God, how guilty I am before you!" he cried in deep sorrow. "Oh, what vile thoughts I had of you in my suspiciousness . . . Forgive me, Arkady Makarovich!"

I suddenly jumped up, wanted to say something to him, stood in front of him, but, having said nothing, ran out of the room and out of the house. I plodded home on foot and barely remember the way. I threw myself on my bed, buried my face in the pillow, in the darkness, and thought and thought. At such moments one's thinking is never orderly and consistent. It was as if the thread of my mind and imagination kept snapping, and, I remember, I would even start dreaming of something totally irrelevant and even of God knows what. But grief and calamity would suddenly come back to my mind with pain and heartache, and I would wring my hands again and exclaim, "Liza, Liza!" and weep again. I don't remember how I fell asleep, but I slept soundly, sweetly.

Chapter Seven

I

I WOKE UP in the morning at around eight o'clock, instantly locked my door, sat by the window, and started to think. I sat like that until ten o'clock. The maid knocked at my door twice, but I sent her away. Finally, between ten and eleven, there came another knock. I shouted again, but it was Liza. Along with her the maid came in, brought me coffee, and set about lighting the stove. To send the maid away was impossible, and all the while Fekla was putting in the wood and blowing up the fire, I paced my small room with big strides, not starting a conversation and even trying not to look at Liza. The maid worked with inexpressible slowness, and that on purpose, as all maids do in such cases, when they notice that their presence is keeping the masters from talking. Liza sat on a chair by the window and watched me.

"Your coffee will get cold," she said suddenly.

I looked at her: not the least embarrassment, perfect calm, and even a smile on her lips.

"Women!" I couldn't stand it and heaved my shoulders. Finally the maid got the stove lighted and began tidying up, but I hotly chased her out and locked the door at last.

"Tell me, please, why you locked the door again?" asked Liza.

I planted myself in front of her:

"Liza, I would never have thought you could deceive me like this!" I exclaimed suddenly, not even thinking at all that I would begin that way, and it was not tears this time, but almost some sort of spiteful feeling that suddenly stung my heart, so much so that I didn't even expect it. Liza blushed, yet did not answer, but only went on looking me straight in the eye.

"Wait, Liza, wait, oh, how stupid I was! But was I? The hints all came together into one heap only yesterday, and before that how could I have known? From the fact that you went to see Mrs. Stolbeev and this...Darya Onisimovna? But I looked upon you as the sun, Liza, and how could anything have occurred to me? Remember how I met you that time, two months ago, in *his* apartment, and how we walked in the sun then and rejoiced...was it already then? Was it?"

She responded by inclining her head affirmatively.

"So you were already deceiving me then! Here it's not from my stupidity, Liza, the reason here is sooner my egoism, not stupidity, my heart's egoism and—and, perhaps, the certainty of your holiness. Oh, I was always certain that you were all infinitely higher than I, and—now look! Finally, yesterday, in the course of one day, I didn't manage to figure it out, despite all the indications... But that's not at all what I was occupied with yesterday!"

Here I suddenly remembered Katerina Nikolaevna, and again something stung my heart painfully, as with a pin, and I blushed all over. Naturally, I couldn't be kind at that moment.

"But why are you justifying yourself? It seems you're in a hurry to justify yourself for something, Arkady—what is it?" Liza asked softly and meekly, but in a very firm and convinced voice.

"What is it? Why, what am I to do now?—there's at least that question! And you say 'what is it?' I don't know how to act! I don't know how brothers act on such occasions... I know marriages can be forced with a pistol in the hand... I'll act as an honorable man should! But, you see, I don't know how an honorable man should act here!... Why? Because we're not nobility, but he's a prince and is making his career; he won't listen to us honorable people. We're not even brother and sister, but some sort of illegitimates, without a family name, a household serf's children. Do princes marry household serfs? Oh, how vile! And, on top of that, you sit there and get surprised at me."

"I believe that you're suffering," Liza blushed again, "but you're in a rush and make yourself suffer."

"In a rush? So I'm really not behind enough, in your opinion! Is it for you, for you, Liza, to speak to me like that?" I got carried away, finally, by total indignation. "And how much disgrace I endured, and how this prince must have despised me! Oh, it's all clear to me now, and the whole picture stands before me: he fully imagined that I had guessed about his liaison with you long ago, but that I was keeping quiet or even putting on airs and boasting about 'honor'—he might even have thought that of me! And that I was taking money for my sister, for my sister's disgrace! That's what he found so repulsive to see, and I fully justify him: to see and receive a scoundrel every day, because he's her brother, and what's more, he talks about honor... it could make the heart wither, even his heart! And you allowed all that, you didn't warn me! He despised me so much that he talked about me with

Stebelkov, and yesterday he told me himself that he wanted to throw both me and Versilov out. And that Stebelkov! 'Anna Andreevna is as much a sister to you as Lizaveta Makarovna,' and then he shouts after me: 'My money's better.' And me, me, sprawling insolently on *his* sofas and foisting myself on his acquaintances as an equal, devil take them! And you allowed all that! Perhaps Darzan knows now, too, at least judging by his tone yesterday evening . . . Everybody, everybody knows, except me!"

"Nobody knows anything, he hasn't and *couldn't* have told any of his acquaintances," Liza interrupted me, "and about this Stebelkov I know only that Stebelkov torments him, and that this Stebelkov could only have guessed it . . . And I told him about you several times, and he believed me completely that you didn't know anything, and I simply don't know why and how it came out between you yesterday."

"Oh, at least I paid him back yesterday, and that's a load off my heart anyway! Liza, does mama know? But how could she not know? Yesterday, yesterday, how she rose up against me! . . . Ah, Liza! Can it be that you consider yourself right in decidedly everything, that you don't blame yourself the tiniest bit? I don't know how these things are judged nowadays and of what thoughts you are—that is, as regards me, mama, your brother, your father . . . Does Versilov know?"

"Mama hasn't said anything to him; he doesn't ask; it must be that he doesn't want to ask."

"He knows, but he doesn't want to know, that's so, that's like him! Well, you can make fun of your brother's role, your stupid brother, talking about pistols, but your mother, your mother! Can it be that you didn't think, Liza, how this is a reproach to mama? I was suffering over that all night. Mama's first thought will be, 'It's because I was also guilty, and like mother, like daughter!' "

"Oh, how spitefully and cruelly you said that!" Liza cried with tears bursting from her eyes, got up, and went quickly towards the door.

"Wait, wait!" I caught hold of her, sat her back down, and sat down beside her, my arm still around her.

"I just thought it would all be like this, as I was coming here, and that you were sure to want to make sure that I acknowledge my guilt. As you wish, I acknowledge it. It was only out of pride that I was silent just now and didn't say anything, but I pity you and mama much more than I do myself..." She didn't finish, and suddenly burst into hot tears.

"Come, Liza, don't, don't say anything. I'm not your judge. Liza, how is mama? Tell me, has she known for long?"

"I think so; but I told her myself not long ago, when *this* happened," she said quietly, lowering her eyes.

"And what did she say?"

"She said, 'Keep it!'" Liza said still more softly.

"Ah, yes, Liza, 'keep it'! Don't do anything to yourself, God forbid!"

"I won't," she replied firmly and again raised her eyes to me. "Don't worry," she added, "that's not it at all."

"Liza, dear, I see only that I don't know anything here, but instead I've only now found out how much I love you. There's only one thing I don't understand, Liza: it's all clear to me, there's only one thing I can't understand at all: what makes you love him? How could you have fallen in love with such a man? That's the question!"

"And you probably also suffered over that at night?" Liza smiled gently.

"Wait, Liza, it's a stupid question, and you're laughing; laugh, then, but it's impossible not to be surprised: you and *he* are such opposites! He—I've studied him—he's gloomy, suspicious, maybe he's very kind, let it be so, but he's highly inclined to see evil in everything first of all (in that, however, he's quite like me!). He passionately respects nobility—I admit that, I see it—but only, it seems, in the ideal. Oh, he's inclined to repentance, he spends all his life constantly blaming himself and repenting, but on the other hand he never improves; however, maybe that's also like me. A thousand prejudices and false thoughts and—no thoughts at all! He seeks a great deed and does dirty little tricks. Forgive me, Liza, anyhow I'm a fool: I say this, I hurt you and know it; I understand that..."

"The portrait would be true," Liza smiled, "but you're too angry with him over me, and therefore none of it is true. He's been mistrustful of you from the beginning, and you couldn't see the whole of him, but with me even in Luga... He's seen only me alone, ever since Luga. Yes, he's suspicious and morbid, and without me he would have lost his mind; and if he leaves me, he will lose his mind or shoot himself; it seems he's realized that and knows it," Liza added as if to herself and pensively. "Yes, he's constantly weak, but these weak ones are occasionally capable of doing something very strong... How strangely you said that about the pistol, Arkady; there's no need for any of that, and I know what will happen myself. It's not I who am after him, but he who is after me. Mama weeps, she says, 'If you marry him, you'll be unhappy, he'll stop loving you.' I don't believe that. Maybe I'll be unhappy, but he won't stop loving me. That's not why I haven't accepted him all along, but for another reason. For two months now I haven't given him my acceptance, but today I told him, '*Yes,* I'll marry you.' Arkasha, you know, yesterday" (her eyes shone and she suddenly put her arms around my neck), "yesterday he went to Anna Andreevna and told her directly, in all sincerity, that he couldn't love her... Yes, he gave a complete explanation, and that thought is now finished! He never had any part in that thought, it was all dreamed up by Prince Nikolai Ivanovich, and those tormentors, Stebelkov and another one, kept pushing him... And so for that I said *yes* to him today. Dear Arkady, he's calling for you very much, and don't be offended with him for yesterday; he's not feeling well today, and will be at home all day. He's really unwell, Arkady, don't think it's a pretext. He sent me specially and asked me to tell you that he 'needs' you, that he has much to tell you, and it wouldn't be convenient here in this apartment. Well, good-bye! Ah, Arkady, I'm ashamed even to say it, but as I was coming here, I was terribly afraid that you had stopped loving me, I kept crossing myself on the way, but—you're so kind, so sweet! I'll never forget it! I'm going to see mama. And you try to love him a little, hm?"

I embraced her warmly and told her:

"I think, Liza, that you're a strong character. Yes, I believe it's not you who are after him, but he who is after you, only still..."

"Only still, 'What makes you love him—that's the question!'" Liza picked up with a suddenly mischievous smile, as she used to, and said "that's the question!" terribly like me. And what's more, exactly as I do with this phrase, she raised her index finger in front of her. We kissed each other, but when she left, my heart was wrung again.

II

I'LL NOTE HERE just for myself: there were, for instance, moments after Liza left when a whole crowd of the most unexpected thoughts came to my head, and I was even very pleased with them. "Well, why do I fuss so," I thought, "what is it to me? It's the same with everyone, or almost. So what if it happened with Liza? Do I have to save 'the family honor' or what?" I mark all these meannesses in order to show how poorly fortified I was in the understanding of evil and good. The only saving thing was feeling: I knew that Liza was unhappy, that mama was unhappy, and I knew it through feeling, when I remembered about them, and therefore I felt that all that had happened must not be good.

Now I'll state beforehand that from this day right up to the catastrophe of my illness, events raced on so quickly that, recalling them now, I'm even surprised myself at how I could hold out against them, how fate failed to crush me. They weakened my mind and even my feelings, and if, in the end, I hadn't held out and had committed a crime (and a crime almost was committed), the jury might very well have acquitted me. But I will try to describe it all in strict order, though I tell you beforehand that there was little order in my thoughts then. Events came pressing like the wind, and thoughts whirled in my mind like dry leaves in autumn. Since I consisted entirely of other people's thoughts, where could I get my own, when I needed them for an independent decision? And I had no guide at all.

I decided to go to see the prince in the evening, so that we could discuss everything in perfect freedom, and until evening I stayed at home. But at twilight I again received a note from Stebelkov by the city mail, three lines, with an insistent and "earnest" request to call on him the next morning at around eleven o'clock on "most important business, and you will see yourself that it is business." Having thought it over, I decided to act according to the circumstances, since tomorrow was still a long way off.

It was already eight o'clock. I would have left long ago, but I kept waiting for Versilov; there was much I wanted to express to him, and my heart was burning. But Versilov wouldn't come and didn't come. For the time being I couldn't show myself at mama's and Liza's, and I had a feeling that Versilov probably hadn't been there all day. I went on foot, and it occurred to me on the way to peek into yesterday's tavern on the canal. Versilov happened to be sitting in yesterday's place.

"I just thought you'd come here," he said, smiling strangely and looking at me strangely. His smile was unkind, such as I hadn't seen on his face in a long time.

I sat down at his table and first told him all the facts about the prince and Liza from the beginning, and about my scene yesterday at the prince's after the roulette; and I didn't forget my winning at roulette. He listened very attentively and asked again about the prince's decision to marry Liza.

"*Pauvre enfant*, maybe she won't gain anything by that. But most likely it won't happen... though he's capable..."

"Tell me, as a friend: you did know about it, you had a presentiment?"

"My friend, what could I do here? It's all a matter of feelings and another person's conscience, if only on the side of this poor little girl. I repeat to you: I did enough poking into other people's consciences once upon a time—it's a most inconvenient maneuver! I won't refuse to help in misfortune, as much as my strength allows and if I can sort it out myself. And you, my dear, you really suspected nothing all the while?"

"But how could you," I cried, flushing all over, "how could you, with even a drop of suspicion that I knew about Liza's liaison with the prince, and seeing that at the same time I was taking the prince's money—how could you talk to me, sit with me, offer me your hand—me, whom you should have considered a scoundrel! Because I bet you certainly suspected that I knew everything and was knowingly taking the prince's money for my sister!"

"Once again it's a matter of conscience," he smiled. "And how do you know," he added distinctly, with a certain enigmatic feeling, "how do you know that I wasn't afraid, too, like you yesterday on a different occasion, to lose my 'ideal' and, instead of my ardent and honest boy, to confront a blackguard? Fearing it, I postponed the moment. Why not suppose in me, instead of laziness or perfidy, something more innocent, well, stupid perhaps, but of a more noble sort? *Que diable!* I'm all too often stupid and without nobility. What use would you be to me, if you had the same inclinations? To persuade and reform in such cases is mean; you'd have lost all value in my eyes, even if you were reformed..."

"And Liza—are you sorry, are you sorry for her?"

"Very sorry, my dear. What makes you think I'm so unfeeling?... On the contrary, I'll try as hard as I can... Well, and how are *you*? How are *your* affairs?"

"Let's leave my affairs out of it; I have no affairs of *my own* now. Listen, why do you doubt that he'll marry her? Yesterday he was at Anna Andreevna's and positively renounced... well, I mean, that a stupid idea... conceived by Prince Nikolai Ivanovich—to get them married. He renounced it positively."

"Oh? When was that? And from whom precisely did you hear it?" he inquired with curiosity. I told him all I knew.

"Hm..." he said pensively and as if figuring something out for himself, "meaning that it happened precisely an hour... before a certain other talk. Hm... well, yes, of course, such a talk could have taken place between them... though, incidentally, I'm informed that so far nothing has been said or done on one side or the other... Of course, two words are enough for such a talk. But, look here," he suddenly smiled strangely, "I have a piece of quite extraordinary information, which will, of course, interest you right now: even if your prince had made a proposal to Anna Andreevna yesterday (which I, suspecting about Liza, would have done everything in my power to prevent, *entre nous soit dit**), Anna Andreevna would certainly and in any case have refused him at once. You seem to love Anna Andreevna very much, to respect and value her? That's very nice on your part, and therefore you will probably be very glad for her: she's getting married, my dear, and, judging by her character, it seems she will certainly get married, and I—well, I, of course, will give her my blessing."

"Getting married? To whom?" I cried, terribly surprised.

"Try to guess. But I won't torment you: to Prince Nikolai Ivanovich, your dear old man."

I stared at him all eyes.

"She must have been nursing this idea for a long time, and, of course, she worked it out artistically on all sides," he went on lazily and distinctly. "I suppose it happened exactly an hour after the visit of 'Prince Seryozha.' (See how inopportunely he came galloping!) She simply went to Prince Nikolai Ivanovich and made him a proposal."

"How, 'made him a proposal'? You mean he proposed to her?"

"He? Come now! It was she, she herself. That's just it, that he's perfectly delighted. They say he sits there now, surprised at how it hadn't occurred to him. I've heard he's even slightly ill... also from delight, it must be."

"Listen, you speak so mockingly... I almost can't believe it. And how could she propose? What did she say?"

"Rest assured, my friend, that I'm sincerely glad," he replied,

*Be it said between us.

suddenly assuming a terribly serious air. "He's old, of course, but he can marry, according to all laws and customs, while she—here again it's a matter of another person's conscience, something I've already repeated to you, my friend. However, she's more than competent enough to arrive at her own view and her own decision. As for the details proper and the words in which she expressed it, I'm unable to tell you, my friend. But she, of course, was able to do it, and maybe in a way such as you and I would never have come up with. The best thing in all this is that there's no scandal involved, everything's *très comme il faut** in the world's eyes. Of course, it's only too clear that she wanted a position for herself in the world, but then, too, she deserves it. All this, my friend, is a completely worldly thing. And she must have proposed splendidly and gracefully. She's a stern type, my friend, a girl-nun, as you once defined her; a 'calm young lady,' as I've long been calling her. She's almost his ward, you know, and has seen his kindness towards her more than once. She's been assuring me for a long time now that she 'so respects and values, so pities and sympathizes with him,' well, and all the rest, that I was even partly prepared. I was told of it all this morning, on her behalf and at her request, by my son and her brother, Andrei Andreevich, with whom it seems you're not acquainted, and with whom I meet regularly twice a year. He respectfully approbates her step."

"Then it's already public? God, I'm so amazed!"

"No, it's not public at all yet, not for some time . . . I don't know about them, generally I'm quite outside of it. But it's all true."

"But now Katerina Nikolaevna . . . What do you think, is Bjoring going to like this little snack?"

"That I don't know . . . what, essentially, there is for him not to like; but, believe me, Anna Andreevna is a highly decent person in that sense as well. And what a one she is, though, this Anna Andreevna! Yesterday morning, just before that, she inquired of me whether I was or was not in love with the widow Akhmakov! Remember, I told you that yesterday with surprise: she wouldn't be able to marry the father if I married the daughter. Do you understand now?"

"Ah, indeed!" I cried. "But can it be, indeed, that Anna Andreevna supposed you . . . might wish to marry Katerina Nikolaevna?"

"It looks that way, my friend, however . . . however, it seems it's

*Very proper.

time you went wherever you're going. You see, I keep having these headaches. I'll tell them to play *Lucia.* I love the solemnity of boredom—however, I've already told you that... I repeat myself unpardonably... However, maybe I'll leave here. I love you, my dear, but good-bye; when I have a headache or a toothache, I always yearn for solitude."

Some tormented wrinkle appeared on his face; I believe now that his head did ache then, his head especially...

"See you tomorrow," I said.

"What about tomorrow, what's happening tomorrow?" he smiled crookedly.

"I'll come to you, or you to me."

"No, I won't come to you, but you'll come running to me..."

There was something all too unkind in his face, but I had other things to think about: such an event!

III

THE PRINCE WAS actually unwell and was sitting at home alone, his head wrapped in a wet towel. He was waiting very much for me; but it was not his head alone that ached, but rather he ached all over morally. Again I'll state beforehand: all this time lately, and right up to the catastrophe, I was somehow forced to meet nothing but people who were so agitated that they were almost crazy, so that I myself must have been as if involuntarily infected. I confess, I came with bad feelings, and I was very ashamed that I had burst into tears in front of him the day before. And anyway he and Liza had managed to deceive me so skillfully that I couldn't help seeing myself as a fool. In short, when I went in, there were false strings sounding in my soul. But all that was affected and false quickly dropped away. I must do him justice: as soon as his suspiciousness fell and broke to pieces, he gave himself definitively, displaying features of an almost infantile affection, trustfulness, and love. He kissed me tearfully and at once began talking business... Yes, he really needed me very much; there was an extremely great disorder in his words and flow of ideas.

He announced to me quite firmly his intention to marry Liza and as soon as possible. "That she's not of the nobility, believe me, has never embarrassed me for a moment," he said to me. "My grandfather was married to a household serf, a singer from a neighboring landowner's private serf theater. Of course, my family nursed some hopes in my regard, but they'll have to give in now, and there won't be any struggle. I want to break, to break with the whole present definitively! Everything will be different, everything will be in a new way! I don't understand what makes your sister love me; but, of course, without her maybe I wouldn't be living in the world now. I swear to you from the bottom of my heart that I now look at my meeting her in Luga as at the finger of Providence. I think she loves me for the 'boundlessness of my fall'... though, can you understand that, Arkady Makarovich?"

"Perfectly!" I said in a highly convinced voice. I was sitting in an armchair by the table, and he was pacing the room.

"I must tell you this whole fact of our meeting without reserve. It began with my soul's secret, which she alone has learned, because she's the only one I've ventured to entrust it to. And to this day no one else knows it. I found myself in Luga then with despair in my soul and was living at Mrs. Stolbeev's, I don't know why, maybe I was seeking the most complete solitude. At that time I had just retired from service in the ——— regiment. I had entered that regiment when I came back from abroad, after that meeting abroad with Andrei Petrovich. I had money then, I squandered it in the regiment, lived openhandedly; but my officer comrades didn't like me, though I tried not to insult anyone. And I confess to you that no one has ever liked me. There was an ensign there, Stepanov or something, I confess to you, an extremely empty, worthless, and even as if downtrodden man, in short, not distinguished by anything. Indisputably honest, however. He began calling on me, I wasn't ceremonious with him, he spent whole days sitting in the corner of my room, silently but with dignity, though he didn't bother me at all. Once I told him a certain current anecdote, which I embellished with a lot of nonsense, such as that the colonel's daughter was not indifferent to me and that the colonel, who was counting on me, would of course do whatever I liked... In short, I'll omit the details, but from all this later came a very complex and vile piece of gossip. It came not from Stepanov, but from my orderly, who had been eavesdropping and remembered everything, because it involved an anecdote compromising to the young lady. When the gossip went around, this orderly, at the officers' interrogation, pointed the finger at Stepanov, that is, that I had told it to this Stepanov. Stepanov was put in such a position that he simply couldn't deny having heard it; it was a matter of honor. And since I had lied for two-thirds of the anecdote, the officers were indignant, and the regimental commander, summoning us to him, was forced to have it out. It was here that the question was put to Stepanov in front of everyone: had he or had he not heard it? And the man told the whole truth. Well, sir, what did I do then, I, a thousand-year prince? I denied it and told Stepanov to his face that he was lying, told him politely, that is, in the sense that he had 'misunderstood' it, and so on . . . Again, I'll omit the details, but the advantage of my position was that, since Stepanov frequented me, I could present the matter, not without some probability, so that it would look as if he had connived with my orderly with a view to some advantage. Stepanov only looked at me silently and shrugged. I remember his look and will never forget it. Then he immediately sent in his resignation, but what do you think happened? The officers, all of them at once, to a man, paid him a visit and persuaded him not to resign. Two weeks later I also left the regiment. Nobody drove me out, nobody asked me to leave, I gave family circumstances as a pretext. That was the end of the matter. At first I was perfectly all right and was even angry with them; I lived in Luga, made the acquaintance of Lizaveta Makarovna, but then, a month later, I began looking at my revolver and thinking about death. I look at everything darkly, Arkady Makarovich. I prepared a letter to the regimental commander and my comrades, with a full confession of my lie, restoring Stepanov's honor. Having written the letter, I posed myself a problem: 'Send it and live, or send it and die?' I wouldn't have been able to resolve this problem. Chance, blind chance, after one quick and strange conversation with Lizaveta Makarovna, suddenly brought us close. Before then she had come to see Mrs. Stolbeev; we met, greeted each other, and even spoke occasionally. I suddenly revealed everything to her. And it was then that she gave me her hand."

"How did she resolve the problem?"

"I didn't send the letter. She decided against sending it. She motivated it like this: if I did send the letter, I would, of course, be committing a noble act, enough to wash away all the dirt and even much more, but could I bear it myself? Her opinion was that no one could bear it, because the future would be ruined then, and resurrection into a new life would be impossible. And besides, it would have been one thing if Stepanov had suffered; but he had been vindicated by all the officers without that. In short—a paradox; but she held me back, and I gave myself to her completely."

"She resolved it in a Jesuitical way, but like a woman!" I cried. "She already loved you then!"

"And with that I was reborn into a new life. I gave myself a promise to remake myself, to change my life, to be worthy of it before myself and before her, and—look what we ended with! It ended with you and me going to the roulette houses, playing faro; I couldn't stand up to the inheritance, was glad for my career, all these people, the trotters... I tormented Liza—a disgrace!"

He rubbed his forehead with his hand and paced the room.

"You and I have been overtaken by the same Russian fate, Arkady Makarovich: you don't know what to do, and I don't know what to do. Once a Russian man gets slightly out of the ordinary rut that custom lays down for him—he immediately doesn't know what to do. In the rut, everything is clear: income, rank, position in the world, equipage, visits, service, wife—but the slightest something, and what am I? A leaf driven by the wind. I don't know what to do! These two months I've stuggled to keep in the rut, I've come to love the rut, I've been drawn into the rut. You still don't know all the depths of my fall here: I loved Liza, sincerely loved her, and at the same time had thoughts of Mme. Akhmakov!"

"Is it possible?" I cried in pain. "By the way, Prince, what did you tell me yesterday about Versilov, that he set you on to some sort of meanness against Katerina Nikolaevna?"

"Maybe I exaggerated and am as guilty in my suspiciousness before him as before you. Let's drop that. What, can you really think that for all this time, ever since Luga, I haven't been nursing a lofty ideal of life? I swear to you, it never left me and was with me constantly, not losing the least of its beauty in my soul. I remembered the oath I had given Lizaveta Makarovna to be reborn. Andrei Petrovich, speaking here yesterday about nobility, didn't say anything new to me, I assure you. My ideal was firmly established: a few score acres of land (and only a few score, because I already have almost nothing left of the inheritance); then a complete, the most complete, break with society and career; a house in the country, a family, and myself—a plowman or something of the sort. Oh, in our family it's nothing new; my father's brother plowed with his own hands, so did my grandfather. We're only thousand-year-old princes and as noble as the Rohans,[24] but we're paupers. And this is what I'd teach my children: 'Always remember all your life that you are a nobleman, that the sacred blood of Russian princes flows in your veins, but do not be ashamed that your father plowed the earth himself: he did it *like a prince.*' I wouldn't leave them any fortune except for this piece of land, but instead I'd give them a higher education, I'd consider it my duty. Oh, here Liza could help me. Liza, the children, work—oh, how we both dreamed of it all, dreamed of it here, right in these rooms, and what then? At the same time I had thoughts of Mme. Akhmakov, without loving this person at all, and of the possibility of a wealthy society marriage! And only after the news Nashchokin brought yesterday, about this Bjoring, did I decide to go to Anna Andreevna."

"But didn't you go to renounce her? That was already an honorable act, I think."

"You think so?" he stopped in front of me. "No, you still don't know my nature! Or... or there's something here that I don't know myself, because here, it must be, there's not just nature. I love you sincerely, Arkady Makarovich, and, besides that, I've been deeply guilty before you for all these two months, and therefore I want you, as Liza's brother, to know everything: I went to propose to Anna Andreevna, and not to renounce her."

"Can it be? But Liza said..."

"I deceived Liza."

"I beg your pardon: you made a formal proposal and Anna Andreevna refused you? Is that it? Is that it? The details are extremely important for me, Prince."

"No, I didn't make any proposal, but only because I had no time; she let me know beforehand—not directly, of course, but nevertheless in very transparent and clear terms, she 'delicately' gave me to understand that the idea was henceforth impossible."

"That means it's the same as if you didn't make the proposal, and your pride hasn't suffered!"

"How can you possibly reason like that! And the judgment of my own conscience? And Liza, whom I deceived and... therefore wanted to abandon? And the vow I made to myself and all the generations of my ancestors—to be reborn and to redeem all my former baseness! I beg you not to tell her about it. Maybe it's the one thing she'd be unable to forgive me! I've been sick since that business yesterday. And the main thing is that it's all over now, and the last of the Princes Sokolsky will go to hard labor. Poor Liza! I've been waiting all day for you, Arkady Makarovich, to reveal to you, as Liza's brother, something she doesn't know yet. I am a criminal and a partner in the counterfeiting of shares in the ——sky railroad."

"What's this now! Why to hard labor?" I jumped up, looking at him in horror. His face expressed the most deep, dark, and hopeless grief.

"Sit down," he said, and sat down himself in the facing armchair. "First of all, learn this fact: a little over a year ago, that same summer of Ems, Lydia and Katerina Nikolaevna, and then Paris, precisely at the time when I went to Paris for two months, in Paris, of course, I didn't have enough money. Just then Stebelkov turned up, whom, incidentally, I had known before. He gave me some money and promised to give more, but for his part also asked me to help him: he had need of an artist, a draftsman, an engraver, a lithographer, and so on, a chemist, and a technician—and all that for certain purposes. About the purposes, even from the first, he spoke quite transparently. And what then? He knew my character—all this only made me laugh. The thing was that since my schooldays I had been acquainted with a certain man, at the present time a Russian émigré, not of Russian origin, however, and living somewhere in Hamburg. In Russia he had already been mixed up once in a story to do with forged documents. It was this man Stebelkov was counting on, but he needed a recommendation, and he turned to me. I gave him two lines and forgot about it at once. Later he met me once more and then again, and I got as much as three thousand from him then. I literally forgot about this whole affair. Here I kept taking money from him on promissory notes and pledges, and he twisted before me like a slave, and suddenly yesterday I find out from him for the first time that I'm a criminal."

"When yesterday?"

"Yesterday morning, when we were shouting in my study before Nashchokin's arrival. For the first time, and perfectly clearly now, he dared to bring up Anna Andreevna with me. I raised my hand to strike him, but he suddenly stood up and announced to me that I was solidary with him and that I should remember that I was a partner and as much of a swindler as he—in short, that was the idea, though not in those words."

"What nonsense, but is this a dream?"

"No, it's not a dream. He was here today and explained in more detail. These shares have been circulating for a long time, and more are going to be put into circulation, but it seems they've already begun to be picked up here and there. Of course, I'm on the sidelines, but 'all the same, you kindly furnished that letter then, sir'—that's what Stebelkov told me."

"But you didn't know what it was for, or did you?"

"I knew," the prince replied softly and lowered his eyes. "That is, you see, I knew and didn't know. I laughed, I found it funny. I didn't think about anything then, the less so as I had no need at all for counterfeit shares and it wasn't I who was going to make them. But, all the same, the three thousand he gave me then, he didn't even set down to my account afterwards, and I allowed that. And, anyway, how do you know, maybe I, too, was a counterfeiter? I couldn't help knowing—I'm not a child; I knew, but I found it amusing, and so I helped scoundrels and jailbirds... and did it for money! Which means that I, too, am a counterfeiter!"

"Oh, you're exaggerating; you were wrong, but you're exaggerating!"

"Above all, there's a certain Zhibelsky here, still a young man, in the legal line, something like a lawyer's assistant. He was also some sort of partner in these shares, and later he came to me from that gentleman in Hamburg, with trifles, naturally, and I didn't even know why myself, there was no mention of shares... But, anyhow, he saved two documents written in my hand, both two-line notes, and, of course, they are also evidence; today I understood that very well. Stebelkov explains that this Zhibelsky is hindering everything: he stole something there, somebody's money, public money, it seems, but he intends to steal more and then to emigrate; so he needs eight thousand, not less, to help him emigrate. My share of the inheritance satisfies Stebelkov, but Stebelkov says that Zhibelsky also has to be satisfied... In short, I must give up my share of the inheritance, plus ten thousand more—that's their final word. And then they'll give me back my two notes. They're in it together, it's clear."

"An obvious absurdity! If they denounce you, they'll betray themselves! They won't denounce you for anything."

"I realize that. They're not threatening me with denunciation at all; they merely say: 'We won't denounce you, of course, but if the affair happens to be discovered, then...'—that's what they say, and that's all; but I think it's enough! That's not the thing: whatever may come of it, and even if those notes were in my pocket now, but to be solidary with those swindlers, to be comrades with them eternally, eternally! To lie to Russia, to lie to my children, to lie to Liza, to lie to my own conscience!..."

"Does Liza know?"

"No, she doesn't know everything. She couldn't bear it in her condition. I now wear the uniform of my regiment, and every time I meet a soldier of my regiment, every second, I'm conscious in myself that I dare not wear this uniform."

"Listen," I cried suddenly, "there's nothing to talk about here; you have only one way of salvation: go to Prince Nikolai Ivanovich, borrow ten thousand from him, ask without revealing anything, then summon those two swindlers, settle with them finally, and buy your notes back... and that will be the end of it! That will be the end of it all, and—off to the plowing! Away with fantasies and trust yourself to life!"

"I've thought about that," he said firmly. "I spent the whole day today deciding, and finally decided. I've only been waiting for you. I'll go. Do you know that I've never borrowed a kopeck from Prince Nikolai Ivanovich in my life? He's kind towards our family and has even... contributed, but I myself, I personally, have never taken money from him. But now I've decided... Note that our branch of the Sokolskys is older than Prince Nikolai Ivanovich's branch: they're a younger branch, even a collateral one, even a questionable one... Our ancestors were enemies. At the beginning of Peter's reforms, my great-grandfather, also Peter, was and remained a schismatic[25] and wandered in the forests of Kostroma. That Prince Peter was also married a second time to a non-noble girl... It was then that these other Sokolskys advanced themselves, but I... what am I talking about?"

He was very tired and talking as if at random.

"Calm yourself," I stood up, taking my hat, "go to bed, that's the first thing. And Prince Nikolai Ivanovich won't refuse you for anything, especially now, in his joy. Do you know the story there? You really don't? I've heard a wild thing, that he's getting married; it's a secret, but not from you, naturally."

And I told him everything, already standing hat in hand. He knew nothing. He quickly inquired about the details, primarily the time, the place, and the degree of reliability. Of course, I didn't conceal from him that, according to the story, this had happened immediately after his visit yesterday to Anna Andreevna. I can't express what a painful impression this news made on him; his face became distorted, as if twisted, and a crooked smile convulsively contracted his lips; in the end he turned terribly pale and lapsed into deep thought, his eyes lowered. I suddenly saw all too clearly that his self-love had been terribly stricken by Anna Andreevna's refusal yesterday. Maybe, in his morbid mood, he pictured all too vividly at that moment his ridiculous and humiliating role yesterday before this girl, of whose acceptance, it now turned out, he had been so calmly assured all along. And, finally, maybe the thought that he had done such a mean thing to Liza, and for nothing! It's curious how these society fops regard each other, and on what basis they can respect each other; this prince might have supposed that Anna Andreevna already knew of his liaison with Liza—with her sister, in fact—and if she didn't, she was sure to find out one day; and yet he "had no doubt of her decision"!

"Could you really think," he suddenly raised his eyes to me proudly and haughtily, "that I, I am capable of going now, after your communication, and asking Prince Nikolai Ivanovich for money? Asking him who is the fiancé of the girl who has just refused me—how beggarly, how servile! No, now all is lost, and if the help of this old man was my last hope, then let that last hope, too, be lost!"

I agreed with him in my heart; but still, one must take a broader view of reality: was the little old prince a man, a fiancé? Several ideas began seething in my head at once. Even without that, however, I had decided earlier that tomorrow I would visit the old man without fail. But now I tried to soften the impression and put the poor prince to bed: "You'll have a good sleep, and your ideas will brighten up, you'll see for yourself!" He shook my hand warmly, but didn't kiss me. I gave him my word that I'd come the next evening and "we'll talk, we'll talk: all too much has accumulated for us to talk about." At these words of mine he smiled somehow fatally.

Chapter Eight

I

ALL THAT NIGHT I dreamed of roulette, gambling, gold, calculations. I kept calculating something, as if I was at the gaming table, some stake, some chance, and it oppressed me all night like a nightmare. To tell the truth, that whole previous day, despite all my extraordinary impressions, I kept recalling my win at Zershchikov's. I suppressed the thought, but could not suppress the impression and trembled at the mere recollection. That win had stung my heart. Could it be I was a born gambler? At least it was certain that I had the qualities of a gambler. Even now, as I'm writing all this, I like at moments to think about gambling! It sometimes happens that I spend whole hours sitting silently, making gambling calculations in my mind and dreaming of how it will all go, how I'll stake and win. Yes, there are many different "qualities" in me, and my soul is restless.

At ten o'clock I intended to set off for Stebelkov's, and that on foot. I sent Matvei home as soon as he appeared. While having my coffee, I tried to collect my thoughts. For some reason I was pleased; instantly looking into myself, I realized that I was mainly pleased with the fact that "today I would be in the home of Prince Nikolai Ivanovich." But this day of my life was fateful and unexpected and began at once with a surprise.

At exactly ten o'clock my door was flung open and in flew—Tatyana Pavlovna. I might have expected anything but that woman's appearance, and I jumped up before her in fright. Her face was ferocious, her gestures disordered, and, if asked, she might not have been able to say herself why she had rushed in on me. I'll say beforehand: she had just received an extraordinary piece of news which had crushed her, and was under the very first impression of it. And the news touched me as well. However, she spent just half a minute with me, or say a whole minute, but not more. She just fastened on to me.

"So that's how you are!" she stood in front of me, all thrust forward. "Ah, you puppy! What have you done? Or don't you know yet? He's having his coffee! Ah, you babbler, ah, you windmill, ah, you paper lover . . . the likes of you ought to be birched, birched, birched!"

"Tatyana Pavlovna, what's happened? What's wrong? Mama? . . ."

"You'll find out!" she cried menacingly and rushed from the room—that was all I saw of her. Of course, I would have chased after her, but I was stopped by a thought, or not a thought, but some dark anxiety: I had a presentiment that "paper lover" was the chief phrase in her shouting. Of course, I would have guessed nothing on my own, but I quickly left, in order to finish the sooner with Stebelkov and go to Prince Nikolai Ivanovich's. "The key to everything is there!" I thought instinctively.

It was astonishing how, but Stebelkov already knew everything about Anna Andreevna, and even in detail; I won't describe his conversation and gestures, but he was in rapture, in an ecstasy of rapture, from the "artistry of the deed."

"There's a person, sir! No, sir, there's quite a person!" he exclaimed. "No, sir, that's not our way; we just sit here and nothing more, but she wanted to drink water from a true source—and she did. It's . . . it's an ancient statue! It's an ancient statue of Minerva, sir, only she walks around and wears modern dress!"

I asked him to get down to business. The whole business, as I fully anticipated, consisted merely in inducing and persuading the prince to go and ask for ultimate aid from Prince Nikolai Ivanovich. "Otherwise it may be very, very bad for him, and not by my will; is that so or not?"

He peeked into my eyes, but didn't seem to suppose that I knew anything more than I had the day before. And he couldn't have supposed anything: needless to say, I didn't betray by a word or a hint that I knew "about the shares." We didn't talk long, he at once began promising me money, "and a considerable amount, sir, a considerable amount, only help to make the prince go. It's an urgent matter, very urgent, there's the force of it, that it's all too urgent!"

I didn't want to argue and wrangle with him like the day before, and I got up to go, letting drop to him in any case that I'd "try." But he suddenly astonished me inexpressibly: I was already going to the door when, putting his arm affectionately around my waist, he unexpectedly began telling me . . . the most incomprehensible things.

I'll omit the details and not recount the whole thread of the conversation, so as not to be tiresome. The gist of it was that he made me a proposition "to acquaint him with Mr. Dergachev, since you do go there"!

I instantly became quiet, trying as hard as I could not to betray myself by some gesture. I replied at once, however, that I was a complete stranger there, and if I had been there, it was only once by chance.

"But if you were *admitted* once, then you can go another time, is that so or not?"

I asked him directly, but very coolly, what he needed it for. And to this day I cannot understand how such a degree of naïveté was possible in a seemingly "practical" and not stupid man, as Vasin defined him. He explained to me quite directly that at Dergachev's, as he suspected, "most likely something forbidden, strictly forbidden, is going on, and so, having investigated, I might make myself a little profit from it." And, smiling, he winked at me with his left eye.

I answered precisely nothing in the affirmative, but pretended I was thinking it over and "promised to think," after which I quickly left. Things were getting complicated: I flew to Vasin's and just caught him at home.

"Ah, and you, too!" he said mysteriously on seeing me.

Not picking up his phrase, I went straight to the point and told him. He was visibly struck, though he didn't lose his equanimity. He asked me to repeat it all in detail.

"Might it not well be that you misunderstood?"

"No, I understood correctly, the meaning was perfectly straightforward."

"In any case I'm extremely grateful to you," he added sincerely. "Yes, indeed, if that's how it all was, then he supposed you wouldn't be able to hold out against a certain sum."

"And besides, he knew my situation all too well: I've been gambling, I've behaved badly, Vasin."

"I heard about that."

"The most puzzling thing of all for me is that he knows about you, that you go there, too," I risked asking.

"He knows only too well," Vasin replied quite simply, "that I have nothing to do with them. And all these young people are mostly babblers—and nothing more. You, however, may remember that better than anyone."

It seemed to me as if he was not trusting me with something.

"In any case I'm extremely grateful to you."

"I've heard that Mr. Stebelkov's affairs are somewhat in

disorder," I made another attempt to ask. "At least I've heard about some shares..."

"What shares have you heard about?"

I deliberately mentioned the "shares," but, naturally, not in order to tell him the prince's secret from yesterday. I only wanted to drop a hint and see by his face, by his eyes, whether he knew anything about the shares. I achieved my goal: by an imperceptible and instant movement in his face, I guessed that he might know something here as well. I didn't reply to his question, "What shares?" but remained silent; and he, curiously, didn't pursue it.

"How is Lizaveta Makarovna's health?" he inquired with concern.

"She's well. My sister has always respected you..."

Pleasure flashed in his eyes: I had guessed long ago that he was not indifferent to Liza.

"Prince Sergei Petrovich came to see me the other day," he suddenly imparted.

"When?" I cried.

"Exactly four days ago."

"Not yesterday?"

"No, not yesterday." He looked at me questioningly.

"Later maybe I'll tell you about this meeting in more detail, but now I find it necessary to warn you," Vasin said enigmatically, "that he appeared to me then to be in an abnormal state of spirit and...even of mind. However, I've had yet another visit," he suddenly smiled, "just before you, and I was also forced to conclude that the visitor was not quite in a normal state."

"The prince was just here?"

"No, not the prince, I'm not talking about the prince now. Andrei Petrovich Versilov was just here and...do you know anything? Has anything happened to him?"

"Maybe so, but what precisely went on between you and him?" I asked hastily.

"Of course, I ought to keep this a secret...We're having a strange conversation, you and I, all too secretive," he smiled again. "However, Andrei Petrovich didn't order me to keep it a secret. But you're his son, and since I know your feelings for him, this time it even seems I'll do well to warn you. Imagine, he came to me with a question: 'If it so happens, one of these days, very soon, that he needs to fight a duel, would I agree to play the role of his second?' Naturally, I roundly refused him."

I was infinitely amazed; this news was the most alarming of all: something had come out, something had gone on, something had certainly happened that I still didn't know about! I suddenly had a fleeting recollection of Versilov saying to me yesterday, "I won't come to you, but you'll come running to me." I flew to Prince Nikolai Ivanovich's, with a still greater presentiment that the answer was there. Vasin, saying good-bye, thanked me once more.

II

THE OLD PRINCE was sitting in front of the fireplace, his legs wrapped in a plaid. He met me even with some sort of questioning look, as if surprised that I had come, and yet he himself sent to invite me almost every day. However, he greeted me affectionately, though he answered my first questions as if somewhat squeamishly and somehow terribly distractedly. Every now and then it was as if he realized something and peered at me intently, as if he had forgotten something and was trying to recall this something that undoubtedly had to be related to me. I told him directly that I had heard everything and was very glad. A cordial and kindly smile immediately appeared on his lips, and he became animated; his wariness and mistrust dropped away at once, as if he had forgotten them. And, of course, he had.

"My dear friend, I just knew you'd be the first to come and, you know, only yesterday I had this thought about you: 'Who will be glad? He will.' Well, and really nobody else; but never mind that. People have wicked tongues, but that's insignificant... *Cher enfant*, this is all so sublime and so lovely... But you know her only too well yourself. And Anna Andreevna even has the highest notions of you. It's... it's a stern and lovely face, a face out of an English keepsake.[26] The loveliest English engraving that could ever be... Two years ago I had a whole collection of these engravings... I always, always had this intention, always; I'm only surprised that I never thought of it."

"As far as I remember, you always loved and distinguished Anna Andreevna so."

"My friend, we don't want to harm anybody. Life with our friends, with our family, with those dear to our hearts—this is paradise. Everyone is a poet... In short, it's all been known from prehistoric times. You know, in the summer we'll go first to Soden and then to Bad-Gastein.[27] But you haven't come for so long, my friend; what's the matter with you? I've been expecting you. And isn't it true, so much, so much has gone on since then. It's only a pity I get restless; as soon as I'm left alone, I get restless. That's why I shouldn't be left alone, isn't it true? It's two times two. I understood it at once from her first words. Oh, my friend, she said only two words, but it... it was like a magnificent poem. But anyhow, you're her brother, almost a brother, isn't it true? My dear, it's not for nothing that I loved you so! I swear, I anticipated it all. I kissed her little hand and wept."

He pulled out his handkerchief as if he was going to weep again. He was badly shaken and seemed to be in one of the worst "states" I could remember him being in during all the time of our acquaintance. Ordinarily, and even almost always, he was incomparably more fresh and hearty.

"I would forgive everyone, my friend," he prattled on. "I want to forgive everyone, and I haven't been angry with anyone for a long time. Art, *la poésie dans la vie*,* helping the poor, and she, a biblical beauty. *Quelle charmante personne, eh? Les chants de Salomon... non, ce n'est pas Salomon, c'est David qui mettait une jeune fille dans son lit pour se chauffer dans sa vieillesse. Enfin David, Salomon*,† [28] it's all going around in my head—some sort of jumble. Each and every thing, *cher enfant*, can be both majestic and at the same time ridiculous. *Cette jeune belle de la vieillesse de David—c'est tout un poème*,‡ but Paul de Kock[29] would make some *scène de bassinoire*§ out of it, and we'd all laugh. Paul de Kock has neither measure nor taste, though he is talented... Katerina Nikolaevna smiles... I told her we wouldn't bother anybody. We've begun our romance, and they should let us finish it. Let it be a dream, but let them not take this dream away from us."

"How is it a dream, Prince?"

"A dream? How a dream? Well, let it be a dream, only let them allow us to die with this dream."

"Oh, Prince, what's this about dying? Live, only live now!"

*The poetry in life.

†What a charming person, eh? The songs of Solomon... no, it's not Solomon, it's David who put a young girl in his bed to warm him in his old age. Anyhow, David, Solomon...

‡That young beauty of David's old age—it's a whole poem.

§Warming-pan scene.

"But what am I saying? That's all I keep repeating. I decidedly don't know why life is so short. So as not to be boring, of course, for life is also a work of art by the Creator himself, in the finished and impeccable form of a Pushkin poem. Brevity is the first condition of artistry. But if there are some who aren't bored, they should be allowed to live longer."

"Tell me, Prince, is it already public?"

"No, my dear, by no means! We all agreed on that. It's a family matter, a family matter, a family matter. For now I've only revealed it fully to Katerina Nikolaevna, because I consider myself guilty before her. Oh, Katerina Nikolaevna is an angel, she's an angel!"

"Yes, yes!"

"Yes? You, too, say 'yes'? And I precisely thought you were her enemy. Ah, yes, incidentally, she asked me not to receive you anymore. And imagine, when you came in, I suddenly forgot it."

"What are you saying?" I jumped up. "What for? When?"

(My presentiment had not deceived me; yes, I had had precisely that presentiment ever since Tatyana!)

"Yesterday, my dear, yesterday. I don't even understand how you came in, for measures were taken. How did you come in?"

"I simply came in."

"Most likely. If you had come in cunningly, they would certainly have caught you, but since you simply came in, they let you in. Simplicity, *mon cher*, is in fact the highest form of cunning."

"I don't understand anything. So you, too, have decided not to receive me?"

"No, my friend, I said I'd keep out of it... That is, I gave my full consent. And you may be sure, my dear boy, that I love you very much. But Katerina Nikolaevna demanded it all very, very insistently... Ah, there!"

At that moment Katerina Nikolaevna suddenly appeared in the doorway. She was dressed to go out, and, as she used to do before, had come to kiss her father. Seeing me, she stopped, became embarrassed, turned quickly, and left.

"*Voilà!*" cried the prince, struck and terribly alarmed.

"It's a misunderstanding!" I cried. "It's some sort of momentary... I... I'll be right back, Prince!"

And I ran after Katerina Nikolaevna.

Everything that followed after that happened so quickly that I was not only unable to collect my thoughts, but couldn't even prepare in the least how to behave. If I could have prepared myself,

I would, of course, have behaved differently. But I was at a loss, like a little boy. I was rushing to her rooms, but a footman on the way told me that Katerina Nikolaevna had already gone out and was getting into the carriage. I rushed headlong to the front stairway. Katerina Nikolaevna was going down the stairs in her fur coat, and beside her, or, better to say, leading her, was a tall, trim officer in uniform, without a greatcoat, wearing a saber; a footman behind him was carrying his greatcoat. This was the baron, a colonel, about thirty-five, the foppish type of officer, lean, with a slightly too-elongated face, with a reddish moustache and even eyelashes. His face, though not at all handsome, had a sharp and defiant physiognomy. I'm describing him hastily, as I noticed him at that moment. I had never seen him before. I ran down the stairs after them, without hat or coat. Katerina Nikolaevna noticed me first and quickly whispered something to him. He made as if to turn his head, but nodded at once to the servant and the porter. The servant was stepping towards me just at the front door, but I moved him aside with my arm and jumped out after them onto the porch. Bjoring was helping Katerina Nikolaevna into the carriage.

"Katerina Nikolaevna! Katerina Nikolaevna!" I exclaimed senselessly (like a fool! Like a fool! Oh, I remember it all, I had no hat on!).

Bjoring again turned fiercely to the servant and loudly shouted something to him, one or two words, I didn't make it out. I felt someone seize me by the elbow. At that moment the carriage started; I cried out again and rushed after the carriage. Katerina Nikolaevna, I saw this, peeked out the window of the carriage and seemed to be greatly troubled. But in my quick movement as I rushed, I suddenly gave Bjoring a strong shove, not thinking of it at all, and, it seems, stepped very painfully on his foot. He cried out slightly, gnashed his teeth, and with his strong hand seized me by the shoulder and spitefully shoved me away, so that I went flying two or three paces. At that moment they handed him his greatcoat, he threw it on, got into a sledge, and shouted menacingly once more, pointing me out to the lackeys and the porter. Here they seized me and held me back. One servant threw my coat over my shoulders, the other handed me my hat, and—I don't remember what they said then; they were saying something, and I stood and listened to them without understanding anything. But suddenly I abandoned them and ran off.

III

SEEING NOTHING AND bumping into people as I ran, I finally reached Tatyana Pavlovna's apartment, not even thinking of hiring a cab on the way. Bjoring had shoved me aside in her presence! Of course, I had stepped on his foot, and he had shoved me aside instinctively, like a man whose corn has been stepped on (and maybe I had indeed squashed his corn!). But she had seen it, and had seen the servants seize me, and it had all happened in front of her, in front of her! When I came running into Tatyana Pavlovna's apartment, for the first minute I couldn't say anything, and my lower jaw trembled as in a fever. And I was in a fever and, on top of that, I was weeping... Oh, I had been so insulted!

"Eh! What! Kicked out? Serves you right, serves you right!" said Tatyana Pavlovna. I lowered myself silently onto the sofa and looked at her.

"But what's the matter with him?" she looked me over intently. "Here, drink this glass, drink some water, drink it! Speak, what other mischief have you been up to?"

I murmured that I had been thrown out, and Bjoring had pushed me in the street.

"Are you able to understand anything yet, or not? Here, read and admire." And taking a note from the table, she handed it to me and stood in front of me expectantly. I at once recognized Versilov's hand, there were just a few lines: it was a note to Katerina Nikolaevna. I gave a start, and understanding immediately came back to me in full force. Here are the contents of this terrible, outrageous, preposterous, and villainous note, word for word:

> Dear Madam, Katerina Nikolaevna,
>
> However depraved you are, by your nature and by your art, still I always thought that you would restrain your passion and at least not make attempts on children. But even of that you were not ashamed. I inform you that the document known to you has certainly not been burned in a candle and was never with Kraft, so you will not gain anything here. And therefore do not corrupt the youth for nothing. Spare him, he is still under age, almost a boy, undeveloped mentally and physically, what use is he to you? I have sympathy for him, and therefore I have

risked writing to you, though I have no hope of success. I have the honor of forewarning you that I am simultaneously sending a copy of this present to Baron Bjoring.

A. Versilov.

I turned pale as I read, but then suddenly flushed, and my lips trembled with indignation.

"He means me! It's about what I revealed to him two days ago!" I cried in fury.

"That's just it—revealed!" Tatyana Pavlovna tore the note from my hands.

"But... that's not, that's not at all what I said! Oh, my God, what can she think of me now! But isn't this mad? Yes, he's mad... I saw him yesterday. When was the letter sent?"

"It was sent yesterday afternoon, it came in the evening, and today she gave it to me personally."

"But I saw him yesterday myself. He's mad! Versilov couldn't have written like that, it was written by a madman! Who can write like that to a woman?"

"Such madmen write like that in a fury, when they go blind and deaf from jealousy and spite, and their blood turns to poisonous arsenic... But you still didn't know about him, what kind he is! They'll swat him for that now, there'll be nothing left but a wet spot. He's put himself under the axe! Better go to the Nikolaevsky railroad at night, lay his head on the rails, and get it lopped off, since he finds it so heavy to carry around! What drove you to tell him? What drove you to tease him? Did you want to boast?"

"But what hatred! What hatred!" I slapped myself on the head with my hand. "And what for, what for? Towards a woman! What has she done to him? What kind of relations did they have, that he can write such letters?"

"Ha-a-atred!" Tatyana Pavlovna imitated me with furious mockery.

The blood rose to my face again; it was as if I suddenly realized something quite new; I looked at her questioningly as hard as I could.

"Get out of here!" she shrieked, quickly turning away and waving her hand at me. "I've bothered enough with all of you! That will do now! You can all fall through the earth!... It's only your mother I'm still sorry for..."

Naturally, I went running to Versilov. But such perfidy! Such perfidy!

IV

Versilov was not alone. I'll explain beforehand: having sent such a letter to Katerina Nikolaevna the day before, and having actually (God only knows why) sent a copy of it to Baron Bjoring, he naturally had to expect that day, in the course of the day, certain "consequences" of his act, and therefore had taken measures of a sort. In the morning he had transferred mama and Liza (who, as I learned later, on coming back in the morning, had felt unwell and was lying in bed) upstairs to the "coffin," and the rooms, especially our "drawing room," had been thoroughly tidied up and cleaned. And indeed, at two o'clock in the afternoon, he had been visited by a certain Baron R., an army colonel, a gentleman of about forty, of German origin, tall, dry, with the look of a man of great physical strength, also with reddish hair like Bjoring, and slightly bald. He was one of those Barons R., of whom there are so many in the Russian army, all people of strong baronial arrogance, utterly without fortune, who live on their pay alone and are extremely soldierly and disciplinarian. I didn't catch the beginning of their talk; they were both very animated, and how could they not be. Versilov was sitting on the sofa in front of the table, and the baron in an armchair to the side. Versilov was pale, but spoke with restraint and through his teeth, while the baron kept raising his voice and was obviously inclined to impulsive gestures, restrained himself with effort, but had a stern, haughty, and even scornful look, though not without a certain surprise. Seeing me, he frowned, but Versilov was almost glad of me:

"Greetings, my dear. Baron, this is that same very young man who is mentioned in the note, and believe me, he won't hinder us, and may even be needed." (The baron looked me over scornfully.) "My dear," Versilov added to me, "I'm even glad you've come, so sit in the corner, I beg you, while the baron and I finish here. Don't worry, Baron, he'll just sit in the corner."

It was all the same to me, because I had made up my mind, and besides, all this struck me; I sat silently in the corner, as far as possible in the corner, and sat without batting an eye or stirring till the end of their talk...

"I repeat to you once more, Baron," Versilov said, firmly rapping out the words, "that I consider Katerina Nikolaevna Akhmakov, to whom I wrote that unworthy and morbid letter, not only the noblest being, but also the height of all perfections!"

"Such a refutation of your own words, as I've already observed to you, looks like a new confirmation of them," grunted the baron. "Your words are decidedly disrespectful."

"But, all the same, it would be most correct if you took them in their precise sense. You see, I suffer from fits and... various disorders, and am even being treated, and so it happened that in one such moment..."

"These explanations can in no way enter in. I have told you again and again that you stubbornly go on being mistaken, and maybe you deliberately want to be mistaken. I already warned you at the very beginning that the whole question concerning this lady, that is, about your letter to Mme. Akhmakov proper, must be definitively eliminated from our present conversation; yet you keep returning to it. Baron Bjoring asked me and charged me particularly to clarify, properly speaking, only that which concerns him, that is, your brazen communicating of this 'copy' and then your postscript, that 'you are prepared to answer for it in whatever way he pleases.'"

"But it seems the last part is already clear without explanations."

"I understand, I've heard. You do not even apologize, but just go on insisting that 'you are prepared to answer in whatever way he pleases.' But that would be too cheap. And therefore I now find myself right, in view of the turn you so stubbornly want to give our talk, to tell you everything from my side without constraint; that is, I have come to the conclusion that Baron Bjoring cannot possibly have any dealings with you... on an equal footing."

"Such a decision is, of course, one of the more advantageous for your friend, Baron Bjoring, and, I confess, you haven't surprised me in the least: I was expecting that."

I'll note in parenthesis: it was all too evident to me from the first words, the first look, that Versilov was even seeking an outburst, that he was provoking and teasing this irritable baron, and maybe trying his patience too much. The baron winced.

"I have heard that you can be witty, but wit is not yet intelligence."

"An extremely profound observation, Colonel."

"I did not ask for your praise," cried the baron, "and I have not come to pour through a sieve! Be so good as to listen: Baron

Bjoring was in great doubt on receiving your letter, because it testified to the madhouse. And, of course, means could have been found at once to... calm you down. But, owing to certain special considerations, you were granted indulgence, and inquiries were made about you. It turned out that, though you belonged to good society and had once served in the guards, you have been excluded from society, and your reputation is more than dubious. However, even despite that, I have come here to ascertain personally, and here, on top of everything else, you allow yourself to play with words and yourself assert that you are subject to fits. Enough! Baron Bjoring's position and his reputation cannot indulge you in this affair... In short, dear sir, I am authorized to announce to you that if this is followed by a repetition or merely by anything resembling the previous action, means will immediately be found to pacify you, quite quick and reliable ones, I can assure you. We do not live in the forest, but in a well-organized state!"

"Are you so sure of that, my good Baron R.?"

"Devil take it," the baron suddenly stood up, "you tempt me too much to prove to you right now that I am hardly your 'good Baron R.'"

"Ah, once again I warn you," Versilov also got up, "that my wife and daughter are not far from here... and therefore I would beg you not to speak so loudly, because your shouts may reach them."

"Your wife... the devil... If I sat and talked with you now, it was solely with the aim of clarifying this vile affair," the baron went on with the same wrath and not lowering his voice in the least. "Enough!" he cried out furiously. "You are not only excluded from the circle of decent people, but you are a maniac, a real crazy maniac, and so you have been attested! You are not worthy of indulgence, and I announce to you that this very day measures will be taken regarding you, and you will be invited to one such place, where they will know how to restore your reason... and they will remove you from town!"

With big and rapid strides he left the room. Versilov didn't see him off. He stood, gazed at me distractedly, and seemed not to notice me; suddenly he smiled, shook his hair, and, taking his hat, also started towards the door. I seized him by the arm.

"Ah, yes, you're here, too? You... heard?" he stopped in front of me.

"How could you have done it? How could you so distort, so disgrace!... With such perfidy!"

He gazed intently, but his smile extended more and more and decidedly turned to laughter.

"But I've been disgraced... in front of her! In front of her! I was derided in her eyes, and he... shoved me!" I cried, beside myself.

"Really? Ah, poor boy, I'm so sorry for you... So they... de-ri-ded you there!"

"You're laughing, you're laughing at me! You think it's funny!"

He quickly tore his arm from my hand, put his hat on, and laughing, laughing with genuine laughter now, left the apartment. Why should I go after him? What for? I had understood everything and—lost everything in a single moment! Suddenly I saw mama; she had come down from upstairs and was timidly looking around.

"He's gone?"

I silently embraced her, and she me, tightly, tightly, pressing herself against me.

"Mama, my own, can you possibly stay here? Let's go now, I'll protect you, I'll work for you like at hard labor, for you and for Liza... Let's leave them all, all, and go away. We'll be by ourselves. Mama, do you remember how you came to see me at Touchard's and how I refused to recognize you?"

"I remember, my own, all my life I've been guilty before you, I gave birth to you, but I didn't know you."

"He's the guilty one, mama, it's he who is guilty of everything; he never loved us."

"No, he did love us."

"Let's go, mama."

"How can I go away from him, is he happy, do you think?"

"Where's Liza?"

"Lying down. She came back and felt unwell; I fear for her. What, are they very angry with him there? What will they do with him now? Where did he go? What was this officer threatening here?"

"Nothing will happen to him, mama, nothing will ever happen to him, and nothing can, he's that kind of man! Here's Tatyana Pavlovna, ask her, if you don't believe me, here she is." (Tatyana Pavlovna suddenly came into the room.) "Good-bye, mama. I'll come back to you right away, and when I do, I'll ask you the same thing again..."

I ran off; I couldn't see anybody at all, not only Tatyana Pavlovna, and mama tormented me. I wanted to be alone, alone.

V

BUT BEFORE I reached the end of the street, I felt that I couldn't walk around senselessly bumping into these alien, indifferent people; but what to do with myself? Who needs me and—what do I need now? Mechanically, I trudged to Prince Sergei Petrovich's, without thinking of him at all. He wasn't home. I told Pyotr (his man) that I'd wait in the study (as I had done many times). His study was a big, very high room, cluttered with furniture. I wandered into the darkest corner, sat down on the sofa, and, placing my elbows on the table, propped my head in both hands. Yes, that was the question: "What do I need now?" And if I could have formulated the question then, the last thing I could have done was answer it.

But I was no longer able either to think or to ask properly. I've already made known above that by the end of those days I was "crushed by events"; I sat there now and everything was spinning like chaos in my mind. "Yes, I failed to see everything in him and perceived nothing," I fancied at moments. "He laughed in my face just now: it wasn't at me; it's all Bjoring here, and not me. Two days ago, over dinner, he already knew everything and was gloomy. He picked up my stupid confession in the tavern and distorted all that concerned any truth, only what did he need the truth for? He doesn't believe half a word of what he wrote to her. He only needed to insult her, to insult her senselessly, not even knowing what for, snatching at a pretext, and I gave him a pretext... The act of a rabid dog! Does he want to kill Bjoring now, or what? Why? His heart knows why! And I know nothing of what's in his heart... No, no, even now I don't know. Can he love her with so much passion? Or hate her with so much passion? I don't know, but does he know himself? What was that I said to mama, that 'nothing can happen to him'? What did I mean to say by that? Have I lost him or not?

"... She saw how he shoved me... Did she also laugh or not? I'd have laughed! The spy's been beaten, the spy!...

"What does it mean" (it suddenly flashed in me), "what does it mean, his including in that nasty letter that the document hasn't been burned at all, but still exists?...

"He won't kill Bjoring, but he's certainly sitting in the tavern now, listening to *Lucia*! And maybe after *Lucia* he'll go and kill Bjoring. Bjoring shoved me, almost hit me; did he hit me? Bjoring scorns to fight even with Versilov, how can he go fighting with me? Maybe I should kill him tomorrow with a revolver, waiting in the street..." And I let this thought pass through my head quite mechanically, without lingering over it in the least.

At moments it was as if I dreamed that the door would open now, Katerina Nikolaevna would come in, give me her hand, and we'd both laugh... Oh, my dear student! I imagined it, that is, wished for it, when it was already very dark in the room. "But was it so long ago that I stood before her, saying good-bye to her, and she gave me her hand and laughed? How could it happen that in such a short time such a terrible distance appeared! Simply go to her and talk it over right now, this minute, simply, simply! Lord, how is it that a totally new world has begun so suddenly! Yes, a new world, totally, totally new... And Liza, and the prince, that's still the old... Here I am now at the prince's. And mama—how could she live with him, if it's so? I could, I can do anything, but she? What will happen now?" And here, as in a whirl, the figures of Liza, Anna Andreevna, Stebelkov, the prince, Aferdov, everybody flashed tracelessly in my sick brain. But my thoughts were growing more formless and elusive; I was glad when I managed to comprehend one of them and get hold of it.

"I have my 'idea'!" I thought suddenly. "But is that so? Don't I just repeat it by rote? My idea is darkness and solitude, but is it possible now to crawl back into the former darkness? Ah, my God, I haven't burned the 'document'! I simply forgot to burn it two days ago. I'll go back and burn it in a candle, precisely in a candle; I don't know whether what I think now..."

It had long been dark, and Pyotr brought in candles. He stood over me and asked whether I had eaten. I only waved my hand. However, an hour later he brought me tea, and I greedily drank a big cup. Then I inquired what time it was. It was half-past eight, and I wasn't even surprised that I had been sitting there for five hours already.

"I've come to you three times now," said Pyotr, "but it seemed you were asleep."

I didn't remember him coming in. I don't know why, but I suddenly felt terribly frightened at having "slept," got up and began pacing the room so as not to "fall asleep" again. Finally, my head began to ache badly. At exactly ten o'clock the prince came in, and

I was surprised that I had waited for him; I had totally forgotten about him, totally.

"You're here, and I went to your place looking for you," he said to me. His face was dark and stern, without the slightest smile. There was a fixed idea in his eyes.

"I've struggled all day and used all measures," he went on focusedly. "Everything kept collapsing, and there's horror to come..." (N.B. He never went to Prince Nikolai Ivanovich.) "I saw Zhibelsky, he's an impossible man. You see: first I must have the money, and then we'll see. And if, with the money, it still doesn't work out, then... But today I decided not to think about it. Let's just get the money today, and tomorrow we'll see about it all. Your winnings from three days ago are still intact to the kopeck. It's three thousand minus three roubles. Subtracting your debt, you're left with three hundred and forty in change. Take that and another seven hundred to make a thousand, and I'll take the remaining two thousand. Then we'll sit down at Zershchikov's at two different ends and try to win ten thousand—maybe we'll do something, and if we don't win, then... Anyhow, that's the only way left."

He gave me a fateful look.

"Yes, yes!" I cried suddenly, as if resurrecting. "Let's go! I've only been waiting for you..."

I'll note that I hadn't thought about roulette for a moment in all those hours.

"But the baseness? But the meanness of the act?" the prince asked suddenly.

"That we're going to play roulette? No, that's everything!" I cried. "Money is everything! It's only we who are saints, and Bjoring has sold himself. Anna Andreevna has sold herself, and Versilov—have you heard that Versilov's a maniac? A maniac! A maniac!"

"Are you well, Arkady Makarovich? Your eyes are somehow strange."

"Are you saying that in order to go without me? But I won't leave you now. Not for nothing was I dreaming about gambling all night. Let's go, let's go!" I kept crying, as if I had suddenly found the solution to everything.

"Let's go, then, though you're in a fever, but there..."

He didn't finish. His face looked heavy, terrible. We were already going out.

"Do you know," he said suddenly, pausing in the doorway, "there's yet another way out of my trouble besides gambling?"

"Which?"

"The princely way!"

"But what? But what?"

"Later you'll find out what. Only know that I'm no longer worthy of it, because it's too late. Let's go, and remember my words. Let's try the lackey's way out... As if I don't know that I am consciously, of my own full will, going and acting like a lackey!"

VI

I FLEW TO the roulette table as if my whole salvation, my whole way out, was focused in it, and yet, as I've already said, before the prince came, I hadn't even thought of it. And I was going to play, not for myself, but for the prince, on the prince's money; I can't conceive what drew me on, but it drew me irresistibly. Oh, never had these people, these faces, these croupiers, these gambling cries, this whole squalid hall at Zershchikov's, never had it all seemed so loathsome to me, so dismal, so coarse and sad, as this time! I remember only too well the grief and sadness that seized my heart at times during all those hours at the table. But what made me not leave? What made me endure, as if I had taken a fate, a sacrifice, a heroic deed upon myself? I'll say one thing: I can scarcely say of myself that I was in my right mind then. And yet I had never played so intelligently as that evening. I was silent and concentrated, attentive and terribly calculating; I was patient and stingy and at the same time decided in decisive moments. I placed myself again by the *zéro*, that is, again between Zershchikov and Aferdov, who always sat next to Zershchikov on the right; I detested that place, but I wanted absolutely to stake on *zéro*, and all the other places by the *zéro* were taken. We had been playing for over an hour; finally, from my place, I saw the prince suddenly get up, pale, and walk over to us, and stand facing me across the table. He had lost everything and silently watched my game, though he probably understood nothing in it and was no longer thinking about the game. By that time I was just beginning to win, and Zershchikov counted out money to me. All at once Aferdov, silently, before my eyes, in the most brazen way, took one of my hundred-rouble notes and added it to his pile of money lying in front of him. I cried out and seized him by the hand. Here something unexpected happened to me: it was as if I snapped my chain, as if all the horrors and injuries of that day were suddenly focused on this one instant, on this disappearance of a hundred-rouble note. As if all that was stored up and suppressed in me had only been waiting for this moment to break out.

"He's a thief! He just stole a hundred-rouble note from me!" I exclaimed, looking around, beside myself.

I won't describe the tumult that arose; such an incident was a complete novelty here. People behaved decently at Zershchikov's, and the place was known for that. But I forgot myself. Amidst the noise and shouting, Zershchikov's voice was suddenly heard:

"And by the way, there's money missing, and it was lying right here! Four hundred roubles!"

Another incident took place at once: money had disappeared from the bank, under Zershchikov's nose, a roll of four hundred roubles. Zershchikov pointed to the spot where it was lying, "was lying just now," and that spot turned out to be right next to me, adjoining me, the place where my money lay, meaning much closer to me than to Aferdov.

"Here's the thief! It's him stealing again, search him!" I exclaimed, pointing at Aferdov.

"It's all because unknown people are let in," someone's thundering and impressive voice rang out amidst the general outcry. "They get in without any recommendation! Who brought him? Who is he?"

"Some Dolgoruky."

"Prince Dolgoruky?"

"Prince Sokolsky brought him," somebody cried.

"Listen, Prince," I screamed to him across the table in a frenzy, "they consider me a thief, when it's I who have just been robbed here! Tell them, tell them about me!"

And here something took place that was the most terrible of all that had happened that whole day... even in my whole life: the prince disavowed me. I saw him shrug his shoulders and, in reply to the flood of questions, utter sharply and clearly:

"I don't answer for anyone. I beg you to leave me alone."

Meanwhile Aferdov stood amidst the crowd and loudly demanded to be searched. He turned out his pockets himself. His demand was answered with shouts: "No, no, the thief is known!" Two summoned lackeys seized me by the arms from behind.

"I will not let you search me, I will not allow it!" I shouted, struggling to free myself.

But they dragged me to the next room, and there, amidst the crowd, they searched me down to the last fold. I shouted and struggled.

"Dropped it, must be, have to look on the floor," somebody decided.

"Go now and look on the floor!"

"Under the table, must be he managed to throw it there!"

"Of course, the trail's cold..."

They led me out, but I somehow managed to stand in the doorway and shout with senseless fury to the whole hall:

"Roulette is forbidden by law. Today I shall denounce you all!"

They took me downstairs, dressed me, and... opened the door to the street before me.

Chapter Nine

I

THE DAY ENDED with catastrophe, but there remained the night, and this is what I remembered from that night.

I think it was just past midnight when I found myself in the street. The night was clear, still, and frosty. I almost ran, was hurrying terribly, but—certainly not for home. "Why home? Can there be a home now? At home you live, I'd wake up tomorrow to live—but is that possible now? Life is over, it's no longer possible to live now." And so I plodded along the streets, not knowing where I was going, and I doubt that I wanted to get anywhere. I felt very hot and kept throwing open my heavy raccoon coat. "Now no sort of action," it seemed to me at that moment, "can have any purpose." And, strangely, I kept fancying that everything around me, even the air I breathed, was as if from another planet, as though I suddenly found myself on the moon. All of it—the city, the passersby, the sidewalk I was running along—all of it was suddenly *not mine* anymore. "This is the Palace Square, this is St. Isaac's," went through my head, "but now I have nothing to do with them." Everything somehow forsook me, suddenly became *not mine*. "I have mama, Liza—well, what of it, what are Liza and my mother to me now? Everything is over, everything is over all at once, except one thing: that I am a thief forever.

"How can I prove that I'm not a thief? Is it possible now? Shall I go to America? Well, what would I prove by that? Versilov will be the first to believe that I stole! My 'idea'? What 'idea'? What of that now? In fifty years, in a hundred years, I'll be walking along, and a man will always turn up who will point at me and say: 'Look at that thief. He began his "idea" by stealing money at roulette'..."

Was there anger in me? I don't know, maybe there was. Strangely, there had always been this feature in me, maybe ever since earliest childhood: once evil had been done to me, fulfilled to the utmost, and I had been offended to the final limits, there always appeared in me at once an unquenchable desire to submit passively to the offense and even to outstrip the offender's desires: "There, you've humiliated me, so I'll humiliate myself still more, look here, admire!" Touchard used to beat me and wanted to show that I was a lackey and not a senator's son, and so I myself at once entered into the role of lackey then. I not only helped him to dress, but would seize the brush myself and begin brushing the last specks of dust off him, without any request or order from him, sometimes ran after him, in the heat of my lackey zeal, to brush off some last speck of dust from his tailcoat, so that he himself sometimes stopped me: "Enough, enough, Arkady, enough." He used to come and take off his street clothes—and I would clean them, fold them carefully, and cover them with a checked silk handkerchief. I knew that my comrades laughed and despised me for that, I knew it perfectly well, but that was what I liked: "You wanted me to be a lackey, well, so I'm a lackey, a boor—yes, a boor." I could keep up this passive hatred and underground spite for years. And what then? At Zershchikov's I had shouted to the whole hall, in complete frenzy: "I shall denounce you all, roulette is forbidden by law!" And I swear that here, too, there was something as if similar: I had been humiliated, searched, declared a thief, destroyed—"well, then know, all of you, that you've guessed right, I'm not only a thief, I'm an informer as well!" Recalling it now, I sum it up and explain it in precisely that way; but then I couldn't be bothered with analyzing; then I shouted without any intention; even a moment before, I hadn't known I'd shout that; it shouted itself—there was that *streak* in my soul.

While I ran, the delirium was undoubtedly already starting, but I remember very well that I was acting consciously. And yet I will say firmly that there was a whole cycle of ideas and conclusions that was impossible for me then; even in those minutes, I felt about myself that "certain thoughts I can have, but others I can't possibly have." So, too, certain of my decisions, though made with clear awareness, might not have the least logic in them. Not only that: I remember very well that at some moments I could be fully aware of the absurdity of some decision, and at the same time, with full awareness, set about realizing it. Yes, a crime was hatching that night, and it is only by chance that it wasn't committed.

Tatyana Pavlovna's phrase about Versilov suddenly flashed in me then: "He should go to the Nikolaevsky railroad and lay his head on the rails: he'd get it lopped off for him." This thought momentarily took hold of all my feelings, but I instantly and painfully drove it away: "I'll lay my head on the rails and die, and tomorrow they'll say: he did it because he stole, he did it out of shame—no, not for anything!" And then, at that moment, I remember, I suddenly felt an instant of terrible anger. "What then?" raced through my mind. "There's no way I can vindicate myself, to start a new life is also impossible, and so—submit, become a lackey, a dog, an insect, an informer, a real informer now, but at the same time quietly make preparations, and one day—blow it all sky high, destroy everything, everybody—the guilty and the not-guilty, and then suddenly they'll all find out that it's the same one they called a thief... and only then kill myself."

I don't remember how I ran into a lane somewhere near the Konnogvardeisky Boulevard. In this lane there were high stone walls on both sides, for almost a hundred paces—the enclosures of backyards. Behind one wall to the left I saw an enormous woodpile, a long woodpile, as in a lumberyard, and higher than the wall by some seven feet. I suddenly stopped and began to ponder. In my pocket I had wax matches in a small silver matchbox. I repeat, I was fully and distinctly aware then of what I was pondering and what I wanted to do, as I am in recollecting it now, but why I wanted to do it—I have no idea, none at all. I only remember that I suddenly wanted it very much. "It's very possible to climb onto the wall," I reasoned. Just two steps away there was a gate in the wall, which must have been tightly shut for months. "If I step on the ledge below," I reflected further, "I can get hold of the top of the gate and climb onto the wall—and nobody will notice, there's nobody here, silence! And then I'll sit on top of the wall and set fire to the wood quite excellently, possibly even without getting down, because the wood is almost touching the wall. It will burn still better from the cold, all I have to do is take one birch log... and there's even no need to take a log: simply sit on the wall, peel some bark off a birch log with my hand, and set fire to it with a match, set fire to it, and shove it between the logs—and there's your fire. And I'll jump down and leave; there's even no need to run, because they won't notice for a long time..." So I reasoned it all out and—suddenly became quite decided. I felt extreme pleasure, delight, and began to climb. I was an excellent climber: gymnastics had been my specialty back in high school, but I was wearing galoshes, and the thing proved difficult. Nevertheless I did manage to get hold of a barely perceptible ledge above and pull myself up, while swinging my other arm to grab at the top of the wall, but here I suddenly lost hold and fell backwards. I suppose I hit the ground with the back of my head and must have lain unconscious for a minute or two. Coming to, I mechanically wrapped myself in my fur coat, suddenly feeling unbearably cold, and, still not fully conscious of what I was doing, crawled into the corner of the gateway and sat down there, huddling and crouching in the nook between the gate and the projecting wall. My thoughts were confused, and I probably dozed off very quickly. I now remember as if through sleep that a deep, heavy bell suddenly rang in my ears, and I began listening to it with delight.

II

THE BELL STRUCK firmly and distinctly once every two or even three seconds, but it was not a tocsin, but some pleasant, smooth ringing, and I suddenly realized that it was familiar, that it was ringing in the red church of St. Nicholas opposite Touchard's—the ancient Moscow church that I remember so well, built in the time of Alexei Mikhailovich,[30] fretty, many-domed, and "all in pillars," and that Holy Week[31] was just over, and the newborn little green leaves were already trembling on the scrawny birches in the front garden of Touchard's house. The bright late-afternoon sun is pouring its slanting rays into our classroom, and in my little room to the left, where Touchard had put me a year before, away from the "princely and senatorial children," a visitor is sitting. Yes, I, the kinless one, suddenly have a visitor—for the first time since I've been at Touchard's. I recognized this visitor as soon as she came in: it was mama, though I hadn't seen her even once since the time she brought me to communion in the village church and the dove flew across the cupola. We were sitting together, and I was watching her strangely. Afterwards, many years later, I learned that, having been left then without Versilov, who had suddenly gone abroad, she had come to Moscow on her own pitiful means, *without leave*, almost in secret from those who were then charged with taking care of her, and had done it solely in order to see me. Another strange thing was that, having come in and spoken with Touchard, she had not even said a word to me about being my mother. She sat by me and, I remember, I was even surprised that she spoke so little. She had a small bundle with her, and she untied it: there were six oranges in it, several gingerbreads, and two loaves of ordinary French bread. I was offended by the French bread and, with a wounded look, replied that our "food" here was very good and that we were given a whole loaf of French bread with tea every day.

"Never mind, darling, I just thought in my simplicity, 'Maybe they feed them poorly in that school.' Don't hold it against me, dearest."

"And Antonina Vassilievna" (Touchard's wife) "will be offended. My comrades will also laugh at me..."

"Don't you want to take them, maybe you'll eat them?"

"Leave them, if you like, ma'am..."

I didn't even touch the treats; the oranges and gingerbreads lay in front of me on the little table, and I sat looking down, but with a great air of personal dignity. Who knows, maybe I also wanted very much not to conceal from her that her visit even shamed me in the eyes of my comrades; to show it to her at least a little, so that she'd understand: "You see, you shame me and don't even understand it yourself." Oh, I was already running after Touchard with a brush then, whisking specks of dust off him! I also pictured how much mockery I'd have to endure from the boys as soon as she left, and maybe from Touchard himself—and there was not the slightest kind feeling for her in my heart. I only looked out of the corner of my eye at her dark old dress, her rather coarse, almost working-woman's hands, her completely coarse shoes, and her very thin face; little wrinkles already ran across her forehead, though Antonina Vassilievna told me later in the evening, when she had left: "Your *maman* must have been very good-looking once."

We were sitting like that, and suddenly Agafya came in with a cup of coffee on a tray. It was after dinner, and the Touchards always had coffee in their living room at that time. But mama thanked her and did not take the cup: as I learned later, she didn't drink coffee at all then, because it gave her heart palpitations. The thing was that to themselves the Touchards probably considered her visit and the permission for her to see me an extraordinary indulgence on their part, so that the cup of coffee they sent to mama was, so to say, a deed of humaneness, comparatively speaking, which did extraordinary credit to their civilized feelings and European notions. And, as if on purpose, mama refused it.

I was summoned to Touchard, and he told me to take all my books and notebooks to show mama: "So that she can see how much you've managed to acquire in my institution." Here Antonina

Vassilievna, pursing her lips, said to me for her part, touchily and mockingly, through her teeth:

"It seems your *maman* didn't like our coffee."

I gathered a pile of notebooks and carried them to my waiting mama, past the "princely and senatorial children," who were crowding in the classroom and spying on mama and me. And I even liked fulfilling Touchard's order with literal precision. I methodically began to open my notebooks and explain, "This is a lesson in French grammar, this is an exercise from dictation, here is the conjugation of the auxiliary verbs *avoir* and *être*, here's something from geography, a description of the major cities of Europe and all parts of the world," and so on, and so forth. For half an hour or more I went on explaining in an even little voice, looking down like a well-behaved boy. I knew that mama understood nothing in my studies, maybe couldn't even write, but it was here that my role pleased me. But I couldn't weary her—she went on listening without interrupting me, with extraordinary attention and even awe, so that I myself finally became bored and stopped; her look was sad, however, and there was something pitiful in her face.

She finally got up to leave. Suddenly Touchard himself came in and, with a foolishly important air, asked her: "Was she pleased with her son's progress?" Mama began murmuring and thanking him incoherently; Antonina Vassilievna came in, too. Mama started asking them both "not to abandon the little orphan, he's the same as an orphan now, be his benefactors..." and with tears in her eyes she bowed to them both, each separately, with a deep bow, precisely as "simple folk" bow when they come to ask important people about something. The Touchards weren't even expecting that, and Antonina Vassilievna was visibly softened and, of course, at once changed her conclusion about the cup of coffee. Touchard, with increased importance, replied humanely that he "made no distinction among the children, that here they were all his children, and he their father, and that he held me on almost the same footing with princely and senatorial children, and that that should be appreciated," and so on, and so forth. Mama only kept bowing, but with embarrassment, finally turned to me, and with tears glistening in her eyes, said, "Good-bye, darling!"

And she kissed me—that is, I allowed myself to be kissed. She obviously would have liked to kiss me again and again, to embrace me, to hug me, but whether she was ashamed to do it in front of people, or was bitter about something else, or realized that I was ashamed of her, in any case, having bowed once more to the Touchards, she hastily started for the door. I just stood there.

"*Mais suivez donc votre mère*," said Antonina Vassilievna. "*Il n'a pas de coeur cet enfant!*"*

Touchard shrugged his shoulders in reply, which, of course, signified: "It's not for nothing I treat him as a lackey."

I obediently followed mama downstairs; we went out to the porch. I knew they were now all watching from the window. Mama turned to the church and crossed herself deeply three times before it, her lips twitched, the bell tolled densely and measuredly from the belfry. She turned to me and—couldn't help herself, she laid both hands on my head and wept over it.

"Mama, come on... it's shameful... they can see me from the window..."

She roused herself and began to hurry:

"Well, the Lord... well, the Lord be with you... the angels in heaven, the most-pure Mother, Saint Nicholas protect you... Lord, Lord!" she repeated in a quick patter, crossing me all the while, trying quickly to make as many crosses as possible, "my darling, my dear. But wait, darling..."

She hurriedly put her hand in her pocket and took out a handkerchief, a blue checked handkerchief tightly knotted at the corner, and began to untie the knot... but it wouldn't come untied...

"Well, it makes no difference, take it with the handkerchief, it's clean, maybe you can use it, there are maybe four twenty-kopeck pieces in it, maybe you'll need it, forgive me, darling, it's all I have... forgive me, darling."

I accepted the handkerchief, was about to observe that we "were very well kept here by Mr. Touchard and Antonina Vassilievna, and that we didn't need anything," but I restrained myself and took the handkerchief.

Once more she crossed me, once more she whispered some prayer, and suddenly—and suddenly she bowed to me, too, just as she had to the Touchards upstairs—a deep, long, slow bow—I'll never forget it! I just shuddered, and didn't know why myself. What did she mean to say by this bow: that she "acknowledged her guilt before me," as I once thought up long afterwards? I don't know. But then I at once felt still more ashamed, because "they

*But follow your mother, then [...] He has no heart, this child.

were watching from up there, and Lambert might even start beating me."

She finally left. The princely and senatorial children had eaten the oranges and gingerbreads before I came back, and Lambert took the four twenty-kopeck pieces from me at once; they bought pastry and chocolate with them in a pastry shop and didn't even offer me any.

A whole half-year went by, and a windy and foul October came. I completely forgot about mama. Oh, by then hatred, a dull hatred for everything, had already penetrated my heart, saturating it completely; though I brushed Touchard off as before, I already hated him with all my might, and more and more every day. And it was then, once in the sad evening twilight, that I began rummaging in my little drawer for some reason, and suddenly saw her blue cambric handkerchief in the corner. It had lain like that ever since I stuffed it there then. I took it out and looked it over even with a certain curiosity; the end of the handkerchief still kept traces of the former knot and even the clearly outlined round imprint of a coin; however, I put the handkerchief back in its place and closed the drawer. It was the eve of a holiday, and the bell began ringing for the vigil. The pupils had gone home after dinner, but this time Lambert had stayed for Sunday, I don't know why no one had sent for him. Though he still beat me then, as before, he used to tell me a great deal, and he needed me. We talked all evening about Lepage pistols, which neither one of us had seen, about Circassian sabers and how they cut, and about how good it would be to start a band of robbers, and in the end Lambert got on to his favorite conversation about a certain smutty subject, and though I wondered to myself, I liked listening very much. But this time I suddenly couldn't stand it, and I told him I had a headache. At ten o'clock we went to bed; I pulled the covers over my head and took the blue handkerchief from under the pillow: for some reason I had gone an hour earlier to take it from the drawer, and as soon as our beds were made, had put it under the pillow. I pressed it to my face at once and suddenly began kissing it. "Mama, mama," I whispered, remembering, and my whole breast was clenched as in a vise. I closed my eyes and saw her face with trembling lips, when she crossed herself before the church, then crossed me, and I said to her, "It's shameful, they're watching." "Mama, dearest mama, just once in my life you came to me... Dearest mama, where are you now, my faraway visitor? Do you remember your poor boy now, the one you came to see?... Show yourself to me now just one little time, come to me just only in a dream, only so I can tell you how I love you, only so I can embrace you and kiss your blue eyes, and tell you that I'm not ashamed of you at all now, and that I loved you then, too, and that my heart ached then, but I only sat there like a lackey. You'll never know how I loved you then, mama! Dearest mama, where are you now, can you hear me? Mama, mama, do you remember the little dove, in the village?..."

"Ah, the devil... What ails him!" Lambert grumbles from his bed. "Wait, I'll show you! Won't let me sleep..." He finally jumps out of bed, runs over to me, and starts tearing the blanket off me, but I hold very, very tightly to the blanket, covering my head with it.

"Whimpering, what are you whimpering for, cretin, cghretin! Take that!" and he beats me, he hits me painfully with his fist on the back, on the side, more and more painfully, and... and I suddenly open my eyes...

It's already bright dawn, needles of frost sparkle on the snow, on the wall... I'm sitting, crouched, barely alive, frozen in my fur coat, and someone is standing over me, rousing me, abusing me loudly, and kicking me painfully in the side with the toe of his right boot. I raise myself, look: a man in a rich bearskin coat, a sable hat, with black eyes, pitch-black foppish side-whiskers, a hooked nose, his white teeth bared at me, a white and ruddy face like a mask... He has bent down very close to me, and cold steam comes from his mouth with each breath:

"Frozen, the drunken mug, the cghretin! You'll freeze like a dog! Get up! Get up!"

"Lambert!" I shout.

"Who are you?"

"Dolgoruky!"

"What the hell kind of Dolgoruky?"

"*Simply* Dolgoruky!... Touchard... The one you stuck in the side with a fork in the tavern!..."

"Ha-a-a!" he cries out, smiling some sort of long, recollecting smile (but he can't have forgotten me!). "Ha! So it's you, you!"

He pulls me up, sets me on my feet; I can barely stand, barely move, he leads me, supporting me on his arm. He peers into my eyes, as if pondering and recalling and listening to me with all his might, and I babble on, also with all my might, ceaselessly, without pause, and I'm so glad, so glad I'm talking, and glad that it's

Lambert. Whether he appeared to me somehow as my "salvation," or I rushed to him at that moment because I took him for a man from an entirely different world—I don't know, I didn't reason then, but rushed to him without reasoning. What I said then I don't remember at all, and I hardly spoke coherently, hardly even articulated the words clearly; but he listened intently. He grabbed the first cab that came along, and a few moments later I was sitting in the warmth, in his room.

III

EVERY PERSON, WHOEVER he may be, certainly preserves some recollection of something that has happened to him which he regards or is inclined to regard as fantastic, remarkable, out of the ordinary, almost miraculous, whether it's a dream, a meeting, a divination, a presentiment, or something of the sort. To this day I am inclined to regard this meeting of mine with Lambert as something even prophetic... judging at least by the circumstances and consequences of the meeting. It all happened, however, on the one hand at least, in the most natural way: he was simply coming back from one of his nighttime occupations (which one will become clear later) half drunk, and, stopping for a moment by the gate in the lane, saw me. He had been in Petersburg for only a few days then.

The room I found myself in was a small, quite unassumingly furnished example of ordinary Petersburg *chambres garnies** of the middling sort. Lambert himself, however, was excellently and expensively dressed. On the floor lay two suitcases only half unpacked. A corner of the room was partitioned off by a screen, concealing a bed.

"Alphonsine!" cried Lambert.

"*Présente!*"† a cracked female voice replied in a Parisian accent from behind the screen, and in no more than two minutes out popped Mlle. Alphonsine, hastily dressed in a bed jacket, only just risen—a strange sort of being, tall and lean as a splinter, a young girl, a brunette, with a long waist, a long face, darting eyes, and sunken cheeks—an awfully worn-out creature!

*Furnished rooms.
†Here!

"Quick!" (I'm translating, but he spoke to her in French.) "They must have a samovar going, fetch some boiling water, red wine and sugar, and a glass here, quick, he's frozen, this is a friend of mine... he slept all night in the snow."

"*Malheureux!*"* she cried out, clasping her hands with a theatrical gesture.

"Uh-uh!" Lambert shouted at her as at a little dog, and shook his finger; she stopped gesturing at once and ran to fulfill his order.

He examined and palpated me; he felt my pulse, touched my forehead, my temples.

"Strange," he muttered, "how you didn't freeze... though you were all covered up in your fur coat, including your head, like sitting in a fur hole..."

The hot glass arrived, I gulped it down greedily, and it revived me at once; I started babbling again; I was half-reclining on the sofa in the corner and talking away—I was spluttering as I talked—but of precisely what and how I was speaking, once again I have almost no recollection; there are moments and even whole stretches that I've completely forgotten. I repeat: whether he understood anything then from what I was telling, I don't know; but one thing I realized clearly afterwards—namely, that he managed to understand me well enough to draw the conclusion that he ought not to disregard his meeting with me... Later I'll explain in its place what reckoning he might have made here.

I was not only terribly animated, but at moments, it seems, quite merry. I remember the sun suddenly lighting up the room when the blinds were raised, and the stove crackling when someone lit it—who and how, I don't remember. I also have the memory of a tiny black dog that Mlle. Alphonsine held in her arms, coquettishly pressing it to her heart. This lapdog somehow diverted me very much, even so much that I stopped talking and twice reached out for it, but Lambert waved his hand, and Alphonsine and her lapdog instantly effaced themselves behind the screen.

He was very silent himself, sat facing me and, leaning strongly towards me, listened without tearing himself away; at times he smiled a long, drawn-out smile, baring his teeth and narrowing his eyes, as if making an effort to think and wishing to guess. I've kept a clear recollection only of the fact that, when I was telling him about the "document," I simply couldn't express myself understand-

*Poor boy!

ably and make a coherent story of it, and by his face I could see only too well that he couldn't understand me, but that he wanted very much to understand, so that he even risked stopping me with a question, which was dangerous, because as soon as I was interrupted, I at once interrupted the subject and forgot what I was talking about. How long we sat and talked like that I don't know and can't even reckon. He suddenly got up and called Alphonsine:

"He needs rest; he may also need a doctor. Do whatever he asks, that is... *vous comprenez, ma fille? Vous avez de l'argent,** no? Here!" And he took out a ten-rouble note for her. He started whispering to her: "*Vous comprenez! Vous comprenez!*" he repeated to her, shaking his finger at her and frowning sternly. I saw that she trembled frightfully before him.

"I'll be back, and you'd best have a good sleep," he smiled to me and took his hat.

"*Mais vous n'avez pas dormi du tout, Maurice!*"† Alphonsine cried out pathetically.

"*Taisez-vous, je dormirai après,*"‡ and he left.

"*Sauvée!*"§ she whispered pathetically, pointing after him to me with her hand.

"*Monsieur, monsieur!*" she began declaiming at once, assuming a pose in the middle of the room. "*Jamais homme ne fut si cruel, si Bismarck, que cet être, qui regarde une femme comme une saleté de hasard. Une femme, qu'est-ce que ça dans notre époque? 'Tue-la'—voilà le dernier mot de l'Académie française!...*"‖

I goggled my eyes at her; I was seeing double, there seemed to be two Alphonsines in front of me... Suddenly I noticed that she was weeping, gave a start, and realized that she had been talking to me for a very long time now, which meant that during that time I had been asleep or unconscious.

"...*Hélas! de quoi m'aurait servi de le découvrir plutôt,*" she exclaimed, "*et n'aurais-je pas autant gagné à tenir ma honte cachée toute ma vie? Peut-être, n'est-il pas honnête à une demoiselle de s'expliquer si*

*You understand, my girl? You have money ...
†But you haven't slept at all, Maurice!
‡Shut up, I'll sleep afterwards.
§Saved!
‖Never was a man so cruel, so Bismarck, as this being, who looks at a woman as a chance bit of filth. A woman, what is she in our epoch? "Kill her!"—that's the last word of the Académie Française.

*librement devant monsieur, mais enfin je vous avoue, que s'il m'était permis de vouloir quelque chose, oh, ce serait de lui plonger au coeur mon couteau, mais en détournant les yeux, de peur que son regard exécrable ne fît trembler mon bras et ne glaçât mon courage! Il a assassiné ce pope russe, monsieur, il lui arracha sa barbe rousse pour la vendre à un artiste en cheveux au pont des Maréchaux, tout près de la Maison de monsieur Andrieux—hautes nouveautés, articles de Paris, linge, chemises, vous savez, n'est-ce pas?... Oh, monsieur, quand l'amitié rassemble à table épouse, enfants, soeurs, amis, quand une vive allégresse enflamme mon coeur, je vous le demande, monsieur: est-il bonheur préférable à celui dont tout jouit? Mais il rit, monsieur, ce monstre exécrable et inconcevable et si ce n'était pas par l'entremise de monsieur Andrieux, jamais, oh, jamais je ne serais... Mais quoi, monsieur, qu'avez vous, monsieur?"**[*]

She rushed to me: it seems I had a chill, and maybe had also swooned. I can't express what a painful, morbid impression this half-crazed being made on me. Maybe she imagined that she had been ordered to entertain me; at any rate she never left me for a moment. Maybe she had been on the stage once; she declaimed awfully, fidgeted, talked nonstop, while I had long been silent. All I could understand from her stories was that she was closely connected with some "*Maison de M. Andrieux—hautes nouveautés, articles de Paris, etc.*" and maybe even came from *la Maison de M. Andrieux*, but she had somehow been torn forever from *M. Andrieux par ce monstre furieux et inconcevable,*[†] and this was what the tragedy consisted in... She sobbed, but it seemed to me that it was only as a

*Alas, what good would it have done me to reveal it sooner... and wouldn't I have gained just as much by keeping my shame hidden all my life? Perhaps it's not honorable for a young woman to explain herself so freely in front of *monsieur*, but finally I'll admit to you that if I were allowed to wish for something, oh, it would be to plunge my knife into his heart, but with my eyes averted, for fear that his execrable look would make my arm tremble and freeze my courage! He killed that Russian priest, *monsieur*, he tore out his red beard to sell it to a hair artist on the Blacksmiths' [i.e., Kuznetsky] Bridge, just near the *Maison* of Monsieur Andrieux—the latest novelties, articles from Paris, linen, shirts, you know it, don't you?... Oh, *monsieur*, when friendship gathers wife, children, sisters, friends around the table, when a lively happiness enflames my heart, I ask you, *monsieur*; is any happiness preferable to that which everyone enjoys? But he laughs, *monsieur*, this execrable and inconceivable monster, and if it weren't through the agency of Monsieur Andrieux, never, oh, never would I be... But what is it, *monsieur*, what's wrong with you, *monsieur*?

†By this furious and inconceivable monster.

matter of course and that she wasn't crying at all; at times I fancied that she was suddenly going to fall apart like a skeleton; she articulated her words in some crushed, cracked voice; the word *préférable*, for instance, she pronounced *préfér-a-able* and on the syllable *a* bleated like a sheep. Coming to my senses once, I saw her making a pirouette in the middle of the room, yet she wasn't dancing, but this pirouette also had some relation to the story, and she was only doing an impersonation. Suddenly she rushed and opened the small, old, out-of-tune piano that was in the room, started strumming on it and singing... It seems that for ten minutes or more I became completely unconscious, fell asleep, but the lapdog squeaked and I came to: full consciousness suddenly returned to me for a moment and lit me up with all its light. I jumped up in horror.

"Lambert, I'm at Lambert's!" I thought and, seizing my hat, I rushed for my fur coat.

"*Où allez-vous, monsieur?*"* cried the keen-eyed Alphonsine.

"I want to get out, I want to leave! Let me go, don't keep me..."

"*Oui, monsieur!*" Alphonsine concurred with all her might, and rushed to open the door to the corridor for me herself. "*Mais ce n'est pas loin, monsieur, c'est pas loin du tout, ça ne vaut pas la peine de mettre votre chouba, c'est ici près, monsieur!*"† she exclaimed to the whole corridor. Running out of the room, I turned to the right.

"*Par ici, monsieur, c'est par ici!*"‡ she exclaimed with all her might, clutching at my coat with her long, bony fingers, and with her other hand pointing me to the left somewhere down the corridor, where I had no wish to go. I tore myself free and ran for the door to the stairs.

"*Il s'en va, il s'en va!*"§ Alphonsine raced after me, shouting in her cracked voice. "*Mais il me tuera, monsieur, il me tuera!*"‖ But I had already run out to the stairs, and though she even raced after me down the stairs, I managed to open the outside door, run out to the street, and jump into the first cab. I gave mama's address...

*Where are you going, *monsieur*?

†But it isn't far, *monsieur*, it's not far at all, it's not worth the trouble of putting on your *shuba*, it's nearby, *monsieur*.

‡This way, *monsieur*, it's this way!

§He's leaving, he's leaving!

‖But he'll kill me, *monsieur*, he'll kill me!

IV

But consciousness, having flashed for a moment, quickly went out. I still have a slight memory of how I was brought in and taken to mama's, but there I fell almost at once into complete oblivion. The next day, as I was told later (though this I also remembered myself), my reason became clear again for a moment. I remembered myself in Versilov's room on his sofa; I remember the faces of Versilov, mama, Liza around me, remember very well how Versilov spoke to me about Zershchikov, about the prince, showed me some letter, reassured me. They told me later that I kept asking in horror about some Lambert, and kept hearing the barking of some lapdog. But the faint light of consciousness quickly dimmed; by evening of this second day I was already totally delirious. But I'll forestall events and explain them beforehand.

When I ran out of Zershchikov's that evening and everything calmed down somewhat there, Zershchikov, having started the game, suddenly announced in a loud voice that a lamentable error had occurred: the lost money, the four hundred roubles, had been found in a pile of other money and the accounts of the bank proved to be perfectly correct. Then the prince, who had remained in the hall, accosted Zershchikov and demanded insistently that he make a public declaration of my innocence and, besides that, offer his apologies in the form of a letter. Zershchikov, for his part, found the demand worthy of respect and gave his word, in front of everybody, to send me a letter of explanation and apology the next day. The prince gave him Versilov's address, and indeed the very next day Versilov personally received from Zershchikov a letter in my name and over thirteen hundred roubles that belonged to me and that I had forgotten on the roulette table. Thus ended the affair at Zershchikov's. This joyful news contributed greatly to my recovery when I regained consciousness.

The prince, on coming back from gambling, wrote two letters that same night, one to me, and the other to his former regiment, where he had had the incident with Ensign Stepanov. He sent both letters the next morning. After which he wrote a report to his superiors, and with this report in hand, early in the morning, he went in person to the commander of his regiment and announced to him that he, "a common criminal, a partner in counterfeiting the ——sky shares, surrenders himself into the hands of justice and asks to be put on trial." With that he handed over the report, in which it was all explained in writing. He was arrested.

Here is the letter he wrote to me that night, word for word:

Priceless Arkady Makarovich,

Having tried the lackeyish "way out," I have thereby lost the right to comfort my soul at least somewhat with the thought that I, too, was finally able to venture upon a righteous deed. I am guilty before my fatherland and before my family, and for that, as the last of my family, I am punishing myself. I do not understand how I could have seized upon the base thought of self-preservation and dreamed for some time of buying myself back from them with money. All the same, I myself, before my own conscience, would have remained forever a criminal. Those people, even if they did return the compromising notes to me, would never have left me all my life! What remained then: to live with them, to be one with them all my life—that was the lot that awaited me! I could not accept it, and finally found in myself enough firmness, or maybe just despair, to act as I am acting now.

I have written a letter to my former regiment, to my former comrades, and vindicated Stepanov. In this act there is not and cannot be any redeeming deed: it is all just the dying bequest of tomorrow's dead man. That is how it must be regarded.

Forgive me for turning away from you in the gambling house; it was because I was not sure of you at that moment. Now that I am a dead man, I can make such confessions . . . from the other world.

Poor Liza! She knows nothing of this decision; may she not curse me, but judge for herself. I cannot justify myself and do not even find words to explain anything to her. Know also, Arkady Makarovich, that yesterday, in the morning, when she came to me for the last time, I revealed my deceit to her and confessed that I had gone to Anna Andreevna with the intention of proposing to her. I could not leave that on my conscience before the last, already taken decision, seeing her love, and so I revealed it to her. She forgave me, forgave me everything, but I did not believe her; it was not forgiveness; in her place I would not be able to forgive.

Remember me.

Your unfortunate last Prince *Sokolsky.*

I lay unconscious for exactly nine days.

PART THREE

Chapter One

I

Now about something completely different.

I keep announcing: "something different, something different," and I keep scribbling away about myself alone. Yet I've already declared a thousand times that I don't want to describe myself at all, and I firmly didn't want to when I began my notes; I understand only too well that the reader hasn't got the slightest need of me. I'm describing and want to describe others, and not myself, and if I keep turning up all the time, that is a sad mistake, because I simply can't avoid it, however much I wish to. Above all, it vexes me that, in describing my own adventures with such ardor, I thereby give reason for thinking that I'm the same now as I was then. The reader will remember, however, that I've already exclaimed more than once: "Oh, if only one could change the former and start completely anew!" I wouldn't be able to exclaim like that if I hadn't changed radically now and become a totally different person. That is all too obvious; and you can't imagine how sick I am of all these apologies and prefaces that I'm forced to squeeze every minute even into the very middle of my notes!

To business.

After nine days of unconsciousness, I came to my senses regenerated, but not reformed; my regeneration, however, was stupid, naturally, if it's taken in the vast sense, and maybe if it were now, it wouldn't be so. The idea, that is, the feeling, again consisted (as a thousand times before) only in the fact that I should leave them completely, but this time leave without fail, and not as before, when I set myself the same topic a thousand times and never could do it. I didn't want revenge on anyone, and I give my word of honor on that—though I had been offended by everyone. I was going to leave without disgust, without curses, but I wanted my own strength, and genuine this time, not dependent on any of them or the whole world; for I was all but reconciled with everything in the world! I record this dream of mine not as a thought, but as an irresistible feeling at that time. I didn't want to formulate it yet, while I was in bed. Sick and without strength, lying in Versilov's room, which they set aside for me, I was painfully aware of what a low degree of strengthlessness I had come to: some sort of little straw, not a man, lolled there in bed, and not only on account of illness—and how offensive that was to me! And so, from the very depths of my being, from all my strength, a protest began to rise, and I choked with a feeling of boundlessly exaggerated arrogance and defiance. I don't even remember a time in my whole life when I was more filled with arrogant feelings than in those first days of my recovery, that is, when the little straw lolled in bed.

But for the moment I was silent and even decided not to think about anything! I kept peeking into their faces, trying to guess everything I needed by them. It was evident that they did not wish to ask questions or show curiosity either, but talked to me about completely irrelevant things. I liked that and at the same time it upset me; I won't explain this contradiction. I saw Liza more rarely than mama, though she came to see me every day and even twice a day. From bits of their conversation and from the whole look of them I concluded that Liza had accumulated an awful lot of cares, and that she was even frequently away from home because of her affairs. For me it was as if the mere idea of the possibility of "her own affairs" already contained something offensive; however, these were all just sick, purely physiological feelings, which are not worth describing. Tatyana Pavlovna also came to see me almost daily, and though she wasn't gentle with me at all, at least she didn't abuse me as before, which vexed me in the extreme, so that I simply said to her, "Tatyana Pavlovna, when you're not abusing me, you're a great bore." "Well, then I won't come to see you," she snapped, and left. And I was glad to have chased at least one of them away.

Most of all I tormented mama and got very irritated with her. I suddenly had a terrible appetite, and I grumbled a lot that the food came late (but it never came late). Mama didn't know how to please me. Once she brought me soup and, as usual, began to feed me herself, but I kept grumbling while I ate. And suddenly I became vexed that I was grumbling: "She's maybe the only one I love, and it's her that I torment." But my anger wouldn't subside, and I suddenly burst into tears from anger, and she, poor dear, thought I was weeping from tenderness, leaned over, and started kissing me. I restrained myself and somehow endured it and actually hated her in that second. But I always loved mama, loved her then, too, and didn't really hate her, but it was what always happens: the one you love most is the first one you insult.

The only one I did hate in those first days was the doctor. This doctor was a young man with a presumptuous air, who spoke sharply and even impolitely. As if all those people in science, just yesterday and suddenly, had found out something special, whereas nothing special had happened yesterday; but "the middle" and "the street" are always that way. I endured for a long time, but in the end suddenly burst out and declared to him, before all our people, that he needn't drag himself here, that I'd get well without him, that he, though he had the look of a realist, was filled with nothing but prejudice and didn't understand that medicine had never yet cured anyone; that finally, in all probability, he was grossly uneducated, "like all our present-day engineers and specialists, who have lately started turning up their noses at us." The doctor was very offended (proving what he was by that alone), yet he continued to visit. I finally announced to Versilov that if the doctor did not stop coming, I'd tell him something ten times more unpleasant. Versilov only observed that it was impossible to say anything even twice more unpleasant than what had been said, let alone ten times. I was glad he had noticed that.

What a man, though! I'm speaking of Versilov. He, he alone, was the cause of it all—and yet he was the only one I wasn't angry with then. It wasn't only his manner with me that won me over. I think we felt mutually then that we owed each other many explanations . . . and that, precisely for that reason, it would be best never to explain. It is extremely agreeable, on such occasions in life, to run into an intelligent person! I have already mentioned in the second part of my story, running ahead, that he gave me a very brief and clear account of the arrested prince's letter to me, about Zershchikov, about his explanation in my favor, and so on. Since I had decided to be silent, I put to him, with all possible dryness, only two or three very brief questions; he answered them clearly and precisely, but entirely without superfluous words and, what was best of all, without superfluous feelings. I was afraid of superfluous feelings then.

About Lambert I say nothing, but the reader has, of course, guessed that I thought all too much about him. In my delirium, I spoke several times about Lambert; but once I came out of my delirium and could observe attentively, I quickly realized that everything about Lambert remained a secret, and that they knew nothing, not excepting Versilov. I was glad then, and my fear went away, but I was mistaken, as I found out later, to my astonishment:

he had come to see me during my illness, but Versilov said nothing about it, and I concluded that for Lambert I had already sunk into oblivion. Nevertheless I often thought about him; what's more, I thought not only without disgust, not only with curiosity, but even with concern, as if anticipating here something new, a way out that corresponded to the new feelings and plans that were being born in me. In short, I proposed to think Lambert over first of all, once I decided to start thinking. I'll add one strange thing: I had completely forgotten where he lived and on what street it had all happened then. The room, Alphonsine, the little dog, the corridor—all that I remembered; I could paint a picture of it all now; but where it had all happened, that is, on what street and in what house—I had completely forgotten. And what's strangest of all, I figured it out only on my third or fourth day of full consciousness, when I had long begun to be concerned with Lambert.

And so, such were my first sensations upon my resurrection. I've indicated only the most superficial, and very probably was unable to indicate the important. In fact, maybe it was precisely then that everything important was being defined and formulated in my heart; surely I didn't spend the whole time being vexed and angry only because they hadn't served me my broth. Oh, I remember how sad I could be then, and how grieved I sometimes was in those moments, especially when I was left alone for a long time. And they, as if on purpose, quickly understood that I felt oppressed with them and that their sympathy annoyed me, and they started leaving me alone more and more often: an unnecessarily subtle perceptivity.

II

On my fourth day of consciousness, I was lying in my bed between two and three o'clock in the afternoon, and there was no one with me. It was a clear day, and I knew that after three, when the sun would be setting,[1] its slanting red ray would strike straight into the corner of my wall, and there would be a bright spot of light there. I knew it from the previous days, and the fact that it would unfailingly happen in an hour, and, above all, that I knew it beforehand, like two times two, angered me to the point of spite. I turned my whole body convulsively, and suddenly, amidst the deep silence, clearly heard the words: "Lord Jesus Christ, our God, have mercy on us." The words were pronounced in a half-whisper, followed by a deep, full-chested sigh, and then everything became perfectly still again. I quickly raised my head.

Earlier, that is, the day before, and even two days before, I had begun to notice something peculiar in our three downstairs rooms. In that little room across the drawing room, which used to be mama's and Liza's, there was apparently someone else. More than once I had heard some sort of sounds during the daytime and at night, but it was all for moments, the briefest moments, then total silence would set in again at once for several hours, so that I paid no attention. The day before, the thought had occurred to me that it was Versilov there, the more so as he had come to my room soon afterwards, though I knew for certain from their own conversations that Versilov had moved somewhere to another apartment during the time of my illness, and spent his nights there. And about mama and Liza I had long known that (for the sake of my tranquillity, I thought) they had both moved upstairs, to my former "coffin," and I had even thought once to myself, "How can the two of them have enough room there?" And now it suddenly turns out that some man is living in their old room and that the man is not Versilov at all. With an ease I wouldn't have supposed I had (imagining till then that I was totally strengthless), I lowered my feet from the bed, put them into my slippers, threw on a gray lambskin robe that lay next to me (and had been donated to me by Versilov), and set out across our living room to mama's former bedroom. What I saw there totally confounded me; I had never anticipated anything like it, and stopped as if rooted to the threshold.

There sat a very gray-haired old man with a big, awfully white beard, and it was clear that he had been sitting there for a long time. He sat not on the bed but on mama's little bench, and only leaned his back against the bed. However, he held himself so straight that it seemed he didn't need any support, though he was obviously ill. Over his shirt he wore a jacket lined with sheepskin, his knees were covered with mama's plaid, there were slippers on his feet. One could tell that he was tall and broad-shouldered, and he looked quite hale, despite his illness, though somewhat pale and thin. He had an oblong face, very thick hair, but not too long, and he seemed to be over seventy. Beside him on a little table, within his reach, lay three or four books and a pair of silver spectacles. Though I hadn't had the least thought of meeting him,

I guessed that same moment who he was, only I still couldn't figure out how he had sat there all those days, almost next to me, so quietly that up to then I had never heard a thing.

He didn't stir when he saw me, but gazed at me intently and silently, as I did at him, with the difference that I gazed with boundless astonishment, and he without the least. On the contrary, having scrutinized the whole of me, to the last line, in those five or ten seconds of silence, he suddenly smiled and even laughed softly and inaudibly, and though the laughter passed quickly, its bright, mirthful trace remained on his face, and above all in his eyes, very blue, radiant, big, but with lids slightly drooping and swollen with age and surrounded by countless tiny wrinkles. This laughter of his affected me most of all.

I think that when a person laughs, in the majority of cases he becomes repulsive to look at. Most often something banal is revealed in people's laughter, something as if humiliating for the laugher, though the laughing one almost always knows nothing of the impression he makes. Just as he doesn't know, as nobody generally knows, what kind of face he has when he's asleep. Some sleepers have intelligent faces even in sleep, while other faces, even intelligent ones, become very stupid in sleep and therefore ridiculous. I don't know what makes that happen; I only want to say that a laughing man, like a sleeping one, most often knows nothing about his face. A great many people don't know how to laugh at all. However, there's nothing to know here: it's a gift, and it can't be fabricated. It can only be fabricated by re-educating oneself, developing oneself for the better, and overcoming the bad instincts of one's character; then the laughter of such a person might quite possibly change for the better. A man can give himself away completely by his laughter, so that you suddenly learn all his innermost secrets. Even indisputably intelligent laughter is sometimes repulsive. Laughter calls first of all for sincerity, but where is there any sincerity in people? Laughter calls for lack of spite, but people most often laugh spitefully. Sincere and unspiteful laughter is mirth, but where is there any mirth in our time, and do people know how to be mirthful? (About mirth in our time—that was Versilov's observation, and I remembered it.) A man's mirth is a feature that gives away the whole man, from head to foot. Someone's character won't be cracked for a long time, then the man bursts out laughing somehow quite sincerely, and his whole character suddenly opens up as if on the flat of your hand. Only a man of the loftiest and happiest development knows how to be mirthful infectiously, that is, irresistibly and goodheartedly. I'm not speaking of his mental development, but of his character, of the whole man. And so, if you want to discern a man and know his soul, you must look, not at how he keeps silent, or how he speaks, or how he weeps, or even how he is stirred by the noblest ideas, but you had better look at him when he laughs. If a man has a good laugh, it means he's a good man. Note at the same time all the nuances: for instance, a man's laughter must in no case seem stupid to you, however merry and simplehearted it may be. The moment you notice the slightest trace of stupidity in someone's laughter, it undoubtedly means that the man is of limited intelligence, though he may do nothing but pour out ideas. Or if his laughter isn't stupid, but the man himself, when he laughs, for some reason suddenly seems ridiculous to you, even just slightly—know, then, that the man has no real sense of dignity, not fully in any case. Or, finally, if his laughter is infectious, but for some reason still seems banal to you, know, then, that the man's nature is on the banal side as well, and all the noble and lofty that you noticed in him before is either deliberately affected or unconsciously borrowed, and later on the man is certain to change for the worse, to take up what's "useful" and throw his noble ideas away without regret, as the errors and infatuations of youth.

I am intentionally placing this long tirade about laughter here, even sacrificing the flow of the story, for I consider it one of the most serious conclusions of my life. And I especially recommend it to those would-be brides who are ready to marry their chosen man, but keep scrutinizing him with hesitation and mistrust, and can't make the final decision. And let them not laugh at the pathetic adolescent for poking with his moral admonitions into the matter of marriage, of which he doesn't understand the first thing. But I understand only that laughter is the surest test of a soul. Look at a child: only children know how to laugh perfectly—that's what makes them seductive. A crying child is repulsive to me, but a laughing and merry child is a ray from paradise, a revelation from the future, when man will finally become as pure and simplehearted as a child. And so something childlike and incredibly attractive also flashed in the fleeting laughter of this old man. I went up to him at once.

III

"Sit, sit a while, must be your legs don't stand firm yet," he invited me affably, pointing to the place next to him and continuing to look into my face with the same radiant gaze. I sat down next to him and said:

"I know you, you're Makar Ivanovich."

"So I am, dear heart. And it's a fine thing that you got up. You're a young man, it's a fine thing for you. An old man looks towards the grave, but a young man must live."

"But are you ill?"

"I am, my friend, the legs mostly; they brought me as far as the doorstep, but once I sat down here, they got swollen. It came over me last Thursday, when the degrees set in" (N.B.—that is, when the frost set in). "I've been rubbing them with ointment so far, you see; two years ago Lichten, the doctor, Edmund Karlych, prescribed it to me in Moscow, and the ointment helped, oh, it helped; well, but now it's stopped helping. And my chest is blocked up, too. And since yesterday it's the back as well, like dogs nipping at me... I don't sleep nights."

"How is it I haven't heard you here at all?" I interrupted. He looked at me as if he was trying to figure something out.

"Just don't wake your mother," he added, as if recalling something. "She fussed around me all night here, and so inaudibly, like a fly; but now I know she's lying down. Ah, it's bad for a sick old man," he sighed. "Not much for the soul to hang on to, it seems, but still it holds on, but still it's glad of the world; and, it seems, if you were to begin your whole life over again, the soul mightn't fear even that; though maybe such a thought is sinful."

"Why sinful?"

"It's a dream, this thought, and an old man ought to depart in a handsome way. Again, if you meet death with murmuring or displeasure, it's a great sin. Well, but if you love life out of spiritual mirth, then I suppose God will forgive, even if you're an old man. It's hard for a man to know about every sin, what's sinful and what's not; there's a mystery here that passes human reason. An old man should be pleased at all times, and he should die in the full flower of his mind, blessedly and handsomely, full of days, sighing at his last hour and rejoicing, departing like the ear to its sheaf, and fulfilling his mystery."

"You keep saying 'mystery'; what is this 'fulfilling his mystery'?" I asked, and looked back at the door. I was glad that we were alone and that there was undisturbed silence around us. The sun was shining brightly through the window before sunset. He spoke somewhat grandiloquently and imprecisely, but very sincerely and with some strong excitement, as if he was indeed so glad of my coming. But I noticed that he was undoubtedly in a feverish condition and even a strong one. I was also sick, also in a fever, from the moment I went in to him.

"What is a mystery? Everything is a mystery, my friend, there is God's mystery in everything. Every tree, every blade of grass contains this same mystery. Whether it's a small bird singing or the whole host of stars shining in the sky at night—it's all one mystery, the same one. And the greatest mystery of all is what awaits the human soul in the other world. That's how things are, my friend!"

"I don't know in what sense... Of course, I'm not saying it to tease you, and, believe me, I do believe in God, but all these mysteries have long been revealed by the human mind, and what hasn't been revealed will be revealed, quite certainly and maybe in the nearest time. Botany has perfect knowledge of how trees grow, physiologists and anatomists even know why birds sing, or will know it soon, and as for the stars, they've not only all been counted, but all their movements have been calculated to the minute, so that it's possible to predict the appearance of some comet a thousand years ahead... and now even the composition of the remotest stars has become known. Take a microscope—it's like a magnifying glass that magnifies objects a million times—and examine a drop of water through it, and you'll see a whole new world there, a whole life of living beings, and yet this was also a mystery, but now it has been revealed."

"I've heard of that, dear heart, more than once I've heard it from people. There's nothing to say, it's a great and glorious thing; everything has been given over to man by the will of God; it's not for nothing that God blew into him the breath of life: 'Live and know.'"

"Well, that's a commonplace. Anyhow, you're not an enemy of science, not a clericalist? That is, I don't know if you'll understand..."

"No, dear heart, from my youth I've respected learning, and though I have no knowledge myself, I don't murmur about that; if I don't have it, someone else does. And maybe it's better that way, because to each his own. Because, my dear friend, not everyone profits from learning. They're all intemperate, they all want to astonish the whole universe, and I might want it more than anyone, if I were clever. But not being clever at all now, how can I exalt myself, when I don't know anything? You're young and sharp, and that's the lot that has fallen to you, you must study. Learn everything, so that when you meet a godless or mischievous man, you can give him answers, so that he won't hurl insensate words at you and confuse your immature thoughts. And that glass I saw not so long ago."

He paused for breath and sighed. I had decidedly given him great pleasure by coming. He had a morbid desire for communication. Besides that, I will decidedly not be mistaken if I maintain that he looked at me, at moments, even with some extraordinary love: he placed his hand on my arm caressingly, stroked my shoulder . . . well, but at moments, I must confess, he seemed to forget all about me, as though he were sitting alone, and while he went on speaking ardently, it was as if somewhere into the air.

"In St. Gennady's hermitage, my friend," he went on, "there's a man of great intelligence. He's of a noble family and a lieutenant-colonel by rank, and he possesses great wealth. While he lived in the world, he did not want to commit himself to marriage; he withdrew from the world ten years ago now, loving peace and silent havens and resting his senses from worldly vanities. He observes the whole monastic rule, but he doesn't want to be tonsured. And of books, my friend, he has so many, I've never seen anyone have so many—he told me himself it was eight thousand roubles' worth. Pyotr Valeryanych he's called. He taught me much at various times, and I loved listening to him exceedingly. I said to him once, 'How is it, sir, that with such great intelligence as yours, and living for ten years now in monastic obedience and the complete cutting off of your will—how is it that you don't accept honorable tonsuring so as to be more perfect?' And to that he replied, 'How can you go talking about my intelligence, old man? Maybe it's my intelligence that holds me captive, and not I who control it. And how can you discuss my obedience? Maybe I lost my measure long ago. And about the cutting off of my will? I could give away my money this very moment, and give up my rank, and put all my medals on the table this very moment, but for ten years I've struggled to give up my tobacco pipe, and I can't. What kind of monk am I after that, and what is this cutting off of my will that you praise?' And I was astonished then at this humility. Well, so last summer, during the Peter and Paul fast,[2] I came to that hermitage again—the Lord brought me—and I saw that very thing—a microscope—standing in his cell—he had ordered it from abroad for a lot of money. 'Wait, old man,' he says, 'I'll show you an astonishing thing, because you've never seen it before. You see a drop of water pure as a tear, well, then look at what there is in it, and you'll see that the mechanics will soon search out all the mysteries of God and won't leave a single one for you and me'—that's what he said. I remember it. And I had already looked through a microscope thirty-five years ago, at Alexander Vladimirovich Malgasov's, our master, Andrei Petrovich's uncle on his mother's side, whose estate went to Andrei Petrovich after his death. He was an important squire, a big general, and kept a big pack of hounds, and I lived for many years as his huntsman. It was then that he also set up this microscope, he brought it with him and told all the servants to come and look, one by one, both the male and the female sex, and they were shown a flea, and a louse, and the point of a needle, and a hair, and a drop of water. And it was funny: they were afraid to go look, and they were afraid of the master, too—he was hot-tempered. Some didn't even know how to look, they squinted one eye but didn't see anything, others got scared and shouted, and the headman Savin Makarov covered his eyes with both hands and shouted, 'Do what you want with me—I won't look!' There was a lot of empty laughter. However, I didn't tell Pyotr Valeryanych that I had seen this same wonder before, thirty-five years ago, because I saw the man took great pleasure in showing it, so I began, on the contrary, to marvel and be terrified. He waited a while and then asked, 'Well, old man, what do you say now?' And I straightened myself up and said, 'The Lord said: Let there be light, and there was light.' But to that he suddenly replied, 'And wasn't there darkness?' And he said it so strangely, not even smiling. I was astonished at him then, but he even seemed a little angry and fell silent."

"Quite simply, your Pyotr Valeryanych eats *kutya*[3] in the monastery and bows, but doesn't believe in God, and you happened onto such a moment—that's all," I said. "And on top of that, he's a rather ridiculous man: he had probably already seen a microscope ten times before, why did he lose his mind the eleventh time? Some sort of nervous impressionability... worked up in the monastery."

"He's a pure man and of lofty mind," the old man said imposingly, "and he's not godless. He has a solid mind, but his heart is uneasy. There are a great many such people now, come from gentlefolk and of learned rank. And I'll say this as well: the man punishes himself. But you avoid them and don't vex them, and remember them in your prayers before sleep at night, for such men seek God. Do you pray before sleep?"

"No, I consider it empty ritualism. I must confess, however, that I like your Pyotr Valeryanych: at least he's not made of straw, but a human being, somewhat resembling a certain man close to us both, whom we both know."

The old man paid attention only to the first part of my answer.

"It's too bad you don't pray, my friend; it's a good thing, it gladdens the heart, before sleep, and rising from sleep, and waking up in the night. That I can tell you. In summer, in the month of July, we were hastening to the Bogorodsky Monastery for the feast. The closer we came to the place, the more people joined us, and finally almost tenscore people came together, all hurrying to kiss the holy and incorrupt relics of two great wonder-workers, Aniky and Grigory. We spent the night in the fields, brother, and I woke up early in the morning, everybody was still asleep, and the sun hadn't even peeked out from behind the forest yet. I raised my head, my dear, gazed about me, and sighed: inexpressible beauty everywhere! All's still, the air's light; the grass is growing—grow, grass of God; a bird's singing—sing, bird of God; a baby squeals in a woman's arms—the Lord be with you, little person, grow and be happy, youngling! And for the first time in my life it was as if I contained it all in myself... I lay down again and fell asleep so easily. It's good in the world, my dear! If I mended a bit, I'd go again in the spring. And that it's a mystery makes it even better; your heart fears and wonders, and this fear gladdens the heart: 'All is in thee, Lord, and I am in thee, and so receive me!' Don't murmur, young one: it's all the more beautiful that it's a mystery," he added tenderly.

"'It's even more beautiful that it's a mystery...' I'll remember those words. You express yourself terribly imprecisely, but I understand... It strikes me that you know and understand much more than you can express; only it's as if you're in delirium..." escaped me, looking at his feverish eyes and pale face. But it seems he didn't hear my words.

"Do you know, my dear young one," he began again, as if continuing his former speech, "do you know that there's a limit to the memory of a man on this earth? The limit to the memory of a man is set at just a hundred years. A hundred years after a man's death, his children or grandchildren, who have seen his face, can still remember him, but after that, though his memory may persist, it's just orally, mentally, for all who have seen his face will have passed on. And his grave in the cemetery will overgrow with grass, its white stone will chip away, and all people will forget him, even his own posterity, then his very name will be forgotten, for only a few remain in people's memory—and so be it! And let me be forgotten, my dears, but I'll love you even from the grave. I hear your merry voices, little children, I hear your footsteps on your parents' graves on forefathers' day;[4] live under the sun meanwhile, rejoice, and I'll pray to God for you, I'll come to you in a dream . . . it's all the same and there is love after death! . . ."

Mainly, I was in as much of a fever as he was; and instead of leaving or persuading him to calm down, and maybe putting him on the bed, because he seemed to be quite delirious, I suddenly seized him by the hand and, leaning towards him and pressing his hand, said in an excited whisper and with tears in my soul:

"I'm glad of you. Maybe I've been waiting for you a long time. I don't love any of them; they have no seemliness . . . I won't go after them, I don't know where I'll go, I'll go with you . . ."

But, fortunately, mama suddenly came in, otherwise I don't know where it would have ended. She came in with a just-awakened and alarmed face, a vial and a tablespoon in her hands. Seeing us, she exclaimed:

"I just knew it! I'm late giving him his quinine, he's all in a fever! I overslept, Makar Ivanovich, dear heart!"

I got up and left. She gave him the medicine anyway and laid him down in bed. I also lay down in mine, but in great agitation. I went back with great curiosity and thought as hard as I could about this encounter. What I expected from it then—I don't know. Of course, I was reasoning incoherently, and not thoughts but only fragments of thoughts flashed through my mind. I lay with my face to the wall, and suddenly in the corner I saw the bright spot of light from the setting sun, the one I had been waiting for earlier with such a curse, and I remember it was as if my whole soul leaped up and a new light penetrated my heart. I remember that sweet moment and do not want to forget it. It was just a moment of new hope and new strength... I was recovering then, and therefore such impulses might have been the inevitable consequence of the state of my nerves; but I believe in that bright hope even now—that's what I want to write down now and remember. Of course, I also knew firmly then that I wouldn't go wandering with Makar Ivanovich and that I myself didn't know what this new yearning was that had come over me, but I had uttered one phrase, though in delirium: "There's no seemliness in them!" "That's it," I thought, beside myself, "from this moment on I'm seeking 'seemliness,' but they don't have it, and for that I'll leave them."

Something rustled behind me. I turned: mama stood bending over me and peeking into my eyes with timid curiosity. I suddenly took her by the hand.

"And why didn't you tell me anything about our dear guest, mama?" I asked suddenly, myself almost not expecting I'd say it. All anxiety left her face at once, and it was as if joy lit up in it, but she answered me with nothing except a single phrase:

"Liza, don't forget Liza either; you've forgotten Liza."

She spoke it in a quick patter, blushing, and wanted to leave quickly, because she also awfully disliked smearing feelings around, and in this respect was just like me, that is, shy and chaste; besides, naturally, she wouldn't have wanted to start on the theme of Makar Ivanovich with me; what we could say by exchanging looks was enough. But I, who precisely hated any smearing around of feelings, it was I who stopped her forcefully by the hand; I looked sweetly into her eyes, laughed softly and tenderly, and with my other hand stroked her dear face, her sunken cheeks. She bent down and pressed her forehead to mine.

"Well, Christ be with you," she said suddenly, straightening up and beaming all over, "get well. I'll credit you with that. He's sick, very sick... Life is in God's will... Ah, what have I said, no, it can't be that!..."

She left. All her life, in fear and trembling and awe, she had greatly respected her lawful husband, the wanderer Makar Ivanovich, who had magnanimously forgiven her once and for all.

Chapter Two

I

BUT I HAD NOT "forgotten" Liza, mama was mistaken. The sensitive mother saw what seemed to be a cooling off between brother and sister, but it was not a matter of not loving, but sooner of jealousy. In view of what follows, I'll explain in a couple of words.

Ever since the prince's arrest, a sort of arrogant pride had appeared in poor Liza, a sort of unapproachable haughtiness, almost unbearable; but everyone in the house understood the truth and how she was suffering, and if I pouted and frowned in the beginning at her manner with us, it was solely from my own petty irritability, increased tenfold by illness—that's how I think of it now. No, I never stopped loving Liza but, on the contrary, loved her still more, only I didn't want to approach her first, though I understood that she wouldn't come to me first for anything.

The thing was that as soon as everything was revealed about the prince, right after his arrest, Liza, first of all, hastened to assume such a position with regard to us and to anyone you like, as though she couldn't admit even the thought that she could be pitied or in any way comforted, or the prince justified. On the contrary—trying not to have any explanations or arguments with anyone—it was as if she were constantly proud of her unfortunate fiancé's action as of the highest heroism. It was as if she were saying to us all every moment (I repeat: without uttering a word): "No, none of you would do such a thing, none of you would give yourself up from the demands of honor and duty; none of you has such a sensitive and pure conscience! And as for his deeds, who doesn't have bad deeds on his soul? Only everybody hides them, and this man wished rather to ruin himself than remain unworthy in his own eyes." That is what her every gesture apparently expressed. I don't know, but I would have done exactly the same thing in her place. I also don't know whether she had the same thoughts in her soul, that is, to herself; I suspect not. With the other, clear half of her mind, she must certainly have perceived all the worthlessness of her "hero"; for who would not agree now that this unfortunate and even magnanimous man was at the same time in the highest degree a worthless man? Even this very arrogance and snappishness, as it were, with all of us, this constant suspicion that we thought differently of him, partly allowed for the surmise that in the secret places of her heart she might have formed another opinion of her unfortunate friend. I hasten to add, however, for my own part, that in my opinion she was at least half right; for her it was even more forgivable than for the rest of us to hesitate in her ultimate conclusion. I myself confess with all my heart that, to this day, when everything has already passed, I absolutely do not know how or at what to ultimately evaluate this unfortunate man, who set us all such a problem.

Nevertheless, on account of it the house nearly became a little hell. Liza, who loved so strongly, must have suffered very much. By her character, she preferred to suffer silently. Her character was like mine, that is, domineering and proud, and I always thought, both then and now, that she came to love the prince precisely because, having no character, he submitted fully to her domination, from the first word and hour. That happens in one's heart somehow of itself, without any preliminary calculation; but such love, of a strong person for a weak one, is sometimes incomparably stronger and more tormenting than the love of equal characters, because one involuntarily takes upon oneself the responsibility for one's weak friend. So I think at least. All of us, from the very beginning, surrounded her with the tenderest care, especially mama; but she didn't soften, didn't respond to sympathy, and as if rejected all help. At first she still spoke with mama, but every day she grew more and more sparing of words, more abrupt and even hard. She asked Versilov's advice at first, but soon she chose Vasin as her adviser and helper, as I was surprised to learn later... She went to see Vasin every day, also went to the courts, to the prince's superiors, went to the lawyers, the prosecutor; in the end she spent almost whole days away from home. Naturally, twice every day she visited the prince, who was confined in prison, in a section for the nobility, but these meetings, as I became fully convinced later, were very painful for Liza. Naturally, a third person cannot know fully what goes on between two lovers. But it is known to me that the prince deeply insulted her all the time—and how, for instance? Strangely enough, by constant jealousy; however, of that later; but I'll add one thought to it: it's hard to decide which of them tormented the other more. Proud of her hero among us, Liza may have treated him quite differently when they were alone, as I firmly suspect, on the basis of certain facts, of which, however, also later.

And so, as for my feelings and relations with Liza, everything that was on the surface was only an affected, jealous falsehood on both sides, but never did the two of us love each other more strongly than at that time. I'll add, too, that towards Makar Ivanovich, from his very appearance among us, Liza, after the first surprise and curiosity, began for some reason to behave herself almost disdainfully, even condescendingly. It was as if she deliberately paid not the slightest attention to him.

Having promised myself to "keep silent," as I explained in the previous chapter, in theory, of course, that is, in my dreams, I thought to keep my promise. Oh, with Versilov, for instance, I would sooner speak about zoology or the Roman emperors than, for instance, about *her*, or about, for instance, that most important line in his letter to her, where he informed her that "the document has not been burned, but is alive and will emerge"—a line I immediately began to ponder to myself again, as soon as I managed to recover and come to reason after my fever. But alas! with my first steps in practice, and almost before any steps, I realized how difficult and impossible it was to keep myself to such a predetermination: on the very next day after my first acquaintance with Makar Ivanovich, I was awfully disturbed by one unexpected circumstance.

II

I WAS DISTURBED by the unexpected visit of Nastasya Egorovna,[5] the mother of the deceased Olya. I had heard from mama that she had come twice during my illness and was very interested in my health. Whether this "good woman," as my mother always referred to her, came specifically on my account, or was simply visiting mama, following the previously established order—I didn't ask. Mama always told me about everything at home, usually when she came with soup to feed me (when I still couldn't eat by myself), in order to entertain me; while I persistently tried to show each time that this information had little interest for me, and therefore I didn't ask for any details about Nastasya Egorovna, and even remained quite silent.

It was around eleven o'clock. I was just about to get out of bed and move to the armchair by the table when she came in. I purposely stayed in bed. Mama was very busy with something upstairs and did not come down when she arrived, so that we suddenly found ourselves alone with each other. She sat down facing me, on a chair by the wall, smiling and not saying a word. I anticipated a game of silence; and generally her coming made a most irritating impression on me. I didn't even nod to her and looked directly into her eyes; but she also looked directly at me.

"It must be boring for you alone in that apartment, now that the prince is gone?" I asked suddenly, losing patience.

"No, sir, I'm no longer in that apartment. Through Anna Andreevna, I'm now looking after his baby."

"Whose baby?"

"Andrei Petrovich's," she said in a confidential whisper, looking back at the door.

"But Tatyana Pavlovna's there..."

"Tatyana Pavlovna and Anna Andreevna, the both of them, sir, and Lizaveta Makarovna also, and your mother... everybody, sir. Everybody's taking part. Tatyana Pavlovna and Anna Andreevna are now great friends with each other, sir."

News to me. She became very animated as she spoke. I looked at her with hatred.

"You've become very animated since the last time you called on me."

"Oh, yes, sir."

"Grown fat, it seems."

She looked at me strangely.

"I've come to like her very much, sir, very much."

"Who's that?"

"Why, Anna Andreevna. Very much, sir. Such a noble young lady, and so sensible..."

"Just so. And how is she now?"

"She's very calm, sir, very."

"She's always been calm."

"Always, sir."

"If you've come to gossip," I suddenly cried, unable to stand it, "know that I don't meddle with anything, I've decided to drop... everything, everybody, it makes no difference to me—I'm leaving!..."

I fell silent, because I came to my senses. It was humiliating to me that I had begun as if to explain my new goals to her. She listened to me without surprise and without emotion, but silence ensued again. Suddenly she got up, went to the door, and peeked out into the next room. Having made sure there was no one there and we were alone, she quite calmly came back and sat down in her former place.

"Nicely done!" I suddenly laughed.

"That apartment of yours, at the clerk's, are you going to keep it, sir?" she asked suddenly, leaning towards me slightly and lowering her voice, as if this was the main question she had come for.

"That apartment? I don't know. Maybe I'll vacate it . . . How do I know?"

"And your landlords are waiting very much for you; that clerk is in great impatience, and so is his wife. Andrei Petrovich assured them that you'd certainly come back."

"But why did you ask?"

"Anna Andreevna also wanted to know; she was very pleased to learn that you're staying."

"And how does she know so certainly that I'll be sure to stay in that apartment?"

I was about to add, "And what is it to her?"—but I refrained from asking questions out of pride.

"And Mr. Lambert confirmed the same thing to them."

"Wha-a-at?"

"Mr. Lambert, sir. And to Andrei Petrovich, too, he confirmed as hard as he could that you would stay, and he assured Anna Andreevna of it."

I was as if all shaken. What wonders! So Lambert already knows Versilov, Lambert has penetrated as far as Versilov—Lambert and Anna Andreevna—he has penetrated as far as her! Heat came over me, but I said nothing. An awful surge of pride flooded my whole soul, pride or I don't know what. But it was as if I suddenly said to myself at that moment, "If I ask for just one word of explanation, I'll get mixed up with this world again and never break with it." Hatred kindled in my heart. I resolved with all my might to keep silent and lay there motionlessly; she also fell silent for a whole minute.

"What about Prince Nikolai Ivanovich?" I asked suddenly, as if losing my reason. The thing was that I asked decidedly in order to divert the theme, and once more, unwittingly, posed the most capital question, returning again like a madman to that same world from which I had just so convulsively resolved to flee.

"He's in Tsarskoe Selo, sir.[6] He's been a bit unwell, and there's fever going around the city now, so everybody advised him to move to Tsarskoe, to his own house there, for the good air, sir."

I did not reply.

"Anna Andreevna and Mme. Akhmakov visit him every three days, they go together, sir."

Anna Andreevna and Mme. Akhmakov (that is, *she*) are friends! They go together! I kept silent.

"They've become such friends, sir, and Anna Andreevna speaks so well of Katerina Nikolaevna..."

I still kept silent.

"And Katerina Nikolaevna has 'struck' into society again, fête after fête, she quite shines; they say even all the courtiers are in love with her... and she's quite abandoned everything with Mr. Bjoring, and there'll be no wedding; everybody maintains the same... supposedly ever since that time."

That is, since Versilov's letter. I trembled all over, but didn't say a word.

"Anna Andreevna is so sorry about Prince Sergei Petrovich, and Katerina Nikolaevna also, sir, and everybody says he'll be vindicated, and the other one, Stebelkov, will be condemned..."

I looked at her hatefully. She got up and suddenly bent over me.

"Anna Andreevna especially told me to find out about your health," she said in a complete whisper, "and very much told me to ask you to call on her as soon as you start going out. Good-bye, sir. Get well, sir, and I'll tell her so..."

She left. I sat up in bed, cold sweat broke out on my forehead, but it wasn't fear I felt: the incomprehensible and outrageous news about Lambert and his schemes did not, for instance, fill me with horror at all, compared to the fright—maybe unaccountable—with which I had recalled, both in my illness and in the first days of recovery, my meeting with him that night. On the contrary, in that first confused moment in bed, right after Nastasya Egorovna's departure, I didn't even linger over Lambert, but... I was thrilled most of all by the news about *her*, about her break-up with Bjoring, and about her luck in society, about the fêtes, about her success, about her "shining." "She shines, sir"—I kept hearing Nastasya Egorovna's little phrase. And I suddenly felt that I did not have strength enough to struggle out of this whirl, though I had been able to restrain myself, keep silent, and not question Nastasya Egorovna after her wondrous stories! A boundless yearning for this life, *their* life, took all my breath away and... and also some other sweet yearning, which I felt to the point of happiness and tormenting pain. My thoughts were somehow spinning, but I let them spin. "What's the point of reasoning!"—was how I felt. "Though even mama didn't let on to me that Lambert came by," I thought in incoherent fragments, "it was Versilov who told them not to let on... I'll die before I ask Versilov about Lambert!" "Versilov," flashed in me again, "Versilov and Lambert—oh, so much is new with them! Bravo, Versilov! Frightened the German Bjoring with that letter; he slandered her; *la calomnie... il en reste toujours quelque chose*,* and the German courtier got scared of a scandal—ha, ha... there's a lesson for her!" "Lambert... mightn't Lambert have gotten in with her as well? What else! Why couldn't she get 'connected' with him as well?"

Here I suddenly left off thinking all this nonsense and dropped my head back on the pillow in despair. "But that won't be!" I exclaimed with unexpected resolution, jumped up from the bed, put on the slippers, the robe, and went straight to Makar Ivanovich's room, as if there lay the warding off of all obsessions, salvation, an anchor I could hold on to.

In fact it may be that I felt that thought then with all the forces of my soul; otherwise why should I jump up from my place so irrepressibly then, and in such a moral state rush to Makar Ivanovich?

III

But at Makar Ivanovich's, quite unexpectedly, I found people—mama and the doctor. Since for some reason I had imagined to myself, going there, that I would certainly find the old man alone, as the day before, I stopped on the threshold in dumb perplexity. Before I had time to frown, Versilov at once came to join them, and after him suddenly Liza as well... Everybody, that is, gathered for some reason at Makar Ivanovich's and "just at the wrong time!"

"I've come to inquire about your health," I said, going straight to Makar Ivanovich.

*Calumny... something of it always remains.

"Thank you, dear, I was expecting you, I knew you'd come! I thought about you during the night."

He looked tenderly into my eyes, and it was evident to me that he loved me almost best of all, but I instantly and involuntarily noticed that, though his face was cheerful, the illness had made progress overnight. The doctor had only just examined him quite seriously. I learned afterwards that this doctor (the same young man with whom I had quarreled and who had been treating Makar Ivanovich ever since his arrival) was quite attentive to his patient and—only I can't speak their medical language—supposed that he had a whole complication of various illnesses. Makar Ivanovich, as I noticed at first glance, had already established the closest friendly relations with him. I instantly disliked that; but anyhow, I, too, of course, was in a bad way at that moment.

"Indeed, Alexander Semyonovich, how is our dear patient today?" Versilov inquired. If I hadn't been so shaken, I would have been terribly curious, first thing, to follow Versilov's relations with this old man, which I had already thought about the day before. I was struck most of all now by the extremely soft and pleasant expression on Versilov's face; there was something perfectly sincere in it. I have already observed, I believe, that Versilov's face became astonishingly beautiful as soon as he turned the least bit simple-hearted.

"We keep on quarreling," replied the doctor.

"With Makar Ivanovich? I don't believe it; it's impossible to quarrel with him."

"He won't obey me; he doesn't sleep at night..."

"Stop it now, Alexander Semyonovich, enough grumbling," laughed Makar Ivanovich. "Well, Andrei Petrovich, dear heart, what have they done with our young lady? Here she's been clucking and worrying all morning," he added, pointing to mama.

"Oh, Andrei Petrovich," mama exclaimed, greatly worried indeed, "tell us quickly, don't torment us: what did they decide about the poor thing?"

"Our young lady has been sentenced!"

"Oh!" mama cried out.

"Not to Siberia, don't worry—only to a fifteen-rouble fine. It turned into a comedy!"

He sat down, the doctor sat down, too. They were talking about Tatyana Pavlovna, and I still knew nothing at all about this story. I was sitting to the left of Makar Ivanovich, and Liza sat down opposite me to the right; she evidently had her own special grief today, with which she had come to mama; the expression on her face was anxious and annoyed. At that moment we somehow exchanged glances, and I suddenly thought to myself, "We're both disgraced, and I must make the first step towards her." My heart suddenly softened towards her. Versilov meanwhile began telling about the morning's adventure.

The thing was that Tatyana Pavlovna had gone before the justice of the peace that morning with her cook. The case was trifling in the highest degree; I've already mentioned that the spiteful Finn would sometimes keep angrily silent even for whole weeks, not answering a word to her lady's questions; I've also mentioned that Tatyana Pavlovna had a weakness for her, endured everything from her, and absolutely refused to dismiss her once and for all. In my eyes, all these psychological caprices of old maids and old ladies are in the highest degree worthy of contempt, and by no means of attention, and if I venture to mention this incident here, it is solely because later on, in the further course of my story, this cook is destined to play a certain not inconsiderable and fateful role. And so, having lost patience with this stubborn Finn, who hadn't responded to her for several days already, in the end Tatyana Pavlovna suddenly struck her, which had never happened before. The Finn did not emit the slightest sound even then, but that same day she got in touch with the retired midshipman Ossetrov, who lived on the same back stairway somewhere in a corner below, and who occupied himself with soliciting various sorts of cases, and, naturally, with bringing such cases to court, in his struggle for existence. It ended with Tatyana Pavlovna being summoned to the justice of the peace, and Versilov for some reason had to give testimony at the hearing as a witness.

Versilov recounted it all jokingly and with extraordinary merriment, so that even mama burst out laughing; he impersonated Tatyana Pavlovna, and the midshipman, and the cook. The cook announced to the court right from the start that she wanted a fine in money, "otherwise, if you put the lady in prison, who am I going to cook for?" Tatyana Pavlovna answered the judge's questions with great haughtiness, not even deigning to justify herself; on the contrary, she concluded with the words, "I beat her and I'll beat her more," for which she was immediately fined three roubles for insolent answers in court. The midshipman, a lean and lanky young man, began a long speech in defense of his client, but got shamefully confused and made the whole courtroom laugh. The hearing soon ended, and Tatyana Pavlovna was sentenced to pay the injured Marya fifteen roubles. Without delay, she took out her purse on the spot and started handing her the money. The midshipman turned up at once and reached out his hand, but Tatyana Pavlovna almost struck his hand aside and turned to Marya. "Never mind, ma'am, you needn't trouble yourself, add it to the accounts, and I'll pay this one myself." "See, Marya, what a lanky fellow you picked for yourself!" Tatyana Pavlovna pointed to the midshipman, terribly glad that Marya had finally started to speak. "Lanky he is, ma'am," Marya replied coyly. "Did you order cutlets with peas for today? I didn't quite hear earlier, I was hurrying here." "Oh, no, Marya, with cabbage, and please don't burn it as you did yesterday." "I'll do my best today especially, ma'am. Your hand, please"—and she kissed her mistress's hand as a sign of reconciliation. In short, she made the whole courtroom merry.

"What a one, really!" Mama shook her head, very pleased both by the news and by Andrei Petrovich's account, but casting anxious glances at Liza on the sly.

"She's been a willful young lady from early on," Makar Ivanovich smiled.

"Bile and idleness," the doctor retorted.

"Me willful, me bile and idleness?" Tatyana Pavlovna suddenly came in, apparently very pleased with herself. "Alexander Semyonovich, you of all people shouldn't go talking nonsense; you knew when you were ten years old what sort of idle woman I was, and as for my bile, you've been treating it for a whole year and can't cure it, so shame on you. Well, enough of your jeering at me. Thank you, Andrei Petrovich, for taking the trouble to come to court. Well, how are you, Makarushka, it's you I've come to see, not this one" (she pointed at me, but at the same time gave me a friendly pat on the shoulder; I'd never seen her in such a merry state of mind before).

"Well, so?" she concluded, suddenly turning to the doctor and frowning worriedly.

"This one doesn't want to stay in bed, but sitting up like this only wears him out."

"I'll just sit a wee bit with people," Makar Ivanovich murmured, his face as pleading as a child's.

"Yes, we love that, we do; we love chatting in a little circle, when people gather round us; I know Makarushka," said Tatyana Pavlovna.

"And, oh, what a speedy one he is," the old man smiled again, turning to the doctor. "And you don't give ear to speech; wait, let me say it. I'll lie down, dear heart, I've heard, but to our minds what it means is, 'Once you lie down, you may not get up again'—that, my friend, is what's standing back of me."

"Well, yes, I just knew it, a popular prejudice: 'I'll lie down, yes,' they say, 'and for all I know, I won't get up again'—that's what people are very often afraid of, and they'd rather spend the time of their illness on their feet than go to the hospital. And you, Makar Ivanovich, are simply yearning, yearning for your dear freedom, for the open road; that's all your illness; you're not used to living in the same place for long. Aren't you what's known as a wanderer? Well, and with our people vagrancy almost turns into a passion. I've noticed it more than once in our people. Our people are mostly vagrants."

"So Makar is a vagrant, in your opinion?" Tatyana Pavlovna picked up.

"Oh, not in that sense; I was using the word in its general sense. Well, so he's a religious vagrant, a pious one, but a vagrant all the same. In a good, respectable sense, but a vagrant . . . From a medical point of view, I . . ."

"I assure you," I suddenly addressed the doctor, "that the vagrants are sooner you and I, and everybody else here, and not this old man, from whom you and I have something to learn, because there are firm things in his life, and we, all of us here, have nothing firm in our lives . . . However, you could hardly understand that."

It appears I spoke cuttingly, but that's what I had come for. In fact, I don't know why I went on sitting there and was as if out of my mind.

"What's with you?" Tatyana Pavlovna looked at me suspiciously. "So, how did you find him, Makar Ivanovich?" she pointed her finger at me.

"God bless him, a sharp boy," the old man said with a serious air; but at the word "sharp" almost everybody burst out laughing. I restrained myself somehow; the doctor laughed most of all. It was bad enough that I didn't know then about their preliminary agreement. Three days earlier, Versilov, the doctor, and Tatyana Pavlovna had agreed to try as hard as they could to distract mama from bad anticipations and apprehensions for Makar Ivanovich, who was far more ill and hopeless than I then suspected. That's why everybody joked and tried to laugh. Only the doctor was stupid and, naturally, didn't know how to joke: that's why it all came out as it did later on. If I had also known about their agreement, I wouldn't have done what came out. Liza also knew nothing.

I sat and listened with half an ear; they talked and laughed, but in my head was Nastasya Egorovna with her news, and I couldn't wave her away. I kept picturing her sitting and looking, getting up cautiously and peeking into the other room. Finally they all suddenly laughed. Tatyana Pavlovna, I have no idea on what occasion, had suddenly called the doctor a godless person: "Well, you little doctors, you're all godless folk! . . ."

"Makar Ivanovich!" the doctor cried out, pretending most stupidly that he was offended and was seeking justice, "am I godless or not?"

"You, godless? No, you're not godless," the old man replied sedately, giving him an intent look. "No, thank God!" he shook his head. "You're a mirthful man."

"And whoever is mirthful isn't godless?" the doctor observed ironically.

"That's a thought—in its own way!" Versilov observed, but not laughing at all.

"It's a powerful thought!" I exclaimed inadvertently, struck by the idea. The doctor looked around questioningly.

"These learned people, these same professors," Makar Ivanovich began, lowering his eyes slightly (they had probably been saying something about professors before then), "oh, how afraid of them I was at first: I didn't dare before them, for I feared the godless man most of all. There's one soul in me, I thought; if I lose it, there's no other to find. Well, but then I took heart. 'So what,' I thought, 'they're not gods, they're like us, fellow-sufferering men the same as us.' And I had great curiosity: 'I must find out what this godlessness is!' Only later, my friend, this same curiosity also went away."

He fell silent, though intending to continue with that quiet and sedate smile. There is a simpleheartedness that trusts each and everyone, unsuspecting of mockery. Such people are always limited, for they're ready to bring out the most precious thing from their hearts before the first comer. But in Makar Ivanovich, it seemed to me, there was something else, and it was something else that moved him to speak, not merely the innocence of simpleheartedness. It was as if a propagandist peeped out of him. I had the pleasure of catching a certain as if sly smile that he directed at the doctor, and maybe at Versilov as well. The conversation was evidently a continuation of their previous arguments during the week; but into it, to my misfortune, there again slipped that same fatal little phrase that had so electrified me the day before, and it led me to an outburst that I regret to this day.

"I might be afraid of the godless man even now," the old man went on with concentration, "only the thing is, my friend Alexander Semyonovich, that I've never once met a godless man, what I've met instead is vain men—that's how they'd better be called. They're all sorts of people; there's no telling what people: big and small, stupid and learned, even some of the simplest rank, and it's all vanity. For they read and talk all their lives, filled with bookish sweetness, but they themselves dwell in perplexity and cannot resolve anything. One is all scattered, no longer noticing himself. Another has turned harder than stone, but dreams wander through his heart. Yet another is unfeeling and light-minded and only wants to laugh out his mockery. Another has merely plucked little flowers from books, and even that by his own opinion; he's all vanity himself, and there's no judgment in him. Again I'll say this: there is much boredom. A small man may be needy, have no crust, nothing to feed his little ones, sleep on prickly straw, and yet his heart is always merry and light; he sins, he's coarse, but still his heart is light. But the big man drinks too much, eats too much, sits on a heap of gold, yet there's nothing but anguish in his heart. Some have gone through all learning—and are still anguished. And my thinking is that the more one learns, the more boredom there is. Take just this: they've been teaching people ever since the world was made, but where is the good they've taught, so that the world might become the most beautiful, mirthful, and joy-filled dwelling place? And I'll say another thing: they have no seemliness, they don't even want it; they've all perished, and each one only praises his perdition, but doesn't even think of turning to the one truth; yet to live without God is nothing but torment. And it turns out that what gives light is the very thing we curse, and we don't know it ourselves. And what's the point? It's impossible for a man to exist without bowing down; such a man couldn't bear himself, and no man could. If he rejects God, he'll bow down to an idol—a wooden one, or a golden one, or a mental one. They're all idolaters, not godless, that's how they ought to be called. Well, but how could there not be godless people as well? There are such as are truly godless, only they're much more frightening than these others, because they come with God's name on their lips. I've heard of them more than once, but I've never met any. There are such, my friend, and I think there must needs be."

"There are, Makar Ivanovich," Versilov suddenly confirmed, "there are such, and 'there must needs be.'"

"There certainly are and 'there must needs be'!" escaped from me irrepressibly and vehemently, I don't know why; but I was carried away by Versilov's tone and was captivated as if by some sort of idea in the words "there must needs be." This conversation was totally unexpected for me. But at that moment something suddenly happened that was also totally unexpected.

IV

IT WAS AN extremely bright day; the blinds in Makar Ivanovich's room were usually not raised all day, on the doctor's orders; but there was not a blind but a curtain over the window, so that the uppermost part of the window was uncovered; this was because the old man had been upset, with the former blind, at not seeing the sun at all. And we just went on sitting there till the moment when a ray of sunlight suddenly struck Makar Ivanovich right in the face. He paid no attention at first, while he was talking, but several times as he spoke he mechanically inclined his head to the side, because the bright ray strongly troubled and irritated his ailing eyes. Mama, who was standing next to him, had already glanced worriedly at the window several times; she had simply to cover the window completely with something, but, so as not to hinder the conversation, she decided to try and pull the little bench Makar Ivanovich was sitting on a bit to the right. She only had to move it five inches, six at the most. She had bent down several times and taken hold of the bench, but she coudn't pull it; the bench, with Makar Ivanovich sitting on it, wouldn't move. Feeling her effort, but being in the heat of conversation, Makar Ivanovich, quite unconsciously, tried several times to raise himself, but his legs wouldn't obey him. Mama nevertheless went on straining and pulling, and all this finally angered Liza terribly. I remember her several flashing, irritated glances, only in the first moment I didn't know what to ascribe them to; besides, I was distracted by the conversation. And then suddenly we heard her almost shout sharply at Makar Ivanovich:

"At least raise yourself a little, you can see how hard it is for mama!"

The old man quickly glanced at her, understood at once, and instantly hastened to raise himself, but nothing came of it; he rose a couple of inches and fell back on the bench.

"I can't, dear heart," he answered Liza as if plaintively, looking at her somehow all obediently.

"You can talk whole books full, but you haven't got the strength to stir yourself?"

"Liza!" cried Tatyana Pavlovna. Makar Ivanovich again made an extreme effort.

"Take your crutch, it's lying beside you, you can raise yourself with your crutch!" Liza snapped once more.

"Right you are," said the old man, and at once hurriedly seized his crutch.

"We simply have to lift him!" Versilov stood up, the doctor also moved, Tatyana Pavlovna also jumped up, but before they had time to approach him, Makar Ivanovich leaned on the crutch with all his strength, suddenly rose, and stood where he was, looking around in joyful triumph.

"And so I got up!" he said with all but pride, smiling joyfully. "Thank you, dear, for teaching me reason, and I thought my little legs wouldn't serve me at all..."

But he didn't go on standing for long. He hadn't even managed to finish speaking when his crutch, on which he had rested the whole weight of his body, suddenly slipped on the rug, and as his "little legs" hardly supported him at all, he toppled from his full height onto the floor. This was almost terrible to see, I remember. Everybody gasped and rushed to lift him up, but, thank God, he hadn't hurt himself; he had only struck the floor heavily, noisily, with both knees, but he had managed to put his right hand in front of him and brace himself with it. He was picked up and seated on the bed. He was very pale, not from fright, but from shock. (The doctor had also found a heart ailment in him, along with everything else.) But mama was beside herself with fright. And suddenly Makar Ivanovich, still pale, his body shaking, and as if not yet quite recovered, turned to Liza and in an almost tender, quiet voice, said to her:

"No, dear, my little legs just won't stand up!"

I cannot express my impression at the time. The thing was that there wasn't the slightest sound of complaint or reproach in the poor old man's words; on the contrary, you could see straight off that, from the very beginning, he had decidedly noticed nothing spiteful in Liza's words, but had taken her shouting at him as something due, that is, that he ought to have been "reprimanded" for his fault. All this affected Liza terribly as well. At the moment of his fall, she had jumped up, like everybody else, and stood all mortified and, of course, suffering, because she had been the cause of it all, but, hearing such words from him, she suddenly, almost instantly, became flushed all over with the color of shame and repentance.

"Enough!" Tatyana Pavlovna suddenly commanded. "It all comes from talk! Time we were in our places; what's the good of it if the doctor himself starts babbling!"

"Precisely," Alexander Semyonovich picked up, bustling around the patient. "I'm to blame, Tatyana Pavlovna, he needs rest!"

But Tatyana Pavlovna wasn't listening: for half a minute she had been silently and intently watching Liza.

"Come here, Liza, and kiss me, old fool that I am—if you want to," she said unexpectedly.

And she kissed her, I don't know what for, but that was precisely what needed to be done; so that I almost rushed myself to kiss Tatyana Pavlovna. It was precisely necessary not to crush Liza with reproach, but to greet with joy and felicitation the new beautiful feeling that undoubtedly must have been born in her. But, instead of all these feelings, I suddenly stood up and began, firmly rapping out the words:

"Makar Ivanovich, you have again used the word 'seemliness,' and just yesterday and for all these days I've been suffering over that word... and all my life I've been suffering, only before I didn't know over what. I consider this coincidence of words fateful, almost miraculous... I announce it in your presence..."

But I was instantly stopped. I repeat: I didn't know about their agreement concerning mama and Makar Ivanovich; and judging by my former doings, they certainly considered me capable of any scandal of that sort.

"Stifle him, stifle him!" Tatyana Pavlovna turned utterly ferocious. Mama began to tremble. Makar Ivanovich, seeing everyone's fright, also became frightened.

"Arkady, enough!" Versilov cried sternly.

"For me, ladies and gentlemen," I raised my voice still more, "for me to see you all next to this babe" (I pointed to Makar) "is unseemly. There's only one saint here, and that's mama, but she, too..."

"You'll frighten him!" the doctor said insistently.

"I know I'm the whole world's enemy," I began to babble (or something of the sort), but, turning around once more, I looked defiantly at Versilov.

"Arkady," he cried again, "there has already been exactly the same scene here between us! I beg you, restrain yourself now!"

I cannot express with what strong feeling he uttered this. Extreme sadness, the most sincere, the fullest, was expressed in his features. Most surprising of all was that he looked as if he were guilty: I was the judge, and he was the criminal. All this finished me off.

"Yes!" I cried to him in reply, "there has already been exactly the same scene, when I buried Versilov and tore him out of my heart... But then there followed the resurrection from the dead, while now... now there will be no dawn! but... but all of you here will see what I'm capable of! You don't even expect what I can prove!"

Having said this, I rushed to my room. Versilov ran after me...

V

I SUFFERED A relapse of my illness; I had a very strong attack of fever, with delirium towards nightfall. But it was not all delirium: there were countless dreams, a whole series and without measure, among which there was one dream or fragment of a dream that I've remembered all my life. I'll recount it without any explanations. It was prophetic and I cannot omit it.

I suddenly found myself, with some grand and proud design in my heart, in a big and lofty room; but not at Tatyana Pavlovna's: I remember the room very well; I make note of that, running ahead. But though I'm alone, I constantly feel, with uneasiness and torment, that I'm not alone at all, that I'm expected and that something is expected of me. Somewhere behind the doors, people sit and expect me to do something. The sensation is unbearable: "Oh, if only I were alone!" And suddenly *she* comes in. She looks timid, she's terribly afraid, she peeks into my eyes. *The document is in my hand.* She smiles in order to charm me, she fawns on me; I'm sorry, but I begin to feel disgust. Suddenly she covers her face with her hands. I fling the "document" on the table with inexpressible contempt: "Don't beg, take it, I need nothing from you! I revenge myself for all my insults with contempt!" I walk out of the room, breathless with immeasurable pride. But in the doorway, in the darkness, Lambert seizes me: "Cghretin, cghretin!" he whispers, holding me back by the arm with all his might. "She'll have to open a boarding school for high-born girls on Vassilievsky Island" (N.B. that is, to support herself, if her father, learning about the document from me, deprives her of her inheritance and drives her out of the house. I set down Lambert's words literally as I dreamed them).

"Arkady Makarovich is searching for 'seemliness,'" comes Anna Andreevna's little voice, somewhere nearby, right there on the stairs; but it is not praise but unbearable mockery that sounds in her words. I return to the room with Lambert. But, seeing Lambert, *she* suddenly begins to guffaw. My first impression is horrible fright, such fright that I stop and do not want to go closer. I look at her and can't believe it; it's as if she has suddenly taken a mask from her face: the same features, but as if each line of her face has been distorted by boundless impudence. "The ransom, lady, the ransom!" shouts Lambert, and the two of them guffaw still more, and my heart sinks: "Oh, can this shameless woman possibly be the same one at whose mere glance my heart boiled over with virtue?"

"That's what they're capable of, these proud ones, in their high society, for money!" exclaims Lambert. But the shameless woman is not embarrassed even by that; she guffaws precisely because I'm so frightened. Oh, she's ready for the ransom, I can see that and . . . and what's with me? I no longer feel either pity or loathing; I tremble as never before . . . I'm overcome by a new, inexpressible feeling, such as I've never known, and strong as the whole world . . . Oh, I'm no longer able to go away now for anything! Oh, how I like that it's so shameless! I seize her by the hands, the touch of her hands makes me shiver painfully, I bring my lips to her impudent crimson lips, trembling with laughter and inviting me.

Oh, away with this base memory! A cursed dream! I swear that before this loathsome dream there had been nothing in my mind even resembling this disgraceful thought! There hadn't even been any involuntary thought of that sort (though I kept the "document" sewn up in my pocket, and I would sometimes snatch at my pocket with a strange smile). Where did this all come from, quite ready-made? It's because I had the soul of a spider! It means that everything was already born and lying in my depraved heart, lying in my *desire*, but in a waking state my heart was ashamed and my mind still didn't dare to imagine anything like that consciously. But in a dream my soul herself presented and laid out all that was in my heart, with perfect precision and in the fullest picture and—in prophetic form. And can it have been *this* that I wanted to *prove* to them when I ran out of Makar Ivanovich's room that morning? But enough, nothing of that for the time being! This dream I dreamed is one of the strangest adventures of my life.

Chapter Three

I

THREE DAYS LATER I got up in the morning and suddenly felt, standing on my legs, that I wouldn't stay in bed anymore. I fully felt the nearness of recovery. All these little details are maybe not worth including, but then came several days which, though nothing special happened, have all remained in my memory as something delightful and calm, and that is a rare thing in my memories. My inner state I will not meanwhile formulate; if the reader learned what it consisted in, he certainly wouldn't believe it. Better if everything becomes clear later from the facts. And meanwhile I'll just say one thing: let the reader remember about *the soul of a spider*. And that in a man who wanted to go away from them all and from the whole world in the name of "seemliness"! The yearning for seemliness was there in the highest degree, that was certainly so, but how it could be combined with God knows what other yearnings—is a mystery to me. And it has always been a mystery, and I've marveled a thousand times at this ability of man (and, it seems, of the Russian man above all) to cherish the highest ideal in his soul alongside the greatest baseness, and all that in perfect sincerity. Whether it's a special breadth in the Russian man, which will take him far, or simply baseness—that's the question!

But let's leave that. One way or another, a lull came. I simply understood that I had to get well at all costs and as soon as possible, so that I could begin to act as soon as possible, and therefore I resolved to live hygienically and obey the doctor (whoever he was), and with extreme reasonableness (the fruit of breadth) I put off stormy designs till the day of my going out, that is, till my recovery. How all these peaceful impressions and the enjoyment of the lull could combine with a painfully sweet and anxious throbbing of the heart at the anticipation of imminent, stormy decisions—I don't know, but, again, I attribute it all to "breadth." But the former recent restlessness was no longer in me; I put it all off for a while, no longer trembling before the future as just recently, but like a rich man assured of his means and powers. My arrogance and defiance of the fate awaiting me swelled more and more, partly,

I suppose, from my now actual recovery and the quick return of my vital forces. It is these several days of final and even actual recovery that I recall now with full pleasure.

Oh, they forgave me everything, that is, my outburst, and these were the very same people I had called unseemly to their faces! I like that in people, I call it intelligence of the heart; at least it attracted me at once—to a certain degree, of course. Versilov and I, for instance, went on speaking like the best acquaintances, but to a certain degree: as soon as there was a glimpse of too much expansiveness (and there were glimpses), we both restrained ourselves at once, as if a bit ashamed of something. There are occasions when the victor can't help being ashamed before the one he has vanquished, precisely for having overcome him. The victor was obviously I; and I was ashamed.

That morning, that is, when I got out of bed after the relapse of my illness, he came to see me, and then I learned from him for the first time about their agreement concerning mama and Makar Ivanovich; he also observed that, though the old man felt better, the doctor would not answer positively for him. I gave him my heartfelt promise to behave more prudently in the future. As Versilov was telling me all that, I then suddenly noticed for the first time that he himself was extremely and sincerely concerned for this old man, that is, far more than I would have expected from a man like him, and that he looked upon him as a being for some reason especially dear to him, and not only because of mama. This interested me at once, almost surprised me, and, I confess, without Versilov I might out of inattention have missed and failed to appreciate much in this old man, who left one of the most lasting and original impressions in my heart.

Versilov seemed to have fears about my attitude towards Makar Ivanovich; that is, he trusted neither my intelligence nor my tact, and therefore he was extremely pleased later, when he discerned that I could occasionally understand how to treat a person of totally different notions and views—in short, that I was able to be both yielding and broad when necessary. I also confess (without humiliating myself, I think) that in this being who was from the people I found something totally new for me in regard to certain feelings and views, something unknown to me, something much clearer and more comforting than the way I myself had understood these things before. Nevertheless, it was sometimes impossible not to get simply beside oneself from certain decided prejudices which he believed with the most shocking calmness and steadfastness. But here, of course, only his lack of education was to blame, while his soul was rather well organized, even so well that I've never yet come across anything better of its kind in people.

II

WHAT WAS MOST attractive about him, as I've already noted above, was his extreme candor and the absence of the slightest self-love; the feeling was of an almost sinless heart. There was "mirth" of heart, and therefore also "seemliness." He loved the word "mirth" very much and used it often. True, one sometimes found a sort of morbid rapture in him, as it were, a sort of morbidity of tenderness—in part, I suppose, due also to the fever which, truly speaking, never left him all that time; but that did not interfere with the seemliness. There were also contrasts: alongside an astonishing simpleheartedness, sometimes completely unaware of irony (often to my vexation), there also lived in him a sort of clever subtlety, most often in polemical clashes. And he liked polemics, but only occasionally and in his own way. It was evident that he had walked a lot through Russia, had heard a lot, but, I repeat, he liked tender feeling most of all, and therefore all that led to it, and he himself liked to tell things that moved people to tenderness. Generally he liked telling stories. I heard a lot from him both about his own wanderings and various legends from the lives of the most ancient "ascetics." I'm not familiar with these things, but I think he distorted a lot in these legends, having learned them mostly by word of mouth from simple folk. It was simply impossible to accept certain things. But alongside obvious alterations or simple lies, there were always flashes of something astonishingly wholesome, full of popular feeling, and always conducive to tenderness... Among these stories, for instance, I remember a long one, "The Life of Mary of Egypt."[7] Up to that time I had had no conception of this "Life," nor of almost any like it. I'll say outright: it was almost impossible to endure it without tears, and not from tender feeling, but from some sort of strange rapture. You felt something extraordinary and hot, like that scorching sandy desert with its lions, in which the saint wandered. However, I don't want to speak of it, and am also not competent.

Besides tenderness, I liked in him certain sometimes extremely original views of certain still quite disputable things in modern reality. He once told, for instance, a recent story about a discharged soldier; he was almost a witness to this event. A soldier came home from the service, back to the peasants, and he didn't like living with the peasants again, and the peasants didn't like him either. The man went astray, took to drinking, and robbed somebody somewhere; there was no firm evidence, but they seized him anyhow and took him to court. In court his lawyer all but vindicated him—there was no evidence, and that was that—when suddenly the man listened, listened, and suddenly stood up and interrupted the lawyer: "No, you quit talking." And he told everything "to the last speck"; he confessed everything, with tears and repentance. The jury went and locked themselves in for the decision, then suddenly they all come out: "No, not guilty." Everybody shouted, rejoiced, and the soldier just stood rooted to the spot, as if he'd turned into a post, didn't understand anything; nor did he understand anything from what the magistrate told him in admonition as he let him go. The soldier was set free again, and still didn't believe it. He began to be anguished, brooded, didn't eat, didn't drink, didn't speak to people, and on the fifth day he up and hanged himself. "That's how it is to live with a sin on your soul!" Makar Ivanovich concluded. This story is, of course, a trifling one, and there's an endless number of them now in all the newspapers, but I liked the tone of it, and most of all a few little phrases, decidedly with a new thought in them. Speaking, for instance, of how the soldier returned to his village and the peasants didn't like him, Makar Ivanovich said, "And you know what a soldier is: a soldier is *a peasant gone bad*." Speaking later about the lawyer who all but won the case, he also said: "And you know what a lawyer is: a lawyer is *a hired conscience*." He uttered both of these expressions without any effort and unaware of having done so, and yet in these two expressions there is a whole special view of both subjects, and though, of course, it doesn't belong to the whole people, still it's Makar Ivanovich's own and not borrowed! These ready notions among the people to do with certain subjects are sometimes wonderful in their originality.

"And how do you look at the sin of suicide, Makar Ivanovich?" I asked him on the same occasion.

"Suicide is the greatest human sin," he answered with a sigh, "but the Lord alone is the only judge here, for He alone knows everything—every limit and every measure. But we're bounden to pray for such a sinner. Each time you hear of such a sin, then before you go to sleep, pray for the sinner tenderly; at least sigh for him to God; even if you didn't know him at all—your prayer for him will get through the better."

"But will my prayer help him if he's already condemned?"

"But how do you know? There are many, oh, many who don't believe and deafen ignorant people's ears with it; but don't listen, for they don't know where they're straying themselves. A prayer from a still-living person for a condemned one truly gets through. How is it for someone who has nobody to pray for him? So when you stand and pray before you go to sleep, add at the end: 'And have mercy, Lord Jesus, on all those who have nobody to pray for them.' This prayer really gets through and is pleasing. And also for all the sinners who are still living: 'Lord, who knowest all destinies, save all the unrepentant'—that's also a good prayer."

I promised him that I would pray, feeling that by this promise I would give him the greatest satisfaction. And in fact joy shone in his face; but I hasten to add that he never treated me condescendingly on such occasions, that is, as an old man would treat some adolescent; on the contrary, he quite often liked listening to me himself, even listened with delight, on various themes, supposing that, though he had to do with a "young one," as he put it in his lofty style (he knew very well that the way to put it would be "youth," and not "young one"), at the same time this "young one," as he understood, was infinitely higher than he in education. He liked, for instance, to speak very often about the hermitic life and placed the "hermitage" incomparably higher than "wanderings." I hotly objected to him, insisting on the egoism of those people, who abandon the world and the benefit they might produce for mankind solely for the egoistic idea of their own salvation. At first he didn't understand, I even suspect he didn't understand at all; but he defended the hermitic life very strongly: "At first you're sorry for yourself, of course (that is, when you've settled in the hermitage)—well, but after that you rejoice more and more every day, and then you see God." Here I developed before him a full picture of the useful activity in the world of the scholar, the doctor, or the friend of mankind in general, and I brought him to real ecstasy, because I myself spoke ardently; he yessed me every minute: "Right, dear, right, God bless you, you think according to the truth." But when I finished, he still did not quite agree: "That's all so," he sighed deeply, "but how many are there who will endure and not get distracted? Though money is not a god yet, it's at least a half-god—a great temptation; and then there's the female sex, there's self-conceit and envy. So they'll forget the great cause and busy themselves with the little one. A far cry from the hermitic life. In the hermitage a man strengthens himself even for every sort of deed. My friend! What is there in the world?" he exclaimed with great feeling. "Isn't it only a dream? Take some sand and sow it on a stone; when yellow sand sprouts for you on that stone, then your dream will come true in this world—that's the saying among us. Not so with Christ: 'Go and give away your riches and become the servant of all.' And you'll become inestimably richer than before; for not only in food, nor in costly clothing, nor in pride nor envy will you be happy, but in immeasurably multiplied love. Not little riches now, not a hundred thousand, not a million, but you'll acquire the whole world! Now we gather without satiety and squander senselessly, but then there will be no orphans or beggars, for all are mine, all are dear, I've acquired them all, bought them all to a man! Now it's not a rare thing that a very rich and noble man is indifferent to the number of his days, and doesn't know what amusement to think up; but then our days will multiply as if a thousandfold, for you won't want to lose a single minute, but will feel each one in your heart's mirth. And then you'll acquire wisdom, not from books only, but you'll be with God himself face to face; and the earth will shine brighter than the sun, and there will be neither sadness nor sighing, but only a priceless paradise..."

It was these ecstatic outbursts that Versilov seemed to like greatly. That time he was there in the room.

"Makar Ivanovich!" I interrupted him suddenly, growing excited myself beyond all measure (I remember that evening), "but in that case it's communism you're preaching, decidedly communism!"

And as he knew decidedly nothing about communist doctrine, and was hearing the word itself for the first time, I immediately began to expound for him everything I knew on the subject. I confess I knew little and that confusedly, and I'm not quite competent now either, but what I knew I expounded with great ardor, heedless of anything. To this day I recall with pleasure the extraordinary impression I made on the old man. It wasn't even an impression, but almost a shock. At the same time he was terribly interested in the historical details: "Where? How? Who set it up? Who said it?" Incidentally, I've noticed that this is generally a quality of simple people: they won't be satisfied with a general idea, if they get very interested, but will unfailingly demand the most firm and precise details. I was confused about the details, though, and as Versilov was there, I was a little embarrassed before him, and that made me still more excited. The end was that Makar Ivanovich, moved to tenderness, finally could only repeat "Right, right!" after each word, obviously without understanding and having lost the thread. I became vexed, but Versilov suddenly interrupted the conversation, stood up, and announced that it was time to go to bed. We were all together then, and it was late. When he peeked into my room a few minutes later, I asked him at once how he looked at Makar Ivanovich in general, and what he thought of him. Versilov smiled merrily (but not at all at my mistakes about communism—on the contrary, he didn't mention them). I repeat again: he decidedly cleaved, as it were, to Makar Ivanovich, and I often caught an extremely attractive smile on his face as he listened to the old man. However, the smile did not prevent criticism.

"Makar Ivanovich, first of all, is not a peasant, but a household serf," he pronounced with great readiness, "a former household serf and a former servant, born a servant and from a servant. Household serfs and servants shared a great deal in the interests of their masters' private, spiritual, and intellectual life in the old days. Note that Makar Ivanovich to this day is interested most of all in the events of life among the gentry and in high society. You don't know yet to what degree he's interested in certain recent events in Russia. Do you know that he's a great politician? He'd give anything to know who is at war, and where, and whether we'll go to war. In former times I used to bring him to a state of bliss with such conversations. He has great respect for science, and of all sciences he likes astronomy the most. For all that, he has worked out something so independent in himself that he won't be budged from it for anything. He has convictions, firm ones, rather clear... and true. For all his perfect ignorance, he's capable of astounding you by being unexpectedly familiar with certain notions you wouldn't suppose him to have. He delights in praising the hermitic life, but not for anything would he go to a hermitage or a monastery, because he is in the highest degree a 'vagrant,' as Alexander Semyonovich nicely called him—with whom, to mention it in passing, you needn't be angry. Well, what else, finally: he's something of an artist, has many words of his own, but also not of his own. He's somewhat lame in logical explanations, at times very abstract; has fits of sentimentality, but of a completely popular sort, or, better, has fits of that generally popular tenderness that our people introduce so broadly into their religious feeling. Of his purity of heart and lack of malice I won't speak: it's not for us to get started on that theme..."

III

To finish with the characterization of Makar Ivanovich, I shall tell one of his stories from his own private life. His stories had a strange character, or rather, they had no general character at all; it was impossible to squeeze any moral or any general trend out of them, unless it was that they were all more or less moving. But there were also some that were not moving, that were even quite merry, that even made fun of wayward monks, so that he directly harmed his idea by telling them—which I pointed out to him; but he didn't understand what I meant to say. Sometimes it was hard to make out what prompted him to this storytelling, so that I even wondered at such loquacity and ascribed it in part to old age and to his ailing condition.

"He's not what he used to be," Versilov once whispered to me, "he used to be not at all like this. He'll die soon, much sooner than we think, and we must be prepared."

I forgot to mention that something like "evenings" had been established among us. Besides mama, who wouldn't leave Makar Ivanovich's side, Versilov always came to his little room in the evenings; I, too, always came, and couldn't be anywhere else; during the last few days, Liza almost always came, though later than everyone else, and almost always sat silently. Tatyana Pavlovna also came sometimes, though rarely, and sometimes the doctor. It suddenly happened somehow that I became friends with the doctor; not very much, but at least there were none of my former outbursts. I liked his simplicity, as it were, which I finally discerned in him, and the certain attachment he had to our family, so that I finally ventured to forgive him his medical arrogance and, on top of that, taught him to wash his hands and clean his fingernails, if he was incapable of wearing clean linen. I explained to him directly that it was not at all for the sake of foppishness or any sort of fine arts, but that cleanliness was a natural part of a doctor's profession, and I proved it to him. Finally, Lukerya often came to the door from her kitchen and, standing behind it, listened to Makar Ivanovich's stories. Versilov once called her out from behind the door and invited her to sit with us. I liked that; but from then on she stopped coming to the door. Their ways!

I include one of his stories, without choosing, solely because I remember it more fully. It's a story about a merchant, and I think that in our towns, big and small, such stories occur by the thousand, if only we know how to look. Those who wish to can skip the story, the more so as I tell it in his style.

IV

AND IN THE town of Afimyevsk, I'll tell you now, here's what a wonder we had. There lived a merchant named Skotoboinikov,[8] Maxim Ivanovich, and there was nobody richer than he in the whole region. He built a calico factory and employed several hundred workers; and he became conceited beyond measure. And it must be said that everything walked at a sign from him, and the authorities themselves didn't hinder him in anything, and the abbot of the monastery thanked him for his zeal: he donated a lot to the monastery, and when the fancy took him, he sighed greatly for his soul and had no little concern for the age to come. He was a widower and childless; about his wife, rumor had it that he sweetened her away in the first year and that since his youth he had always liked making free with his hands; only that was a very long time back; he never wanted to enter the bonds of matrimony again. He also had a weakness for drink, and when the time came on him, he would run drunkenly around town, naked and yelling; the town was nothing grand, but still it was a shame. When the time was over, he'd get irate, and then everything he decided was good, and everything he ordered was wonderful. And he settled accounts with people arbitrarily; he'd take an abacus, put his spectacles on: "How much for you, Foma?" "Haven't had anything since Christmas, Maxim Ivanovich, there's thirty-nine roubles owing to me." "Oof, that's a lot of money! It's too much for you; the whole of you isn't worth such money; it doesn't suit you at all; let's knock off ten roubles, and you'll get twenty-nine." The man says nothing; and nobody else dares to make a peep, they all say nothing.

"I know how much he should be given," he says. "It's impossible to deal with the people here any other way. The people here are depraved; without me they'd all have died of hunger, however many there are. I say again, the people here are thieves, whatever they see, they filch, there's no manliness in them. And again take this, that he's a drunkard; give him money, he'll bring it to the pot-house and sit there naked, not a stitch left, he goes home stripped. Again, too, he's a scoundrel: he'll sit on a stone facing the pot-house and start wailing: 'Mother, dear, why did you give birth to me, bitter drunkard that I am? It would be better if you'd smothered me, bitter drunkard that I am, at birth!' Is this a man? This is a beast, not a man; he should be eddicated first of all and then be given money. I know when to give it to him."

So Maxim Ivanovich spoke about the people of Afimyevsk; though it was bad what he said, all the same it was the truth: they were slack, unsteady folk.

There lived in that same town another merchant, and he died; he was a young and light-minded man, he went broke and lost all his capital. During the last year he struggled like a fish on dry land, but his life had come full term. He had been on bad terms with Maxim Ivanovich all the time, and remained roundly in debt to him. In his last hour he still cursed Maxim Ivanovich. And he left behind a widow, still young, and five children with her. And to be left a solitary widow after your husband is like being a swallow without a nest—no small ordeal, the more so with five little ones and nothing to feed them: their last property, a wooden house, Maxim Ivanovich was taking for debt. And so she lined them all up in a row by the church porch; the eldest was a boy of eight, the rest were all girls with a year's difference between them, each one smaller than the next; the eldest was four and the youngest was still nursing in her mother's arms. The liturgy was over, Maxim Ivanovich came out, and all the children knelt before him in a row—she had taught them beforehand—and they pressed their little palms together in front of them all as one, and she herself behind them, with the fifth child in her arms, bowed down to the ground before him in front of all the people: "Dear father, Maxim Ivanovich, have mercy on the orphans, don't take our last crust of bread, don't drive us out of our own nest!" And everybody there waxed tearful—she had taught them so well. She thought, "He'll take pride in front of the people, and forgive us, and give the house back to the orphans," only it didn't turn out that way. Maxim Ivanovich stopped: "You're a young widow," he said, "you want a husband, it's not the orphans you're weeping about. And the deceased man cursed me on his deathbed." And he walked on and didn't give them back the house. "Why be indigent" (that is, indulgent) "of their foolishness? I'll do them a good turn, and they'll berate me still more; nothing will be accomplished, except that a great rumor will spread." And there was, in fact, a rumor that he had sent to this widow when she was still a young girl, ten years before, and offered her a large sum (she was very beautiful), forgetting that this sin was the same as desecrating God's church; but he hadn't succeeded then. And he did not a few such abominations, in town and even all over the province, and on this occasion even lost all measure.

The mother and her fledglings howled when he drove them orphaned from the house, and not only out of wickedness, but like a man who sometimes doesn't know himself what makes him stand his ground. Well, people helped her at first, and then she went to look for work. Only what kind of work was there, except for the factory? She'd wash the floors here, weed the vegetable patch there, stoke the stove in a bathhouse, all with the baby in her arms, and start wailing, while the other four ran around outside in nothing but their shirts. When she made them kneel by the church porch, they still had some sort of shoes and some sort of coats, because anyhow they were a merchant's children; now they ran around barefoot: clothes burn up on children, that's a known fact. Well, what is that to children? As long as the sun shines, they rejoice, they don't sense their ruin, they're like little birds, their voices are like little bells. The widow thinks, "Winter will come, and what am I going to do with you? If only God would take care of you by then!" Only she didn't have to wait till winter. There's a children's disease in our parts, the whooping cough, that goes from one to another. First of all the nursing girl died, after her the rest fell ill, and that same autumn all four girls, one after the other, were carried off. True, one was run over by horses in the street. And what do you think? She buried them and started wailing; she had cursed them before, but once God took them, she was sorry. A mother's heart!

The only one left alive to her was the oldest boy, and she doted on him, trembled over him. He was weak and delicate, and had a pretty face like a girl's. And she took him to the factory, to his godfather, who was a manager, and got herself hired in the official's family as a nanny. One day the boy was running in the yard, and here suddenly Maxim Ivanovich came driving up with a pair, and just then he was tipsy; and the boy ran down the stairs straight at him, slipped accidentally, and bumped straight into him as he was getting out of his droshky, punching him in the belly with both hands. He seized the boy by the hair: "Whose boy is he? The birch! Whip him right now, in front of me!" he yelled. The boy went numb, they started thrashing him, he screamed. "So you scream, too? Whip him till he stops screaming!" Maybe they whipped him a lot, maybe not, but he didn't stop screaming till he looked quite dead. Then they left off whipping him, they got frightened, the boy wasn't breathing, he lay there unconscious. Later they said they hadn't whipped him much, but he was very fearful. Maxim Ivanovich also got frightened. "Whose boy is he?" he asked; they told him. "Really now! Take him to his mother. Why was he loitering around the factory?" For two days afterwards he said nothing and then asked again, "How's the boy?" And things were bad with the boy: he was sick, lying in his mother's corner, she left her job at the official's because of it, and he had an inflammation in his lungs. "Really now!" he said. "And why do you think that is? It's not that they whipped him painfully: they just gave him a little treatment. I've ordered the same kind of beatings for others; it went over without any such nonsense." He expected the mother to go and make a complaint, and, being proud, said nothing; only how could she, the mother didn't dare to make a complaint. And then he sent her fifteen roubles and a doctor from himself; not because he was afraid or anything, but just so, from pondering. And soon after that his time came, and he went on a three-week binge.

Winter passed, and on the bright day of Christ's resurrection itself, on the great day itself, Maxim Ivanovich asked again, "And how's that same boy?" And for the whole winter he had said nothing, hadn't asked. They say to him, "He's recovered, he's with his mother, and she still does day labor." That very day Maxim Ivanovich drove to the widow's, he didn't go into the house, but called her out to the gate, sitting in the droshky himself: "Here's what, honest widow," he says, "I want to be a true benefactor to your son and do no end of good things for him: from now on I'm taking him to live with me, in my own house. And if he pleases me the least bit, I'll make over a sufficient capital to him; and if he really pleases me, I may set him up as the heir to my whole fortune at my death, as if he were my own son, on condition, however, that your honor doesn't visit my house except on great feast days.[9] If that's agreeable to you, bring the boy tomorrow morning, he can't go on playing knucklebones." And having said that, he drove off, leaving the mother as if out of her mind. People heard about it and said to her, "The lad will grow up and reproach you that you deprived him of such a destiny." She spent the night weeping over him and in the morning she brought the child. And the boy was more dead than alive.

Maxim Ivanovich dressed him like a young gentleman and hired a tutor, and from that hour on had him sitting over books; and it reached the point that he wouldn't let him out of his sight, but always kept him with him. As soon as the boy starts gaping, he shouts, "To your books! Study! I want to make a man of you." And the boy was sickly, he had been coughing ever since that time, after the beating. "As if it's not a fine life with me!" Maxim Ivanovich marveled. "With his mother he just ran around barefoot, chewed on crusts, why is he more sickly than ever?" And the tutor says to him, "Every boy needs to romp and play," he says, "he shouldn't study all the time, movement is necessary for him," and he deduced it all for him reasonably. Maxim Ivanovich thought, "It's true what you say." And this tutor, Pyotr Stepanovich, God rest his soul, was like a holy fool;[10] he drank ver-ry much, so that it was even too much, and for that reason had long been removed from any position, and he lived about town like a beggar, but he had great intelligence and a solid education. "I shouldn't have been here," he used to say of himself, "I should have been a professor at the university, and here I sink into the mud and 'even my garments hate my flesh.' "[11] Maxim Ivanovich sits and shouts at the boy, "Romp!"—and the boy can barely breathe before him. It reached the point that the child couldn't bear his voice—he just started trembling all over. And Maxim Ivanovich was still more surprised: "He's neither this nor that; I took him up from the dirt, dressed him in *drap de dames*; he's got nice cloth bootikins, an embroidered shirt, I keep him like a general's son, why isn't he well disposed towards me? Why is he silent as a wolf cub?" And though people had long ceased marveling at Maxim Ivanovich, here again they began to wonder: the man's out of his mind; latched onto the little child and won't let him be. "Upon my life, I'll eradicate his character. His father cursed me on his deathbed, after taking holy communion; he has his father's character." He didn't use the birch rod even once (was afraid ever since that time). He intimidated him, that's what. Intimidated him without the birch rod.

And then the thing happened. Once he went out, and the boy

left his book and climbed on a chair. Earlier he had thrown a ball up onto the chiffonier, and he wanted to get his ball, but he caught his sleeve on a china lamp that stood on the chiffonier; the lamp crashed to the floor and broke into smithereens, the clatter was heard all over the house, and it was a costly object—Saxony china. And here suddenly Maxim Ivanovich heard it three rooms away and yelled. The child rushed out and ran in fear wherever his legs would take him, ran out to the terrace, and across the garden, and through the back gate, straight to the riverbank. And there was a boulevard along the bank, old willows, a cheerful spot. He ran down to the water, people saw, clasped his hands, at the very place where the ferry docks, maybe terrified of the water—and stood as if rooted to the spot. And it was a wide place, the river swift, barges going past, on the other side there are shops, a square, the church of God shines with its golden domes. And just then the wife of Colonel Ferzing—an infantry regiment was stationed in town—was hurrying to catch the ferry. Her daughter, also a little child of about eight, walks along in a white dress, looks at the boy and laughs, and she's carrying a little country basket, and in the basket there's a hedgehog. "Look, mummy," she says, "how the boy is looking at my hedgehog." "No," says the colonel's wife, "he's frightened of something. What are you so afraid of, pretty boy?" (So they told it afterwards.) "And what a pretty boy he is, and how well he's dressed; whose boy are you?" she says. And he had never seen a hedgehog before, he came closer and looked, and he had already forgotten—childhood! "What's that you've got?" he says. "This," says the young miss, "is our hedgehog, we just bought it from a village peasant, he found it in the forest." "What's a hedgehog like?" he says, and he's laughing now, and he begins poking his finger at it, and the hedgehog bristles up, and the girl is glad of the boy. "We're taking it home," she says, "we want to tame it." "Ah," he says, "give me your hedgehog!" And he asked her so touchingly, and no sooner had he said it than Maxim Ivanovich descended on him: "Ah! Here's where you are! Take him!" (He was so enraged that he had run out of the house without his hat to chase him.) The boy, the moment he remembered everything, cried out, rushed to the water, pressed his little fists to his breast, looked up at the sky (they saw it, they saw it!) and—splash into the water! Well, people shouted, rushed from the ferry, tried to pull him out, but the current was swift, it carried him away, and when they pulled him out he was already dead—drowned. He had a weak chest, he couldn't endure the water, and how much does it take for such a boy? And in people's memories in those parts there had never yet been such a small child to take his own life! Such a sin! And what can so small a soul say to the Lord God in the other world!

This was what Maxim Ivanovich brooded over ever after. And the man changed beyond recognition. He was sorely grieved then. He took to drinking, drank a lot, but stopped—it didn't help. He stopped going to the factory as well, and paid no heed to anybody. They say something to him—he keeps silent or waves his hand. He went about like that for a couple of months, then began talking to himself. He goes about and talks to himself. An outlying village, Vaskova, caught fire, nine houses burned down; Maxim Ivanovich went to have a look. The burnt-out people surrounded him, wailing—he promised to help and gave orders, then summoned his steward and canceled it all: "No need to give them anything," he said, and didn't say why. "The Lord gave me over to all people," he says, "to trample me down like some monster, so let it be so. Like the wind," he says, "my glory has been scattered." The abbot himself called on him, a stern old man who had introduced cenobitic order in the monastery.[12] "What's with you?" he says, so sternly. "Here's what," and Maxim Ivanovich opened the book for him and pointed to the place:

"But whoso shall offend one of these little ones which believe in me, it were better for him that a millstone were hanged about his neck and that he were drowned in the depth of the sea" (Matthew 18:6).

"Yes," said the abbot, "though it's not said directly about that, still it touches upon it. It's bad if a man loses his measure—he's a lost man. And you've become conceited."

Maxim Ivanovich sat as if dumbstruck. The abbot looked and looked.

"Listen," he said, "and remember. It is said, 'The words of a desperate man fly on the wind.' And also remember that even the angels of God are not perfect, but the only perfect and sinless one is Jesus Christ our God, whom the angels also serve. You didn't want the death of that child, you were merely unreasonable. Only," he says, "here is what I even marvel at: you've uttered so many worse outrages, you've sent so many people into poverty, corrupted so many, ruined so many—isn't it the same as if you'd killed them? Hadn't his sisters died even before then, all four little babies, almost in front of your eyes? Why does this one disturb you so much? For

I suppose you've forgotten, not only to regret, but even to think about the previous ones? Why are you so frightened of this child, before whom you're not even so guilty?"

"I see him in my dreams," said Maxim Ivanovich.

"And what of it?"

But the man revealed no more, he sat and said nothing. The abbot wondered, but with that he left; there was nothing more to be done here.

And Maxim Ivanovich sent for the tutor, for Pyotr Stepanovich; they hadn't seen each other since that occasion.

"Do you remember?" he says.

"I do," he says.

"You've painted oil paintings for the tavern here," he says, "and made a copy of the bishop's portrait. Can you paint a picture for me?"

"I can do everything," he says. "I," he says, "have all talents and can do everything."

"Then paint me a very big picture, over the whole wall, and first of all paint the river on it, and the landing, and the ferry, and so that all the people who were there will be in the picture. The colonel's wife, and the little girl, and that hedgehog. And paint me the whole other bank as well, so that it's seen as it was—the church, the square, the shops, and the cab stand—paint it all as it was. And there by the ferry, paint the boy, just over the river, on that very spot, and he must have his two fists pressed to his breast, to both nipples. That without fail! And open up the sky before him on the other side over the church, and have all the angels in the heavenly light come flying to meet him. Can you satisfy me or not?"

"I can do everything."

"I could invite the foremost painter from Moscow, or even from London itself, instead of a bumpkin like you, only you remember his face. If it comes out not like or a little like, I'll only give you fifty roubles, but if it comes out very much like, I'll give you two hundred. Remember, blue eyes . . . And the painting should be very, very big."

They prepared everything; Pyotr Stepanovich started painting, then suddenly he comes:

"No," he says, "it's impossible to paint it like that."

"How so?"

"Because this sin, suicide, is the greatest of all sins. So how would angels come to meet him after such a sin?"

"But he's a child, he's not responsible."

"No, he's not a child, but already a boy; he was eight years old when this happened. He has to give at least some sort of answer."

Maxim Ivanovich was still more terrified.

"But," says Pyotr Stepanovich, "here's what I've thought up: we won't open the sky or paint the angels; but I'll bring a ray of light down from the sky as if to meet him; one bright ray of light: it will be as if there's something all the same."

So they brought down the ray of light. And I myself saw this painting afterwards, much later, and that same ray, and the river stretched across the whole wall, all blue; and the dear young boy right there, both hands pressed to his breast, and the young miss, and the hedgehog—he did it all satisfactorily. Only Maxim Ivanovich didn't show the painting to anybody then, but locked it up in his study, away from all eyes. And they really were eager to have a look at it in town. He ordered everybody to be chased away. There was a lot of talk. And Pyotr Stepanovich was as if out of his mind then: "I can do everything now," he says, "it's proper for me to be at the court in St. Petersburg." He was a most amiable man, but he had an inordinate love of extolling himself. And fate caught up with him: as soon as he received all two hundred roubles, he immediately started drinking and showing the money to everybody, boasting; and he was killed during the night, drunk, by one of our tradesmen, whom he had been drinking with, and robbed of his money. All this became known the next morning.

And it all ended in such a way that even now it's the first thing they remember. Suddenly Maxim Ivanovich turns up at that same widow's: she rented in a tradeswoman's cottage at the edge of town. This time he went into the yard, stood before her, and bowed to the ground. And since those events the woman had been sick, could scarcely move. "Dear heart," he cried, "honest widow, marry me, monster that I am, let me live in the world!" She looks at him, more dead than alive. "I want," he says, "another boy to be born to us, and if he gets born, it would mean that that boy has forgiven us both, you and me. The boy told me to do it." She can see the man is not in his right mind, he's as if in a frenzy, but still she can't help herself.

"That's all trifles," she said, "and nothing but faintheartedness. On account of this faintheartedness, I lost all my little ones. I can't even bear the sight of you before me, still less take such an everlasting torment on myself."

Maxim Ivanovich drove off, but he didn't calm down. The whole town rumbled at such a wonder. And Maxim Ivanovich sent matchmakers. He summoned two aunts of his from the provincial capital, tradeswomen. Aunts or no aunts, they were relations, meaning it was honest; they started persuading her, turning her head, wouldn't leave the cottage. He sent women from the townsfolk, from the merchants, sent the archpriest's wife, and some wives of officials; the whole town surrounded her, but she even scorns them: "If," she says, "my orphans could come back to life, but now what? To take such a sin on myself before my little orphans?" He persuaded the abbot, and he blew it into her ear: "You," he says, "can call up a new man in him." She was horrified. And people are astonished at her: "How is it even possible that she refuses such happiness!" And here's what he tamed her with: "After all," he says, "he's a suicide, and not as a child, but already as a boy, and owing to his years, he couldn't be admitted to holy communion directly,[13] and so he still has to give some sort of answer. If you marry me, I'll make you a great promise: I'll build a new church only for the eternal commemoration of his soul." She couldn't stand up against that, and accepted him. So they were married.

And it turned out to everyone's amazement. They began to live from the first day in great and unfeigned harmony, carefully preserving their marriage and like one soul in two bodies. She conceived that same winter, and they started going around to the churches of God and trembling before the wrath of the Lord. They visited three monasteries and heard prophecies. He constructed the promised church and built a hospital and an almshouse for the town. He allotted capital for widows and orphans. And he remembered everyone he had injured, and wished to recompense them; he started giving money away without stint, so that his spouse and the abbot restrained his hands, for "this," they said, "is already enough." Maxim Ivanovich obeyed: "I cheated Foma that time." Well, so they paid Foma back. And Foma even wept: "I," he says, "I'm so . . . There's so much I'm content with even without that, and I'm eternally bounden to pray to God for you." So everyone was touched by it, and that means it's true what they say, that man will live by a good example. And they're good people there.

His wife began to manage the factory herself, and in such a way that people still remember it. He didn't stop drinking, but she took care of him on those days, and then also tried to cure him. His speech became decorous, and his voice itself even changed. He became filled with boundless pity, even for animals: from his window he saw a peasant beating his horse outrageously on the head and at once sent to him and bought the horse for twice the price. And he received the gift of tears:[14] someone would start talking to him, and he'd just dissolve in tears. When her time came, the Lord finally heeded their prayers and sent them a son, and Maxim Ivanovich brightened up for the first time since those events; he gave away a lot of alms, forgave many debts, invited the whole town for the baptism. He invited the town, but the next day he came out black as night. His wife saw something had happened to him, she went up to him with the newborn. "The boy," she says, "has forgiven us, and heeded our tears and prayers for him." And it must be said that they hadn't said a word about the matter for that whole year, but had kept it to themselves. And Maxim Ivanovich looked at her black as night. "Wait," he says, "just consider, for the whole year he hasn't come, but last night I saw him in a dream again." "Here, for the first time, terror also entered my heart, after those strange words," she remembered later.

And it was not for nothing that he had dreamed of the boy. As soon as Maxim Ivanovich mentioned it, almost, so to speak, that very minute, something happened to the newborn: he suddenly fell ill. And the baby was sick for eight days, they prayed tirelessly and invited doctors, and they sent for the foremost doctor to come by train from Moscow. The doctor arrived and was angry. "I," he said, "am the foremost doctor, the whole of Moscow is waiting for me." He prescribed some drops and left hurriedly. Took eight hundred roubles with him. And the baby died towards evening.

And what then? Maxim Ivanovich wrote a will leaving all his property to his gentle wife, handed all the capital and papers over to her, completed everything properly and in lawful order, then stood before her and bowed to the ground. "Let me go, my priceless wife, to save my soul while it's still possible. If I spend my time without progress for my soul, I won't come back anymore. I was hard and cruel, and imposed heavy burdens, but I imagine that the Lord will not leave me unrewarded for my future sorrows and wanderings, for to leave it all is no small cross and no small sorrow." And his wife tried to soothe him with many tears: "You're the only one I have on earth now, who can I stay with? I," she says, "have laid up mercy in my heart during this year." And all the town admonished him for the whole month, and begged him, and decided to keep him by force. But he didn't listen to them, and left secretly at night, and never came back. And we hear that he performs his deeds of wandering and patience even to this day, and sends news to his dear wife every year...

Chapter Four

I

Now I'm approaching the final catastrophe, which concludes my notes. But in order to continue further, I must first run ahead of myself and explain something I had no idea of at the time of the action, but that I learned of and fully explained to myself only much later, that is, when everything was over. Otherwise I won't be able to be clear, since I would have to write in riddles. And therefore I will give a direct and simple explanation, sacrificing so-called artistic quality, and I will do so as if it were not I writing, without the participation of my heart, but as if in the form of an *entrefilet** in the newspapers.

The thing was that my childhood friend Lambert may very well have belonged, even directly, to those vile gangs of petty crooks who communicate among themselves for the sake of what is now called blackmail, and for which they now seek legal definitions and punishments in the code of law. The gang Lambert was part of had begun in Moscow and had already done enough mischief there (afterwards it was partly uncovered). I heard later that in Moscow they had for a while an extremely experienced and clever, and no longer young, leader. They embarked on their ventures as a whole gang or in parts. Along with the most dirty and unprintable things (of which, however, information did appear in the newspapers), they also carried out rather complex and even clever ventures, under the leadership of their chief. I learned about some of them later, but I won't go into the details. I will only mention that the main feature of their method consisted in finding out certain secrets of people, sometimes very honest and highly placed people; then they went to these persons and threatened to reveal the documents (which they sometimes didn't have at all), and demanded a ransom to keep silent. There are things that are not sinful and not at all criminal, the revealing of which might frighten even a respectable and firm man. They mostly aimed at family secrets. To indicate how deftly their chief sometimes acted, I will tell, with no details

*Notice.

and in only three lines, about one of their tricks. In a certain very honorable house something in fact both sinful and criminal occurred: namely, the wife of a well-known and respected man entered into a secret amorous liaison with a young and rich officer. They got wind of it, and here is what they did: they directly gave the young man to know that they were going to inform the husband. They had not the slightest proof, and the young man knew that perfectly well, and they themselves made no secret of it with him; but all the deftness of the method and the cleverness of the calculation in this case consisted merely in the consideration that the informed husband, even without any proof, would act in the same way and take the same steps as if he had received the most mathematical proof. They aimed here at a knowledge of the man's character and a knowledge of his family circumstances. The main thing was that one member of the gang was a young man from a very decent circle, who had managed to obtain the preliminary information. They fleeced the lover for a very tidy sum, and that without any danger to themselves, because the victim himself desired secrecy.

Lambert, though he took part, did not belong entirely to that Moscow gang; having acquired a taste for it, he gradually began, by way of trial, to act on his own. I'll say beforehand: he was not quite up to it. He was calculating and by no means stupid, but he was hot-tempered and, what's more, simplehearted, or, better to say, naïve—that is, he had no knowledge either of people or of society. For instance, he seemed not to understand at all the significance of their Moscow chief and supposed it was very easy to direct and organize such ventures. Finally, he assumed that almost everyone was the same sort of scoundrel as himself. Or, for instance, once having imagined that so-and-so was afraid or ought to be afraid for such-and-such reason, he no longer doubted that the man was indeed afraid, as in an axiom. I don't know how to put it; later on I'll explain it more clearly with facts, but in my opinion he was rather crudely developed, and there were certain good, noble feelings which he not only did not believe in, but maybe even had no conception of.

He had come to Petersburg because he had long been thinking of it as a vaster field than Moscow, and also because in Moscow he had gotten into a scrape somewhere and somehow, and somebody was looking for him with the most ill intentions in his regard. On coming to Petersburg, he immediately contacted a former comrade, but he found the field scant, the affairs petty. His acquaintance later widened, but nothing came of it. "People here are trashy, nothing but kids," he himself said to me later. And then, one bright morning, at dawn, he suddenly found me freezing under the wall and fell directly onto the trail of the "richest," in his opinion, of "affairs."

The whole affair rested on what I had babbled as I thawed out in his apartment then. Oh, I was nearly delirious then! But still it came out clearly from my words that, of all my offenses on that fateful day, the one I remembered most and took closest to heart was the offense from Bjoring and from *her*: otherwise I wouldn't have raved about that alone at Lambert's, but would also have raved, for example, about Zershchikov; yet it turned out to be only the first, as I learned afterwards from Lambert himself. And besides, I was in ecstasy and looked upon Lambert and Alphonsine that terrible morning as some sort of liberators and saviors. Later, while recovering, I tried to figure out as I lay in bed what Lambert might have learned from my babble and precisely to what degree I had babbled—but I never once even suspected that he could have learned so much then! Oh, of course, judging by my pangs of conscience, I already suspected even then that I must have told a lot that was unnecessary, but, I repeat, I could never have supposed it was to such a degree! I also hoped and counted on the fact that I had been unable to articulate clearly at his place then, I had a firm memory of that, and yet it turned out in fact that I had articulated much more clearly than I supposed and hoped afterwards. But the main thing was that it was all revealed only later and long after, and that's where my trouble lay.

From my raving, babbling, prattling, raptures, and so on, he had learned, first, almost all the family names accurately, and even some addresses. Second, he had formed a rather approximate notion of the significance of these persons (the old prince, her, Bjoring, Anna Andreevna, and even Versilov); third, he had learned that I had been offended and was threatening revenge; and finally, fourth and most important, he had learned that this document existed, mysterious and hidden, this letter which, if shown to the half-mad old prince, he, having read it and learned that his own daughter considered him mad and had already "consulted lawyers" about how to lock him up, would either lose his mind definitively or drive her out of the house and disinherit her, or marry a certain Mlle. Versilov, whom he already wanted to marry but had not been allowed to. In short, Lambert understood a great deal; without doubt terribly much remained obscure, but still the blackmailing artificer had fallen onto a sure trail. When I fled from Alphonsine then, he immediately found my address (by the simplest means: through the information bureau), then immediately made the proper inquiries, from which he learned that all these persons I had babbled about actually existed. Then he proceeded directly to the first step.

The main thing was that there existed a *document*, and it was in my possession, and this document was of great value; of that Lambert had no doubt. Here I will omit one circumstance, which it would be better to speak of later and in its place, but I will just mention that this circumstance was what most chiefly confirmed Lambert in his conviction of the real existence and, above all, the value of the document. (A fateful circumstance, I say it beforehand, which I could never have imagined, not only then, but even till the very end of the whole story, when everything suddenly began to collapse and got explained by itself.) And so, convinced of the chief thing, as a first step he went to see Anna Andreevna.

And yet for me there's a puzzle to this day: how could he, Lambert, infiltrate and stick himself to such an unapproachable and lofty person as Anna Andreevna? True, he made inquiries, but what of it? True, he was excellently dressed, spoke Parisian French, and was the bearer of a French name, but how could it be that Anna Andreevna did not discern the swindler in him at once? Or we may suppose that a swindler was just what she needed then. But can it be so?

I was never able to find out the circumstances of their meeting, but later I imagined the scene many times. Most likely Lambert, from the first word and gesture, had played my childhood friend before her, trembling for his beloved and dear comrade. But, of course, in that first meeting he managed to hint very clearly that I also had a "document," to let her know that this was a secret, and that only he, Lambert, was in possession of this secret, and that with this document I was going to take revenge on Mme. Akhmakov, and so on, and so forth. Above all, he could explain to her, as pointedly as possible, the significance and value of this paper. As for Anna Andreevna, she was precisely in such a position that she could not help snatching at the news of something like that, could not help listening with extreme attention, and . . . could not help getting caught on the bait—"out of the struggle for existence."

Just at that time, she had precisely had her fiancé canceled and taken under tutelage to Tsarskoe, and she herself had been taken under tutelage as well. And suddenly such a find: here it was no longer old wives whispering in each other's ears, or tearful complaints, or calumny and gossip, here was a letter, a manuscript, that is, a mathematical proof of the perfidy of his daughter's intentions, and of all those who had taken him from her, and that, therefore, he had to save himself at least by fleeing again to her, the same Anna Andreevna, and marrying her even within twenty-four hours; otherwise they would up and confiscate him to a madhouse.

But it also may be that Lambert used no cunning with the girl at all, not even for a moment, but just blurted out with the first word: "Mademoiselle, either remain an old maid, or become a princess and a millionaire: there is this document, I'll steal it from the adolescent and hand it over to you . . . on a promissory note from you for thirty thousand." I even think that's precisely how it was. Oh, he considered everyone the same sort of scoundrel as himself. I repeat, there was in him a sort of scoundrel's simpleheartedness, a scoundrel's innocence . . . Be that as it may, it's quite possible that Anna Andreevna, even in the face of such an assault, was not thrown off for a minute, but was perfectly able to control herself and hear out the blackmailer, who spoke in his own style—and all that out of "breadth." Well, naturally, at first she blushed a little, but then she got hold of herself and heard him out. And when I picture that unapproachable, proud, truly dignified girl, and with such a mind, hand in hand with Lambert, then . . . a mind, yes! A Russian mind, of such dimensions, a lover of breadth; and moreover a woman's, and moreover in such circumstances!

Now I'll make a résumé. By the day and hour of my going out after my illness, Lambert stood on the two following points (this I now know for certain): first, to take a promissory note from Anna Andreevna for no less than thirty thousand in exchange for the document; and then to help her frighten the prince, abduct him, and suddenly get him married to her—in short, something like that. Here a whole plan had even been formed; they were only waiting for my help, that is, for the document itself.

The second plan: to betray Anna Andreevna, abandon her, and sell the paper to Mme. Akhmakov, if it proved more profitable. Here account was also taken of Bjoring. But Lambert had not yet gone to Mme. Akhmakov, but had only tracked her down. Also waiting for me.

Oh, he did need me, that is, not me but the document! Concerning me, he had also formed two plans. The first consisted in acting in concert with me, if it really was impossible otherwise, and going halves with me, after first subjecting me morally and physically. But the second plan was much more to his liking; it consisted in hoodwinking me like a little boy and stealing the document from me, or even simply taking it from me by force. He loved this plan and cherished it in his dreams. I repeat: there was one circumstance owing to which he had almost no doubt of the success of the second plan, but, as I've already said, I will explain it later. In any case, he was waiting for me with convulsive impatience: everything depended on me, all the steps and what to decide on.

And I must do him justice: for a while he controlled himself, despite his hot temper. He didn't come to my house during my illness—he came only once and saw Versilov; he didn't disturb or frighten me, he preserved an air of the most total detachment before me, up to the day and hour of my going out. With regard to the fact that I might give away, or tell about, or destroy the document, he was at ease. From what I had said at his place, he was able to conclude how much I myself valued secrecy and how afraid I was that someone might learn of the document. And that I would go to him first, and to no one else, on the first day of my recovery, he did not doubt in the least: Nastasya Egorovna came to see me partly on his orders, and he knew that my curiosity and fear were already aroused, that I wouldn't be able to stand it . . . And besides, he took every measure, might even know the day of my going out, so that there was no way I could turn my back on him, even if I wanted to.

But if Lambert was waiting for me, then maybe Anna Andreevna was waiting for me still more. I'll say directly: Lambert might have been partly right in preparing to betray her, and the fault was hers. In spite of their undoubted agreement (in what form I don't know, but I have no doubt of it), Anna Andreevna down to the very last minute was not fully candid with him. She didn't open herself all the way. She hinted to him about all agreements and all promises on her part—but only hinted; she listened, maybe, to his whole plan in detail, but gave only silent approval. I have firm grounds for concluding so, and the reason was that she was *waiting for me*. She liked better to have dealings with me than with the scoundrel Lambert—that was an unquestionable fact for me! I understand that; but her mistake was that Lambert finally understood it as well. And it would have been too disadvantageous for him if she, bypassing him, wheedled the document out of me, and we entered into an agreement. Besides, at that time he was already certain of the solidity of the "affair." Another in his place would have been afraid and would still have had doubts; but Lambert was young, bold, with a most impatient desire for gain, had little knowledge of people, and undoubtedly regarded them all as base; such a man could have no doubts, especially as he had already elicited all the main confirmations from Anna Andreevna.

A last and most important little word: did Versilov know anything by that day and had he already participated then in some, however remote, plans with Lambert? No, no, no, not yet *then*, though perhaps a fateful little word had been dropped... But enough, enough, I'm running too far ahead.

Well, and what about me? Did I know anything, and what did I know by the day I went out? At the beginning of this *entrefilet* I announced that I knew nothing by the day I went out, that I learned about it all much later and even at a time when everything was already accomplished. That's true, but is it fully? No, it's not; I undoubtedly already knew something, knew even all too much, but how? Let the reader remember the *dream*! If there could be such a dream, if it could burst from my heart and formulate itself that way, it meant that I—didn't know, but *anticipated*—an awful lot of those things I have just explained and actually learned only "when everything was already over." There was no knowledge, but my heart throbbed with anticipations, and evil spirits already possessed my dreams. And this was the man I was eager to see, knowing full well what sort of man he was and even anticipating the details! And why was I eager to see him? Imagine: now, in this very moment as I write, it seems to me that I knew in all its details why I was eager to see him, whereas at the time, again, I still knew nothing. Maybe the reader will understand that. But now—to business, fact by fact.

II

IT BEGAN, STILL two days before my going out, with Liza coming home in the evening all in alarm. She was awfully insulted; and indeed something insufferable had happened to her.

I've already mentioned her relations with Vasin. She went to him not only to show us that she didn't need us, but also because she really appreciated Vasin. Their acquaintance had already begun in Luga, and it had always seemed to me that Vasin was not indifferent to her. In the misfortune that struck her, it was natural that she might wish for advice from a firm, calm, always elevated mind, which she supposed Vasin to have. Besides, women are not great masters at evaluating the male mind, if they like the man, and they gladly take paradoxes for strict deductions, if they agree with their own wishes. What Liza liked in Vasin was his sympathy with her position, and, as it had seemed to her from the first, his sympathy for the prince as well. Besides, suspecting his feelings towards her, she could not help appreciating his sympathy for his rival. The prince, whom she herself had told that she sometimes went to Vasin for advice, had taken this news with extreme uneasiness from the very first; he had begun to be jealous. This had offended her, so that she had deliberately continued her relations with Vasin. The prince said nothing, but was gloomy. Liza herself confessed to me (very long afterwards) that she had very soon stopped liking Vasin; he was calm, and precisely this eternal, smooth calm, which she had liked so much in the beginning, later seemed rather unsightly to her. It seemed he was practical, and, indeed, several times he gave her advice that appeared good, but all this advice, as if on purpose, turned out to be unfeasible. He sometimes judged too haughtily and without the least embarrassment before her—becoming less embarrassed as time went on, which she ascribed to his growing and involuntary contempt for her position. Once she thanked him for being constantly good-natured with me and for talking with me as with an equal, though he was so superior to me in intelligence (that is, she conveyed my own words to him). He replied:

"That's not so, and it's not for that. It's because I don't see any difference in him from the others. I don't consider him either stupider than the smart ones or wickeder than the good ones. I'm the same with everybody, because in my eyes everybody's the same."

"You mean you really can't see any differences?"

"Oh, of course, they're all different from each other in some way, but in my eyes the differences don't exist, because the differences between people are of no concern to me; for me they're all the same and it's all the same, and so I'm equally nice to everybody."

"And you don't find it boring?"

"No, I'm always content with myself."

"And you don't desire anything?"

"Of course I do, but not very much. I need almost nothing, not a rouble more. Myself in golden clothes and myself as I am—it's all the same; golden clothes will add nothing to Vasin. Morsels don't tempt me: can positions or honors be worth the place I'm worth?"

Liza assured me on her honor that he once uttered this literally. However, it's impossible to judge like that here; one must know the circumstances under which it was uttered.

Liza gradually came to the conclusion that his attitude towards the prince was indulgent maybe only because everybody was the same to him and "differences did not exist," and not at all out of sympathy for her. But in the end he began somehow visibly to lose his indifference, and his attitude towards the prince changed to one not only of condemnation, but also of scornful irony. This made Liza angry, but Vasin wouldn't let up. Above all, he always expressed himself so softly, he even condemned without indignation, but simply made logical deductions about her hero's total nonentity; but in this logic lay the irony. Finally he deduced for her almost directly all the "unreasonableness" of her love, all the stubborn forcedness of this love. "You erred in your feelings, and errors, once recognized, ought unfailingly to be corrected."

This was just on that very day. Liza got up indignantly in order to leave, but what did this reasonable man do and how did he end? With a most noble air and even with feeling, he offered her his hand. Liza at once called him a fool to his face and left.

To suggest betraying an unfortunate man because this unfortunate man was "not worthy" of her and, above all, to suggest it to a woman who was pregnant by this unfortunate man—there's the mind of these people! I call that being awfully theoretical and completely ignorant of life, which comes from a boundless self-love. And on top of all that, Liza discerned in the clearest way that he was even proud of his act, if only because, for example, he already knew about her pregnancy. With tears of indignation she hurried to the prince, and he—he even outdid Vasin: it would seem he might have been convinced after she told him that there was no point in being jealous now; but it was here that he went out of his mind. However, jealous people are all like that! He made an awful scene and insulted her so much that she decided to break all relations with him at once.

She came home, however, still keeping hold of herself, but she couldn't help telling mama. Oh, that evening they became close again, absolutely as before: the ice was broken; they both naturally wept their fill, embracing each other as they used to do, and Liza apparently calmed down, though she was very gloomy. She sat that evening with Makar Ivanovich, not saying a word, but not leaving the room either. She listened very hard to what he was saying. Since the occasion with the little bench, she had become extremely and somehow timidly respectful towards him, though she still remained taciturn.

But this time, Makar Ivanovich somehow gave the conversation an unexpected and astonishing turn. I'll note that in the morning Versilov and the doctor had spoken very frowningly of his health. I'll also note that for several days preparations had been under way in our house for the celebration of mama's birthday, which was to take place in five days, and we often spoke of it. Apropos of that day, Makar Ivanovich for some reason suddenly embarked on reminiscences and recalled mama's childhood and the time when she still "couldn't stand on her little legs." "She never left my arms," the old man recalled. "I used to teach her to walk, I'd put her in the corner three steps away and call her, and she comes swaying to me across the room, and she's not afraid, she laughs, and when she reaches me, she throws her arms around my neck and embraces me. I also told you fairy tales, Sofya Andreevna; you were a great lover of fairy tales; for two hours you'd sit on my knee listening. They marveled in the cottage: 'See how attached she is to Makar.' Or else I'd take you to the forest, find a raspberry bush, sit you down there, and start cutting wooden whistles for you. We'd have a good walk, and I'd carry you back in my arms—the baby's asleep. And once you got frightened by a wolf, ran to me all trembling, and there wasn't any wolf."

"That I remember," said mama.

"Do you really?"

"I remember a lot. From as early as I can remember myself in life, ever since then I've seen your love and mercy over me," she said in a heartfelt voice and suddenly blushed all over.

Makar Ivanovich paused briefly.

"Forgive me, little children, I'm going. Now the term of my life is upon me. In my old age I have found comfort from all sorrows. Thank you, my dears."

"Come now, Makar Ivanovich, dear heart," Versilov exclaimed, somewhat alarmed, "the doctor told me today that you were incomparably better . . ."

Mama was listening fearfully.

"Well, what does he know, your Alexander Semyonych?" Makar Ivanovich smiled. "He's a dear man, but no more than that. Come, friends, do you think I'm afraid to die? Today, after my morning prayer, I had the feeling in my heart that I wouldn't leave here anymore; it was told me. Well, and what of it, blessed be the name of the Lord; only I'd like to have a good look at you all again. The much-suffering Job, too, was comforted, looking at his new children, but that he forgot the former ones, and that he could have forgotten them—is impossible![15] Only over the years sorrow seems to mingle with joy and turn into a bright sighing. That's how it is in the world: every soul is both tested and comforted. I've decided, little children, to tell you a word or two, not much," he went on with a gentle, beautiful smile, which I will never forget, and suddenly turned to me: "You, my dear, be zealous for the holy Church, and if the time calls for it, also die for her; but wait, don't be frightened, not now," he smiled. "Now maybe you're not thinking of it, but later maybe you will. Only there's this as well: whatever good you intend to do, do it for God, and not for the sake of envy. Hold firmly to what you do, and don't give up out of any sort of faintheartedness; and do it gradually, without rushing or throwing yourself about; well, that's all you need, save maybe also getting used to praying every day and steadfastly. I say it just so, in case you remember it one day. I was going to say something to you, too, Andrei Petrovich, sir, but God will find your heart even without me. And it's long ago now that you and I stopped talking of such things, ever since that arrow pierced my heart. And now, as I'm going, I'll just remind you . . . of what you promised then . . ."

He almost whispered the last words, looking down.

"Makar Ivanovich!" Versilov said in embarrassment, and got up from his chair.

"Well, well, don't be embarrassed, sir, I'm only reminding you . . . It's I who am guiltiest of all before God in this matter; for, though you were my master, I still shouldn't have condoned this weakness. So you, too, Sofya, don't trouble your soul too much, for your whole sin is mine, and in you, as I think, there was hardly any understanding then, and perhaps in you also, sir, along with her," he smiled, his lips trembling with some sort of pain, "and though I might have taught you then, my spouse, even with a rod, and so I should have, I pitied you as you fell down before me in tears and concealed nothing... and kissed my feet. I recall that, my beloved, not as a reproach to you, but only as a reminder to Andrei Petrovich... for you yourself, sir, remember your nobleman's promise, and marriage covers everything... I'm saying it in front of the children, sir, my dear heart."

He was extremely agitated, and looked at Versilov as if expecting words of confirmation from him. I repeat, all this was so unexpected that I sat motionless. Versilov was even no less agitated than he was: he silently went over to mama and embraced her tightly; then mama, also silently, went up to Makar Ivanovich and bowed down at his feet.

In short, the scene turned out to be stupendous; this time there was only our family in the room, not even Tatyana Pavlovna was there. Liza somehow straightened up in her place and listened silently; suddenly she rose and said firmly to Makar Ivanovich:

"Bless me, too, Makar Ivanovich, for a great torment. Tomorrow my whole fate will be decided... and so pray for me today."

And she left the room. I know that Makar Ivanovich already knew everything about her from mama. But that evening for the first time I saw Versilov and mama together; till then I had just seen his slave beside him. There was an awful lot that I didn't know or hadn't noticed yet in this man, whom I had already condemned, and therefore I went back to my room in confusion. And it must be said that precisely by that time all my perplexities about him had thickened; never yet had he seemed so mysterious and unfathomable as precisely at that time; but that's just what the whole story I'm writing is about. All in good time.

"However," I thought to myself then, as I was going to bed, "it turns out that he gave his 'nobleman's word' to marry mama in case she was left a widow. He said nothing about it when he told me earlier about Makar Ivanovich."

The next day Liza was gone the whole day, and coming back quite late, she went straight to Makar Ivanovich. At first I didn't want to go in, so as not to bother them, but I soon noticed that mama and Versilov were already there, and I went in. Liza was sitting next to the old man and weeping on his shoulder, and he, with a sad face, was silently stroking her head.

Versilov explained to me (later in my room) that the prince insisted on having his way and proposed to marry Liza at the first opportunity, before the decision of the court. It was hard for Liza to decide on it, though she now almost had no right not to. Besides, Makar Ivanovich had "ordered" her to marry. Of course, all this would have come out right later by itself, and she would undoubtedly have married on her own, without any orders and hesitations, but at the present moment she was so insulted by the one she loved, and so humiliated by this love even in her own eyes, that it was hard for her to decide. But, besides the insult, there was a new circumstance mixed into it, which I couldn't have begun to suspect.

"Have you heard that all those young people from the Petersburg side were arrested last night?" Versilov added suddenly.

"What? Dergachev?" I cried.

"Yes, and Vasin also."

I was struck, especially on hearing about Vasin.

"But is he mixed up with anything? My God, what will happen to them now? And, as if on purpose, at the very time when Liza was accusing Vasin so! . . . What do you think may happen to them? It's Stebelkov! I swear to you, it's Stebelkov!"

"Let's drop it," said Versilov, looking at me strangely (precisely as one looks at an uncomprehending and unsuspecting man). "Who knows what they've got there, and who knows what will happen to them? There's something else: I hear you want to go out tomorrow. Won't you be going to Prince Sergei Petrovich?"

"First thing—though, I confess, it's very hard for me. Why, do you have some message for him?"

"No, nothing. I'll see him myself. I'm sorry for Liza. And what advice can Makar Ivanovich give her? He himself understands nothing in people or in life. There's another thing, my dear" (he hadn't called me "my dear" for a long time), "there are also . . . certain young men here . . . one of whom is your former schoolmate, Lambert . . . It seems to me they're all great scoundrels . . . I say it just to warn you . . . Anyhow, of course, all that is your business, I understand that I have no right . . ."

"Andrei Petrovich," I seized his hand without thinking and almost in inspiration, as often happened with me (we were almost in the dark), "Andrei Petrovich, I've been silent—you've seen that, I've kept silent up to now, and do you know why? To avoid your secrets. I've simply resolved never to know them. I'm a coward, I'm afraid that your secrets will tear you out of my heart completely, and I don't want that. And if so, then why should you know my secrets? Let it be all the same to you, wherever I may go! Isn't it so?"

"You're right, but not a word more, I beg you!" he said, and left my room. Thus we accidentally had a bit of a talk. But he only added to my agitation before my new step in life the next day, so that I spent the whole night constantly waking up. But I felt good.

III

THE NEXT DAY, though I left the house at ten o'clock in the morning, I tried as hard as I could to leave on the quiet, without saying good-bye or telling anybody—to slip away, as they say. Why I did that I don't know, but if even mama had seen me going out and started talking to me, I would have answered with something angry. When I found myself outside and breathed the cold outdoor air, I shuddered from a very strong sensation—almost an animal one, and which I'd call *carnivorous*. Why was I going, where was I going? It was completely indefinite and at the same time *carnivorous*. I felt frightened and joyful—both at once. "And will I dirty myself today, or not?" I thought dashingly to myself, though I knew all too well that today's step, once taken, would be decisive and irreparable for my whole life. But there's no use speaking in riddles.

I went straight to the prince's prison. For three days already I had had a note from Tatyana Pavlovna to the warden, and he gave me an excellent reception. I don't know whether he's a good man, and I don't think it matters; but he allowed me to meet with the prince and arranged it in his own room, kindly yielding it to us. The room was like any room—an ordinary room in the government apartment of an official of a known sort—that also, I think, we can omit describing. So the prince and I were left alone.

He came out to me in some half-military housecoat, but with a very clean shirt, a fancy necktie, washed and combed, and along with that terribly thin and yellow. I noticed this yellowness even in his eyes. In short, his looks were so changed that I even stopped in perplexity.

"How changed you are!" I cried.

"Never mind! Sit down, my dear," he half-foppishly showed me to an armchair and sat down facing me. "Let's go on to the main thing: you see, my dear Alexei Makarovich..."

"Arkady," I corrected.

"What? Ah, yes—well, well, it makes no difference. Ah, yes!"

he suddenly realized, "excuse me, dear heart, let's go on to the main thing..."

In short, he was in a terrible hurry to go on to something. He was all pervaded with something, from head to foot, with some sort of main idea, which he wished to formulate and present to me. He talked terribly much and quickly, with strain and suffering, explaining and gesticulating, but in the first moments I understood decidedly nothing.

"To put it briefly" (he had already used the phrase "to put it briefly" ten times before then), "to put it briefly," he concluded, "if I have troubled you, Arkady Makarovich, and summoned you so insistently yesterday through Liza, then, though things are ablaze, still, since the essence of the decision should be extraordinary and definitive, we..."

"Excuse me, Prince," I interrupted, "did you summon me yesterday? Liza told me precisely nothing."

"What!" he cried, suddenly stopping in great bewilderment, even almost in fright.

"She told me precisely nothing. Last night she came home so upset that she didn't even manage to say a word to me."

The prince jumped up from his chair.

"Can this be true, Arkady Makarovich? In that case, it's... it's..."

"But, anyhow, what of it? Why are you so disturbed? She simply forgot or something..."

He sat down, but it was as if stupefaction came over him. The news that Liza hadn't told me anything simply crushed him. He suddenly began speaking quickly and waving his arms, but again it was terribly difficult to understand.

"Wait!" he said suddenly, falling silent and holding up his finger. "Wait, it's... it's... unless I'm mistaken... these are—tricks, sir!..." he murmured with a maniac's smile. "And it means that..."

"It means precisely nothing!" I interrupted. "And I only don't understand why such an empty circumstance torments you so... Ah, Prince, since that time, ever since that night—remember..."

"Since what night, and what of it?" he cried fussily, obviously vexed that I had interrupted him.

"At Zershchikov's, where we saw each other for the last time—well, before your letter? You were also terribly disturbed then, but between then and now there's such a difference that I'm even horrified at you... Or don't you remember?"

"Ah, yes," he said, in the voice of a worldly man, and as if suddenly recalling, "ah, yes! That evening... I heard... Well, how is your health, and how are you now after all this, Arkady Makarovich?... But, anyway, let's go on to the main thing. You see, I am essentially pursuing three goals; there are three tasks before me, and I..."

He quickly began speaking again about his "main thing." I realized, finally, that I saw before me a man who ought at least to have a napkin with vinegar put to his head at once, if not to have his blood let. His whole incoherent conversation, naturally, turned around his trial, around the possible outcome; also around the fact that the regimental commander himself had visited him and spent a long time talking him out of something, but that he had not obeyed; around a note he had just written and submitted somewhere; around the prosecutor; about the fact that he would probably be stripped of his rights and exiled somewhere to the northern reaches of Russia; about the possibility of becoming a colonist and earning back his rights in Tashkent;[16] that he would teach his son (the future one, from Liza) this, and pass on that, "in the backwoods, in Arkhangelsk, in Kholmogory."[17] "If I wished for your opinion, Arkady Makarovich, then believe me, I value so much the feeling... If you only knew, if you only knew, Arkady Makarovich, my dear, my brother, what Liza means to me, what she has meant to me here, now, all this time!" he cried suddenly, clutching his head with both hands.

"Sergei Petrovich, can it be that you'll ruin her and take her away? To Kholmogory!" suddenly burst from me irrepressibly. Liza's lot with this maniac all her life suddenly presented itself to my consciousness clearly and as if for the first time. He looked at me, stood up again, took a step, turned around, and sat down again, still holding his head with his hands.

"I keep dreaming of spiders!" he said suddenly.

"You're terribly agitated, Prince, I'd advise you to lie down and send for the doctor at once."

"No, excuse me, that can wait. I mainly asked you to come so that I could explain to you about the marriage. The marriage, you know, will take place right here in the church, I've already said so. Approval has been granted, and they even encourage... As for Liza..."

"Prince, have mercy on Liza, my dear," I cried, "don't torment her now at least, don't be jealous!"

"What!" he cried, looking at me point-blank, his eyes almost popping out, and his face twisted into some sort of long, senselessly questioning smile. It was clear that the words "don't be jealous" for some reason struck him terribly.

"Forgive me, Prince, it was inadvertent. Oh, Prince, I've come to know an old man recently, my nominal father... Oh, if you could see him you'd be calmer... Liza also appreciates him so."

"Ah, yes, Liza... ah, yes, it's your father? Or... *pardon, mon cher,*[*] something like that... I remember... she told me... a little old man... To be sure, to be sure. I also knew a little old man... *Mais passons,*[†] the main thing, in order to clarify the whole essence of the moment, we must..."

I got up to leave. It was painful for me to look at him.

"I do not understand!" he uttered sternly and imposingly, seeing that I had gotten up to leave.

"It's painful for me to look at you," I said.

"Arkady Makarovich, one word, one word more!" He suddenly seized me by the shoulders with a completely different look and gesture, and sat me down in the armchair. "Have you heard about those... you understand?" he leaned towards me.

"Ah, yes, Dergachev. It must be Stebelkov!" I cried, unable to restrain myself.

"Yes, Stebelkov and... you don't know?"

He stopped short and again stared at me with the same popping eyes and the same long, convulsive, senselessly questioning smile, which spread wider and wider. His face gradually grew pale. It was as if something suddenly shook me: I remembered Versilov's look the day before, when he was telling me about Vasin's arrest.

"Oh, can it be?" I cried fearfully.

"You see, Arkady Makarovich, this is why I summoned you, in order to explain... I wanted..." he was whispering quickly.

"It was you who denounced Vasin!" I cried.

"No, you see, there was this manuscript. Before the very last day, Vasin gave it to Liza... for safekeeping. And she left it here for me to look at, and then it so happened that they quarreled the next day..."

"You turned the manuscript over to the authorities!"

"Arkady Makarovich! Arkady Makarovich!"

*Excuse me, my dear.
†But let's leave that.

"And so you," I cried, jumping up and rapping out the words, "you, with no other motive, with no other purpose, but solely because the unfortunate Vasin is *your rival*, solely out of jealousy, you gave the *manuscript entrusted to Liza*... gave it to whom? To whom? To the prosecutor?"

But he didn't have time to answer, and he hardly would have answered anything, because he stood before me like an idol, still with the same morbid smile and fixed gaze; but suddenly the door opened and Liza came in. She almost fainted, seeing us together.

"You here? So you are here?" she cried with a suddenly distorted face and seizing me by the hands. "So you... *know*?"

But she had already read in my face that I "knew." I quickly and irrepressibly embraced her, tightly, tightly! And only at that moment did I grasp for the first time, in its full force, what hopeless, endless grief, with no dawn, lay forever over the whole destiny of this... voluntary seeker of suffering!

"But is it possible to speak with him now?" she suddenly tore herself away from me. "Is it possible to be with him? Why are you here? Look at him! Look! And is it possible, is it possible to judge him?"

Endless misery and commiseration were in her face as she exclaimed this, pointing to the unfortunate man. He was sitting in the armchair, covering his face with his hands. And she was right: this was a man in high delirium and irresponsible; and maybe for three days now he had already been irresponsible. That same morning he had been put in the hospital, and by evening he had come down with brain fever.

IV

FROM THE PRINCE, whom I left then with Liza, I went at around one o'clock to my former apartment. I forgot to mention that it was a damp, dull day, with the beginnings of a thaw and with a warm wind, capable of upsetting even an elephant's nerves. The landlord met me rejoicing, hustling and bustling, something I terribly dislike precisely at such moments. I treated him drily and went straight to my room, but he followed me, and though he didn't dare ask any questions, curiosity simply shone in his eyes, and at the same time he looked as if he even had some right to be curious. I had to treat him politely for my own good; but though it was all too necessary for me to find out a thing or two (and I knew I would), still I was loath to start asking questions. I inquired after his wife's health, and we went to see her. She met me courteously, though with an extremely businesslike and taciturn air; this reconciled me a little. Briefly, this time I learned some quite wondrous things.

Well, naturally, Lambert had been there, but then he had come twice more and "looked the rooms all over," saying he might rent them. Nastasya Egorovna had come several times, God alone knew why. "She was also very curious," the landlord added, but I didn't gratify him, I didn't ask what she was curious about. In general, I didn't ask any questions, it was he who spoke, and I pretended to be rummaging in my suitcase (in which there was almost nothing left). But the most vexing thing was that he also decided to play mysterious and, noticing that I refrained from asking questions, also thought it his duty to become more clipped, almost enigmatic.

"The young lady was also here," he added, looking at me strangely.

"What young lady?"

"Anna Andreevna. She came twice; got acquainted with my wife. Very nice person, very agreeable. Such an acquaintance one can appreciate only too well, Arkady Makarovich..." And, having brought that out, he even took a step towards me: so much did he want me to understand something.

"Twice, really?" I was surprised.

"The second time she came with her brother."

"Meaning with Lambert," occurred to me involuntarily.

"No, sir, not with Mr. Lambert," he guessed at once, as if jumping into my soul with his eyes, "but with her brother, the real one, the young Mr. Versilov. A kammerjunker,[18] it seems?"

I was very embarrassed; he looked on, smiling terribly affectionately.

"Ah, there was someone else here asking for you—that mamzelle, the Frenchwoman, Mamzelle Alphonsine de Verdaigne. Ah, how well she sings, and she also declaims beautifully in verse! She was on her way in secret to see Prince Nikolai Ivanovich then, in Tsarskoe, to sell him a little dog, she said, a rarity, black, no bigger than your fist..."

I begged him to leave me alone, excusing myself with a headache. He instantly satisfied me, not even finishing the phrase, and not only without the least touchiness, but almost with pleasure, waving his hand mysteriously and as if saying, "I understand, sir, I understand," and though he didn't say it, instead he left the room on tiptoe, he gave himself that pleasure. There are very vexatious people in this world.

I sat alone, thinking things over for about an hour and a half—not thinking things over, however, but just brooding. Though I was confused, I was not in the least surprised. I even expected something more, some still greater wonders. "Maybe they've already performed them by now," I thought. I had been firmly and long convinced, still at home, that their machine was wound up and running at full speed. "It's only me they lack, that's what," I thought again, with a sort of irritable and agreeable smugness. That they were waiting for me with all their might—and setting something up to happen in my apartment—was clear as day. "Can it be the old prince's wedding? The beaters are all after him. Only will I allow it, gentlemen, that's the thing," I concluded again with haughty satisfaction.

"Once I start, I'll immediately get drawn into the whirlpool again, like a chip of wood. Am I free now, this minute, or am I no longer free? Going back to mama tonight, can I still say to myself, as in all these past days, 'I am on my own'?"

That was the essence of my questions or, better, of the throbbings of my heart, during that hour and a half that I spent then in the corner on the bed, my elbows resting on my knees, my head propped in my hands. But I knew, I already knew even then, that all these questions were complete nonsense, and I was drawn only by *her*—her and her alone! At last I've said it straight out and written it with pen on paper, for even now, as I write, a year later, I still don't know how to call my feeling of that time by its name!

Oh, I felt sorry for Liza, and there was a most unhypocritical pain in my heart! Just by itself this feeling of pain for her might, it seems, have restrained and effaced, at least for a time, the *carnivorousness* in me (again I mention that word). But I was drawn by boundless curiosity and a sort of fear, and some other feeling as well—I don't know which; but I know, and already knew then, that it was not good. Maybe I yearned to fall at *her* feet, or maybe I wanted to give her over to every torment and "quickly, quickly" prove something to her. No pain and no compassion for Liza could stop me now. Well, could I get up and go home... to Makar Ivanovich?

"But is it really impossible simply to go to them, find out everything from them, and suddenly go away from them forever, passing unharmed by the wonders and monsters?"

At three o'clock, catching myself and realizing that I was almost late, I quickly went out, caught a cab, and flew to Anna Andreevna.

Chapter Five

I

As soon as I was announced, Anna Andreevna dropped her sewing and hurriedly came out to meet me in her front room—something that had never happened before. She held out both hands to me and quickly blushed. Silently she led me to her room, sat down to her handwork again, sat me down beside her; but she didn't take her sewing now, but went on examining me with the same warm concern, not saying a word.

"You sent Nastasya Egorovna to me," I began directly, somewhat burdened by this all-too-spectacular concern, though it pleased me.

She suddenly spoke, not answering my question.

"I've heard everything, I know everything. That terrible night... Oh, how you must have suffered! Is it true, is it true that you were found unconscious in the freezing cold?"

"You got that... from Lambert..." I murmured, reddening.

"I learned everything from him right then; but I've been waiting for you. Oh, he came to me so frightened! At your apartment... where you were lying ill, they didn't want to let him in to see you... and they met him strangely... I really don't know how it was, but he told me all about that night; he said that, having just barely come to your senses, you mentioned me to him and... your devotion to me. I was moved to tears, Arkady Makarovich, and I don't even know how I deserved such warm concern on your part, and that in such a situation as you were in! Tell me, is Mr. Lambert your childhood friend?"

"Yes, but this incident... I confess, I was imprudent, and maybe told him far too much then."

"Oh, I would have learned of this black, terrible intrigue even without him! I always, always had a presentiment that they would drive you to that. Tell me, is it true that Bjoring dared to raise his hand against you?"

She spoke as if it was only because of Bjoring and *her* that I had wound up under the wall. And it occurred to me that she was right, but I flared up:

"If he had raised his hand against me, he wouldn't have gone unpunished, and I wouldn't be sitting in front of you now unavenged," I replied heatedly. Above all, it seemed to me that she wanted to provoke me for some reason, to rouse me up against somebody (however, it was clear whom); and all the same I succumbed.

"If you say you had a presentiment that they would drive me *to that*, then on Katerina Nikolaevna's part, of course, there was only a misunderstanding... though it's also true that she was all too quick in exchanging her good feelings towards me for this misunderstanding..."

"That's precisely it, that she was all too quick!" Anna Andreevna picked up, even in some sort of rapture of sympathy. "Oh, if you knew what an intrigue they've got there now! Of course, Arkady Makarovich, it's hard for you now to understand all the ticklishness of my position," she said, blushing and looking down. "Since that same morning when we saw each other last, I have taken a step that not every person can understand and grasp as one with your as-yet-uncontaminated mind, with your loving, unspoiled, fresh heart would understand it. Rest assured, my friend, that I am capable of appreciating your devotion to me, and I will repay you with eternal gratitude. In society, of course, they will take up stones against me, and they already have. But even if they were right, from their vile point of view, which of them could, which of them dared even then to condemn me? I have been abandoned by my father since childhood; we Versilovs—an ancient, highborn Russian family—are all strays, and I eat other people's bread on charity. Wouldn't it be natural for me to turn to the one who ever since childhood has replaced my father, whose kindness towards me I have seen for so many years? God alone can see and judge my feelings for him, and I do not allow society to judge me for the step I've taken! And when, on top of that, there is the darkest, most perfidious intrigue, and a daughter conspires to ruin her own trusting, magnanimous father, can that be endured? No, let me even ruin my reputation, but I will save him! I am ready to live in his house simply as a nurse, to watch over him, to sit by his sickbed, but I will not give the triumph to cold, loathsome society calculation!"

She spoke with extraordinary animation, very possibly half-affected, but nevertheless sincere, because it could be seen to what degree she had been wholly drawn into this affair. Oh, I could feel that she was lying (though sincerely, because one can also lie sincerely) and that she was now bad; but it's astonishing how it happens with women: this air of respectability, these lofty forms, this unapproachability of social heights and proud chastity—all this threw me off, and I began to agree with her in everything, that is, while I sat with her; at least I didn't dare contradict her. Oh, man is decidedly in moral slavery to woman, especially if he is magnanimous! Such a woman can convince a magnanimous man of anything. "She and Lambert—my God!" I thought, looking at her in bewilderment. However, I'll say all: even to this day I don't know how to judge her; indeed God alone could see her feelings, and besides, a human being is such a complex machine that in some cases there's no figuring him out, and all the more so if that being is—a woman.

"Anna Andreevna, precisely what do you expect of me?" I asked, however, rather resolutely.

"How's that? What does your question mean, Arkady Makarovich?"

"It seems to me by all . . . and by certain other considerations . . ." I explained, getting confused, "that you sent to me expecting something from me. So what was it precisely?"

Not answering my question, she instantly began speaking again, just as quickly and animatedly:

"But I cannot, I'm too proud to enter into discussions and deals with unknown persons like Mr. Lambert! I've been waiting for you, not for Mr. Lambert. My position is extreme, terrible, Arkady Makarovich! Surrounded by that woman's schemes, I'm obliged to be devious—and it's unbearable for me. I almost stoop to intrigues, and I've been waiting for you as for a savior. I cannot be blamed that I look eagerly around me to find at least one friend, and so I couldn't help rejoicing over a friend: one who, even on that night, nearly frozen, could remember me and repeat only my name alone, is of course devoted to me. So I've been thinking all this time, and therefore I put my hopes in you."

She looked into my eyes with impatient inquiry. And here again I lacked the courage to dissuade her and to explain to her directly that Lambert had deceived her and that I had never told him then that I was so especially devoted to her, and hadn't remembered "only her name alone." Thus, by my silence, it was as if I confirmed Lambert's lie. Oh, I'm sure she herself understood very well that Lambert had exaggerated and even simply lied to her, solely in order to have a decent pretext for coming to see her and establishing contacts with her; and if she looked into my eyes as though convinced of the truth of my words and of my devotion, then, of course, she knew that I wouldn't have dared deny it, so to speak, out of delicacy and on account of my youth. But, anyhow, whether this guess of mine is right or wrong—I don't know. Maybe I'm terribly depraved.

"My brother will stand up for me," she pronounced suddenly with ardor, seeing that I didn't want to reply.

"I was told that you came to my apartment with him," I murmured in embarrassment.

"But poor Prince Nikolai Ivanovich has almost nowhere to escape to now from the whole intrigue, or, better, from his own daughter, except to your apartment, that is, to a friend's apartment; for he does have the right to consider you at least a friend! . . . And then, if only you want to do something for his benefit, you can do it—if only you can, if only there is magnanimity and courage in you . . . and, finally, if it's true that you *can do something*. Oh, it's not for me, not for me, but for a poor old man, who alone loved you sincerely, who managed to become attached to you in his heart as to his own son, and who longs for you even to this day! For myself I expect nothing, even from you—if even my own father has played such a perfidious, such a malicious escapade with me!"

"It seems to me that Andrei Petrovich . . ." I tried to begin.

"Andrei Petrovich," she interrupted with a bitter smile, "Andrei Petrovich, to my direct question, answered me then on his word of honor that he never had the least intentions towards Katerina Nikolaevna, which I fully believed when taking my step; and yet it turned out that he was calm only until the first news about some Mr. Bjoring."

"It's not that!" I cried. "There was a moment when I, too, believed in his love for this woman, but it's not that . . . and even if it was that, it would seem he could be perfectly calm now . . . since this gentleman has been dismissed."

"What gentleman?"

"Bjoring."

"Who told you about his dismissal? This gentleman has perhaps never been in so strong a position," she smiled caustically; it even seemed to me that she gave me a mocking look.

"Nastasya Egorovna told me," I murmured in embarrassment, which I was unable to conceal and which she noticed only too well.

"Nastasya Egorovna is a very sweet person, and I certainly cannot forbid her to love me, but she has no means of knowing what doesn't concern her."

My heart was wrung; and since she was counting precisely on firing my indignation, indignation did boil up in me, not against *that* woman, but so far only against Anna Andreevna herself. I got up from my place.

"As an honest man, I must warn you, Anna Andreevna, that your expectations . . . concerning me . . . may prove vain in the highest degree . . ."

"I expect you to stand up for me," she looked at me firmly, "for me, who am abandoned by everyone . . . your sister, if you want that, Arkady Makarovich!"

Another moment and she would have started crying.

"Well, it would be better not to, because 'maybe' nothing will happen," I babbled with an inexpressibly heavy feeling.

"How am I to take your words?" she asked somehow too warily.

"Like this, that I will leave you all and—*basta!*" I suddenly exclaimed almost in fury. "And as for the *document*—I'll tear it up! Farewell!"

I bowed to her and left silently, at the same time almost not daring to glance at her; but I had not yet reached the bottom of the stairs when Nastasya Egorovna overtook me with a folded half-page of note paper. Where Nastasya Egorovna had come from, and where she had been sitting while I was talking with Anna Andreevna—I can't even comprehend. She didn't say a single word, but only handed me the paper and ran back. I unfolded it: Lambert's address was written on it legibly and clearly, and it had been prepared, obviously, several days earlier. I suddenly remembered that on the day when Nastasya Egorovna had come to see me, I had let slip to her that I didn't know where Lambert lived, but in the sense that "I didn't know and didn't want to know." But by that time I had already learned Lambert's address through Liza, whom I had asked especially to make inquiries at the information bureau. Anna Andreevna's escapade seemed to me too resolute, even cynical: despite my refusal to assist her, she, as if not believing me a whit, was sending me straight to Lambert. It became only too clear to me that she had already learned all about the document—and from whom else if not from Lambert, to whom she was therefore sending me to arrange things?

"Decidedly every last one of them takes me for a little boy with no will or character, with whom anything can be done!" I thought with indignation.

II

Nevertheless I went to Lambert's anyway. How could I overcome my curiosity at that time? Lambert, it turned out, lived very far away, in Kosoy Lane, by the Summer Garden, incidentally in the same furnished rooms; but the other time, when I had fled from him, I had been so oblivious of the way and the distance that, when I got his address from Liza four days earlier, I was even surprised and almost didn't believe he lived there. While still going up the stairs, I noticed two young men at the door to his rooms, on the third floor, and thought they had rung before me and were waiting to be let in. As I came up the stairs, they both turned their backs to the door and studied me carefully. "These are furnished rooms, and they, of course, are going to see other lodgers," I frowned as I approached them. It would have been very unpleasant for me to find somebody at Lambert's. Trying not to look at them, I reached out my hand for the bell-pull.

"*Atanday*,"* one of them shouted at me.

"Please wait to ring," the other young man said in a ringing and gentle little voice, drawing the words out somewhat. "We'll finish this, and then we can all ring together if you like."

I stopped. They were both still very young men, about twenty or twenty-two years old; they were doing something strange there by the door, and in surprise I tried to grasp what it was. The one who had shouted *atanday* was a very tall fellow, about six foot six, not less, gaunt and haggard, but very muscular, with a very small head for his height, and a strange, sort of comically gloomy expression on his somewhat pockmarked but not at all stupid and even pleasant face. His eyes looked with a somehow excessive intentness, and even a sort of unnecessary and superfluous resolution. He was quite vilely dressed, in an old quilted cotton overcoat with a small, shabby raccoon collar, too short for his height—obviously from someone else's back—and vile, almost peasant boots, and with a terribly crumpled, discolored top hat on his head. In all he was clearly a sloven: his gloveless hands were dirty, and his long nails were in mourning. His comrade, on the contrary, was foppishly dressed, judging by his light polecat coat, his elegant hat, and the

*Wait (in mispronounced French).

light, fresh gloves on his slender fingers; he was the same height as I, but with an extremely sweet expression on his fresh and young little face.

The long fellow was pulling off his necktie—a completely tattered and greasy ribbon or almost tape—and the pretty boy, having taken from his pocket another new, black tie, just purchased, was tying it around the neck of the long fellow, who obediently and with a terribly serious face, was stretching out his very long neck, throwing his overcoat back from his shoulders.

"No, it's impossible if the shirt's so dirty," the young man thus occupied said. "There not only won't be any effect, but it will seem still dirtier. I told you to put on a collar . . . I can't do it . . . Maybe you can?" he suddenly turned to me.

"Do what?" I asked.

"Here, you know, tie his necktie. You see, it has to be done in some way so that his dirty shirt doesn't show, otherwise there'll be no effect, no matter what. I just bought him a necktie from Filipp, the barber, for a rouble."

"Was it that rouble?" the long one murmured.

"Yes, that one; now I don't even have a kopeck. So you can't do it? In that case we'll have to ask Alphonsinka."

"To see Lambert?" the long one suddenly asked me abruptly.

"To see Lambert," I replied with no less resolution, looking him in the eye.

"*Dolgorowky?*"[19] he repeated in the same tone and the same voice.

"No, not Korovkin," I replied just as abruptly, having misheard.

"*Dolgorowky?!*" the long one almost shouted, repeating himself, and coming at me almost menacingly. His comrade burst out laughing.

"He's saying *Dolgorowky*, not Korovkin," he clarified. "You know how the French in the *Journal des débats* often distort Russian last names . . ."

"In the *Indépendance*,"[20] the long one grunted.

". . . Well, in the *Indépendance*, too, it makes no difference. Dolgoruky, for instance, is written Dolgorowky, I've read it myself, and *V—v* is always *Comte Wallonieff*."

"*Doboyny!*" cried the long one.

"Yes, there's also some *Doboyny*. I read it myself and we both laughed: some Russian *Mme. Doboyny*, abroad . . . only, you see, why mention them all?" he suddenly turned to the long one.

"Excuse me, are you Mr. Dolgoruky?"

"Yes, I'm Dolgoruky, but how do you know?"

The long one suddenly whispered something to the pretty boy, who frowned and made a negative gesture; but the long one suddenly turned to me:

"*Monsieur le prince, vous n'avez pas de rouble d'argent pour nous, pas deux, mais un seul, voulez-vous?*"*

"Ah, how vile you are!" cried the boy.

"*Nous vous rendons,*"† the long one concluded, pronouncing the French words crudely and awkwardly.

"He's a cynic, you know," the boy smiled to me. "And do you think he doesn't know how to speak French? He speaks like a Parisian, and he's only mocking those Russians who want to speak French aloud among themselves in society, but don't know how..."

"*Dans les wagons,*"‡ the long one clarified.

"Well, yes, in railway carriages, too—ah, what a bore you are, there's nothing to clarify! A nice fancy to pretend you're a fool."

Meanwhile I took out a rouble and offered it to the long one.

"*Nous vous rendons,*" the man said, pocketing the rouble, and, suddenly turning to the door, with a perfectly immobile and serious face he began banging on it with the toe of his enormous, crude boot and, above all, without the slightest irritation.

"Ah, you're going to have a fight with Lambert again!" the boy observed uneasily. "You'd better ring!"

I rang, but the long one still went on banging with his boot.

"*Ah, sacré...*"§ Lambert's voice suddenly came from behind the door, and he quickly opened it.

"*Dites donc, voulez-vous que je vous casse la tête, mon ami!*"‖ he shouted at the long one.

"*Mon ami, voilà Dolgorowky, l'autre mon ami,*"¶ the long one pronounced importantly and seriously, looking point-blank at Lambert, who had turned red with anger. As soon as he saw me, he was as if all transformed at once.

"It's you, Arkady! At last! So you're well now, you're well at last?"

*Mister prince, do you have a silver rouble for us, not two, but only one, if you will?

†We pay you back.

‡In railway carriages.

§Ah, you damned...

‖Say, then, would you like me to crack your skull, my friend!

¶My friend, here's Dolgorovky, the other my friend [*sic*].

He seized me by the hands, pressing them hard; in short, he was so sincerely delighted that I instantly felt terribly pleased, and even began to like him.

"You're the first one I'm calling on!"

"Alphonsine!" cried Lambert.

The woman instantly leaped out from behind the screen.

"*Le voilà!*"*

"*C'est lui!*"† exclaimed Alphonsine, clasping her hands, and, spreading them wide again, she rushed to embrace me, but Lambert came to my defense.

"No, no, no, down!" he shouted at her as if she were a puppy. "You see, Arkady, a few of us fellows have arranged to have dinner at the Tartar's today. I won't let you off, come with us. We'll have dinner; I'll chase these boys out at once—and then we can talk as much as we like. But do come in! We're leaving right away, just stay for a little minute..."

I went in and stood in the middle of that room, looking around and remembering. Lambert was hastily changing his clothes behind the screen. The long one and his comrade also came in with us, despite Lambert's words. We all remained standing.

"*Mlle. Alphonsine, voulez-vous me baiser?*"‡ the long one grunted.

"*Mlle. Alphonsine,*" the younger one made a movement, pointing to the little tie, but she fell fiercely on them both.

"*Ah, le petit vilain!*" she cried to the younger one. "*Ne m'approcher pas, ne me salissez pas, et vous, le grand dadais, je vous flanque à la porte tous les deux, savez-vous cela!*"§

The younger one, in spite of her waving him away scornfully and squeamishly, as if she really was afraid to dirty herself by touching him (which I couldn't understand, because he was so pretty and turned out to be so well dressed when he threw off his fur coat)—the younger one began begging her insistently to tie the necktie on his long friend, after first tying one of Lambert's clean collars on him. She almost started beating them, she was so indignant at this suggestion, but Lambert, having heard it, cried to her from behind the screen that she shouldn't hamper them and should do as she

*Here he is!

†It's him!

‡Mlle. Alphonsine, do you want to kiss me?

§Ah, the little rogue!... Don't come near me, don't dirty me, and you, you big booby, I'll chuck you both out the door, do you know that!

was asked, "otherwise they won't leave you alone," he added, and Alphonsine instantly seized the collar and began tying it on the long one, now without the slightest squeamishness. Just as on the stairs, the man stretched his neck out for her while she tied it.

"*Mlle. Alphonsine, avez-vous vendu votre bologne?*"* he asked.

"*Qu'est-ce que ça, ma bologne?*"†

The younger one explained that *ma bologne* signified her little Bolognese lap dog.

"*Tiens, quel est ce baragouin?*"‡

"*Je parle comme une dame russe sur les eaux minérales,*"§ observed *le grand dadais*, his neck still stretched out.

"*Qu'est-ce que ça qu'une dame russe sure les eaux minérales et... où est donc votre jolie montre, que Lambert vous a donné?*"‖ she suddenly turned to the younger one.

"What, no watch again?" Lambert echoed irritably from behind the screen.

"We ate it up!" *le grand dadais* grunted.

"I sold it for eight roubles. It was gilded silver, and you told me it was gold. Ones like that, in a shop now, cost only sixteen roubles," the younger one replied to Lambert, justifying himself with reluctance.

"We must put an end to this!" Lambert went on still more irritably. "I don't buy you clothes, my young friend, and give you beautiful things, so that you can waste it all on your long friend... What's this tie you've bought?"

"That was only a rouble; it wasn't yours. He didn't have any tie at all, and he still needs to buy a hat."

"Nonsense!" Lambert was now angry indeed. "I gave him enough for a hat as well, and he up and bought oysters and champagne. He smells; he's a sloven; he can't be taken anywhere. How can I take him to dinner?"

"In a cab," the *dadais* grunted. "*Nous avons un rouble d'argent que nous avons prêté chez notre nouvel ami.*"¶

"Don't give them anything, Arkady!" Lambert cried again.

*Mlle. Alphonsine, have you sold your *bologne* [deformation of *bolognais*]?

†What's my *bologne*?

‡Say, what is this gibberish?

§I talk like a Russian lady on the mineral waters [*sic*].

‖What's a Russian lady on the mineral waters and... so where's your pretty watch that Lambert gave you?

¶We have a silver rouble that we lent [*sic*] from our new friend.

"Excuse me, Lambert, I demand outright that you give me ten roubles here and now," the boy suddenly became angry and even turned all red, which made him twice as good-looking, "and don't you ever dare to say foolish things, as you just did to Dolgoruky. I demand ten roubles, one rouble to give back to Dolgoruky right now, and the rest to buy Andreev a hat at once—you'll see for yourself."

Lambert came from behind the screen:

"Here's three yellow notes, three roubles, and nothing more till Tuesday, and don't you dare . . . or else . . ."

Le grand dadais snatched the money from him.

"Dolgorowky, here's the rouble, *nous vous rendons avec beaucoup de grâce.** Petya, let's go!" he cried to his comrade, and then, holding up the two notes, waving them and looking point-blank at Lambert, he suddenly screamed with all his might:

"*Ohé, Lambert! où est Lambert, as-tu vu Lambert?*"†

"Don't you dare, don't you dare!" Lambert also screamed in the most terrible wrath. I saw that there was something previous in all this, totally unknown to me, and I gazed in astonishment. But the long one wasn't frightened in the least by Lambert's wrath; on the contrary, he screamed still louder: "*Ohé, Lambert!*" and so on. With this shouting they went out to the stairs. Lambert started after them, but then came back.

"Eh, soon I'll thr-r-row them out on their ears! They cost more than they bring in . . . Come on, Arkady! I'm late. There's yet another necessary man . . . waiting for me . . . Also a brute . . . They're all brutes! Tghrash, tghrash!" he cried again and almost ground his teeth; but all at once he came fully to his senses. "I'm glad you finally came. Alphonsine, not a step from the house! Let's go!"

By the porch, a smart trotter was waiting for him. We got in; but even all the way he still couldn't recover from some sort of fury against those young men and calm down. I marveled that it was so serious, and that, besides, they were all so irreverent with Lambert, while he all but even cowered before them. To me, by an ingrown old impression from childhood, it always seemed that everyone must fear Lambert, so that, despite all my independence, I myself probably cowered before Lambert at that moment.

"I tell you, they're all terrible tghrash," Lambert couldn't calm

*We pay you back with much thanks.

†Hey, Lambert! where's Lambert, have you seen Lambert?

down. "Would you believe it, that tall, vile one tormented me three days ago, in good society. He stands in front of me and shouts: '*Ohé, Lambert!*' In good society! Everybody laughs and knows that it's to get money from me—can you imagine. I gave it. Oh, they're scoundrels! Would you believe it, he was a junker[21] in a regiment and got thrown out, and, can you imagine, he's educated; he was brought up in a good home, can you imagine! He has thoughts, he could... Eh, the devil! And he's strong as *Hercule*. He's useful, but not very. And you can see he doesn't wash his hands. I recommended him to a certain lady, an old noble lady, saying that he had repented and wanted to kill himself from remorse, and he came to her, sat down, and whistled. And the other, the pretty one, is a general's son; the family's ashamed of him, I pulled him out of a trial, I saved him, and this is how he repays me. There are no people here! On their ears, on their ears!"

"They know my name; did you speak to them about me?"

"I had the stupidity. Please sit through dinner, brace yourself... Another awful canaille is coming. This one is really an awful canaille, and he's terribly cunning; they're all scum here; not a single honest man! Well, so we'll finish—and then... What do you like to eat? Well, it makes no difference, they have good food there. I'm paying, don't worry. It's a good thing you're well dressed. I can give you money. Come any time. Imagine, I wined and dined them here, there was cabbage pie every day; that watch he sold, it's the second time. The little one, Trishatov—you saw him, Alphonsine even scorns to look at him and forbids him to come near her—and suddenly, in a restaurant, in front of some officers, he says, 'I'll have snipe.' I gave him snipe! Only I'll get my revenge."

"Remember, Lambert, how we drove to a tavern in Moscow, and in the tavern you stabbed me with a fork, and how you had five hundred roubles then?"

"Yes, I remember! Eh, the devil, I do! I like you... Believe that. Nobody likes you, but I do; I'm the only one, remember... The one who's coming, the pockmarked one, is the most cunning canaille; don't say anything to him if he starts talking, and if he starts asking questions, answer with nonsense, keep mum..."

At any rate, on account of his excitement, he didn't ask me anything on the way. I even felt offended that he was so sure of me and didn't even suspect any mistrust in me; it seemed to me that he had the stupid notion that he could still order me around. "And besides, he's terribly uneducated," I thought, going into the restaurant.

III

I USED TO go to this restaurant on Morskaya[22] before, during the time of my infamous decadence and depravity, and therefore the impression of these rooms, these waiters, looking me over and recognizing me as a familiar visitor, the impression, finally, of this mysterious company of Lambert's friends, in which I had so suddenly found myself and to which I already seemed to belong indivisibly, and above all—the dark foreboding that I was voluntarily heading for some sort of vileness and would undoubtedly end up in bad business—it was as if all this suddenly pierced me. There was a moment when I almost left; but the moment passed and I stayed.

That "pockmarked one" Lambert was so afraid of for some reason was already waiting for us. He was a small man with one of those stupidly businesslike appearances, a type I've hated almost since childhood; about forty-five years old, of medium height, with some gray in his hair, with a face clean-shaven to the point of vileness, and with small, regular, gray, trimmed side-whiskers in the form of two little sausages on the two cheeks of an extremely flat and wicked face. Naturally, he was dull, serious, taciturn, and even, as is usual with all these wretched little people, for some reason arrogant. He scrutinized me very attentively but didn't say a word, and Lambert was so stupid that, in seating us at the same table, he felt no need to introduce us, so that the man might have taken me for one of Lambert's blackmailing associates. To those young people (who arrived almost at the same time as we did) he also said nothing all through dinner, but it could be seen, nevertheless, that he knew them closely. He talked about something only with Lambert, and then almost in a whisper, and then it was almost only Lambert who talked, while the pockmarked one just got off with fragmentary and angry ultimatums. He behaved superciliously, was spiteful and jeering, whereas Lambert, on the contrary, was in great agitation and evidently kept persuading him, probably trying to win him over to some venture. Once I reached for the bottle of red wine; the pockmarked one suddenly took a bottle of sherry and handed it to me, having not said a word to me till then.

"Try this," he said, offering me the bottle. Here I suddenly realized that he must already know everything in the world about me—my story, and my name, and maybe why Lambert was counting on me. The thought that he might take me for someone in Lambert's service infuriated me again, and Lambert's face expressed a very strong and stupid alarm as soon as the man addressed me. The pockmarked one noticed it and laughed. "Lambert decidedly depends on everybody," I thought, hating him at that moment with all my soul. Thus, though we sat through the whole dinner at one table, we were divided into two groups: the pockmarked one and Lambert nearer the window, facing each other, and I next to the greasy Andreev, with Trishatov facing me. Lambert hurried with the meal, urging the waiter to serve every minute. When champagne was served, he suddenly reached out his glass to me.

"To your health, let's clink!" he said, interrupting his conversation with the pockmarked one.

"And will you allow me to clink with you?" The pretty Trishatov reached out his glass to me across the table. Before the champagne he had been somehow very pensive and silent. The *dadais* said nothing at all, but ate silently and a lot.

"With pleasure," I replied to Trishatov. We clinked glasses and drank.

"And I won't drink to your health," the *dadais* suddenly turned to me, "not because I wish for your death, but so that you won't drink anymore here today." He uttered it gloomily and weightily. "Three glasses are enough for you. I see you're looking at my unwashed fist?" he went on, displaying his fist on the table. "I don't wash it, and rent it out to Lambert unwashed as it is, for crushing other people's heads on occasions that Lambert finds ticklish." And, having said that, he suddenly banged his fist on the table with such force that all the plates and glasses jumped. Besides us, there were people dining at four other tables in this room, all of them officers and various imposing-looking gentlemen. It was a fashionable restaurant; for a moment everybody stopped talking and looked at our corner. And it seems we had long been arousing some curiosity. Lambert turned all red.

"Hah, he's at it again! I believe I asked you to behave yourself, Nikolai Semyonovich," he said to Andreev in a fierce whisper. The man looked him over with a long and slow stare:

"I don't want my new friend *Dolgorowky* to drink much wine here today."

Lambert turned still more red. The pockmarked one listened

silently, but with visible pleasure. For some reason he liked Andreev's escapade. I was the only one who didn't understand why I shouldn't drink.

"He only does it to get money! You'll get another seven roubles, do you hear, after dinner—only let us finish eating, don't disgrace us," Lambert rasped to him.

"Aha!" the *dadais* grunted victoriously. This quite delighted the pockmarked one, and he sniggered maliciously.

"Listen, you're much too..." Trishatov said to his friend with uneasiness and almost with suffering, evidently wishing to restrain him. Andreev fell silent, but not for long; that was not how he reckoned. At a table about five steps away from us, two gentlemen were dining and having a lively conversation. They were both middle-aged gentlemen of an extremely ticklish appearance. One was tall and very fat, the other also very fat but small. They were talking in Polish about the current Parisian events. The *dadais* had long been glancing at them curiously and listening. The little Pole obviously struck him as a comic figure, and he hated him at once, after the manner of all bilious and liverish people, to whom this always happens suddenly even without any cause. Suddenly the little Pole spoke the name of the deputy Madier de Montjau,[23] but following the habit of a great many Poles, he pronounced it in a Polish manner, that is, with the stress on the next-to-last syllable, and it came out not as Madiér de Montjáu, but as Mádier de Móntjau. That was all the *dadais* needed. He turned to the Poles and, drawing himself up importantly, suddenly said distinctly and loudly, as though asking them a question:

"Mádier de Móntjau?"

The Poles turned to him fiercely.

"What do you want?" the big fat Pole cried menacingly in Russian. The *dadais* bided his time.

"Mádier de Móntjau?" he suddenly repeated for the whole room to hear, without giving any further explanations, just as he had stupidly repeated "*Dolgorowky?*" as he came at me earlier by the door. The Poles jumped up from their places, Lambert jumped up from the table, rushed first to Andreev, but then abandoned him, leaped over to the Poles, and humbly began apologizing to them.

"They're buffoons, *panie*,* buffoons!" the little Pole repeated contemptuously, all red as a carrot with indignation. "Soon it will

*Sir (polite form of direct address in Polish).

be impossible to come here!" There was a stirring in the room, some murmuring was heard, but more laughter.

"Leave . . . please . . . let's go now!" Lambert murmured, completely at a loss, trying somehow to get Andreev out of the room. Giving Lambert a searching look and figuring that at this point he could get money from him, the man agreed to follow him. It was probably not the first time he had used this shameless method to knock money out of Lambert. Trishatov also made as if to run after them, but looked at me and stayed.

"Ah, how nasty!" he said, covering his eyes with his slender fingers.

"Very nasty, sirs," the pockmarked one whispered this time with a very angered air. Meanwhile Lambert came back almost completely pale and, with lively gesticulations, began whispering something to the pockmarked one. The latter meanwhile ordered the waiter to quickly serve coffee. He listened squeamishly; he evidently wanted to leave quickly. And, nevertheless, the whole incident was merely a schoolboy prank. Trishatov, with his cup of coffee, came over from his place and sat next to me.

"I like him very much," he began, addressing me with such a candid air as though he had always been talking to me about it. "You wouldn't believe how unhappy Andreev is. He ate and drank up his sister's dowry, and ate and drank up everything they had, the year he served in the army, and I can see how he suffers now. And as for his not washing—it's from despair. And he has terribly strange thoughts: he suddenly tells you that a scoundrel and an honest man are all the same and there's no difference; and that there's no need to do anything, either good or bad, or it's all the same—you can do either good or bad, but the best thing of all is to lie there without taking your clothes off for a month at a time, drink, eat, sleep—and that's all. But, believe me, he just says it. And you know, I even think he carried on like that just now because he wanted to finish completely with Lambert. He spoke of it yesterday. Believe me, sometimes at night or when he's been sitting alone for a long time, he begins to weep, and, you know, when he weeps, it's in some special way, as no one else weeps: he starts howling, howling terribly, and that, you know, is still more pitiful . . . And besides, he's so big and strong, and suddenly—he's just howling. Such a poor fellow, isn't it so? I want to save him, but I'm such a nasty, lost little brat myself, you wouldn't believe it! Will you let me in, Dolgoruky, if I ever come to see you?"

"Oh, do come, I even like you."

"What on earth for? Well, but thank you. Listen, let's drink another glass. Though—what's the matter with me?—you'd better not drink. It's true what he said, that you mustn't drink more," he suddenly winked at me significantly, "but I'll drink even so. I'm all right now, but, believe me, I can't restrain myself in anything. Just tell me I'm not to dine in restaurants anymore, and I'm ready for anything just to go and do it. Oh, we sincerely want to be honest, I assure you, only we keep postponing it.

And the years go by—all the best years![24]

And I'm terribly afraid he'll hang himself. He'll go and not tell anybody. He's like that. Nowadays they all hang themselves; who knows—maybe there are a lot like us? I, for instance, simply can't live without spare cash. The spare cash is much more important for me than the necessary. Listen, do you like music? I'm terribly fond of it. I'll play something for you when I come to see you. I play the piano very well, and I studied for a long time. I studied seriously. If I were to write an opera, you know, I'd take the subject from *Faust*.[25] I like that theme very much. I keep creating the scene in the cathedral, just so, imagining it in my head. A Gothic cathedral, inside, choirs, hymns, Gretchen enters, and, you know, the choirs are medieval, so that you can just hear the fifteenth century. Gretchen is in grief, first there's a recitative, quiet but terrible, tormenting, but the choirs rumble gloomily, sternly, indifferently:

Dies irae, dies illa![26]

And suddenly—the devil's voice, the devil's song. He's invisible, it's just a song, alongside the hymns, together with the hymns, it almost coincides with them, and yet it's quite different—it has to be done that way somehow. The song is long, tireless, it's a tenor, it must be a tenor. He starts quietly, tenderly: 'Remember, Gretchen, how you, still innocent, still a child, used to come with your mama to this cathedral and prattle out your prayers from an old book?' But the song grows stronger, more passionate, more impetuous; the notes get higher: there are tears in it, anguish, tireless, hopeless, and, finally, despair: 'There is no forgiveness, Gretchen, there is no forgiveness for you here!' Gretchen wants to pray, but only cries burst from her breast—you know, when your breast is contracted with tears—but Satan's song doesn't stop, ever more deeply it pierces the soul, like a sharp point, ever higher—and suddenly it breaks off almost with a shout: 'It's all over, you are cursed!' Gretchen falls on her knees, clasps her hands before her—and here comes her prayer, something very short, half recitative, but naïve, without any polish, something medieval in the highest degree, four lines, only four lines in all—there are several such notes in Stradella[27]—and at the last note she swoons! Commotion. She's lifted, borne up—and here suddenly a thundering choir. It's like an assault of voices, an inspired chorus, victorious, overwhelming, something like our 'Up-borne-by-the-an-gel-ic-hosts'[28]—so that everything's shaken to its foundations, and everything changes into an ecstatic, exultant, universal exclamation—'Hosanna!'—as if it were the cry of the whole universe, and she's borne up, borne up, and here the curtain falls! No, you know, if I could, I'd have done something! Only I can't do anything now, but only keep dreaming. I keep dreaming and dreaming; my whole life has turned into a dream, I even dream at night. Ah, Dolgoruky, have you read Dickens's *Old Curiosity Shop*?"

"I have. What about it?"

"Do you remember... Wait, I'll drink another glass... Do you remember that place at the end, when they—that crazy old man and that lovely thirteen-year-old girl, his granddaughter—after their fantastic flight and wanderings, finally find refuge somewhere on the edge of England, near some medieval Gothic cathedral, and the girl obtains some post there, showing the cathedral to visitors... And then, once, the sun is setting, and this child is standing on the porch of the cathedral, all bathed in the last rays, standing and watching the sunset with quiet, pensive contemplation in her child's soul, a soul astonished as before some riddle, because the one and the other are like a riddle—the sun as God's thought, and the cathedral as man's thought... isn't it so? Oh, I don't know how to express it, only God likes such first thoughts from children... And there, next to her on the steps, this mad old man, the grandfather, stares at her with a fixed gaze... You know, there's nothing special in this picture from Dickens, absolutely nothing, but you'll never forget it, and this remains in all of Europe—why? Here is the beautiful! Here is innocence! Eh! I don't know what it is, only it's good. I was always reading novels in high school. You know, I have a sister in the country, only a year older than me... Oh, it's all been sold there now, and there's no longer any estate! We sat on the terrace, under our old lindens, and read that novel, and the sun was also setting, and suddenly we stopped reading and said to each other that we, too, would be good, and we, too, would be beautiful—I was preparing for the university then and . . . Ah, Dolgoruky, you know, each of us has his memories! . . ."

And suddenly he leaned his pretty little head on my shoulder—and wept. I felt very, very sorry for him. True, he had drunk a lot of wine, but he had talked so sincerely with me, like a brother, with such feeling . . . Suddenly, at that moment, a shout came from the street and a strong rapping of knuckles on our window (the windows here are one-piece, big, and it was on the ground floor as well, so that it's possible to knock from the street). It was the ejected Andreev.

"*Ohé, Lambert! Où est Lambert? As-tu vu Lambert?*" his wild shout resounded in the street.

"Ah, but he's here! So he hasn't gone?" exclaimed my boy, tearing from his place.

"The check!" Lambert rasped to the waiter. His hands even trembled with anger as he went to pay, but the pockmarked one wouldn't let Lambert pay for him.

"But why? Didn't I invite you, didn't you accept the invitation?"

"No, permit me." The pockmarked one took out his purse and, having calculated his share, paid separately.

"You offend me, Semyon Sidorych!"

"That's how I want it, sir," Semyon Sidorovich snapped and, taking his hat and not saying good-bye to anyone, walked out of the room alone. Lambert threw the money at the waiter and hastily ran out after him, even forgetting about me in his confusion. Trishatov and I went out after all the rest. Andreev was standing by the entrance like a milepost, waiting for Trishatov.

"Blackguard!" Lambert couldn't keep from saying.

"Uh-uh!" Andreev growled at him, and with one swing of his arm he knocked off his round hat, which rolled along the pavement. The humiliated Lambert rushed to pick it up.

"*Vingt-cinq roubles!*"* Andreev showed Trishatov the banknote he had wrested from Lambert earlier.

"Enough," Trishatov cried to him. "Why do you keep making a row? . . . And why did you skin him for twenty-five roubles? You only had seven coming."

"What do you mean, skin him? He promised we'd dine in a

*Twenty-five roubles.

private room with Athenian women, and he served up the pock-marked one instead of the women, and, besides that, I didn't finish eating and froze in the cold a sure eighteen roubles' worth. He had seven roubles outstanding, which makes exactly twenty-five for you."

"Get the hell out of here, both of you!" yelled Lambert. "I'm throwing you both out, and I'll tie you in little knots..."

"Lambert, I'm throwing you out, and I'll tie you in little knots!" cried Andreev. "*Adieu, mon prince*,* don't drink any more wine! Off we go, Petya! *Ohé, Lambert! Où est Lambert? As-tu vu Lambert?*" he roared one last time, moving off with enormous strides.

"So I'll come to see you, may I?" Trishatov hastily babbled to me, hurrying after his friend.

Lambert and I remained alone.

"Well... let's go!" he uttered, as if he had difficulty catching his breath and even as if demented.

"Where should I go? I'm not going anywhere with you!" I hastened to cry in defiance.

"How do you mean, not going?" he roused himself up fearfully, coming to his senses all at once. "But I've only been waiting for us to be left alone!"

"But where on earth can we go?" I confess, I also had a slight ringing in my head from the three glasses of champagne and two of sherry.

"This way, over this way, you see?"

"But the sign says fresh oysters, you see? It's a foul-smelling place..."

"That's because you've just eaten, but it's Miliutin's shop; we won't eat oysters, I'll give you champagne..."

"I don't want it! You want to get me drunk."

"They told you that; they were laughing at you. You believe the scoundrels!"

"No, Trishatov is not a scoundrel. But I myself know how to be careful—that's what!"

"So you've got your own character?"

"Yes, I've got character, a bit more than you have, because you're enslaved to the first comer. You disgraced us, you apologized to the Poles like a lackey. You must have been beaten often in taverns?"

*Farewell, my prince.

"But we have to have a talk, cghretin!" he cried with that scornful impatience which all but said, "And you're at it, too?" "What, are you afraid or something? Are you my friend or not?"

"I'm not your friend, and you're a crook. Let's go, if only to prove that I'm not afraid of you. Ah, what a foul smell, it smells of cheese! What nastiness!"

Chapter Six

I

I ASK YOU once more to remember that I had a slight ringing in my head; if it hadn't been for that, I would have talked and acted differently. In the back room of this shop one could actually eat oysters, and we sat down at a little table covered with a foul, dirty cloth. Lambert ordered champagne; a glass of cold, golden-colored wine appeared before me and looked at me temptingly; but I was vexed.

"You see, Lambert, what mainly offends me is that you think you can order me around now, as you used to at Touchard's, while you yourself are enslaved by everybody here."

"Cghretin! Eh, let's clink!"

"You don't even deign to pretend before me; you might at least conceal that you want to get me drunk."

"You're driveling, and you're drunk. You have to drink more, and you'll be more cheerful. Take your glass, go on, take it!"

"What's all this 'go on, take it'? I'm leaving, and that's the end of it."

And I actually made as if to get up. He became terribly angry.

"It's Trishatov whispering to you against me: I saw the two of you whispering there. You're a cghretin in that case. Alphonsine is even repulsed when he comes near her . . . He's vile. I'll tell you what he's like."

"You've already said it. All you've got is Alphonsine, you're terribly narrow."

"Narrow?" He didn't understand. "They've gone over to the pockmarked one now. That's what! That's why I threw them out. They're dishonest. That pockmarked villain will corrupt them, too. But I always demanded that they behave nobly."

I sat down, took the glass somehow mechanically, and drank a gulp.

"I'm incomparably superior to you in education," I said. But he was only too glad that I had sat down, and at once poured me more wine.

"So you're afraid of them?" I went on teasing him (and at that point I was certainly more vile than he was himself). "Andreev knocked your hat off, and you gave him twenty-five roubles for it."

"I did, but he'll pay me back. They're rebellious, but I'll tie them into . . ."

"You're very worried about the pockmarked one. And you know, it seems to me that I'm the only one you've got left now. All your hopes are resting on me alone now—eh?"

"Yes, Arkashka, that's so: you're my only remaining friend; you put it so well!" he slapped me on the shoulder.

What could be done with such a crude man? He was totally undeveloped and took mockery for praise.

"You could save me from some bad things, if you were a good comrade, Arkady," he went on, looking at me affectionately.

"In what way could I save you?"

"You know what way. Without me you're like a cghretin, and you're sure to be stupid, but I'd give you thirty thousand, and we'd go halves, and you yourself know how. Well, who are you, just look: you've got nothing—no name, no family—and here's a pile all at once; and on such money you know what a career you can start!"

I was simply amazed at such a method. I had decidedly assumed he would dodge, but he began with such directness, such boyish directness, with me. I decided to listen to him out of breadth and . . . out of terrible curiosity.

"You see, Lambert, you won't understand this, but I agree to listen to you because I'm broad," I declared firmly and took another sip from the glass. Lambert at once refilled it.

"Here's the thing, Arkady: if a man like Bjoring dared to heap abuse on me and strike me in front of a lady I adored, I don't know what I'd do! But you took it, and I find you repulsive, you're a dishrag!"

"How dare you say Bjoring struck me!" I cried, turning red. "It's rather I who struck him, and not he me."

"No, he struck you, not you him."

"Lies, I also stepped on his foot!"

"But he shoved you with his arm and told the lackeys to drag you away . . . and she sat and watched from the carriage and laughed at you—she knows you have no father and can be insulted."

"I don't know, Lambert, we're having a schoolboy conversation, which I'm ashamed of. You're doing it to get me all worked up, and so crudely and openly, as if I were some sort of sixteen-year-old. You arranged it with Anna Andreevna!" I cried, trembling with anger and mechanically sipping wine all the while.

"Anna Andreevna is a rascal! She'll hoodwink you, and me, and the whole world! I've been waiting for you, because you're better able to finish with the other one."

"What other one?"

"With *Madame* Akhmakov. I know everything. You told me yourself that she's afraid of the letter you've got..."

"What letter... you're lying... Have you seen her?" I muttered in confusion.

"I've seen her. She's good-looking. *Très belle*,* and you've got taste."

"I know you've seen her; only you didn't dare to speak with her, and I want you also not to dare to speak *of* her."

"You're still little, and she laughs at you—that's what! We had a pillar of virtue like her in Moscow! Oh, how she turned up her nose! But she trembled when we threatened to tell all, and she obeyed at once; and we took the one and the other: both the money and the other thing—you understand what? Now she's back in society, unapproachable—pah, the devil, how high she flies, and what a carriage, and if only you'd seen in what sort of back room it all went on! You haven't lived enough; if you knew what little back rooms they'll venture into..."

"So I've thought," I murmured irrepressibly.

"They're depraved to the tips of their fingers; you don't know what they're capable of! Alphonsine lived in one such house; she found it quite repulsive."

"I've thought about that," I confirmed again.

"They beat you, and you feel sorry..."

"Lambert, you're a villain, curse you!" I cried out, suddenly somehow understanding and trembling. "I saw it all in a dream, you stood there, and Anna Andreevna... Oh, curse you! Did you really think I was such a scoundrel? I saw it in a dream, because I just knew you were going to say it. And, finally, all this can't be so simple that you'd tell me about it all so simply and directly!"

"Look how angry he is! Tut-tut-tut!" Lambert drawled, laughing and triumphant. "Well, brother Arkashka, now I've learned all I needed to know. That's why I was waiting for you. Listen, it means you love her and want to take revenge on Bjoring—that's what I

*Very beautiful.

needed to know. I suspected it all along, while I was waiting for you. *Ceci posé, celà change la question.** And so much the better, because she loves you herself. So get married, don't delay, that's the best. And you can't possibly do otherwise, you've hit on the right thing. And then know, Arkady, that you have a friend—me, that is—whom you can saddle and ride on. This friend will help you and get you married; I'll leave no stone unturned, Arkasha! And afterwards you can give your old friend thirty thousand for his labors, eh? But I will help you, don't doubt that. I know all the fine points in these matters, and they'll give you a whole dowry, and you'll be a rich man with a career!"

Though my head was spinning, I looked at Lambert in amazement. He was serious, that is, not really serious, but I could see clearly that he fully believed in the possibility of getting me married, and even accepted the idea with rapture. Naturally, I also saw that he was trying to ensnare me like a little boy (I saw it right then for certain), but the thought of marrying her so pierced me through that, though I was astonished at Lambert's ability to believe in such a fantasy, at the same time I rushed to believe it myself, though without losing even for a moment the awareness that, of course, it couldn't be realized for anything. It somehow all sank in together.

"Can it be possible?" I babbled.

"Why not? You'll show her the document—she'll turn coward and marry you so as not to lose the money."

I decided not to stop Lambert in his meanness, because he laid it out for me so simpleheartedly that he didn't even suspect I might suddenly become indignant; but I murmured, nevertheless, that I wouldn't want to marry only by force.

"Not for anything do I want to use force; how can you be so mean as to suppose that in me?"

"Ehh! She'll marry you of herself: it won't be your doing, she'll get frightened herself and marry you. And she'll also do it because she loves you," Lambert caught himself.

"That's a lie. You're laughing at me. How do you know she loves me?"

"Absolutely. I know. And Anna Andreevna thinks so, too. I'm telling you seriously and truthfully that Anna Andreevna thinks so. And then I'll also tell you another thing, when you come to my

*Put that in, and it changes the question.

place, and you'll see that she loves you. Alphonsine was in Tsarskoe; she also found things out there..."

"What could she have found out there?"

"Let's go to my place. She'll tell you herself, and you'll be pleased. What makes you worse than another man? You're handsome, you're well bred..."

"Yes, I'm well bred," I whispered, barely pausing for breath. My heart was throbbing and, of course, not from wine alone.

"You're handsome. You're well dressed."

"Yes, I'm well dressed..."

"And you're kind..."

"Yes, I'm kind."

"Then why shouldn't she agree? After all, Bjoring won't take her without money, and you can deprive her of money—so she'll get frightened; you'll marry her, and that will be your revenge on Bjoring. You told me yourself that night, after you froze, that she was in love with you."

"Did I tell you that? Surely I didn't put it that way."

"No, that way."

"I was delirious. Surely I must also have told you then about the document?"

"Yes, you said you had this letter, and I thought: since he has such a letter, why should he lose what's his?"

"This is all fantasy, and I'm by no means so stupid as to believe it," I muttered. "First, there's the difference in age, and, second, I have no name."

"She'll marry you; she can't do otherwise when so much money's to be lost—I'll arrange that. And besides, she loves you. You know, that old prince is quite well disposed towards you; through his patronage you know what sort of connections you could make; and as for the fact that you have no name, nowadays that's all unnecessary: once you've grabbed the money, you'll get on, you'll get on, and in ten years you'll be such a millionaire that all Russia will be talking, and what name do you need then? You can buy up a baron in Austria. But once you marry her, you'll have to keep her in hand. They need it good and proper. A woman, if she's in love, likes to be kept in a tight fist. A woman likes character in a man. But once you frighten her with the letter, from that time on you'll also show her your character. 'Ah,' she'll say, 'so young, but he's got character.'"

I was sitting there as if bemused. Never would I have stooped to such a stupid conversation with anyone else. But here some sweet longing drew me into continuing it. Besides, Lambert was so stupid and mean that it was impossible to be ashamed before him.

"No, Lambert, you know," I said suddenly, "as you like, but there's a lot of nonsense here; I'm talking to you because we're comrades, and there's nothing for us to be ashamed of; but with anyone else I wouldn't have demeaned myself for anything. And, above all, why do you insist so much that she loves me? You spoke very well about capital just now, but you see, Lambert, you don't know high society: with them it all rests on the most patriarchal, familial, so to speak, relations, so that now, when she still doesn't know my abilities and how far I may get in life—now in any case she'll be ashamed. But I won't conceal from you, Lambert, that there is indeed one point here which may give hope. You see: she might marry me out of gratitude, because then I'd rid her of a certain man's hatred. And she's afraid of that man."

"Ah, you mean your father? And what, does he love her very much?" Lambert suddenly roused himself with extraordinary curiosity.

"Oh, no!" I cried. "And how frightening you are, and at the same time how stupid, Lambert! I mean, if he was in love with her, how could I want to marry her? After all, a son and a father—that would be shameful. It's mama he loves, mama, and I saw him embrace her, and before that I myself thought he loved Katerina Nikolaevna, but now I know clearly that he maybe loved her once, but for a long time now he's hated her... and wanted revenge, and she's afraid, because, I'll tell you, Lambert, he's terribly frightening once he starts on revenge. He almost turns into a madman. When he's angry with her, he can go to any lengths. It's an enmity of the old kind over lofty principles. In our time we spit on all general principles; in our time it's not general principles, it's only special cases. Ah, Lambert, you understand nothing, you're as stupid as my big toe: I'm talking to you about these principles, but you surely understand none of it. You're terribly uneducated. Do you remember beating me? I'm now stronger than you—do you know that?"

"Arkashka, let's go to my place! We'll spend the evening and drink another bottle, and Alphonsine will play the guitar and sing."

"No, I won't go. Listen, Lambert, I have an 'idea.' If things don't work out and I don't get married, then I'll go into my idea; but you have no idea."

"All right, all right, you'll tell me, let's go."

"I'm not going!" I got up. "I don't want to and I won't. I'll come to see you, but you're a scoundrel. I'll give you the thirty thousand—so be it, but I'm purer and higher than you . . . I can see that you want to deceive me in everything. And about her I even forbid you to think: she's higher than everyone, and your plans are so base that I'm even surprised at you, Lambert. I want to get married—that's another matter, but I don't need capital, I despise capital. If she gives me her capital on her knees, I won't take it . . . But getting married, getting married, that's—another matter. And you know, you said it well about keeping her in a tight fist. To love, to love passionately, with all a man's magnanimity, which can never be found in a woman, but also to be despotic—that's a good thing. Because, Lambert, you know what—women love despotism. You know women, Lambert. But you're astonishingly stupid in everything else. And, you know, Lambert, you're not at all as vile as you seem, you're—simple. I like you. Ah, Lambert, why are you such a knave? Otherwise we could live so merrily! You know, Trishatov's a dear man."

I babbled these last incoherent phrases when we were already in the street. Oh, I'm recalling it all in detail, to let the reader see that, for all my raptures and for all my vows and promises to be regenerated for the better and to seek seemliness, I could fall so easily then, and into such mire! And I swear, if I weren't fully and completely certain that I'm not at all like that now and that I have developed my character through practical life, I would not have confessed all this to the reader for anything.

We came out of the shop, and Lambert supported me, putting his arm lightly around me. Suddenly I looked at him and saw almost the same expression in his eyes—intent, scrutinizing, terribly attentive, and at the same time sober in the highest degree—as on that morning when I was freezing and he led me to a cab, with his arm around me in exactly the same way, and listened, all ears and eyes, to my incoherent babble. People who are getting drunk, but are not quite drunk yet, can suddenly have moments of the fullest sobriety.

"I won't go to your place for anything!" I uttered firmly and coherently, looking at him mockingly and pushing him away with my hand.

"Ah, come on, I'll tell Alphonsine to make tea, come on!"

He was terribly certain that I wouldn't escape; he held and supported me with relish, like a dear little victim, and I, of course, was just what he needed, precisely that evening and in that condition! Why—will be explained later.

"I'm not going!" I repeated. "Cabbie!"

Just then a cab came trotting up, and I hopped into the sledge.

"Where are you going? What's with you?" yelled Lambert, in terrible alarm, seizing my fur coat.

"And don't you dare follow me," I cried, "don't try to overtake me!" At that moment the cab started, and my coat was torn from Lambert's hand.

"You'll come anyway!" he shouted after me in an angry voice.

"I'll come if I want to—by my own will!" I turned to him from the sledge.

II

He didn't pursue me, of course, because there happened to be no other cab at hand, and I managed to disappear from his sight. I drove only as far as the Haymarket, and there I got out and dismissed the sledge. I wanted terribly to go by foot. I felt no fatigue, no great drunkenness, but was just full of vigor; there was an influx of strength, there was an extraordinary ability for any undertaking, and an endless number of pleasant thoughts in my head.

My heart was pounding intensely and distinctly—I could hear each beat. And everything seemed so nice to me, everything was so easy. Walking past the guardhouse on the Haymarket, I wanted terribly to go up to the sentry and kiss him. There was a thaw, the square turned black and smelly, but the square, too, I liked very much.

"I'll go to Obukhovsky Prospect now," I thought, "then turn left and come out in the Semyonovsky quarter, I'll make a detour, it's excellent, it's all excellent. My fur coat's unbuttoned—why doesn't anybody take it off me, where are the thieves? They say there are thieves in the Haymarket, let them come, maybe I'll give them my fur coat. What do I need a fur coat for? A fur coat is property. *La propriété, c'est le vol.**[29] But anyhow, what nonsense, and how good everything is. It's good that there's a thaw. Why frost? There's no need at all for frost. It's also good to talk nonsense. What was it I said to Lambert about principles? I said there are no general

*Property is theft.

principles, but only special cases. That's nonsense, that's arch-nonsense! I said it on purpose, to show off. It's a bit shameful, but anyhow—never mind, I'll smooth it over. Don't be ashamed, don't torment yourself, Arkady Makarovich. Arkady Makarovich, I like you. I even like you very much, my young friend. It's too bad you're a little knave . . . and . . . and . . . ah, yes . . . ah!"

I suddenly stopped, and again my whole heart was wrung in ecstasy:

"Lord! What was it he said? He said she loves me. Oh, he's a crook, he told a lot of lies here; it was so that I'd go and spend the night with him. But maybe not. He said Anna Andreevna thought so, too . . . Bah! Nastasya Egorovna could also find out a thing or two here: she pokes around everywhere. And why didn't I go to his place? I'd learn everything. Hm! he's got a plan, and I anticipated it all to the last stroke. A dream. It's broadly conceived, Mr. Lambert, only you're wrong, it won't be that way. But maybe it will! Maybe it will! And can he really get me married? But maybe he can. He's naïve and credulous. He's stupid and impudent, like all practical people. Stupidity and impudence, joined together, are a great force. And confess that you were in fact afraid of Lambert, Arkady Makarovich! What does he need honest people for? He says it so seriously: there's not one honest man here! And you yourself—who are you? Eh, never mind me! Don't scoundrels need honest people? In knavery, honest people are more needed than anywhere else. Ha, ha! You're the only one who didn't know that before, Arkady Makarovich, with your total innocence. Lord! What if he really gets me married!"

I paused again. Here I must confess one stupidity (since it happened so long ago), I must confess that I had already wanted to marry long before—that is, I didn't want to and it would never have happened (and it won't in the future, I give my word), but already more than once and long before then I had dreamed of how nice it would be to get married—that is, terribly many times, especially on going to sleep each night. This began with me when I was almost sixteen. I had a schoolmate, Lavrovsky, the same age as me—such a nice, quiet, pretty boy, though not distinguished in any way. I hardly ever spoke to him. Suddenly one day we were sitting next to each other alone, and he was very pensive, and suddenly he says to me, "Ah, Dolgoruky, what do you think about getting married now? Really, when should one get married if not now? Now would be the very best time, and yet it's quite impossible!" And he said it so candidly. And I suddenly agreed with him wholeheartedly, because I myself had dreamed of something like it. Then we came together for several days in a row and kept talking about it, as if in secret, though only about that. And then, I don't know how it happened, but we drifted apart and stopped talking. But ever since then I began to dream. This, of course, would not be worth recalling, but I only wanted to show how far back these things can sometimes go . . .

"There's only one serious objection here," I went on dreaming as I walked. "Oh, of course, the insignificant difference in age would be no obstacle, but there's this: she's such an aristocrat, and I'm—simply Dolgoruky! Awfully nasty! Hm! Surely Versilov, once he's married my mother, could ask the authorities for permission to adopt me . . . for the father's services, so to speak . . . He was in the service, so of course there were services; he was an arbiter of the peace . . . Oh, devil take it, what vileness!"

I suddenly exclaimed that and suddenly stopped for the third time, but now as if squashed on the spot. All the painful feeling of humiliation from the consciousness that I could wish for such a disgrace as a change of name through adoption, this betrayal of my whole childhood—all this in almost one instant destroyed my whole previous mood, and all my joy vanished like smoke. "No, I won't tell this to anyone," I thought, blushing terribly. "I stooped so low because I'm . . . in love and stupid. No, if Lambert is right about anything, it's that nowadays all this foolishness is simply not required, and that the main thing in our age is the man himself, and then his money. That is, not his money, but his power. With my capital I'll throw myself into the 'idea,' and in ten years all Russia will be talking, and I'll have my revenge on everyone. And there's no need to be ceremonious with her, here again Lambert is right. She'll turn coward and simply marry me. In the simplest and most banal way, she'll accept and marry me. 'You don't know, you don't know in what sort of back room it went on!' " Lambert's words came to my mind. "And that's so," I confirmed, "Lambert is right in everything, a thousand times righter than I, and Versilov, and all these idealists! He's a realist. She'll see that I have character and say, 'Ah, he has character!' Lambert is a scoundrel, and all he wants is to fleece me of thirty thousand, and yet he's the only friend I've got. There is no other friendship and cannot be, that was all invented by impractical people. And I don't even humiliate her; do I humiliate her? Not a bit: women are all like that! Can there be a woman without meanness? That's why she needs to have man over her, that's why she was created a subordinate being. Woman is vice and temptation, and man is nobility and magnanimity. And so it will be unto ages of ages. And never mind that I'm preparing to use the 'document.' That won't prevent either nobility or magnanimity. Schillers in a pure form don't exist—they've been invented. Never mind a little dirt, if the goal is splendid! Afterwards it will all be washed away, smoothed over. And now it's only—breadth, it's only—life, it's only—life's truth—that's what they call it now!"

Oh, again I repeat: may I be forgiven for citing to the last line all this drunken raving from that time. Of course, this is only the essence of my thoughts from that time, but I believe I did speak in those very words. I had to cite them, because I sat down to write in order to judge myself. And what am I to judge, if not that? Can there be anything more serious in life? Wine is no justification. *In vino veritas.**

Dreaming thus and all buried in fantasy, I didn't notice that I had finally reached home, that is, mama's apartment. I didn't even notice how I entered the apartment; but as soon as I stepped into our tiny front hall, I understood at once that something extraordinary had happened. In the rooms they were talking loudly, exclaiming, and mama could be heard weeping. In the doorway I was almost knocked off my feet by Lukerya, who ran swiftly from Makar Ivanovich's room to the kitchen. I threw off my coat and went into Makar Ivanovich's room, because everyone was crowded there.

There stood Versilov and mama. Mama lay in his arms, and he pressed her tightly to his heart. Makar Ivanovich was sitting, as usual, on his little bench, but as if in some sort of strengthlessness, so that Liza had to support him by the shoulders with her arms to keep him from falling; and it was even obvious that he was all leaning over so as to fall. I swiftly stepped closer, gave a start, and realized that the old man was dead.

He had only just died, about a minute before my arrival. Ten minutes earlier he had felt as much himself as ever. Only Liza was with him; she was sitting with him and telling him about her grief, and he was stroking her hair as the day before. Suddenly he trembled all over (Liza told us), made as if to stand up, made as if to cry out, and silently began to fall towards the left. "Heart failure!" said Versilov. Liza cried out for the whole house to hear, and

*The truth's in wine.

it was then that they came running—all that about a minute before my arrival.

"Arkady!" Versilov shouted to me. "Run instantly to Tatyana Pavlovna's. She should certainly be at home. Ask her to come at once. Take a cab. Quickly, I beg you!"

His eyes were flashing—I remember that clearly. I didn't notice in his face anything like pure pity, tears—only mama, Liza, and Lukerya were weeping. On the contrary, and this I recall very well, what was striking in his face was some extraordinary excitement, almost ecstasy. I ran for Tatyana Pavlovna.

The way, as is known from the foregoing, wasn't long. I didn't take a cab, but ran all the way without stopping. There was confusion in my mind, and also even almost something ecstatic. I realized that a radical event had happened. The drunkenness had disappeared completely in me, to the last drop, and along with it all ignoble thoughts, by the time I rang at Tatyana Pavlovna's.

The Finnish woman unlocked the door: "Not at home!" and wanted to lock it at once.

"What do you mean, not at home?" I burst into the front hall by force. "It can't be! Makar Ivanovich is dead!"

"Wha-a-at?" Tatyana Pavlovna's cry suddenly rang out through the closed door of her drawing room.

"Dead! Makar Ivanovich is dead! Andrei Petrovich asks you to come this minute."

"No, you're lying! . . ."

The latch clicked, but the door opened only an inch: "What is it, tell me!"

"I don't know myself, I just arrived and he was already dead. Andrei Petrovich says it's heart failure!"

"At once, this minute. Run, tell them I'll be there. Go on, go on, go on! Well, what are you standing there for?"

But I saw clearly through the half-opened door that someone had come out from behind the curtain that screened Tatyana Pavlovna's bed and was standing there in the room behind Tatyana Pavlovna. Mechanically, instinctively, I seized the latch and would not let her close the door.

"Arkady Makarovich! Is it really true that he's dead?" the familiar, soft, smooth, metallic voice rang out, at which everything began to tremble in my soul all at once: in the question something could be heard that had penetrated and stirred *her* soul.

"In that case," Tatyana Pavlovna suddenly abandoned the door, "in that case—settle it between you as you like. You want it that way!"

She rushed impetuously out of the apartment, putting on her kerchief and coat as she ran, and started down the stairs. We were left alone. I threw off my coat, stepped in, and closed the door behind me. She stood before me as she had when we met the other time, with a bright face, a bright gaze, and, as then, reached both hands out to me. As if cut down, I literally fell at her feet.

III

I WAS BEGINNING to weep, I don't know why; I don't remember how she sat me down beside her, I only remember, in a memory that is priceless for me, how we sat next to each other, hand in hand, and talked impetuously: she was asking about the old man and his death, and I was telling her about him—so that one might have thought I was weeping over Makar Ivanovich, whereas that would have been the height of absurdity; and I know that she could never have supposed in me such a thoroughly childish banality. At last I suddenly recollected myself and felt ashamed. Now I suppose that I wept then solely out of ecstasy, and I think she understood it very well herself, so that with regard to this memory I'm at peace.

It suddenly seemed very strange to me that she should keep asking like that about Makar Ivanovich.

"Did you know him?" I asked in surprise.

"For a long time. I've never seen him, but he has played a role in my life, too. At one time the man I'm afraid of told me a great deal about him. You know who that man is."

"I only know now that 'the man' was much nearer to your soul than you revealed to me before," I said, not knowing myself what I meant to express by it, but as if in reproach and frowning deeply.

"You say he was kissing your mother just now? Embracing her? You saw it yourself?" she went on asking without listening to me.

"Yes, I saw it; and, believe me, it was all sincere and magnanimous in the highest degree!" I hastened to confirm, seeing her joy.

"God grant it!" She crossed herself. "Now he's unbound. That beautiful old man only bound his life. With his death, duty and... dignity will resurrect in him again, as they already resurrected once. Oh, he's magnanimous before all else, he'll give peace to the heart of your mother, whom he loves more than anything on earth, and he himself will finally be at peace, and thank God—it's high time."

"Is he very dear to you?"

"Yes, very dear, though not in the sense in which he himself would wish and in which you're asking."

"So are you afraid now for him or for yourself?" I asked suddenly.

"Well, these are intricate questions, let's drop them."

"Let's drop them, of course; only I was ignorant of that, all too much so, maybe; but let it be, you're right, everything's new now, and if anyone is resurrected, it's me first of all. I've been mean in my thoughts before you, Katerina Nikolaevna, and maybe no more than an hour ago I committed a meanness against you in deed as well, but you know, here I am sitting next to you, and I feel no remorse. Because everything has vanished now, and everything is new, and that man who was plotting a meanness against you an hour ago, I don't know and do not want to know!"

"Come to your senses," she smiled, "it's as if you're slightly delirious."

"And how can a man possibly judge himself sitting next to you," I went on, "whether he's honest or mean? You're like the sun, unattainable... Tell me, how could you come out to me after all that's happened? If you knew what happened an hour ago, only an hour? What sort of dream was coming true?"

"I probably know everything," she smiled gently. "You wanted to take revenge on me for something just now, swore to ruin me, and certainly would have killed or beaten anyone who uttered even one bad word about me in your presence."

Oh, she was smiling and joking; but it was only from her immeasurable kindness, because her whole soul was filled at that moment, as I later realized, with such enormous care of her own and such strong and powerful feeling, that she could talk with me and answer my trifling, irksome questions only as one answers a little boy who has asked some importunate, childish question, in order to get rid of him. I suddenly understood that and felt ashamed, but I was no longer able to stop.

"No," I cried, losing control of myself, "no, I didn't kill the one who spoke badly of you, but, on the contrary, I even seconded him!"

"Oh, for God's sake, don't, there's no need, don't tell me anything," she suddenly reached her hand out to stop me, and even with a sort of suffering in her face, but I had already jumped up from my seat and stood before her in order to speak everything out, and if I had spoken it out, what happened later wouldn't have happened, because it would certainly have ended with my confessing everything and returning the document to her. But she suddenly laughed:

"Don't, don't say anything, no details! I know all your crimes myself. I'll bet you wanted to marry me or something like that, and were just talking it over with one of your accomplices, a former schoolmate of yours... Ah, it seems I've guessed right!" she cried, peering gravely into my face.

"How... how could you guess?" I stammered like a fool, terribly struck.

"Well, what else! But enough, enough! I forgive you, only stop talking about it," she waved her hand again, now with visible impatience. "I'm a dreamer myself, and if you knew what means I resort to in my dreams when nothing holds me back! Enough, you keep confusing me. I'm very glad that Tatyana Pavlovna left; I wanted very much to see you, and with her here it would be impossible to speak as we're doing now. It seems I'm guilty before you for what happened then. Right? Am I right?"

"You, guilty? But I betrayed you to *him* then and—what can you have thought of me! I've been thinking about that all this time, all these days, ever since then, every moment, thinking and feeling." (I wasn't lying to her.)

"You needn't have tormented yourself so much, I understood only too well then how it all happened; you simply blurted out to him in joy that you were in love with me and that I... well, that I had listened to you. That's twenty years old for you. You do love him more than anything in the world, you're looking for a friend, an ideal in him? I understood that only too well, but it was too late. Oh, yes, I was the guilty one then: I should have sent for you right then and put you at ease, but I was vexed; and I requested that you not be received in the house; and what came of it was that scene at the front door, and then that night. And you know, all this time, just like you, I've dreamed of meeting you secretly, only I didn't know how to arrange it. And what do you think I feared most? That you would believe his slander against me."

"Never!" I cried.

"I value our former meetings; your youth is dear to me, and even, perhaps, this sincerity itself... For I'm a most serious character. I'm the most serious and scowling character of all modern women, know that . . . ha, ha, ha! We'll talk our fill some other time, but now I'm a bit out of sorts, I'm agitated and . . . it seems I'm in hysterics. But at last, at last, *he* will let me live in the world, too!"

This exclamation escaped involuntarily; I understood that at once and didn't want to pick it up, but I trembled all over.

"He knows I've forgiven him!" she suddenly exclaimed again, as if to herself.

"Could you really have forgiven him that letter? And how can he know that you've forgiven him?" I exclaimed, no longer restraining myself.

"How does he know? Oh, he knows," she went on answering me, but looked as if she had forgotten me and was talking to herself. "He's come to his senses now. And how could he not know I've forgiven him, since he knows my soul by heart? He knows I'm somewhat of the same sort as he."

"You?"

"Well, yes, he's aware of that. Oh, I'm not passionate, I'm calm: but, like him, I also want everybody to be good . . . He does love me for something after all."

"Then how is it he said you have all the vices?"

"He just said that; he's keeping another secret to himself. And isn't it true that the way he wrote his letter is terribly funny?"

"Funny?" (I was listening to her with all my might; I suppose she really was as if in hysterics and . . . maybe wasn't speaking for me at all; but I couldn't keep myself from asking.)

"Oh, yes, funny, and how I'd laugh if . . . if I wasn't afraid. Though I'm not such a coward, don't think it; but on account of that letter I didn't sleep all that night, it's written as if with some sort of sick blood . . . and after such a letter, what's left? I love life, I'm terribly afraid for my life, I'm terribly pusillanimous about it . . . Ah, listen!" she suddenly roused herself. "Go to him! He's alone now, he can't be there all the time, he must have gone somewhere alone. Find him quickly, you must, run to him quickly, show him you're his loving son, prove to him that you're a dear, kind boy, my student, whom I . . . Oh, God grant you happiness! I don't love anyone, and it's better that way, but I wish everyone happiness, everyone, and him first, and let him know of it . . . even right now, I'd be very pleased . . ."

She got up and suddenly disappeared behind the portière; tears glistened on her cheeks at that moment (hysterical, after laughing). I remained alone, agitated and confused. I positively did not know to what to ascribe such agitation in her, which I could never have supposed in her. It was as if something contracted in my heart.

I waited five minutes, and finally ten; I was suddenly struck by the profound silence, and I ventured to peek through the door and call out. At my call, Marya appeared and declared to me in the most calm voice that the lady had long since dressed and gone out by the back door.

Chapter Seven

I

THAT WAS ALL I needed. I grabbed my fur coat and, putting it on as I went, ran outside, thinking, "She told me to go to him, but where am I going to get him?"

But, apart from everything else, I was struck by the question, "Why does she think something's come now and *he* will give her peace? Of course, because he's going to marry mama, but what about her? Is she glad that he's marrying mama, or, on the contrary, is that what makes her unhappy? Is that why she's in hysterics? Why can't I resolve this?"

I note this second thought that flashed in me then literally, as a reminder: it's important. That evening was fateful. And here, perhaps, against one's will, one comes to believe in predestination: I hadn't gone a hundred steps in the direction of mama's apartment, when I suddenly ran into the man I was looking for. He seized my shoulder and stopped me.

"It's you!" he cried joyfully and at the same time as if in the greatest astonishment. "Imagine, I went to your place," he spoke quickly, "looking for you, asking for you—you're the only one I need now in the whole universe! Your official told me God knows what lies; but you weren't at home, and I left, even forgetting to ask him to tell you to run to me at once—and what then? I was going along in the unshakable conviction that fate couldn't help sending you now, when I need you most, and here you're the first one I meet! Let's go to my place. You've never been to my place."

In short, the two of us had been looking for each other, and something similar, as it were, had happened to each of us. We walked on, hurrying very much.

On the way he just uttered a few short phrases about having left mama with Tatyana Pavlovna, and so on. He led me, holding on to my arm. He lived not far away, and we got there quickly. I had, in fact, never been to his place. It was a small apartment of three rooms, which he rented (or, more correctly, Tatyana Pavlovna rented) solely for that "nursing baby." This apartment had always been under Tatyana Pavlovna's supervision, and was inhabited by a nanny with the baby (and now also by Nastasya Egorovna); but there had always been a room for Versilov as well—namely, the very first one, by the front door, rather spacious and rather well and plushly furnished, a sort of study for bookish and scribal occupations. In fact, there were many books on the table, in the bookcase, and on the shelves (while at mama's there were almost none at all); there were pages covered with writing, there were tied-up bundles of letters—in short, it all had the look of a corner long lived in, and I know that, before as well, Versilov had sometimes (though rather rarely) moved to this apartment altogether and stayed in it even for weeks at a time. The first thing that caught my attention was a portrait of mama that hung over the desk, in a magnificent carved frame of costly wood—a photograph, taken abroad, of course, and, judging by its extraordinary size, a very costly thing. I hadn't known and had never heard of this portrait before, and the main thing that struck me was the extraordinary likeness in the photograph, a spiritual likeness, so to speak—in short, as if it was a real portrait by an artist's hand, and not a mechanical print. As soon as I came in, I stopped involuntarily before it.

"Isn't it? Isn't it?" Versilov suddenly repeated over me.

That is, "Isn't it just like her?" I turned to look at him and was struck by the expression of his face. He was somewhat pale, but with an ardent, intense gaze, as if radiant with happiness and strength. I had never known him to have such an expression.

"I didn't know you loved mama so much!" I suddenly blurted out, in rapture myself.

He smiled blissfully, though there was a reflection as if of some suffering in his smile, or, better, of something humane, lofty... I don't know how to say it; but highly developed people, it seems to me, cannot have triumphant and victoriously happy faces. Without answering me, he took the portrait from the rings with both hands, brought it close, kissed it, then quietly hung it back on the wall.

"Notice," he said, "it's extremely rare that photographic copies bear any resemblance, and that's understandable: it's extremely rare that the original itself, that is, each of us, happens to resemble itself. Only in rare moments does a human face express its main feature, its most characteristic thought. An artist studies a face and divines its main thought, though at the moment of painting it might be absent from the face. A photograph finds the man as he is, and it's quite possible that Napoleon, at some moment, would come out stupid, and Bismarck tenderhearted. But here, in this portrait, the sun, as if on purpose, found Sonya in her main moment—of modest, meek love and her somewhat wild, timorous chastity. And how happy she was then, when she was finally convinced that I was so eager to have her portrait! This picture was taken not so long ago, but all the same she was younger and better looking then; though there were already those sunken cheeks, those little wrinkles on her forehead, that timorous shyness in her eyes, which seems to be increasing in her more and more with the years. Would you believe it, my dear? I can hardly imagine her now with a different face, and yet once she was young and lovely! Russian women lose their looks quickly, their beauty is fleeting, and in truth that's not only owing to the ethnographic properties of the type, but also to the fact that they're capable of loving unreservedly. A Russian woman gives everything at once if she loves—moment and destiny, present and future. They don't know how to economize, they don't lay anything aside, and their beauty quickly goes into the one they love. Those sunken cheeks—that is also a beauty gone into me, into my brief bit of fun. You're glad I loved your mother, and maybe you didn't even believe I loved her? Yes, my friend, I loved her very much, yet I did her nothing but harm... There's another portrait here—look at it as well."

He took it from the desk and handed it to me. It was also a photograph, of an incomparably smaller size, in a slender oval wooden border—the face of a girl, thin and consumptive and, for all that, beautiful; pensive and at the same time strangely devoid of thought. Regular features, of a type fostered over generations, yet leaving a painful impression: it looked as though this being had suddenly been possessed by some fixed idea, tormenting precisely because it was beyond this being's strength.

"This... this is the girl you wanted to marry there and who died of consumption... *her* stepdaughter?" I said somewhat timidly.

"Yes, wanted to marry, died of consumption, *her* stepdaughter. I knew you knew... all that gossip. However, apart from gossip, you couldn't have known anything here. Let the portrait be, my friend, this is a poor madwoman and nothing more."

"Quite mad?"

"Or else an idiot. However, I think she was mad as well. She had a child by Prince Sergei Petrovich (out of madness, not out of love; that was one of Sergei Petrovich's meanest acts); the child is here now, in the other room, I've long wanted to show it to you.

Prince Sergei Petrovich didn't dare to come here and look at the baby; I made that stipulation with him while we were still abroad. I took it under my care with your mama's permission. With your mama's permission I also wanted then to marry that... unfortunate woman..."

"Was such permission possible?" I uttered hotly.

"Oh, yes! she gave it to me. One gets jealous of a woman, and that was not a woman."

"Not a woman for anybody except mama! Never in my life will I believe that mama wasn't jealous!" I cried.

"And you're right. I realized it only when it was all over—that is, when she had given her permission. But let's drop it. The affair didn't work out on account of Lydia's death, and maybe it wouldn't have worked out even if she had remained alive, but even now I don't let mama see the child. It was merely an episode. My dear, I've long been waiting for you to come here. I've long been dreaming of how we'd get together here. Do you know how long? For two years now."

He looked at me sincerely and truthfully, with an unreserved warmth of heart. I seized his hand:

"Why were you so slow, why didn't you invite me long ago? If you knew what has happened... and what wouldn't have happened if you had called me long ago!..."

At that moment the samovar was brought in, and Nastasya Egorovna suddenly brought in the baby, asleep.

"Look at him," said Versilov. "I love him, and I had him brought now on purpose, so that you could also look at him. Well, take him away again, Nastasya Egorovna. Sit down to the samovar. I'm going to imagine that we've lived like this forever and have come together every evening, never parting. Let me look at you; sit like this, so that I can see your face! How I love your face! How I kept imagining your face to myself, as I was waiting for you to come from Moscow! You ask why I didn't send for you long ago? Wait, maybe now you'll understand."

"But can it be only this old man's death that has loosened your tongue now? It's strange..."

But though I did say that, I still looked at him with love. We talked like two friends in the highest and fullest sense of the word. He had brought me here to explain, to recount, to justify something to me; and yet everything was already explained and justified before any words. Whatever I was to hear from him now, the result had already been achieved, and we both happily knew it and looked at each other that way.

"It's not exactly this old man's death," he replied, "not only his death; there's something else now that has hit on the same spot... May God bless this moment and our life, for a long time to come! Let's talk, my dear! I keep getting broken up, diverted, I want to talk about one thing and get sidetracked into a thousand other details. That always happens when one's heart is full... But let's talk; the time has come, and I've long been in love with you, my boy..."

He leaned back in his armchair and looked me over once more.

"How strange! How strange it is to hear that!" I repeated, drowning in ecstasy.

And then, I remember, in his face there suddenly flashed the usual wrinkle—as if of sadness and mockery together—which I knew so well. He controlled himself and, as if with a certain strain, began.

II

"HERE'S THE THING, Arkady: if I had invited you earlier, what would I have said to you? In this question lies my whole answer."

"That is, you mean to say that you're now mama's husband and my father, while then... You wouldn't have known before what to say about my social position? Is that it?"

"That's not the only thing I wouldn't have known what to say about, my dear; there's much here that I would have had to pass over in silence. There's even much here that's ridiculous and humiliating, because it looks like a trick—really, like a most farcical trick. Well, how could we have understood each other before, if I understood myself only today, at five o'clock in the afternoon, exactly two hours before Makar Ivanovich's death? You look at me with unpleasant perplexity? Don't worry, I'll explain the trick; but what I said is quite right: life is all wanderings and perplexities, and suddenly—the resolution, on such-and-such a day, at five o'clock in the afternoon! It's even offensive, isn't it? In the still-recent old days I'd have been quite offended."

I was actually listening in painful perplexity; there was a strong presence of the former Versilovian wrinkle, which I had no wish to encounter that evening, after the words that had been spoken. Suddenly I exclaimed:

"My God! You got something from her... at five o'clock today?"

He looked at me intently and was evidently struck by my exclamation, and maybe also by my saying "from her."

"You'll learn everything," he said with a pensive smile, "and, of course, I won't conceal from you what you need to know, because that's what I brought you here for; but let's set it aside for now. You see, my friend, I've long known that we have children who brood about their families from childhood on, who are outraged by the unseemliness of their fathers and their surroundings. I noticed these brooders while I was still in school, and concluded then that it was all because they became envious very early on. Note, however, that I myself was one of these brooding children, but... excuse me, my dear, I'm surprisingly distracted. I only wanted to say how constantly I've been afraid for you here almost all this time. I always imagined you as one of those little beings who are conscious of their giftedness and given over to solitude. Like you, I also never cared for my comrades. Woe to those beings who are left only to their own powers and dreams, and with a passionate, all too premature, and almost vengeful longing for seemliness—precisely 'vengeful.' But enough, my dear, I'm digressing again... Even before I began to love you, I had already imagined you and your solitary, wild dreams... But enough; in fact, I've forgotten what I started to say. However, all that still had to be spoken out. But before, before, what could I have said to you? Now I see your gaze upon me and know that it's my *son* looking at me; while even yesterday I couldn't have believed I'd ever be sitting and talking with my boy as I am today."

He was indeed becoming very distracted, but at the same time was as if touched by something.

"Now I have no need for dreams and reveries, now you are enough for me! I will follow you!" I said, giving myself to him with all my soul.

"Follow me? But my wanderings have just ended, and just today as it happens. You're too late, my dear. Today is the finale of the last act, and the curtain is coming down. This last act dragged on for a long time. It began very long ago—when I fled abroad for the last time. I abandoned everything then, and know, my dear, that I unmarried your mother then, and told her so myself. You should know that. I explained to her then that I was going away forever, and that she would never see me again. Worst of all, I even forgot to leave her any money then. Nor did I think of you for a minute. I left with the intention of remaining in Europe, my dear, and never coming home. I emigrated."

"To Herzen?[30] To take part in foreign propaganda? You've probably taken part in some conspiracy all your life?" I cried, not restraining myself.

"No, my friend, I never took part in any conspiracy. But your eyes are even flashing; I like your exclamations, my dear. No, I simply left then from yearning. From a sudden yearning. This was the yearning of a Russian nobleman—I truly can't put it any better. A nobleman's yearning—and nothing more."

"Serfdom . . . the emancipation of the people?"[31] I murmured, breathless.

"Serfdom? You think I was yearning for serfdom? Couldn't bear the emancipation of the people? Oh, no, my friend, it was we who were the emancipators. I emigrated without any spite. I had just been an arbiter of the peace and had struggled with all my might; I had struggled disinterestedly, and didn't even leave because I had gotten too little reward for my liberalism. None of us got anything then—that is, again, the ones like me. I left rather in pride than in repentance, and, believe me, quite far from thinking it was time to end my life as a humble bootmaker. *Je suis gentilhomme avant tout et je mourrai gentilhomme!** But even so I felt sad. There are maybe about a thousand men of our sort in Russia; maybe no more, in fact, but that's quite enough for an idea not to die. We are the bearers of an idea, my dear! . . . My friend, I'm talking in some strange hope that you'll understand all this gibberish. I invited you on a whim of my heart: I've long been dreaming of how I might say something to you . . . to you, precisely to you! But, anyhow . . . anyhow . . ."

"No, speak," I cried, "I see sincerity in your face again . . . So what, did Europe resurrect you then? And what was your 'nobleman's yearning'? Forgive me, dear heart, I still don't understand."

"Did Europe resurrect me? But I myself was going then to bury her!"

"To bury her?" I repeated in surprise.

He smiled.

"Arkady, my friend, my soul has waxed tender now, and my spirit

*I'm a gentleman before all and I'll die a gentleman!

is stirred. I'll never forget my first moments in Europe that time. I had lived in Europe before, but that was a special time, and I had never arrived there with such inconsolable sadness and... such love as at that time. I'll tell you one of my first impressions then, one of the dreams I had then, an actual dream. It was still in Germany. I had just left Dresden and, in my absentmindedness, had missed the station at which I should have changed direction and wound up on another branch line. They got me off at once; it was past two in the afternoon, a bright day. It was a little German town. They directed me to a hotel. I had to wait: the next train came through at eleven o'clock at night. I was even pleased to have an adventure, because I was in no particular hurry. I was wandering, my dear, just wandering. The hotel turned out to be wretched and small, but it was all covered in greenery and surrounded with beds of flowers, as always there. I was given a little room and, as I had spent the whole night on the road, I fell asleep after dinner, at four o'clock in the afternoon.

"I dreamed a dream that was completely unexpected for me, because I had never had one like it. In Dresden, in the gallery, there's a painting by Claude Lorrain—*Acis and Galatea*[32] according to the catalog, but I've always called it *The Golden Age*, I don't know why myself. I had seen it before, and then, some three days earlier, I had noticed it once again in passing. I saw this painting in my dream, but not as a painting, but as if it were something happening. However, I don't know precisely what I dreamed; it was exactly as in the painting—a corner of the Greek archipelago, and time, too, seemed to have shifted back three thousand years; gentle blue waves, islands and rocks, a flowering coast, a magic panorama in the distance, the inviting, setting sun—words can't express it. Here European mankind remembered its cradle, and the thought of it seemed to fill my soul with a kindred love. This was the earthly paradise of mankind: the gods came down from heaven and were united with people... Oh, beautiful people lived here! They woke up and fell asleep happy and innocent; the meadows and groves were filled with their songs and merry shouts; a great surplus of untouched forces went into love and simple-hearted joy. The sun poured down warmth and light on them, rejoicing over its beautiful children... A wonderful reverie, a lofty delusion of mankind! The golden age—the most incredible dream of all that have ever been, but for which people have given all their lives and all their strength, for which prophets have died and been slain, without which the peoples do not want to live and cannot even die! And it was as if I lived through this whole feeling in my dream; the cliffs and the sea and the slanting rays of the setting sun—it was as if I could still see it all when I woke up and opened my eyes, literally wet with tears. I remember that I was glad. A feeling of happiness unknown to me before went through my heart, even to the point of pain; this was an all-human love. It was already full evening; a sheaf of slanting rays came in the window of my little room, breaking through the greenery of the plants on the windowsill, pouring its light over me. And then, my friend, and then—this setting sun of the first day of European mankind, which I had seen in my dream, turned for me as soon as I woke up, in reality, into the setting sun of the last day of European mankind! At that time especially it was as if a death knell could be heard over Europe. I'm not just speaking of the war, or of the Tuileries;[33] I knew even without that that it would all pass away, the whole countenance of the old European world—sooner or later; but as a Russian European I couldn't accept it. Yes, they had just burned the Tuileries then...Oh, don't worry, I know it was 'logical,' and I understand only too well the irresistibility of the current idea, but as a bearer of the highest Russian cultural thought I couldn't accept it, because the highest Russian thought is the all-reconciliation of ideas. And who in the whole world could understand such a thought then? I wandered alone. I'm not talking about myself personally—I'm talking about Russian thought. There, there was strife and logic; there the Frenchman was only a Frenchman, and the German only a German, and that with a greater intensity than at any time in their entire history; meaning that a Frenchman never did more harm to France, or a German to his Germany, than at that time! In the whole of Europe then there wasn't a single European! I alone among all those *pétroleurs*[34] could tell them to their faces that their Tuileries was a mistake, and I alone among all the avenging conservatives could tell the avengers that the Tuileries, though a crime, still had its logic. And that was so, my boy, because I alone, as a Russian, was then *the only European* in Europe. I'm not talking about myself—I'm talking about all of Russian thought. I wandered, my friend, I wandered and knew firmly that I had to keep silent and wander. But still I felt sad. My boy, I cannot help respecting my nobility. It seems you're laughing?"

"No, I'm not laughing," I said in a deeply moved voice, "I'm not laughing at all. You've shaken my heart with your vision of the golden age, and be assured that I'm beginning to understand you. But most of all I'm glad that you respect yourself so much. I hasten to tell you so. That's something I never expected of you!"

"I've already told you that I like your exclamations, my dear," he smiled again at my naïve exclamation and, getting up from his armchair, began pacing the room without noticing it. I also got up. He went on speaking in his strange language, but with deeply penetrating thought.

III

"YES, MY BOY, I repeat to you that I can't help respecting my nobility. Over the centuries we have developed a high cultural type never seen before, which does not exist anywhere else in the world—the type of universal suffering for all. It's a Russian type, but since it's taken from the highest cultural stratum of the Russian people, that means I have the honor of belonging to it. It preserves in itself the future of Russia. There are perhaps only a thousand of us—maybe more, maybe less—but the whole of Russia has lived up to now only to produce this thousand. Too few, they'll say, indignant that so many centuries and so many millions of people have been spent for a thousand men. In my opinion, it's not too few."

I listened with strained attention. A conviction was emerging, the tendency of a whole lifetime. This "thousand men" betrayed him in such high relief! I felt that his expansiveness with me came from some external shock. He made all these ardent speeches while loving me; but the reason why he suddenly began speaking, and why he wished to speak this way precisely with me, still remained unknown to me.

"I emigrated," he went on, "and I didn't regret anything I left behind. I had served Russia then with all that was in my power, while I lived there; having left, I also continued to serve her, but only expanded the idea. But serving her in that way, I served her far more than if I had been merely a Russian, as a Frenchman then was merely a Frenchman, and a German a German. In Europe that has not yet been understood. Europe created noble types of the Frenchman, the Englishman, the German, but of her future man she still knows almost nothing. And it seems she doesn't want to know yet. And that's understandable: they're not free, and we are free. I, with my Russian yearning, was the only free man in Europe then.

"Make note of a strange thing, my friend: any Frenchman can serve not only his France, but even mankind, solely on condition that he remains most of all a Frenchman; the same applies to the Englishman and the German. Only the Russian, even in our time, that is, long before the general summing up, is capable of becoming most Russian precisely only when he is most European. That is our most essential national distinction from all the rest, and in this respect Russia is like nowhere else. In France I'm a Frenchman, with a German I'm a German, with an ancient Greek a Greek, and by that very fact I'm most Russian. By that very fact I am a real Russian, and I serve Russia most, for I put forward her chief thought. I am a pioneer of that thought. I emigrated then, but did I leave Russia? No, I continued to serve her. Granted, I did nothing in Europe; granted, I went only to wander (and I knew I went only to wander), but it was enough that I went with my thought and my consciousness. I took my Russian yearning there. Oh, it wasn't only the blood of that time that alarmed me so much, and not even the Tuileries, but all that was bound to follow. They're doomed to go on fighting for a long time, because they're still all too German and all too French, and they haven't finished their work in those roles. But I regret the destruction on the way. For a Russian, Europe is as precious as Russia; for him, every stone in her is dear and beloved. Europe was just as much our fatherland as Russia. Oh, even more! It's impossible to love Russia more than I do, but I never reproached myself for the fact that Venice, Rome, Paris, the treasures of their science and art, their whole history—are dearer to me than Russia. Oh, Russians cherish those old foreign stones, those wonders of God's old world, those fragments of holy wonders; and they're even dearer to us than to them! They have other thoughts and other feelings now, and they've ceased to cherish the old stones... A conservative there merely struggles for existence; and the *pétroleur* acts up only over the right to a crust of bread. Russia alone lives not for herself, but for thought, and you must agree, my friend, with the portentous fact that, for almost a hundred years, Russia has lived decidedly not for herself, but for Europe alone! And they? Oh, they are doomed to terrible torments before they reach the Kingdom of God."

I confess, I listened in great confusion; even the tone of his speech alarmed me, though I couldn't help being struck by the thoughts. I had a morbid fear of falseness. Suddenly I remarked to him in a stern voice:

"You just said 'the Kingdom of God.' I've heard you preached God there, and wore chains?"

"Let my chains be," he smiled, "that's something else entirely. I was not yet preaching anything then, but I was yearning for their God—that's true. They proclaimed atheism then... a small bunch of them, but that makes no difference; these were only the front-runners, but this was their first *executive* step—that's the important thing. Here again it's their logic; but there is always anguish in logic. I was of a different culture, and my heart couldn't accept it. The ingratitude with which they parted with the idea, the whistling and mudslinging were unbearable to me. The bootishness of the process alarmed me. However, reality always smacks of the boot, even with the brightest striving towards the ideal, and I, of course, should have known that. But even so, I was a man of a different type: I was free in choosing, but they were not—and I wept, wept for them, wept over the old idea, and maybe wept real tears, without any pretty words."

"You believed so strongly in God?" I asked mistrustfully.

"My friend, that question is perhaps superfluous. Let's suppose I didn't believe very much, but still I couldn't help yearning for the idea. I couldn't help imagining to myself at times how man was going to live without God and whether it would ever be possible. My heart always decided it was impossible; but a certain period was perhaps possible... For me, there is even no doubt that it will come; but here I've always imagined another picture to myself..."

"Which?"

True, he had said earlier that he was happy; of course, there was a good deal of rapturousness in his words; that is how I take much of what he said then. Without doubt, respecting this man as I do, I will not venture now to set down on paper all that we talked about then; but I will present here several strokes from the strange picture I managed to coax out of him. Above all, always and all the time before then, I had been tormented by these "chains," and I wanted to clear them up—that was why I persisted. Several fantastic and extremely strange ideas that he uttered then have remained in my heart forever.

"I imagine to myself, my dear," he began with a pensive smile, "that the battle is over and the fighting has subsided. After the curses, the mudslinging and whistling, a calm has come, and people are left *alone*, as they wished: the great former idea has left them; the great source of strength that had nourished and warmed them till then is departing, like that majestic, inviting sun in Claude Lorrain's painting, but it already seemed like the last day of mankind. And people suddenly realized that they remained quite alone, and at once felt a great orphancy. My dear boy, I've never been able to imagine people ungrateful and grown stupid. The orphaned people would at once begin pressing together more closely and lovingly; they would hold hands, understanding that they alone were now everything for each other. The great idea of immortality would disappear and would have to be replaced; and all the great abundance of the former love for the one who was himself immortality, would be turned in all of them to nature, to the world, to people, to every blade of grass. They would love the earth and life irrepressibly and in the measure to which they gradually became aware of their transient and finite state, and it would be with a special love now, not as formerly. They would begin to observe and discover such phenomena and secrets in nature as they had never supposed before, because they would look at nature with new eyes, the eyes with which a lover looks at his beloved. They would wake up and hasten to kiss each other, hurrying to love, conscious that the days were short, and that that was all they had left. They would work for each other, and each would give all he had to everyone, and would be happy in that alone. Every child would know and feel that each person on earth was like a father and mother to him. 'Tomorrow may be my last day,' each of them would think, looking at the setting sun, 'but all the same, though I die, they will all remain, and their children after them'—and this thought that they would remain, loving and trembling for each other in the same way, would replace the thought of a meeting beyond the grave. Oh, they would hasten to love, in order to extinguish the great sadness in their hearts. They would be proud and brave for themselves, but would become timorous for one another. Each would tremble for the life and happiness of each. They would become tender to each other and would not be ashamed of it, as now, and would caress each other like children. Meeting each other, they would exchange deep and meaningful looks, and there would be love and sadness in their eyes...

"My dear," he suddenly broke off with a smile, "this is all a fantasy, even quite an incredible one; but I have imagined it only too often, because all my life I've been unable to live without it and not to think of it. I'm not talking about my faith: I have no great faith, I'm a deist, a philosophical deist, like all the thousand of us, as I suppose, but . . . but it's remarkable that I've always ended my picture with a vision, as in Heine, of 'Christ on the Baltic Sea.'[35] I couldn't do without him, I couldn't help imagining him, finally, amidst the orphaned people. He would come to them, stretch out his arms to them, and say, 'How could you have forgotten me?' And here it would be as if a veil fell from everyone's eyes, and the great exultant hymn of the new and last resurrection would ring out . . .

"Let's drop it, my friend; and my 'chains' are nonsense; don't worry about them. And here's another thing: you know that I'm modest and sober of speech; if I fell to talking now, it's . . . from various feelings, and because it's with you; I'll never say it to anyone else. I add that to reassure you."

But I was even touched; the falseness I had feared wasn't there, and I was especially glad, because it became clear to me that he really was yearning and suffering and really, undoubtedly, had loved much—and for me that was the most precious thing of all. I told him so with enthusiasm.

"But you know," I suddenly added, "it seems to me that despite all your yearning, you must have been extremely happy then."

He laughed gaily.

"You're particularly apt in your observations today," he said. "Well, yes, I was happy, and how could I be unhappy with such yearning? There's no one freer and happier than a Russian European wanderer from our thousand. I say it, truly, without laughing, and there's much that's serious here. Yes, I wouldn't exchange my yearning for any other happiness. In this sense I've always been happy, my dear, all my life. And out of happiness I came to love your mama then for the first time in my life."

"How, for the first time in your life?"

"Precisely so. In my wandering and yearning, I suddenly came to love her as never before, and sent for her at once."

"Oh, tell me about that, too, tell me about mama!"

"But that's why I invited you, and, you know," he smiled gaily, "I was afraid you'd forgiven me mama on account of Herzen or some sort of little conspiracy . . ."

Chapter Eight

I

SINCE WE WENT on talking all evening then and sat till it was night, I won't quote the whole conversation, but will just set down something that explained to me, finally, one mysterious point in his life.

I'll begin by saying that for me there's no doubt that he loved mama, and if he abandoned her and "unmarried" her when he went away, it was, of course, because he had become too bored or something of the sort, which, however, happens with everyone in the world, but which is always hard to explain. Abroad, however, after a long while, he suddenly began to love mama again from afar, that is, in thought, and sent for her. "Whimsicality," they may say, but I say something else: in my opinion, here was all that can possibly be serious in human life, despite the apparent slip-slop, which I, perhaps, partly make allowances for. But I swear that I put this European yearning of his beyond question and not only on a par with, but incomparably higher than, any contemporary practical activity in the building of railroads. His love for mankind I acknowledge as a most sincere and profound feeling, without any tricks; and his love for mama as something completely unquestionable, though maybe a bit fantastic. Abroad, "in yearning and happiness," and, I'll add, in the strictest monastic solitude (this particular information I received later through Tatyana Pavlovna), he suddenly remembered mama—remembered precisely her "sunken cheeks"—and sent for her at once.

"My friend," escaped him, among other things, "I suddenly realized that my serving the idea did not free me, as a moral and reasonable being, from the duty of making at least one person happy in practice during the course of my life."

"Can such a bookish thought really have been the cause of it all?" I asked in perplexity.

"It's not a bookish thought. However, perhaps it is. Here, though, everything comes together, for I did love your mama really, sincerely, not bookishly. If I hadn't loved her so much, I wouldn't have sent for her, but would have 'made happy' some passing

German man or woman, once I had thought up the idea. And I would set it down as a commandment for any developed man to make at least one being happy in his life, unfailingly and in something, but to do it in practice, that is, in reality; just as I would set it down as a law or an obligation for every peasant to plant at least one tree in his life, in view of the deforestation of Russia; though one tree would be too little, he can be ordered to plant a tree every year. The superior and developed man, pursuing a superior thought, sometimes departs entirely from the essential, becomes ridiculous, capricious, and cold, I'd even simply say stupid, and not only in practical life, but, in the end, even stupid in his theories. Thus, the duty of occupying oneself with the practical, and of making at least one existing being happy, would in fact set everything right and refresh the benefactor himself. As a theory, it's very funny; but if it became a practice and turned into a custom, it wouldn't be stupid at all. I experienced it for myself: as soon as I began to develop this idea of a new commandment—at first, naturally, as a joke—I suddenly began to realize the full extent of my love for your mother, which lay hidden in me. Till then I had never realized that I loved her. While I lived with her I merely enjoyed her, while she had her good looks, but then I became capricious. Only in Germany did I realize that I loved her. It began with her sunken cheeks, which I could never remember and sometimes couldn't even see without a pain in my heart—a literal pain, real, physical. There are painful memories, my dear, which cause actual pain; nearly everyone has them, only people forget them; but it happens that they suddenly remember later, even only some feature, and then they can't get rid of it. I began to recall a thousand details of my life with Sonya; in the end they came to my memory of themselves, pouring in a mass, and all but tormented me while I waited for her. Most of all I was tormented by the memory of her eternal abasement before me, and of her eternally considering herself infinitely inferior to me in all respects—imagine, even the physical. She became ashamed and blushed when I sometimes looked at her hands and fingers, which were not at all aristocratic. And not her fingers only, she was ashamed of everything in herself, despite the fact that I loved her beauty. She had always been shy with me to the point of wildness, but the bad thing was that a glimpse of some sort of fear, as it were, showed in this shyness. In short, she considered herself a worthless or even almost indecent thing next to me. Truly, once in a while, at the beginning, I sometimes thought she still considered me her master and was afraid, but it wasn't that at all. And yet I swear she was better able than anyone else to understand my shortcomings, and never in my life have I met a woman with such a subtle and discerning heart. Oh, how unhappy she was in the beginning, while she was still so good looking, when I demanded that she dress up. There was self-love in it, and also some other offended feeling: she realized that she could never be a lady, and that wearing clothes that weren't for her only made her ridiculous. As a woman, she didn't want to feel ridiculous in her clothes, and she realized that every woman had to wear dresses that were *hers*—something that thousands and hundreds of thousands of women will never realize, so long as they're dressed fashionably. She was afraid of my mocking look—that's what it was! But it was especially sad for me to recall her deeply astonished look, which I often caught on me during all our time. It bespoke a perfect understanding of her fate and of the future in store for her, so that it even made me feel bad, though, I confess, I didn't get into any conversations with her then, and treated it all somehow condescendingly. And, you know, she wasn't always so timorous and wild as she is now; even now it happens that she suddenly gets as merry and pretty as a twenty-year-old; and then, when she was young, she sometimes liked very much to chatter and laugh, in her own company, of course—with the girls, with the women of the household; and how startled she'd be when I unexpectedly found her laughing sometimes, how quickly she'd blush and look at me timorously! Once, not long before I left for abroad, that is, almost on the eve of my unmarrying her, I came into her room and found her alone, at the little table, without any work, leaning her elbow on the table, and deep in thought. It almost never happened with her that she would sit like that, without work. By then I had long ceased to caress her. I managed to approach very softly, on tiptoe, and suddenly embrace and kiss her... She jumped up—and I'll never forget that rapture, that happiness on her face, and suddenly it all changed quickly to a blush, and her eyes flashed. Do you know what I read in that flashing glance? 'You're giving me charity—that's what!' She sobbed hysterically, under the pretext that I had frightened her, but even then I fell to thinking. And in general, all such recollections are a very hard thing, my friend. It's the same as how, in a great artist's poems, there are sometimes such *painful* scenes that you remember them with pain all your life afterwards—for instance, Othello's last monologue in Shakespeare, Evgeny at Tatyana's feet, or the escaped convict meeting a child, a little girl, on a cold night, by a well, in Victor Hugo's *Les Misérables*.[36] It pierces your heart once, and the wound remains forever after. Oh, how I waited for Sonya and how I wanted to embrace her quickly! I dreamed with convulsive impatience of a whole new program of life; I dreamed of destroying gradually, through methodical effort, this constant fear she had of me in her soul, of explaining her own worth to her and everything in which she was even superior to me. Oh, I knew only too well then that I always began to love your mother as soon as we parted, and always cooled towards her when we came together again; but here it wasn't that, this time it wasn't that."

I was surprised. "And *she*?" the question flashed in me.

"Well, and how was your meeting with mama then?" I asked warily.

"Then? But I didn't meet her then at all. She barely got as far as Königsberg then, and she stayed there, while I was on the Rhine. I didn't go to her, but told her to stay and wait. We saw each other much later, oh, a long time later, when I went to ask her permission to marry..."

II

HERE I'LL CONVEY the essence of the matter, that is, only what I myself could take in; and he also began telling me things incoherently. His speech suddenly became ten times more incoherent and disorderly, just as he reached this point.

He met Katerina Nikolaevna suddenly, precisely when he was expecting mama, at the most impatient moment of expectation. They were all on the Rhine then, at the waters, all taking the cure. Katerina Nikolaevna's husband was almost dying by then, or at least he had already been sentenced to death by the doctors. From the first meeting she struck him as with some sort of sorcery. It was a *fatum*.* It's remarkable that, writing it down and recalling it now, I don't remember him once using the word "love" or saying he was "in love" in his account then. The word *fatum* I do remember.

And it certainly was a *fatum*. He *did not want it*, "did not want to love." I don't know whether I can convey it clearly; only his

*Decree of fate.

whole soul was indignant precisely at the fact that this could have happened to him. All that was free in him was annihilated at once in the face of this meeting, and the man was forever fettered to a woman who wanted nothing at all to do with him. He had no wish for this slavery of passion. I will say straight out now: Katerina Nikolaevna is a rare type of society woman—a type which maybe doesn't exist in that circle. It is the type of the simple and straightforward woman in the highest degree. I've heard, that is, I know for certain, that this was what made her irresistible in society when she appeared in it (she often withdrew from it completely). Versilov, naturally, did not believe then, on first meeting her, that she was that way, but believed precisely the opposite, that is, that she was a dissembler and a Jesuit. Skipping ahead, I will quote here her own opinion of him: she maintained that he couldn't think of her in any other way, "because an idealist, when he runs his head into reality, is always inclined, before anybody else, to assume all sorts of vileness." I don't know whether that is true of idealists in general, but of him, of course, it was fully true. Here, perhaps, I'll set down my own opinion as well, which flashed through my mind as I listened to him then: it occurred to me that he loved mama with a more humane and generally human love, so to speak, than the simple love with which one loves women in general, and, as soon as he met a woman whom he loved with that simple love, he immediately refused that love—most likely because he was unaccustomed to it. However, maybe this is a wrong thought; of course, I didn't say it to him. It would have been indelicate; and I swear, he was in such a state that he almost had to be spared: he was agitated; at some points of his story he suddenly just broke off and was silent for several minutes, pacing the room with an angry face.

She soon penetrated his secret then. Oh, maybe she also flirted with him on purpose. Even the most shining women are mean on such occasions; that is their irrepressible instinct. It ended with an embittered break between them, and it seems he wanted to kill her; he frightened her and maybe would have killed her; "but it all suddenly turned to hatred." A strange period ensued. He suddenly came up with the strange thought of tormenting himself with discipline, "the same sort that monks exercise. Gradually and by methodical practice, you overcome your will, beginning with the most ridiculous and petty things, and ending by overcoming your will entirely and becoming free." He added that among monks this is a serious matter, because it has been raised to the level of a science through a thousand years of experience. But the most remarkable thing was that he came up with this idea of "discipline" then, not at all in order to get rid of Katerina Nikolaevna, but in the fullest certainty that he not only did not love her anymore, but even hated her in the highest degree. He believed in his hatred of her to such an extent that he even suddenly thought of falling in love with and marrying her stepdaughter, who had been deceived by the prince, persuaded himself completely of this new love, and got the poor idiot girl to fall in love with him irresistibly, making her completely happy by this love during the last months of her life. Why, instead of her, he didn't remember then about mama, who was waiting for him all the while in Königsberg, remained unclear to me . . . On the contrary, he suddenly and entirely forgot about mama, didn't even send her money to live on, so that it was Tatyana Pavlovna who saved her then. Suddenly, however, he went to mama to "ask her permission" to marry that girl, under the pretext that "such a bride isn't a woman." Oh, maybe this is all merely the portrait of a "bookish man," as Katerina Nikolaevna said of him afterwards; however, why is it that these "paper people" (if it's true that they are paper) are able to suffer in such a real way and reach the point of such tragedies? Though then, that evening, I thought somewhat differently, and was shaken by a certain thought:

"All your development, all your soul came to you through suffering and through your whole life's struggle—while all her perfection came to her gratis. There's inequality here . . . Women are outrageous in that," I said, not at all to ingratiate myself with him, but with fervor and even with indignation.

"Perfection. Her perfection? Why, there's no perfection in her!" he said suddenly, all but astonished at my words. "She's a most ordinary woman, she's even a trashy woman . . . But she's obliged to have every perfection!"

"Why obliged?"

"Because, having such power, she's obliged to have every perfection!" he cried spitefully.

"The saddest thing is that you're so tormented even now!" suddenly escaped me involuntarily.

"Now? Tormented?" he repeated my words again, stopping before me as if in some perplexity. And then suddenly a quiet, long, thoughtful smile lit up his face, and he raised his finger before him as if reflecting. Then, recovering completely, he snatched an unsealed letter from the table and flung it down before me.

"Here, read it! You absolutely must know everything . . . and why did you let me rummage around so much in that old rubbish! . . . I've only defiled and embittered my heart! . . ."

I'm unable to express my astonishment. It was a letter from *her* to him, written that day, received at around five o'clock in the afternoon. I read it almost trembling with excitement. It wasn't long, but was written so directly and candidly that, as I read it, it was as if I could see her before me and hear her words. Truthfully in the highest degree (and therefore almost touchingly), she confessed to him her fear and then simply entreated him "to leave her in peace." In conclusion, she informed him that she was now positively going to marry Bjoring. Until that occasion, she had never written to him.

And here is what I understood then from his explanations:

As soon as he read this letter earlier, he suddenly sensed a most unexpected phenomenon in himself: for the first time in those fateful two years, he felt neither the slightest hatred for her nor the slightest shock, similar to the way he had "gone out of his mind" not long ago at the mere rumor about Bjoring. "On the contrary, I sent her a blessing from my whole heart," he said to me with deep feeling. I listened to these words with delight. It meant that everything there was in him of passion, of torment, had disappeared all at once, of itself, like a dream, like a two-year-long enchantment. Still not believing himself, he rushed to mama—and what then: he came in precisely at the moment when she became *free*, and the old man who had bequeathed her to him the day before died. These two coincidences shook his soul. A little later he rushed to look for me—and his thinking of me so soon I will never forget.

Nor will I forget the end of that evening. This man became all and suddenly transformed again. We sat late into the night. About how all this "news" affected me, I will tell later, in its place, but now—just a few concluding words about him. Reflecting now, I understand that what charmed me most then was his humility, as it were, before me, his so-truthful sincerity before such a boy as I! "It was all fumes, but blessings on it!" he cried. "Without that blindness I might never have discovered in my heart so wholly and forever my sole queen, my sufferer—your mother!" I make special note of these rapturous words that escaped him uncontrollably, with a view to what followed. But then he conquered and overcame my soul.

I remember, towards the end we became terribly merry. He ordered champagne brought, and we drank to mama and to "the future." Oh, he was so full of life and so bent on living! But it wasn't the wine that made us terribly merry; we drank only two glasses each. I don't know why, but towards the end we laughed almost uncontrollably. We started talking about totally unrelated things; he got to telling jokes, and so did I. Neither our laughter nor our jokes were the least bit spiteful or jeering, we were simply merry. He kept refusing to let me go: "Stay, stay a while longer!" he repeated, and I stayed. He even went out to see me off; it was a lovely evening, there was a slight frost.

"Tell me, have you already sent *her* a reply?" I suddenly asked quite inadvertently, pressing his hand for the last time at the intersection.

"Not yet, no, and it makes no difference. Come tomorrow, come early... And another thing: drop Lambert altogether, and tear up the 'document,' and soon. Good-bye!"

Having said that, he suddenly left. I remained standing there, and in such confusion that I didn't dare call him back. The expression "the document" especially staggered me; from whom could he have learned of it, and in such a precise expression, if not from Lambert? I returned home in great confusion. And how could it happen, the thought flashed in me suddenly, that such a "two-year-long enchantment" could vanish like a dream, like fumes, like a phantom?

Chapter Nine

I

BUT I WOKE UP the next morning feeling fresher and heartier. I even reproached myself, involuntarily and sincerely, for the certain levity and haughtiness, as it were, with which I recalled listening yesterday to certain parts of his "confession." If it was partially disordered, if certain revelations were as if somewhat fumy and even incoherent, he hadn't really been prepared for an oration when he invited me to his place yesterday. He only did me a great honor, turning to me as to an only friend at such a moment, and I will never forget it. On the contrary, his confession was "touching," however much I may be laughed at for the expression, and if there was an occasional flash of the cynical or even of something seemingly ridiculous, I was too broad not to understand and not to allow for realism—without, however, besmirching the ideal. Above all, I had finally comprehended this man, and I even felt partly sorry and as if vexed that it had all turned out so simple. In my heart I had always placed this man extremely high, in the clouds, and had unfailingly clothed his destiny in something mysterious, so that I naturally wished that the key wouldn't fit the lock so easily. However, in his meeting *with her* and in his two-year-long suffering there was also much that was complicated: "He refused the *fatum* of life; what he needed was freedom, not slavery to the *fatum*; through slavery to the *fatum* he had been obliged to offend mama, who was sitting in Königsberg..." Besides, I considered this man, in any case, a preacher: he bore the golden age in his heart and knew the future of atheism; and then the meeting with her had shattered everything, perverted everything! Oh, I didn't betray her, but still I took his side. Mama, I reasoned, for instance, wouldn't hinder anything in his destiny, not even marriage to mama. That I understood; that was quite other than the meeting with *that one*. True, all the same, mama would not have given him peace, but that would even have been better: such people ought to be judged differently, and let their life always be like that; and there's nothing unseemly in it; on the contrary, it would be unseemly if they settled down, or generally became similar to all average people. His praise of the nobility and his words, "*Je mourrai gentilhomme*," didn't confound me in the least; I perceived what sort of *gentilhomme* he was; he was the type who gives everything away and becomes the herald of world citizenship and the main Russian thought of the "all-unification of ideas." And though that, too, was even all nonsense, that is, the "all-unification of ideas" (which, of course, is unthinkable), still there was one good thing, that all his life he had worshipped an idea, and not the stupid golden calf. My God! I, I myself, when I conceived my "idea"— was I bowing down to the golden calf? Was it money I wanted then? I swear I wanted only the idea! I swear I wouldn't have a single chair or sofa upholstered in velvet, and if I had a hundred million, I'd eat the same bowl of beef soup as now!

I was dressing and hurrying to him irrepressibly. I will add: concerning his outburst yesterday about the "document," I was also five times more at ease than yesterday. First, I hoped to clarify things with him, and, second, so what if Lambert had filtered through to him and they had talked something over? But my chief joy was in one extraordinary sensation; this was the thought that he "didn't love *her*" now; I believed in that terribly, and felt as if someone had rolled an awful stone off my heart. I even remember the flash of a certain surmise then: precisely the ugliness and senselessness of his last fierce outburst at the news about Bjoring and the sending of that insulting letter then; precisely that extremity could also have served as a prophecy and precursor of the most radical change in his feelings and of his approaching return to common sense. It must have been almost as with an illness, I thought, and he precisely had to reach the opposite extreme—a medical episode and nothing more! This thought made me happy.

"And let her, let her dispose of her fate as she likes, let her marry her Bjoring as much as she likes, only let him, my father, my friend, not love her anymore," I exclaimed. However, there was in it a certain secret of my own feelings, but I don't wish to smear it around here in my notes.

Enough of that. And now I will tell all the horror that followed, and all the machinations of the facts, without any discussions.

II

AT TEN O'CLOCK, just as I was ready to go out—to see him, of course—Nastasya Egorovna appeared. I asked her joyfully if she was coming from him, and heard with vexation that it was not from him at all, but from Anna Andreevna, and that she, Nastasya Egorovna, had "left the apartment at first light."

"Which apartment?"

"The same one as yesterday. Yesterday's apartment, the one with the little baby, is rented in my name now, and Tatyana Pavlovna pays . . ."

"Ah, well, it makes no difference to me!" I interrupted with vexation. "Is he at home at least? Will I find him in?"

And to my astonishment I heard from her that he had left the premises even before she had—meaning that she had left "at first light," and he still earlier.

"Well, so now he's come back?"

"No, sir, he certainly hasn't come back, and he may not come back at all," she said, looking at me with the same keen and furtive eye, and not taking it off me, just as she had done when she visited me while I lay sick. What mainly made me explode was that here again some secrets and stupidities emerged, and that these people apparently couldn't do without secrets and slyness.

"Why did you say he certainly won't come back? What are you implying? He went to mama's, that's all!"

"I d-don't know, sir."

"And why were you so good as to come?"

She told me that she had come now from Anna Andreevna, who was sending for me and expected me at once, otherwise "it would be too late." This further mysterious phrase drove me completely beside myself.

"Why too late? I don't want to go and I won't go! I won't let myself be taken over again! I spit on Lambert—tell her that, and that if she sends Lambert to me, I'll chuck him out—just tell her that!"

Nastasya Egorovna was terribly frightened.

"Ah, no, sir!" she stepped towards me, pressing her hands together as if entreating me, "take your time before you go hurrying so. This is an important matter, very important for you yourself, and also for the lady, and for Andrei Petrovich, and for your mama, for everybody... Do go to Anna Andreevna at once, because she simply can't wait any longer... I assure you on my honor... and then you can make your decision."

I stared at her in amazement and disgust.

"Nonsense, nothing will happen, I won't go!" I cried stubbornly and gleefully. "Now everything will be a new way! And how can you understand that? Good-bye, Nastasya Egorovna, I purposely won't go, I purposely won't ask you any questions. You only throw me off. I don't want to enter into your riddles."

But as she wouldn't leave and went on standing there, I grabbed my coat and hat and went out myself, leaving her there in the middle of the room. There were no letters or papers in my room, and previously I had almost never locked my door when I left. But before I reached the front door, my landlord, Pyotr Ippolitovich, came running down the stairs after me, hatless and in his uniform.

"Arkady Makarovich! Arkady Makarovich!"

"What is it now?"

"Have you no orders on leaving?"

"None."

He looked at me with a stabbing glance and with evident uneasiness.

"Concerning the apartment, for instance?"

"What about the apartment? Didn't I send you the money on time?"

"No, sir, I'm not talking about money," he suddenly smiled a long smile and went on stabbing me with his glance.

"What's the matter with you all?" I finally cried, almost totally ferocious. "What are *you* after?"

He waited for another few seconds, as if he still expected something from me.

"Well, so you can give the orders later... if you're not in the mood now," he murmured, with an even longer grin. "Go on, sir, and I myself have my duties."

He ran upstairs to his apartment. Of course, all that could set one to thinking. I'm purposely not leaving out the slightest stroke from all that petty nonsense, because every little stroke of it later went into the final bouquet, where it found its proper place, as the reader will ascertain. But it was true that they really threw me off then. If I was so agitated and annoyed, it was precisely because I again heard in their words that tiresome tone of intrigue and riddling that reminded me of the old days. But to continue.

Versilov turned out not to be at home, and he had indeed gone out at first light. "To mama's, of course," I stubbornly stood my ground. I asked no questions of the nanny, a rather stupid woman, and there was no one else in the apartment. I ran to mama's, and, I confess, I was so worried that halfway there I grabbed a cab. *He hadn't been at mama's since last evening.* Only Tatyana Pavlovna and Liza were with mama. As soon as I came in, Liza started preparing to leave.

They were all sitting upstairs in my "coffin." In our drawing room downstairs, Makar Ivanovich was laid out on the table,[37] and some old man was measuredly reading the psalter over him. I won't describe anything now that is not directly related to the matter, but will just observe that the coffin, which they had already had time to make and was standing right there in the room, was not simple, though black, but was lined with velvet, and the shroud on the deceased was an expensive one—a magnificence not suited to the old man or his convictions, but such was the express wish of both mama and Tatyana Pavlovna.

Naturally, I didn't expect to find them cheerful; but the peculiarly oppressive anguish, with concern and uneasiness, that I read in their eyes, struck me immediately, and I instantly concluded that "here, surely, the deceased is not the only cause." All this, I repeat, I remember perfectly well.

Despite all, I embraced mama tenderly and asked at once *about him*. An alarmed curiosity instantly flashed in mama's eyes. I hastily mentioned that he and I had spent the whole last evening together, till late into the night, but that today he hadn't been at home since daybreak, whereas just yesterday he had invited me himself, as we were parting, to come today as early as possible. Mama made no reply, and Tatyana Pavlovna, seizing the moment, shook her finger at me.

"Good-bye, brother," Liza suddenly cut off, quickly going out of the room. I naturally went after her, but she had stopped right at the front door.

"I thought it might occur to you to come down," she said in a quick whisper.

"Liza, what's going on here?"

"I don't know myself, only there's a lot of something. Probably the dénouement of the 'eternal story.' He hasn't come, but they have some sort of information about him. They won't tell you, don't worry, and you won't ask, if you're smart; but mama is crushed. I didn't ask about anything either. Good-bye."

She opened the door.

"But, Liza, what about you?" I sprang after her into the hallway. Her terribly crushed, desperate air pierced my heart. She gave me a look, not so much angry as even almost somehow embittered, grinned biliously, and waved her hand.

"If he died—it would be a godsend!" she flung at me from the stairs, and went out. She said this of Prince Sergei Petrovich, who at the time was lying in delirium and unconscious. "Eternal story! What eternal story?" I thought with defiance, and then suddenly I absolutely wanted to tell them at least part of my impressions yesterday from his night confession, and the confession itself. "They think something bad about him now—let them know all!" flew through my head.

I remember that I managed somehow very deftly to begin my story. Their faces instantly showed a terrible curiosity. This time Tatyana Pavlovna simply fastened her eyes on me, but mama was more restrained; she was very serious, but a light, beautiful, though somehow quite hopeless smile came to her face and almost never left it all the while I was talking. I spoke well, of course, though I knew that for them it was almost incomprehensible. To my surprise, Tatyana Pavlovna did not pick on me, did not insist on exactitude, did not try to catch me up, as she was accustomed to do whenever I began saying something. She only pressed her lips occasionally and narrowed her eyes, as if making an effort to comprehend. At times it even seemed to me that they understood everything, but that was all but impossible. I talked, for instance, about his convictions, but, above all, about his rapture yesterday, about his rapture over mama, about his love for mama, about how he kissed her portrait... Listening to that, they exchanged quick and silent glances, and mama turned all red, though they both went on being silent. Then... then, of course, I couldn't touch on the main point *before mama*, that is, the meeting with *her* and all the rest, and, above all, *her* letter to him yesterday and his moral "resurrection" after the letter; but that was the main thing, so that all his feelings yesterday, with which I had thought to gladden mama, naturally remained incomprehensible, though, of course, through no fault of my own, because all that could be told, I told beautifully. I ended in total perplexity; their silence remained unbroken, and it became very oppressive for me to be with them.

"Surely he's come back by now, or maybe he's sitting at my place and waiting," I said, and got up to leave.

"Go, go!" Tatyana Pavlovna firmly agreed.

"Have you been downstairs?" mama asked me in a half-whisper, as I was taking my leave.

"Yes, I bowed down to him and prayed for him. Such a calm, seemly face he has, mama! Thank you, mama, for not sparing on his coffin. First I found it strange, but then I thought at once that I would have done the same myself."

"Will you come to church tomorrow?" she asked, and her lips trembled.

"What are you asking, mama?" I was surprised. "I'll come to the *panikhida*[38] today, too, and I'll come again; and... besides, tomorrow is your birthday, mama, my dearest! He didn't live the three days till then!"

I left in painful astonishment. How could she ask such questions—whether I'd come to the funeral at the church or not? "And if it's so about me, then what do they think about *him*?"

I knew that Tatyana Pavlovna would come running after me, and I purposely lingered in the front doorway; but she, having overtaken me, pushed me out onto the stairway with her hand, came out after me, and closed the door behind her.

"Tatyana Pavlovna, you mean you don't expect Andrei Petrovich either today or tomorrow? I'm alarmed..."

"Quiet. Much it matters that you're alarmed. Speak—what was it you didn't finish saying when you told about yesterday's balderdash?"

I found no need to conceal it, and, almost annoyed with Versilov, told her all about Katerina Nikolaevna's letter to him yesterday, and about the effect of the letter, that is, his resurrection into a new life. To my surprise, the fact of the letter didn't surprise her in the least, and I guessed that she already knew about it.

"You're not lying?"

"No, I'm not."

"Well, now," she smiled venomously, as if pondering, "resurrected! Just what he'd do! Is it true that he kissed the portrait?"

"It's true, Tatyana Pavlovna."

"Did he kiss it with feeling, without pretending?"

"Pretending? Does he ever pretend? Shame on you, Tatyana Pavlovna; you have a coarse soul, a woman's soul."

I said it heatedly, but it was as if she didn't hear me. She again seemed to be figuring something out, despite the intense cold on the stairway. I was wearing a fur coat, but she was wearing only a dress.

"I'd entrust you with an errand, but the trouble is you're very stupid," she said with contempt and as if with vexation. "Listen, go to Anna Andreevna's and see what's happening there... Ah, no, don't go; a dolt is a dolt! Leave, be off, don't stand there like a post!"

"I'm just not going to go to Anna Andreevna's! And Anna Andreevna sent for me herself."

"Herself? Sent Nastasya Egorovna?" she quickly turned to me. She was on the point of leaving and had even opened the door, but she slammed it shut again.

"I won't go to Anna Andreevna's for anything!" I repeated with spiteful glee. "I won't go, because you just called me a dolt, while I've never been so perspicacious as today. I can see all your doings as if on the palm of my hand; and even so I won't go to Anna Andreevna's!"

"I just knew it!" she exclaimed, but, again, not in response to my words, but continuing to think her own thoughts. "They'll ensnare *her* completely now, and tighten the deadly noose!"

"Anna Andreevna?"

"Fool!"

"Whom do you mean, then? Not Katerina Nikolaevna? What deadly noose?" I was terribly frightened. Some vague but terrible idea passed through my soul. Tatyana Pavlovna looked at me piercingly.

"And what are you doing in it?" she asked suddenly. "What's your part? I did hear something about you—oh, watch out!"

"Listen, Tatyana Pavlovna, I'll tell you a terrible secret, only not now, I have no time now, but tomorrow, when we're alone, but in return tell me the whole truth now, and what this is about the deadly noose... because I'm trembling all over..."

"I spit on your trembling!" she exclaimed. "What secret do you want to tell me tomorrow? Can it really be that you know something?" she fixed me with her questioning gaze. "Didn't you swear to her yourself that you had burned Kraft's letter?"

"Tatyana Pavlovna, I repeat, don't torment me," I went on with my own thing, ignoring her question in turn, because I was beside myself, "watch out, Tatyana Pavlovna, what you hide from me may lead to something worse... why, yesterday he was in full, in the fullest resurrection!"

"Eh, away with you, buffoon! You must be in love like a sparrow yourself—father and son with the same object! Pah, outrageous creatures!"

She disappeared, slamming the door in indignation. Infuriated by the impudent, shameless cynicism of her very last words—a cynicism that only a woman is capable of—I rushed off, deeply offended. But I won't describe my vague sensations, as I've already promised; I will continue with just the facts, which will now resolve everything. Naturally, I ran over to his place for a moment, and again heard from the nanny that he hadn't been there.

"And he won't come at all?"

"God knows."

III

FACTS, FACTS!...But does the reader understand anything? I myself remember how these same facts weighed on me then and kept me from comprehending anything, so that by the end of that day my head was totally thrown off. And therefore I'll run ahead for two or three words!

All my torments consisted in this: if yesterday he had resurrected and stopped loving *her*, then in that case where should he have been today? Answer: first of all with me, since he had spent last night embracing me, and then right away with mama, whose portrait he had kissed yesterday. And yet, instead of these two natural steps, suddenly, at "first light," he's not at home and has disappeared somewhere, and Nastasya Egorovna raves, for some reason, that "he most likely won't come back." What's more, Liza assures me of some dénouement to an "eternal story" and of mama's having some information about him, and of the very latest; on top of that, they undoubtedly knew about Katerina Nikolaevna's letter as well (I noticed it myself), and still they didn't believe in his "resurrection into a new life," though they listened to me attentively. Mama is crushed, and Tatyana Pavlovna jokes caustically about the word "resurrection." But if that's all so, then it means he had another turnabout during the night, another crisis, and that—after yesterday's rapture, tenderness, pathos! It means that all this "resurrection" popped like a blown-up bubble, and at the moment he might be knocking around somewhere in the same rage as the other time, after the news about Bjoring! One might ask, what would become of mama, of me, of us all, and . . . and, finally, what would become of *her*? What "deadly noose" had Tatyana let on about, sending me to Anna Andreevna? It means the "deadly noose" is there—at Anna Andreevna's! Why at Anna Andreevna's? Naturally, I'll run to Anna Andreevna's; I said purposely, out of vexation, that I wouldn't go; I'll run right now. But what was Tatyana Pavlovna saying about the "document"? And didn't he himself say to me yesterday, "Burn the document"?

These were my thoughts, this was what also weighed on me like a deadly noose; but above all I wanted *him*. With him I'd resolve everything at once—I could feel it; we'd understand each other after two words! I'd seize his hands, press them; I'd find ardent words in my heart—that was my irresistible dream. Oh, I would subdue his madness! . . . But where was he? Where? And just then, at such a moment, Lambert had to appear, when I was so worked up! A few steps from home I suddenly met Lambert; he yelled joyfully when he saw me and seized me by the arm:

"It's the thighrd time I've come to see you . . . *Enfin!* Let's go and have lunch."

"Wait! Were you at my place? Is Andrei Petrovich there?"

"Nobody's there. Drop them all! You got angry yesterday, you cghretin; you were drunk, but I have something important to tell you; today I heard some lovely news about what we were discussing yesterday . . ."

"Lambert," I interrupted, breathless and hurrying and involuntarily declaiming a little, "if I've stopped with you, it's only in order to be done with you forever. I told you yesterday, but you still don't understand. Lambert, you're a child and as stupid as a Frenchman. You still think you're as you were at Touchard's and I'm as stupid as at Touchard's . . . But I'm not as stupid as at Touchard's . . . I was drunk yesterday, but not from wine, but because I was excited to begin with; and if I went along with what you were driveling, it was from cunning, in order to worm your thoughts out of you. I deceived you, and you were glad, and believed, and driveled. Know that marrying her is such nonsense that a first-year schoolboy wouldn't believe it. Could anyone think I believed it? But you did! You believed it, because you're not received in high society and know nothing of how things are done in high society. Things aren't done so simply in high society, and it's impossible that a woman should so simply—up and get married . . . Now I'll tell you clearly what you want: you want to invite me to your place and get me drunk, so that I'll hand over the document to you, and together we'll pull some sort of swindle on Katerina Nikolaevna! What rubbish! I'll never go to your place, and know also that by tomorrow, or the day after without fail, this paper will be in her own hands, because this document belongs to her, because she wrote it, and I'll hand it to her personally, and if you want to know where, know that I'll do it through Tatyana Pavlovna, her acquaintance, in Tatyana Pavlovna's apartment—I'll hand it to her in Tatyana Pavlovna's presence, and take nothing from her for it . . . And now—off with you, forever, or else . . . or else, Lambert, I'll deal with you less politely . . ."

When I finished, I was trembling all over. The main thing and the nastiest habit in life, which harms every manner of business, is . . . is when you start showing off. The devil pushed me to get so worked up in front of him that, as I finished speaking, rapping out the words with pleasure, and raising my voice more and more, I suddenly got so heated that I threw in this totally unnecessary detail about handing over the document through Tatyana Pavlovna and in her apartment! But I suddenly wanted so much to disconcert him then! When I burst out so directly about the document and suddenly saw his stupid fright, I wanted to crush him still more with precise details. And this boastful, womanish babble later became the cause of terrible misfortunes, because this detail about Tatyana Pavlovna and her apartment lodged at once in his mind, the mind of a swindler and practical petty dealer; in higher and more important matters he's worthless and understands nothing, but still he does have a flair for these petty things. If I had kept quiet about Tatyana Pavlovna, great misfortunes would not have occurred. However, on hearing me, for the first moment he was terribly at a loss.

"Listen," he muttered, "Alphonsina . . . Alphonsina will sing . . . Alphonsina went to see *her*; listen, I have a letter, almost a letter, where Mme. Akhmakov talks about you, the pockmarked one got it for me—remember the pockmarked one?—you'll see now, you'll see, come on!"

"Lies! Show me the letter!"

"It's at home, Alphonsina has it, come on!"

Of course, he was lying and raving, trembling for fear I might run away from him; but I suddenly abandoned him in the middle of the street, and when he made as if to follow me, I stopped and shook my fist at him. But he already stood thinking—and let me go: maybe a new plan was already flashing in his head. But for me the surprises and encounters weren't over... And when I remember that whole unfortunate day, it seems to me that all these surprises and accidents had as if conspired together then to come pouring down on my head at once from some cursed cornucopia. I had hardly opened the door to my apartment when, in the front hall, I ran into a tall young man with an elongated and pale face, of imposing and "graceful" appearance, and wearing a magnificent fur coat. He had a pince-nez on his nose; but as soon as he saw me, he pulled it off his nose (apparently out of courtesy) and, politely raising his top hat with his hand, though without stopping, said to me with a graceful smile, "*Ha, bonsoir*,"* and walked past me to the stairs. We recognized each other immediately, though I had seen him fleetingly only once in my life, in Moscow. It was Anna Andreevna's brother, the kammerjunker, the young Versilov, Versilov's son and therefore almost my brother. He was being shown out by the landlady (the landlord hadn't come home from work yet). When he left, I simply fell upon her:

"What was he doing here? Was he in my room?"

"Not at all. He came to see me..." she broke off quickly and drily and turned to go to her room.

"No, not like that!" I shouted. "Kindly answer: what did he come for?"

"Ah, my God! so I'm to tell you all about what people come for! I believe we, too, can have our concerns. The young man may have wanted to borrow money, to find out an address from me. I may have promised him last time..."

"Last time when?"

"Ah, my God, but it's not the first time he's come!"

She left. Above all, I understood that the tone was changing here: they were beginning to speak rudely to me. It was clear that this was again a secret; secrets accumulated with every step, every hour. The young Versilov came the first time with his sister, Anna Andreevna, while I was sick; I remembered it only too well, as I did the fact that Anna Andreevna had let drop to me yesterday an extraordinary little phrase, that the old prince might stay in my apartment... but it was all so jumbled and so grotesque that I could come up with almost no thoughts in that regard. Slapping myself on the forehead and not even sitting down to rest, I ran to

*Ah, good evening.

Anna Andreevna's. She was not at home, and the answer I got from the porter was that "she had gone to Tsarskoe, would be back around the same time tomorrow."

"She goes to Tsarskoe, to the old prince, of course, while her brother inspects my apartment! No, this will not be!" I rasped. "And if there is indeed some deadly noose here, I'll protect the 'poor woman'!"

I didn't return home from Anna Andreevna's, because there suddenly flashed in my inflamed head the memory of the tavern on the canal where Andrei Petrovich was accustomed to go in his dark moments. Delighted with my surmise, I instantly ran there; it was past three o'clock and dusk was gathering. In the tavern I was told that he had come: "He stayed a little while and left, but maybe he'll come again." I suddenly resolved with all my might to wait for him, and ordered dinner; at least there was a hope.

I ate dinner, even ate too much, so as to have the right to stay as long as possible, and sat there, I think, for some four hours. I won't describe my sadness and feverish impatience; it was as if everything in me was shaking and trembling. The barrel organ, the customers—oh, all that anguish left an imprint on my soul, maybe for my whole life! I won't describe the thoughts that arose in my head like a cloud of dry leaves in autumn after a gust of wind; it really was something like that, and, I confess, I felt at times as if reason was beginning to betray me.

But what tormented me to the point of pain (in passing, naturally, on the side, past the main torment), was one nagging, venomous impression—as nagging as a venomous autumn fly, which you give no thought to, but which circles around you, pestering you, and suddenly gives you a very painful bite. It was just a memory, a certain event, of which I had not yet told anyone in the world. Here's what it was, for this, too, has to be told somewhere or other.

IV

WHEN IT WAS decided in Moscow that I would go to Petersburg, I was given to know through Nikolai Semyonovich that I should expect money to be sent for the trip. Who the money would come from, I didn't ask; I knew it was from Versilov, and since I dreamed day and night then, with a leaping heart and high-flown plans, about my meeting with Versilov, I completely stopped speaking of him aloud, even with Marya Ivanovna. Remember, however, that I had my own money for the trip; but I decided to wait anyway; incidentally, I assumed the money would come by post.

Suddenly one day Nikolai Semyonovich came home and informed me (briefly, as usual, and without smearing it around) that I should go to Miasnitskaya Street the next day, at eleven o'clock in the morning, to the home and apartment of Prince V——sky, and that there the kammerjunker Versilov, Andrei Petrovich's son, who had come from Petersburg and was staying with his lycée comrade, Prince V——sky, would hand me the sum sent for my moving expenses. It seemed quite a simple matter: Andrei Petrovich might very well charge his son with this errand instead of sending it by post; but this news crushed me and alarmed me somehow unnaturally. There was no doubt that Versilov wanted to bring me together with his son, my brother; thus the intentions and feelings of the man I dreamed of were clearly outlined; but an enormous question presented itself to me: how would and how should I behave myself in this quite unexpected meeting, and would my own dignity not suffer in some way?

The next day, at exactly eleven o'clock, I came to Prince V——sky's apartment—bachelor's quarters, but, as I could guess, magnificently furnished, with liveried lackeys. I stopped in the front hall. From the inner rooms came the sounds of loud talk and laughter: besides the visiting kammerjunker, the prince had other guests. I told the lackey to announce me, evidently in rather proud terms: at least, on going to announce me, he looked at me strangely, as it seemed to me, and even not as respectfully as he should have. To my surprise, he took a very long time announcing me, some five minutes, and meanwhile the same laughter and the same sounds of talk came from inside.

I, naturally, stood while I waited, knowing very well that for me, as "just as much a gentleman," it was unfitting and impossible to sit in the front hall where there were lackeys. I myself, of my own will, without a special invitation, would not have set foot in the reception room for anything, out of pride—out of refined pride, maybe, but so it had to be. To my surprise, the remaining lackeys (two) dared to sit down in my presence. I turned away so as not to notice it, but nevertheless I began trembling all over, and suddenly, turning and stepping towards one of the lackeys, I *ordered* him to go "at once" and announce me again. In spite of my stern gaze and my extreme agitation, the lackey looked at me lazily, without getting up, and the other one answered for him:

"You've been announced, don't worry!"

I decided to wait only one minute more, or possibly even less than a minute, and then—*leave without fail.* The main thing was that I was dressed quite decently; my suit and overcoat were new, after all, and my linen was perfectly fresh, Marya Ivanovna had purposely seen to that for the occasion. But about these lackeys I learned *for certain* much later, and already in Petersburg, that they had learned the day before, through the servant who came with Versilov, that "so-and-so would be coming, the natural brother and a student." That I now know for certain.

A minute passed. It's a strange feeling, when you're making up your mind and can't make it up: "To leave or not, to leave or not?" I repeated every second, almost in a cold fit. Suddenly the servant who had gone to announce me reappeared. In his hand, between finger and thumb, dangled four red banknotes, forty roubles.

"Here, sir, kindly take these forty roubles!"

I boiled over. This was such an insult! All the past night I had dreamed of the meeting of the two brothers arranged by Versilov; all night I had feverishly imagined how I should behave so as not to abase myself—not to abase the whole cycle of ideas I had lived out in my solitude and which I could be proud of even in any circle. I had imagined how I would be noble, proud, and sad, maybe even in the company of Prince V——sky, and thus would be introduced straight into that world—oh, I'm not sparing myself, and so be it, so be it: it must be written down exactly in these details! And suddenly—forty roubles through a lackey, in the front hall, and what's more, after ten minutes of waiting, and what's more, straight from his hand, from his lackeyish fingers, not on a salver, not in an envelope!

I shouted so loudly at the lackey that he gave a start and recoiled; I immediately told him to take the money back, and so that "his master should bring it himself"—in short, my demand was, of course, incoherent and, of course, incomprehensible for a lackey. However, I shouted so loudly that he went. Moreover, it seems my shouting was heard in the reception room, and the talk and laughter suddenly died down.

Almost at once I heard footsteps, imposing, unhurried, soft, and the tall figure of a handsome and haughty young man (he seemed to me still paler and leaner then than at today's meeting) appeared on the threshold of the front hall—even five feet before the threshold. He was wearing a magnificent red silk dressing gown and slippers, and had a pince-nez on his nose. Without saying a word, he turned his pince-nez on me and began to study me. I, like a beast, took a step towards him and stood there in defiance, staring at him point-blank. But he studied me for just a moment, ten seconds at most; suddenly a most imperceptible smile appeared on his lips, and yet a most caustic one, caustic precisely in being almost imperceptible. He silently turned and went back inside, as unhurriedly, as quietly and smoothly, as he had come. Oh, these offenders from childhood, who still in the bosom of their families are taught by their mothers to offend! Naturally, I was at a loss... Oh, why was I at a loss then!

Almost at the same moment, the same lackey reappeared with the same banknotes in his hand:

"Kindly take this, it has been sent to you from Petersburg, and the master cannot receive you himself; 'perhaps some other time, when he's more free'"—I felt he added these last words on his own. But my lostness still persisted; I took the money and went to the door; took it precisely because I was at a loss, because I should have refused it; but the lackey, of course, wishing to wound me, allowed himself a most lackeyish escapade: he suddenly thrust the door open emphatically before me and, holding it open, said imposingly and deliberately, as I went past him:

"If you please, sir!"

"Scoundrel!" I roared at him, and suddenly raised my arm, but didn't bring it down. "And your master's a scoundrel, too! Report that to him at once!" I added, and quickly went out to the stairs.

"You daren't do that! If I report it to the master right now, you could be sent with a note to the police this very minute. And you daren't raise your arm..."

I was going down the stairs. It was a grand stairway, all open, and I was fully visible from above as I went down the red carpet. All three lackeys came out and stood looking over the banister. I, of course, resolved to keep silent; it was impossible to squabble with lackeys. I went all the way down without quickening my pace, and maybe even slowing it.

Oh, there may be philosophers (and shame on them!) who will say that this is all trifles, the vexation of a milksop—there may be, but for me it was a wound, a wound that hasn't healed even to this minute, as I write, when everything is over and even avenged. Oh,

I swear, I'm not rancorous or vengeful! Unquestionably, I always want revenge, even to the point of pain, when I'm offended, but I swear—only with magnanimity. Let me repay him with magnanimity, but so that he feels it, so that he understands it—and I'm avenged! Incidentally, I'll add that I'm not vengeful, but I am rancorous, though also magnanimous. Does that happen to others? But then, oh, then I had come with magnanimous feelings, maybe ridiculous, but let it be. Better let them be ridiculous and magnanimous than not ridiculous but mean, humdrum, and average! I never revealed anything about that meeting with my "brother" to anyone, not even to Marya Ivanovna, or to Liza in Petersburg; that meeting was the same as receiving a shameful slap in the face. And now suddenly I meet this gentleman when I least expect to meet him; he smiles at me, tips his hat, and says with perfect amiability: "*Bonsoir.*" Of course, that was worth pondering . . . But the wound was reopened!

V

HAVING SAT FOR some four hours in the tavern, I suddenly rushed out as if in a fit—naturally, again to Versilov's and, naturally, again I didn't find him at home; he hadn't come back at all. The nanny was bored and asked me to send Nastasya Egorovna—oh, as if I could be bothered with that! I ran by mama's, too, but I didn't go in, but asked Lukerya to come out to the hallway; from her I learned that he hadn't come and that Liza wasn't there either. I saw that Lukerya would also have liked to ask something and maybe also to have sent me on some errand—as if I could be bothered with that! There remained a last hope, that he had been at my place; but I no longer believed in it.

I have already let it be known that I was almost losing my reason. And then in my room I suddenly found Alphonsinka and my landlord. True, they were on their way out, and Pyotr Ippolitovich had a candle in his hand.

"What is this?" I yelled almost senselessly at my landlord. "How dared you bring this rascally woman to my room?"

"*Tiens!*" Alphonsinka cried out, "*et les amis?*"*

"Out!" I bellowed.

*Well! . . . and what about friends?

"*Mais c'est un ours!*"* she fluttered out to the corridor, pretending to be frightened, and instantly disappeared into the landlady's room. Pyotr Ippolitovich, still holding the candle, approached me with a stern look.

"Allow me to observe to you, Arkady Makarovich, that you have grown too hot-tempered; much as we respect you, Mamzelle Alphonsine is not a rascally woman, but even quite the contrary, she is here as a guest, and not yours, but my wife's, with whom she has been mutually acquainted for some time now."

"But how dared you bring her to my room?" I repeated, clutching my head, which almost suddenly began to ache terribly.

"By chance, sir. I went in to close the vent window, which I myself had opened for the fresh air; and since Alphonsina Karlovna and I were continuing our previous conversation, in the midst of this conversation she, too, went into your room, solely to accompany me."

"Not true, Alphonsinka's a spy, Lambert's a spy! Maybe you're a spy yourself! And Alphonsinka came to steal something from me."

"That's as you like. Today you're pleased to say one thing, tomorrow another. And my apartment I've rented out for a while, and will move with my wife into the storeroom; so Alphonsina Karlovna is now almost as much of a tenant here as you are, sir."

"You've rented out the apartment to Lambert?" I cried in fear.

"No, sir, not to Lambert," he smiled his previous long smile, in which, however, firmness could now be seen instead of the morning's perplexity. "I suppose you're so good as to know to whom, and are only putting on a vain air of not knowing, solely for the beauty of it, sir, and that's why you're angry. Good night, sir!"

"Yes, yes, leave me, leave me in peace!" I waved my hands, all but weeping, so that he suddenly looked at me in surprise; however, he left. I fastened the latch on the door and collapsed on my bed, face to the pillow. And so there passed for me the first terrible day of those three fateful last days with which my notes conclude.

*What a bear!

Chapter Ten

I

But again, anticipating the course of events, I find it necessary to explain at least something to the reader beforehand, for here so many chance things mingled with the logical sequence of this story that it is impossible to make it out without explaining them beforehand. Here the matter consisted in that same "deadly noose" that Tatyana Pavlovna had let on about. The noose consisted in Anna Andreevna risking, finally, the boldest step that could be imagined in her situation. True character! Though the old prince, under the pretext of health, had been opportunely confiscated to Tsarskoe Selo then, so that the news of his marriage to Anna Andreevna might not spread in society and for a time would be snuffed out, so to speak, in the bud, nevertheless, the feeble old man, with whom anything could be done, would not for any reason in the world abandon his idea and betray Anna Andreevna, who had proposed to him. On this account he was chivalrous; so that sooner or later he might suddenly rise up and set about fulfilling his intention with irrepressible force, which is quite, quite likely to happen precisely with weak characters, for they have this limit, to which they ought not to be driven. Besides, he was perfectly aware of all the ticklishness of the position of Anna Andreevna, for whom he had boundless respect, aware of the possibility of society rumors, mockery, and bad fame on her account. The only thing that had restrained and stopped him so far was that in his presence Katerina Nikolaevna had never once, either by a word or a hint, allowed herself to mention Anna Andreevna in a bad sense, or betray anything at all against his intention to marry her. On the contrary, she displayed extreme cordiality and attentiveness towards her father's fiancée. Thus Anna Andreevna was put in an extremely awkward position, sensing with her subtle feminine flair that the slightest calumny against Katerina Nikolaevna, before whom the prince also stood in awe, and now more than ever, precisely because she so goodnaturedly and respectfully allowed him to marry—the slightest calumny against her would offend all his tender feelings and arouse mistrust of her in him and even, perhaps, indignation. Thus it was in this field that the battle had gone on so far: the two rivals were as if rivaling each other in delicacy and patience, and in the end the prince no longer knew which of them to be more surprised at, and, as is usual with all weak but tenderhearted people, ended by beginning to suffer and blame himself alone for everything. His anguish, they said, reached the point of illness; his nerves were indeed upset, and instead of recovering in Tsarskoe, he was, as they assured me, ready to take to his bed.

Here I'll note in parenthesis something I learned much later: that Bjoring had supposedly proposed directly to Katerina Nikolaevna that they take the old man abroad, persuading him to go by some sort of deceit, meanwhile make it known privately in society that he had completely lost his reason, and obtain a doctor's certificate for it abroad. But Katerina Nikolaevna wouldn't do that for anything—so at least they maintained afterwards. She supposedly rejected the plan with indignation. All this is only the most distant rumor, but I believe it.

And so, when the matter had reached, so to speak, the point of ultimate hopelessness, Anna Andreevna suddenly learns through Lambert that there exists this letter in which the daughter had consulted a lawyer about the means of declaring her father insane. Her vengeful and proud mind was aroused in the highest degree. Remembering her former conversations with me, and grasping a multitude of the tiniest circumstances, she could not doubt the correctness of the information. Then, in that firm, inexorable feminine heart, the plan for a bold stroke ripened irrepressibly. The plan consisted in suddenly telling the prince everything outright, without preliminaries and calumnies, frightening him, shocking him, pointing out that the madhouse inevitably awaited him, and when he resisted, became indignant, refused to believe it—showing him his daughter's letter, as if to say, "since there once was an intention of declaring him insane, so now it was all the more likely, in order to prevent the marriage." After which they would take the frightened and crushed old man and move him to Petersburg—*straight to my apartment*.

This was a terrible risk, but she trusted firmly in her power. Here, departing from my story for a moment, I'll say, running very far ahead, that she was not deceived in the effect of her stroke; moreover, the effect went beyond all her expectations. The news of this letter affected the old prince maybe several times more strongly than she or any of us had supposed. I never knew until then that the prince had known something about this letter before; but, as is usual with all weak and timid people, he hadn't believed the rumor and had warded it off with all his might, so as to remain at peace; what's more, he blamed himself for his ignoble gullibility. I'll also add that the fact of the letter's existence affected Katerina Nikolaevna, too, incomparably more strongly than I myself then expected... In short, this document turned out to be much more important than I myself, who was carrying it in my pocket, had supposed. But here I've run too far ahead.

But why, I'll be asked, to my apartment? Why move the prince to our pathetic little rooms and maybe frighten him with our pathetic furnishings? If it was impossible to go to his house (because there the whole thing could be hindered at once), then why not to a special "rich" apartment, as Lambert had suggested? But here lay the whole risk of Anna Andreevna's extraordinary step.

The main thing was to present the prince with the document immediately on his arrival; but I wouldn't hand over the document for anything. Since there was no more time to lose, Anna Andreevna, trusting in her power, ventured to start the business without the document, but by having the prince delivered directly to me instead. Why? Precisely in order to catch me in the same step as well, so to speak, and, as the saying goes, kill two birds with one stone. She counted on affecting me as well with the jolt, the shock, the unexpectedness. She reasoned that when I saw the old man at my place, saw his fear, his helplessness, heard their joint entreaties, I'd give in and produce the document! I admit her reckoning was cunning and clever, and psychological—what's more, she nearly succeeded... As for the old man, Anna Andreevna led him on then, made him believe her, if only on her word, by telling him outright that she would take him *to me*. I learned all that afterwards. Even the news alone that the document was with me destroyed in his timid heart the last doubts as to the verity of the fact—so greatly did he love and respect me!

I'll also note that Anna Andreevna herself didn't doubt for a moment that the document was still with me and that I hadn't let it slip out of my hands. Above all, she misunderstood my character and cynically counted on my innocence, simpleheartedness, even sentimentality; and, on the other hand, she supposed that, even if I had ventured to give the letter, for instance, to Katerina Nikolaevna, then it could not have been otherwise than under some special circumstances, and it was those circumstances she was hastening to prevent by unexpectedness, a swoop, a stroke.

And, finally, she was confirmed in all this by Lambert. I've already said that Lambert's situation then was a most critical one: traitor as he was, he wished with all his might to lure me away from Anna Andreevna, so that the two of us together could sell the document to Mme. Akhmakov, which for some reason he found more profitable. But since I wouldn't hand over the document for anything down to the last moment, he ultimately decided even to throw in with Anna Andreevna, so as not to lose all profit, and therefore he foisted his services on her with all his might, till the very last hour, and I know that he even offered, if need be, to procure a priest... But Anna Andreevna, with a scornful smile, asked him not to mention it. Lambert seemed terribly crude to her and aroused her deepest loathing; but, being prudent, she still accepted his services, which consisted, for instance, in spying. Incidentally, I don't know for certain even to this day whether they bribed Pyotr Ippolitovich, my landlord, or not, and whether he received at least something for his services, or simply joined their company for the joy of intrigue; but he, too, spied on me, and his wife as well—that I do know for certain.

The reader will now understand that, though I had been partly forewarned, I really couldn't have guessed that tomorrow or the day after I would find the old prince in my apartment and in such circumstances. Nor could I ever have imagined such boldness from Anna Andreevna! In words you can say and imply anything you like; but to decide, to begin, and in fact to carry through—no, that, I tell you, is character!

II

To continue.

I woke up late the next morning, and had slept unusually soundly and without dreams, I recall that with surprise, so that on awakening, I again felt unusually cheerful morally, as if the whole previous day had never been. I decided not to stop at mama's but to go directly to the cemetery church, with the intention of returning to mama's apartment later, after the ceremony, and not leaving her side for the rest of the day. I was firmly convinced that in any case I would meet him today at mama's, sooner or later, but without fail.

Neither Alphonsinka nor the landlord had been at home for a long time. I didn't want to question the landlady about anything, and had generally resolved to stop all contacts with them and even to move out of the apartment as soon as possible; and therefore, the moment my coffee was brought, I latched the door again. But suddenly there was a knock at the door; to my surprise it turned out to be Trishatov.

I opened the door for him at once and very gladly asked him to come in, but he didn't want to come in.

"I'll only say a couple of words from the threshold . . . or, no, I'll come in, because it seems one has to speak in whispers here; only I won't sit down. You're looking at my wretched coat: it's because Lambert took my fur coat away."

Indeed he was wearing a shabby old coat that was too long for him. He stood before me somehow gloomy and sad, his hands in his pockets, and without taking off his hat.

"I won't sit down, I won't sit down. Listen, Dolgoruky, I know nothing in detail, but I do know that Lambert is preparing some treachery against you, imminent and inevitable—and that is certain. So be careful. The pockmarked one let it slip to me—remember the pockmarked one? But he said nothing about what it has to do with, so I can't say anything more. I only came to warn you. Good-bye."

"But do sit down, dear Trishatov! Though I'm in a hurry, I'm so glad to see you . . ." I cried.

"I won't sit, I won't sit; but I'll remember that you were glad to see me. Eh, Dolgoruky, why deceive people: consciously, of my own free will, I've agreed to do all sorts of nastiness, and such meanness that it's shameful to speak of it here with you. We're with the pockmarked one now . . . Good-bye. I'm not worthy of sitting with you."

"Come now, Trishatov, dear . . ."

"No, you see, Dolgoruky, I'm a bold fellow in front of everybody, and I'll start carousing now. Soon I'll have a fur coat better than the old one made for me, and I'll go around driving trotters. But I'll know within myself that still I didn't sit down here, because that's how I've judged myself, because I'm low compared to you. I'll still find it pleasant to remember it when I'm carousing dishonestly. Well, good-bye, good-bye; I won't offer you my hand; even

Alphonsinka doesn't take my hand. And please don't follow me, and don't come to see me; we have a contract."

The strange boy turned and left. I had no time then, but I resolved that I'd be sure to seek him out quickly, as soon as our affairs were settled.

I won't describe the rest of that morning, though there's much that might be recalled. Versilov wasn't in church for the funeral, and, by the look of them, one might have concluded that he wasn't expected in church even before the coffin was taken out. Mama prayed reverently and, apparently, was wholly given over to prayer. Only Tatyana Pavlovna and Liza stood by the coffin. But no, no, I won't describe anything. After the burial, everyone came back and sat down at the table, and once again, by the look of them, I concluded that they didn't expect him at the table either. When we got up from the table, I went over to mama, embraced her warmly, and wished her a happy birthday. After me, Liza did the same.

"Listen, brother," Liza whispered on the sly, "they're expecting him."

"I guessed that, Liza, I can see it."

"He's sure to come."

That means they have precise information, I thought, but I didn't ask any questions. Though I'm not describing my feelings, this whole riddle, despite all my cheerfulness, again suddenly lay its weight like a stone on my heart. We all sat down in the drawing room at the round table, around mama. Oh, how I liked being with her then and looking at her! Mama suddenly asked me to read something from the Gospel. I read a chapter from Luke. She didn't weep and wasn't even very sad, but never had her face seemed so full of spiritual meaning. An idea shone in her quiet gaze, but I was simply unable to make out that she was anxiously expecting anything. The conversation never flagged. There were many reminiscences about the deceased; Tatyana Pavlovna told many stories about him that had been quite unknown to me before. And generally, if it were all written down, many curious things would be found. Even Tatyana Pavlovna seemed to have completely changed her usual look; she was very quiet, very tender, and, above all, also very calm, though she talked a lot to distract mama. But one detail I remember only too well: mama was sitting on the sofa, and to the left of the sofa, on a special round table, as if prepared for something, lay an image—an old icon, with no casing, but just with crowns over the heads of the saints, of whom there were two. This icon had belonged to Makar Ivanovich—that I knew, and I also knew that the deceased had never parted with this icon and considered it miracle-working. Tatyana Pavlovna glanced at it several times.

"Listen, Sofya," she said suddenly, changing the subject, "instead of the icon lying here, wouldn't it be better to stand it on a table against the wall and light an icon lamp in front of it?"

"No, it's better the way it is now," said mama.

"You're right. Otherwise it would seem too solemn . . ."

I understood nothing then, but the thing was that Makar Ivanovich had long ago bequeathed this icon, verbally, to Andrei Petrovich, and mama was now preparing to give it to him.

It was five o'clock in the afternoon; our conversation went on, and suddenly I noticed as if a slight tremor in mama's face; she quickly straightened up and began listening, while Tatyana Pavlovna, who was speaking just then, went on with what she was saying, not noticing anything. I turned to the door at once and, a moment later, saw Andrei Petrovich in the doorway. He had come in not from the porch, but by the back stairs, through the kitchen and the corridor, and mama was the only one of us who had heard his footsteps. I will now describe the whole insane scene that followed, gesture by gesture, word by word. It was brief.

First of all, in his face, at least at first glance, I didn't notice the slightest change. He was dressed as always, that is, almost foppishly. In his hand was a small but expensive bouquet of fresh flowers. He went over and gave it to mama with a smile; she looked at him with timorous perplexity, but then accepted the bouquet, and color suddenly enlivened her pale cheeks slightly, and joy flashed in her eyes.

"I just knew you'd take it that way, Sonya," he said. As we had all risen when he came in, he went to the table, took Liza's chair, which stood to mama's left, and, not noticing that he was occupying someone else's place, sat down on it. Thus he found himself directly in front of the little table on which the icon lay.

"Greetings to you all. Sonya, I wanted to bring you this bouquet today without fail, for your birthday, and therefore I didn't appear at the funeral, so as not to come to the dead man with a bouquet; and you didn't expect me at the funeral, I know. The old man surely won't be angry over these flowers, because he himself bequeathed us joy, isn't it so? I think he's here in the room somewhere."

Mama looked at him strangely; Tatyana Pavlovna seemed to cringe.

"Who's here in the room?" she asked.

"The deceased. Never mind. You know that a man who doesn't fully believe in all these wonders is always the more inclined to prejudices... But I'd better speak of the bouquet: how I got it here, I don't know. Three times on the way I wanted to drop it in the snow and trample it with my feet."

Mama shuddered.

"I wanted to terribly. Pity me, Sonya, and my poor head. But I wanted to, because it's too beautiful. Of anything in the world, what is more beautiful than a flower? I was carrying it, and here there was snow and frost. Our frost and flowers—what a contrast! However, that's not what I'm getting at: I wanted to crush it because it was beautiful. Sonya, I'm going to disappear again now, but I'll come back very soon, because it seems I'll be afraid. I'll be afraid—and who will cure me of my fear, where will I get hold of an angel like Sonya?... What's this icon you have here? Ah, it's the old man's, I remember. It came to him from his family, his forefathers; he never parted with it all his life; I know, I remember, he bequeathed it to me; I remember very well... and it seems it's an Old Believers' icon[39]... let me look at it."

He took the icon in his hand, brought it to a candle, and studied it intently, but after holding it for just a few seconds, he set it down on the table in front of him. I wondered, but he uttered all these strange speeches so unexpectedly that I could make no sense of them yet. All I remember is that a morbid fear was coming into my heart. Mama's fear was changing to perplexity and compassion; before all, she saw just an unhappy man in him; it happened that formerly as well he had sometimes spoken almost as strangely as now. Liza suddenly became very pale for some reason and strangely nodded her head towards him to me. But Tatyana Pavlovna was the most frightened of all.

"What's wrong with you, dearest Andrei Petrovich?" she spoke cautiously.

"I really don't know what's wrong with me, my dear Tatyana Pavlovna. Don't worry, I still remember that you are Tatyana Pavlovna and that you are dear. However, I've dropped in just for a minute; I'd like to say something nice to Sonya, and I'm looking for the right word, though my heart is filled with words which I'm unable to utter; truly, they're all somehow such strange words. You know, it seems to me as if I'm divided in two," he looked us all over with a terribly serious face and with the most sincere communicativeness. "Truly, mentally divided in two, and I'm terribly afraid of that. Just as if your double were standing next to you; you yourself are intelligent and reasonable, but that one absolutely wants to do something senseless next to you, and sometimes something very amusing, and you suddenly notice that it's you who want to do this amusing thing, and, God knows why, that is, somehow unwillingly you want it, resisting with all your might, you want it. I once knew a doctor who suddenly started whistling in church at his father's funeral. Truly, I was afraid to come to the funeral today, because for some reason the absolute conviction came into my head that I would suddenly start whistling or guffawing, like that unfortunate doctor, who ended rather badly... And, truly, I don't know why I keep remembering that doctor today—so much so that there's no getting rid of him. You know, Sonya, here I've picked up this icon again" (he had picked it up and was turning it in his hands), "and you know, I want terribly much to smash it against the stove now, this second, on this very corner. I'm sure it will split at once into two halves—no more, no less."

Above all, he said all this without any air of pretense or even of some sort of prank; he spoke quite simply, but that was the more terrible; and it seemed he really was terribly afraid of something; I suddenly noticed that his hands were trembling slightly.

"Andrei Petrovich!" mama cried, clasping her hands.

"Let it alone, let the icon alone, Andrei Petrovich, put it down!" Tatyana Pavlovna jumped up. "Get undressed and go to bed. Arkady, fetch the doctor!"

"But no... but no, why are you fussing so?" he said softly, looking around at us all with an intent gaze. Then he suddenly put both elbows on the table and rested his head in his hands.

"I'm frightening you, but I tell you what, my friends: indulge me a little, sit down again and be more calm, all of you—at least for one minute! Sonya, that's not at all what I came here to talk about; I came to tell you something, but quite different. Goodbye, Sonya, I'm setting out on my wanderings again, as I've set out from you several times already... Well, of course, someday I'll come back to you, in this sense you're inevitable. To whom am I to come when it's all over? Believe me, Sonya, I've come to you now as to an angel, and not at all as to an enemy: what sort of enemy, what sort of enemy are you to me! Don't think it's in order to break this icon, because, do you know, Sonya, I still want to break it..."

When Tatyana Pavlovna had cried before then, "Let the icon alone!"—she had snatched the image out of his hands and was holding it herself. Suddenly, at his last words, he quickly jumped up, instantly snatched the icon out of Tatyana's hands, and, swinging ferociously, smashed it with all his might against the corner of the tile stove. The icon split exactly into two pieces... He suddenly turned to us, and his pale face suddenly turned all red, almost purple, and every feature of his face trembled and twitched:

"Don't take it as an allegory, Sonya, it's not Makar's inheritance I've broken, I only did it in order to break... And even so I'll come back to you, my last angel! But, anyhow, why not take it as an allegory; it certainly must have been!..."

And he suddenly hurried out of the room, again through the kitchen (where he had left his fur coat and hat). I won't describe in detail what happened with mama: scared to death, she stood with her hands raised and clasped above her and suddenly called out after him:

"Andrei Petrovich, come back at least to say good-bye, dear!"

"He'll come, Sofya, he'll come! Don't worry!" Tatyana cried, trembling all over in a terrible fit of anger, ferocious anger. "You heard, he himself promised to come back! Let the madcap run loose for one last time. He'll get old, and who indeed will nurse him then, when he's broken down, except you, his old nurse? He says it straight out himself, without shame..."

As for us, Liza was in a faint. I was about to run after him, but then I rushed to mama. I put my arms around her and held her in my embrace. Lukerya came running with a glass of water for Liza. But mama soon recovered; she sank onto the sofa, covered her face with her hands, and wept.

"But no, but no... catch up with him!" Tatyana Pavlovna suddenly cried out with all her might, as if coming to her senses. "Go... go... catch up with him, don't let him get a step ahead of you—go, go!" She was pulling me away from mama with all her might. "Ah, I'll run myself!"

"Arkasha, ah, run after him quickly!" mama suddenly cried as well.

I ran out headlong, also through the kitchen and the yard, but he was nowhere to be seen. Far down the sidewalk I made out the black figures of passersby in the darkness; I started running after them and, catching up with them, looked each one in the face as I ran past. In this way I ran as far as the intersection.

"You don't get angry with madmen," suddenly flashed in my head, "but Tatyana was ferociously angry with him, which means he's not mad at all..." Oh, I kept thinking that it was an *allegory* and that he absolutely wanted to have done with something, as with that icon, and to show it to us, to mama, to everybody. But the "double" was also undoubtedly next to him; of that there was no doubt at all...

III

HE DIDN'T TURN up anywhere, however, and there was no point in running to his place; it was hard to imagine that he had just simply gone home. Suddenly a thought began to gleam before me, and I rushed headlong to Anna Andreevna's.

Anna Andreevna had already returned, and I was admitted at once. I went in, controlling myself as far as I could. Without sitting down, I told her directly about the scene that had just taken place, that is, precisely about the "double." I will never forget nor forgive her the greedy but mercilessly calm and self-assured curiosity with which she listened to me, also without sitting down.

"Where is he? Maybe you know?" I concluded insistently. "Tatyana Pavlovna sent me to you yesterday..."

"I sent for you yesterday. Yesterday he was in Tsarskoe, and he was here as well. And now," she glanced at the clock, "now it's seven o'clock... That means he's probably at home."

"I see you know everything—so speak, speak!" I cried.

"I know a good deal, but I don't know everything. Of course, there's no need to conceal it from you..." She measured me with a strange look, smiling and as if reflecting. "Yesterday morning, in response to Katerina Nikolaevna's letter, he made her a formal proposal of marriage."

"That's not true!" I goggled my eyes.

"The letter went through my hands; I myself took it to her, unopened. This time he acted 'chivalrously' and concealed nothing from me."

"Anna Andreevna, I don't understand anything!"

"Of course, it's hard to understand, but it's like a gambler who throws his last gold coin on the table and has a revolver ready in his pocket—that's the meaning of his proposal. The chances are nine out of ten that she won't accept his proposal; but it means that he's counting on that one-tenth chance, and, I confess, that's very curious, in my opinion, though... though there might also be frenzy in it, that same 'double,' as you said so well just now."

"And you laugh? And how can I believe that the letter was conveyed through you? Aren't you her father's fiancée? Spare me, Anna Andreevna!"

"He asked me to sacrifice my destiny to his happiness, though he didn't really ask; it was all done quite silently, I merely read it all in his eyes. Ah, my God, what more do you want? Didn't he go to your mother in Königsberg to ask her permission to marry Mme. Akhmakov's stepdaughter? That goes very well with the way he chose me yesterday as his representative and confidante."

She was slightly pale. But her calmness only reinforced her sarcasm. Oh, I forgave her much during that minute when I gradually came to grasp the matter. For a minute I thought it over; she waited in silence.

"You know," I smiled suddenly, "you conveyed the letter, because for you there was no risk, because there will be no marriage, but what about him? And her, finally? Of course, she'll turn down his proposal, and then... what may happen then? Where is he now, Anna Andreevna?" I cried. "Here every minute is precious, any minute there may be trouble!"

"He's at home, I told you. In his letter to Katerina Nikolaevna yesterday, which I conveyed, he asked her, *in any event*, for a meeting at his apartment, today, at exactly seven o'clock in the evening. She gave her promise."

"She'll go to his apartment? How is it possible?"

"Why not? The apartment belongs to Nastasya Egorovna; they both could very well meet there as her guests..."

"But she's afraid of him... he may kill her!"

Anna Andreevna only smiled.

"Katerina Nikolaevna, despite all her fear, which I've noticed in her myself, has always nursed, since former times, a certain reverence and awe for the nobility of Andrei Petrovich's principles and the loftiness of his mind. She's trusting herself to him this time so as to have done with him forever. In his letter he gave her his most solemn, most chivalrous word that she had nothing to fear... In short, I don't remember the terms of his letter, but she's trusting herself... so to speak, for the last time... and, so to speak, responding with the most heroic feelings. There may be some sort of chivalrous struggle here on both sides."

"But the double, the double!" I exclaimed. "He really has lost his mind!"

"On giving her word yesterday that she would come to meet him, Katerina Nikolaevna probably didn't suppose the possibility of such a case."

I suddenly turned and broke into a run... To him, to them, of course! But I came back from the front room for a second.

"Maybe that's just what you want, that he should kill her!" I cried, and ran out of the house.

Though I was trembling all over as if in a fit, I entered the apartment silently, through the kitchen, and asked in a whisper to have Nastasya Egorovna come out to me; but she came out at once herself and silently fixed me with a terribly questioning look.

"He's not at home, sir."

But I explained to her directly and precisely, in a quick whisper, that I knew everything from Anna Andreevna and had just come from her.

"Where are they, Nastasya Egorovna?"

"They're in the drawing room, sir, where you were sitting two days ago, at the table..."

"Let me in there, Nastasya Egorovna!"

"How is that possible, sir?"

"Not there, but the room next to it. Nastasya Egorovna, it may be that Anna Andreevna herself wants it. If she didn't, she wouldn't have told me they were here. They won't hear me... she wants it herself..."

"And what if she doesn't?" Nastasya Egorovna kept her gaze fixed on me.

"Nastasya Egorovna, I remember your Olya... let me in."

Her lips and chin suddenly began to tremble:

"Dear heart, maybe for Olya's sake... for your feeling... Don't abandon Anna Andreevna, dear heart! You won't abandon her, eh? You won't?"

"I won't!"

"Give me your great word, then, that you won't rush in on them and start shouting, if I put you in there?"

"I swear on my honor, Nastasya Egorovna!"

She took hold of my frock coat, let me into the dark room adjacent to the one they were sitting in, led me barely audibly over the soft rug to the door, placed me just at the lowered portière and, lifting a tiny corner of the portière, showed me both of them.

I stayed and she left. Naturally, I stayed. I realized that I was eavesdropping, eavesdropping on other people's secrets, but I stayed. How could I not stay—what of the double? Hadn't he smashed an icon before my eyes?

IV

THEY WERE SITTING opposite each other at the same table at which he and I had drunk wine yesterday to his "resurrection." I could see their faces very well. She was in a simple black dress, beautiful, and apparently calm, as always. He was speaking, and she was listening to him with extreme and obliging attention. Maybe a certain timidity could be seen in her. He was terribly agitated. I arrived when the conversation had already begun, and therefore understood nothing for a certain time. I remember she suddenly asked:

"And I was the cause?"

"No, it was I who was the cause," he replied, "and you were only blamelessly to blame. Do you know that one can be blamelessly to blame? That is the most unpardonable blame, and it almost always gets punished," he added, laughing strangely. "And I really thought for a moment that I had quite forgotten you, and I quite laughed at my stupid passion... but you know that. And, anyhow, what do I care about the man you're about to marry? I proposed to you yesterday, forgive me for that, it was absurd, and yet there was no alternative... what could I have done except that absurdity? I don't know..."

He laughed perplexedly at these words, suddenly raising his eyes to her; till that time he had spoken as if looking away. If I had been in her place, I would have been frightened by that laughter, I could feel it. He suddenly got up from his chair.

"Tell me, how could you have agreed to come here?" he asked suddenly, as if remembering the main thing. "My invitation and my whole letter were absurd... Wait, I may still guess how it happened that you agreed to come, but—why have you come?—that's the question. Can it be that you came only out of fear?"

"I came to see you," she said, studying him with timid wariness. They were both silent for half a minute. Versilov lowered himself onto the chair again and began in a meek but deeply moved, almost trembling voice:

"I haven't seen you for a terribly long time, Katerina Nikolaevna, so long that I almost considered it impossible ever to be sitting beside you as I am now, looking into your face and listening to your voice... For two years we haven't seen each other, for two years we haven't talked. I didn't think I'd ever be talking to you. Well, so be it, what's past is past, and what there is now will vanish tomorrow like smoke—so be it! I accept, because once again there's no alternative, but don't just go away now for nothing," he suddenly added almost beseechingly, "since you've done me the charity of coming, don't go away for nothing: answer me one question!"

"What question?"

"You and I will never see each other again and—what is it to you? Tell me the truth once and for all, to the one question intelligent people never ask: did you ever love me, or was I... mistaken?"

She blushed.

"I did love you," she said.

I was just waiting for her to say that—oh, the truthful one, oh, the sincere one, oh, the honest one!

"And now?" he continued.

"Now I don't."

"And you laugh?"

"No, I just smiled inadvertently, because I knew you'd ask, 'And now?' And I smiled because... because when you guess something, you always smile..."

It was even strange. I had never yet seen her so wary, even almost timid, and so abashed. He was devouring her with his eyes.

"I know you don't love me... and—you don't love me at all?"

"Maybe I don't love you at all. I don't love you," she added firmly, not smiling now and not blushing. "Yes, I did love you, but not for long. I very soon stopped loving you then..."

"I know, I know, you saw it wasn't what you wanted, but... what do you want? Explain it to me once more..."

"Did I already explain it to you sometime? What I want? But I'm a most ordinary woman; I'm a calm woman, I like... I like merry people."

"Merry?"

"You see, I don't even know how to speak with you. It seems to me that if you could love me less, then I could come to love you," she again smiled timidly. The fullest sincerity flashed in her reply, and could she possibly not have understood that her reply was the most definitive formula of their relations, which explained and resolved everything? Oh, how he must have understood that! But he looked at her and smiled strangely.

"Is Bjoring merry?" he went on asking.

"Oh, he shouldn't trouble you at all," she answered with a certain haste. "I'm marrying him only because with him it will be calmest for me. My soul will remain entirely my own."

"They say you've again come to like society, the world?"

"Not society. I know that in our society there's the same disorder as everywhere; but the external forms are still beautiful, so that if one lives only so as to pass by, it's better here than anywhere else."

"I've begun hearing the word 'disorder' quite often. Were you also frightened then by my disorder, the chains, the ideas, the stupidities?"

"No, it wasn't quite that..."

"Then what was it? For God's sake, say it all straight out."

"Well, I'll tell you straight out, because I consider you of the greatest intelligence...I always thought there was something ridiculous in you."

Having said that, she suddenly blushed, as if realizing that she had done something extremely imprudent.

"I can forgive you a great deal for telling me that," he said strangely.

"I didn't finish," she hurried on, turning more red. "It's I who am ridiculous...for talking to you like a fool."

"No, you're not ridiculous, you're merely a depraved society woman!" He turned terribly pale. "I also didn't finish earlier, when I asked you why you came. Would you like me to finish? There exists a certain letter, a document, and you are terribly afraid of it, because your father, with that letter in his hands, might curse you while he lives and legally deprive you of your inheritance in his will. You are afraid of that letter, and you have come for that letter," he spoke nearly trembling all over, and his teeth even almost chattering. She listened to him with a wistful and pained expression on her face.

"I know that you can cause me considerable unpleasantness," she said, as if warding off his words, "but I've come not so much to persuade you not to persecute me, as to see you yourself. I've even wished very much to meet you for a long time now, I myself... But I find you the same as you were before," she suddenly added, as if carried away by a particular and decisive thought and even by some strange and sudden feeling.

"And you hoped to see me different? This—after that letter of mine about your depravity? Tell me, did you come here without any fear?"

"I came because I once loved you; but, you know, I beg you, please, don't threaten me with anything while we're together now, don't remind me of my bad thoughts and feelings. If you could talk to me about something else, I'd be very glad. Let there be threats afterwards, but something different now... I truly came to see and hear you for a moment. Well, but if you can't, then kill me straight out, only don't threaten me and don't torture yourself before me," she concluded, looking at him in strange expectation, as if she really supposed he might kill her. He got up from his chair again and, looking at her with an ardent gaze, said firmly:

"You will leave here without the slightest offense."

"Ah, yes, your word of honor!" she smiled.

"No, not only because I gave my word of honor in the letter, but because I want to and shall think about you all night..."

"To torment yourself?"

"I always imagine you when I'm alone. All I do is talk to you. I go into slums and dens and, as a contrast, you appear before me at once. But you always laugh at me, as now..." he said as if beside himself.

"Never, never have I laughed at you!" she exclaimed in a deeply moved voice and as if with the greatest compassion showing on her face. "If I came, I tried as hard as I could to do it so as not to hurt you in any way," she suddenly added. "I came here to tell you that I almost love you... Forgive me, I may not have said it right," she added hastily.

He laughed.

"What makes you unable to pretend? What makes you such a simpleton, what makes you unlike everyone else... Well, how can you say to a man you're driving away, 'I almost love you'?"

"I just didn't know how to put it," she hurried on, "I didn't say it right; it's because I've always been abashed in your presence and have never known how to speak, ever since our first meeting. And if I used the wrong words when I said I 'almost love you,' in my thought it was almost so—that's why I said it, though I love you with that... well, that *general* love with which one loves everyone and which there's no shame in confessing..."

He listened silently, not taking his ardent gaze off her.

"I, of course, offend you," he went on as if beside himself. "This must indeed be what they call passion... I know one thing, that with you I'm finished; without you also. It's all the same with you or without you, wherever you are, you're always with me. I also know that I can hate you very much, more than I love you... However, I've long ceased thinking of anything—it's all the same to me. I'm only sorry that I love a woman like you..."

His voice faltered; he went on as if breathless:

"What's the matter? You find what I'm saying wild?" He smiled a pale smile. "I think that, if only it would attract you, I could stand on one leg on a pillar somewhere for thirty years... I see you pity me, your face says, 'I'd love you if I could, but I can't...' Yes? Never mind, I have no pride. I'm ready, like a beggar, to take any charity from you—any... do you hear?... What pride can a beggar have?"

She got up and went over to him.

"My friend!" she said, touching his shoulder with her hand and with inexpressible feeling in her face. "I cannot listen to such words! I'll think of you all my life as of the most precious of men, as of the greatest of hearts, as of something sacred out of all that I can respect and love. Andrei Petrovich, understand my words: there's something I came for now, dear man, dear before and now! I'll never forget how you shook my mind during our first meetings. Let's part as friends, and you will be my most serious and most dear thought in all my life!"

"'Let's part and then I'll love you,' I'll love you, only let's part. Listen," he said, quite pale, "give me more charity: don't love me, don't live with me, let's never see each other; I'll be your slave, if you call me, I'll vanish instantly if you don't want to see or hear me, only... *only don't marry anyone!*"

My heart was wrung painfully when I heard such words. This naïvely humiliating request was the more pathetic, it pierced the heart the more strongly, for being so naked and impossible. Yes, of course, he was asking for charity! Well, but could he think she'd agree? And yet he stooped to the attempt: he attempted to ask! This last degree of dispiritedness was unbearable to see. All the features of her face suddenly twisted as if with pain; but before she had time to say a word, he suddenly came to his senses:

"I'll *exterminate* you!" he said suddenly in a strange, distorted voice, not his own.

But her answer was also strange, also in an unexpected voice, not at all her own:

"If I were to give you charity," she suddenly said firmly, "you'd revenge yourself on me for it afterwards still worse than you're threatening now, because you'd never forget that you stood before me as such a beggar . . . I cannot listen to threats from you!" she concluded almost with indignation, looking at him all but in defiance.

" 'Threats from you,' that is, from such a beggar! I was joking," he said softly, smiling. "I won't do anything to you, don't be afraid, go now . . . and I'll do all I can to send you that document—only go, go! I wrote you a stupid letter, and you responded to the stupid letter and came—we're quits. Go this way," he pointed to the door (she was about to pass through the room where I was standing behind the portière).

"Forgive me if you can," she stopped in the doorway.

"Well, what if we meet as quite good friends someday and remember this scene with bright laughter?" he said suddenly; but all the features of his face trembled, as in a man overcome by a fit.

"Oh, God grant it!" she cried, pressing her hands together before her, but peering timorously into his face and as if trying to guess what he meant to say.

"Go. Much sense there is in the two of us, but you . . . Oh, you're my kind of person! I wrote a crazy letter, and you agreed to come and say that you 'almost love me.' No, you and I—we're people of the same madness! Always be mad like that, don't change, and we'll meet as friends—that I predict to you, I swear it to you!"

"And then I'll certainly love you, because I feel it even now!" The woman in her couldn't help herself and threw him these last words from the threshold.

She went out. I hastily and inaudibly moved to the kitchen and, almost without looking at Nastasya Egorovna, who was waiting for me, set off down the back stairs and across the courtyard to the street. But I only had time to see her get into a hired carriage that was waiting for her by the porch. I ran down the street.

Chapter Eleven

I

I WENT RUNNING to Lambert. Oh, how I wish I could give a semblance of logic and seek out the least bit of common sense in my acts that evening and all that night, but even now, when I can grasp everything, I'm in no way able to present the matter in proper and clear connection. There was a feeling here, or, better, a whole chaos of feelings, among which I was naturally bound to get lost. True, there was one chiefest feeling that overwhelmed me and commanded everything, but... need I confess it? The more so as I'm not certain...

I ran to Lambert, naturally, beside myself. I even frightened him and Alphonsinka at first. I've always noticed that the most lost, most crapulous Frenchmen are exceedingly attached, in their domestic life, to some sort of bourgeois order, to some sort of most prosaic daily routine of life established once and for all. However, Lambert very soon realized that something had happened and went into raptures, seeing me finally at his place, finally *possessing* me. That was all he thought about, day and night, those days! Oh, how he needed me! And now, when he had already lost all hope, I suddenly come on my own, and in such madness—precisely the state he needed.

"Wine, Lambert!" I shouted. "Let's drink, let's storm it up. Alphonsina, where's your guitar?"

I won't describe the scene—it's superfluous. We drank, and I told him everything, everything. He listened greedily. I—and I was the first—directly suggested a plot to him, a conflagration. First of all, we must invite Katerina Nikolaevna here by letter...

"That can be done," Lambert confirmed, snatching at every word I said.

Second, to be convincing, we must send a complete copy of her "document" with the letter, so that she can see straight off that she's not being deceived.

"So we should, so we must!" Lambert confirmed, constantly exchanging glances with Alphonsinka.

Third, the one to invite her must be Lambert himself, on his own, in the manner of some unknown person just arrived from Moscow, and I must bring Versilov...

"Versilov can be done..." Lambert confirmed.

"Must be, not can be!" I cried. "It's necessary! The whole thing's being done for him!" I explained, sipping gulp after gulp from my glass. (All three of us were drinking, but it seems I alone drank the whole bottle of champagne, while they only made a show of it.) "Versilov and I will sit in the other room (we have to secure the other room, Lambert!), and when she suddenly agrees to everything—to the ransom in cash and to the *other* ransom, because they're all mean—then Versilov and I will come out and catch her in all her meanness, and Versilov, seeing how loathsome she is, will be cured at once and will kick her out. But we need to have Bjoring there as well, so that he, too, can have a look at her!" I added in a frenzy.

"No, we don't need Bjoring," Lambert observed.

"We do, we do!" I yelled again. "You understand nothing, Lambert, because you're stupid! On the contrary, let the scandal spread through high society—that way we'll be revenged both on high society and on her, and let her be punished! She'll give you a promissory note, Lambert... I don't need money, I spit on money; you'll stoop down to pick it up and put it in your pocket along with my spit, but instead I will crush her!"

"Yes, yes," Lambert kept confirming, "it's all as you..." He kept exchanging glances with Alphonsinka.

"Lambert! She's terribly in awe of Versilov; I've just been convinced of it," I babbled to him.

"It's good that you spied it all out. I never supposed you were such a spy and had so much sense!" He said that in order to flatter me.

"Lies, Frenchman, I'm not a spy, but there is a lot of sense in me! And you know, Lambert, she loves him!" I went on, trying with all my might to speak myself out. "But she won't marry him, because Bjoring's an officer of the guards and Versilov is only a magnanimous man and friend of mankind, a comical person, in their opinion, and nothing more! Oh, she understands this passion and enjoys it, she flirts, she entices, but she won't marry him! She's a woman, she's a serpent! Every woman is a serpent, and every serpent is a woman! He's got to be cured; he's got to have the scales torn off. Let him see what she's like, and he'll be cured. I'll bring him to you, Lambert!"

"So you must," Lambert kept confirming, pouring more for me every minute.

Above all, he simply trembled over not angering me with something, over not contradicting me, and getting me to drink more. This was so crude and obvious that even I couldn't help noticing it then. But I myself couldn't leave for anything; I kept drinking and talking, and I wanted terribly to speak myself out finally. When Lambert went for another bottle, Alphonsinka played some Spanish motif on the guitar; I almost burst into tears.

"Lambert, you don't know all!" I exclaimed with deep feeling. "This man absolutely must be saved, because he's surrounded by... sorcery. If she married him, the next morning, after the first night, he'd kick her out... because that does happen. Because such violent, wild love works like a fit, like a deadly noose, like an illness, and—as soon as you reach satisfaction—the scales fall at once and the opposite feeling appears: disgust and hatred, the wish to exterminate, to crush. Do you know the story of Abishag,[40] Lambert, have you read it?"

"No, I don't recall. A novel?" murmured Lambert.

"Oh, you know nothing, Lambert! You're terribly, terribly uneducated... but I spit on that. It makes no difference. Oh, he loves mama; he kissed her portrait; he'll drive the other woman out the next morning and go to mama himself; but it will be too late, and that's why we must save him now..."

Towards the end I started weeping bitterly; but I still went on talking, and I drank terribly much. The most characteristic feature consisted in the fact that Lambert, all evening, never once asked about the "document," that is, where it was. That is, that I should show it to him, lay it on the table. What, it seems, would have been more natural than to ask about it, when we were arranging to act together? Another feature: we only said it must be done, that we must do "it" without fail, but where it would be, how and when—of that we also didn't say a word! He only yessed me and exchanged glances with Alphonsinka—nothing more! Of course, I couldn't put anything together then, but all the same I remember it.

I ended by falling asleep on his sofa without undressing. I slept for a very long time and woke up very late. I remember that, on waking up, I lay for some time on the sofa, as if stunned, trying to remember and put things together and pretending I was still asleep. But Lambert turned out not to be in the room: he had left. It was going on ten o'clock; the stove was burning and crackling, exactly as then, after that night, when I found myself at Lambert's for the first time. But Alphonsinka was keeping watch on me from behind the screen. I noticed it at once, because she peeked out a couple of times and checked on me, but I closed my eyes each time and pretended I was still asleep. I did that because I was crushed and had to make sense of my situation. I felt with horror the whole absurdity and loathsomeness of my night's confession to Lambert, my complicity with him, my mistake in having run to him! But, thank God, the document still remained with me, was still sewn up in my side pocket; I felt it with my hand—it was there! So all I had to do right then was jump up and run away, and there was no point in being ashamed of Lambert afterwards; Lambert wasn't worth it.

But I was also ashamed of myself! I was my own judge, and—God, what there was in my soul! But I'm not going to describe that infernal, unbearable feeling and that consciousness of filth and vileness. But all the same I must confess it, because it seems the time has come for that. It should be pointed out in my notes. And so, let it be known that I wanted to disgrace her and witness her giving the ransom to Lambert (oh, baseness!), not because I wanted to save the mad Versilov and return him to mama, but because... maybe I myself was in love with her, in love and jealous! Jealous of whom? Of Bjoring? Of Versilov? Of all those she would look at or talk with at a ball, while I stood in the corner, ashamed of myself?... Oh, unseemliness!

In short, I don't know whom I was jealous of; I only felt and had become convinced during the past evening, like two times two, that for me she was lost, that this woman would spurn and deride me for my falseness and absurdity. She was truthful and honest, while I—I was a spy, and with documents!

All this I've kept hidden in my heart ever since, but now the time has come, and I'm drawing the bottom line. But, once again and for the last time: maybe I've heaped lies on myself by a whole half or even seventy-five percent! That night I hated her, like a man beside himself, and later like a raging drunkard. I've already said it was a chaos of feelings and sensations in which I myself could make out nothing. But, all the same, they had to be spoken out, because at least a part of these feelings was certainly there.

With irrepressible disgust and with the irrepressible intention of smoothing everything over, I suddenly jumped up from the sofa;

but just as I jumped up, Alphonsinka instantly jumped out. I grabbed my coat and hat, and told her to tell Lambert that I was raving the night before, that I had slandered the woman, that I was deliberately joking, and that Lambert should never dare come to me... All this I brought out anyhow, haphazardly, hastily, in French, and, of course, awfully unclearly, but, to my surprise, Alphonsinka understood it all terribly well. But, what was most surprising, she was even as if glad of something.

"*Oui, oui,*" she agreed with me, "*c'est une honte! Une dame... Oh, vous êtes généreux, vous! Soyez tranquille, je ferai voir raison à Lambert...*"*

So that even at that moment I should have been thrown into perplexity, seeing such an unexpected turnabout in her feelings, which meant, perhaps, in Lambert's as well. I went out silently, however; my soul was troubled and I wasn't reasoning well. Oh, afterwards I considered it all, but by then it was too late! Oh, what an infernal machination came out here! I'll stop and explain everything beforehand; otherwise it will be impossible for the reader to understand.

The thing was that, back at my first meeting with Lambert, while I was thawing out in his apartment, I had murmured to him, like a fool, that the document was sewn up in my pocket. Then I had suddenly fallen asleep for a while on the sofa in the corner, and Lambert had immediately felt my pocket then and made sure that a piece of paper was actually sewn up in it. Several times later he had made sure that the paper was still there: so, for instance, during our dinner at the Tartars', I remember he purposely put his arm around my waist several times. Realizing, finally, how important this paper was, he put together his own totally particular plan, which I never supposed he had. Like a fool, I imagined all the while that he was so persistently inviting me to his place solely to persuade me to join company with him and not act otherwise than together. But, alas! he invited me for something quite different! He invited me in order to get me dead drunk and, when I was sprawled out there, unconscious and snoring, to cut my pocket open and take possession of the document. That's just what he and Alphonsinka did that night; it was Alphonsinka who cut open the pocket. Having taken out the letter, *her letter*, my Moscow docu-

*Yes, yes... it's a shame! A lady... Oh, you're generous, you are! Don't worry, I'll make Lambert see reason ...

ment, they took a simple sheet of note paper of the same size, put it into the cut pocket, and sewed it up again as if nothing had happened, so that I wouldn't notice anything. Alphonsinka also did the sewing up. And I, almost to the very end, I—for a whole day and a half—went on thinking that I was in possession of the secret, and that Katerina Nikolaevna's destiny was still in my hands!

A last word: this theft of the document was the cause of it all, all the remaining misfortunes!

II

NOW COME THE last twenty-four hours of my notes, and I'm at the final end!

It was, I think, around half-past ten when, agitated and, as far as I remember, somehow strangely distracted, but with a definitive resolve in my heart, I came trudging to my apartment. I was not in a hurry, I already knew how I was going to act. And suddenly, just as I entered our corridor, I understood at once that a new calamity had befallen and an extraordinary complication of matters had occurred: the old prince, having just been brought from Tsarskoe Selo, was in our apartment, and Anna Andreevna was with him!

He had been put not in my room, but in the two rooms next to mine, which belonged to the landlord. The day before, as it turned out, certain changes and embellishments, though of a minimal sort, had been carried out in these rooms. The landlord and his wife had moved to the tiny closet occupied by the fussy pockmarked tenant whom I have mentioned before, and the pockmarked tenant had been confiscated for the time being—I don't know where to.

I was met by the landlord, who at once darted into my room. He did not have the same resolute air as the day before, but he was in an extraordinarily agitated state, equal, so to speak, to the event. I said nothing to him, but went to the corner and, clutching my head with my hands, stood there for about a minute. At first he thought I was "putting it on," but in the end he couldn't stand it and became alarmed.

"Is anything wrong?" he murmured. "I've been waiting to ask you," he added, seeing that I didn't answer, "whether you wouldn't like to open this door, for direct communication with the prince's rooms... rather than through the corridor?" He was pointing to the side door, which was always locked, and which communicated with his own rooms and now, therefore, with the prince's quarters.

"Look here, Pyotr Ippolitovich," I addressed him with a stern air, "I humbly beg you to go and invite Anna Andreevna here to my room for a talk. Have they been here long?"

"Must be nearly an hour."

"So go."

He went and brought back the strange reply that Anna Andreevna and Prince Nikolai Ivanovich were impatiently awaiting me in their rooms—meaning that Anna Andreevna did not wish to come. I straightened and cleaned my frock coat, which had become wrinkled during the night, washed, combed my hair, all of that unhurriedly, and, aware of how necessary it was to be cautious, went to see the old man.

The prince was sitting on the sofa at a round table, and Anna Andreevna was preparing tea for him in another corner, at another table covered with a tablecloth, on which the landlord's samovar, polished as it had never been before, was boiling. I came in with the same stern look on my face, and the old man, instantly noticing it, gave a start, and the smile on his face quickly gave way to decided alarm. But I couldn't keep it up, laughed at once, and held out my arms to him. The poor man simply threw himself into my embrace.

Unquestionably, I realized at once whom I was dealing with. First of all, it became as clear to me as two times two that, during the time since I last saw him, they had made the old man, who had even been almost hale and still at least somewhat sensible and with a certain character, into a sort of mummy, a sort of perfect child, fearful and mistrustful. I will add that he knew perfectly well why he had been brought here, and that everything had happened exactly as I explained above, when I ran ahead of myself. He was suddenly struck, broken, crushed by the news of his daughter's betrayal and of the madhouse. He had allowed himself to be brought, so frightened that he scarcely knew what he was doing. He had been told that I was in possession of the secret, and held the key to the ultimate solution. I'll say beforehand: it was this ultimate solution and key that he feared more than anything in the world. He expected that I'd just walk in there with some sort of sentence on my forehead and a paper in my hand, and he was awfully glad that I was prepared meanwhile to laugh and chatter about other things. When we embraced, he wept. I confess, I wept a bit, too. But I suddenly felt very sorry for him... Alphonsinka's little dog went off into a high, bell-like barking and strained towards me from the sofa. He hadn't parted from this tiny dog since the day he acquired it, and even slept with it.

"*Oh, je disais qu'il a du coeur!*"* he exclaimed, pointing at me to Anna Andreevna.

"But how you've improved, Prince, what a fine, fresh, healthy look you have!" I observed. Alas! it was all quite the opposite: this was a mummy, and I only said it to encourage him.

"*N'est-ce pas, n'est-ce pas?*"† he repeated joyfully. "Oh, my health has improved astonishingly."

"Anyhow, have your tea, and if you offer me a cup, I'll drink with you."

"Marvelous! 'Let us drink and enjoy...' or how does the poem go? Anna Andreevna, give him tea, *il prend toujours par les sentiments*‡ ... give us tea, my dear."

Anna Andreevna served us tea, but suddenly turned to me and began with extreme solemnity:

"Arkady Makarovich, both of us, I and my benefactor, Prince Nikolai Ivanovich, have taken refuge with you. I consider that we have come to you, to you alone, and we are both asking you for shelter. Remember that almost the whole destiny of this saintly, this most noble and offended man is in your hands... We await the decision of your truthful heart!"

But she was unable to finish; the prince was horrified and almost trembled with fear:

"*Après, après, n'est-ce pas? Chère amie!*"§ he repeated, holding his hands up to her.

I can't express how unpleasantly her outburst also affected me. I said nothing in reply and contented myself only with a cold and grave bow; then I sat down at the table and even deliberately began talking about other things, about some foolishness, started laughing and cracking jokes... The old man was obviously grateful to me and became rapturously merry. But his merriment, though rapturous, was somehow fragile and might be supplanted at any moment by complete dispiritedness; that was clear from the first glance.

*Oh, I said he had a heart!
†Isn't it so, isn't it so?
‡He always appeals to one's feelings ...
§Afterwards, afterwards, don't you think? My dear friend!

"*Cher enfant*, I hear you were ill...Ah, *pardon*! I hear you've been occupied all the while with spiritism?"[41]

"Never dreamed of it," I smiled.

"No? Then who was talking about spir-it-ism?"

"That clerk here, Pyotr Ippolitovich, spoke to you about it earlier," Anna Andreevna explained. "He's a very merry man and knows lots of anecdotes; would you like me to invite him here?"

"*Oui, oui, il est charmant** ... he knows anecdotes, but we'd better invite him later. We'll invite him, and he'll tell us everything, *mais après*. Imagine, earlier they were setting the table, and he says, 'Don't worry, it won't fly away, we're not spiritists.' Can spiritists make tables fly?"

"I really don't know; they say they get all four legs off the ground."

"*Mais c'est terrible ce que tu dis*,"† he looked at me in fright.

"Oh, don't worry, it's nonsense."

"I say so myself. Nastasya Stepanovna Salomeeva...you do know her...ah, no, you don't know her...imagine, she also believes in spiritism, and imagine, *chère enfant*," he turned to Anna Andreevna, "I tell her there are tables in the ministry as well, with eight pairs of clerkly hands lying on them, all writing documents—why don't the tables dance there? Imagine if they suddenly started dancing! A revolt of the tables in the Ministry of Finance or National Education—just what we need!"

"What nice things you say, Prince, as always," I exclaimed, trying to laugh sincerely.

"*N'est-ce pas? Je ne parle pas trop, mais je dis bien.*"‡

"I'll bring Pyotr Ippolitovich," Anna Andreevna got up. Her face shone with pleasure; she was glad to see how affectionate I was with the old man. But as soon as she went out, the old man's face changed instantly. He glanced back hastily at the door, looked around, and, leaning towards me from the sofa, whispered in a frightened voice:

"*Cher ami!* Oh, if only I could see the two of them here together! *Oh, cher enfant!*"

"Calm yourself, Prince..."

"Yes, yes, but...we'll reconcile them, *n'est-ce pas*? It's an empty

*Yes, yes, he's charming ...
†But it's terrible what you say.
‡Isn't it so? I don't talk much, but I speak well.

little quarrel of two most worthy women, *n'est-ce pas*? I put my hopes in you alone... We'll straighten it all out here; and what a strange apartment you have here," he looked around almost fearfully, "and, you know, this landlord... he's got such a face... Tell me, he's not dangerous?"

"The landlord? Oh, no! how could he be dangerous?"

"*C'est ça*.* So much the better. *Il semble qu'il est bête, ce gentilhomme*.† *Cher enfant*, for Christ's sake, don't tell Anna Andreevna that I'm afraid of everything here; I praised everything here from the first, I praised the landlord, too. Listen, you know the story of von Sohn[42]—remember?"

"What about it?"

"*Rien, rien du tout... Mais je suis libre ici, n'est-ce pas?*‡ What do you think, can anything happen to me here... of the same sort?"

"But I assure you, dearest Prince... for pity's sake!"

"*Mon ami! Mon enfant!*" he exclaimed suddenly, clasping his hands before him and no longer hiding his fear. "If you do indeed have something... documents... in short, if you have anything to tell me, then don't tell me; for God's sake, don't tell me anything; better not tell me at all... for as long as you can, don't tell me..."

He was about to rush and embrace me; tears poured down his face; I can't express how my heart was wrung: the poor old man was like a pathetic, weak, frightened child, stolen from his own nest by gypsies and taken to strangers. But we were kept from embracing: the door opened, and in came Anna Andreevna, not with the landlord, but with her brother, the kammerjunker. This novelty astounded me; I got up and made for the door.

"Arkady Makarovich, allow me to introduce you," Anna Andreevna said loudly, so that I involuntarily had to stop.

"I'm *only too well* acquainted with your dear brother already," I said distinctly, especially emphasizing the words "only too well."

"Ah, there's a terrible mistake here! And I do apo-lo-gize, my dear And... Andrei Makarovich," the young man began to maunder, approaching me with an extraordinarily casual air and taking hold of my hand, which I was unable to withdraw. "It's all my Stepan's fault. He announced you so stupidly then that I took you for someone else—this was in Moscow," he clarified for his sister,

*That's right.
†He seems to be stupid, this gentleman.
‡Nothing, nothing at all... But I'm free here, am I not?

"then I tried my best to find you and explain, but I fell ill, ask her . . . *Cher prince, nous devons être amis même par droit de naissance . . .*"*

And the brazen young man even dared to put one arm around my shoulder, which was the height of familiarity. I drew back, but, in my embarrassment, preferred to leave quickly without saying a word. Going into my room, I sat down on the bed, thoughtful and agitated. The intrigue was suffocating me, yet I couldn't just dumbfound Anna Andreevna and cut her down. I suddenly felt that she, too, was dear to me, and that her position was terrible.

III

As I EXPECTED, she came into my room herself, having left the prince with her brother, who began telling him some society gossip, the most recent and fresh-baked, and instantly cheered up the impressionable old man. I got up from the bed silently and with a questioning look.

"I've told you everything, Arkady Makarovich," she began directly. "Our fate is in your hands."

"But I also warned you that I can't . . . The most sacred duties prevent me from fulfilling your expectations . . ."

"Oh? So that's your answer? Well, let me perish, but what of the old man? What are your expectations: will he lose his mind by evening?"

"No, he'll lose his mind if I show him his daughter's letter, in which she consults a lawyer about declaring her father insane!" I exclaimed vehemently. "That's what he won't be able to bear. You should know that he doesn't believe this letter, he's already told me!"

I lied about his telling me; but it was opportune.

"Already told you? Just as I thought! In that case, I'm lost. He was weeping just now and asking to be taken home."

"Tell me, what does your plan in fact consist in?" I asked insistently.

She blushed, from wounded arrogance, so to speak, though she controlled herself:

"With this letter of his daughter's in our hands, we are justified in the eyes of the world. I'll send word at once to Prince V——sky and Boris Mikhailovich Pelishchev, his childhood friends; they're

*Dear Prince, we should be friends even by right of birth.

both respectable men with influence in the world, and I know that two years ago they were already indignant at certain actions of his merciless and greedy daughter. They will, of course, reconcile him with his daughter, at my request, and I myself will insist on it; but, on the other hand, the state of affairs will change completely. Besides, then my relations, the Fanariotovs, as I expect, will venture to support my rights. But for me his happiness comes before everything; let him understand, finally, and appreciate who is really devoted to him! Unquestionably, I'm counting most of all on your influence, Arkady Makarovich; you love him so much... And who else loves him except you and I? You're all he talked about these last few days; he pined for you, you're 'his young friend'... It goes without saying that, for the rest of my life, my gratitude will know no bounds..."

This meant she was now offering me a reward—money, maybe. I interrupted her sharply.

"No matter what you say, I can't," I said with an air of unshakable resolution. "I can only repay you with the same frankness and explain to you my latest intentions: I will, in the nearest future, hand this fatal letter over to Katerina Nikolaevna, but with the understanding that no scandal will be made of all that has just happened, and that she gives her word beforehand that she will not interfere with your happiness. That is all I can do."

"This is impossible!" she said, blushing all over. The mere thought that Katerina Nikolaevna would *spare* her, made her indignant.

"I will not alter my decision, Anna Andreevna."

"Maybe you will."

"Turn to Lambert!"

"Arkady Makarovich, you don't know what misfortunes may come of your stubbornness," she said sternly and bitterly.

"Misfortunes will come—that's certain... my head is spinning. Enough talk; my mind is made up and that's the end of it. Only for God's sake, I beg you, don't bring your brother to me."

"But he precisely wishes to smooth over..."

"There's nothing to smooth over! I don't need it, I don't want it, I don't want it!" I exclaimed, clutching my head. (Oh, maybe I treated her too haughtily then!) "Tell me, however, where will the prince spend the night tonight? Surely not here?"

"He'll spend the night here, in your place and with you."

"By evening I'll have moved to another apartment!"

And after these merciless words, I seized my hat and began putting on my coat. Anna Andreevna watched me silently and sternly. I felt sorry—oh, I felt sorry for this proud girl! But I ran out of the apartment, not leaving her a word of hope.

IV

I'LL TRY TO make it short. My decision was taken irrevocably, and I went straight to Tatyana Pavlovna. Alas! a great misfortune could have been prevented if I had found her at home then; but, as if by design, I was especially pursued by bad luck that day. Of course, I went by mama's as well, first of all to see how poor mama was, and, second, counting almost certainly on meeting Tatyana Pavlovna there. But she wasn't there either; she had just gone somewhere, mama was sick in bed, and Liza alone remained with her. Liza asked me not to come in and waken mama: "She didn't sleep all night and was suffering; thank God, now at least she's fallen asleep." I embraced Liza and told her in only a word or two that I had taken an enormous and fateful decision, and that I would presently carry it out. She listened without any special surprise, as if to the most usual words. Oh, they were all accustomed then to my ceaseless "final decisions" and to their fainthearted cancellation afterwards. But now—now it was a different matter! I did stop by at the tavern on the canal, though, and sat there to while away the time, and then certainly catch Tatyana Pavlovna. However, I should explain why I suddenly needed this woman so much. The thing was that I wanted to send her at once to Katerina Nikolaevna, to invite her to her apartment and in Tatyana Pavlovna's presence return the document to her, having explained everything once and for all... In short, I wanted what was only fitting: I wanted to justify myself once and for all. On finishing with that point, I had absolutely and now imperatively resolved to put in a few words right then in favor of Anna Andreevna, and, if possible, to take Katerina Nikolaevna and Tatyana Pavlovna (as a witness), bring them to my place, that is, to the prince, and there reconcile the hostile women, resurrect the prince, and... and... in short, make everyone happy this very day, at least here in this little bunch, so that only Versilov and mama would be left. I could have no doubt of success. Katerina Nikolaevna, grateful for the return of the letter, for which I would not ask her anything, could not refuse me such a request. Alas, I still imagined that I was in possession of the document! Oh, what a stupid and undignified position I was in, without knowing it myself!

It was already quite dark and around four o'clock when I again dropped in at Tatyana Pavlovna's. Marya answered rudely that she "hasn't come back." I well recall Marya's strange, furtive glance now; but then, naturally, nothing could have entered my head. On the contrary, another thought suddenly pricked me: as I was going down Tatyana Pavlovna's back stairs, vexed and somewhat dejected, I remembered the poor prince, who had reached out his hands to me today—and I suddenly reproached myself painfully for having abandoned him, maybe even out of personal vexation. I worriedly began imagining that something even very bad might have happened to them in my absence, and I hastily headed for home. At home, however, only the following circumstances occurred.

Anna Andreevna, having left me in wrath earlier, had not yet lost heart. It must be said that she had already sent to Lambert in the morning, then sent to him once again, and since Lambert had still not turned up at home, she finally sent her brother to look for him. The poor girl, seeing my resistance, placed her last hopes in Lambert and his influence on me. She was waiting impatiently for Lambert, and only marveled that he, who wouldn't leave her side and had fawned on her till today, had suddenly abandoned her entirely and vanished. Alas! it couldn't even enter her head that Lambert, now in possession of the document, had taken quite different decisions, and therefore, of course, was avoiding her and even purposely hiding from her.

Thus, worried and with increasing anxiety in her soul, Anna Andreevna was almost unable to divert the old man; and meanwhile his worry had grown to threatening proportions. He asked strange and fearful questions, started casting suspicious glances even at her, and several times began to weep. Young Versilov hadn't stayed long then. After he left, Anna Andreevna finally brought Pyotr Ippolitovich, in whom she placed such hopes, but the man was not found pleasing at all, and even provoked disgust. In general, the prince for some reason looked at Pyotr Ippolitovich with ever-growing mistrust and suspicion. And the landlord, as if on purpose, again started his talk about spiritism and some tricks he himself had supposedly seen performed, namely, how some itinerant charlatan had supposedly cut people's heads off before the whole public, so that the blood flowed and everyone could see it, and then put them back onto the necks, and they supposedly grew on again, also before the whole public, and all this had supposedly taken place in the year fifty-nine. The prince was so frightened, and at the same time became so indignant for some reason, that Anna Andreevna was forced to remove the narrator immediately. Fortunately, dinner arrived, ordered specially the day before somewhere in the neighborhood (through Lambert and Alphonsinka) from a remarkable French chef, who was without a post and was seeking to place himself in an aristocratic house or club. Dinner with champagne diverted the old man extremely; he ate a great deal and was very jocular. After dinner, of course, he felt heavy and wanted to sleep, and as he always slept after dinner, Anna Andreevna prepared a bed for him. As he was falling asleep, he kept kissing her hands, said that she was his paradise, his hope, his houri, his "golden flower"—in short, he went off into the most Oriental expressions. At last he fell asleep, and it was just then that I returned.

Anna Andreevna hurriedly came into my room, pressed her hands together before me, and said, "no longer for her own sake, but for the prince's," that she "begs me not to leave, and to go to him when he wakes up. Without you, he'll perish, he'll have a nervous breakdown; I'm afraid he won't last till nighttime . . ." She added that she herself absolutely had to be absent, "maybe even for two hours," which meant that she was "leaving the prince to me alone." I warmly gave her my word that I'd stay till evening, and that when he woke up, I'd do all I could to divert him.

"And I will do my duty!" she concluded energetically.

She left. I'll add, running ahead, that she herself went looking for Lambert; this was her last hope. On top of that, she visited her brother and her Fanariotov family; it's clear what state of mind she must have come back in.

The prince woke up about an hour after she left. I heard him groan through the wall and ran to him at once. I found him sitting on his bed in a dressing gown, but so frightened by the solitude, by the light of the single lamp, and by the strange room, that when I came in he gave a start, jumped up, and cried out. I rushed to him, and when he made out that it was I, he began to embrace me with tears of joy.

"And they told me you had moved somewhere, to another apartment, that you got frightened and ran away."

"Who could have told you that?"

"Who could? You see, I may have thought it up myself, or maybe someone told me. Imagine, I just had a dream: in comes an old man with a beard and with an icon, an icon that's split in two, and he suddenly says, 'That's how your life will be split!'"

"Ah, my God, you must have heard from someone that Versilov broke an icon yesterday?"

"*N'est-ce pas?* I heard, I heard! I heard it this morning from Nastasya Egorovna. She moved my trunk and my little dog over here."

"Well, and so you dreamed of it."

"Well, it makes no difference. And imagine, this old man kept shaking his finger at me. Where is Anna Andreevna?"

"She'll be back presently."

"From where? Has she also gone?" he exclaimed with pain.

"No, no, she'll be back presently, and she asked me to sit with you."

"*Oui*, to come here. And so our Andrei Petrovich has gone off his head—'so inadvertently and so swiftly!'[43] I always predicted to him that he'd end up that way. My friend, wait..."

He suddenly seized me by the frock coat with his hand and pulled me towards him.

"Today," he began to whisper, "the landlord suddenly brought me photographs, vile photographs of women, all naked women in various Oriental guises, and began showing them to me through a glass... You see, I praised them reluctantly, but that's just how they brought vile women to that unfortunate man, to make it easier to get him drunk..."

"You keep on about von Sohn, but enough, Prince! The landlord is a fool and nothing more!"

"A fool and nothing more! *C'est mon opinion!** My friend, save me from this place if you can!" he suddenly pressed his hands together before me.

"Prince, I'll do everything I can! I'm all yours... Dear Prince, wait, and maybe I'll settle everything!"

"*N'est-ce pas?* We'll up and run away, and we'll leave the trunk for appearances, so that he'll think we're coming back."

"Run away where? And Anna Andreevna?"

"No, no, together with Anna Andreevna... Oh, *mon cher*, I've got some sort of jumble in my head... Wait—there, in my bag, to

*That's my opinion!

the right, is Katya's portrait; I put it there on the sly, so that Anna Andreevna and especially this Nastasya Egorovna wouldn't notice. Take it out, for God's sake, quickly, carefully, watch out that they don't find us... Can't we put the hook on the door?"

Indeed, I found in the bag a photographic portrait of Katerina Nikolaevna in an oval frame. He took it in his hands, brought it to the light, and tears suddenly poured down his gaunt yellow cheeks.

"*C'est un ange, c'est un ange du ciel!*"* he exclaimed. "All my life I've been guilty before her... and now, too! *Chère enfant*, I don't believe anything, anything! My friend, tell me: well, is it possible to imagine that they want to put me in a madhouse? *Je dis des choses charmantes et tout le monde rit*† ... and suddenly this man is taken to the madhouse?"

"That was never so!" I cried. "That is a mistake! I know her feelings!"

"And you also know her feelings? Why, that's wonderful! My friend, you've resurrected me. What was all that they were telling me about you? My friend, invite Katya here, and let the two of them kiss each other before me, and I'll take them home, and we'll chase the landlord away!"

He stood up, pressed his hands together before me, and suddenly knelt before me.

"*Cher*," he whispered, now in some sort of insane fear, all shaking like a leaf, "my friend, tell me the whole truth: where are they going to put me now?"

"God!" I cried, raising him up and sitting him on the bed, "you finally don't believe me either; you think I'm also in the conspiracy? But I won't let anyone here even lay a finger on you!"

"*C'est ça*, don't let them," he babbled, seizing me firmly by the elbows with both hands, and continuing to tremble. "Don't let anybody! And don't tell me any lies... because can it be that they'll take me away from here? Listen, this landlord, Ippolit, or whoever he is, he's not... a doctor?"

"What sort of doctor?"

"This... this isn't a madhouse, I mean here, in this room?"

But at that moment the door suddenly opened and Anna Andreevna came in. She must have been eavesdropping by the door and,

*She's an angel, she's an angel of heaven!

†I say charming things and everybody laughs ...

unable to help herself, opened it too abruptly—and the prince, who jumped at every creak, cried out and threw himself facedown on the pillow. He finally had some sort of fit, which resolved itself in sobbing.

"Here are the fruits of *your* work," I said to her, pointing to the old man.

"No, these are the fruits of *your* work!" she raised her voice sharply. "I turn to you for the last time, Arkady Makarovich: do you want to reveal the infernal intrigue against the defenseless old man and sacrifice your 'insane and childish amorous dreams' in order to save *your own* sister?"

"I'll save you all, but only in the way I told you before! I'm running off again; maybe in an hour Katerina Nikolaevna herself will be here! I'll reconcile everybody, and everybody will be happy!" I exclaimed almost with inspiration.

"Bring her, bring her here," the prince roused himself. "Take me to her! I want Katya, I want to see Katya and bless her!" he exclaimed, raising his arms and trying to get out of bed.

"You see," I pointed at him to Anna Andreevna, "you hear what he says: now in any case no 'document' will help you."

"I see, but it could still help to justify my action in the opinion of the world, while now—I'm disgraced! Enough; my conscience is clear. I've been abandoned by everyone, even my own brother, who is afraid of failure... But I will do my duty and stay by this unfortunate man as his nurse, his attendant!"

But there was no time to be lost, and I ran out of the room.

"I'll come back in an hour, and I won't come back alone!" I called out from the threshold.

Chapter Twelve

I

I FINALLY CAUGHT Tatyana Pavlovna! I explained everything to her at once—everything about the document, and everything, to the last shred, about what was happening in our apartment. Though she understood these events only too well herself and could have grasped the matter after two words, the explanation nevertheless took us, I think, about ten minutes. I alone spoke, I spoke the whole truth, and I wasn't ashamed. She sat silent and motionless on her chair, drawn up straight as a poker, her lips pressed together, not taking her eyes off me, and listening with all her might. But when I finished, she suddenly jumped up from her chair, and so precipitously that I jumped up, too.

"Ah, you little cur! So you've really got that letter sewn in, and it was that fool Marya Ivanovna who did the sewing! Ah, you outrageous scoundrels! So you came here to conquer hearts, to win over high society, to take revenge on Devil Ivanovich because you're an illegitimate son, is that what you wanted?"

"Tatyana Pavlovna," I cried, "don't you dare abuse me! It may be you, with your abuse, who from the very beginning were the cause of my bitterness here. Yes, I'm an illegitimate son, and maybe I did indeed want to take revenge for being an illegitimate son, and maybe indeed on some Devil Ivanovich, because the devil himself won't find who's to blame here; but remember that I rejected an alliance with the scoundrels and overcame my passions! I will silently place the document before her and leave without even waiting for a word from her; you yourself will be the witness!"

"Give me the letter, give it to me right now, put it here on the table! Or maybe you're lying?"

"It's sewn into my pocket; Marya Ivanovna herself did the sewing. And here, when I had a new frock coat made, I took it from the old one and sewed it into this new frock coat myself; it's here, feel it, I'm not lying, ma'am!"

"Give it to me, take it out!" Tatyana Pavlovna stormed.

"Not for anything, ma'am, I repeat it to you. I'll place it before her in your presence and leave, without waiting for a single word;

but it's necessary that she know and see with her own eyes that it is I, I myself, who am giving it to her, voluntarily, without compulsion and without reward."

"Showing off again? Are you in love, you little cur?"

"Say as many nasty things as you like. Go on, I deserve it, but I'm not offended. Oh, let me look like a paltry little brat to her, who spied on her and plotted a conspiracy, but let her recognize that I conquered myself and placed *her* happiness higher than anything in the world! Never mind, Tatyana Pavlovna, never mind! I cry out to myself: courage and hope! Let this be my first step on life's path, but then it has ended well, ended nobly! And what if I do love her," I went on inspiredly and flashing my eyes, "I'm not ashamed of it: mama is a heavenly angel, but *she* is an earthly queen! Versilov will go back to mama, and I'm not going to be ashamed before her; I did hear what she and Versilov said then, I was standing behind the curtain . . . Oh, all three of us are 'people of the same madness'! Do you know whose phrase that is—'people of the same madness'? It's his phrase, Andrei Petrovich's! Do you know, maybe there are more than three of us here who are of the same madness? I'll bet you're a fourth one of the same madness! Want me to say it? I'll bet you yourself have been in love with Andrei Petrovich all your life and maybe still are . . ."

I repeat, I was inspired and in some sort of happiness, but I had no time to finish. She suddenly seized me by the hair with some unnatural swiftness and tugged me downwards twice with all her might . . . then suddenly left me, went into the corner, stood facing the corner, and covered her face with a handkerchief.

"Little cur! Don't you ever dare say that to me again!" she said, weeping.

This was all so unexpected that I was naturally dumbfounded. I stood and gazed at her, not yet knowing what I should do.

"Pah, you fool! Come here, kiss me, foolish woman that I am!" she said suddenly, weeping and laughing. "And don't you dare, don't you ever dare repeat that to me . . . But I love you and have loved you all your life . . . fool that you are."

I kissed her. I will add in parenthesis: from then on Tatyana Pavlovna and I became friends.

"Ah, yes! But what's the matter with me!" she suddenly exclaimed, slapping herself on the forehead. "What were you saying? The old prince is there in your apartment? Is it true?"

"I assure you."

"Ah, my God! Oh, I'm sick!" she whirled and rushed about the room. "And they order him around! Eh, there's no lightning to strike the fools! Ever since morning? That's Anna Andreevna! That's the nun! And the other one, Militrisa,[44] doesn't know anything!"

"What Militrisa?"

"The earthly queen, the ideal! Eh, but what are we to do now?"

"Tatyana Pavlovna!" I cried, coming to my senses. "We've been saying foolish things, and we've forgotten the main thing: I ran here precisely to fetch Katerina Nikolaevna, and they're all waiting for me to come back."

And I explained that I would hand the document over only if she gave her word to make peace with Anna Andreevna immediately and even agree to her marriage...

"And that's splendid," Tatyana Pavlovna interrupted, "and I, too, have repeated it to her a hundred times. He'll die before the wedding—anyway he won't marry her, and if it's about him leaving her money in his will—Anna, I mean—it's been written in and left to her even without that..."

"Can it be that Katerina Nikolaevna is only sorry about the money?"

"No, she was afraid all along that she had the document—Anna, I mean—and I was, too. So we kept watch on her. The daughter didn't want to shock the old man, but, true, the little German, Bjoring, was also sorry about the money."

"And she can marry Bjoring after that?"

"What can you do with a foolish woman? As they say, once a fool, always a fool. You see, he's going to give her some sort of calm. 'I must marry somebody,' she says, 'so I suppose he'd be the most suitable one.' We'll see just how suitable it will be. She'll slap her sides afterwards, but it will be too late."

"Then why do you allow it? Don't you love her; didn't you tell her to her face that you're in love with her?"

"And I am in love with her, I love her more than all of you taken together, but still she's a senseless fool!"

"Then run and fetch her now, and we'll resolve everything and take her in person to her father."

"But it's impossible, impossible, you little fool! That's the point! Ah, what to do! Ah, I'm sick!" She rushed about again, though she did snatch up her shawl. "E-eh, if only you had come four hours earlier, it's past seven now, and she went to dine with the Pelishchevs some time ago, and then to go with them to the opera."

"Lord, can't we run over to the opera . . . no, we can't! What's going to happpen to the old man? He may die during the night!"

"Listen, don't go there, go to your mama, sleep there, and tomorrow early . . ."

"No, I won't leave the old man for anything, whatever may come of it."

"Don't leave him; that's good of you. And, you know . . . I'll run to her place anyhow and leave her a note . . . you know, I'll write it in our own words (she'll understand!), that the document is here, and that tomorrow at exactly ten o'clock in the morning she must be at my place—on the dot! Don't worry, she'll come, she'll listen to me—then we'll settle everything at once. And you go there and fuss over the old man as much as you can, put him to bed, chances are he'll survive till morning! Don't frighten Anna either; I love her, too. You're unfair to her, because you can't understand these things: she's offended, she's been offended since childhood. Oh, you all pile up on me! And don't forget, tell her from me that I've taken this matter up myself, with all my heart, and that she should be at peace, and there will be no damage to her pride . . . Over the past few days she and I have squabbled, quarreled—fallen out completely! Well, off you run . . . wait, show me the pocket again . . . is it true, is it true? Oh, is it true? Give me the letter for the night, what is it to you? Leave it, I won't eat it. You may let it slip out of your hands during the night . . . do change your mind?"

"Not for anything!" I cried. "There, feel it, look, but I won't leave it with you for anything."

"I see there's a piece of paper," she felt it with her fingers. "E-eh, all right, go, and I may even swing by the theater for her, that was a good idea! But run, run!"

"Wait, Tatyana Pavlovna, how's mama?"

"Alive."

"And Andrei Petrovich?"

She waved her hand.

"He'll come round!"

I ran off encouraged, reassured, though it hadn't turned out the way I had reckoned. But, alas, fate had determined differently, and something else awaited me—truly, there is a *fatum* in the world!

II

While still on the stairs, I heard noise in our apartment, and the door turned out to be open. In the corridor stood an unknown lackey in livery. Pyotr Ippolitovich and his wife, both frightened by something, were also in the corridor and waiting for something. The door to the prince's room was open and a voice was thundering there, which I recognized at once—the voice of Bjoring. I hadn't managed to step two steps when I suddenly saw the prince, tearful and trembling, being taken out to the corridor by Bjoring and his companion, Baron R., the same one who had come to Versilov for a talk. The prince was sobbing loudly, embracing and kissing Bjoring. Bjoring's shouting was addressed to Anna Andreevna, who also came out to the corridor after the prince; he threatened her and, I believe, stamped his feet—in short, the coarse German soldier told in him, despite all his "high society." Later it was discovered that for some reason it had come into his head then that Anna Andreevna was even guilty of something criminal and now unquestionably had to answer for her action even before the court. In his ignorance of the matter, he exaggerated it, as happens to many, and therefore began to consider it his right to be unceremonious in the highest degree. Above all, he had had no time to go into it. He had been informed of it all anonymously, as it turned out later (and of which I will make mention later), and had flown at them in that state of the enraged gentleman, in which even the most intelligent people of his nation are sometimes ready to start brawling like cobblers. Anna Andreevna had met this whole swoop with the highest degree of dignity, but I missed that. I only saw that, having taken the old man out to the corridor, Bjoring suddenly left him in the hands of Baron R. and, turning swiftly to Anna Andreevna, shouted at her, probably in response to some remark she had made:

"You are an intriguer! You want his money! From this moment on you are disgraced in society, and you will answer before the court! . . ."

"It's you who are exploiting an unfortunate invalid and driving him to madness . . . and you shout at me because I'm a woman and have no one to defend me . . ."

"Ah, yes! you are his fiancée, his fiancée!" Bjoring guffawed spitefully and furiously.

"Baron, Baron... *Chère enfant, je vous aime*,"* the prince wept out, reaching his arms towards Anna Andreevna.

"Go, Prince, go, there has been a conspiracy against you and maybe even a threat to your life!" cried Bjoring.

"*Oui, oui, je comprends, j'ai compris au commencement*..."†

"Prince," Anna Andreevna raised her voice, "you insult me and allow me to be insulted!"

"Away with you!" Bjoring suddenly shouted at her.

That I could not endure.

"Blackguard!" I yelled at him. "Anna Andreevna, I'll be your defender!"

Here I will not and cannot describe anything in detail. A terrible and ignoble scene took place, and it was as if I suddenly lost my reason. It seems I leaped over and struck him, or at least shoved him hard. He also struck me with all his might on the head, so that I fell to the floor. Coming to my senses, I started after them down the stairs; I remember that my nose was bleeding. A carriage was waiting for them at the entrance, and while the prince was being put into it, I ran up to the carriage and, despite the lackey, who was pushing me away, again threw myself on Bjoring. I don't remember how the police turned up. Bjoring seized me by the scruff of the neck and sternly told the policeman to take me to the precinct. I shouted that he had to go with me, so that he could file a statement with me, and that they couldn't take me like that, almost from my own apartment. But since it had happened in the street and not in my apartment, and since I shouted, swore, and fought like a drunk man, and since Bjoring was in his uniform, the policeman arrested me. Here I became totally furious and, resisting with all my might, it seems I struck the policeman as well. Then, I remember, two of them suddenly appeared, and I was taken away. I barely remember being brought to some smoke-filled room, with a lot of different people sitting and standing around, waiting and writing. I went on shouting here, I demanded to file a statement. But the case no longer consisted only in a statement, but was complicated by violence and resistance to the authority of the police. And my appearance was all too unseemly. Someone suddenly shouted menacingly at me. The policeman had meanwhile accused me of fighting, had told about the colonel...

*Dear child, I love you.
†Yes, yes, I understand, I understood at the beginning ...

"Your name?" someone cried to me.

"Dolgoruky," I roared.

"Prince Dolgoruky?"

Beside myself, I responded with quite a nasty curse word, and then . . . and then I remember they dragged me to some dark little room "for sobering up." Oh, I'm not protesting. The public all read in the newspapers not long ago the complaint of some gentleman who sat all night under arrest, bound, and also in a sobering-up room, but he, it seems, wasn't even guilty; while I was guilty. I collapsed on a bunk in the company of some two unconsciously sleeping people. My head ached, there was a throbbing in my temples, a throbbing in my heart. It must be that I became oblivious and, it seems, I raved. I remember only that I woke up in the middle of the deep night and sat up on the bunk. All at once I remembered everything and grasped everything, and, putting my elbows on my knees, propping my head in my hands, I sank into deep thought.

Oh! I'm not going to describe my feelings, and I also have no time, but I will note just one thing: maybe never have I experienced more delightful moments in my soul than in those minutes of reflection in the depths of the night, on the bunk, under arrest. This may seem strange to the reader, a sort of ink-slinging, a wish to shine with originality—and yet it was all just as I say. It was one of those minutes that, perhaps, occur with everyone, but that come only once in a lifetime. In such moments you decide your fate, determine your worldview, and say to yourself once and for all your life: "Here is where the truth lies, and here is where I should go to reach it." Yes, those moments were the light of my soul. Insulted by the arrogant Bjoring, and hoping to be insulted by that high-society woman tomorrow, I knew only too well that I could take terrible revenge on them, but I decided that I would not take revenge. I decided, despite all temptation, that I would not reveal the document, would not make it known to the whole world (as had already spun round in my mind); I repeated to myself that tomorrow I would place the letter before her and, if necessary, even endure a mocking smile from her instead of gratitude, but still I would not say a word and would leave her forever . . . However, there's no point in expanding on it. Of all that would happen to me here tomorrow, of how I'd be brought before the authorities and what would be done to me, I almost forgot to think. I crossed myself lovingly, lay down on the bunk, and fell into a serene, childlike sleep.

I awoke late, when it was already light. I was now the only one in the room. I sat up and began silently waiting, a long time, about an hour; it must have been about nine o'clock when I was suddenly summoned. I could go into greater detail, but it's not worth it, for it's all extraneous now; all I want to do is finish telling the main thing. I'll only point out that, to my greatest amazement, I was treated with unexpected politeness: they asked me something, I answered something, and I was at once let go. I went out silently, and it was with pleasure that I read in their looks even a certain surprise at a man who, even in such a position, was capable of not losing his dignity. If I hadn't noticed it, I wouldn't have written it down. At the exit, Tatyana Pavlovna was waiting for me. I'll explain in two words why I got off so easily then.

Early in the morning, maybe at eight o'clock, Tatyana Pavlovna came flying to my apartment, that is, to Pyotr Ippolitovich's, still hoping to find the prince there, and suddenly learned about all of yesterday's horrors, and above all that I had been arrested. She instantly rushed to Katerina Nikolaevna (who, the evening before, on returning from the theater, had met with her father, who had been brought to her), woke her up, frightened her, and demanded that I be released immediately. With a note from her, she flew at once to Bjoring and immediately obtained another note from him, to "the proper person," with an urgent request from Bjoring himself that I be released, "having been arrested through a misunderstanding." With this note she arrived at the precinct, and his request was honored.

III

Now I'll go on with the main thing.

Tatyana Pavlovna, having picked me up, put me in a cab, brought me to her place, immediately ordered the samovar, and washed me and scrubbed me in the kitchen herself. Also in the kitchen, she loudly told me that at half-past eleven Katerina Nikolaevna herself would come—as the two had already arranged earlier—in order to meet me. And this Marya also heard. After a few minutes she brought the samovar, but after another two minutes, when Tatyana Pavlovna suddenly summoned her, she did not respond. It turned out that she had gone somewhere. I ask the reader to note that very well; it was then, I suppose, about a quarter to ten. Though

Tatyana Pavlovna was angry at her disappearing without asking, she merely thought she had gone to the shop, and at once forgot about it for a while. And we couldn't be bothered with that; we talked nonstop, because we had things to discuss, so that I, for instance, paid almost no attention to Marya's disappearance; I ask the reader to remember that as well.

Needless to say, I was as if in a daze; I was explaining my feelings, and above all—we were waiting for Katerina Nikolaevna, and the thought that in an hour I would finally meet with her, and at such a decisive moment of my life, made me tremble and quake. Finally, when I had drunk two cups, Tatyana Pavlovna suddenly got up, took a pair of scissors from the table, and said:

"Give me your pocket, we must take out the letter—we can't cut it with her here!"

"Right!" I exclaimed, and unbuttoned my frock coat.

"What's all this tangle here? Who did the sewing?"

"I did, I did, Tatyana Pavlovna."

"That's obvious. Well, here it is..."

The letter was taken out; it was the same old envelope, but with a blank piece of paper stuck into it.

"What's this?..." Tatyana Pavlovna exclaimed, turning it over. "What's got into you?"

But I stood there speechless, pale... and suddenly sank strengthlessly onto the chair; truly, I almost fainted away.

"What on earth is this?" Tatyana Pavlovna yelled. "Where is your note?"

"Lambert!" I jumped up suddenly, realizing and slapping myself on the forehead.

Hurrying and breathless, I explained everything to her—the night at Lambert's, and our conspiracy at the time; however, I had already confessed this conspiracy to her the day before.

"They stole it! They stole it!" I cried, stamping the floor and seizing myself by the hair.

"Trouble!" Tatyana Pavlovna suddenly decided, grasping what it meant. "What time is it?"

It was about eleven.

"Eh, Marya's not here!... Marya, Marya!"

"What is it, ma'am?" Marya suddenly responded from the kitchen.

"You're here? So what are we to do now? I'll fly to her... Ah, you dodderer, you dodderer!"

"And I'll go to Lambert!" I yelled. "And I'll strangle him, if need be!"

"Ma'am!" Marya suddenly squeaked from the kitchen. "There's some woman here asking for you very much..."

But before she finished speaking, the "some woman" herself burst precipitously from the kitchen with cries and screams. It was Alphonsinka. I won't describe the scene in full detail; the scene was a trick and a fake, but it should be noted that Alphonsinka played it splendidly. With tears of repentance and with violent gestures, she rattled out (in French, naturally) that she herself had cut out the letter then, that it was now with Lambert, and that Lambert, with "that brigand," *cet homme noir*,* wanted to lure *madame la générale*† and shoot her, right now, in an hour... that she had learned it all from them and had suddenly become terribly frightened, because she saw they had a pistol, *le pistolet*, and had now rushed to us, so that we could go, save, prevent... *Cet homme noir*...

In short, it was all extremely plausible; the very stupidity of some of Alphonsinka's explanations even increased the plausibility.

"What *homme noir*?" cried Tatyana Pavlovna.

"*Tiens, j'ai oublié son nom... Un homme affreux... Tiens, Versiloff.*"‡

"Versilov! It can't be!" I yelled.

"Oh, yes, it can!" shrieked Tatyana Pavlovna. "But speak, dearie, without jumping, without waving your arms. What is it they want? Talk sense, dearie. I refuse to believe they want to shoot her!"

The "dearie" talked the following sense (NB: it was all a lie, I warn you again): *Versiloff* would sit behind the door, and Lambert, as soon as she came in, would show her *cette lettre*, here *Versiloff* would jump out, and they... *Oh, ils feront leur vengeance!*§ That she, Alphonsinka, was afraid of trouble, because she had taken part herself, and *cette dame, la générale*, was sure to come "right now, right now," because they had sent her a copy of the letter, and she would see at once that they really had the letter and go to them, and that it was Lambert alone who had written to her, and she knew nothing about Versilov; but Lambert had introduced himself

*That black man.
†Madame the general's wife.
‡Wait, I've forgotten his name... A dreadful man... Wait, Versiloff.
§Oh, they will take their revenge!

as a visitor from Moscow, from a certain Moscow lady, *une dame de Moscou* (NB: Marya Ivanovna!).

"Ah, I'm sick! I'm sick!" Tatyana Pavlovna kept exclaiming.

"*Sauvez-la, sauvez-la!*"* cried Alphonsinka.

Of course, there was something incongruous in this crazy news, even at first glance, but there was no time to think it over, because essentially it was all terribly plausible. It might still be supposed, and with great probability, that Katerina Nikolaevna, having received Lambert's invitation, would first come to us, to Tatyana Pavlovna, to explain the matter; but, on the other hand, that might well not happen, and she might go directly to them, and then—she was lost! It was also hard to believe that she would just rush to the unknown Lambert at the first summons; but again, it might happen for whatever reason, for instance, seeing the copy and being convinced that they indeed had her letter, and then—the same trouble! Above all, we didn't have a drop of time left, even in order to consider.

"And Versilov will do her in! If he's stooped to Lambert, he'll do her in! It's the double!" I cried.

"Ah, this 'double'!" Tatyana Pavlovna wrung her hands. "Well, no help for it," she suddenly made up her mind, "take your hat and coat and off we go. Take us straight to them, dearie. Ah, it's so far! Marya, Marya, if Katerina Nikolaevna comes, tell her that I'll be back presently and that she should sit and wait for me, and if she refuses to wait, lock the door and force her to stay. Tell her I said so! A hundred roubles for you, Marya, if you do me this service."

We ran out to the stairs. No doubt it would have been impossible to think up anything better, because in all events the main trouble was at Lambert's apartment, and if Katerina Nikolaevna indeed came to Tatyana Pavlovna first, Marya could always keep her there. And yet, having already hailed a cab, Tatyana Pavlovna suddenly changed her mind.

"You go with her!" she told me, leaving me with Alphonsinka, "and die there if need be, understand? And I'll follow you at once, but I'll swing by her place beforehand, on the chance that I'll find her, because, say what you will, but I find it suspicious!"

And she flew to Katerina Nikolaevna. Alphonsinka and I set off for Lambert's. I kept urging the cabbie on, and as we flew, I went

*Save her, save her!

on questioning Alphonsinka, but Alphonsinka mostly got off with exclamations, and finally with tears. But God kept and preserved us all, when everything was hanging by a thread. Before we'd gone a quarter of the way, I suddenly heard a shout behind me: someone called my name. I turned to look—Trishatov was overtaking us in a cab.

"Where to?" he shouted in alarm. "And with her, with Alphonsinka!"

"Trishatov!" I cried to him. "What you said is true—bad trouble! I'm going to that scoundrel Lambert! Let's go together, there'll be more of us!"

"Turn back, turn back right now!" shouted Trishatov. "Lambert's deceiving you, and so is Alphonsinka. The pockmarked one sent me. They're not at home; I've just met Versilov and Lambert; they were driving to Tatyana Pavlovna's . . . they're there now . . ."

I stopped the cab and jumped over to Trishatov. To this day I don't understand how I could have decided so suddenly, but I suddenly believed and suddenly decided. Alphonsinka screamed terribly, but we abandoned her, and I don't know whether she turned to follow us or went home, but anyhow I never saw her again.

In the cab, Trishatov haphazardly and breathlessly told me that there was some machination, that Lambert had come to an agreement with the pockmarked one, but that the pockmarked one had betrayed him at the last minute, and had just sent Trishatov to Tatyana Pavlovna to inform her that she should not believe Lambert and Alphonsinka. Trishatov added that he knew nothing more, because the pockmarked one hadn't told him any more, because he'd had no time, that he himself had hurried off somewhere, and that it had all been done hastily. "I saw you driving," Trishatov went on, "and chased after you." Of course, it was clear that this pockmarked one also knew everything, because he had sent Trishatov straight to Tatyana Pavlovna; but this was a new riddle.

But to avoid confusion, before describing the catastrophe, I'll explain the whole real truth and run ahead of myself for the last time.

IV

HAVING STOLEN THE letter then, Lambert at once joined with Versilov. Of how Versilov could have coupled himself with Lambert, I will not speak now; that's for later; above all, it was the "double" here! But having coupled himself with Versilov, Lambert was faced with luring Katerina Nikolaevna as cleverly as possible. Versilov told him outright that she wouldn't come. But Lambert, ever since I had met him in the street that evening two days before and, to show off, had told him I would return the letter to her in Tatyana Pavlovna's apartment and in Tatyana Pavlovna's presence—Lambert from that moment on had set up some sort of espionage on Tatyana Pavlovna's apartment—namely, he had bribed Marya. He had given Marya twenty roubles, and then, a day later, when the theft of the document had been accomplished, he had visited Marya for a second time and come to a radical agreement with her, promising her two hundred roubles for her services.

That was why, when she heard earlier that Katerina Nikolaevna would be at Tatyana Pavlovna's at half-past eleven and that I would be there as well, Marya immediately rushed out of the house and went galloping in a cab to Lambert with the news. This was precisely what she was to inform Lambert of—it was in this that her service consisted. Just at that moment, Versilov, too, was at Lambert's. In one second Versilov came up with this infernal combination. They say that madmen can be terribly clever at certain moments.

The combination consisted in luring the two of us, Tatyana and me, out of the apartment, at all costs, for at least a quarter of an hour, but before Katerina Nikolaevna's arrival. Then—to wait outside, and as soon as Tatyana Pavlovna and I left, to run into the apartment, which Marya would open for them, and wait for Katerina Nikolaevna. Meanwhile, Alphonsinka was to do her best to keep us wherever she liked and however she liked. Katerina Nikolaevna was to arrive, as she had promised, at half-past eleven, meaning at least twice sooner than we could return. (Needless to say, Katerina Nikolaevna had not received any invitation from Lambert, and Alphonsinka had told a pack of lies, and it was this trick that Versilov had thought up in all its details, while Alphonsinka had only played the role of the frightened traitress.) Of course, there was a risk, but their reasoning was correct: "If it works—good; if not—nothing's lost, because the document is still in our hands." But it did work, and it couldn't help working, because we couldn't help running after Alphonsinka, if only on the supposition, "And what if it's all true!" Again I repeat, there was no time to consider.

V

TRISHATOV AND I CAME running into the kitchen and found Marya in a fright. She had been struck because, as she let Lambert and Versilov in, she suddenly somehow noticed a revolver in Lambert's hand. Though she had taken the money, the revolver had not entered into her calculations. She was bewildered and, as soon as she saw me, rushed to me:

"Mme. Akhmakov has come, and they've got a pistol!"

"Trishatov, wait here in the kitchen," I ordered, "and the moment I shout, come running as fast as you can to help me."

Marya opened the door to the little corridor for me, and I slipped into Tatyana Pavlovna's bedroom—that same tiny room in which there was only space enough for Tatyana Pavlovna's bed and in which I had once eavesdropped inadvertently. I sat on the bed and at once found myself an opening in the portière.

But there was already noise and loud talk in the room. I'll note that Katerina Nikolaevna had entered the apartment exactly one minute after them. I had already heard noise and talk from the kitchen; it was Lambert shouting. She was sitting on the sofa, and he was standing in front of her and shouting like a fool. Now I know why he so stupidly lost his wits: he was in a hurry and was afraid they would be caught; later I'll explain precisely whom he was afraid of. The letter was in his hand. But Versilov was not in the room. I prepared myself to rush in at the first sign of danger. I give only the meaning of what was said, maybe there's much that I don't remember correctly, but I was too agitated then to memorize it with final precision.

"This letter is worth thirty thousand roubles, and you're surprised! It's worth a hundred thousand, and I'm asking only thirty!" Lambert said loudly and in awful excitement.

Katerina Nikolaevna, though obviously frightened, looked at him with a sort of scornful surprise.

"I see some trap has been set here, and I don't understand anything," she said, "but if you really have that letter..."

"Here it is, you can see for yourself! Isn't this it? A promissory note for thirty thousand and not a kopeck less!" Lambert interrupted her.

"I have no money."

"Write a promissory note—here's some paper. Then go and get the money, and I'll wait, but a week—no longer. You bring the money, I'll give you back the promissory note, and then I'll give you the letter."

"You speak to me in such a strange tone. You're mistaken. If I go and complain, this document will be taken from you today."

"To whom? Ha, ha, ha! And the scandal? And if we show the letter to the prince? Taken from me how? I don't keep documents in my apartment. I'll show it to the prince through a third person. Don't be stubborn, lady, say thank you that I'm not asking much, somebody else would ask for certain favors besides... you know what kind... something no pretty woman refuses in embarrassing circumstances, that's what kind... Heh, heh, heh! *Vous êtes belle, vous!*"*

Katerina Nikolaevna impetuously got up from her place, blushed all over, and—spat in his face. Then she quickly made for the door. It was here that the fool Lambert snatched out the revolver. He had blindly believed, like a limited fool, in the effect of the document, that is—above all—he hadn't perceived whom he was dealing with, precisely because, as I've already said, he considered that everyone had the same mean feelings as himself. From the very first word, he had irritated her with his rudeness, whereas she might not have declined to enter into a monetary deal.

"Don't move!" he yelled, enraged at being spat upon, seizing her by the shoulder and showing her the revolver—naturally just to frighten her. She cried out and sank onto the sofa. I rushed into the room; but at the same moment, Versilov, too, came running into the room from the door to the corridor. (He had been standing there and waiting.) Before I could blink an eye, he snatched the revolver from Lambert and hit him on the head with it as hard as

*You're a pretty one, you are!

he could. Lambert staggered and fell senseless; blood gushed from his head onto the carpet.

She, on seeing Versilov, suddenly turned as white as a sheet; for a few moments she looked at him fixedly, in inexpressible horror, and suddenly fell into a swoon. He rushed to her. All this seems to flash before me now. I remember with what fear I then saw his red, almost purple, face and bloodshot eyes. I think that, though he noticed me in the room, it was as if he didn't recognize me. He picked her up, unconscious, lifted her with incredible strength, like a feather in his arms, and began carrying her senselessly around the room like a child. The room was tiny, but he wandered from corner to corner, obviously not knowing why he was doing it. In one single moment he had lost his reason. He kept looking at her face. I ran after him and was mainly afraid of the revolver, which he had simply forgotten in his right hand and was holding right next to her head. But he pushed me away, first with his elbow, then with his foot. I wanted to call out to Trishatov, but was afraid to vex the madman. In the end, I suddenly opened the portière and started begging him to put her down on the bed. He went and put her down, stood over her himself, looked intently into her face for about a minute, and suddenly bent down and kissed her twice on her pale lips. Oh, I understood, finally, that this was a man who was totally beside himself. Suddenly he went to swing the revolver at her, but, as if realizing, turned the revolver around and aimed it at her face. I instantly seized his arm with all my might and shouted to Trishatov. I remember we both struggled with him, but he managed to free his arm and shoot at himself. He had wanted to shoot her and then himself. But when we didn't let him have her, he pressed the revolver straight to his heart, but I managed to push his hand up and the bullet struck him in the shoulder. At that moment, Tatyana Pavlovna burst in with a shout; but he was already lying senseless on the carpet beside Lambert.

Chapter Thirteen

Conclusion

I

THAT SCENE IS now almost six months in the past, and much has flowed by since then, much is quite changed, and for me a new life has long begun... But I will set the reader free as well.

For me, at least, the first question, both then and long afterwards, was: how could Versilov join with such a man as Lambert, and what aim did he have in view then? I have gradually arrived at some sort of explanation: in my opinion, Versilov, in those moments, that is, in all that last day and the day before, could not have had any firm aim, and I don't think he even reasoned at all here, but was under the influence of some whirlwind of feelings. However, I do not admit of any genuine madness, the less so as he is not mad at all now. But I do unquestionably admit of the "double." What essentially is a double? A double, at least according to a certain medical book by a certain expert, which I later read purposely, a double is none other than the first step in a serious mental derangement, which may lead to a rather bad end. And Versilov himself, in the scene at mama's, had explained to us the "doubling" of his feelings and will with awful sincerity. But again I repeat: that scene at mama's, that split icon, though it undoubtedly occurred under the influence of a real double, still has always seemed to me in part a sort of malicious allegory, a sort of hatred, as it were, for the expectations of these women, a sort of malice towards their rights and their judgment, and so, half-and-half with his double, he smashed the icon! It meant, "Thus I'll split your expectations as well!" In short, if there was a double, there was also simply a whim... But all this is only my guess; to decide for certain is difficult.

True, despite his adoration of Katerina Nikolaevna, there was always rooted in him a most sincere and profound disbelief in her moral virtue. I certainly think that he was just waiting behind the door then for her humiliation before Lambert. But did he want it, even if he was waiting? Again I repeat: I firmly believe that he didn't want anything then, and wasn't even reasoning. He simply wanted to be there, to jump out later, to say something to her, and maybe—maybe to insult her, maybe also to kill her... Anything might have happened then; only, as he was coming there with Lambert, he had no idea what would happen. I'll add that the revolver belonged to Lambert, and he himself came unarmed. But seeing her proud dignity, and, above all, unable to bear the scoundrel Lambert's threatening her, he jumped out—and then lost his reason. Did he want to shoot her at that moment? In my opinion, he didn't know himself, but he certainly would have shot her if we hadn't pushed his hand away.

His wound turned out not to be fatal and it healed, but he spent a long time in bed—at mama's, of course. Now, as I write these lines, it is spring outside, the middle of May, a lovely day, and our windows are open. Mama is sitting beside him; he strokes her cheeks and hair and looks into her eyes with tender feeling. Oh, this is only half of the former Versilov, he no longer leaves mama's side and never will again. He has even received "the gift of tears," as the unforgettable Makar Ivanovich put it in his story about the merchant; however, it seems to me that Versilov will live a long time. With us he's now quite simplehearted and sincere, like a child, without losing, however, either measure or restraint, or saying anything unnecessary. All his intelligence and all his moral cast have remained with him, though all that was ideal in him stands out still more strongly. I'll say directly that I've never loved him as I do now, and I'm sorry that I have neither time nor space to say more about him. However, I will tell one recent anecdote (and there are many): by Great Lent he had recovered, and during the sixth week he announced that he would prepare for communion.[45] He hadn't done that for some thirty years or more, I think. Mama was glad; they started cooking lenten meals, though quite costly and refined. From the other room I heard him on Monday and Tuesday hum to himself "Behold, the Bridegroom cometh"[46]—and admire the melody and the poetry. Several times during those two days he talked very beautifully about religion; but on Wednesday the preparation suddenly ceased. Something had suddenly irritated him, some "amusing contrast," as he put it, laughing. Something had displeased him in the appearance of the priest, in the surroundings; but he only came back and said with a quiet smile, "My friends, I love God very much, but—I'm incapable of these things." The same day roast beef was served at dinner. But I know that even now mama often sits down beside him and in a quiet voice and with a quiet smile begins to talk to him sometimes about the most abstract things: she has suddenly become somehow *bold* with him now, but how it happened I don't know. She sits by him and talks to him, most often in a whisper. He listens with a smile, strokes her hair, kisses her hands, and the most complete happiness shines in his face. Sometimes he also has fits, almost hysterical ones. Then he takes her photograph, the one he kissed that evening, looks at it with tears, kisses it, remembers, calls us all to him, but he says little at such moments... He seems to have forgotten Katerina Nikolaevna completely, and has never once mentioned her name. Of his marriage with mama, nothing has been said yet either. We wanted to take him abroad for the summer, but Tatyana Pavlovna insisted that we not take him, and he didn't want it himself. They'll spend the summer in a country house somewhere in a village in the Petersburg region. Incidentally, we're all meanwhile living at Tatyana Pavlovna's expense. I'll add one thing: I'm awfully sorry that in the course of these notes I have frequently allowed myself to refer to this person disrespectfully and haughtily. But as I wrote, I imagined myself exactly as I was at each of the moments I was describing. On finishing my notes and writing the last line, I suddenly felt that I had re-educated myself precisely through the process of recalling and writing down. I disavow much that I've written, especially the tone of certain phrases and pages, but I won't cross out or correct a single word.

I said that he has never uttered a single word about Katerina Nikolaevna; but I even think maybe he has been cured completely. Only Tatyana Pavlovna and I talk occasionally about Katerina Nikolaevna, and even that in secret. Katerina Nikolaevna is now abroad; I saw her before her departure and visited her several times. I've already received two letters from her from abroad, and have answered them. But of the content of our letters and of what we discussed as we said good-bye before her departure, I will not speak; that is another story, a quite *new* story, and even maybe all still in the future. Even with Tatyana Pavlovna there are certain things I keep silent about. But enough. I'll only add that Katerina Nikolaevna is not married and is traveling with the Pelishchevs. Her father is dead, and she is the wealthiest of widows. At the present moment she's in Paris. Her break with Bjoring occurred quickly and as if of itself, that is, with the highest degree of naturalness. However, I will tell about that.

On the morning of that terrible scene, the pockmarked one, to whom Trishatov and his friend had gone over, managed to inform Bjoring of the imminent evildoing. It happened in the following way: Lambert had after all inclined him to take part with him and, getting hold of the document then, had told him all the details and all the circumstances of the undertaking, and, finally, the last moment of the plan as well, that is, when Versilov thought up the combination of deceiving Tatyana Pavlovna. But at the decisive moment, the pockmarked one preferred to betray Lambert, being the most sensible of them all and foreseeing the possible criminality in their projects. Above all, he considered Bjoring's gratitude a much surer thing than the fantastic plan of the inept but hot-tempered Lambert and a Versilov nearly insane with passion. All this I learned later from Trishatov. Incidentally, I do not know or understand Lambert's relation with the pockmarked one, and why Lambert couldn't do without him. But much more curious for me was the question of why Lambert needed Versilov, when Lambert, who already had the document in his hands, could have done perfectly well without his help. The answer is now clear to me: he needed Versilov, first, because he knew the circumstances, but above all he needed Versilov in case of an alarm or some sort of trouble, so that he could shift all the responsibility onto him. And since Versilov wanted no money, Lambert considered his help even far from superfluous. But Bjoring didn't manage to get there in time. He arrived an hour after the shot, when Tatyana Pavlovna's apartment already had a totally different look. Namely, about five minutes after Versilov fell bleeding to the carpet, Lambert, whom we all thought had been killed, rose and stood up. He looked around in surprise, suddenly figured things out, went to the kitchen without saying a word, put his coat on there, and vanished forever. He left the "document" on the table. I've heard that he wasn't even sick, but just slightly unwell for a while; the blow with the revolver had stunned him and drawn blood, without causing any greater harm. Meanwhile, Trishatov had already run for a doctor; but before the doctor arrived, Versilov came to, and before that Tatyana Pavlovna, having brought Katerina Nikolaevna to her senses, had managed to take her home. Thus, when Bjoring came running in on us, he found in Tatyana Pavlovna's apartment only me, the doctor, the sick Versilov, and mama, who, though still sick, had come to him beside herself, brought by the same Trishatov. Bjoring stared in bewilderment, and, as soon as he learned that Katerina

Nikolaevna had already left, went to her at once, without saying a word to us.

He was put out; he saw clearly that scandal and publicity were now almost inevitable. No big scandal occurred, however, only rumors came of it. They didn't manage to conceal the shot—that's true—but the whole main story, in its main essence, went almost unknown. The investigation determined only that a certain V., a man in love, a family man at that and nearly fifty years old, beside himself with passion and while explaining his passion to a person worthy of the highest respect, but who by no means shared his feelings, had shot himself in a fit of madness. Nothing more came to the surface, and in this form the news, as dark rumors, penetrated the newspapers, without proper names, only with initials. At least I know that Lambert, for instance, wasn't bothered at all. Nevertheless, Bjoring, who knew the truth, was frightened. Just then, as if by design, he suddenly managed to learn that a meeting, tête-à-tête, of Katerina Nikolaevna and Versilov, who was in love with her, had taken place two days before the catastrophe. This made him explode, and he rather imprudently allowed himself to observe to Katerina Nikolaevna that, after that, he was no longer surprised that such fantastic stories could happen to her. Katerina Nikolaevna rejected him at once, without wrath, but also without hesitation. Her whole preconceived opinion about some sort of reasonableness in marrying this man vanished like smoke. Maybe she had already figured him out long before, or maybe, after the shock she had received, some of her views and feelings had suddenly changed. But here again I will keep silent. I will only add that Lambert vanished to Moscow, and I've heard that he got caught at something there. As for Trishatov, I lost sight of him long ago, almost from that same time, despite my efforts to find his trail even now. He vanished after the death of his friend, *le grand dadais*, who shot himself.

II

I've mentioned the death of old Prince Nikolai Ivanovich. This kindly, sympathetic old man died soon after the event, though, anyhow, a whole month later—died at night, in bed, of a nervous stroke. After that same day he spent in my apartment, I never saw him again. It was told of him that during that month he had supposedly become incomparably more reasonable, even more stern, was no longer frightened, did not weep, and in all that time never once uttered a single word about Anna Andreevna. All his love turned to his daughter. Once, a week before his death, Katerina Nikolaevna suggested inviting me for diversion, but he even frowned. I communicate this fact without any explanations. His estate turned out to be in order and, besides that, there turned out to be quite a considerable capital. Up to a third of this capital had, according to the old man's will, to be divided up among his countless goddaughters; but what everyone found extremely strange was that in this will there was no mention at all of Anna Andreevna: her name was omitted. But, nevertheless, I know this as a most trustworthy fact: just a few days before his death, the old man, having summoned his daughter and his friends, Pelishchev and Prince V——sky, told Katerina Nikolaevna, in the likely chance of his imminent demise, to be sure to allot sixty thousand roubles of this capital to Anna Andreevna. He expressed his will precisely, clearly, and briefly, not allowing himself a single exclamation or clarification. After his death, and when matters had become clear, Katerina Nikolaevna informed Anna Andreevna, through her attorney, that she could receive the sixty thousand whenever she liked; but Anna Andreevna, drily and without unnecessary words, declined the offer: she refused to receive the money, despite all assurances that such was indeed the prince's will. The money is still lying there waiting for her, and Katerina Nikolaevna still hopes she will change her mind; but that won't happen, and I know it for certain, because I'm now one of Anna Andreevna's closest acquaintances and friends. Her refusal caused some stir, and there was talk about it. Her aunt, Mme. Fanariotov, first vexed by her scandal with the old prince, suddenly changed her opinion and, after the refusal of the money, solemnly declared her respect. On the other hand, her brother quarreled with her definitively because of it. But, though I often visit Anna Andreevna, I can't say that we get into great intimacies. We don't mention the old times at all; she receives me very willingly, but speaks to me somehow abstractly. Incidentally, she firmly declared to me that she will certainly go to a convent; that was not long ago; but I don't believe her and consider it just bitter words.

But bitter, truly bitter, are the words I'm now faced with saying in particular about my sister Liza. Here is real unhappiness, and what are all my failures beside her bitter fate! It began with Prince Sergei Petrovich not recovering and dying in the hospital without waiting for the trial. He passed away before Prince Nikolai Ivanovich. Liza was left alone with her future child. She didn't weep and, by the look of it, was even calm; she became meek, humble; but all the former ardor of her heart was as if buried at once somewhere in her. She humbly helped mama, took care of the sick Andrei Petrovich, but she became terribly taciturn, did not even look at anyone or anything, as if it was all the same to her, as if she was just passing by. When Versilov got better, she began to sleep a lot. I brought her books, but she didn't want to read them; she began to get awfully thin. I somehow didn't dare to start comforting her, though I often came precisely with that intention; but in her presence I somehow had difficulty approaching her, and I couldn't come up with the right words to begin speaking about it. So it went on until one awful occasion: she fell down our stairs, not all the way, only three steps, but she had a miscarriage, and her illness lasted almost all winter. Now she has gotten up from bed, but her health has suffered a long-lasting blow. She is silent and pensive with us as before, but she has begun to talk a little with mama. All these last days there has been a bright, high spring sun, and I kept remembering that sunny morning last autumn when she and I walked down the street, both rejoicing and hoping and loving each other. Alas, what happened after that? I don't complain, for me a new life has begun, but her? Her future is a riddle, and now I can't even look at her without pain.

Some three weeks ago, however, I managed to get her interested in news about Vasin. He was finally released and set completely free. This sensible man gave, they say, the most precise explanations and the most interesting information, which fully vindicated him in the opinion of the people on whom his fate depended. And his notorious manuscript turned out to be nothing more than a translation from the French—material, so to speak, that he had gathered solely for himself, intending afterwards to compose from it a useful article for a magazine. He has now gone to ——— province, but his stepfather, Stebelkov, still goes on sitting in prison on his case, which, I've heard, keeps growing and gets more and more complicated as time goes on. Liza listened to the news about Vasin with a strange smile and even observed that something like that was bound to happen to him. But she was obviously pleased by the fact that the late Prince Sergei Petrovich's interference had done Vasin no harm. I have nothing to tell here about Dergachev and the others.

I have finished. Maybe some readers would like to know what became of my "idea" and what this new life is that is beginning for me now and that I've announced so mysteriously. But this new life, this new path that has opened before me, is precisely my "idea," the same as before, but under a totally different guise, so that it's no longer recognizable. But it can't be included in my "Notes" now, because it's something quite different. The old life has totally passed, and the new has barely begun. But I will nevertheless add something necessary: Tatyana Pavlovna, my intimate and beloved friend, pesters me almost every day with exhortations that I enter the university without fail and as soon as possible. "Later, when you've finished your studies, you can think up other things, but now go and complete your studies." I confess, I'm pondering her suggestion, but I have no idea what I'll decide. Among other things, my objection to her has been that I don't even have the right to study now, because I should work to support mama and Liza; but she offers her money for that and assures me that there's enough for my whole time at the university. I decided, finally, to ask the advice of a certain person. Having looked around me, I chose this person carefully and critically. It was Nikolai Semyonovich, my former tutor in Moscow, Marya Ivanovna's husband. Not that I needed anyone's advice so much, but I simply and irrepressibly wanted to hear the opinion of this total outsider, even something of a cold egoist, but unquestionably an intelligent man. I sent him my whole manuscript, asking him to keep it a secret, because I had not yet shown it to anyone and especially not to Tatyana Pavlovna. The manuscript came back to me two weeks later with a rather long letter. I'll make only a few excerpts from this letter, finding in them a sort of general view and something explanatory, as it were. Here are these excerpts.

III

"...AND NEVER, my unforgettable Arkady Makarovich, could you have employed your leisure time more usefully than now, having written these 'Notes' of yours! You've given yourself, so to speak, a conscious account of your first stormy and perilous steps on your career in life. I firmly believe that by this account you could indeed 're-educate yourself' in many ways, as you put it yourself. Naturally, I will not allow myself the least thing in the way of critical observations per se; though every page makes one ponder... for instance, the fact that you kept the 'document' so long and so persistently is in the highest degree characteristic... But out of hundreds of observations, that is the only one I will allow myself. I also greatly appreciate that you decided to tell, and apparently to me alone, the 'secret of your idea,' according to your own expression. But your request that I give my opinion of this idea per se, I must resolutely refuse: first, there would not be room enough for it in a letter, and second, I am not ready for an answer myself and still need to digest it. I will only observe that your 'idea' is distinguished by its originality, whereas the young men of the current generation fall mainly upon ideas that have not been thought up but given beforehand, and their supply is by no means great, and is often dangerous. Your 'idea,' for instance, preserved you, at least for a while, from the ideas of Messrs. Dergachev and Co., undoubtedly not so original as yours. And, finally, I concur in the highest degree with the opinion of the much-esteemed Tatyana Pavlovna, whom, though I know her personally, till now I had never been able to appreciate in the measure that she deserves. Her idea about your entering the university is in the highest degree beneficial for you. Learning and life will, in three or four years, undoubtedly open the horizon of your thoughts and aspirations still more widely, and if, after the university, you propose to turn again to your 'idea,' nothing will hinder that.

"Now allow me on my own, and without your request, to lay out for you candidly several thoughts and impressions that came to my mind and soul as I was reading your so candid notes. Yes, I agree with Andrei Petrovich that one might indeed have had fears for you and your *solitary* youth. And there are not a few young men like you, and their abilities always threaten to develop for the worse—either into a Molchalin-like obsequiousness[47] or into a secret desire for disorder. But this desire for disorder—and even most often—comes, maybe, from a secret thirst for order and 'seemliness' (I am using your word). Youth is pure if only because it is youth. Maybe in these so early impulses of madness there lies precisely this desire for order and this search for truth, and whose fault is it that some modern young men see this truth and this order in such silly and ridiculous things that it is even incomprehensible how they could believe in them! I will note, incidentally, that before, in the quite recent past, only a generation ago, these interesting young men were not to be so pitied, because in those days they almost always ended by successfully joining our higher cultivated strata and merging into one whole with them. And if, for instance, they were aware, at the beginning of the road, of all their disorderliness and fortuitousness, of all the lack of nobility, say, in their family surroundings, the lack of a hereditary tradition and of beautiful, finished forms, it was even so much the better, because later they themselves would consciously strive for these things and learn to appreciate them. Nowadays it is somewhat different—precisely because there is almost nothing to join.

"I will explain by a comparison or, so to speak, an assimilation. If I were a Russian novelist and had talent, I would be sure to take my heroes from the hereditary Russian nobility, because it is only in that type of cultivated Russian people that there is possible at least the appearance of a beautiful order and a beautiful impression, so necessary in a novel if it is to graciously affect the reader. I am by no means joking when I say this, though I myself am not a nobleman at all, which, however, you know yourself. Pushkin already sketched out the subjects of his future novels in his 'Traditions of the Russian Family,'[48] and, believe me, it indeed contains all we have had of the beautiful so far. At least all we have had that has been somewhat completed. I do not say this because I agree so unconditionally with the correctness and truthfulness of this beauty; but here, for instance, there were finished forms of honor and duty, which, except among the nobility, are not only not finished anywhere in Russia, but are not even begun. I speak as a peaceful man and seeking peace.

"Whether this honor is good and this duty right—is another question; but for me it is more important that the forms precisely be finished and that there be at least some sort of order that is not prescribed, but that we ourselves have finally developed. God, the most important thing for us is precisely at least some order of our own! In this has lain our hope and, so to speak, our rest; finally at least something built, and not this eternal smashing, not chips flying everywhere, not trash and rubbish, out of which nothing has come in the last two hundred years.

"Do not accuse me of Slavophilism; I am saying it just so, from misanthropy, because my heart feels heavy! Nowadays, in recent times, something quite the opposite of what I have described above has been happening among us. It is no longer rubbish that grows on to the higher stratum of people, but, on the contrary, bits and pieces are torn with merry haste from the beautiful type, and get stuck into one heap with the disorderly and envious. And it is a far from isolated case that the fathers and heads of former cultivated families themselves laugh at something that their children may still want to believe in. What's more, they enthusiastically do not conceal from their children their greedy joy at the unexpected right to dishonor, which a whole mass of them suddenly deduced from something. I am not speaking about the true progressists, my dearest Arkady Makarovich, but only about the riffraff, who have turned out to be numberless, of whom it is said: *'Grattez le russe et vous verrez le tartare.'** And, believe me, the true liberals, the true and magnanimous friends of mankind, are by no means so many among us as it suddenly seemed to us.

"But this is all philosophy; let us go back to the imaginary novelist. The position of our novelist in such a case would be quite definite: he would be unable to write in any other genre than the historical, for the beautiful type no longer exists in our time, and if any remnants remain, in the now-dominant opinion, they have not kept their beauty. Oh, in the historical genre it is still possible to portray a great many extremely pleasant and delightful details! One can even carry the reader with one so far that he will take the historical picture for something still possible in the present. Such a work, given great talent, would belong not so much to Russian literature as to Russian history. It would be an artistically finished picture of a Russian mirage, which existed in reality until people realized that it was a mirage. The grandson of the heroes portrayed in the picture portraying a Russian family of the average upper-class cultivated circle over three generations and in connection with Russian history—this descendant of his forebears could not be portrayed as a contemporary type otherwise than in a somewhat misanthropic, solitary, and undoubtedly sad guise. He should even appear as a sort of eccentric, whom the reader could recognize at first glance as someone who has quit the field, and be convinced that the field is no longer his. A bit further, and even this misanthropic grandson will vanish; new, as yet unknown persons will appear, and a new mirage; but what kind of persons? If they are not beautiful, then the Russian novel will no longer be possible.

*Scratch a Russian and you'll find a Tartar.

But, alas! is it only the novel that will turn out then to be impossible?

"Rather than go far, I will resort to your own manuscript. Look, for instance, at Mr. Versilov's two families (this time allow me to be fully candid). First of all, I will not expand on Andrei Petrovich himself; but, anyhow, he still belongs among the ancestors. He is a nobleman of very ancient lineage, and at the same time a Parisian communard.[49] He is a true poet and loves Russia, but on the other hand he totally denies her. He is without any religion, but is almost ready to die for something indefinite, which he cannot even name, but which he passionately believes in, after the manner of a multitude of Russian-European civilizers of the Petersburg period of Russian history. But enough of the man himself; here, however, is his hereditary family. I will not even speak of his son, and he does not deserve the honor. Those who have eyes know beforehand what such rascals come to among us, and incidentally what they bring others to. But his daughter Anna Andreevna—is she not a young lady of character? A person on the scale of the mother superior Mitrofania[50]—not, of course, to predict anything criminal, which would be unfair on my part. Tell me now, Arkady Makarovich, that this family is an accidental phenomenon, and my heart will rejoice. But, on the contrary, would it not be more correct to conclude that a multitude of such unquestionably hereditary Russian families are, with irresistible force, going over *en masse* into *accidental* families and merging with them in general disorder and chaos? In your manuscript you point in part to the type of this accidental family. Yes, Arkady Makarovich, you are *a member of an accidental family*, as opposed to our still-recent hereditary types, who had a childhood and youth so different from yours.

"I confess, I would not wish to be a novelist whose hero comes from an accidental family!

"Thankless work and lacking in beautiful forms. And these types in any case are still a current matter, and therefore cannot be artistically finished. Major mistakes are possible, exaggerations, oversights. In any case, one would have to do too much guessing. What, though, is the writer to do who has no wish to write only in the historical genre and is possessed by a yearning for what is current? To guess . . . and be mistaken.

"But 'Notes' such as yours could, it seems to me, serve as material for a future artistic work, for a future picture—of a disorderly but already bygone epoch. Oh, when the evil of the day is past and the future comes, then the future artist will find beautiful forms even for portraying the past disorder and chaos. It is then that 'Notes' like yours will be needed and will provide material—as long as they are sincere, even despite all that is chaotic and accidental about them... They will preserve at least certain faithful features by which to guess what might have been hidden in the soul of some adolescent of that troubled time—a not-entirely-insignificant knowledge, for the generations are made up of adolescents..."

NOTES

PART ONE

1. The princely family of Dolgoruky belonged to the oldest Russian nobility. Yuri Dolgoruky founded the princedom of Suzdal in the twelfth century.
2. At that time there were seven classes in the Russian gymnasium (high school), the seventh being the last. Graduates would generally be between nineteen and twenty years old.
3. *Anton the Wretch*, a novella by Dostoevsky's old school friend D. V. Grigorovich (1822–1899), and *Polinka Sachs*, a novella by A. V. Druzhinin (1824–1864), were both published in the journal *The Contemporary* in 1847. The former portrays peasant life in the darkest colors; the latter, written under the influence of George Sand, tells of a loving husband who, when betrayed by his wife, grants her the freedom to marry his rival. Both are sentimental tales in the liberal taste of the period.
4. The Semyonovsky quarter in Petersburg was named for the illustrious Semyonovsky Guards regiment, which was stationed there.
5. In the table of fourteen civil ranks established by the emperor Peter the Great, the rank of privy councillor was third, equivalent to the military rank of lieutenant general.
6. Dostoevsky himself was sent to a boarding school run (in K. Mochulsky's phrase) by "a poorly enough educated Frenchman" named Souchard. He stayed there for only a year, but the experience clearly left its mark on him. In his notes for the novel, he first uses the name Souchard and later alters it to Touchard.
7. The Senate in Petersburg also served as the highest Russian court; hence the opportunities for bribery.
8. The German romantic poet and playwright Friedrich Schiller (1759–1805) stood, in Dostoevsky's keyboard of references, for notions of the ideal, the "great and beautiful," and a simplified struggle for freedom. Having loved Schiller's works as a young man, Dostoevsky indulged in a good deal of indirect mockery of him in his later works.
9. The Summer Garden in Petersburg is on the left bank of the

Neva, a short distance from the imperial Winter Palace. Copies of antique sculptures were placed in it, on the orders of the tsar Peter the Great (1672–1725), for the edification of the public that went strolling there.

10. Lambert, being French, is a Catholic. In the Catholic Church at that time, first communion followed and was directly connected with confirmation in the faith, and was received at the age of ten or twelve, usually accompanied by a family celebration. (In the Orthodox Church, communion is given immediately after baptism to infants as well as adults.)

11. The relics of a saint are "revealed" when they start producing miracles of one sort or another—giving off a sweet fragrance, healing the sick, and so on.

12. One form of mortification of the flesh among ascetics was (and perhaps still is) the wearing of heavy iron chains wrapped about the waist under one's clothing.

13. Baron James Rothschild (1792–1868), the "moneylender to kings," died a few years before the events described in the novel. His "coup" had to do, however, with advance knowledge of Napoleon's defeat at Waterloo in 1815, not of the assassination of the Duc de Berry in 1820.

14. Dostoevsky modeled Dergachev and his associates on an actual conspiratorial group of some ten members, led by an engineer named Dolgushin, which called for the overthrow of the landowners and the tsar, the extermination of the bourgeoisie, and the redistribution of the land under an elected government. Dostoevsky closely followed their trial in July 1874. Among Dolgushin's people there was a Kramer and a Vasnin, corresponding to the Kraft and Vasin of the novel. Kraft's fate exactly parallels Kramer's, as described in the memoirs of Dostoevsky's friend, the famous jurist A. F. Koni.

15. The police found several inscriptions in Dolgushin's house, in English, French, Italian, and among them this one in Latin; they also found a large wooden cross with *Liberté, Égalité, Fraternité* carved on it.

16. One slogan of the Dolgushin group was: "Man should live according to truth and nature." The words have a long history both in enlightened social thought and in Dostoevsky's work, where they go back to the narrator's sarcastic play in *Notes from Underground* on the prefatory note to the *Confessions* of Jean-Jacques Rousseau (1712–1778), in which Rousseau claims to offer his readers "the only

portrait of a man, painted exactly from nature and in all its truth, that exists and probably ever will exist."

17. The "calendars" published in Russia at that time, like the American *Farmer's Almanac*, included stories, lore, advice, and statistics.

18. The term "phalanstery" (*phalanstère* in French) was coined by the French utopian socialist thinker Charles Fourier (1772–1837) to designate the physical and productive arrangements of the future communal life. "Barracks communism" is another term for the same idea. Here and further on, Arkady Makarovich plays ironically on various radical notions of the time, including the "rational egoism" of the radical ideologist N. G. Chernyshevsky (1828–1889) and the social structures envisioned in his novel *What Is to Be Done?* Dostoevsky's interest in "Fourierism" as a young man led to his arrest by the tsar's agents in 1849.

19. The Kalmyks are a nomadic Buddhist Mongol people, originally from Dzungaria in western China, who migrated to the steppes between the Don and the Volga, and also to Siberia.

20. The Crimean War (1854–1856) was fought by Russia against an alliance of Turkey, England, France, and the Piedmont.

21. Arbiter of the peace was one of the government posts established in Russia after the emancipation of the serfs by the "tsar-liberator" Alexander II in 1861. Arbiters of the peace were elected by the nobility from among local landowners and were mainly responsible for questions of land division between peasants and landowners. The function, taken earnestly at first, later became subject to abuses and was finally abolished in 1874.

22. Harpagon and Plyushkin are both famous misers, the former from the comedy *L'Avare* ("The Miser") by Molière (1622–1673), the latter from the novel *Dead Souls*, by Nikolai Gogol (1809–1852).

23. Historically, Russia had two capitals: Moscow, dating back to the thirteenth century, and St. Petersburg, founded by Peter the Great in 1703. Dostoevsky later refers to the period following 1703 as "the Petersburg period of Russian history."

24. Names of well-known Russian tycoons of the period following the abolition of serfdom in 1861, when mining, industry, railroads, and banking developed at a great pace. Polyakov and Gubonin were mainly builders of railroads.

25. John Law (1671–1729), a Scottish financier, became comptroller general of French finances, created the French Indies Company, and in 1719, having offered the plan unsuccessfully to Scotland, England, and Savoy, managed to persuade the Regency govern-

ment to create a Banque Générale of France, based on the selling of shares and the issuing of paper money. Extremely popular and successful at first, the system soon led to runaway inflation and ended in a catastrophic bankruptcy. Law was forced to flee France, and died in poverty in Venice.

26. Charles Maurice de Talleyrand-Périgord (1754–1838), prince of Bénévent, bishop of Autun, an ambitious, intelligent, and extremely witty man, was one of the most skillful French diplomats and politicians of his time, during which he served under the king, the constitutional assembly, the Directoire, the consulate, the empire, and finally the restoration of the Bourbons. Alexis Piron (1689–1773) was a poet, known mainly for his satires and often licentious songs. Denied admission to the French Academy, he wrote his own epitaph, which is also his most famous piece of verse: *Ci-gît Piron, qui ne fut rien, / Pas même académicien* ("Here lies Piron, who was nothing, / Not even an academician").

27. These lines come from the central monologue of the Baron in *The Covetous Knight*, one of the "little tragedies" by the poet Alexander Pushkin (1799–1837). Arkady Makarovich's "Rothschild idea" has been strongly influenced by the Baron's own "idea"—that the awareness of the power money brings is superior to the need to exercise it.

28. God commanded the ravens to feed the prophet Elijah when he went into hiding in the wilderness after denouncing the wicked King Ahab for abandoning the God of Israel (I Kings 17:4–6).

29. The Prussian statesman Otto von Bismarck (1815–1898), the "Iron Chancellor," was one of the main architects of German unification. In 1871, after defeating France, he proclaimed the German Empire, of which he became the first chancellor in that same year. The early period of Bismarck's *Kulturkampf* against the Catholics and social democrats coincided with the writing of *The Adolescent*, and Dostoevsky kept a close eye on the successes of this man who was famous for having said, "The questions of the time will be decided not by speeches and resolutions of the majority, but by blood and iron."

30. See note 16 above. Rousseau's *Confessions* were published posthumously in 1782 and 1789. Arkady Makarovich makes explicit what Rousseau describes more circumspectly at the beginning of Book III: "I sought out dark alleys, hidden redoubts, where I could expose myself from afar to persons of the fair sex in the state in which I should have liked to be able to be up close to them."

31. This painting of the Mother of God by Raphael Sanzio (1483–1520), usually known as the Sistine Madonna because it was painted for the church of St. Sixtus in Piacenza, belongs to the collection of the Dresden Pinakothek. For Dostoevsky, who had seen the painting a number of times during his visits to Dresden, it represented the ideal of pure beauty. In the last years of his life, he himself had a large engraving of it hanging in his study in Petersburg.
32. Arkady Makarovich probably means the famous doors of the Florentine Baptistry, the work of Lorenzo Ghiberti (1378–1455), which Michelangelo, in admiration, called "the doors of paradise." Dostoevsky's wife, Anna Grigorievna, recalls in her memoirs that her husband, during their stay in Florence (1868–1869), often made a special detour to look at these doors, before which he would stand in ecstasy.
33. Versilov is probably referring to the ideas of Rousseau (who was born in Geneva) and his followers, including the early utopian socialists. In Part Two of the novel, he will explain to Arkady that by "Geneva ideas" he means "virtue without Christ . . . today's ideas . . . the idea of the whole of today's civilization" (in the notebooks for the novel, Dostovsky has him say more specifically "the French ideas of today").
34. Eliseevs' was and still is a fine delicatessen and wine shop on Nevsky Prospect in Petersburg. Ballet's was a confectioner's shop, also on Nevsky Prospect, still mentioned in Baedecker's guide for 1897.
35. This is the first line of a folk song made popular by the singer and amateur of folk music M. V. Zubova (d. 1779). There is mention of the lady and the song in a book titled *Modern Russian Women*, by P. D. Mordovtsev, published in 1874, when Dostoevsky was working on the novel.
36. The allusion is to the famous reply of Voltaire (1694–1778), when he was asked which literary genre was the best: "*Tous les genres sont bons hors le genre ennuyeux*" ("All genres are good, except the boring genre").
37. The poet Ivan Krylov (1769–1844), Russia's greatest fabulist, is often referred to as the Russian La Fontaine (many of whose fables he translated or adapted into Russian). Arkady will quote from his fable "The Fussy Bride" a little further on.
38. *Woe from Wit*, a comedy by the Russian poet and diplomat Alexander Griboedov (1795–1829), is the first masterpiece of the

Russian theater; many lines from the play became proverbial in Russia and have remained so.

39. Chatsky is the disillusioned protagonist of *Woe from Wit*, and the first in the series of "superfluous men" in nineteenth-century Russian literature. He is often likened to Alceste, the hero of Molière's *Misanthrope*. Zhileiko was a well-known actor of the time, who played in the private theaters of the nobility as well as on the public stage.

40. The linked short stories of *A Hunter's Sketches*, by Ivan Turgenev (1818–1883), were published in one volume in 1852.

41. As the son of a serf, Arkady Makarovich would not have had the possibility of attending high school and university and would not have enjoyed the legal rights of a gentleman.

42. The wanderer (*strannik*) is a well-known figure in Russian religious life. Such spiritual wandering meant abandoning a fixed home and undertaking a sort of perpetual pilgrimage from monastery to monastery, as is described most memorably in *The Way of a Pilgrim*, an anonymous book published in the nineteenth century.

43. The Slavophiles ("lovers of the Slavs") were a group of writers and thinkers of the nineteenth century (the most important were Alexei Khomyakov, Konstantin and Ivan Aksakov, and Yuri Samarin) who believed that Russia should follow her own way of development, based on the structures of the rural community and the Orthodox Church, instead of imitating the West, as their opponents, the Westernizers, advocated. The Slavophile-Westernizer controversy dominated Russian social thought throughout the nineteenth century. Dostoevsky appeared, at various times, to take both sides in it.

44. This combination of terms goes back ultimately to such eighteenth-century treatises as *A Philosophical Enquiry into the Origin of Our Ideas of the Sublime and Beautiful*, by the Anglo-Irish philosopher and statesman Edmund Burke (1729–1797) and *Observations on the Feeling of the Beautiful and Sublime*, by the German philosopher Immanuel Kant (1724–1804). The Russian phrase, replacing "sublime" with the less rhetorical "lofty," became a critical commonplace in the 1840s, but acquired an ironic tone in the utilitarian and anti-aesthetic 1860s. The narrator of Dostoevsky's *Notes from Underground* makes much sarcastic play with it.

45. See II Samuel 11. Uriah the Hittite was the husband of Bathsheba; King David arranged for him to be killed in battle, so that he could take his wife.

46. A line from the poem "Vlas," by Nikolai Nekrasov (1821–1878), an old acquaintance and longtime ideological opponent of Dostoevsky's, editor of the journal *Notes of the Fatherland* at the time that *The Adolescent* was appearing in it. The poem describes a greedy and pitiless peasant who ends his days as a wanderer collecting money for churches. Dostoevsky wrote about the poem in his *Diary of a Writer* for 1873, quoting many passages, including this same line, which he describes as "wonderfully well-put." Incidentally, Vlas wore iron chains "for his soul's perfection" as he went on his wanderings.
47. Pushkin's story "The Queen of Spades," published in 1834, is one of the key works of Russian literature; in its atmosphere and in the character of its hero, Hermann, it prefigured the depiction of Petersburg in the works of Gogol, Dostoevsky, Andrei Bely, and others.
48. The reference is to the equestrian statue of Peter the Great by the French sculptor Etienne-Maurice Falconet (1716–1791), which stands on Senate Square in Petersburg, and to Pushkin's poem "The Bronze Horseman," which describes the same statue come to life in the delirium of its hero.
49. An allusion to shares in the "Brest-Graev" railway, referring to an actual forgery scandal of the day, involving shares in the Tambov-Kozlov line. The forger, Kosolov, prototype of Dostoevsky's Stebelkov, was prosecuted by A. F. Koni (see note 14).
50. The quotation is from Pushkin's poem "The Black Shawl" (1820).
51. It was indeed possible to rent not a whole room but only a corner of a room, which would be partitioned off by a hanging sheet or the like.
52. See Hamlet's soliloquy about the player (Act II, Scene ii, ll. 553–563): "Tears in his eyes, distraction in's aspect / A broken voice, and his whole function suiting / With forms to his conceit? and all for nothing! / For Hecuba? / What's Hecuba to him or he to Hecuba / That he should weep for her?" The comparison does not quite fit Kraft's case.
53. See Luke 15:11–32, the parable of the prodigal son. Arkady totally confuses the meaning of the parable.
54. Rurik (d. 879), chief of the Scandinavian rovers known as Varangians, founded the Russian principality of Novgorod at the invitation of the local populace, thus becoming the ancestor of the

oldest Russian nobility. The dynasty of Rurik ruled Russia from 862 to 1598, when it was succeeded by the Romanovs.

55. Court councillor was seventh in the table of ranks established by Peter the Great, equivalent to the military rank of major.

56. A condensed quotation of Matthew 5:25–26 (King James Version).

57. Céladon, the hero of the pastoral novel *Astrée*, by Honoré d'Urfé (1607–1628), is a platonic and sentimental lover.

58. See Luke 15:32 (King James Version). This is now Arkady's third reference to the parable of the prodigal son. In the parable, however, these words are spoken of the son by the father; Arkady reverses the relations.

59. The lines are from Pushkin's poem "The Hero" (1830).

60. The fig (*figue* in French, *fica* in Italian) is a contemptuous gesture made by inserting the thumb between the first and second fingers of the fist; also used in verbal form, as in the saying, "I don't care a fig." Obsolete in English, according to the *Oxford English Dictionary*, its use has continued in Russia, where a special covert form known as "a fig in the pocket" was developed, especially among intellectuals, as a sign of dissent during Soviet times.

PART TWO

1. Borel's restaurant in Petersburg, named for its French founder, was already famous in Pushkin's time. The plural implies "Borel and the like."

2. Titular councillor was ninth in the table of ranks, equivalent to the military rank of staff-captain. The type of the titular councillor entered Russian literature in the person of the wretched copying clerk Akaky Akakievich Bashmachkin, hero of Gogol's story "The Overcoat."

3. That is, under the emperor Nicholas I (1796–1855).

4. The Duma referred to in this case is the city council, elected from the nobility.

5. The first railway in Russia, the Tsarskoe Selo line from Petersburg to Pavlovsk, was opened in 1838. Tsarskoe Selo (literally "Tsar's Village") was an aristocratic suburb about fifteen miles south of Petersburg; Pavlovsk, named for the emperor Paul (1754–1801), who had a palace there, is slightly further south.

6. The Cathedral of St. Isaac in Petersburg was begun in 1819 and

completed in 1858, on plans by the French architect Auguste Ricard de Montferrand (1756–1858).
7. Alexander Suvorov (1729–1800), who served under Catherine the Great (1729–1796), was the only Russian military man to bear the title of generalissimo until Joseph Stalin (1879–1953) awarded himself the title during World War II. Suvorov's successes against the French revolutionary army in Italy gained him the additional titles of count of Italy and prince of Rimini, but they were not hereditary.
8. Zavyalov was a Russian merchant and manufacturer.
9. King Charles XI of Sweden (1655–1697) was said to have had a vision of an assembly in a brightly lit hall in which unknown men were cutting the throats of a great number of young people under the eyes of a fifteen-year-old king seated on his throne. The vision was spread through the Russian court under Alexander I (1777–1825) by the Swedish ambassador, a freemason by the name of Stedding.
10. See Part One, note 7. According to a popular anecdote, the "somebody" was in fact the emperor Alexander I himself.
11. Pavel Bashutsky (1771–1836) was an officer who fought in the campaigns against the French, was promoted to general, and from 1814 until his death served as military commandant of Petersburg.
12. Alexander Chernyshov (1785–1857), who distinguished himself at Austerlitz and as a partisan leader in 1812, went on diplomatic missions for Alexander I, was made a count by Nicholas I, and served as minister of war from 1827 to 1852.
13. A quotation from Luke 8:17 (King James Version).
14. See Matthew 4:3, Christ's temptation in the wilderness, where the devil asks him to prove he is the son of God by turning stones into bread.
15. See Part One, note 33.
16. According to legend, during the reign of the third king of Rome, Tullus Hostilius (seventh century B.C.), the three sons of Horatius fought for Rome against three champions of the city of Alba Longa, in the presence of the two armies, to decide which of the two peoples would command the other. The only survivor of the six was one of the Horatii, who thus gave the victory to Rome.
17. See Part One, note 11.
18. Vissarion Belinsky (1811–1848) was the most influential liberal critic and Westernizer of his time, an advocate of socially committed literature. He championed Dostoevsky's first novel, *Poor Folk* (1845), and exerted a strong influence on the young writer, but they

soon disagreed and parted ways. Dostoevsky's inner debate with Belinsky continued throughout his life.

19. Bolshaya Millionnaya is an older name for the present Millionnaya Street, which runs through what was then an aristocratic neighborhood between the Summer Garden and Palace Square in Petersburg.

20. See Part One, note 47.

21. The period of Tartar occupation of Russia, known as the "Tartar Yoke," in fact lasted from the conquest of 1237–1240 to around 1480, when Prince Ivan III of Moscow removed the last traces of Muscovite dependence on the khanate of the Golden Horde.

22. That is, from *Lucia di Lammermoor*, an opera by Gaetano Donizetti (1797–1848).

23. According to the Gospels, the court of the Sanhedrin in Jerusalem convicted Christ of blasphemy, which carried a sentence of death, and turned him over to the Roman procurator Pontius Pilate for sentencing. Pilate, who found no fault in him, washed his hands of the guilt and, yielding to the demands of the crowd, gave him over to be crucified.

24. The princely family of Rohan, one of the most ancient and illustrious in France, has as its motto, *Premier ne puis, second ne daigne, Rohan suis* ("I cannot be first, I scorn to be second, I am Rohan").

25. In 1720, Peter the Great abolished the position of patriarch, the administrative head of the Orthodox Church, chosen by and from the clergy, and established a standing council to administer Church affairs, presided over by a lay procurator appointed by the emperor himself. The term "schismatic" (*raskolnik*) refers to the so-called Old Believers, who split off from the Orthodox Church in disagreement over the reforms of the patriarch Nikon in the mid-seventeenth century.

26. Russian borrowed the word "keepsake" (*kipsek*) from English. It was the trade name of a literary annual or miscellany, finely bound and illustrated, intended for gift-giving.

27. Soden is a German watering-place at the foot of the Taunus Mountains, ten miles west of Frankfurt-am-Main. Bad-Gastein is a watering-place near Salzburg in Austria.

28. The biblical Song of Solomon, or Song of Songs, is a collection of mystical-erotic bridal poems written down in about the third century B.C. The opening of the first Book of Kings tells how King

David in his old age took a young virgin, Abishag the Shunammite, to his bed to keep him warm and minister to him, though he "knew her not" (I Kings 1:1–15).
29. The French writer Paul de Kock (1794–1871) was the author of innumerable novels depicting petit-bourgeois life, some of them considered risqué.
30. Alexei Mikhailovich Romanov (1629–1676), tsar of Russia, was the father of Peter the Great.
31. Holy Week is the week between Palm Sunday and Easter Sunday.

PART THREE

1. In Petersburg, owing to its northern latitude, the sun sets in midafternoon during the winter.
2. The two-week fast preceding the feast of Saints Peter and Paul on June 29.
3. *Kutya* (accented on the last syllable) is a special dish offered to people in church at the end of a memorial service, and in some places on Christmas Eve, made from rice, barley, or wheat and raisins, sweetened with honey.
4. This day of commemoration of the dead, also known as *Krasnaya gorka* ("Pretty Little Hill"), falls on the Tuesday following Saint Thomas's Sunday, the first Sunday after Easter. The Russian name probably comes from the custom of decorating the graves ("little hills") for the occasion.
5. In Part Three of both editions of *The Adolescent* published during Dostoevsky's lifetime, the name of this character changes from Darya Onisimovna to Nastasya Egorovna. The same shift occurs in the notebooks for the novel, and evidently slipped from there into the final draft and hence into print. We follow the definitive Russian edition in preserving the change.
6. See Part Two, note 5.
7. Saint Mary of Egypt, a fifth-century saint greatly venerated in Orthodoxy, was a prostitute who was miraculously converted and spent the last forty-seven years of her life in the desert, in prayer and repentance.
8. The merchant's name, though a plausible one in Russian, is suggestive of his character: it means "cattle slaughterer."
9. There are twelve great feasts in the Orthodox liturgical year.
10. A "holy fool" (or "fool in God," or "fool for Christ's sake"—

yurodivy in Russian) is a saintly person or ascetic whose saintliness is expressed in a certain "folly" of behavior. Holy fools were known early in Christian tradition. However, the term may also be applied to a harmless village idiot.

11. A distorted quotation of the Epistle of Jude: "hating even the garment spotted by the flesh" (Jude 23).

12. Cenobitic order means a life in common (from the Greek *koinobion*, "common life") for all the monks in a monastery, as opposed to the "idiorhythmic" life in which each monk is responsible for his own maintenance.

13. In the Orthodox Church, young children are allowed to take communion without prior preparation, but after a certain age they are expected to prepare, like adults, by attendance at services, confession, and fasting.

14. In Orthodox piety, the "gift of tears" is a sign of profound spiritual development. In *The Brothers Karamazov* the elder Zosima will say: "Water the earth with the tears of your joy, and love those tears."

15. In the Book of Job, God in his wager with Satan allows him to destroy Job's seven sons and three daughters. Having won the wager by proving Job's righteousness, God gives him another seven sons and three daughters. It is never said, however, that Job "forgot the former ones."

16. A nobleman convicted of a crime would be stripped of his legal and hereditary rights, but it was possible to have them restored in return for service to the state, for instance, in one of the new Russian "colonies" in Turkestan, which was being settled at the time.

17. Arkhangelsk is in the northwest of Russia on the White Sea; Kholmogory is a small village about fifty miles south of Arkhangelsk on the Dvina River.

18. The German title *Kammerjunker* ("gentleman of the bedchamber") was adopted by the Russian court. It was a high distinction for a young man.

19. This is an example of the long fellow's (or Dostoevsky's) absurd humor: the French often substitute a *w* for a *v* in writing German or Russian names, but the *w* is still pronounced as a *v*. However, Arkady's name transliterated into French would be "Dolgorouky," not "Dolgorowky." What's more, the long fellow obviously pronounces his fanciful version "Dolgorovky," which is why Arkady thinks he has said "Korovkin."

20. The *Journal des débats* was a French daily newspaper founded in 1789 and continuously published until 1944, always with a moderate liberal tendency; the *Indépendance belge* was published in Brussels from 1830 to 1937.
21. In Russian, the German *Junker*, meaning "young lord," referred to a lower officer's rank open only to the nobility.
22. That is, Bolshaya Morskaya Street, which runs from Palace Square to Senate Square in Petersburg, parallel to the Moyka River. It was a wealthy street with many fine houses on it, including the mansion belonging to Vladimir Nabokov's family.
23. Noël-François-Alfred Madier de Montjau (1814–1892) was a French lawyer who became a people's representative after the establishment of the Second Republic in 1848. Banished following Napoleon III's coup d'état in 1852, his name became news again in 1874, when his election as a deputy of the extreme left caused a considerable stir. The "current Parisian events" were the declaration of the Third Republic, the elections, and the drafting of a new constitution. The Poles, who had been under Russian domination since the partition of Poland in 1772, were often ardent republican sympathizers.
24. An imprecise quotation from the poem "I feel dull and sad..." by the Russian poet Mikhail Lermontov (1814–1841).
25. The monumental two-part drama by the German poet Johann Wolfgang von Goethe (1749–1852), based on the much older legend of the philosopher Faust, who sells his soul to the devil in exchange for earthly power. Gretchen is a young girl seduced and abandoned by Faust.
26. The first words (and title) of the great hymn from the *missa pro defunctis* (requiem mass): *Dies irae, dies illa / solvet saeclum in favilla, / teste David cum Sibylla* ("Day of wrath, day that will / dissolve the world to burning coals, / as witnessed David and the Sibyl"), a meditation on the Last Judgment attributed to Tommaso da Celano (1190–1260), one of the first disciples and also the first biographer of Saint Francis of Assisi.
27. Alessandro Stradella (1644–1682) was an Italian singer and composer of cantatas, operas, oratorios, and instrumental music.
28. In the Orthodox liturgy, these words are sung by the choir at the end of the Cherubic Hymn, which accompanies the entrance of the priest bearing the bread and wine of the eucharist: "Let us lay aside all earthly cares...That we may receive the King of all, who comes invisibly upborne by the angelic hosts. Alleluia!

Alleluia! Alleluia!" Trishatov recites the scene in the cathedral from the opera *Faust*, by French composer Charles Gounod (1818–1893), but adds his own uplifting "hosanna" at the end.
29. This famous phrase comes from the book *What Is Property?* (1840), by the French socialist philosopher Pierre-Joseph Proudhon (1809–1865).
30. Alexander Herzen (1812–1870), a radical publicist and an acquaintance of Dostoevsky's in the 1840s, went into self-imposed exile in 1847. In London, from 1857 to 1869, he published a revolutionary Russian-language weekly called *The Bell*, and also wrote two important books: *From the Other Shore*, a series of letters on socialism, and *My Past and Thoughts*.
31. See Part One, note 21.
32. Dostoevsky first intended this dream for the chapter entitled "At Tikhon's" in his previous novel, *Demons* (1871–1872). That chapter was suppressed by his publisher, and the dream was then reincorporated into *The Adolescent* with modifications. Dostoevsky knew this painting from his own visits to the Dresden Pinakothek. Claude Gellée, called Le Lorrain (1600–1682), was a master of sun and light, and one of the greatest French painters of landscape. The Sicilian shepherd Acis, who was loved by the nymph Galatea, was crushed under a huge rock by the jealous cyclops Polyphemus. The cyclops in the picture makes the age a little less golden than Versilov likes to think.
33. The allusions are to the Franco-Prussian War (1870–1871) and the burning of the Tuileries (and much of the Louvre) in Paris under the Commune (1871).
34. *Pétroleurs* were incendiaries who used oil or kerosene (*pétrole*) to start fires.
35. The reference is to the poem "*Frieden*" ("Peace"), from the cycle *Die Nordsee* ("The North Sea") in *Das Buch der Lieder* ("The Book of Songs"), by the German poet Heinrich Heine (1797–1856), which describes Christ's return to earth and the regeneration of people under his love. Versilov (or Dostoevsky) changes the North Sea to the Baltic.
36. Versilov is probably referring to the soliloquy that opens Act V, Scene ii of *Othello* ("It is the cause, it is the cause, my soul"), not Othello's last speech in lines 338–56 of the same scene ("Soft you! A word or two before you go"). "Evgeny at Tatyana's feet" refers to stanza XLI in the eighth and final chapter of Pushkin's novel in verse *Evgeny Onegin*. The episode from *Les Misérables*

(Part Two, Book Three) describes the meeting of the little girl Cosette with the escaped convict Jean Valjean.
37. It was customary in Russia to lay a dead person out on a table while waiting for the coffin to be prepared.
38. A *panikhida* is a memorial service for the dead, which may be held before as well as after the actual burial service.
39. See Part Two, note 25. The Old Believers, in their wish to hold on to all that had characterized the Russian Orthodox Church before the reforms of the patriarch Nikon, managed to preserve some of the finest old Russian icons.
40. See Part Two, note 28. As is often the case with Arkady's allusions, the story of Abishag has no relation at all to what he is describing here.
41. A vogue for spiritualism, or spiritism, as it was originally called, swept through upper-class Europe, including the courts, in the late 1860s and early 1870s, when mediums and table-rapping séances became socially respectable. Tolstoy also refers mockingly to the vogue for spiritism in *Anna Karenina*, which was written at the same period as *The Adolescent*.
42. The von Sohn murder trial caused a stir in Petersburg in 1869–1870. The elderly von Sohn was murdered in a brothel to the dancing and singing of the prostitutes; he was then put in a trunk and shipped to Moscow as baggage. Dostoevsky refers to the case again in *The Brothers Karamazov*.
43. An imprecise quotation of a line spoken apropos of Chatsky by the old lady Khlyostova in *Woe from Wit* (see Part One, notes 38 and 39).
44. Militrisa is the daughter of King Kirbit in *The Tale of Prince Bova*, a sixteenth-century Russian version of *Beuves d'Hanstone*, a thirteenth-century French *chanson de geste* that was widely spread in Europe. Dostoevsky refers to the same tale again in *The Brothers Karamazov*.
45. In the Orthodox Church, Great Lent is the forty-day period of fast that precedes Holy Week (see Part Two, note 31). Preparation for communion at Easter would include eating lenten meals (no meat, eggs, or dairy products), confessing, and attending the services of Lent and Holy Week.
46. During the Bridegroom services that fall on the first three days of Holy Week, the hymn is sung which gives these services their name: "Behold! the Bridegroom comes at midnight, and blessed is the servant whom He shall find watching..."

47. Molchalin is the trivial and servile private secretary in *Woe from Wit* (see Part One, notes 38 and 39). Dostoevsky mentions Molchalin in his *Diary of a Writer* for October 1876 (Chapter One, section 3), and adds parenthetically, "Some day I am going to dwell on Molchalin. It is a great theme."
48. Nikolai Semyonovich is referring to Chapter Three, stanzas XIII–XIV, of *Evgeny Onegin*, where Pushkin says he may cease to be a poet and "descend to humble prose" in order to describe the "traditions of a Russian family, / love's captivating dreams, / and manners of our ancientry," and so on (Nabokov translation). Pushkin already speaks with a hint of irony here of the kind of novel that Nikolai Semyonovich advocates, and that Leo Tolstoy would go on to write. Dostoevsky was, of course, writing precisely the opposite kind of novel, and therefore appreciates Pushkin's irony, which escapes both Tolstoy and Nikolai Semyonovich.
49. The radical socialist communards seized control of Paris following the insurrection of March 18, 1871, when the Prussians lifted their siege of the city after the defeat of France. They were overthrown in May of the same year.
50. Mother Mitrofania (Baroness Praskovya Grigoryevna Rosen in the world), the superior of a convent in Serpukhov, was convicted of passing counterfeit promissory notes for enormous sums and of forging a will, and sentenced to three years of exile in Siberia. According to the memoirs of Dostoevsky's friend, the lawyer A. F. Koni, she was a woman of great intelligence and of a strongly masculine and practical character. Her trial caused a sensation in Petersburg.

ABOUT THE TRANSLATORS

RICHARD PEVEAR has published translations of Alain, Yves Bonnefoy, Alberto Savinio, Pavel Florensky, and Henri Volohonsky, as well as two books of poetry. He has received fellowships or grants for translation from the National Endowment for the Arts, the Ingram Merrill Foundation, the Guggenheim Foundation, the National Endowment for the Humanities, and the French Ministry of Culture.

LARISSA VOLOKHONSKY was born in Leningrad. She has translated works by the prominent Orthodox theologians Alexander Schmemann and John Meyendorff into Russian.

Together, Pevear and Volokhonsky have translated *Dead Souls* and *The Collected Tales* by Nikolai Gogol, and *The Brothers Karamazov*, *Crime and Punishment*, *Notes from Underground*, *Demons*, *The Idiot*, and *The Adolescent* by Fyodor Dostoevsky. They were awarded the PEN Book-of-the-Month Club Translation Prize for their version of *The Brothers Karamazov*, and more recently *Demons* was one of three nominees for the same prize. They are married and live in France.

NINETEENTH-CENTURY TITLES IN EVERYMAN'S LIBRARY

JANE AUSTEN
Emma
Mansfield Park
Northanger Abbey
Persuasion
Pride and Prejudice
Sanditon and Other Stories
Sense and Sensibility

HONORÉ DE BALZAC
Cousin Bette
Eugénie Grandet
Old Goriot

HECTOR BERLIOZ
The Memoirs of Hector Berlioz

CHARLOTTE BRONTË
Jane Eyre
Villette

EMILY BRONTË
Wuthering Heights

SAMUEL BUTLER
The Way of all Flesh

ANTON CHEKHOV
My Life and Other Stories
The Steppe and Other Stories

CARL VON CLAUSEWITZ
On War

S. T. COLERIDGE
Poems

WILKIE COLLINS
The Moonstone
The Woman in White

CHARLES DARWIN
The Origin of Species
The Voyage of the Beagle
(in 1 vol.)

CHARLES DICKENS
Bleak House
David Copperfield
Dombey and Son
Great Expectations
Hard Times
Little Dorrit
Martin Chuzzlewit
Nicholas Nickleby
The Old Curiosity Shop
Oliver Twist

CHARLES DICKENS (*cont.*)
Our Mutual Friend
The Pickwick Papers
A Tale of Two Cities

FYODOR DOSTOEVSKY
The Adolescent
The Brothers Karamazov
Crime and Punishment
Demons
The Idiot

GEORGE ELIOT
Adam Bede
Daniel Deronda
Middlemarch
The Mill on the Floss
Silas Marner

GUSTAVE FLAUBERT
Madame Bovary

ELIZABETH GASKELL
Mary Barton

IVAN GONCHAROV
Oblomov

THOMAS HARDY
Far From the Madding Crowd
Jude the Obscure
The Mayor of Casterbridge
The Return of the Native
Tess of the d'Urbervilles
The Woodlanders

NATHANIEL HAWTHORNE
The Scarlet Letter

JAMES HOGG
Confessions of a Justified Sinner

VICTOR HUGO
Les Misérables

HENRY JAMES
The Awkward Age
The Bostonians
The Golden Bowl
The Portrait of a Lady
The Princess Casamassima
The Wings of the Dove
Collected Stories (2 vols)

JOHN KEATS
The Poems

SØREN KIERKEGAARD
Fear and Trembling and
The Book on Adler

MIKHAIL LERMONTOV
A Hero of Our Time

HERMAN MELVILLE
The Complete Shorter Fiction
Moby-Dick

JOHN STUART MILL
On Liberty and Utilitarianism

EDGAR ALLAN POE
The Complete Stories

ALEXANDER PUSHKIN
The Collected Stories

WALTER SCOTT
Rob Roy

MARY SHELLEY
Frankenstein

STENDHAL
The Charterhouse of Parma
Scarlet and Black

ROBERT LOUIS STEVENSON
The Master of Ballantrae and
Weir of Hermiston
Dr Jekyll and Mr Hyde
and Other Stories

HARRIET BEECHER STOWE
Uncle Tom's Cabin

W. M. THACKERAY
Vanity Fair

HENRY DAVID THOREAU
Walden

ALEXIS DE TOCQUEVILLE
Democracy in America

LEO TOLSTOY
Collected Shorter Fiction (2 vols)
Anna Karenina
Childhood, Boyhood and Youth
The Cossacks
War and Peace

ANTHONY TROLLOPE
Barchester Towers
Can You Forgive Her?
Doctor Thorne
The Eustace Diamonds
Framley Parsonage
The Last Chronicle of Barset
Phineas Finn
The Small House at Allington
The Warden

IVAN TURGENEV
Fathers and Children
First Love and Other Stories
A Sportsman's Notebook

MARK TWAIN
Tom Sawyer
and Huckleberry Finn

OSCAR WILDE
Plays, Prose Writings and Poems

WILLIAM WORDSWORTH
Selected Poems (UK only)

ÉMILE ZOLA
Germinal

This book is set in CASLON, designed and engraved by William Caslon of WILLIAM CASLON & SON, Letter-Founders in London, around 1740. In England at the beginning of the eighteenth century, Dutch type was probably more widely used than English. The rise of William Caslon put a stop to the importation of Dutch types and so changed the history of English typecutting.